AN ANTHOLOGY

W. W. NORTON & COMPANY   NEW YORK • LONDON

To my children Sarah, Graham, and Mary

Photograph credits: Elvis Presley (Bettmann/Corbis); Chuck Berry
(Barnabas Bosshart/Corbis); Little Richard (Hulton-Deutsch
Collection/Corbis); The Beatles (Bettmann/Corbis); The Supremes
(Bettmann/Corbis); The Rolling Stones (Lewis Gardner); James Brown
(Bettmann/Corbis); Bob Dylan (Bettmann/Corbis); Otis Redding
(Bettmann/Corbis); Aretha Franklin (Bettmann/Corbis); Tina Turner
(Neal Preston/Corbis); Jimi Hendrix (Hulton-Deutsch Collection/Corbis);
The Doors (Henry Diltz/Corbis); Janis Joplin (Hulton-Deutsch
Collection/Corbis); Eric Clapton (Neal Preston/Corbis); Bruce
Springsteen (Corbis); Patti Smith (Lynn Goldsmith/Corbis); Madonna
(Lauren Radack/Corbis); Nirvana (S.I.N./Corbis)

Since this page cannot legibly accommodate all the copyright notices,
pages 645–51 constitute an extension of the copyright page.

The text of this book is composed in 8.5/13.75 Leawood Book
with the display set in Univers Bold Condensed and Octopus
Composition by Allentown Digital Services
Manufacturing by Haddon Craftsmen
Book design by Dana Sloan

Library of Congress Cataloging-in-Publication Data

Rock and roll is here to stay : an anthology / edited by William McKeen ;
introduction by Peter Guralnick.
p.   cm.
Includes index.
ISBN 0-393-04700-8
1. Rock music—History and criticism. I. McKeen, William, 1954– .
ML3534.R613 2000
781.66—DC21   99-31759
                                                     CIP

W. W. Norton & Company, Inc., 500 Fifth Avenue, New York, N.Y. 10110
www.wwnorton.com

W. W. Norton & Company Ltd., 10 Coptic Street, London WC1A 1PU

1 2 3 4 5 6 7 8 9 0

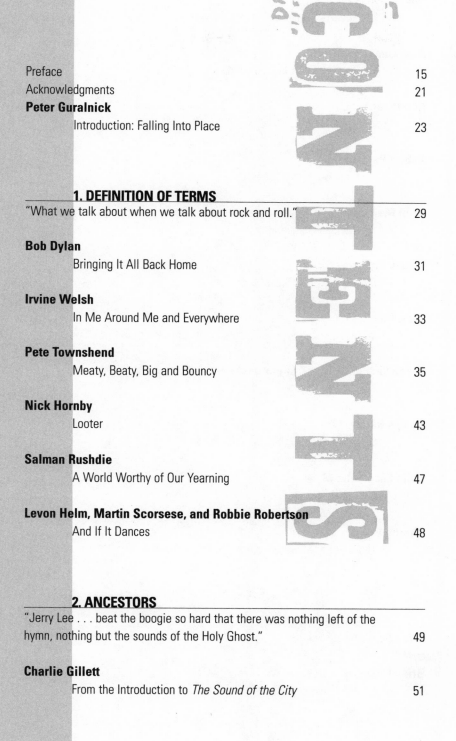

5. PRESENT AT THE CREATION

7. CRITICS

IN THE SUMMER of 1965, when I was ten, my family moved from Miami to Dallas. Imagine this caravan: a moving van, two cars, five people, and five dogs. My father and teenage brother were ahead in the Triumph, packed into the tiny sports car. My mother, my sixteen-year-old sister Suzanne, five poodles, and I followed in the Cadillac, trying to keep up with the little red car and managing our own internal crisis. I sprawled on the back seat with the four female poodles, all of whom were in heat. My mother and sister comforted the remaining poodle, Walter, up front.

It was August and well over a hundred degrees. We managed, for the four days of that epic journey, to keep Walter away from the girls. At rest stops, my sister held Walter while I struggled, like some low-budget Ben-Hur, with four females straining their leashes. Walter moaned and tugged at his collar. His teeth chattered like typewriter keys.

Picture the view from the back seat: Besides the horny poodle, there was my mother, driving, pretending not to notice my sister. Though Suzanne was seated, she was moving, doing whatever dance was popular that summer. Music came in a steady beat from the radio—and what *great* music: Dylan's "Like a Rolling Stone," the Beatles' "Ticket to Ride," James Brown's "Papa's Got a Brand-New Bag." There was also Herman's Hermits' "Henry the Eighth," but still . . . if the summer of '65 wasn't the high-water mark of rock and roll radio, then I'll eat my Chevy. That summer was kind of like the Continental Divide in popular music. We could look back in one direction and see the matching suits, the well-scrubbed faces, and the kind of rock and roll innocence we'd never see again. Looking the other way, we could see the patched jeans, the dope-smoking, the songs about war and injustice that would reach the top ten, and a weariness underneath the thrashing power chords. And they started calling it simply *rock*.

That was a great summer on the radio.

And what song, of all the great songs on the radio that summer, was the soundtrack of Walter's frustrations?

It was a song by England's self-proclaimed "newest hitmakers" that twanged out nearly every hour on the hour. As Suzanne writhed in the front seat and my mother pretended to passing motorists that she didn't notice her daughter's seizures, Walter gazed longingly at four sets of nubile poodle thighs, and an adenoidal wail blared from the tinny speakers, voicing the hound's lament:

> I . . . can't . . . *get no*
> I . . . can't . . . *get no* . . . No sat-iss-*fack-shun*

Over the years, when American mothers and fathers feared for the well-being of their children and regarded Michael Phillip Jagger as rock and roll Lucifer, corrupter of youth, leader of the nation's children down the path toward carnalities too bizarre to imagine, I could never see the grounds for their fears. Whenever vice presidents or members of congress (or their spouses) prated about pop-music vulgarity and lascivious lyrics, they offered as evidence the Jagger-Richards song catalog.

When others conjured visions of evil too horrifying to mention, all the fault of the Rolling Stones, all I could think of was that horny poodle with the chattering teeth.

In spite of the poor dog's frustration, that trip remains one of my favorite memories of childhood and, like so much of my life, it is informed by rock and roll. It's as if my whole life has a soundtrack played by two guitars, bass, and drums.

I was born the summer that Elvis Presley recorded "That's All Right (Mama)," and so I am a true rock and roll baby, and I date myself with the use of that term: ROCK AND ROLL. It's a wonderful name, isn't it? The fact is, no one seems to know what to call this music anymore, but only aging dilletantes such as myself employ the old rock and roll term. *Rock and roll* came into fashion in the 1950s. It became rock in the 1960s, then split into so many factions and divisions that it's hard to keep track. But I want to use rock and roll in this book. It's such a wonderful thing to say. Go on, say it loud: ROCK AND ROLL. As Jerry Lee would say, "MMMmmmmmmmm-mmmmmmm . . . feels good!"

When Elvis and his peers took over radio in the 1950s, the Hillbilly Cat and other early rock and rollers—Chuck Berry, Little Richard, Jerry Lee Lewis, and others—were condemned from pulpits across America and vilified by the press.

Nearly a half century later, rock and roll (in my broad definition: all popular music aimed at the youth market) still makes people mad. Rap has been drawing heat for over a decade and the adjectives that used to be carted out for Elvis were dusted off and refitted for the 1990s: obscene, immoral, disgusting . . . high praise, of course, in the world of rock and roll. Tipper Gore tried to crusade against the bat-eating, blood-spitting headbangers in the early 1980s and rapper Ice-T felt the Time Warner corporate squeeze when he produced a song called "Cop Killer."

But there's nothing really new about all of this. Ice-T and the headbangers and the gangstas went from the magazine covers to the annals of rock and roll history pretty fast, seeming quaint just these few years later. If modern music was simply making people happy, it wouldn't be rock and roll.

Rock and roll's importance goes beyond radio playlists and album sales because it established itself in American culture as a forum for anger and rebellion. And that's one of the reasons it's in college classrooms as the subject of legitimate study.

I teach rock and roll history and defend my job with a straight face. Rock and Roll History is nothing less than a far-ranging cultural history of America. The course exists for a good reason: more than any other form of popular music, rock and roll has embraced social commentary. It has real historic value. From the start, the music made statements about culture. Its very sound—the raucous, anarchistic guitar, the pounding drums, the pulsing, subversive bass—was a protest against the smoother tones of mainstream popular music.

Elvis Presley isn't thought of as a "political" artist, but his first single was a Statement because it combined the music of black America with the music of white America. Radio was segregated in 1954, but when Sun Records released that single, Elvis's reinterpretation of rhythm and blues led listeners to the original sources. Those liberating radio waves didn't recognize whether listeners were black or white. The air did not honor Jim Crow laws.

These musical walls began tumbling down the same year that the

Supreme Court outlawed classroom segregation in *Brown v. the Board of Education.* The next year, when Martin Luther King, Jr., began organizing the Montgomery bus boycott, rock and roll saw its first major performing songwriter, Chuck Berry, trying to consciously knock down racial barriers. Using a narrative style that borrowed a lot from country and western music—and combining that with a love of the blues—Berry created a distinctive syllable-crammed style with songs about experiences he knew both black and white kids shared. Berry's songs were about things rarely considered fodder for pop songs: divorce from the kid's-eye view ("Memphis"), unappreciated Army veterans ("Too Much Monkey Business"), and statements of black pride ("Brown-Eyed Handsome Man"). Berry wanted to entertain, but like a lot of rock and rollers to follow, there was a message in those chords.

Whenever there's talk of rock and roll's social consciousness, it often centers on Bob Dylan, who did not begin recording until the 1960s. Yet before Dylan came along, the songs of Chuck Berry and Eddie Cochran made statements about teenage angst. In "Summertime Blues," Cochran played both kid and tormenting adult (lowering his voice an octave) in this famous passage in which a congressman brushes off a kid's appeal for help:

> "I'd like to help you son
> but you're too young to vote."

So Dylan did not invent social commentary in popular music. It's just that rock and roll embraced the idea more than any other strain of music except folk, and after Dylan came along in the early 1960s, things were never the same in rock and roll. Dylan knocked down walls between folk and rock and upped the ante for songwriters.

But Dylan and other performers of the mid-1960s had an advantage over artists here, at the turn of the century. They had an audience. Back then, radio was not as segmented as today, and listeners could hear rock and roll and soul and pop on the same station, one song right after the other. The Beatles followed by James Brown followed by Bob Dylan followed by Smokey Robinson followed by Frank Sinatra. Today, radio is so format-split that it's a lot like the pre–rock and roll era of radio segregation.

In the 1960s, Dylan used music to chronicle two social movements.

His finger-pointing songs about racial injustice were sung at scores of civil rights rallies, and his anti-war ballads were the soundtrack for the get-us-out-of-Vietnam campus demonstrations (oddly, though, Dylan didn't use the word "Vietnam" in a lyric until 1985).

In the 1970s, the frightening and rebellious music of the Sex Pistols and the other punk bands was another wave of insurrection—this time, in part, against rock music that had become too corporate. Johnny Rotten and his band raged against the fat, happy rock stars who had once symbolized youth and swagger, but who then committed the sin of aging. Now Johnny and his gang are pot-bellied middle-agers.

In the 1980s and the 1990s, we again heard rock as an expression of anger aimed at our social conditions. The music asked whose cultural values were at stake. Rappers inspired the same outrage that got Chuck Berry in so much trouble back in the 1950s. (Berry was persecuted by the white establishment and did two years in prison.) Forty years later, rappers brought ghetto anger into white homes.

That means rock and roll is still on the job, working for you. If the music isn't making people mad, it isn't rock and roll. At least once a decade, rock and roll eats itself, and that process of reinvention is one of the things that makes it so much fun.

This book is not a definitive history of rock and roll. I doubt that such a thing could be done and make any real sense. To do a book like that, you'd need a shovel, not an editor.

What I have included is testimony from some of the creators of rock and roll, some serious historical research, some brilliant criticism, and a few artifacts. There are greatest hits (Jules Siegel's tracking of Brian Wilson), some historical accounts (Peter Guralnick's meticulous recreation of Elvis in mid-1950s Memphis, Alan Lomax's memoir of song-hunting in the Deep South), some rock and roll reminiscences (Chuck Berry, Patti Smith) and some essays by great critics (Dave Marsh, Greil Marcus, Lester Bangs).

I recognize that not all of the great artists are discussed in detail. Alas, we had to leave out that killer profile of Lothar & the Hand People. I wish that all the great rock and rollers could have been mentioned in this book. My guide in selecting the pieces was to walk the line between what was good history and what was good writing. And there had to be significant amounts of fun.

Rock and roll has always been about attitude. This book also has an attitude. The selections were made with an attempt to cover most of the significant developments in rock and roll, but beyond that general plan, I offer no guarantees. The music has inspired dogma, devotion, and doctrine. These pieces reflect that. One of the great pleasures of rock and roll has been reading all of the superb writing the music has inspired. I may question some of the writers' judgments, but there is no doubt about their passion.

ACKNOWLEDGMENTS

THERE ARE a lot of people to thank. My children, Sarah, Graham, and Mary, spent good bits of their summer vacations helping me copy, organize, and fret, all the while stoking the CD player with the tunes that made this book so worthwhile.

I want to thank the honors program at the University of Florida. When I sent in my proposal to revise a media survey course into a rock and roll history course, I got a note to call the honors director. I expected some *are-you-nuts* talk and instead got this. Him: "So you want to teach rock and roll history, huh?" Me: "Yeah." Him: "Cool."

There are a lot of other people at the University of Florida to thank, including my colleagues David Chalmers, John Griffith, and Jon Roosenraad. I also want to thank some of my rock and roll history students who pitched in to help: Rebecca Brauner, Jared Flamm, Paul Ghiotto, Brad Jones, Emily Mendez, Jeff Parker, Paul Ryan, Erin Stoy, and Matt Thompson. My invaluable friend Steve Webb interrupted work on his thesis (a study of Brian Wilson during the *Pet Sounds* era, of course) to track down a couple of hard-to-find articles.

This book exists because of my agent and friend, David Hendin. I owe him so much.

I want to acknowledge the friendship, genius, and long-distance wisdom of Norton editors Amy Cherry and Gerald Howard. Nomi Victor, also of Norton, endured a year with the stuffings of this book spread over her office floor. That some order came out of this chaos is mostly due to Amy and Nomi. Margaret Farley diligently edited the manuscript, and two designers made it so appealing: Dana Sloan (book) and John Gall (jacket).

I want to thank my parents for always being so encouraging and tolerant—especially of the loud music they endured coming from my bedroom when I was in high school.

And thanks to the brilliant and beautiful Kelley Benham, for so many things.

William McKeen

Peter Guralnick

INTRODUCTION: FALLING INTO PLACE

I COULD act as if I don't really know how it happened, but it wouldn't be true. I know exactly how I got to this place, whether for good or for ill, and I can't pretend otherwise.

I wanted to be a writer. Not a rock writer—there was no such thing. I wanted to write novels and stories. And so I did—and occasionally still do. When I was fifteen, I first read the *Paris Review* interview with Ernest Hemingway in which he spoke of his working methods, and I took note of the fact that he set himself a quota of at least 500 words a day. With as much self-doubt as confidence, I did the same, committing myself to the idea that should inspiration ever deign to visit I was not going to be absent from my post. And so I began a daily vigil that has persisted more or less over the last forty years.

When I was around fifteen, too, I fell in love with the blues: Lightnin' Hopkins and Big Bill Broonzy, Leadbelly and Muddy Waters, Howlin' Wolf and Blind Willie McTell. I lived it, breathed it, absorbed it by osmosis, fantasized it—don't ask me why. It was like the writing of Italo Svevo or Henry Green: it just turned me around in a way that I am no more inclined to quantify or explain today than I was then. But I never dreamt of writing about it. There was nowhere to write about it *in*. And besides, I'm not sure I could have imagined a way in which to truly evoke just what I was feeling at the time. *Experience, don't analyze,* my inner voice whispered. Though that didn't stop my friend Bob and me from studying liner notes, poring over the one book we knew on the subject, Sam Charters' *The Country Blues,* and talking about the blues—*all the time.* It was almost as if by the time we saw our first bluesman, Lightnin' Hopkins, live and in person in the spring of 1961, we had created a virtual world that ignored the complexities of the real one. All of a sudden we were forced to adjust to the idea that there were actual people who made the music, subject to neither our preconceptions nor our fantasies and, of course, far more interesting than either.

I won't bore you with all the mundane details of my awakening to that music and that world. Everyone has a similar story. Suffice it to say that I almost literally held my breath every time I went to see Muddy Waters, Big Joe Williams, Sleepy John Estes, Chuck Berry, Bo Diddley, and Mississippi John Hurt in those days, for fear that all of this beauty, all of this wit, all of this gloriously undifferentiated reality might somehow disappear as suddenly as it had first manifested itself in my life.

I was perfectly happy as a mere acolyte, expanding my world to the soul and gospel shows that came through town, when a series of related events conspired to rob me of my innocence. First I stumbled upon the English blues magazines *Blues Unlimited* and *Blues World* in 1964 and 1965. I started writing to the editors of both and, inspired by the recognition that there were others out there like me, began to file reports on the shows I was going to see. It was this sense of a larger community, as hungry as I for insights and information, that led me to approach the great Mississippi bluesman Skip James in the summer of 1965. There could have been no more unlikely interviewer than I, and certainly no one burdened with a greater degree of self-consciousness, but I had witnessed Skip's astonishing performance at Newport the previous summer, just after his rediscovery in a Tunica, Mississippi, hospital, and his even more astonishing reclamation of the weird, almost unearthly sound that characterized his remote 1931 recordings. So I presented myself as best I could, asked questions at whose obviousness I winced even as they were being greeted with a kind of courtly gravity by the person to whom they were addressed, and persisted in this exercise in self-abasement because, I told myself, greatness such as this would not pass my way again.

That was my entire motivation. I wanted to tell the world something of the inimitable nature of Skip James' music, I wanted to proclaim Muddy Waters' and Bo Diddley's genius, I wanted to find some way to describe the transcendent drama of the rhythm and blues revues that I had witnessed, featuring astonishing performances by such virtuosic entertainers as Solomon Burke, Otis Redding, Joe Tex, Jackie Wilson, sometimes on the same bill. When in 1966 an underground music press began to emerge, first with the appearance of *Crawdaddy! The Magazine of Rock 'n' Roll*, Paul Williams' utopian embrace of the revolution, then, in the same year, with the arrival of *Boston After Dark,* "Boston's Only Complete Entertainment Weekly," and finally, in 1967, with *Rolling Stone,* my course was set. In each case someone at the paper knew of my love for the blues (and who within the sound of my voice could *fail* to be aware of it?) and asked if I would like to write about the music. I never saw it as a life decision (I had no intention of abandoning my novels and short stories), but I never hesitated either. How could I refuse the opportunity to tell people about this music that I thought was so great? How could I turn down the chance simply to put some of those names down on paper?

Muddy Waters, Howlin' Wolf, James Brown, Solomon Burke, Robert Pete Williams, Jerry Lee Lewis, Bo Diddley, Elvis Presley, Chuck Berry, and Buddy Guy—these were among the first stories I wrote, some of them no longer than 150 to 200 words. They were intended to *sell,* not a product but an unarticulated belief, a belief in the intrinsic worth of American vernacular culture. Even writing these names down today evokes some of the same secret thrill, but it could never fully suggest the tenor of a time when merely to name was to validate, when so much of this music was not simply ignored but reviled in the mainstream press. To be able to write in my perfectly serious, if not altogether unself-conscious way, of James Brown's "brilliant sense of theatrics," his "genius for showmanship," and the "passionate conviction" with which he transformed his show into something like a religious ritual, to proclaim Solomon Burke an artist "whose every song seems to [possess] the underlying conviction that somehow or other by his investment of emotion he might alter the world's course," to describe Muddy Waters as the creator of a seminal style whose songs were our contemporary classics, to speak of the "existential acts" with which Elvis "helped to liberate a generation"—these were my own intentional acts of subversion, by which I was clearly attempting to undermine ingrained cultural prejudices and, no doubt, declare my own.

The more I wrote, of course, the more I found the need to seek out a vocabulary that could suggest something of the experience that I found so compelling. Writing about music is, as more than one dismissive wag has pointed out, a little like dancing about architecture, and for someone almost entirely lacking in musical training or knowledge, it is even more so. What I was trying to capture, though, I realized from the start, was the *feeling,* not the technique. I was not trying to provide deconstructive analysis of the swoops and glissandos that went into the first few bars of Aretha Franklin's "I Never Loved a Man (The Way I Loved You)" any more than I would have attempted to break down the sentence structure of Henry Green's *Pack My Bag*; what I was interested in was exhortatory writing,

writing that would bring the reader to the same appreciation of Muddy Waters, Skip James, and Charlie Rich that I felt, that would in a sense mimic the same emotions not just that I experienced but that I believed the musician put into the music in the first place. Just how ambivalent I was about this whole enterprise can be gleaned from the opening paragraph of the epilogue to my first book. "I consider this chapter a swan song," I wrote in 1971, "not only to the book but to my whole brief critical career. Next time you see me I hope I will be my younger, less self-conscious and critical self. It would be nice to just sit back and listen to the music again without a notebook always poised or the next interviewing question always in the back of your mind."

Well, perhaps it's unnecessary to admit but, save for a brief interlude, that never really happened. After writing another novel, two years later I was back, lured by the siren song of Bobby "Blue" Bland and Waylon Jennings. My moment of abject self-recognition in fact came while I was writing the Bobby "Blue" Bland story, spending my time shuttling back and forth between teaching Classics at Boston University and hanging out at the somewhat seedy soul club downtown where Bobby was playing a weeklong engagement. My teaching job was running out, and I thought I'd better look for a new one, so I arranged for an interview at a nearby prep school, where I met with the head of the English department and talked about some of my favorite books, like *Tristram Shandy* and Thomas Pynchon's *V.* That night Bobby's bandleader, Mel Jackson, called a horn rehearsal for after the show, and I sat around for an hour or two as the lights were turned up, the club emptied out, and all of its tawdry glitter was unmasked. Finally it became obvious that the rehearsal was never going to happen. Bobby had gone back to the hotel, the horn players had drifted off to various unspecified assignations, and in the end Mel Jackson just shrugged and walked up the stairs to the deserted street.

I was exhausted and, I suppose, frustrated, too. But I realized in that moment that I would rather sit around in this club watching all the transactions that were taking place and waiting for an event that was not going to occur than spend a lifetime teaching English in a muted, well-bred academic setting. And so my fate was sealed. It involved an admission I had never wanted to make: that I was drawn not just to the music but to the life. I had discovered what Murray Kempton called the lure of "going around." That was twenty-five years ago, and since then I have never really tried to escape.

I don't mean to suggest in any way that my experience has been without pitfalls or regrets—but it has been enormous fun. To meet and write about my heroes, figures as diverse as Merle Haggard and Sam Phillips, Ray Charles and Big Joe Turner, Doc Pomus and Charlie Rich, has been as exciting an adventure as anything I could ever have imagined as a kid, except maybe playing big-league baseball. As far as the pitfalls go, they are, I suppose, just the pitfalls of life: as soon as you start out doing *something*, you can no longer do everything. As soon as you set words down on paper (the moment in fact you embark upon any kind of real-life adventure), you have to let go of the dream of perfection, you are forced inevitably to make do with reality.

The reality that anyone who writes about music (or film, or literature) has to make do with is: how do you sustain enthusiasm, how do you avoid repetition, how do you keep from tangling up in the web of your own words and ideas? Maybe that's the dilemma of writing in general—or just of life. I know that early on I stumbled upon a strategy that seemed to accommodate both my strengths and weaknesses. I started writing about people primarily, presenting the music within the context of their background, their aspirations, their cultural traditions. That helped solve a number of problems. It allowed me to seek a colloquial language suited to each subject and better suited, I thought, to the subject as a whole than generational enthusiasm (the "groovy/far out/awesome" syndrome) or academic pretension. It allowed me, in other words, to *reflect* the music without trying to dissect it, something for which I was neither prepared nor in which I believed. It also gave me a fresh path to pursue every time I started a new project, since each artist stakes out his own territory, every artist has his or her own story to tell, no matter how it may connect with a common tradition or fuse in certain elemental ways with that of others. But the pursuit of endless byways can carry with it its own price, as any writer, as anyone who appreciates the digressive and the strange, inevitably finds. You listen to music for a living, and you no longer hear with the ears of the teenager who once discovered it. You pursue your curiosity, and it tends to carry you further and further afield, until the question arises: how do you get back to the place you once were? How do you rekindle that simple enthusiasm for the music, the ardor I sought to describe in that same 1971 epilogue to my first book as "an emotional experience which I could not deny. It expressed for me a sense of sharp release and a feeling of almost savage joy."

The short answer is that you can't—at least not without assuming a kind of disingenuousness as embarrassing as any other transparent attempt at the denial of age or experience. But in another sense, who knows what disingenuousness I was capable of even at fifteen when I first discovered the music or at twenty-seven when I wrote those words? I'm not convinced we are ever wholly ingenuous. But whether we are or not, what other hope is there except in surrender, whatever indignities surrender may entail? So in the end that is my advice: surrender to the music. That is what I imagine the message of much of this book must be. Surrender to Muddy Waters. Surrender to Solomon Burke. Surrender to Jimi Hendrix and Bob Dylan and the Rolling Stones. We are all just looking to get lost.

1. DEFINITION OF TERMS

**"What we talk about
when we talk about rock and roll."**

A collector feels kinship with a man he's never met
and declines to decimate the man's record library
when a scorned wife offers it up cheap. Another
man, seeking to define himself, says that as a rock
and roll singer, his job is to ask questions and not
wait around for answers. Entranced at a rave, a man
wonders if it's the woman or the hypnotic music he
loves most.

Rock and roll is all of these things and more,
defined in lots of ways, in lots of voices, sometimes in
wordless cries, sometimes only in rhythm, relentless
and eloquent.

Life is a succession of epiphanies. For teenage
Bobby Zimmerman, one came the first time he heard
Elvis' voice. "I just knew that I wasn't going to work
for anybody; nobody was going to be my boss," said
the man who became Bob Dylan. "Hearing him the
first time was like busting out of jail."

We offer no standard rock and roll definition, but
the jailbreak analogy works for us. Here are some
other noble efforts.

Bob Dylan

BRINGING IT ALL BACK HOME

Think of this as a job description for being Bob Dylan. He
wrote this prose poem as the album notes for *Bringing It
All Back Home,* the first of his mid-1960s rock and roll
masterpieces (the others being, of course, *Highway 61
Revisited* and *Blonde on Blonde*). To that point, record jackets
had been mere advertisements, with song titles freckling the
cover and album notes the province of record-company
flacks. Dylan was among the first artists to lay claim to the
whole package, and this piece stands as perhaps his best
non-song-lyric writing.

I'M STANDING there watching the parade/feeling combination of sleepy
john estes. jayne mansfield. humphrey bogart/mortimer snurd. murph the
surf and so forth/erotic hitchhiker wearing japanese blanket. gets my attention by asking didn't he see me at this hootenanny down in puerto val-
larta, mexico/i say no you must be mistaken. i happen to be one of the
Supremes/then he rips off his blanket an suddenly becomes a middle-
aged druggist. up for district attorney. He starts screaming at me you're the
one. you're the one that's been causing all them riots over in vietnam. immediately turns t a bunch of people an says if elected, he'll have me electrocuted publicly on the next fourth of july. i look around an all these
people he's talking to are carrying blowtorches/needless t say, i split fast
go back t the nice quiet country. am standing there writing WHAAAT? on
my favorite wall when who should pass by in a jet plane but my recording engineer "i'm here t pick up you and your latest works of art. do you
need any help with anything?"

(pause)

my songs're written with the kettledrum in mind/a touch of any anxious color. unmentionable. obvious. an people perhaps like a soft brazil-
ian singer . . . i have given up at making any attempt at perfection/the fact
that the white house is filled with leaders that've never been t the apollo
theater amazes me. why allen ginsberg was not chosen t read poetry at

the inauguration boggles my mind/if someone thinks norman mailer is more important than hank williams, that's fine. i have no arguments an i never drink milk. i would rather model harmonica holders than discuss aztec anthropology/english literature. or history of the united nations. i accept chaos. i am not sure whether it accepts me. i know there're some people terrified of the bomb. but there are other people terrified t be seen carrying a modern screen magazine. experience teaches that silence terrifies people the most . . . i am convinced that all souls have some superior t deal with/like the school system, an invisible circle of which no one can think without consulting someone/in the face of this, responsibility/security. success mean absolutely nothing . . . i would not want t be bach. mozart. tolstoy. joe hill. gertrude stein or james dean/they are all dead. the Great books've been written. the Great sayings have all been said/I am about t sketch You a picture of what goes on around here sometimes. tho I don't understand too well myself what's really happening. i do know that we're all gonna die someday an that no death has ever stopped the world. my poems are written in a rhythm of unpoetic distortion/divided by pierced ears. false eyelashes/subtracted by people constantly torturing each other. with a melodic purring line of descriptive hollowness—seen at times thru dark sunglasses an other forms of psychic explosion. a song is anything that can walk by itself/i am called a songwriter. a poem is a naked person. . . . some people say that i am a poet.

(end of pause)

an so i answer my recording engineer "yes. well i could use some help in getting this wall in the plane."

Irvine Welsh

IN ME AROUND ME AND EVERYWHERE

This excerpt from Welsh's novel *Ecstasy* briefly takes us into the mind of a raver, and back out again, but not without a few cuts and scrapes and maybe a slight headache.

AH AM FUCKIN well fed up because there's nothing happening and ah've probably done a paracetamol but fuck it you need to have positive vibes and wee Amber, she's rubbing away at the back ay ma neck saying it'll happen when this operatic slab of syth seems to be 3D and ah realise that I'm coming up in a big way as that invisible hand grabs a hud ay me and sticks me onto the roof because the music is in me around me and everywhere, it's just leaking from my body, this is the game this is the game and ah look around and we're all going phoah and our eyes are just big black pools of love and energy and my guts are doing a big turn as the quease zooms through my body and we're up to the floor one by one and ah think I'm going tae need tae shit but ah hold on and it passes and I'm riding this rocket to Russia . . .

—No bad gear, eh, ah say tae Amber, as we dance ourselves slowly into it.

—Aye, sound.

—Awright, eh, says Ally.

Then it's ma main man on the decks, and he's on the form tonight, just pulling away at our collective psychic sex organs as they lay splayed out before us and ah get a big rosy smile off this goddess in a Lycra top, who, with her tanned skin and veneer of sweat, looks as enticing as a bottle of Becks from the cold shelf on a hot, muggy day, and my heart just goes bong bong bong Lloyd Buist reporting for duty, and the dance NRG the dance U4E ahhhh gets a hud ay me and I'm doing a sexy wee shuffle with Ally and Amber and Hazel and this big bone-heided cunt falls into me and gives me a hug and apologies and I'm slapping his hard wall of a stomach and thanking my lucky stars we're E'd and at this club and not pished at The Edge or somewhere brain-dead no that ah would touch that fuckin rubbish . . . whoa rockets . . . whoa it's still coming and I'm think-ing *now* is the time to fall in love now now now but not with the world with that one special *her,* just do it, just do it now, just change your whole fuckin life in the space of a heartbeat, do it *now* . . . but nah . . . this is just entertainment . . .

Pete Townshend

MEATY, BEATY, BIG AND BOUNCY

Quick! Rock and roll's most literate guitarist?

That's right, Pete Townshend. Townshend has always spoken forthrightly and sometimes even eloquently, about the passion and the mission of rock and roll. Townshend took rock and roll to the precipice of high art, with his rock operas *Tommy* and *Quadrophenia*. It's not that other rock and roll guitarists couldn't do that, but they haven't. Townshend was his outspoken self in a series of late-1960s interviews with the rock press and in this career retrospective, which was disguised as a review of an anthology by his band, the Who.

ON LISTENING to this album, it's very easy to imagine that the whole Who world has been made up of singles. Where Tommy and his lengthy and finally expatriated self come in, it's hard to say. Probably nearer the time of the second album, *A Quick One,* or *Happy Jack,* as it was called in the States. Before we even approached the idea of making an album that was an expression of our own feelings, or in the case of *Happy Jack,* an album expression of our own insanity, we believed only in singles. In the Top 10 records and pirate radio. We, I repeat, believed only in singles.

In England albums were what you got for Christmas, singles were what you bought for prestige. It was the whole re-creation of the local dancehall-cum-discotheque in your own sweet front room. You had to have the regulation tin speaker record-player, tin, not twin, housed artistically in a vinyl-covered box under a lid with a two-watt amplifier worthy only of use as a baby alarm, and a record deck on which the current Top 20 singles could be stacked twelve or fifteen high for continuous dancing of the latest dance—which differed only from last week's in the tiniest possible hip-waggling details. A long sentence, but a single sentence. One sentence and you have the truth about singles. We made them tinny to sound tinny. If you made them hi fi to sound tinny you were wasting your time, after all.

Shel Talmy, who produced our first three singles, was a great believer in "making groups who are nothing, stars." He was also a great believer in pretending the group didn't exist when they were in a recording studio. Despite the fact that I go on to say that our first few records are among our best, they were the least fun to make. We only found out recording was fun when we made "Happy Jack" and the ensuing album with our latter-day producer Kit Lambert. However, dear Shel got us our first single hits. So he was as close to being God for a week as any other unworthy soul has been. Of course it was a short week; I quickly realized that it was really the brilliant untapped writing talent of our lead guitarist, needless to say myself, that held the key to our success. Talmy and all following claimers to Who history are imposters.

As you can see, I feel pretty good about my own contributions to this, the greatest of Who albums. John Entwistle's contribution should have been a single too, that's why it's here. Without a hint of guilt I shout aloud that singles just could be what life is all about. What rock is all about. What the Spiritual Path is all about! Ask Kit Lambert about shortening a song two hours long with 24 verses, 6 choruses and 12 over-dubbed guitar solos down to two minutes fifty or preferably shorter. Ask him how he did it without offending the composer. Deceit. Lies. Cheating! That's what rock is all about.

It really is the most incredible thing that after two years of brain-washing himself into being a producer of singles for Top 10 radio play, Kit Lambert actually turned his brain inside out and came up with Rock Opera. Enigmatic paradox. But good thinking for a group who stopped getting hits. Listen to "Magic Bus" and "I Can See For Miles" and tell me why those cuts weren't hits. Tell me why *Tommy* was. Kit Lambert knows some of the answers, and perhaps because this album covers not only a huge chunk of our English success record-wise, but also our evolving relationship with Kit as our producer, it is, in my opinion (doubly prejudiced, and tainted by possible unearned royalties helping to pay for the tactical nuclear missile I am saving up for) the best collection of singles by the Who there is.

It's all our singles, and it includes all our earliest stuff, excluding "I'm The Face" which might be released soon on the Stones label. "I'm The Face" was our very first record on an English label called Phillips. It was "written" by our then-manager Pete Meadon, fashioner of our mod image. He pinched the tune of "Got Love If You Want It" by Slim Harpo and changed the words to fit the groovy group. That is another, even earlier story, which if ever told, would banish the Who mystique forever.

"Can't Explain," more than any other track here, turns me on. We still play this on stage, at the moment we open with it. It can't be beat for straightforward Kinks copying. There is little to say about how I wrote this. It came out of the top of my head when I was eighteen and a half. It seems to be about the frustrations of a young person who is so incoherent and uneducated that he can't state his case to the bourgeois intellectual blah blah blah. Or, of course, it might be about drugs.

"Anyway, Anyhow, Anywhere," our second record, was written mainly by myself, but those were political days in late '64. Or was it '65? Roger helped a lot with the final arrangement and got half the credit. Something he does today for nothing, bless him. I was lying on my mattress on the floor listening to a Charlie Parker record when I thought up the title (it's usually title first with me). I just felt the guy was so free when he was playing. He was a soul without a body, riding, flying, on music. Listening to the compulsory Dizzy Gillespie solo after one by Bird was always a come-down, however clever Gillespie was. No one could follow Bird. Hendrix must have been his reincarnation especially for guitar players. The freedom suggested by the title became restricted by the aggression of our tightly defined image when I came to write the words. In fact, Roger was really a hard nut then, and he changed quite a few words himself to roughen the song up to suit his temperament. It is the most excitingly pigheaded of our songs. It's blatant, proud and—dare I say it—sassy.

Musically it was a step forward. On "Can't Explain" we had been fully manipulated in the studio, the like of which hasn't been seen since (aside from my dastardly treatment of Thunderclap Newman). Jimmy Page played rhythm on the A side and lead on the B, "Bald Headed Woman." He nearly played lead on the A, but it was so simple even I could play it. The Beverly Sisters were brought in to sing backing voices and Keith has done poor imitations on stage ever since. "Can't Explaaaain," he screams, hurling drumsticks at the sound man who turns the mike off because he thinks it's feeding back.

"Anyway" was the first time we encountered the piano playing of Nicky Hopkins, who is a total genius, and likes the Who. He likes John Lennon too and a lot of other people who give him work. A lot of bands breathed a sigh of relief when he and his missus showed their weary cheery faces in England again this summer. We did, and so on. He's still working.

Kit Lambert described "Anyway, Anyhow, Anywhere" to reporters as, "A pop art record, containing pop art music. The sounds of war and chaos and frustration expressed musically without the use of sound effects." A bored and then cynical Nik Cohn—Christ, he was even more cynical than me—said calmly, "That's impressionism, not pop art." I repeated what Kit had briefed me to say, mumbling something about Peter Blake and Lichtenstein and went red. Completely out of order while your record is screaming in the background: "I can go anyway, way I choose. . . . "

Then we released "My Generation." The hymn. The patriotic song they sing at Who football matches. I could say a lot about this, I suppose I should say what hasn't been said, but a lot of what has been said is so hilarious. I wrote it as a throwaway naturally. It was a talking blues thing of the "Talking New York" ilk. This one had come from a crop of songs which I was, by then writing using a tape recorder. Kit Lambert had bought me two good-quality tape decks and suggested I do this; it appealed to me as I had always attempted it using lesser machines and been encouraged by results. But when you sit down and think what to play, it's a little hard. The whole point is that blues patterns, the ones groups use to jam with one another, are somehow the only thing forthcoming when you are gazing at a dial and thinking mainly of how good it's going to be to play this to Beryl and proudly say, "I played all the instruments on this myself." All the instruments being guitar, guitar, bass guitar and maracas.

Anyway, ensconced in my Belgravia two-room tape recorder and hi-fi showroom, I proceeded to enjoy myself writing ditties with which I could later amuse myself, over-dubbing, multi-tracking and adding extra parts. It was the way I practised. I leave to play with myself. Masturbation comes to mind and as a concept making demos is not far off. "Generation" was then praised by Chris Stamp, our "other" manager, who was worshipped only as a source of money from his ever-active roles as assistant director in various film epics. He was convinced it could be the biggest Who record yet. Bearing in mind the state of the demo it shows an astuteness beyond the call. It sounded like (I still, of course, have it) Jimmy Reed at ten years old suffering from nervous indigestion.

Kit made suggestion after suggestion to improve the song. He later said that it was because he was unsure of it. I went on to make two more demos in my den of magnetic iniquity, the first introduced the stutter. The second several key changes, pinched, again, from the Kinks. From then on we knew we had it. I even caught a real stutter which I only lost recently.

Over the period of rewriting I realized that spontaneous words that come out of the top of your head are always the best. I had written the lines of "Generation" without thinking, hurrying them, scribbling on a piece of paper in the back of a car. For years I've had to live by them, waiting for the day someone says, "I thought you said you hope you'd die when you got old in that song. Well, you are old. What now?" Of course, most people are too polite to say that sort of thing to a dying pop star. I say it often to myself. The hypocrisy of accusing hypocrites of being hypocritical is highly hypocritical. See the new Lennon album. See "My Generation."

It's understandable to me, perhaps not to you, that I can only think of inconsequentially detrimental things to say about the emergence of lyrics from my various bodily orifices. "Substitute," for example, was written as a spoof on "Nineteenth Nervous Breakdown." On the demo I sang with an affected Jagger-like accent which Kit obviously liked, as he suggested the song as a follow-up to "My Generation." The lyric has come to be the most quoted Who lyric ever. It somehow goes to show that the "trust the art, not the artist" tag that people put on Dylan's silence about his work could be a good idea. To me, "Mighty Quinn" is about the five Perfect Masters of the age, the best of all being Meher Baba of course, to Dylan it's probably about gardening, or the joys of placing dog shit in the garbage to foul up Alan J. Weberman. "Substitute" makes me recall writing a song to fit a clever and rhythmic-sounding title. A play on words. Again it could mean a lot more to me now than it did when I wrote it. If I told you what it meant to me now, you'd think I take myself too seriously.

The stock, down-beat riff used in the verses, I pinched from a record played to me in "Blind Date," a feature in *Melody Maker*. It was by a group who later wrote to thank me for saying nice things about their record in the feature. The article is set up so that pop stars hear other people's records without knowing who they are by. They say terrible things about their best mates' latest and it all makes the pop scene even snottier and more competitive. Great. The record I said nice things about wasn't a hit, despite an electrifying riff. I pinched it, we did it, you bought it.

"The Kids Are Alright" wasn't a single in England; it was in the States. Funnily enough, this broke really well in Detroit, an area where both Decca Records and the local community were a little more hip to the Who than they were elsewhere. Detroit, or at least Ann Arbor, was the first place in the States we played after New York.

There are a few cuts on this album that are good because they are as simple as nursery rhymes. "Legal Matter," for example, is about a guy on the run from a chick about to pin him down for breach of promise. What this song was screaming from behind lines like, "It's a legal matter baby, marrying's no fun . . . ," was "I'm lonely, I'm hungry, and the bed needs making." I wanted a maid I suppose. It's terrible feeling like an eligible bachelor but with no woman seeming to agree with you. "Pinball Wizard" is, quite simply, quite pimply, from *Tommy*. It's my favourite song on the album and was actually written as a ploy to get Nik Cohn, who is an avid pinball player, to be a little more receptive to my plans for a Rock Opera. Nik writes on and off for *The New York Times*. I know which side my Aronowitz is buttered, mate!

From the superb production of "Pinball" it is hard to imagine that anything produced by Kit Lambert with the Who before "Pinball" could stand up. There are two songs that do. "Pictures of Lily" just jells perfectly somehow. Merely a ditty about masturbation and the importance of it to a young man, I was really digging at my folks who, when catching me at it, would talk in loud voices in the corridor outside my room, "Why can't he go with girls like other boys." The real production masterpiece in the Who/Lambert coalition was, of course, "I Can See For Miles." The version here is not the mono, which is a pity because the mono makes the stereo sound like the Carpenters. We cut the tracks in London at CBS studios and brought the tapes to Gold Star studios in Hollywood to mix and master them. Gold Star have the nicest sounding echo in the world. And there is just a *little* of that on the mono. Plus, a touch of home-made compression in Gold Star's cutting-room. I swoon when I hear the sound. The words, which ageing senators have called "Drug Orientated," are about a jealous man with exceptionally good eyesight. Honest.

Two of the tracks here are produced by the Who, not Kit Lambert. One is "Substitute." We made this straight after "Generation" and Kit wasn't really in a position to steam in and produce, that honour being set aside as a future bunce for Robert Stigwood, God forbid. A blond chap called Chris at Olympic studios got the sound, set up a kinky echo, did the mix etc. I looked on and have taken the credit whenever the opportunity has presented itself ever since. Keith can't even remember doing the session, incidentally, a clue to his condition around that period. The other Who-produced cut was "The Seeker." "The Seeker" is just one of those odd Who records. I suppose I like this least of all the stuff. It suffered from being the first thing we did after *Tommy*, and also from being recorded a few too many times. We did it once at my home studio, then at IBC where we normally worked, then with Kit Lambert producing. Then Kit had a tooth pulled, breaking his jaw, and we did it ourselves. The results are impressive. It sounded great in the mosquito-ridden swamp I made it up in—Florida at three in the morning drunk out of my brain with Tom Wright and John Wolf. But that's always where the trouble starts, in the swamp. The alligator turned into an elephant and finally stampeded itself to death on stages around England. I don't think we even got to play it in the States.

The only non-Townshend track on the album is also a non-single. Politics or my own shaky vanity might be the reason, but "Boris The Spider" was never released as a single and could have been a hit. It was the most requested song we ever played on stage, and if this really means anything to you guitar players, it was Hendrix's favourite Who song. Which rubbed me up well the wrong way, I can tell you. John introduced us to "Boris" in much the same way as I introduced us to our "Generation": through a tape recorder. We assembled in John's three feet by ten feet bedroom and listened incredulously as the strange and haunting chords emerged. Laced with words about the slightly gruesome death of a spider, the song had enough charm to send me back to my pad writing hits furiously. It was a winner, as Harry would say. It still is, for the life of me I don't know why we still don't play it, and the other Entwistle masterpiece "Heaven And Hell," on stage any more. There is no peace for the wicked, John's writing is wicked, his piece here is "Boris."

Of interest to collectors is "I'm A Boy." This is a longer and more relaxed version of the single which was edited and had fancy voices added. The song, of course, is about a boy whose mother dresses him up as a girl and won't let him enjoy all the normal boyish pranks like slitting lizards' tummies and throwing rocks at passing cars. Real Alice Cooper syndrome. Of course, Zappa said it all when he wrote his original Rock Opera. Nobody noticed, so he had to write a satire on the one Rock Opera people did notice. "I'm A Boy" was my first attempt at Rock Opera. Of course the subject matter was a little thin, then what of *Tommy?*

We get right down to the Who nitty-gritty with "Magic Bus." Decca Records really smarmed all over this one. Buses painted like Mickey Mouse's first trip. Album covers featuring an unsuspecting Who endorsing it like it was our idea. "Magic Bus" was a bummer. For one thing, we really like it. It was a gas to record and had a mystical quality to the sound. The first time ever I think that you could hear the room we were recording in when we made it. The words, however, are garbage, again loaded with heavy drug inference. For example, "thruppence and sixpence every way, trying to get to my baby." Obviously a hint at the ever-rising prices of LSD.

When I wrote "Magic Bus," LSD wasn't even invented as far as I knew. Drug songs and veiled references to drugs were not part of the Who image. If you were in the Who and took drugs, you said "I take drugs," and waited for the fuzz to come. We said it but they never came. We very soon got bored with the drugs. No publicity value. Buses, however! Just take another look at Decca's answer to an overdue *Tommy: The Who, Magic Bus, On Tour.* Great title, swinging presentation. Also a swindle as far as insinuating that the record was live. Bastards. They have lived to regret it, but not delete it. This record is what that record should have been. It's the Who at their early best. Merely nippers with big noses and small genitals trying to make the front page of the *Daily News.* Now Peter Max—there's a guy who knows how to use a bus! They pay him to ride on them.

To wind up, this album is a piece of history that we want you to know about. It's really a cross-section of our English successes, and when in the States, and we get compared to come-and-go heavies who, like everyone else, influence us a little, we get paranoid that a lot of American rock fans haven't heard this stuff. They might have heard us churn out a bit on the stage, but not the actual cuts. As groups, Cream, Hendrix and Zeppelin etc., have gotten bigger than the Who ever did and a lot quicker. But they don't have the solid foundation that we have in this album. This album is as much for us as for you, it reminds us who we really are. The Who.

Nick Hornby

There's a brotherhood in rock and roll and no matter how much Rob, rock and roll junkie and record shop owner, may want to violate the covenant, he still will not fall prey to temptation and betray his unknown brother in this excerpt from *High Fidelity*.

EXACTLY one week after Laura has gone, I get a call from a woman in Wood Green who has some singles she thinks I might be interested in. I normally don't bother with house clearance, but this woman seems to know what she's talking about: she mutters about white labels and picture sleeves and all sorts of other things that suggest we're not just talking about half a dozen scratched Electric Light Orchestra records that her son left behind when he moved out.

Her house is enormous, the sort of place that seems to have meandered to Wood Green from another part of London, and she's not very nice. She's mid-to-late forties, with a dodgy tan and a suspiciously taut-looking face; and though she's wearing jeans and a T-shirt, the jeans have the name of an Italian where the name of Mr. Wrangler or Mr. Levi should be, and the T-shirt has a lot of jewelry stuck to the front of it, arranged in the shape of a peace sign.

She doesn't smile, or offer me a cup of coffee, or ask me whether I found the place OK despite the freezing, driving rain that prevented me from seeing the street map in front of my face. She just shows me into a study off the hall, turns the light on, and points out the singles—there are hundreds of them, all in custom-made wooden boxes—on the top shelf, and leaves me to get on with it.

There are no books on the shelves that line the walls, just albums, CDs, cassettes, and hi-fi equipment; the cassettes have little numbered stickers on them, always a sign of a serious person. There are a couple of guitars leaning against the walls, and some sort of computer that looks as though it might be able to do something musical if you were that way inclined.

I climb up on a chair and start pulling the singles boxes down. There are seven or eight in all, and, though I try not to look at what's in them as I put them on the floor, I catch a glimpse of the first one in the last box: it's a James Brown single on King, thirty years old, and I begin to prickle with anticipation.

When I start going through them properly, I can see straightaway that it's the haul I've always dreamed of finding, ever since I began collecting records. There are fan-club-only Beatles singles, and the first half-dozen Who singles, and Elvis originals from the early sixties, and loads of rare blues and soul singles, and . . . *there's a copy of* "God Save the Queen" *by the Sex Pistols on A&M!* I have never even seen one of these! I have never even seen anyone who's seen one! And oh no oh no oh God—"You Left the Water Running" by Otis Redding, released seven years after his death, withdrawn immediately by his widow because she didn't . . .

"What d'you reckon?" She's leaning against the door frame, arms folded, half smiling at whatever ridiculous face I'm making.

"It's the best collection I've ever seen." I have no idea what to offer her. This lot must be worth at least six or seven grand, and she knows it. Where am I going to get that kind of money from?

"Give me fifty quid and you can take every one away with you today."

I look at her. We're now officially in Joke Fantasy Land, where little old ladies pay good money to persuade you to cart off their Chippendale furniture. Except I am not dealing with a little old lady, and she knows perfectly well that what she has here is worth a lot more than fifty quid. What's going on?

"Are these stolen?"

She laughs. "Wouldn't really be worth my while, would it, lugging all this lot through someone's window for fifty quid? No, they belong to my husband."

"And you're not getting on too well with him at the moment?"

"He's in Spain with a twenty-three-year-old. A friend of my daughter's. He had the *fucking* cheek to phone up and ask to borrow some money and I refused, so he asked me to sell his singles collection and send him a check for whatever I got, minus ten percent commission. Which reminds me. Can you make sure you give me a five pound note? I want to frame it and put it on the wall."

"They must have taken him a long time to get together."

"Years. This collection is as close as he has ever come to an achievement."

"Does he work?"

"He calls himself a musician, but . . ." She scowls her disbelief and contempt. "He just sponges off me and sits around on his fat arse staring at record labels."

Imagine coming home and finding your Elvis singles and your James Brown singles and your Chuck Berry singles flogged off for nothing out of sheer spite. What would you do? What would you say?

"Look, can't I pay you properly? You don't have to tell him what you got. You could send the forty-five quid anyway, and blow the rest. Or give it to charity. Or something."

"That wasn't part of the deal. I want to be poisonous but fair."

"I'm sorry, but it's just . . . I don't want any part of this."

"Suit yourself. There are plenty of others who will."

"Yeah, I know. That's why I'm trying to find a compromise. What about fifteen hundred? They're probably worth four times that."

"Sixty."

"Thirteen."

"Seventy-five."

"Eleven. That's my lowest offer."

"And I won't take a penny more than ninety." We're both smiling now. It's hard to imagine another set of circumstances that could result in this kind of negotiation.

"He could afford to come home then, you see, and that's the last thing I want."

"I'm sorry, but I think you'd better talk to someone else." When I get back to the shop I'm going to burst into tears and cry like a baby for a month, but I can't bring myself to do it to this guy.

"Fine."

I stand up to go, and then get back on my knees: I just want one last, lingering look.

"Can I buy this Otis Redding single off you?"

"Sure. Ten pee."

"Oh, come on. Let me give you a tenner for this, and you can give the rest away for all I care."

"OK. Because you took the trouble to come up here. And because you've got principles. But that's it. I'm not selling them to you one by one."

So I go to Wood Green and I come back with a mint-condition "You Left the Water Running," which I pick up for a tenner. That's not a bad morning's work. Barry and Dick will be impressed. But if they ever find out about Elvis and James Brown and Jerry Lee Lewis and the Pistols and the Beatles and the rest, they will suffer immediate and possibly dangerous traumatic shock, and I will have to counsel them, and . . .

How come I ended up siding with the bad guy, the man who's left his wife and taken himself off to Spain with some nymphette? Why can't I bring myself to feel whatever it is his wife is feeling? Maybe I should go home and flog Laura's sculpture to someone who wants to smash it to pieces and use it for scrap; maybe that would do me some good. But I know I won't. All I can see is that guy's face when he gets his pathetic check through the mail, and I can't help but feel desperately, painfully sorry for him.

Salman Rushdie

A WORLD WORTHY OF OUR YEARNING

Salman Rushdie, the new-lease-on-life poster boy, emerged from his years as an unwilling recluse (the Ayatollah had put out a contract on him, you will recall) and appeared center stage at a U2 concert tour. Rushdie wasn't just rocking out; he was doing research. When his novel _The Ground Beneath Her Feet_ was published, its heroine was a rock and roll star.

WHY DO WE care about singers? Wherein lies the power of songs? Maybe it derives from the sheer strangeness of there being singing in the world. The note, the scale, the chord; melodies, harmonies, arrangements; symphonies, ragas, Chinese operas, jazz, the blues: that such things should exist, that we should have discovered the magical intervals and distances that yield the poor cluster of notes, all within the span of a human hand, from which we can build our cathedrals of sound, is as alchemical a mystery as mathematics, or wine, or love. Maybe the birds taught us. Maybe not. Maybe we are just creatures in search of exaltation. We don't have much of it. Our lives are not what we deserve; they are, let us agree, in many painful ways deficient. Song turns them into something else. Song shows us a world that is worthy of our yearning, it shows us our selves as they might be, if we were worthy of the world.

Five mysteries hold the keys to the unseen: the act of love, and the birth of a baby, and the contemplation of great art, and being in the presence of death or disaster, and hearing the human voice lifted in song. These are the occasions when the bolts of the universe fly open and we are given a glimpse of what is hidden; an eff of the ineffable. Glory bursts upon us in such hours.

Levon Helm, Martin Scorsese, and Robbie Robertson
AND IF IT DANCES

Martin Scorsese documented the supposed last concert of the Band, at San Francisco's Winterland in 1976. (Turns out not all members of the Band wanted to retire, so the group returned to performing in the 1980s. But that's another story.) Interspersed with scenes of the all-star concert with the Band and friends Bob Dylan, Joni Mitchell, Ronnie Hawkins, Neil Young, the Staple Singers, Muddy Waters, and Neil Diamond (huh?), were interviews the filmmaker had done with members of the Band. The group was four-fifths Canadian, but the sole American, Levon Helm, was from the heartland, so he more than balanced out his four northern partners. In this interview, Scorsese nudges Helm toward a definition of rock and roll.

Levon Helm: [I'm from] near Memphis. Cotton country. Rice country. The most interesting thing is probably the music.

Martin Scorsese: Levon, who came from around there?

Levon Helm: Carl Perkins.

Martin Scorsese: Carl Perkins . . . sure.

Levon Helm: Muddy Waters. The king of country music.

Robbie Robertson: Elvis Presley. Johnny Cash. Bo Diddley.

Levon Helm: That's kind of the middle of the country right there. So bluegrass, or country music, if it comes down to that area it mixes there with rhythm, and, if it dances . . .

Martin Scorsese: Yeah?

Levon Helm: Then you've got a combination of all these different kinds of music—country, bluegrass, blues music.

Robbie Robertson: The melting pot.

Martin Scorsese: What's it called then?

Levon Helm (smiles): Rock and roll.

Martin Scorsese: Rock and roll. Yes. Exactly.

"Jerry Lee . . . beat the boogie so hard that there was nothing left of the hymn, nothing but the sounds of the Holy Ghost."

Just about all of American culture is hand-me-down, so rock and roll was built on earlier generations of musicians who never knew the big crowds, the limos, the all-areas passes, the backstage buffets. Some artists choose to honor these ancestors, others ignorantly absorb these influences without acknowledgment. Those who know the sources respect and enhance the original work by the pioneers. Rock and roll music has been around since Elvis was a baby immersed in the world of drool and stool; it just wasn't named.

Charlie Gillett

FROM THE INTRODUCTION TO *THE SOUND OF THE CITY*

**This is a brief bit from the beginning of Gillet's great history of
rock and roll. We'll hear more from him later in this section.**

> Calling out around the world,
> Are you ready for a brand new beat?
> —*Martha and the Vandellas*

The city's sounds are brutal and oppressive, imposing themselves on anyone who comes into its streets. Many of its residents, committed by their
jobs to live in the city, measure their freedom by the frequency and ac-
cessibility of departures from it.

But during the mid-fifties, in virtually every urban civilization in the
world, adolescents staked out their freedom in the cities, inspired and reassured by the rock'n'roll beat. Rock'n'roll was perhaps the first form of
popular culture to celebrate without reservation characteristics of city
life that had been among the most criticized. In rock'n'roll, the strident
repetitive sounds of city life were, in effect, reproduced as melody and
rhythm. . . .

With rock'n'roll, major corporations with every financial advantage
were out-maneuvered by independent companies and labels who brought
a new breed of artist into the pop mainstream—singers and musicians
who wrote or chose their own material, whose emotional and rhythmic
styles drew heavily from black gospel and blues music. The corporations
took more than ten years to recover their positions, through artists with
similar autonomy and styles.

Robert Johnson

ME AND THE DEVIL

Much of the vocabulary of rock and roll is found in such early recorded blues musicians as Johnson, who groomed his own legend as protégé of Satan. As the story went, Johnson met the devil at midnight at a crossroads and sold his soul in exchange for supernatural powers of the guitar. Johnson died young, in 1938, poisoned by a jealous husband. It was apparently a good career move but took a long time to pay off—his first gold record, *The Complete Recordings,* did not come until 1990.

Early this mornin'
    when you knocked upon my door
Early this mornin', ooh
    when you knocked upon my door
And I said, "Hello, Satan,
    I believe it's time to go."

Me and the Devil
    was walkin' side by side
Me and the Devil, ooh
    was walkin' side by side
And I'm goin' to beat my woman
    until I get satisfied

She say you don't see why
    that you will dog me 'round
      spoken: Now, babe, you know you ain't doin'
    me right, don'cha
She say you don't see why, ooh
    that you will dog me 'round
It must-a be that old evil spirit
    so deep down in the ground

You may bury my body
> down by the highway side
>> spoken: Baby, I don't care where you bury my
>> body when I'm dead and gone
You may bury my body, ooh
> down by the highway side
So my old evil spirit
> can catch a Greyhound bus and ride

THE LAND WHERE THE BLUES BEGAN

**The legendary Lomax family did American history a great
service with its field recordings for the Library of Congress.
Father John A. Lomax and son Alan Lomax together recorded,
catalogued, and preserved hundreds of American folk and
blues songs. On his own, Alan Lomax gave us *Mister Jelly
Roll,* the story of Jelly Roll Morton, who claimed to have
invented jazz.**

**On one of his missions to the South in the late 1930s,
Lomax tried to find Robert Johnson, to ask him to perform at
John Hammond's "From Spirituals to Swing" concert at
Carnegie Hall in 1938.**

JOHN HAMMOND, the patron of black jazz, put me on to Robert
Johnson. He had discovered the unpublished masters of Johnson when he
went to work for Columbia Records. Later on, one memorable evening in
1939, as I played through Columbia's stock of "race records," I found this
same batch of recordings. All alone that weekend in that New York office
building, I played and replayed these masterworks. Recently, all of
Johnson has been reissued on CD and he has won international recognition. But in 1939 only a handful of us appreciated him. At that time I was
surveying all of the so-called race catalogues of the major record companies, and it was clear that Johnson's recordings stood out as the finest examples of the blues along with those of the great Blind Lemon Jefferson
in the twenties. Blind Lemon's blues sold so well on black-oriented
Paramount Records that he had his own lemon-colored label. At the peak
of his success, a jealous woman put poison in his coffee. His voice still
rings out of the scratchy records of the twenties like a rooster crowing before day, and his guitar, tuned in the neo-African scales of his tunes, is as
subtle as moonlight on the Mississippi. And these recordings inspired rural
blacks to sing the blues all over the South. My guess at the time was that
Robert Johnson probably had been one of Lemon's brilliant disciples, since
Johnson's style seemed to resemble Blind Lemon's—the high-pitched de-

livery, the brilliant countermelodies between phrases, for example. At any rate, it was clear to me then that Johnson was one of the two or three great originals of the blues—as remarkable a singer as he was a lyricist and arranger. Hammond wanted him for his epochal Carnegie Hall Spirituals-to-Swing Concert in 1938, but the South had swallowed him up. No one I knew had a clue as to his whereabouts, until William Brown had said, "Now Robert Johnson's a boy you ought to hear, too. Come from Tunica County. His mama live down there, seem to *me . . .*"

Mrs. Johnson's dwelling was a painted wooden shack, wobbling uncertainly on its cedar-post supports just higher than the sea of ripening cotton that rolled up to the gate. In the narrow dooryard a withered rosebush was dying among the weeds and a slick brown chinaberry tree held out clusters of decaying yellow berries to the sun. A skinny little black woman sat on the gallery watching us. She wore a black sack of a cotton dress, dusty from the fields, her feet were bare, and her face looked out from under a fantastic cap of little grey pigtails like a brown acorn in its cup. She said nothing as I opened the gate, regarding me with a calm gaze that seemed to come from far off.

"Yessuh, I's Mary Johnson. And Robert, he my baby son. But Little Robert, he dead."

She said no more than this; she did not sob or cry out. Her eyes glistened with the dull light of someone whose eye sockets are drained; but slowly she bent forward, her grey head bowing toward her knees, as if grief was weighing her to the earth. Nothing in this place moved. No breath of wind shook the yellow berries of the chinaberry tree or the dead green of the cotton. In the west a mirage lake shimmered in the cotton field like a pool of silver tears.

Country people are not afraid to look Death in the face. He is a familiar in their lives, especially in the violent jungle of the Delta. They have seen him in the houses drowned by the great river and in the towns splintered by tornadoes; they have seen him in the faces of the young men shot down in a gambling hall or in the guise of an old fellow who came home to die after a hard day's plowing, his body on the cooling board still bent from years stooping over the cotton rows.

Mrs. Johnson raised her head, looked into my face shyly, and then said, "I'm mighty happy that someone came to ask about Little Robert. He was a puny baby, but after he could set up, I never had no trouble with him. Always used to be listenin, listenin to the wind or the chickens cluckin in the backyard or me, when I be singin round the house. And he just love church, just love it. Don't care how long the meetin last, long as they sing every once in a while, Little Robert set on my lap and try to keep time, look like, or hold on to my skirt and sort of jig up and down and laugh and laugh.

"I never did have no trouble with him until he got big enough to be round with bigger boys and off from home. Then he used to follow all these harp blowers, mandoleen and guitar pickers. Sometimes he wouldn come home all night, and whippin never did him no good. First time there'd be somebody pickin another guitar, Little Robert follow um off. Look like he was just bent that way, and couldn help hisself. And they tell me he played the first guitar he pick up; never did have to study it, just knew it.

"I used to cry over him, cause I knowed he was playin the devil's instruments, but Little Robert, he'd show me where I was wrong cause he'd sit home and take his little twenty-five cents harp and blow all these old-fashioned church songs of mine till it was better than a meetin and I'd get happy and shout. He was knowed to be the best musicianer in Tunica County, but the more his name got about, the worse I felt, cause I knowed he was gonna git in trouble.

"Pretty soon he begun to leave home for a week at a time, but he always brought me some present back. Then he took to goin off for a month at a time. Then he just stayed gone. I knowed something gonna happen to him. I felt it. And sure enough the word come for me to go to him. First time I ever been off from home, and the last time I'll go till the Lord call me. And, Lord have mercy, I found my little boy dyin. Some wicked girl or her boyfriend had given him poison and wasn no doctor in the world could save him, so they say.

"When I went in where he at, he layin up in bed with his guitar crost his breast. Soon's he saw me, he say, 'Mama, you all I been waitin for. Here,' he say, and he give me his guitar, 'take and hang this thing on the wall, cause I done pass all that by. That what got me messed up, Mama. It's the devil's instrument, just like you said. And I don't want it no more.' And he died while I was hangin his guitar on the wall."

Mrs. Johnson's skinny little body began to tremble and she rose to her feet, clasping and unclasping her hands. Her gaze was no longer directed at my face, but over my head. She came down the steps into the yard and began walking up and down as she finished her story, speaking in short hysterical ejaculations, clapping and almost dancing.

" 'I don't want it no more now, Mama, I done put all that by. I yo child now, Mama, and the Lord's. Yes—the Lord's child and don't belong to the devil no more.' And he pass that way, with his mind on the angels. I know

I'm gonna meet him over yonder, clothed in glory. My little Robert, the Lord's child."

Her slim brown feet, the last vestige of her beauty, raised little puffs of dust as she danced about the yard calling on the Lord and Little Robert. She had forgotten me. She was happy. She was shouting, possessed and in ecstasy. And so I left her.

BLIND WILLIE McTELL

This remarkable song was a statement of humility and unworthiness rare from an artist of Dylan's stature. Though he appears in the final verse the jaded, bored rock star, he can't erase the memory of this man, in whose voice he hears the struggles of black America.

Seen the arrow on the doorpost
Saying, "This land is condemned
All the way from New Orleans
To Jerusalem."
I traveled through East Texas
Where many martyrs fell
And I know no one can sing the blues
Like Blind Willie McTell

Well, I heard the hoot owl singing
As they were taking down the tents
The stars above the barren trees
Were his only audience
Them charcoal gypsy maidens
Can strut their feathers well
But nobody can sing the blues
Like Blind Willie McTell

See them big plantations burning
Hear the cracking of the whips
Smell that sweet magnolia blooming
(And) see the ghosts of slavery ships
I can hear them tribes a-moaning
(I can) hear the undertaker's bell
(Yeah), nobody can sing the blues
Like Blind Willie McTell

There's a woman by the river
With some fine young handsome man
He's dressed up like a squire
Bootlegged whiskey in his hand
There's a chain gang on the highway
I can hear them rebels yell
And I know no one can sing the blues
Like Blind Willie McTell

Well, God is in heaven
And we all want what's his
But power and greed and corruptible seed
Seem to be all that there is
I'm gazing out the window
Of the St. James Hotel
And I know no one can sing the blues
Like Blind Willie McTell

Robert Palmer

FROM THE DELTA TO CHICAGO

Robert Palmer's book *Deep Blues* is nearly impossible to excerpt. It's such a perfect piece of music history, we're tempted to give up and ask the publisher to reprint the whole thing. But they tell us this is supposed to be an anthology, so we'll settle for this morsel, which is about the musical migration from the Deep South to the industrial North. Palmer focuses on McKinley Morganfield, a plantation worker Alan Lomax recorded on Stovall's Plantation near Clarksdale, Mississippi, in 1941. Word of Morganfield's talent spread North, and he moved to Chicago, using the name Muddy Waters.

Palmer was the *New York Times'* first full-time popular music critic and was associated with *Rolling Stone* for more than two decades. In addition to *Deep Blues,* he wrote *Rock and Roll: An Unruly History,* several other books, and produced television documentaries on blues and rock and roll. He died in 1997.

WHEN Muddy Waters left the Delta, in May of 1943, he was still a young man, just turned twenty-eight. But he'd seen the Delta change, and change dramatically, in his lifetime. He rarely heard or saw an automobile when he was a child growing up on Stovall's plantation, and when he did run across one it was often stuck or broken down, for the roads were treacherous, rutted dirt tracks that turned to mud in the Delta's sudden downpours. When the W.P.A. and other federal agencies began putting men to work during the worst years of the Depression, one of Mississippi's first priorities was paved roads, and by 1943 highways crisscrossed the state. Electric lights, found only in the towns when Muddy was growing up, were spreading to the country. There were still plenty of blues musicians playing in the area, but jukeboxes were becoming the rage, not just in downtown taverns but in country stores and even in little juke joints like Muddy's.

Important as these changes were, they were only beginning to alter the texture of day-to-day life. Most blacks were still sharecroppers and lived in shotgun shacks much like the ones their parents had been born in. There were more automobiles, but on Saturdays plenty of black families still rode into town in horse-drawn wagons. After working all week long in the cotton fields, folks still packed into house parties and juke joints on Friday and Saturday nights to dance and party to the blues. Amplified guitars and harmonicas were being introduced, and more and more bluesmen were working with bands that included drummers; the music was getting louder. But melodies, lyrics, guitar parts, even entire songs that had been in vogue when Charley Patton was a young man, more than thirty years earlier, were still common currency.

Phonograph records had been bringing the songs and styles of black and white performers from all over America into Delta shacks and juke joints for more than twenty years, and the Delta had produced musicians who liked these new styles and decided to emulate them—as dance band players, jazz musicians, ballad singers. But the blues that people played and listened to in the country was as isolated from the American mainstream as it had been in Patton's time, perhaps more so. After all, Patton had played deep blues, white hillbilly songs, nineteenth century ballads, and other varieties of black and white country dance music with equal facility; Son House and Muddy Waters could play blues and spirituals and not much else. There was no pressing need for them to learn to play white popular music, as there had been in Patton's time. Black musicians who preferred entertaining whites could now be found in many Delta towns and on most of the larger plantations. They were specialists, unlike the jack-of-all-trades songster-bluesmen of Patton's generation. Most of the younger bluesmen now played mostly or only for blacks. This was one more symptom of the general tendency for whites and blacks in the Delta to draw further and further apart and regard each other with increasing mistrust.

With the aid of hindsight, it's possible to discern a gradual, evolutionary process of change operating in Delta blues during its first few decades. But compared to the rapidity with which jazz changed during the same period of time, Delta blues was practically standing still. Jazz was still developing out of a mix of folk, popular, and European classical influences around the same time blues started to emerge as a clearly definable genre. In 1900, when Patton was learning to play blues from Henry Sloan, jazz was a loose, collective music, still largely unknown outside New Orleans and other Southern cities, played by groups that typically included brass, a clarinet, banjo, guitar, string bass or tuba, and sometimes a piano and/or a set of drums. By 1925 Louis Armstrong, Sidney Bechet, and a few other musicians were radically altering the music's format to make room for improvised solos and establishing exacting standards of virtuosity. By 1935 the New Orleans—style jazz group was considered old hat, and big bands, with sections of brass and saxophones that played written arrangements and a typical rhythm section of piano, string bass, and drums, were in fashion. By 1943, the music of the "swing bands," as Benny Goodman and other white musicians who appropriated the big-band format called them, was beginning to sound dated to younger black jazz musicians in Kansas City and New York, and probably elsewhere. The bebop or modern-jazz movement, spearheaded by Charlie Parker and Dizzy Gillespie, was transforming jazz from a danceable, entertainment-oriented idiom into an art music performed for seated audiences in listening rooms and concert halls.

*　　*　　*

There was still an audience for blues records, but during the thirties and early forties the blues market had become increasingly monopolized by a group of Chicago-based artists. When Muddy got to Chicago, most of the big names in blues recorded either for Columbia or for Victor's celebrated Bluebird label, and both companies depended upon a white record producer, talent scout, and publishing magnate named Lester Melrose for their blues product. Melrose's artists had down-home backgrounds: Tampa Red, a top-selling blues star since the late twenties, was from Georgia; John Lee "Sonny Boy" Williamson, who was largely responsible for transforming the harmonica from an accompanying instrument into a major solo voice, was from Jackson, Tennessee, just north of Memphis; Washboard Sam was from Arkansas; Big Bill Broonzy was a Mississippian by birth. But in the interests of holding onto their increasingly urbanized audience and pleasing Melrose, who was interested both in record sales and in lucrative publishing royalties, they recorded several kinds of material, including jazz and novelty numbers, and began to favor band backing. During the mid-thirties the bands tended to be small—guitar and piano, sometimes a clarinet, a washboard, a string bass. But by the time Muddy arrived in Chicago, the "Bluebird Beat," as it has been called, was frequently carried by bass and drums.

*　　*　　*

Muddy had been a country boy all his life, but he kept his mouth shut and his eyes open and adjusted to Chicago without much trouble. The environment wasn't wholly alien. He started playing his blues at house parties as soon as he arrived, first at the Joneses' and soon in the apartments of other recently transplanted Mississippians. He'd built up quite a reputation as a blues singer during his years in Mississippi—Willie Dixon remembers people talking about him in Chicago as early as the mid-thirties—so the news of his arrival spread through the community. "After about two or three weeks," he says, "I found out I had a bunch of cousins here. Well, really, *they* found out *I* was here, and they come and got me and brought me from the South Side over to the West Side to stay with them. I was there about two or three months, and then I got myself a four-room apartment." Now he was set—his own place, with his woman Annie Mae installed, a regular paycheck, and work playing house parties almost every night. Practically everywhere he went, people fresh up from Mississippi, or people who'd been in Chicago for a while but remembered seeing him play years before, would recognize him and yell out, "Hey! Muddy Waters!"

*   *   *

Once Muddy had settled into his four-room apartment at 1851 West Thirteenth Street, he was living a relatively short distance from the mile-long stretch of Maxwell Street that operated on weekends as a teeming bazaar. Maxwell was a long, wide (sixty feet), straight east-west thor-oughfare bounded by brick and frame buildings, none taller than three sto-ries. Jewish peddlers with pushcarts had started to congregate there some time after the Chicago fire of 1871, and soon a few enterprising souls began putting up wooden stalls at the curbside, paying for the privilege, no doubt, with a tip to the merchant who owned the storefront behind the stall and another tip to the cop on the beat. In 1912 the Chicago City Council officially recognized the Maxwell Street Market, a strip about a mile from Lake Michigan, and before long there were more or less per-manent wooden stands lining the street. Most of the stores had awnings that stretched out to the curbs, so the sidewalks were effectively turned into long, shaded tunnels. The stores, the stands, and the pushcart trade remained overwhelmingly Jewish-operated even after Jewish immigrants began moving out of the neighborhood and blacks began moving in. By the mid-forties the area was mixed residentially, with some lingering Jewish, Mexican, and gypsy enclaves, but it was mostly black.

On a sunny Sunday afternoon one could buy just about anything on Maxwell Street. There were spice stands, used appliances, horse-drawn wagons loaded with country produce, cheap dresses, used socks with the holes carefully folded inside, gypsy fortune-telling parlors, furtive men with watches up and down their arms and legs, even more furtive men con-necting for heroin and morphine in the shadows behind the stands, blan-kets loaded with merchandise of every description spread out on the sidewalks, and an almost limitless variety of individual scams. Ira Berkow, who worked on the street as a child and years later wrote *Maxwell Street,* a fascinating memoir, recalls a legless snake oil salesman whose horse wrote numerals, from one to four, on a blackboard according to how many times the man snapped his whip. He also remembers the frequent violence that earned the street the sobriquet "Bloody Maxwell," center of the roughest police precinct in all Chicago. There were frequent chases, with policemen pursuing thieves and junkies on mad dashes through back alleys or across rooftops. Nobody wanted to end up in the precinct house, which was on Maxwell three blocks west of Halstead. It had its own lockup in the basement, a dingy chamber of horrors where the prisoners urinated and defecated into troughs that ran past the cells and huge rats slept on the hot water pipes near the ceiling, their tails hanging down and flicking languidly.

All along Maxwell Street—on the curbs, on busy corners, in the entrances to alleyways, in the rubble of vacant lots—blues musicians wailed away on guitars, harmonicas, and battered drum sets. Amplification had already made its appearance by 1940. Enterprising guitarists would buy long cords for their amplifiers from one of the cut-rate electrical stores on the street and plug into sockets in convenient stores or ground-floor apartments. Over the hubbub of the bartering and hawking that arose from the market, one could hear the cutting whine of bottleneck guitars, and under it throbbed the bass patterns of "Rollin' and Tumblin' " and "Dust My Broom." The musicians were playing only for tips, but it was possible to make money. Hound Dog Taylor, who grew up near Greenwood, Mississippi, and had learned to play Robert Johnson and Elmore James licks with a bottleneck by the time he arrived in Chicago in 1940, reported to Berkow, "You used to get out on Maxwell Street on a Sunday morning and pick you out a good spot, babe. Dammit, we'd make more money than I ever looked at. Sometimes a hundred dollars, a hundred twenty dollars. Put you out a tub, you know, and put a pasteboard in there, like a newspaper? . . . When somebody throw a quarter or a nickel in there, can't nobody hear it. Otherwise, somebody come by, take the tub and cut out. . . . I'm telling you, Jewtown was jumpin' like a champ, jumpin' like mad on Sunday morning."

Muddy enjoyed visiting Maxwell Street, and he played there on occasion, but he looks back on the experience with evident disdain. "A lot of peoples was down there trying to make a quarter," he told Berkow, "but I didn't like to have to play outside in all the weathers, and I didn't like to pass the hat around and all that bullshit." Nevertheless, in the early forties, right up to the time Muddy arrived, Maxwell Street and informal house parties were the principal sources of musical employment for blues musicians just in from the South. The nightclubs that featured blues artists were dominated by the clique that had risen to prominence through Lester Melrose's connections with Bluebird and Columbia—John Lee "Sonny Boy" Williamson, Big Bill Broonzy, Memphis Minnie, Tampa Red, and their friends. Robert Nighthawk stayed in Chicago off and on and recorded fairly prolifically for Melrose after 1937, but he was an inveterate drifter and kept returning south. Tommy McClennan, Robert Petway, and Arthur "Big Boy" Crudup, the only other Delta musicians on the Melrose roster, would come to Chicago, rehearse at Tampa Red's house, which doubled as the Melrose rehearsal studio, make their recordings, and return home almost immediately. Apparently not all the black blues fans in Chicago appreciated these singers' country ways; in *Chicago Breakdown,* Mike Rowe tells of McClennan being bodily ejected from a Chicago house party, with his guitar broken over his head, for singing emphatically about "niggers."

But as World War II neared its end, more and more of Chicago's blues fans were Mississippi natives who liked their music rural and raw.

* * *

By the end of 1948 Muddy had a steady working band, with Jimmy Rogers on guitar, Little Walter on harmonica, and Baby Face Leroy Foster doubling on guitar and drums. But Leonard Chess refused to record the group until the summer of 1950, and even then he only used Muddy, Jimmy, and Walter—it was several more months before he allowed them to bring in Foster and then Elgin Evans on drums. The generally accepted explanation is that Chess thought he'd found a winning formula in the combination of Muddy's amplified slide guitar and Big Crawford's bass and didn't want to change it, and while a few records were made in 1949 and early 1950 with Leroy on second guitar and, on one session, Johnny Jones on piano, for the most part Muddy's releases did follow the formula. "You're Gonna Miss Me" was a remake of "I Can't Be Satisfied," with the same guitar and bass parts and different words, and Muddy also recorded "Rollin' and Tumblin' " and other traditional material during this period, even though his band was a popular club attraction on the South Side and had already developed the most original and influential ensemble sound in postwar blues. Malcolm Chisholm offers an alternative explanation for Chess's reluctance to record the band—his superstition. "I've been told that once, and it may have been on Muddy's first successful session, the bass player wore a red shirt. The record sold. The next session, Leonard said, 'Get that bass man. And have him wear a red shirt.'

Eventually, I guess his business instincts and the empathy he had for people prevailed. I would argue that Leonard didn't know shit about blues, but he knew an awful lot about feeling. He could *feel* music, although he never learned to read it, and he could feel how people were responding to it. So he *developed* a good feeling for blues, as he went along."

*   *   *

The years 1951–53, when Muddy was consistently hitting the national r&b charts with those overwhelming recordings for Chess, were years of war in Korea and prosperity at home. As Mike Rowe points out in the definitive study of Chicago blues, *Chicago Breakdown,* "The non-white unemployment rate dropped . . . to 4.1% in 1953, the lowest ever recorded." But by the end of 1953 the war was over and a particularly grim recession was setting in. Some of the Delta musicians who were recording in Chicago reflected the change by writing blues that were bitterly outspoken. J. B. Lenoir, who was from Monticello, Mississippi, and had played with Elmore James and Rice Miller down home, warned on his Chess release "Everybody Wants to Know": "You rich people listen, you better listen real deep / If we poor get so hungry, we gonna take some food to eat." Floyd Jones and the Kentucky-born John Brim also made records that explicitly protested the hard times. Muddy sailed through 1954 with the biggest r&b hits of his career—"I'm Your Hoochie Coochie Man," "Just Make Love to Me" (which is better known as "I Just Want to Make Love to You"), and "I'm Ready," all of which were written for him by bassist Willie Dixon. The last two records were the only ones Muddy made that cracked the r&b Top Five.

Dixon, a huge, outgoing bear of a man, is an almost exact contemporary of Muddy's. He was born July 1, 1915, and grew up on a farm near Vicksburg, Mississippi, one of fourteen children. During the late twenties he lived briefly in Chicago, and after returning to Mississippi for several years, he settled in the Windy City for good in 1936. His checkered background included singing spirituals and boxing as a heavyweight, but after he got to Chicago he decided to concentrate on music and took up the string bass. During the forties he worked with two popular, slick club blues groups, the Five Breezes and the Big Three Trio, but he liked to keep up with the newer arrivals from his home state, and when starker, more down-home styles began to dominate the blues recording field in Chicago in the late forties and early fifties, he easily adapted. He listened with interest to the development of Muddy's music, for he'd known Muddy's reputation since the thirties. "There was quite a few people around singin' the blues," he says, "but most of 'em was singin' all *sad* blues. Muddy was givin' his blues a little pep, and ever since I noticed him givin' his blues this kinda pep feelin', I began tryin' to think of things in a peppier form."

*　　*　　*

Living in the city, Muddy adapted to survive. He sang Willie Dixon's songs, which gave him a repertoire loaded with crowd-pleasers and transformed his personal magnetism (which he'd projected in a more understated manner in songs like "Gypsy Woman" and "Louisiana Blues") into a marketable image. For the public, Muddy became the bedroom root doctor, the seer-stud with down-home *power* and urban cool. But he never lost sight of the Delta foundations he mined so deeply in his singing and playing and in lyrics like "Flood," and his audience loved him for that, too. Through all the changes—the rhythmic "pep," the flashier lyrics, and a more and more flamboyant performing style—he kept playing his unmistakable slide guitar and singing his old Delta favorites, and this fidelity to tradition was especially appreciated in the Delta itself, where many of the younger blues musicians were breaking away from the styles and songs that had been the common property of their predecessors for several generations.

Greil Marcus

THE MYTH OF STAGGERLEE

Greil Marcus's 1975 book *Mystery Train* took up the question of rock and roll not as youth culture, or counterculture, but as American culture—as much so as *The Scarlet Letter* or *My Darling Clementine*. This excerpt (from the updated 1997 edition) is taken from the historical notes to the chapter "Sly Stone: The Myth of Staggerlee," where Stone, the great pioneer of interracial pop music, is seen also as a prisoner of the cultural stereotypes—in the form of an implacable hero of black folklore—he meant to transcend.

SOMEWHERE, sometime, a murder took place: a man called Stack-a-lee—or Stacker Lee, Stagolee, or Staggerlee—shot a man called Billy Lyons—or Billy the Lion, or Billy the Liar. It is a story that black America has never tired of hearing and never stopped living out, like whites with their Westerns. Locked in the images of a thousand versions of the tale is an archetype that speaks to fantasies of casual violence and violent sex, lust and hatred, ease and mastery, a fantasy of style and steppin' high. At a deeper level it is a fantasy of no-limits for a people who live within a labyrinth of limits every day of their lives, and who can transgress them only among themselves. It is both a portrait of that tough and vital character that everyone would like to be, and just another pointless, tawdry dance of death.

*　　*　　*

"Stack O'Lee" or "Stagolee" was one of several turn-of-the-century ballads about semilegendary characters (they were real, but their legends were more so): figures like Tom Dula ("Tom Dooley"), John Henry, Casey Jones, Railroad Bill, Frankie and Albert (or Johnnie). Endless variants were popular among both blacks and whites; they were first recorded in profusion in the 1920s, by such songsters as Mississippi John Hurt, Furry Lewis, and countless others (see the *Anthology of American Folk Music, Vol. 1, Ballads,* and *Vol. 3, Songs,* compiled by Harry Smith, 1952, reissued 1997 on Smithsonian Folkways). These tunes form a special genre; characters sometimes jump from song to song. Furry Lewis put Alice Fry (source of the trouble between Frankie and Albert) into his 1928 "Kassie Jones"; in country singer Tom T. Hall's 1972 "More About John Henry," John Henry meets up with Stackerlee, kills him, and throws his body into a river.

Yet while folklorists rather readily tracked down Tom Dula, Railroad Bill, Frankie and Albert (or, at the least, claimants to their names), and Casey Jones, and have come close to identifying a real John Henry, Stack-o-lee remained on the loose for more than eighty years. Even after the historical facts were collected, in 1976, they remained unpublished. Thus a sense of mystery became part of the song; the song became a mystery itself, despite a few folklore-facts that clung to the tale. Most versions of the song share certain details. Stagolee fights Billy Lyons over Stack's Stetson hat (in a version collected by John Lomax, Billy spits in it; as Jeff Bridges' Wild Bill Hickok mutters all through Walter Hill's 1995 *Wild Bill,* "You just don't mess with a man's hat"); Billy begs Stackerlee not to kill him because he has a wife and children to support; Stack-o-lee invariably kills him anyway. In many versions, the crime occurs on Christmas night; always a gun is used (usually a .44), never a knife. But beyond that the story, and Stacker Lee's fate, was up to the singer.

John Lomax seems to have been the first to publish the song; it was given to him in 1910 by one Ella Scott Fisher of San Angelo, Texas, as an account of a murder that had taken place in Memphis about ten years earlier. At the time, some Memphians bragged that their town had the highest murder rate in the world; carnage among blacks was so great that meat wagons were stationed at the end of Beale Street on Saturday night. It seemed odd to me that a single incident, no matter how colorful, would be considered so memorable; that thought, plus the confusion in some early versions of the song as to whether Stagger Lee was black or white, made me wonder if a reversal was hidden in the ambiguities of the story. Perhaps, I speculated, a white man—Stacklee—killed a black man—Billy Lyons. Stagolee was no doubt never even charged, let alone hung. So blacks might have fought back through myth, first exacting justice in song, and then, wishing for a freedom and mastery they could never possess, identifying with their oppressor, subsuming his image into their own culture, taking his name, and sending him out to terrorize the world as one of their own. Inversions of this sort are what myth is all about (according to Harry Smith, regarding the version of "Frankie" included on his *Anthology,* Frankie, always celebrated for killing her unfaithful lover, in fact died by his hand)—but proof that the original Stagolee was white would constitute almost as deep a smearing of cultural identity as Freud's claim that Moses was an Egyptian, and so in 1974 I asked my friend Patrick Thomas, a Kentucky journalist, to go to Memphis and try to dig up the facts. His research established that there were two Stacker Lees: a black man he could not identify, and a white man whom he did.

Samuel Stacker Lee was born on May 5, 1847; he died on April 3, 1890. He was the son of James Lee, Sr. (1808–89), of Memphis, who founded the Lee Steamship line, which ruled the Mississippi from St. Louis to New Orleans after the Civil War. "Father of the river packet service," James Lee began his career as a riverman in 1833, on the Cumberland. He was a friend of Jefferson Davis and Nathan Bedford Forrest, a Confederate hero and a founder of the Ku Klux Klan; in 1863, at the age of sixteen, Samuel Stacker Lee went off to fight at Forrest's side, black manservant in tow. According to Shields McIlwaine's *Memphis Down in Dixie* (New York: Dutton, 1948), which was researched by William McCaskill, Stacker Lee came out of the war ready for bear. He was a rounder, a hell-raiser, a gambler, an all-around tough guy and ladies' man, known up and down the Mississippi once James Lee gave him a boat of his own to pilot. James Lee liked the boy, McCaskill told Pat Thomas; the rest of the Lee family, perhaps because his women were mulatto as often as they were white, spurned him. And though Stacker Lee did have at least one legitimate son—Samuel Stacker Lee, Jr., whom Memphians lost track of when he "moved west"—into the 1970s many black Memphians believed there was a second Stacker Lee, Samuel Stacker Lee's son by a mulatto mistress: according to the legend, his father's son in every way.

The second Stacker Lee, Thomas was told by Thomas Pinkston ("the last man alive to have played with W. C. Handy," Pinkston said), was a roustabout, a waterfront gambler, a legend in his own time; when someone threw a seven, it was called "a Stagolee roll." But Pinkston could offer no more details.*

An early version of the song places Stagger Lee in "The Bend"—the Tennessee penitentiary—but that was a common ending for ballads of the 1910s and '20s. In *Memphis Down in Dixie,* McIlwaine identified Stag-o-lee as a small, dark man from St. Louis who worked the Anchor steamship line, and who took the name of the first Stacker Lee to give himself an

---

*Pinkston (1901–80) was a legendary raconteur, and the flavor of his storytelling, as recorded in 1977 by Memphian Jim Dickinson, can be heard on Dickinson's anthologies *Beale Street Saturday Night* (Memphis Development Foundation LP), for "Ben Griffin Was Killed in the Monarch . . ." and "Mr. Handy Told Me Fifty Years Ago . . . ," and *Down Home* (Fan/Jasrac, Japan) for "Policy Talk: True Story of Machine Gun Kelly and the Memphis Blues," plus Pinkston's backroom, between-the-wars versions of "Dozens" and "Same Man All the Time." "This is bad," he says. "I can't sing this like I wanna . . . but it's too nasty for me."

aura of superiority ("And so it came about that the glamour about the white man's name among Negroes passed to a black with a bad eye who was celebrated in the ballad"), but there was no documentation; in his notes to the *Anthology of American Folk Music*, Harry Smith wrote that the famous murder "probably took place in Memphis in about 1900," and that "Stack Lee seems to have been connected by birth or employment with the Lee family of that city," but this too was only river drifting, even if it occasionally touched the shore.

1900—whether Smith's date or Lomax's—seemed too late as a date for Stacker Lee's encounter with "Billy"; Furry Lewis (1893–1981), who was singing the song well before he recorded it in 1927, recalled nothing of any specific incident. There are claims that the first written version of the Stagger Lee story dates to 1865, but no texts. Lawrence W. Levine notes in his *Black Culture and Black Consciousness* (New York: Oxford, 1977) that "Charles Haffer of Coahoma County, Mississippi, remembered first singing of Stagolee's exploits in 1895, while Will Starks, also a resident of the Mississippi Delta, initially heard the Stagolee saga in 1897 from a man who had learned it in the labor camps near St. Louis." No one seemed to recall anything very clearly about a Billy Lyons, or (as some variants had it) Billy the Lion, or Billy the Liar, though he too had his legends. Billy Lyons, William McCaskill told Pat Thomas, might have been a recasting of Sam de Lyon, a Memphis police officer famous for killing five men in one night. That would have turned my imagined reversal on its head: if the Stagger Lee ballad truly incorporated de Lyon, that would mean that in the fantasy of the song a black man, Stagolee, killed a white sheriff. McCaskill also suggested that in legend de Lyon might have been conflated with "Wild Bill" Latura, a notorious white craps cheat and racketeer—who, Kenneth Neill wrote in "Beale Street Remembered" (*R.P.M.* magazine, January 1984), "blew away five black patrons at Hammitt Ashford's saloon on the corner of Beale and Fourth on December 10, 1908"—an event that could have entered the song after it had taken its initial shape. " 'I just shot 'em,' shrugged Bill when the police arrived, 'and that's all there is to it.' Despite the statement, the all-white jury before which he was tried handed down a verdict of not guilty."

What happened to Stagger Lee? Thomas asked Pinkston. "He just disintegrated; old Joe Turner took him up . . . he took 'em all up." By that, Pinkston meant to prison in Nashville; Sheriff Joe Turner was infamous for running black prisoners, or sometimes simply black men rounded up off the streets, from Memphis to Nashville, where the state sold their labor to white planters. "They tell me Joe Turner come to town, brought one thousand links of chain," Lead Belly sang in "Joe Turner." "Gonna have a nigger for every link." But Thomas's search of prison records, birth records, death records, and burial records, in Memphis and Nashville, turned up nothing. "The Bend," after all, was also "the ben'," as in the river and a "Stack O' Lee" riverboat, in a song quoted by W. C. Handy himself, in his 1941 autobiography, *Father of the Blues*:

> *Oh, the Kate's up the river, Stack O' Lee's in the ben'*
> *Oh, the Kate's up the river, Stack O' Lee's in the ben'*
> *And I ain't seen my baby since I can't tell you when*

As it happened, though, there were hints of a true story in the haze that surrounded Thomas every time he asked a question: "St. Louis," "bad eye," and that most unlikely detail from certain versions, "Christmas night."

It was John David of St. Louis University, in his unpublished Ph.D. dissertation, "Ragtime Tragedies: Black Folklore in St. Louis," who in 1976 first assembled the legal and forensic facts of the historical events behind the legend of Stagger Lee (David's work is available on microfilm, or by individual copy in bound form, from UMI Dissertations Services, 300 N. Zeeb Road, Ann Arbor, MI 48106). David's path was retraced, and greatly extended, by novelist (*The Life and Loves of Mr. Jiveass Nigger*) and memoirist (*Coming Up Down Home*) Cecil Brown in his 1993 Ph.D. dissertation, "Stagolee: from shack bully to culture hero," an infinitely fascinating exploration of nearly all facets of the song, the archetype, the countless tales surrounding both, and their passage through time. (Brown's dissertation is available through UMI Dissertation Services. He first published his findings in *Mojo*, January 1996, as "The Real Stagger Lee"; his *Stagolee Shot Billy* is forthcoming from Harvard University Press.) Brown agrees that the history of the Lee family of Memphis is part of the saga; the name had to come from Samuel Stacker Lee. But the rest of the story goes far past anything anyone has dared invent.

In his reconstruction, Brown describes how, at about 10 P.M. on December 25, 1895, in St. Louis, at Bill Curtis's saloon at Eleventh and Morgan streets, one Lee Shelton—alias Stag Lee, Stack Lee, Lee Stack, and Stack-o-lee—a small man with a crossed left eye, born in Texas in 1865, raised in St. Louis—shot and killed one William Lyons. A bar dustup, one might think; too much liquor, an everyday story. It wasn't that by half.

The incident made the papers—the *Globe-Democrat*, St. Louis's biggest, even the German-language sheet—but it was in the December 29, 1895, issue of the *St. Louis Star Sayings* that Brown found his first hints of a new story. The article centered on a secret society, the "colored 'Four Hundred' " (the name came from the then-current term for New York high society); following the killing, authorities claimed Lee Shelton was the president of the society, and that Lyons' death was the result of a "negro vendetta," with roots in a feud going back to 1890. One J. C. Covington, identifying himself as the financial secretary of the "400," admitted that Shelton was a member of the society (formed only on December 6 of the year, "for the moral and physical culture of young colored men"), indeed its captain, its third-ranking officer, but denounced all talk of a feud: "This vendetta is all bosh, as no such idea has ever been conceived." What, exactly, was being claimed, and what was Covington denying?

"The two negroes," the *Star Sayings* piece began, "were in the saloon drinking and discussing politics" when they "began skylarking. Shelton snatched Lyons' hat and broke it. There was a dispute over this, during which Lyons threatened to kill Shelton. The latter returned Lyons' hat, and then Lyons snatched Shelton's.

"This caused a renewal of the argument and it was said that Lyons was in the act of putting his hand in his pocket threateningly when Shelton stepped back a few paces, drew a forty-four caliber revolver and fired. The bullet entered Lyons' stomach.

"Lyons fell to the floor, and Shelton coolly took his hat out of the prostrate man's hand and walked out of the saloon."

Shelton was arrested the next morning; Lyons died later that day. A crowd of three hundred gathered for the inquest—held, as was the custom, in front of the corpse—and there were fears of a lynching: a black-on-black lynching. Why, for the killing of a notorious local enforcer and knife artist by a reputed "sportsman," that is, a pimp?

Brown sets the scene, re-creating the saloon culture of turn-of-the-century black neighborhoods: they were clubs, often highly politicized, with bitter rivalries, businesspeople tying their ships to one political party or the other. Stag Lee and the 400 were headquartered at Bill Curtis's saloon, where gathered the "hot stuff," men and women dressed to the ceiling (and, matching jailhouse toasting versions of the tale, just down the street from a whorehouse called the Bucket of Blood)—but the ceiling was higher at nearby Bridgewater's, where the real quality held court. Bridgewater's was the headquarters of the black caucus of the Republican Central Committee, and of course almost all blacks voted Republican, faithful to the party of Lincoln since Emancipation; at Curtis's one found renegade black Democrats, those who believed the Republicans took blacks for granted, and who thus thought they might have more leverage with the other party. It was at Bridgewater's that, in 1890, a friend of Lee Shelton's was shot to death by a friend of William Lyons; Stag Lee had vowed revenge. The owner of Bridgewater's, Marie Brown, had powerful political connections; she was also William Lyons' mother-in-law. Word was she paid for Shelton's prosecution. But Shelton had Nathan Drywer, the best black lawyer in the state: "the first lawyer," Brown writes, "to get a white man convicted of killing a black man in the state of Missouri." Ordinarily, a black-on-black killing would have merited little if any jail time; with Marie Brown turning the screws, Shelton was looking at death.

In 1896 Drywer got Stack Lee a hung jury, with three votes for an out-right acquittal. But Drywer died soon after the judge declared a mistrial, a victim of morphine and alcohol addiction; when Shelton went on trial again in 1897, he was convicted and sent to prison—and by that time, Brown writes so magically, with a sense of art overtaking life, "he must have heard the Stagolee songs many times. He would have heard them in the Valley [the nightlife district of black St. Louis], where he had a bar, and he would have heard them when he went to the Silver Dollar saloon, where all the ragtime musicians hung out. Reigning over that group was Tom Turpin, whose father ran the Silver Dollar . . . a few years later Turpin himself would open the Rosebud, the most famous ragtime café in St. Louis. Turpin and Lee Shelton must have become good friends because after Shelton was in prison for a few years, Turpin petitioned the governor to give him parole."

The case didn't die. Year after year, advocates on both sides pressed governor after governor for pardons and refusals of pardons. Petitions for Stag Lee were signed by a state senator and ten of the twelve jurors who convicted him. Finally, in 1909, Shelton was set free. Arrested again for robbery, he was returned to prison, then released because of advanced pneumonia; he died in the state hospital in Jefferson on March 11, 1912. By then he was already a specter in culture, a body irrelevant to the abstractions of his own myth, and nowhere near as real as his legend, with people in Memphis, New Orleans, Chicago, and New York already saying, "Oh, Stacker Lee? Bad man, bad man, lived right here, don't know where he's gone."

The timing was appropriate; black and white sides of the story remained on parallel lines, with the first phases of the saga ending nearly in tandem. In 1902, twelve years after the first, white Stacker Lee was buried (not, for what it's worth, in the Lee family plot), James Lee, Jr., put a boat named for his brother on the Mississippi: the *Stacker Lee.* (In his novel *Another Good Loving Blues,* New York: Viking, 1993, Arthur Flowers has his hero remember "when there wasn't no such thing as blues": when he first started out playing piano, on the *Stacker Lee.*) It was the crack boat of the Lee line, 223 feet long with a 43-foot beam, the most famous boat on the river, known not only as "Stack O'Lee" but as "Stack O'Dollars." In 1916 it dragged a landing and went down; the Lee line itself was soon to be put out of business by land transport. James Lee, Jr., was the last riverman in the family, and he died in 1905; he left well over a million dollars, and the members of his family fought over the money for thirty years. There was a strange match in Southern California almost fifty years after the Lee will was finally settled, with black and white lines long since crossing: "The parents of a college football player who died in 1981 in a jail cell will receive about $1 million in a legal settlement," the *New York Times* reported in 1983; it was Stagger Lee who forced the deal.

Ron Settles, a twenty-one-year-old black man, was arrested for speeding in the private, white community of Signal Hill, and taken to jail; later he was found dead in his cell. His parents, represented by Johnnie Cochran, later world-famous for winning an acquittal for O. J. Simpson on double-murder charges, sued for $62 million, charging their son had been beaten and then strangled to death by Signal Hill police; the police claimed suicide. There never was a trial. The parents settled out of court, "as a result of a high school composition written by Settles his father provided in a deposition" a few days before the case was closed—so said Stephen Yagman, the Signal Hill attorney. "Yagman called the composition 'highly damaging,' saying it demonstrated Ron Settles was 'aware of the notion of jailhouse suicide,' had contemplated it and, in fact, 'admired it,' " the *Times* went on. "Yagman said the composition, which Settles reportedly wrote about four years before his death, concerned the legend of Stagger Lee, a black folk hero of the South. According to legend, Stagger Lee enjoyed superhuman powers. In the paper, Yagman said, 'Settles said he admired Stagger Lee because people had shot at him and he didn't die, but particularly that he had hung himself in a jail cell and hung there for 30 minutes and in the end lived to laugh at everybody.' "

Still, the fight over Stacker Lee's legacy is a fight over meaning, not money; in 1987 blacks tried to take the legend back with the off-Broadway musical *Staggerlee,* written by Vernel Bagneris with a score by Allen Toussaint. Set in New Orleans in the late '50s, during Mardi Gras, the production starred Ruth Brown, in the '50s a top R&B singer. Employing a

Rashomon-style narration ("Stackolee shot Billy Lyons"—"Stag-o-lee fighting with Billy the Lion over a Stetson hat"—"Staggerlee shot Billy Bottom"), the script turned the story around until it swallowed its tale: not only was Bagneris's Stagger Lee innocent of any crime, his "dissatisfaction with his lifestyle and the possibility of being thought a criminal" leads him "to seek redemption" and try "to 'straighten up.' "

The play closed quickly; the legend had never sold tickets to heaven. But there were other plays.

In 1977, in Washington, D.C., a man named Mike Malone was fired as arts director of the Western High School for the Performing Arts. Relying on his ties with the virtually all-black student body, he responded with a street play called *The Life and Times of Stagolee* (the play was originally meant to be staged in a nightclub, but shortly before it was to open, the owner was shot to death and the club closed). The *Washington Star* told the story: "Malone's adaptation of the Stagolee ballad is [a] somewhat allegorical view of the problems at Western . . . To Malone, Stagolee 'represents that part of each of us that strives to be free to live our lives as we wish.' And more than that, said one teacher who worked closely with the production, Stagolee represents Malone himself, who fought unsuccessfully to lift the school for the arts out of the institutional constraints of the school system.

"The symbolism comes out strongest when Stagolee, who has 'shot poor Billy dead' over a gambling argument, is called before the Lord to answer for his sins. The teacher pointed out that the Lord took on the image of Superintendent Vincent E. Reed, who dismissed Malone. The Lord's chief advisor in the play consults a female St. Peter, who was said to represent Superintendent Dorothy L. Johnson, who bumped heads with Malone throughout the Western controversy. In the play, the Lord tells Stagolee: 'You have been disruptive and insubordinate and you ain't got no respect for nothing. So we gone have to get rid of you because if there's one thing we cannot have, it's disorder.' But down on earth, Stagolee's mentor, the Voodoo Woman, complains that the powers that be don't understand Stagolee, because they have 'stopped up their ears and closed their minds,' a charge Malone's supporters have often leveled at school authorities.

"Whether or not the audience understood the allegorical connections, they clearly enjoyed the play, despite the poor acoustics and faulty sound system. The audience was made up mostly of residents and regulars of the 14th and T Street area—children, teenagers on bikes, winos and prostitutes. Some T Street residents had box seats at their bedroom windows and front stoops. Some stood on milk crates or trash cans to watch the action.

"Assistant D.C. Police Chief Tilman O'Bryant, one of the Street Theatre's strongest supporters, said he attends the opening performance every year. 'It takes the kids out of the ghetto, develops their talent, and then brings it back to the ghetto,' he said. 'Who else has nerve enough to bring something into the ghetto? They're all scared to come down here.' "

Year after year, the story returned to its source, the archetype forgotten, the tale surfacing in the papers as an ordinary crime report—except that even then, as in an account from the April 15, 1993, issue of the *Virginian-Pilot,* some hint that the story was more than ordinary, that it demanded more from a writer than facts, was almost always present. Laura LaFay's "Man Guilty of murder in dispute over Stetson" (passed on to me by critic Ricky Wright) had a Norfolk dateline: "Roy Tolbert couldn't find his black cowboy hat at the Fox Trap nightclub last summer," LaFay began. "But he did find his gun.

"It was a .44 Magnum pistol. He used it to murder 21-year-old Kerry Bright, one of three men he suspected of stealing the hat. Before collapsing in the Fox Trap parking lot, Bright took out his gun—a .357 Magnum—and shot once at the fleeing Tolbert, hitting him once in the back of the leg.

"Both men were sailors. Both were at the Fox Trap with friends Aug. 21. And both were armed. On Thursday, a jury convicted Tolbert, 24, of second-degree murder and use of a gun.

" 'This is something that, 20 years ago, would have ended up in a fist-fight, a punch in the nose,' said prosecutor Catherine Dotson. 'But now, with the proliferation of guns, it ended up a . . . murder.'

"According to testimony during the two-day trial, Tolbert was partying at the Fox Trap in the 800 block of E. Little Creek Road, when he noticed that his Stetson was missing. Told by other patrons that Bright and his friends had stolen the hat, he went outside and confronted them.

" 'He asked us, like three times,' testified Osmon El-Wahhibi, a friend of Bright's who was with him at the Fox Trap that night. 'He was like, "I know one of y'all have my hat. I saw you take it off the table." And we were like, "Man, we don't have your hat. Go ahead on." '

"Tolbert, who was stationed aboard the guided missile cruiser San Jacinto, then went to his car and got a gun. A few minutes later, Bright approached him in the parking lot.

" 'Hey bitch,' he said. 'You know you want to talk to me about your hat?'

"Tolbert shot Bright in the chest and ran away.

"He did it, he said, in self-defense. He was afraid Bright was going to shoot him.

" 'I didn't think I was going to make it through the night and I was scared,' he said.

" 'This was not about a hat,' said Tolbert's attorney, Jeffrey Russell.

" 'This is about machoism. It was about some need to prove something. But not on Mr. Tolbert's part.'

"Dotson didn't see it that way.

" 'It wasn't self-defense,' she said during closing arguments. 'It wasn't even close to self-defense.'

" 'Kerry Bright got shot point blank in the chest because Roy Tolbert couldn't handle being called a bitch by someone he thought took his hat.'

" 'We don't want people like Roy Tolbert walking around our community with a loaded .44.'

"The jury recommended a sentence of 12 years. Circuit Judge William F. Rutherford will officially sentence Tolbert on June 17.

"Bright, who was from Greenville, N.C., had been stationed at the Norfolk Naval Base.

" 'Obviously, my client will live to see another day,' Russell said of Tolbert. 'In that respect, at least, he was the more fortunate of the two.'

"Tolbert's hat was never found."*

Cecil Brown surmises that the Stagger Lee ballad emerged in 1896 as a "slow drag" ragtime number, but nothing of the sort was recorded. The first recorded version of the song—of its melody, headed by its motif—may have been by Frank Westphal and His Regal Novelty Orchestra, an "instrumental foxtrot" released in 1923. Another white dance band, Fred Waring and His Pennsylvanians, on television in the '50s, the epitome of square, got a hit out of "Stack O'Lee Blues" in 1924 (his 1928 version, collected on *The Fred Waring Memorial Album,* Viper's Nest, has some of the swing of Handy's "St. Louis Blues" and none of the conviction). The earliest black recording seems to be Ma Rainey's 1925 "Stack O'Lee Blues," a full jazz-band orchestration with Fletcher Henderson on piano and Coleman Hawkins on bass sax (see *Ma Rainey's Black Bottom,* Yazoo). But these were only records.

Frank Hutchison (1897–1945), a white slide guitarist from the West Virginia mountains, cut "Stackalee" in 1927; remarkably, its details (not merely the Stetson hat but the barking bulldog, the fight in the alley) seem

*© 1993 *Virginian-Pilot* (Norfolk, Va.). Used by permission.

to reappear more clearly in Lloyd Price's 1958 pop hit than in any of the countless versions put down in the intervening years. Hutchison makes a good joke out of the story: "God bless your children, I'll take care of your wife," Stack says after Billy begs for mercy. "They taken him to the cemetery," Hutchison sings. "They failed to bring him back." But as the song ends we find Stack in jail—haunted by Billy's shade crawling around his bed (see the *Anthology of American Folk Music, Vol. 1, Ballads,* or Bob Dylan's leaping cover of Hutchison—as "Stack A Lee"—on his 1993 *World Gone Wrong,* Columbia. "what does the song say exactly?" Dylan wrote. "it says no man gains immortality through public acclaim. truth is shadowy. in the pre-postindustrial age, victims of violence were allowed (in fact it was their duty) to be judges over their offenders—parents were punished for their children's crimes (we've come a long way since then) the song says that a man's hat is his crown. futurologists would insist it's a matter of taste. they say 'let's sleep on it' but they're already living in the sanitarium. No Rights Without Duty is the name of the game & fame is a trick. playing for time is only horsing around. Stack's in a cell, no wall phone. he is not some egotistical degraded existentialist dionysian idiot, neither does he represent any alternative lifestyle scam (give me a thousand acres of tractable land & all the gang members that exist & you'll see the Authentic alternative lifestyle, the Agrarian one) Billy didn't have an insurance plan, didnt get airsick yet his ghost is more real and genuine than all the dead souls on the boob tube—a monumental epic of blunder & misunderstanding. a romance tale without the cupidity.")

Beale Street singer Furry Lewis made the delicate "Billy Lyons and Stack O'Lee" (notable for its placing of Billy ahead of Stag), also in 1927; the knowing, stolid refrain, "If you lose your money, learn to lose" kept company with Charlie Poole and the North Carolina Ramblers' "If I Lose Let Me Lose" (for Lewis's version, see Furry Lewis, *Complete Recorded Works in Chronological Order: 1927–1929,* Document, Austria; for Poole's song, which follows the best-known "Stagolee" melody, see *Charlie Poole and the North Carolina Ramblers, Volume 2,* County). 1927 also produced one of the earlier, if not the earliest, black rural recordings of the ballad, the entrancingly lyrical "Original Stack O'Lee Blues" by Long Cleve Reed and the Down Home Boys, collected on *The Songster Tradition: 1927–1935* (Document, Austria). Mississippi John Hurt's "Stack O'Lee Blues," featuring a dramatically hurried, irresistibly pretty guitar intro, is one of the most seductive of his many recordings (see his *Avalon Blues: The Complete 1928 Okeh Recordings,* Columbia Legacy). The 1946 performance by Memphis Slim, Big Bill Broonzy, and Sonny Boy Williamson, with their accompanying conversation on the ballad as nothing more than a version of the next day's labor (on *Blues in the Mississippi Night,* Rykodisc), is probably the most chilling. The most influential postwar version, before that of Lloyd Price, was by the New Orleans singer Archibald; his "Stack-A-Lee I & II" was a top ten R&B hit in 1950 (see his *New Orleans Sessions,* Krazy Kat LP). Archibald offered the complete scenario of Stagger Lee's fight with the devil: here we find not Stack haunted by Billy's ghost, but Stagolee chasing Billy's soul down to hell, where Billy suffers still further tortures. White New Orleans R&B singer Dr. John covered Archibald on his Crescent City tribute, *Gumbo,* in 1972 (Atlantic), retaining the complex lyrics and adding the classic guitar solo from Guitar Slim's 1954 "The Things That I Used to Do," plus a horn intro that can break your heart. It is said Dr. John can sing "Stagger Lee" for half an hour without repeating a lyric.

Lloyd Price, also from New Orleans, put the tale on jukeboxes and car radios across the country in 1958. "Stagger Lee" was his first and only number one pop hit; he had topped the R&B charts in 1952 with his floating "Lawdy, Miss Clawdy." Judging strictly by lyrics, Price's version takes the prize, if only for his completely original introduction; four lines that with the perfection of a haiku set the scene with extraordinary tension and grace.

> *The night was clear*
> *And the moon was yellow*
> *And the leaves . . . came . . . tumbling*
> *Down*

Price's record was all momentum, driven by a wailing sax, and in retrospect his manic enthusiasm seems to be what many earlier versions lacked. However, an interesting thing happened. As "Stagger Lee" was rising up the charts, Dick Clark booked Price onto "American Bandstand"—and then realized he could not possibly expose his millions of young viewers to a song that celebrated gambling and murder. Without missing a beat, Clark had Price change the lyrics. Immediately, Price's label pulled the original record, had Price record the "Bandstand" version, and the result was a story wherein Stack and Billy "argue," not gamble, about a woman, not money or a hat. Stagger Lee and Billy go home, suffer remorse for all the mean things they've said to each other, and then apologize. "Stagger Lee and Billy were no more sore," Price concluded. Paradoxically, Price sounded even more impassioned than he had in the first place, and his band outdid itself. Though Price (or Dick Clark) had succeeded in turning the great tradition not just on its head but inside out, the tradition, as one might have expected, won in the end: ever since 1958, when the radio has called up Price's hit, it is only the once-banned version that is played (both the original and the "Bandstand" variant are on Price's *Greatest Hits—The Original ABC-Paramount Recordings,* MCA).

Wilbert Harrison's 1970 version, which follows Price's story line, is unique among modern treatments for its cautionary tone: "That'll teach ya 'bout gamblin'," he warns (see his *Kansas City: Legendary Golden Classics,* Collectables). The Isley Brothers may have added to the subtradition of Billy's "sickly" wife when in 1963 they cut a raging stomp (withering guitar fire courtesy of a young Jimi Hendrix) that, Dave Marsh swears, has Billy trying to talk Stack out of the inevitable by hinting, "I got four little children and a very *shapely* wife." I confess I don't hear it, but I do like the idea, and it's a great record anyway (on their *Complete UA Sessions*, EMI). Ike and Tina Turner's "Stagger Lee and Billy," from the early '60s (on the anthology *The Sue Records Story: New York City, the Sound of Soul,* EMI box set), tells the story from the perspective of the innocent bystander: when the trouble starts, Tina hides under a table and puts her hands over her ears, but somehow misses nothing.

Because Jamaican rock began in the '50s partly in response to R&B broadcasts originating in New Orleans, it's no surprise Stagger Lee made himself felt in early reggae—but in fact he virtually took it over, ruling the symbolism of the new music at least until the late '60s, when he was ousted by Natty Dread and the Rastafarians, much as Big Red Little was finally buried by Malcolm X. The years between were spent in a long and frequently hilarious cultural struggle, as Stagolee, in the person of the rude boy—the Kingston hooligan who terrorized his own community— claimed his rights, celebrated his prowess, and fought off the inevitable answer records that called for his rehabilitation (or, failing that, his demise). Of the hundreds of discs that tell this story, the most striking were the mid-'60s tunes that made up Prince Buster's "Judge Dread" trilogy ("Judge Dread," "The Appeal," and "Barrister Pardon," the latter also known as "Judge Dread Dance," all collected on *Judge Dread Featuring Prince Buster—Jamaica's Pride*, Melodise/Blue Beat LP), which were naturally accompanied by numerous rudie-talks-back 45s. Buster (who in 1966 recorded a version of "Stagger Lee" itself) produced a set of three-minute morality comedies: a black judge arrives from Ethiopia to clean up the Kingston slums, sentences various rude boys to hundreds of years in prison ("I am the rude boy now," he crows), jails their attorney when he has the temerity to appeal, and then, having reduced all wrongdoers to tears, sets everyone free and steps down from the bench to dance in the courtroom. The final lines—"I am the judge, but I know how to dance"— pretty much sum up the ethos of post-rude-boy-reggae, but Prince Buster was years ahead of his time.

Merging Jamaica's cultural work with the street life of punk-era Great Britain, in 1979 the Clash used the Stagger Lee–rude boy conflict as the underpinning of their epochal *London Calling* (Epic/CBS). Changing names, faces, and races, the old troublemaker appears in "Jimmy Jazz," "Rudie Can't Fail," "The Guns of Brixton," and most powerfully in the shattering "Death or Glory," which was Stagger Lee brought down to earth and made domestic. . . . Stack had surfaced under his own name just a cut earlier, in "Wrong 'em Boyo," originally a Jamaican rock-steady hit by the Rulers. The Clash redid the number with a wildly original introduction based on the old ballad—"Billy said, 'Hey, Stagger! I'm gonna make my big attack / I'm gonna have to leave my knife . . . in your back' "—somehow pulling the knife the real Billy Lyons always carried out of the confusion and forgetting of the intervening eighty-four years before making a heartfelt plea for good behavior.

Those seem to me the most memorable Stagolees, though I've omitted many of the more famous recordings, from Duke Ellington's 1928 "Stack O'Lee Blues" to Cab Calloway's 1931 "Stagger Lee" to P. J. Proby's 1969 "Stagger Lee" (well, the latter not exactly famous, but certainly demented). A version of the tale that marks a tradition in and of itself can be found on *Get Your Ass in the Water and Swim Like Me!—Narrative Poetry from Black Oral Tradition* (Rounder, recorded by folklorist Bruce Jackson) and, skipping over numerous prison recordings of male and female black inmates by the likes of Alan Lomax, on Nick Cave and the Bad Seeds' 1996 *Murder Ballads* (Mute). Both Jackson's jailhouse field recording and Cave's almost Shakespearean rant come from the tradition of prison toasts—ritualized declamatory insults and stories that in some cases have changed barely a word in a hundred years. Nearly all of such toasts, not the least Stackolee's, are so obscene they can sound like an assault not merely on rational discourse (Cave's Stag Lee, or rather "Traditional" 's, orders "Billy Dilly" to perform fellatio on him, then shoots him dead as he complies) but on English itself—though, today, for whites, that may be because few understand Elizabethan obscenity as well as Cave, or enjoy it half so much.

It's out of the toast tradition as much as from the ballad line that the overwhelming reemergence of the Stacker Lee archetype in '80s and '90s rap came: thousands of dope-king brags and gun-thug taunts and dares, self-affirmation all mixed up with the purest nihilism, among them Schoolly D's "Gangster," Ice Cube's "Amerikkka's Most Wanted," and the Geto Boys' "Mind of a Lunatic." "Just like Stagger Lee himself," Nick Cave said, "there seem to be no limits on how evil this song can become."

James Miller

KING OF THE DELTA BLUES

Robert Johnson recorded twenty-nine songs in two hotel rooms, in Dallas and San Antonio, in 1936 and 1937. These went largely unheard until 1961, when John Hammond produced the release of *King of the Delta Blues Singers.* Hearing that album changed the lives of Bob Dylan, Keith Richards, Eric Clapton, and scores of others. Here's an assessment of that record's importance in rock and roll history.

WITHOUT fanfare or publicity, his first album appeared in 1961. The music was strikingly out of place and out of time, particularly in a year when the best-selling album in America was Elvis Presley's *Blue Hawaii.* Still, as one critic has aptly remarked, *King of the Delta Blues Singers* turned Robert Johnson into "a sort of invisible pop star."

The album consisted of sixteen songs, several with starkly evocative, even apocalyptic titles: "Hellhound on My Trail," "If I Had Possession Over Judgment Day," "Me and the Devil Blues." The songs had been recorded in 1936 and 1937. Robert Johnson had been dead for a generation. In 1961, no photographs of him were known to exist. A mysterious and elusive figure, he was—literally—invisible. He nevertheless became a pop star: minor, perhaps, but highly influential just the same.

In his own lifetime, a total of twelve recordings had been released. With the exception of the first one, "Terraplane Blues," none of them had sold well, even in Johnson's home region, the mid-South. From the start, the quality of his music was nevertheless recognized, if only by fellow blues singers, as well as by a handful of respected writers and record collectors.

After the appearance of *King of the Delta Blues Singers,* Johnson's reputation steadily grew. His music was heard, and imitated, by a coterie of prominent young musicians. Among the cognoscenti, his album became a badge of hip taste: in the photo on the cover of Bob Dylan's *Bringing It All Back Home* (1965), the Johnson album is prominent among the emblematic pieces of bohemian bric-a-brac on display. What people like Dylan took away from Johnson's life and work became the source of a tacit ethos, silently transmitted, internationally shared, creating a new mythic measure of what rock and roll could *be*, quite apart from the example of Elvis Presley.

But who *was* Robert Johnson? In an era when worthless teen idols were routinely ballyhooed, Robert Johnson was a mystery, unknown, remote, accessible only through his music. The most storied of the classic Delta bluesmen, his legend had its roots in a failed quest to find him.

The search had begun in 1938. In December of that year, John Hammond was staging the first of his "Spirituals to Swing" concerts at Carnegie Hall (it was this concert that would introduce the jump blues of Big Joe Turner to New York listeners). Hammond was the first important jazz critic and record collector to become an impresario and record producer in his own right, serving as a role model for Ahmet Ertegun when he started Atlantic Records a decade later. An avowed socialist despite his pedigree (his mother was a Vanderbilt), Hammond in the 1930s was committed to advancing the cause of "the people" through a suitably classy presentation of suitably populist strains of music. In an announcement for the Carnegie Hall concert printed in the *New Masses* (a weekly that was an avowed cultural organ of the nation's "class-conscious workers and revolutionary intellectuals"), Hammond promised a program of "American Negro music as it was invented, developed, sung and played by the Negro himself—the true, untainted folk song, spirituals, work songs, songs of protest, chain gang songs, Holy Roller chants, shouts, blues, minstrel music, honky-tonk piano, early jazz and, finally, the contemporary swing of Count Basie." The list of featured artists included Robert Johnson.

A few months before, Hammond had gone to work for Columbia Records, and had chanced upon Johnson's masters, transcriptions of all of his original recordings, many of them still unissued at the time. Transfixed by Johnson's music, Hammond was convinced that he had found an archetypal troubadour—the purest, most powerful (and most authentically populist and proletarian) blues singer in the Deep South.

A call went out. John Hammond wanted to bring Robert Johnson to Carnegie Hall. In Texas and Mississippi, the music men who had first found and recorded Johnson made inquiries. Piecing together information from a variety of itinerant informants, they learned that Johnson had died just weeks before, under uncertain but sinister circumstances.

One search was over. But another was just beginning. In these same months, Hammond played Johnson's unreleased masters for a young friend of his, the Harvard-educated folklorist Alan Lomax. Though he was only twenty-six, Lomax was already a seasoned student of American folk music. In 1934, he had accompanied his father, John, editor of the first major anthology of American folk song, on a trip to the South to record indigenous musicians in the field. Their express purpose had been "to find the Negro who had had the least contact with jazz, the radio, and with the white man." On that trip, they had visited the Louisiana State Penitentiary at Angola, where they had discovered Huddie Ledbetter, aka Leadbelly, whose release they secured, and whom they subsequently took on a well-published tour of Harvard and other college campuses: *Life,* a weekly magazine, covered the phenomenon under the headline "Bad Nigger Makes Good Minstrel."

Leadbelly's tour naturally compromised the authenticity of his claim to be "the Negro who had had the least contact with jazz, the radio, and with the white man." Robert Johnson's recordings, on the other hand, suitably esoteric as they were, suggested someone who came closer to embodying that elusive (and implicitly revolutionary) ideal. Even better, he was dead: so his work would forever remain untainted by contact with "the white man" (never mind that Lomax, like Hammond, was white). But the fact of his death only added urgency to the riddle that now haunted Lomax: who *was* Robert Johnson—who had he been?

In 1941, Lomax headed south, in search now of a ghost. He did not return to New York empty-handed. Assembling evidence and following clues from Memphis back to the Mississippi Delta, Lomax was able to locate Robert Johnson's mother. He discovered Son House, one of Johnson's mentors. And he found one of Johnson's most talented disciples, McKinley Morganfield, later famous as Muddy Waters, who in 1941 was still living on a plantation (he moved to the South Side of Chicago two years later).

From these sources, a legend began to take shape. Some friends said that he'd been shot by a jealous man; others swore that he'd been poisoned by a woman. In his death throes, they said, he crawled on all fours and barked like a dog—the victim of a voodoo curse. In later years, Son House hinted that Robert Johnson had sold his soul to the devil—to House, this was the only conceivable explanation for the man's musical genius.

John Hammond and Alan Lomax first talked about compiling an album of Robert Johnson's music in 1939. But the project was shelved, and evidently forgotten. The rugged beauty of Johnson's recordings, well known by reputation, was rarely experienced firsthand.

Then, in the Fifties, in a paradoxical counterpoint to the simultaneous craze for rock and roll, an international fad for "folk" music took off, stalled, then took off again, finally creating a small but impassioned new market for Robert Johnson's rough-hewn style of music.

In America, the fad had begun in 1950, when the Weavers, led by Pete Seeger, one of Lomax's musical friends and political allies, turned Leadbelly's "Goodnight Irene" into a lushly orchestrated exercise in sentimentality. As a writer remarked at the time in *Billboard*, songs like "Goodnight Irene" and "Tennessee Waltz" were of a piece; the Weavers, like Patti Page, demonstrated the popular appeal of "a bright, homey, simple, folksy melody sort of tune."

This first wave of the America folk revival fell apart in 1951, after the Weavers were prominently mentioned in an FBI publication, *Red Channels: Communist Influence on Radio and Television*. Meanwhile, in England, folk music independently came into vogue in 1956, when the singer Lonnie Donegan took yet another Leadbelly song, "Rock Island Line," and performed it with spirited artlessness, accompanying himself on acoustic guitar. Donegan called his brand of music "skiffle," a term originally used in the late 1920s to describe blues played by so-called jug bands, consisting of guitar, harmonica, kazoo, jug, washtub bass, and washboard drums. It was, in fact, skiffle that John Lennon was playing in 1957 at the church picnic where he first met Paul McCartney.

At first glance, rock and roll and folk music might seem utterly incompatible. Where rock and roll was designed to be popular, folk music evoked a reverie of pastoral populism, untainted by vulgar commercial calculations; where rock and roll was loud and highly amplified, folk was performed on acoustic instruments, an audible emblem of its populist authenticity.

Still, as John Lennon intuitively understood (since his skiffle band performed Elvis Presley songs), rock and folk had some crucial ingredients in common: both genres welcomed, indeed highly prized, the creativity of frank amateurs; both rock and folk were do-it-yourself formats that inspired many listeners to start bands of their own; finally, both rock and folk were simple enough musical forms that even teenagers could, without much practice, successfully approximate the sounds they heard on their radios and record players.

In 1958, the folk fad had resumed in America, and proceeded to blossom, this time fueled by the popularity of the Kingston Trio, a clean-cut (and impeccably apolitical) vocal group. The Kingston Trio wore starched, striped short-sleeve shirts, strummed acoustic guitars quietly, and sang plangent Appalachian ballads with the same kind of deadpan intonation and colorless diction that Ricky Nelson had brought to rockabilly. Across

America, guitar sales soared, as aspiring folk singers joined the ranks of aspiring rock guitarists. And by 1961, when Robert Johnson's first album was belatedly released (thanks, in part, to the continuing interest of John Hammond), there was, at last, a demonstrable market for music that was ostensibly pure, archaic, uncommercial. Out of time, Robert Johnson could at last come into fashion.

For almost everyone who bought *King of the Delta Blues Singers*—the point needs stressing—this was *new* music. In some ways, it was more novel, because more exotic, than anything else readily available in record stores around the world. There had been folk song reissues before, of course, on small American labels like Folkways and RBF, but one had to make a special effort to search them out. There had similarly been blues reissues before, but nothing as raw as *King of the Delta Blues Singers*—and certainly nothing as drenched in romance and mystery.

"The voice sings," Rudi Blesh wrote in 1946, offering the first of countless purple encomiums, "and then—on fateful descending notes—echoes its own phrases. . . . The high, sighing guitar notes vanish suddenly into silence as if swept away by cold autumn wind. Plangent, iron chords intermittently walk, like heavy footsteps, on the same descending minor series. . . . The notes paint a dark wasteland, starless, ululant with bitter wind, swept by the chill rain. Over a hilltop trudges a lonely, ragged, bedeviled figure."

For want of a photograph, the album's cover was a painting. It showed an isolated, featureless black man hunched over his guitar, casting a long shadow over an equally featureless ground the color of parched sand. "Robert Johnson is little, very little more than a name on aging index cards and a few dusty master records in the files of a phonograph company that no longer exists," the album's liner notes began. "A country blues singer from the Mississippi Delta . . . Robert Johnson appeared and disappeared, in much the same fashion as a sheet of newspaper twisting and twirling down a dark and windy midnight street."

Once music has been preserved on recordings, the sounds become available, in principle, to any listener anywhere. When the music thus preserved represents the orally transmitted heritage of an otherwise inaccessible milieu, the effect, paradoxically, is to open up for cosmopolitan appreciation, and imitation, what had been previously segregated, what had been self-contained: the legacy of an organic community of musical craftsmanship. In this way, the Beatles could master from afar a regional American idiom like rockabilly. It was in this way, too, that a new generation of British rock and roll musicians came to study, and copy, a music so tortured in its timbres, and so tormented in its poetic imagery, that Johnson's recordings made "Blue Suede Shoes" sound like "Three Blind Mice"—a simpleminded nursery rhyme.

"I don't think I'd even heard of Robert Johnson when I found the record," Eric Clapton recalled years later. "It was probably just fresh out. I was around fifteen or sixteen," and Clapton's apotheosis as the first widely celebrated demigod of the rock guitar was five years in the future: "It was a real shock that there was something that powerful. . . . It all led me to believe that here was a guy who really didn't want to play for people at all, that his thing was so unbearable for him to have to live with that he was almost ashamed of it. This was an image that I was very, very keen to hang on to."

A similar scene occurred in the spring of 1962, when Keith Richards, then nineteen, visited a fellow rhythm and blues enthusiast named Brian Jones, then twenty—together with Keith's friend Mick Jagger, they would shortly begin to play together as the Rolling Stones. "I'd just met Brian," Richards later recalled, "and I went round to his apartment—crash pad, actually, all he had in it was a chair, a record player, and a few records, one of which was Robert Johnson. He put it on, it was just astounding stuff. . . . To me he was like a comet or a meteor that came along and, BOOM, suddenly he raised the ante, suddenly you just had to aim that much higher."

What Johnson represented to art school students like Clapton and Keith Richards was, to start, a matter of music: a complexity of affect conveyed by guttural vocals, kinetic countermelodies, and a rhythmic attack so relentlessly choppy that, on a recording like "Walkin' Blues," the singer and his guitar achieve a feeling of raw urgency rarely matched by later bands playing with amplified instruments. A model of impassioned artistry, a song like "Walkin' Blues" was also a perfect expression of (among other sentiments) unrequited love; desolation and abandonment; and the untrammeled freedom of a young man unafraid to leave his "lonesome home." For a generation bored by the complacency and comfort of middle-class life, Johnson's songs held out the image of another world— one that was liberated; fearful; thrilling.

It was a music of apparently brute honesty. But as countless later homages would prove, if Johnson's basic sound was imitable, the impression of brute honesty was not. As Greil Marcus remarked in *Mystery Train,* perhaps the first major study of rock as a cultural form, "all of Eric Clapton's love for Johnson's music came to bear not when Clapton sang Johnson's songs"—for example, "Ramblin' on My Mind" in 1966 (with John Mayall), or "Crossroads" in 1968 (with Cream)—"but when, once Johnson's music became part of who Clapton was, Clapton came closest to himself: in the passion of 'Layla' " in 1970 (with Derek and the Dominos).

There was, finally, a certain Gothic beauty about Johnson's legend, which insured that the legend itself became an influence in its own right. By reputation a diabolical and doomed figure, he had died for his art. That creative freedom required a pact with the devil was, of course, a romantic cliché, as well as a major theme in Goethe's *Faust*, Nietzsche's philosophy, and Baudelaire's poetry. But with Johnson's example in mind, the mystique surrounding evil in modern thought acquired a concrete new meaning, transforming the significance of blues borrowings within rock culture.

For Elvis Presley, the blues had been a matter of elemental sensuousness, the kinds of passions that could be routinely evoked by a journeyman like Arthur Crudup: "if I ever got to the place where I could feel all old Arthur felt, I'd be a music man like nobody ever saw." As Elvis proved, one could be "a music man" like Crudup and still embody the virtues of patriotism and a pious reverence for traditional family values.

For Keith Richards and Brian Jones, by contrast, the blues had now to be visibly rooted in "Sympathy for the Devil." Thus was born what has become one of the corniest motifs in subsequent blues-oriented rock and roll, a fascination with evil routinely exploited by so-called heavy metal bands like Black Sabbath in the 1970s, Van Halen in the 1980s, and Metallica in the 1990s. As one academic has solemnly summed up the "discursive practice" of these latter-day rock and roll bands, "Running with the Devil means living in the present, and the music helps us experience the pleasure of the moment. . . . Freedom is presented as a lack of social ties: no love, no law, no responsibility, no delayed gratification."

That such sentiments almost certainly travesty Robert Johnson's life and work does not change the lines of cultural descent connecting Johnson's "Hellhound on My Trail" (recorded in 1937) with Van Halen's "Runnin' With the Devil" (1978); or, for that matter, the parallel lines of cultural descent connecting the gangster folk music of Leadbelly with the gangsta rap of N.W.A. (for "Niggers With Attitude"—compare "Bad Nigger Makes Good Minstrel").

Thanks to the growing influence of country blues, and specifically of Johnson's example, unruliness, already a key component of the rock ethos, acquired the kind of cultural legitimacy Norman Mailer had prophesied in his essay "The White Negro": the cachet of frankly expressing raw desires, deep emotional truths, specifically those too violent for civil society, too ugly for fine art—too dangerous to be condoned.

Nick Tosches

JERRY LEE LEWIS SEES THE BRIGHT LIGHTS OF DALLAS

Hellfire, by Nick Tosches, has been called by no less authority than Greil Marcus "the finest book ever written about a rock'n'roll performer." Written in a blend of literary journalism and history, Tosches tells the foaming-at-the-mouth mad story of Jerry Lee Lewis, a God-fearing young man from Ferriday, Louisiana, who grew up to play the Devil's music. Lewis's story is intertwined with that of his cousins, who grew up to be the Reverend Jimmy Swaggart and country singer Mickey Gilley. In this episode, fourteen-year-old Jerry Lee goes off to be saved at a Bible seminary in Waxahachie, Texas, but finds Satan instead up the road.

SOUTHWESTERN Bible Institute had since 1943 occupied some seventy acres on the northern edge of Waxahachie, the seat of Ellis County, Texas, a rich blackland area of pecan and cotton, abstinence and Jesus. According to its Bulletin,

> Southwestern, being an Assemblies of God school, embraces standards of living and conduct that are the same as those generally accepted by the Pentecostal churches in America. These are characterized by clean conduct and conversation, modest apparel in dress, high standards of moral life, and a deep consecration and devotion in spiritual life. . . . Most certainly will the relationship between sexes reflect moral purity as well as a distaste for promiscuity.

It was here, to this place, that Jerry Lee Lewis came, traveling by bus some four hundred miles, to start life over on the eve of his fifteenth birthday. He looked around him, saw the tan brick buildings, the sparse trees, and the stained-glass chapel from which no sound came. He looked around and saw the young men and women smiling to one another in Christian earnest. He looked around and longed for Haney's Big House.

Most of those attending Southwestern were college students who took courses like Introduction to Missions, Pentecostal Truth, Major Prophets, Elementary Accounting, Exegesis of Isaiah, and Church Business; but many, like Jerry Lee, were enrolled in the Junior College Division. While Jerry Lee was, in his way, an ardent student of the Bible, he found classes here to be no more bearable than they had been at Ferriday High.

Soon he took to creeping out at night, crawling from his dormitory window while his classmates slept. There was not much to do in Waxahachie at night. It was a town of not many more than 8,000 souls, and the majority of those had been saved. There were no nightclubs, no unbuttoned women, no anything as far as Jerry Lee could tell. But lo! some thirty miles north on Highway 75, there she lay with lifted skirt and liquored breath, all flashing lights and fury: Dallas.

He would hitchhike to Dallas and go to the picture shows. He would sneak into nightclubs and hear the bands. He would go to the amusement park, get on the Tilt-a-Whirl, and tell the cowboy who ran it to turn the sucker wide open and let it rip, and he would spin faster and faster, endlessly, feeling all that was within him contract and rise in fluttering escape like a sudden shot of neon from his lungs—like magic.

Jerry Lee lingered at the Bible Institute for about three months, skipping classes and sneaking to Dallas. He was called upon one evening to play piano at chapel service, which he gladly did. But when he began playing the Pentecostal hymn "My God Is Real," the preacher shot him a glance of reproach, for he was playing it boogie-woogie style, and he was playing it faster and faster until it was double tempo, and then an unseen student in the congregation gave a joyous howl, and then there was another, and Jerry Lee heard both of these howls, and he beat the boogie so hard that there was nothing left of the hymn, nothing but the sounds of the Holy Ghost that had inspired it, and he cried out the final lyric and raked the keys violently back and forth.

My God is real, for I can feel Him in my soul!

He was grinning and breathing hard. And then he was expelled from Southwestern Bible Institute. Before leaving Waxahachie, he said what was on his mind to all who would listen. He said, "You can't get the Bible from all these silly books y'all got here." Then he boarded the bus and returned to Ferriday.

Grace Lichtenstein and Laura Dankner

**Equally important with Delta Blues in the birthing of rock and
roll was the New Orleans piano tradition dating from the
whorehouse piano professors of the turn of the century,
including Jelly Roll Morton, and up through the pre–rock and
roll rock of Professor Longhair (Roy Byrd), called by Allen
Toussaint the "Bach of Rock." Antoine "Fats" Domino was
part of that tradition and also one of the first New Orleans-
bred artists to step soundly into the rock and roll arena. This
is from Lichtenstein and Dankner's *Musical Gumbo,* a salute
to the varied music of the Crescent City.**

AROUND THE same time that Professor Longhair recorded "Bald Head"
in a saloon, 21-year-old Fats Domino made his first recording, backed by
Dave Bartholomew's tight band, at J & M. "The Fat Man" began with a
boogie-woogie piano introduction, followed by a higher-pitched version
of a voice that was to become familiar to millions of American teen-agers.
"They call, they call me the fat man 'cause I weigh two hundred pounds,"
he sang. The piano beat was fresh, urgent, toe-tapping; it almost sounded
as if Tuts Washington had latched onto the harder sounds of jump blues.
The Creole-accented vocals were unusual yet assured and inviting. "The
Fat Man" had hooks that grabbed hold of listeners in an instant and
wouldn't let them sit still. It was a sound that with a little modification
would soon sweep the nation, whites as well as blacks, under the banner
of rock'n'roll, laid down by an artist who ultimately would outsell every
founding father except Elvis Presley.

If ever there was an unlikely candidate for such lasting fame, it was
Domino. Neither dynamic nor demented nor dangerous onstage (think of
Elvis, or Little Richard, or Chuck Berry), he was instead a pudgy little guy
with a great smile beaming out beyond the keyboard who won his audience over with a catchy rolling bass line, not swiveling hips. Aided by a
terrific arranger and sharp sidemen, he became, over the next decade,
one of the first and finest masters of the two-and-a-half minute hit. Before

his reign at the top of the charts was over, he had ushered in the golden age of New Orleans R&B.

Born in 1928 in the ninth ward, Antoine "Fats" Domino was the youngest of nine children. His was not one of the prominent New Orleans musical families, but his uncle, Harrison Verret, a guitar player, played with Kid Ory and Papa Celestin. "He just about raised me," Fats said of his uncle. "He showed me the first note I played on the piano." At an early age he quit school to help earn money for his family. By his teens he was playing literally for pennies in local joints while holding down a factory job during the day.

Tuts Washington told an interviewer that when Domino was still "just a lil ole fat boy" he would hang around the Club Desire and beg Tuts to play "The Honeydripper." Other major influences on Fats were the classic boogie-woogie pianists Amos Milburn, Pete Johnson, Meade Lux Lewis, and Albert Ammons. Directly after World War II, the teen-ager started making a name for himself as a member of Billy Diamond's band, a popular local group whose home base was the Hideaway Club in the ninth ward. Patrons liked Domino's rousing version of Ammon's "Swanee River Boogie." He kept his day job at a bedspring factory until a pile of springs fell on him and accidentally cut his hand, temporarily threatening to nip a promising career in the bud. Then one night he went to hear the hottest band in town, under the leadership of Dave Bartholomew. The stage was set for one of the most fruitful musical partnerships of the R&B and rock-'n'roll eras.

Bartholomew, the son of a tuba player well known in local music circles, was born in Edgard, Louisiana, in 1920. As a youngster interested in the trumpet, he took lessons from Peter Davis, the same man who had taught Louis Armstrong when he was in the waifs' home. Before he was out of his teens, Dave was playing with a "reading" band at night while cutting sugarcane by day. He also put in a four-year apprenticeship with Fats Pichon's band playing on the riverboats that plied the Mississippi much as they had done since Armstrong's day. It was an important experience, he explained later, because they "played all types of music . . . jazz, swing, waltzes, you name it. We had rehearsal every morning and if you couldn't read, you'd be in bad shape." Bartholomew's early years also included a stint with Duke Ellington's band.

Discharged from military service after World War II, Bartholomew returned to New Orleans and formed a band that could play jazz, standards, and the new R&B. By 1947, the group—anchored by Herbert Hardesty,

Red Tyler, and Clarence Hall on tenor sax, Salvador Doucette on piano, Frank Fields on bass, and Earl Palmer on drums—had jobs all over the city, in clubs such as the Dew Drop and the Robin Hood and numerous Catholic church halls. The band even cut some records for Jules Braun's Deluxe label (Braun was the New Jerseyan who first recorded Roy Brown) and had a local hit with "Country Boy."

Fats Domino's introduction to the band was not auspicious. It was engineered by Earl Palmer. The drummer, who had tapdanced with his mother's vaudeville troupe as a boy, became a sort of deputy band leader for Bartholomew. On breaks during a club date, Dave "would go socialize and solicit more gigs," Palmer recalled, leaving the band in Palmer's hands onstage to play a bit of bebop. It was during one such break at Al's Starlight Inn that Earl invited Fats to sit in. At the time, according to Palmer, the only thing Fats could play was boogie woogie. He was considered talented but crude. After his short appearance, Bartholomew was cross. "I thought I told you not to let that fat dude up there," he said to Palmer.

Nevertheless, the seed was planted. Dave had previously met Lew Chudd, owner of the Los Angeles-based Imperial record label, who wanted to expand from his Mexican music base into R&B. He carne to New Orleans in search of talent and hired Bartholomew as a scout. One evening in 1949, Chudd and Bartholomew went to hear the young piano player appearing at the Hideaway. As Dave recalled, Fats "was killing them" that night. Chudd immediately signed Domino and arranged for Bartholomew's band to back him at a recording session at Matassa's studio. The first side was "The Fat Man," yet another reworking of "Junker Blues," the same tune that was the basis for Professor Longhair's "Tipitina."

"The Fat Man," with Domino and Bartholomew sharing writing credits, soared to Number 6 on the national R&B charts in 1950. During the next two years, the band backed Fats on several more sides that did well. The early tunes were recorded at J & M with just a small combo—bass, drums, guitar, a couple of saxes (either Herbert Hardesty or Lee Allen contributed the honking tenor solos), and Fats on the piano. As Palmer explained, the recording sessions meant extra money (they were done during the day while the musicians continued to play clubs at night) and the band strove to capture the same "infectious excitement" that punctuated their live appearances. What Fats had that most of his contemporaries did not, however, was a good contract. His brother-in-law convinced him to get a clause paying him royalties based on sales of records, rather than a single flat payment for the right to the song. A common practice today, it was anything but common in those R&B days. The absence of such a clause left numerous artists destitute after their moment in the limelight passed; its inclusion made Fats Domino a millionaire.

Domino was gaining confidence both as a featured performer and as a singer. Finally, in 1952, he reached the Number 1 R&B slot with the tune "Goin' Home." Fats and the band began to go out on tour, promoting their records with successful live shows. Meanwhile, each time they went into the studio, Bartholomew sought to achieve new effects, despite the primitive conditions. Matassa at first recorded directly on vinyl, not tape, with only one microphone. To change the balance on the lone microphone they would turn a drum over or move musicians to the far side of the room. Songs had to be less than three minutes long; sometimes Cosimo would yell, "I'm running out of vinyl."

As an arranger, Bartholomew was searching for a sound that was new yet uncomplicated. "It had to be simple so people could understand it right away. It had to be the kind of thing that a 7-year-old kid could start whistling." And it had to have the big beat—a beat Palmer perfected to such an extent his band mates thought the Palmer-brand metronome had been named for him.

By the time Fats and Bartholomew wrote a mid-tempo ditty called "Ain't It a Shame," they had the formula down cold. The record had an irresistible beat, a memorable rolling left-hand riff, and a sing-along chorus. It was hardly surprising that white audiences began dancing to it. For the first time, a New Orleans R&B hit crossed over to the *Billboard* pop charts, where it reached Number 10 in July 1955. Before Pat Boone had time to surpass its success with his lumbering cover, "Ain't It a Shame" had made Fats Domino a rock'n'roll star.

Domino was hurt by Boone's version. "It took me two months to write 'Ain't It a Shame' and his record comes out around the same time mine did," he commented years later. On the other hand, Pat Boone collected no royalties on it. Nor did Boone have Domino's B-side, "La La." The tune was so catchy, according to Bartholomew, that the Stanford University football team did their warm-up drills to it.

Within a few months, another Domino record, "I'm in Love Again," started to climb up the charts. It was followed by "My Blue Heaven," "Blueberry Hill," "I'm Walkin'," "Blue Monday," "Walkin' to New Orleans," and others. The Fats Domino hit parade, depending on which music history you accept, totaled some 43 chart records, at least 18 gold records, and between 30 million and 65 million discs sold over a 20-year period. Beginning in 1955, Domino shared the glory days of rock'n'roll with the likes of Elvis, Little Richard, Jerry Lee Lewis, the Drifters, Chuck Berry, Bill Haley, and Buddy Holly.

Those days have been sanitized and romanticized; they were rough on performers' stamina and their personal relationships because touring was the one constant in a frenetic existence. A member of Alan Freed's revolutionary package shows, Fats played all over the United States and Canada. Herbert Hardesty, his tenor-sax companion for 35 years, noted that even at such legendary halls as the Apollo Theater in Harlem, conditions were far from perfect. The dressing rooms in the Apollo were eight floors above the stage level, so that after each of the five or more shows a day, everyone would have to hike up flight after flight. In addition, the crowds were so critical you could be stoned off the stage. "If you could make it at the Apollo, you could make it anywhere," said Hardesty. "Pleasing that audience made your career."

Domino was a headliner, but that simply meant he and his band took the stage later than other acts. He was just one of the guys, according to Hardesty. Everyone, stars and sidemen alike, traveled together week after week in buses, with the single exception of Chuck Berry, who preferred to drive his own car. Fats did become the first black star on national television, performing on the Steve Allen Show. That led to dates with Perry Como and Dick Clark's "American Bandstand," two of the mainstays of early television. It was a period in which black artists as well as white could be heard on the biggest radio stations, seen live at the biggest downtown theaters, and even appeared on screen in movies like *The Girl Can't Help It.*

White audiences got to hear Fats's lilting vocals all over the country, from New York's Paramount to casinos in Las Vegas. Fats himself was hardly an incendiary performer compared to fellow pianists Jerry Lee Lewis or Little Richard; he was cuddly, warm, safe. Still, he had his fill of exciting moments. In San Jose, California, Domino was on stage when toughs in the audience at Palomar Gardens threw beer bottles and started a riot. The singer and the band "grabbed their instruments and ran for their lives," according to one account. "The police panicked and lobbed tear gas," Hardesty recalled. Otherwise, the most exciting moments for Domino on the road were those spent gambling. He enjoyed betting on anything; one day he lost all the money in his pockets shooting pool. In Las Vegas, his major activity was craps. The problem was, his luck was bad and he did not know when to quit. "Nobody could tell him that, though," Hardesty noted. Even pit bosses would warn band members: "Get him away from the tables; he's losing too much money."

Fats kept a down-home flavor on tour by packing big pots in which he would cook his own gumbo. "Actually, we all cooked in our rooms. The pay wasn't great, so that was how we survived," said Hardesty. When the band spent one Thanksgiving on the road, Fats and Dave Bartholomew traveled with a huge turkey in their car that Fats roasted following their performance.

In the studio, at first in New Orleans, later in Los Angeles, Domino and Bartholomew strove for new twists to keep their big-beat formula from getting stale. The singer caused Cosimo Matassa grief more than once. "He'd stop right in the middle of the only good tape we had going and say 'how do I sound?'" Matassa said. "It drove you crazy." It did not upset the band members, who lent what one historian called an "off-the-cuff, house-party atmosphere" to the Domino hits. On occasion, Bartholomew would tell Palmer, "Look, just try a different beat." What do you want? Palmer would ask. "I don't know what I want. I want to hear something different," Bartholomew would reply. One result of such improvising was the zippy shuffle of "I'm Walkin'."

In the sixties, with his sound not quite the stuff of surefire Top 40 that it once was, Fats branched out. He was a regular at the biggest Las Vegas rooms, even though he later admitted that his gambling losses totaled over two million dollars. "I was a country boy who didn't know no better," he shrugged. At least he was in good company. During his many Vegas dates, he became friendly with Elvis Presley. Just before Presley's second appearance at a major Vegas hotel, he confessed to Domino that he was nervous because his first date there had not gone over well. "Man, that night he went out and tore the place down," laughed Fats.

*   *   *

He finally deserted Imperial for ABC Records in 1963, then moved on to other labels, but he was never able to duplicate his huge hits of the fifties. In the midst of the psychedelic era, however, he made a comeback with his 1968 album, *Fats Is Back*. An all-star combo played behind him—King Curtis on tenor sax, James Booker on piano, Chuck Rainey on bass, Earl Palmer on drums. One cut in particular—the Beatles' "Lady Madonna"—was a modest hit. It was noblesse oblige; the Beatles loved his music and acknowledged that songs such as "Birthday" on *The White Album* were based on assorted riffs from Fats's records.

An auto accident in Natchitoches in 1970 was the event that really curbed Domino's output. One band member was killed and two were injured; friends said the band was never the same again. Herb Hardesty and Dave Bartholomew continued to work with Fats but his schedule grew quite leisurely. His last big hit was "Whiskey Heaven" in 1980, heard in the movie *Any Which Way You Can*. (He also was among the multitudes who put out a version of the zydeco novelty song "My Toot Toot" in 1985.) Millions of radio listeners in New Orleans did get a taste of the old sound, however, when he did a widely aired jingle for Popeye's Fried Chicken.

*   *   *

What accounted for his enormous popularity? One theory is that in an era of sexually threatening rebels—James Dean and Marlon Brando, as well as Elvis and other rockers—Fats was reassuring and non-threatening. Perhaps, although one could make the same claim for groups like the Platters, who never equaled his popularity. Another theory is that his unusual accent made him sound exotic. That might account for one or two hits, but not for a dozen. As a black performer, he certainly had a manner that whites found comfortable, which helped his crossover appeal. But above all, Fats was a consistently excellent singer who made great Top 40 records. His singles featured tunes from a great variety of sources—standards like "My Blue Heaven," country and western, blues—yet they always sounded like no one else. As Cosimo Matassa told one writer, "He could be singing the national anthem, you'd still know by the time he said two words it was him, obviously, unmistakably and pleasurably him."

UP AGAINST THE WALL WITH LITTLE RICHARD

Little Richard's "Tutti Frutti" is one of rock and roll's first classic recordings. Read this excerpt by Richard's producer, Bumps Blackwell, and you will never think of that song the same way again.

WHEN I GOT to New Orleans, Cosimo Matassa, the studio owner, called and said, "Hey, man, this boy's down here waiting for you." When I walked in, there's this cat in this loud shirt, with hair waved up six inches above his head. He was talking wild, thinking up stuff just to be different, you know? I could tell he was a megapersonality. So we got to the studio, on Rampart and Dumaine. . . .

Well, the first session was to run six hours, and we planned to cut eight sides. Richard ran through the songs on his audition tape. "He's My Star" was very disappointing. I did not even record it. But "Wonderin' " we got in two takes. Then we got "I'm Just a Lonely Guy," which was written by a local girl called Dorothy La Bostrie who was always pestering me to record her stuff. Then "The Most I Can Offer," and then "Baby." So far so good. But it wasn't really what I was looking for. I had heard that Richard's stage act was really wild, but in the studio that day he was very inhibited. Possibly his ego was pushing him to show his spiritual feeling or something, but it certainly wasn't coming together like I had expected and hoped.

The problem was that what he looked like, and what he sounded like didn't come together. If you look like Tarzan and sound like Mickey Mouse it just doesn't work out. So I'm thinking, Oh, Jesus . . . You know what it's like when you don't know what to do? It's "Let's take a break. Let's go to lunch." I had to think. I didn't know what to do. I couldn't go back to Rupe with the material I had because there was nothing there that I could put out. Nothing that I could ask anyone to put a promotion on. Nothing to merchandise. And I was paying out serious money.

So here we go over to the Dew Drop Inn, and, of course, Richard's like any other ham. We walk into the place and, you know, the girls are there and the boys are there and he's got an audience. There's a piano, and that's his crutch. He's on stage reckoning to show Lee Allen his piano style. So WOW! He gets to going. He hits that piano, dididididididididi . . . and starts to sing "Awop-bop-a-Loo-Mop a-good Goddam—Tutti Frutti, good booty . . ." I said, "Wow! That's what I want from you, Richard. That's a hit!" I knew that the lyrics were too lewd and suggestive to record. It would never have got played on the air. So I got hold of Dorothy La Bostrie, who had come over to see how the recording of her song was going. I brought her to the Dew Drop.

Dorothy was a little colored girl so thin she looked like six o'clock. She just had to close one eye and she looked like a needle. Dorothy had songs stacked this high and was always asking me to record them. She'd been singing these songs to me, but the trouble was they all sounded like Dinah Washington's "Blowtop Blues." They were all composed to the same melody. But looking through her words, I could see that she was a prolific writer. She just didn't understand melody. So I said to her, "Look. You come and write some lyrics to this, cos I can't use the lyrics Richard's got." He had some terrible words in there. Well, Richard was embarrassed to sing the song and she was not certain that she wanted to hear it. Time was running out, and I *knew* it could be a hit. I talked, using every argument I could think of. I asked him if he had a grudge against making money. I told her that she was over twenty-one, had a houseful of kids and no husband and needed the money. And finally, I convinced them. Richard turned to face the wall and sang the song two or three times and Dorothy listened.

Break time was over, and we went back to the studio to finish the session, leaving Dorothy to write the words. I think the first thing we did was "Directly from My Heart to You." Now that, and "I'm Just a Lonely Guy," could have made it. Those two I could have gotten by with—just by the skin of my teeth. Fifteen minutes before the session was to end, the chick comes in and puts these little trite lyrics in front of me. I put them in front of Richard. Richard says he ain't got no voice left. I said, "Richard, you've *got* to sing it."

There had been no chance to write an arrangement, so I had to take the chance on Richard playing the piano himself. That wild piano was essential to the success of the song. It was impossible for the other piano players to learn it in the short time we had. I put a microphone between Richard and the piano and another inside the piano, and we started to record. It took three takes, and in fifteen minutes we had it. "Tutti Frutti."

706 UNION AVENUE

Sam Phillips grew up dog poor in Alabama, son of a sharecropper who died young. But Sam was charged by an early visit to Memphis, where the sounds of Beale Street intoxicated him and led him to a career in music. He moved to Memphis, got a start in radio, then opened the Memphis Recording Service at 706 Union Avenue. He made some of the first records by B. B. King and Howlin' Wolf and was the auteur of what is arguably the first real rock and roll record, "Rocket 88" by Jackie Brenston and His Delta Cats.

But Phillips did not have his own record label. "Rocket 88," like many of his earlier productions, was sold to Chess Records in Chicago. Frustrated and envious, Phillips went into hock to start his own label, Sun Records, and find the white singer "with the sound of a Negro." Eventually he found that man in Elvis.

Frederick Jackson Turner's frontier thesis of American history claims that the United States became a leader because the demands of frontier life forced Americans to excel; nations without frontiers were left in Yankee dust. Likewise, that thesis applies to rock and roll. Most of the great innovations occurred on the frontiers of independent record labels, such as Sam Phillips's Sun. With a major label, when an artist showed up with broken equipment, the recording session was cancelled. To Sam Phillips, time was money, and so when a guitarist showed up with a broken amp, there was a chance to make a little history with that fuzztone. That's how Sam Phillips made "Rocket 88."

"THE SUN to me—even as a kid back on the farm—was a universal kind of thing. A new day, a new opportunity," said Sam Phillips, reflecting on the confluence of events that had brought him to the formation of his own label. "I chose the name Sun right at the beginning of 1952, when I had de-termined to try to start issuing my own recordings. It was a frightening experience for me. I had a heavy workload already, and now here I was with lack of time, lack of know-how, and lack of liquidity."

At the same time, having Sun Records meant that Phillips would have to answer only to himself for a record's success or failure. He could release music that others had deemed unworthy, he could hand-carry sample discs to every station within a five-hundred-mile radius, and he could exert pressure on his distributors. Then, if the record succeeded, he would reap the rewards. He was no longer forced to second-guess Chess Records' accountings or to fret that others had won the acclaim for his productions. By the same token, if one of his records bombed, there was only one scapegoat.

"My first step," he continues, "was to sketch out a label design and take it to Memphis Engraving on North Second Street. A man named Parker I had known and played with in the high school band was there. He drew several designs from my sketch and I decided on the one with the sun rays and the rooster. I honestly feel I can say that I know what it's like to have a baby. That's what Sun Records was to me."

* * *

The elemental twelve-bar blues "Hound Dog" has been the subject of an inordinate number of lawsuits since Jerry Leiber and Mike Stoller copyrighted it in early 1953. It was written for Big Mama Thornton (who also claimed to have written it while in the company of her favorite relative, Old Grandad). The latter-day interest, of course, results from the fact that Elvis Presley would make it into one of the most lucrative copyrights in popular music.

But back in March 1953 Elvis was sitting on the side of his bed trying to learn the song, while Sam Phillips was sitting in the studio rewriting it as "Bear Cat." On March 8, only a few weeks after Thornton's version had been released, Phillips called local DJ Rufus Thomas into the studio to cut the song. It entered the national R&B charts on April 18, only two weeks after Thornton's original version, sparking *Billboard* to call it "the fastest answer song to hit the market." It eventually climbed all the way to No. 3 on the R&B charts, becoming Sun Records' first hit.

A lawsuit from Don Robey at Peacock Records/Lion Music, correctly charging copyright infringement, followed in short order. Phillips didn't have a leg to stand on when the case came to trial in July, and he was forced to surrender two cents a song to Lion along with court costs. "I should have known better," Phillips later remarked to Robert Palmer. "The melody was exactly the same as theirs."

The artist, Rufus Thomas, had seen a long career on the periphery of the Memphis music scene before he finally broke through with "Bear Cat." Born in Cayce, Mississippi, on March 26, 1917, Thomas was raised in Memphis and began his career in minstrelsy and vaudeville. In 1935 he started a regular gig at the Palace Theater as a comic with Nat D. Williams, a local high school teacher, as his straight man. Thomas also began singing with the Bill Fort Orchestra, although he has sensibly never made great claims about his singing. "I'm not a singer, I'm an entertainer," he told David Booth. "I've taught a lot of people how to get a song across and project a song, but as a singer myself—no dice."

In 1948 Nat Williams became the first black on-air personality in Memphis, hosting a show called "Brown America Speaks," the success of which prompted WDIA to change format. "Nat got me my job at WDIA," recalled Thomas. "In those days they wouldn't let us twist the knobs. We'd pull the records, give them to the engineer, and give him a sign when we were ready to play another one."

In addition to his daily gig on WDIA, Thomas had worked a day job since January 1941 with an industrial uniform manufacturer. "I was making twenty-five cents an hour," he recounted to Booth. "I'd finish at two-thirty, run home, go to the station, and be on the air at three o'clock. I did that for years and years and years. I also did weekend live shows, and often I'd get home at four o'clock on Monday morning and be punching that clock at six-thirty. It took all of that to make a living."

Thomas made his recording debut in 1950 or 1951 for the Star Talent company from Dallas. In June 1951 he made his first recordings for Sam Phillips, who leased three singles to Chess.

Just under a year after his last session for Chess, Phillips called Thomas back to the studio to cut "Bear Cat." After the record broke, Thomas formed his own group, the Bear Cats, and started touring on weekends. His followup, "Tiger Man," written by Sam Phillips and Joe Hill Louis, was another novelty number that should have done comparably well, but didn't. Thomas was not asked to record for Sun again, a fact that galls him to this day. "I sold a hundred thousand records for him," he told David Booth, "and all the time he was looking for a white boy. Sam never mentions that I was the first to make money for Sun Records either."

Thomas recorded one single for Meteor Records; his recording career then went into abeyance for a few years. In 1959 he and his daughter, Carla, went to the newly formed Satellite label. Their debut, " 'Cause I Love You," was a small hit and was followed by Carla's smash, "Gee Whiz" (recorded in 1961 at Phillips' studio in Nashville). By that point, Satellite had been renamed Stax Records, and Rufus went back in 1963 with a dance number called "The Dog." It became a modest R&B hit and led the way for his biggest hits, "Walkin' the Dog" and the "Funky Chicken." It was the success of "The Dog" that gave Thomas the impetus to finally quit his day job, although he maintained his shows at WDIA until changing times forced him out.

Yet Rufus Thomas, with his first Sun release, had given the label its first national hit—a record tainted with illegitimacy, but, even so, displaying both Phillips' musical values and his business acumen.

Almost as successful on the commercial level—and far more so artistically—was a record Phillips produced in the early summer of 1953 by another waiting-to-break local artist, Little Junior Parker.

Parker had hosted his own show on KWEM in West Memphis, and it was there that Ike Turner recorded him for the Biharis in 1951 or 1952. By that point, Parker had assembled his own band, in which the linchpin was guitarist Floyd Murphy. The brother of another accomplished blues guitarist, Matt "Guitar" Murphy, Floyd was as technically adroit as any picker who ever set up his amp in Phillips' studio. "He had this tremendous ability to make the guitar sound like two guitars," Phillips remembers—an ability that was showcased on Parker's Sun debut.

Parker, with Murphy and the band in tow, had auditioned for Phillips at some point in 1953, playing their brand of slick, uptown R&B. But Phillips wanted to hear something a little rougher, so the group worked up a tune called "Feelin' Good," with a nod to the king of the one-chord boogies, John Lee Hooker. Parker himself apparently despised that simplistic style of music, but Phillips was convinced he heard something marketable in the record; he released it in July 1953. On October 3 it entered the national R&B charts, to Parker's surprise, peaking at No. 5 during its six-week stay.

Called back for another session, Parker brought a moody, elegiac blues called "Mystery Train"—a phrase that appears nowhere in the song but well characterizes the aura Parker and Phillips created in the studio. It is a slow, atmospheric piece in which a loping, syncopated beat, slap bass, and gently moaning tenor sax coalesce to produce a ghostly performance. But at the time, its poise, understatement, and lack of an obvious "hook" were sure predictors of commercial oblivion. Almost as remarkable was the flip side, "Love My Baby," whose pronounced hillbilly flavor might just qualify it as the first black rockabilly record. Released in November, the record failed to sustain the momentum of "Feelin' Good," and Parker began to get itchy feet.

Parker had joined Johnny Ace and Bobby Bland on the Blues

Consolidated tours booked by Don Robey at Duke/Peacock Records. Parker was induced to sign with Duke, prompting Phillips to file a suit against Robey. When the case came to trial, Phillips won a $17,500 settlement—which must have carried some personal gratification after the loss on "Bear Cat." Phillips also seems to have acquired 50 percent of "Mystery Train" at approximately the same time; when Elvis Presley's version appeared as his final Sun single almost two years later, it was published by Phillips' Hi-Lo Music, with Phillips' name appended to the composer credit.

Continuing to record for Robey, Parker worked as part of the Blues Consolidated Revue until Ace killed himself backstage in Houston on Christmas Eve 1954. Parker and Bland continued to work together, touring the black lounges and night spots. Parker scored fairly consistent hits in the R&B market for some years; ironically, after leaving Duke, his music edged closer to the primitive blues feel he had disavowed in Memphis. He died during brain surgery in Chicago on November 18, 1971.

*　　*　　*

By the fall of 1953, even though Sam Phillips was again riding the kind of wave he had enjoyed with "Rocket 88" two summers earlier, he had not found the prosperity he had doubtless anticipated. Phillips' margin per single was small; his profit was tied up in repressings, and with slow-paying distributors.

After "Bear Cat" broke, Sam's first move had been to bring his brother, Jud, into the picture. Jud had the knack for promotion that Sam had for production. He was gregarious, flamboyant, and, given half an opportunity, extravagant. By the time he joined Sam, Jud had worked as a singer, a gospel promoter, a front man for Roy Acuff's tent show, and a production assistant to Jimmy Durante.

*　　*　　*

Despite his perfectionism, the hits he had enjoyed in 1953 showed Phillips that the demographic base he was servicing was simply too narrow. "Keep in mind there were a number of very good R&B labels," he said in 1982. "The base wasn't broad enough because of racial prejudice. It wasn't broad enough to get the amount of commercial play and general acceptance overall—not just in the South. When you're on the road—sixty-five or seventy thousand miles a year—as I was in those days, you get a lot of input from the ground. On Mondays and Wednesdays, when the jukebox operators would come by the distributor for their weekly supply of records, and on Tuesdays and Thursdays, when the smaller retail outlets would come by, I'd be there. They'd tell me, 'These people [the blacks] are ruining our children.' Now these were basically good people, but conceptually they did not understand the kinship between the black and white people in the South. So I knew what I had to do to broaden the base of acceptance."

The path toward commercial salvation was made clear by the success of one young singer who, like Phillips, intuitively understood black music and quickly synthesized both a musical style and an image that would enable Phillips to take yellow Sun records into places where they had never been before.

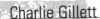
THE FIVE STYLES OF ROCK'N'ROLL

We promised Charlie Gillett would be back. Here, in another excerpt from _The Sound of the City,_ Gillett turns professor to put the manic first years of the rock and roll era into perspective.

IN THE YEARS 1954 to 1956, there were five distinctive styles, developed almost completely independently of one another, that collectively became known as rock'n'roll: northern band rock'n'roll, whose most popular exemplar was Bill Haley; the New Orleans dance blues; Memphis country rock (also known as rockabilly); Chicago rhythm and blues; and vocal group rock'n'roll. All five styles, and the variants associated with each of them, depended for their dance beat on contemporary Negro dance rhythms.

The styles gave expression to moods of their audience that hitherto had not been represented in popular music. Each style was developed in particular regions or locales and expressed personal responses to certain experiences in a way that would make sense to people with comparable experiences. This grass-roots character gave the styles of rock'n'roll their collective identity, putting it in sharp contrast with established modes of popular music, which were conceived in terms of general ideas formulated in ways that made the finished product available for millions of people to accept.

Northern band rock'n'roll, exemplified by Bill Haley and His Comets, was concerned mainly with expressing high-spirited feelings of togetherness. Haley had little of the romantic appeal familiar to the fans of Frankie Laine or Eddie Fisher. More quaint than good looking, Haley rested his appeal on his music, which he had been developing for 10 years before the general audience discovered him in 1953. Haley's earliest records were in conventional country and western style; by 1947 he had begun experimenting with it. As he recalled in an interview much later: ". . . the style we played way back in 1947, 1948, and 1949 was a combination of country and western, Dixieland, and the old style rhythm and blues."

The "old style rhythm and blues" he referred to was probably the roaring, riff-laden music of bands like Lionel Hampton's, itself a simplified descendant of the Kansas City jazz, committed to creating as much excitement as possible, with musicians playing solos on one or two notes lying on their backs or climbing on pianos or basses, or playing their instruments above their heads in search of thrilling visual effects. Contrasting the enjoyment of the audiences at this kind of dance with the staid reaction of audiences where white dance bands played, Haley saw the chance for change. "We decided to try for a new style, mostly using stringed instruments but somehow managing to get the same effect as brass and reeds."

*　　*　　*

It wasn't quite as easy as Haley suggested. Another group, Freddie Bell and the Bellboys, tried the same formula with "Giddy-Up a Ding Dong" (Mercury) but had much less success, despite being featured with Haley, the Platters, and Alan Freed in the film *Rock Around the Clock*. And in 1956 Haley's own Comets left him to form the Jodimars, who sang "Let's All Rock Together" (Capitol) in the prescribed fashion without impressing the customers. (Boyd Bennett's "Seventeen" did confirm, however, that in 1955 a record with little musical quality and banal lyrics could satisfy the popular audience; a singer called Big Moe chanted the words tonelessly, while the band played a rough beat. Bennett, a protege of the Louisiana honky-tonk singer Moon Mullican, had no other hits.)

One of the first of Haley's successors in covering rhythm and blues material for white audiences was Pat Boone, whose first big hit "Ain't That a Shame" (Dot) remained in the top ten for fourteen weeks through the summer of 1955. Whereas Haley had developed his style of rock'n'roll himself, Boone had been surprised and rather shocked when he had been asked to record the uptempo "Two Hearts, Two Kisses" as his first release for Dot, a southern independent company based in Gallatin, Tennessee. He had been accustomed to slow ballads, of the kind well established in the popular and country and western markets. With the rest of middle-class America, Boone regarded rhythm and blues material as being rather crude, musically and lyrically. Nonetheless, he went on to record "Ain't That a Shame," "Tutti Frutti," and a succession of cover versions of other rhythm and blues hits.

In contrast to Bill Haley, Boone was young and good looking and had a more expressive voice. But unlike Haley, he did not seem to be involved with the spirit of the musicians behind him, and he was important to rock'n'roll only in the role he played bringing a little conservative respectability to the music's image. Although his early success delayed the mass public's awareness of real rock'n'roll/rhythm and blues singers, it may also have indirectly generated interest in them. A few disc jockeys, for example, played the original versions of the Boone hits "Tutti Frutti" and "Ain't That a Shame," and when the original singers became better known, Boone retreated to the ballads he seemed from the start to have preferred to record.

"Ain't That a Shame" and "Tutti Frutti" were both originally recorded in the "New Orleans dance blues" style, by Fats Domino and Little Richard, respectively, and Boone's cover versions used instrumentation closely based on the New Orleans arrangements. In these records the rhythms were looser, less mechanical than in the northern band rock'n'roll records, and the singers were more prominent. There was rarely any singing by the band, and the musicians accepted a supportive role.

Fats Domino, working with Dave Bartholomew, a former Duke Ellington trumpeter, as his recording supervisor, co-writer, and session bandleader, helped to evolve the New Orleans dance blues through a remarkable series of records which began with "The Fat Man" (for Imperial), a big hit in the rhythm and blues market in 1949–50. At that time Domino sang in a high, exuberant tenor, and played piano with a distinctive boogie-influenced style that featured chords with both hands. The effervescent good humor of his fast records was eventually discovered by the popular music audience, which, in 1956, after he had achieved many hits in the black market, raised "I'm In Love Again" into *Billboard*'s top ten. Domino's follow-up to "I'm In Love Again" was a slow version of the standard "Blueberry Hill," sung with impressive control and apparently no effort at all. Domino's curious "cajun" accent immediately identified his records, and he maintained a long string of hits, including both infectiously happy songs and plaintive appeals.

A feature of virtually all Domino's records was a tenor-sax solo, taken usually about two thirds of the way through, often by either Lee Allen or Herb Hardesty. These solos were probably shortened versions of the solos that would have been played at dances, and they matched the relaxed control of Domino's voice. Like his singing, the sax tone was melodic, economical, warm, and slightly rough.

Although Little Richard came from Georgia, and did not record for the same company as Domino, he often played with the same musicians. But in contrast to Domino's cool style, Little Richard was intensely involved in everything he sang, exhilarating his audiences with a frantic, sometimes hysterical performance which was distinguished by pure-voiced swoops and whoops out of a raucous shouting style.

With Little Richard, the rock'n'roll audience got the aggressive extrovert to enact their wilder fantasies, and his stage performance set precedents for anyone who followed him. Dressed in shimmering suits with long drape jackets and baggy pants, his hair grown long and slicked straight, white teeth and gold rings flashing in the spotlights, he stood up at, and sometimes on, the piano, hammering boogie chords as he screamed messages of celebration and self-centered pleasure.

. . . [T]he spirit of Little Richard affected and influenced most singers who followed him. Compared to Domino, Little Richard, musically and stylistically speaking, was coarse, uncultured, and uncontrolled, in every way harder for the music establishment to take. Among the white rock-'n'roll singers, Elvis Presley was similarly outrageous as compared with his predecessors Bill Haley and Pat Boone.

Presley was the most commercially successful of a number of Memphis singers who evolved what they themselves called "country rock" and what others, record collectors and people in the industry, have called "rockabilly."

Country rock was the most complete of rock'n'roll's various styles, integrating aspects of rhythm and blues with country and western music in a much more consistent and original way than did Haley's version of northern band rock'n'roll. The style evolved partly from the imaginative guidance of a Memphis record-store owner, Sam Phillips, who entered the recording business by supervising sessions with local blues singers and leasing the masters to a number of independent companies (Chess in Chicago, owned by the Chess brothers, or Modern/RPM in Los Angeles, owned by the Bihari brothers). The success of some of these singers, notably B. B. King and Howlin' Wolf, encouraged Phillips to form his own label, Sun, and two of the singers he recorded for his own label, Little Junior Parker and Rufus Thomas, had hit records in the Negro market.

The Memphis blues singers used small bands which featured piano, guitar, and saxophone. No particular dominant style linked them all, but common to many of their records was a kind of intimate atmosphere created by the singers and enhanced by the careful "documentary" recording technique of Phillips. The singers invariably made their personal presence felt on the records, menacingly in Howlin' Wolf's case, impatiently in Junior Parker's. These recordings, and other more traditional blues and rhythm and blues records issued by Sun, were known to a substantial number of white youths through the South, and presented a source of song material and stylistic inspiration that was in many ways more satisfactory than the orthodox country and western culture.

Elvis Presley seems to have been the first white southern singer to make a record in the "personal" Sun style. According to the legend of his recording debut, his discovery by Sam Phillips was casual and lucky. He is said to have attracted the attention of Phillips when Presley used Sun's studios to cut a record for his mother's birthday present; Phillips encouraged him to make a record with proper accompaniment, and the two men were rewarded with a local hit from one of the sides, "That's All Right."

The story of Presley's discovery has the elements of Romance, coincidence, and fate that legends need, and in fact seems to be true, but it is likely that if Phillips and Presley had not met, two other such people would soon have done what they did—merge rhythm and blues with country and western styles and material and come up with a new style. In the panhandle of west Texas, in Arkansas, in north Louisiana, and in Memphis were other singers whose cultural and musical experience were comparable to Presley's; indeed, some of them followed him into the Sun studios, while others tried studios in Nashville and Clovis, New Mexico.

It is difficult to assess how great a part Sam Phillips played in influencing his singers—among other things, by introducing them to blues records—and how much they already knew.

*   *   *

What Presley achieved was certainly not "the same thing" as the men he copied. On "That's All Right" and "Mystery Train" (written and first recorded by Junior Parker for Sun), he evolved a personal version of this style, singing high and clear, breathless and impatient, varying his rhythmic emphasis with a confidence and inventiveness that were exceptional for a white singer. The sound suggested a young white man celebrating freedom, ready to do anything, go anywhere, pausing long enough for apologies and even regrets and recriminations, but then hustling on toward the new. He was best on fast songs, when his impatient singing matched the urgent rhythm from bass (Bill Black) and guitar (Scotty Moore). Each of his five Sun singles backed a blues song with a country and western song, most of them already familiar to the respective audiences; each sold better than its predecessor, and increasing numbers of people discovered Presley either through radio broadcasts or through his stage appearances.

But Presley did not reach the mass popular music audience with his Sun records, which sold mainly to audiences in the South and to the minority country and western audience elsewhere. Only after Presley's contract was bought by RCA-Victor did his records make the national top ten, and the songs on these records were not in a country rock style. At Victor, under the supervision of Chet Atkins, Presley's records featured vocal groups, heavily electrified guitars, and drums, all of which were considered alien by both country and western audiences and by the audience for country rock music. Responding to these unfamiliar intrusions in his accompaniment, Presley's voice became much more theatrical and self-conscious as he sought to contrive excitement and emotion which he had seemed to achieve on his Sun records without any evident forethought.

Presley's success for Sun, and later for RCA-Victor, encouraged Phillips to try other singers with comparable styles and material, and attracted to his studios young southerners with similar interests. Carl Perkins and Warren Smith from the Memphis area, Roy Orbison from west Texas, Johnny Cash, Conway Twitty, and Charlie Rich from Arkansas, and Jerry Lee Lewis from northern Louisiana brought songs, demonstration tapes, and their ambitions to Phillips, who switched almost completely from black singers to white singers once the latter became commercially successful.

Not all of the singers were as obviously influenced by blues styles as Presley was. Carl Perkins and Johnny Cash, for example, both sang in a much more predominantly country and western style. But, as with Bill Haley, the music and particularly the rhythms of all of them had the emphatic dance beat of rhythm and blues. "Rockabilly" effectively describes this style, which differed from the northern band rock'n'roll of the Comets. Rockabilly has much looser rhythms, no saxophones, nor any chorus singing. Like the New Orleans dance blues singers, the rockabilly singers were much more personal—confiding, confessing—than Haley could ever be, and their performances seemed less calculated and less prepared. But unlike the lyrical, warm instrumentalists in the dance blues, the instrumentalists in rockabilly responded more violently to unpredictable inflections in the singer's voice, shifting into double-time for a few bars to blend with a sudden acceleration in the singer's tempo. Presley's "You're a Heartbreaker" (his third single for Sun) typifies this style, as does Carl Perkins's "Blue Suede Shoes." The latter was the first million-selling record in the rockabilly style, and brought a new dimension to popular music in its defiant pride for the individual's cultural choice.

Later, in 1956, Johnny Cash made *Billboard*'s top twenty with another Sun record, "I Walk the Line," much closer to conventional country and western music in both style and material, and in 1957, the Louisiana pianist-singer Jerry Lee Lewis, heavily influenced by Little Richard, had the first of several big hits with "Whole Lotta Shakin' Goin' On" (also for Sun). Rockabilly became a major part of American popular music, as much in its continuing inspiration for singers from outside the South as in the occasional commercial successes enjoyed by the rockabilly singers other than Presley.

The nearest equivalent to rockabilly among black styles was the "Chicago rhythm and blues" style of Chuck Berry, perhaps the major figure of rock'n'roll, and Bo Diddley. Many of the black singers who had recorded around Memphis before Presley (among them Howlin' Wolf, Elmore James, and James Cotton) moved to Chicago during the early fifties, where they helped Muddy Waters and others develop the Chicago bar blues style—loud, heavily amplified, shouted to a socking beat.

Chicago became the hotbed for any black musician trying to make a living from the blues, many of whom hoped to work for Muddy Waters or Howlin' Wolf and to record for Chess or for its subsidiary Checker. Muddy's harmonica player Little Walter gave Checker two of its biggest rhythm and blues hits in the early fifties with "My Babe" (1952) and "Juke" (1955), and the Chess labels's big rhythm and blues hits of the period were by the soft-voiced club pianist, Willie Mabon: "I Don't Know" (1953) and "I'm Mad" (1954). In 1955 the company became one of the first rhythm and blues indies to break into the pop market with Chuck Berry and Bo Diddley, two guitar-playing singers who recorded with blues musicians but aimed their lyrics and dance rhythms at a younger audience.

"Maybellene" was a "formula" song carefully constructed to meet the apparent taste of the recently emerged mass audience for rock'n'roll. . . .

Berry has since said that he conceived "Maybellene" as a country and western song which he originally called "Ida May." But disc jockeys Alan Freed and Russ Fratto were apparently present at the recording session—both are credited as part-authors—and the result was instant rock'n'roll. The beat was much cruder than any Berry ever used again, echoing Bill Haley more than anyone else, and the shouted-back chorus lines were also derived from the Comets' style. Berry's clear enunciation probably enabled his record to "pass for white" on the radio stations that generally kept such stuff off the air.

The stations could not have made the same mistake with "Bo Diddley." Even worse, the rhythm was a bump-and-grind shuffle, which could not be rendered any the more innocent by such lines as: "Bo Diddley bought-a-baby a diamond ring. . . ." The record hardly had the impact on radio stations that "Maybellene" had, but it ensured demand for Bo

Diddley at high school dances. Both singers had immeasurable influence on other rock'n'roll singers and styles, Berry particularly as a songwriter and guitarist, Diddley as the interpreter of one of the most distinctive rhythms of rock'n'roll. [The syncopation of this rhythm almost certainly derives from an African drum rhythm, and one example of it was recorded in the Deep South in 1951, for Alan Lomax by Lonnie and Ed Young whose "Oree," using this syncopation, was released on an album, *Roots of The Blues* (Atlantic)].

The general preoccupation with rhythm was less important in the last of the five early variants of rock'n'roll, the vocal group style. But of all the variants, the group style was in many ways the most important as an agent of change in the music industry, and therefore played a vital role in the rock'n'roll revolution. The contribution of most groups to the emergence of rock'n'roll lay in the enlargement of the musical scene not the music.

The distinctive features of the vocal group style were in the vocal harmonies and in the tone of the lead singer; from 1956 onward most uptempo records also included a sax solo. There were many ways of singing lead, and an infinite range of harmony patterns. . . . But there was a strong tendency for the songs of the groups to be much more sentimental than those of the other rock'n'roll styles, and this affected the tone of the singers, who drenched their songs with devout humility and melodramatic reverence.

There was a rough correlation between the quality of the group's best singer, the tempo at which the group generally sang, and the intensity of the harmonic support. With a good lead singer, the rest of the group could afford to be muted and songs could be taken slowly; weak control of the lead singer had to be hidden under a fast rhythm and plenty of loud noises from the group.

Black vocal groups were the first representatives of the black musical culture to appear on television and to be played by disc jockeys on the major radio stations. They thus simultaneously introduced the popular music audience to another mode of music and showed the music industry that rhythm and blues could be socially acceptable and commercially successful, if the lyrics were sufficiently innocent.

Ironically, although several of the early rock'n'roll hits were by black groups, almost none of these groups was able to make a permanent career as a major recording act.

Usually they were successful in the mass market with one record—or, rarely, two—and then lapsed back into obscurity. The more fortunate were able to maintain a loyal following among the black audience, but the majority disbanded, sometimes within a year after having a major hit.

The appeal of many of the groups was based largely on some novelty effect, in either their style or their material. This novelty aspect of the music was precisely the problem. Few singers have ever been able to keep a regular record-buying public if their appeal is primarily some oddity in their performance. Yet often a sound that seemed weird to the white audience was a conventional style to the black audience. The Orioles, pioneers of the group style, had several hits in the black market beginning in 1948 and culminating in 1953, with their very successful version of the country and western hit "Crying in the Chapel." Lead singer Sonny Til's wavering tenor and the sighs and cries of the group were familiar to the black audience, but sounded appealingly strange to the popular music audience. Perhaps aided by the fact that Til didn't sound very "black," the record broke into the white popular music market, thereby establishing a precedent for independently produced records featuring black singers. But the Orioles had no more hits in the white market; their strangeness no longer found a response.

Other black groups with hits were the Crows ("Gee"), the Chords ("Sh-Boom"), the Penguins ("Earth Angel"), and the Charms ("Hearts of Stone"). Only the Charms were able to follow up their first success (with "Ling Ting Tong"), and a little later their lead singer, Otis Williams, was successful with "Ivory Tower." But in general, there was no automatic interest in the follow-up records of a successful black group—until the Platters left the independent King and started recording for Mercury.

The first record for Mercury was "Only You," which was structurally similar to hits achieved earlier in the year by two non–rock'n'roll singers, Roy Hamilton (Epic) and Al Hibbler (Decca), with "Unchained Melody." The difference was the rhythm of the record, which helped put the song in the top ten and qualified the Platters for inclusion as a rock'n'roll group in the film Rock Around the Clock. The group's second record was a better song, "The Great Pretender," which exploited the melodramatic qualities of Williams's voice with a series of dramatic stops in the singing.

From the appearance of "Only You" in the fall of 1955, the group was consistently in the top ten until 1960. Their main appeal was the lead tenor of Tony Williams, whose voice soared above the murmuring of the rest of the group, keeping a relaxed rhythm at even the most intense moments of the performance. The Platters presented sentimental songs in a dramatic manner, adeptly combining two of the three kinds of material which dominated the popular music of the time. Later records by the group degenerated into conventional pop material, and even their best records were spoiled by unimaginative harmonizing from the rest of the group, which now locks their records much more firmly to the style of the era than do the more imaginative arrangements of the records by Fats Domino and Elvis Presley.

By the end of 1956, four years after Alan Freed had discovered a group of white kids in Cleveland who liked music with excitement and personal feelings, the music industry was offering, along with its more traditional fare, several other kinds of music designed to suit the demands of an audience seeking excitement and personal expression in its music.

In some cases, the singers and styles that came into national attention were simply achieving belated recognition for something they had been doing all along. Fats Domino, with Dave Bartholomew's arrangements, had achieved the spirit of rock'n'roll from his first records, and he did not have to change much to meet his new audience.

In other cases, singers and producers had been working out experiments, trying new sounds, and merging old ones, without expecting necessarily to do well with what they produced. Sam Phillips was intrigued by the relationship between the blues and country and western music. Elvis Presley, and later Johnny Cash, Carl Perkins, and Jerry Lee Lewis, created individual variants of such a synthesis which intersected with the taste of the audience.

Other producers and singers aimed more deliberately at mass success. Bill Haley, who seems to have been among the few singers who effectively produced his own records with only nominal supervision from a record company executive, and Little Richard (with the help of Bumps Blackwell) were conscious of the audience's taste for music with rhythm and excitement when they planned their records, yet both managed to create styles that retained personal qualities.

But whatever hopes were held for the future of popular music on the basis of the few promising signs that it was becoming more personal had to be countered by the observation that the greatest successes in the new music were enjoyed by Elvis Presley's Victor records—rock'n'roll off the production line.

"We sing the guitar electric."

Too many died young and tragically: Buddy Holly, Janis Joplin, Jimi Hendrix, Kurt Cobain . . . the list goes on. But remember them this way, on the crest of fame, fresh-faced and young. Here's Elvis, with his pals Scotty and Bill, playing their first gigs, two decades away from tragedy down at the end of Lonely Street, dead of too much fame and cholesterol at Graceland. Here's the Grateful Dead, a few months removed from the Merry Pranksters, long before they became a Fortune 500 company. But youth can be overrated. There's nothing better than seeing a rock star pull off a good second act. So here's Eric Clapton at midpassage, and Bob Dylan onstage in the 1990s, raging against the dying of the light. Here are some snapshots of superstars the way we want to remember them.

Brian Wilson

DO YOU REMEMBER?

A member of rock and roll's second generation, Brian Wilson here honors those who went before. Wilson, leader, songwriter, high-voiced singer, producer, bassist, Mr. Everything for the Beach Boys, wrote much better songs than this, but it's nice to have at least one piece in this book containing the phrase "hum diddy wadda."

Wilson, a legendary recluse once called the Howard Hughes of rock and roll, retired from live performing with his band in 1965, to produce such masterpieces as *Pet Sounds* and *Smile*. When he stopped producing masterpieces, Wilson just stayed in bed for a couple of decades, getting up occasionally to take drugs. He finally emerged from his room in the late 1980s, clean, sober, and productive as a solo artist.

Little Richard sang it and Dick Clark brought it to
    life
Danny and the Juniors hit a groove, stuck as sharp
    as a knife
Well now do you remember all the guys that gave
    us rock and roll

Chuck Berry's gotta be the greatest thing that's
    come along
(Hum diddy waddy, hum diddy wadda)
He made the guitar beats and wrote the all-time
    greatest song
(Hum diddy waddy, hum diddy wadda)

Well now do you remember all the guys that gave
    us rock and roll
(Hum diddy waddy doo)

Elvis Presley is the king
He's the giant of the day

Paved the way for the rock and roll stars
Yeah the critics kept a knockin'
But the stars kept a rockin'
And the choppin didn't get very far

Goodness gracious great balls of fire

Nothin's really movin' till the saxophone's ready to
    blow
(Do you remember, do you remember)
And the beat's not jumpin' till the drummer says
    he's ready to go
(Do you remember, do you remember)
Well now do you remember all the guys that gave
    us rock and roll
(Do you remember)

Let's hear the high voice wail (ooooooooooo)
And hear the voice down low (wah-ah ah-ah)
Let's hear the background
Um diddy wadda, Um diddy wadda
Um diddy wadda, Um diddy wadda
They gave us rock and roll
Um diddy wadda, Um diddy wadda
They gave us rock and roll
Um diddy wadda, Um diddy wadda
They gave us rock and roll

Peter Guralnick

ELVIS, SCOTTY, AND BILL

Guralnick has written often, and lovingly, about Elvis Presley, occasionally prefacing his articles with a favored quote from poet William Carlos Williams: "The pure products of America go crazy." This selection comes from the first volume of Guralnick's detailed Presley bio (*Last Train to Memphis*), perhaps the first major book to take Presley seriously as a historical figure. We pick up the story as Sam Phillips and his devoted assistant, Marion Keisker, are on the verge of discovering Elvis.

THAT AFTERNOON a young guitarist named Scotty Moore stopped by 706 Union, ostensibly to find out how his record was doing. He had been coming by the studio for several months now, trying to get somewhere with his group, the Starlite Wranglers, trying to get a leg up in the business. The group, which had existed in various configurations since Scotty's discharge from the navy in early 1952, consisted of fellow guitarist Clyde Rush, steel guitarist Millard Yow, and bass player Bill Black, all of whom worked at Firestone, and a variety of interchangeable vocalists. Scotty, who worked as a hatter at his brothers' dry cleaning establishment at 613 North McLean, had recently brought in Doug Poindexter, a baker with a penchant for Hank Williams tunes, as permanent lead singer, and he had had a big star made up with Christmas lights that flashed on and off to advertise the band's name on the bandstand. They had a few regular bookings through the spring—they continued to play the same rough club out toward Somerville where Scotty and Bill had backed up Dorsey Burnette—and they played a couple of clubs around town. They landed a radio spot on West Memphis station KWEM, and Scotty got them a regular booking at the Bon Air, which had previously featured nothing but pop. The next step, clearly, was to make a record.

That was what led the Starlite Wranglers to the Memphis Recording Service. Doug Poindexter asked Bill Fitzgerald at Music Sales, the local independent record distributor, how they "could get on MGM like Hank

Williams," and Fitzgerald, who distributed the Sun label among others, suggested that they try Sam Phillips. It was Scotty, as manager of the band and prime instigator of their upward professional mobility, who did this, with some trepidation, one afternoon after he got off work.

He and Sam hit it off almost instantly. Sam saw in Scotty an ambitious young man of twenty-two, not content with the limited vistas that lay before him—he didn't know what he wanted exactly, but he wanted something more than a lifetime of blocking hats or playing clubs eventually giving it up to go into some little retail business. Scotty was looking for something different, Sam sensed, and he was a good listener besides. Soon the two of them got into the habit of meeting several days a week at 2 in the afternoon when Scotty got off work—Scotty would just stop by, and they would go next door to Miss Taylor's restaurant for a cup of coffee and talk about the future. To Sam, who at thirty-one had seen more than his share of ups and downs, it was an opportunity to expound upon his ideas to an audience that was not only sympathetic: Scotty clearly enjoyed plotting and scheming and dreaming about the changes that were just around the comer. To Scotty, who had grown up on a farm in Gadsden with the feeling that the world had passed him by (his father and his three older brothers had had a band, but by the time Scotty came along, fifteen years after the next-youngest brother, they had given it up) and who had joined the navy at sixteen, this was heaven. He was married for the second time, had two kids living out in Washington with his first wife, and aspired to playing jazz, like Barney Kessel, Tal Farlow, or country virtuosos Merle Travis and Chet Atkins. He was serious but self-taught, he had quit in the middle of his second year of high school, and here was somebody in Memphis telling him, with a conviction that defied gainsaying, that there was a chance that something could happen, that change was on the way. "Sam had an uncanny knack for pulling things out of people that they didn't even know they had. He knew there was a crossover coming. He foresaw it. I think that recording all those black artists had to give him an insight; he just didn't know where that insight would lead. Sam came from pretty much the same background as the rest of us, basically. We were just looking for some thing, we didn't know quite what it was, we would just sit there over coffee and say to each other, 'What is it? What should we do? How can we do it?' "

Eventually Scotty persuaded Sam to record the Wranglers, and on May 25, 1954, they recorded two sides, which Scotty wrote (he gave half of the credit for one song to Doug Poindexter because he was the vocalist and a third of the other to his brother for writing the lead sheet). The record was released at the beginning of June and never went anywhere—by the end of summer it had sold approximately three hundred copies—but Scotty continued to stop by the studio, knowing that the record wasn't his ticket to the future, the Starlite Wranglers were just a hillbilly band, but feeling somehow that if he stuck close to Sam Phillips he would find out what the future was.

Sometime around the middle of May he started hearing about a young ballad singer with possibilities. There was something different about his voice, Sam said; Sam was interested in trying him out on this one song he had picked up on his latest trip to Nashville to record the Prisonaires [a singing group comprised of inmates at the Tennessee state prison]. At some point Marion mentioned his name, Elvis Presley—to Scotty it sounded like "a name out of science fiction"—but since Sam kept talking about him, he asked Sam to dig up a telephone number and address maybe they could get together, maybe this kid really had something. Somehow Sam never seemed to have the information on hand, he always said he'd have Marion look it up the next day, and Scotty was keenly disappointed on this Saturday afternoon to find out that the boy had actually been in the studio just a week before and that they had worked unsuccessfully on the Nashville song. "This particular day," Scotty said, "It was about five in the afternoon—Marion was having coffee with us, and Sam said, 'Get his name and phone number out of the file.' Then he turned to me and said, 'Why don't you give him a call and get him to come over to your house and see what you think of him?' Bill Black lived just three doors down from me on Belz that ran into Firestone—I had actually moved just to be near Bill—and Sam said, 'You and Bill can just give him a listen, kind of feel him out.' "

Scotty called Elvis that evening, right after supper. His mother answered and said that Elvis was at the movies, at the Suzore No. 2. Scotty said that he "represented Sun Records," and Mrs. Presley said that she would get him out of the movies. There was a call back within an hour; Scotty explained who he was and what he wanted to do. The boy seemed to take it all in stride—his voice sounded confident enough, but wary. "I told him I was working with Sam Phillips and possibly would like to audition him if he was interested, and he said he guessed so. So we made an appointment for the next day at my house."

On Sunday, July 4, Elvis showed up at Scotty's house on Belz in his old Lincoln. He was wearing a black shirt, pink pants with a black stripe, white shoes, and a greasy ducktail, and asked "Is this the right place?" when Scotty's wife, Bobbie, answered the door. Bobbie asked him to have a seat and went to get Scotty. "I said, 'That boy is here.' He said, 'What boy?' I said, 'I can't remember his name, it's the one you're supposed to see today.' Scotty asked me to go down to Bill's house and see if Bill would come practice with them—Bill's bass was already in our apartment, because Bill and Evelyn had two kids, and there was more room there."

After a few minutes of awkward small talk, Bill showed up and they got down to business. Elvis hunched over his guitar and mumbled something about not really knowing what to play, then launched into disconnected fragments, seemingly, of every song he knew. Scotty and Bill fell in behind him on numbers like Billy Eckstine's "I Apologize"; the Ink Spots' "If I Didn't Care"; "Tomorrow Night"; Eddy Arnold's latest hit, "I Really Don't Want to Know"; Hank Snow's "I Don't Hurt Anymore"; and a Dean Martin-styled version of Jo Stafford's "You Belong to Me." They were all ballads, all sung in a yearning, quavery tenor that didn't seem ready to settle anywhere soon and accompanied by the most rudimentary strummed guitar. At some point Bill flopped down on the sofa and there was some talk about how Elvis lived on Alabama, just across from Bill's mother, and how Elvis knew Bill's brother Johnny. Bill, the most affable man in the world and the clown of the Starlite Wranglers ("He never met a stranger," Scotty has said in seeking to describe him) said he had heard from Johnny just the other day, Johnny had been in Corpus Christi since he got laid off from Firestone. They talked a little about the football games down at the Triangle, and Bill said it was funny they had never formally met before, but, of course, he had left home before the Presleys moved into the Courts, he had gone into the army at eighteen, and when he got out in 1946 he was already married. There were a lot of musicians in Memphis, and you couldn't know them all—Elvis didn't happen to know a guitar player named Luther Perkins who lived just around the corner, did he? Elvis met all of Bill's attempts at conversation with perfunctory nods and stammered little asides of agreement that you could barely make out—he was polite enough, but it was almost as if he was filled with a need to say something that couldn't find proper expression, and he couldn't stop fidgeting. "He was as green as a gourd," Scotty would recall, with amusement, at his reaction at the time.

When Bobbie came back with Evelyn and Bill's sister, Mary Ann, they were still playing, but "all of a sudden there was a crowd, we probably scared Elvis," said Bobbie. "It was almost all slow ballads. 'I Love You Because' is the one that I remember." Eventually Elvis left, trailing clouds of oily smoke behind him in the humpbacked old Lincoln. "What'd you think?" Scotty asked, hoping that Bill might have seen something in the boy he didn't. "Well, he didn't impress me too damn much," said Bill. "Snotty-nosed kid coming in here with those wild clothes and everything." But what about his singing? Scotty asked, almost desperately—he *wanted* the kid to be good for reasons that he didn't even care to examine. "Well, it was all right, nothing out of the ordinary—I mean, the cat can sing. . . ."

That was Scotty's opinion, too. It was all right, nothing special—he couldn't see where the boy had added all that much to the songs that he had sung; Scotty didn't think he was going to make the world forget about Eddy Arnold or Hank Snow. But he called Sam anyway, what else was he going to do after making such a fuss about meeting the kid? What did you think? Sam asked.

"I said, 'He didn't really knock me out.' I said, 'The boy's got a good voice.' I told him a lot of the songs he sang. Sam said, 'Well, I think I'll call him, get him to come down to the studio tomorrow, we'll just set up an audition and see what he sounds like coming back off of tape.' I said, 'Shall we bring in the whole band?' And he said, 'Naw, just you and Bill come over, just something for a little rhythm. No use making a big deal out of it.' "

The next night everybody showed up around 7. There was some desultory small talk, Bill and Scotty joked nervously among themselves, and Sam tried to make the boy feel at ease, carefully observing the way in which he both withheld himself and tried to thrust himself into the conversation at the same time. He reminded Sam so much of some of the blues singers he had recorded, simultaneously proud and needy. At last, after a few minutes of aimless chatter and letting them all get a little bit used to being in the studio, Sam turned to the boy and said, "Well, what do you want to sing?" This occasioned even more self-conscious confusion as the three musicians tried to come up with something that they all knew and could play—all the way through—but after a number of false starts, they finally settled on "Harbor Lights," which had been a big hit for Bing Crosby in 1950, and worked it through to the end, then tried Leon Payne's "I Love You Because," a beautiful country ballad that had been a No. 1 country hit for its author in 1949 and a No. 2 hit for Ernest Tubb on the hillbilly charts the same year. They tried up to a dozen takes, running through the song again and again—sometimes the boy led off with several bars of whistling, sometimes he simply launched into the verse. The recitation altered slightly each time that he repeated it, but each time he flung himself into it, seemingly trying to make it new. Sometimes he simply blurted out the words, sometimes his singing voice shifted to a thin, pinched, almost nasal tone before returning to the keening tenor in which he sang the rest of the song—it was as if, Sam thought, he wanted to put everything he had ever known or heard into one song. And Scotty's guitar part was too damn complicated, he was trying too damn hard to sound like Chet Atkins, but there was that strange sense of inconsolable desire in the voice, there was *emotion* being communicated.

Sam sat in the control room, tapping his fingers absentmindedly on the console. All his attention was focused on the studio, on the interaction of the musicians, the sound they were getting, the feeling that was behind the sound. Every so often he would come out and change a mike placement slightly, talk with the boy a little, not just to bullshit with him but to make him feel at home, to try to make him feel really at home. It was always a question of how long you could go on like this, you wanted the artist to get familiar with the studio, but being in the studio could take on a kind of mind-numbing quality of its own, it could smooth over the rough edges, you could take refuge in the little space that you had created for yourself and banish the very element of spontaneity you were seeking to achieve.

For Elvis it seemed like it had been going on for hours, and he began to get the feeling that nothing was ever going to happen. When Mr. Phillips had called, he had taken the news calmly to begin with, he had tried to banish all thoughts of results or consequences, but now it seemed as if he could think of nothing else. He was getting more and more frustrated, he flung himself desperately into each new version of "I Love You Because," trying to make it live, trying to make it new, but he saw his chances slipping away as they returned to the beginning of the song over and over again with numbing familiarity. . . .

Finally they decided to take a break—it was late, and everybody had to work the next day. Maybe they ought to just give it up for the night, come back on Tuesday and try it again. Scotty and Bill were sipping Cokes, not saying much of anything, Mr. Phillips was doing something in the control room, and, as Elvis explained it afterward, "this song popped into my mind that I had heard years ago, and I started kidding around with [it]." It was a song that he told Johnny Black he had written when he sang it at the Courts, and Johnny believed him. The song was "That's All Right (Mama)," an old blues number by Arthur "Big Boy" Crudup.

"All of a sudden," said Scotty, "Elvis just started singing this song, jumping around and acting the fool, and then Bill picked up his bass, and he started acting the fool, too, and I started playing with them. Sam, I think, had the door to the control booth open—I don't know, he was either editing some tape, or doing something—and he stuck his head out and said, 'What are you doing?' And we said, 'We don't know.' 'Well, back up,' he said, 'try to find a place to start, and do it again.' "

Sam recognized it right away. He was amazed that the boy even knew Arthur "Big Boy" Crudup—nothing in any of the songs he had tried so far gave any indication that he was drawn to this kind of music at all. But this was the sort of music that Sam had long ago wholeheartedly embraced, this was the sort of music of which he said, "This is where the soul of man never dies." And the way the boy performed it, it came across with a freshness and an exuberance, it came across with the kind of clear-eyed, unabashed originality that Sam sought in all the music that he recorded—it was "different," it was itself.

They worked on it. They worked hard on it, but without any of the laboriousness that had gone into the efforts to cut "I Love You Because." Sam tried to get Scotty to cut down on the instrumental flourishes— "Simplify, simplify!" was the watchword. "If we wanted Chet Atkins," said Sam good-humoredly, "we would have brought him up from Nashville and gotten him in the damn studio!" He was delighted with the rhythmic propulsion Bill Black brought to the sound. It was a slap beat and a total beat at the same time. He may not have been as good a bass player as his brother Johnny; in fact, Sam said, "Bill was one of the worst bass players in the world, technically, but, man, could he slap that thing!" And yet that wasn't it either—it was the chemistry. There was Scotty, and there was Bill, and there was Elvis scared to death in the middle, "but sounding so fresh, because it was fresh to him."

They worked on it over and over, refining the song, but the center never changed. It always opened with the ringing sound of Elvis' rhythm guitar, up till this moment almost a handicap to be gotten over. Then there was Elvis' vocal, loose and free and full of confidence, holding it together. And Scotty and Bill just fell in with an easy, swinging gait that was the very epitome of what Sam had dreamt of but never fully imagined. The first time Sam played it back for them, "we couldn't believe it was us," said Bill. "It just sounded sort of raw and ragged," said Scotty. "We thought it was exciting, but what was it? It was just so completely different. But it just really flipped Sam—he felt it really had something. We just sort of shook our heads and said, 'Well, that's fine, but good God, they'll run us out of town!' " And Elvis? Elvis flung himself into the recording process. You only have to listen to the tape to hear the confidence grow. By the last take (only two false starts and one complete alternate take remain), there is a different singer in the studio than the one started out the evening—nothing had been said, nothing had been articulated, but everything had changed.

Sam Phillips sat in the studio after the session was over and everyone had gone home. It was not unusual for him to hang around until two or three in the morning, sometimes recording, sometimes just thinking about what was going to become of his business and his family in these perilous times, sometimes mulling over his vision of the future. He knew that something was in the wind. He knew from his experience recording blues, and from his fascination with black culture, that there was something intrinsic to the music that could translate, that did translate. "It got so you could sell a half million copies of a rhythm and blues record," Sam told a Memphis reporter in 1959, reminiscing about his overnight success. "These records appealed to white youngsters just as Uncle Silas [Payne's] songs and stories used to appeal to me. . . . But there was something in many of those youngsters that resisted buying this music. The Southern ones especially felt a resistance that even they probably didn't quite understand. They liked the music, but they weren't sure whether they ought to like it or not. So I got to thinking how many records you could sell if you could find white performers who could play and sing in this same exciting, alive way."

The next night everyone came to the studio, but nothing much happened. They tried a number of different songs—they even gave the Rodgers and Hart standard "Blue Moon" (a 1949 hit for Billy Eckstine) a passing try—but nothing really clicked, and both that evening and the next were spent in more or less getting to know one another musically. Nonetheless, Sam had little doubt of what had transpired in the studio that first night. There was always the question of whether or not it was a fluke, as far as that went, only time would tell. But Sam Phillips was never one to hold back, when he believed in something he just plunged ahead. And so, on Wednesday night, after calling an early halt to the proceedings, he telephoned Dewey Phillips down at the new WHBQ studio in the Hotel Chisca. "Get yourself a wheelbarrow full of goober dust," Dewey was very likely announcing when Sam made the call, "and roll it in the door [of whatever sponsor Dewey happened to be representing], and tell 'em Phillips sent you. *And call Sam!*"

Dewey Phillips in 1954 was very nearly at the apogee of his renown and glory. From a fifteen-minute unpaid spot that he had talked his way into while managing the record department at W. T. Grant's, he had graduated to a 9:00-to-midnight slot six nights a week. According to the

Memphis papers he would get as many as three thousand letters a week and forty to fifty telegrams a night, a measure not just of his audience but of the *fervor* of that audience. When, a year or two later, he asked his listeners to blow their horns at 10 in the evening, the whole city, it was said, erupted with a single sound, and when the police chief, who was also listening, called to remind Dewey of Memphis' antinoise ordinance and begged him not to do it again, Dewey announced on the air, "Well, good people, Chief MacDonald just called me, and he said we can't do that anymore. Now I was going to have you do it at eleven o'clock, but the chief told me we couldn't do it, so whatever you do at eleven o'clock, don't blow your horns." The results were predictable.

One night an assistant started a fire in the wastebasket and convinced Dewey that the hotel was on fire, but Dewey, a hero of the Battle of Hurtgen Forest, kept right on broadcasting, directing the fire department down to the station and staying on the air until the hoax was discovered. He broadcast in stereo before stereo was invented, playing the same record on two turntables which never started or ended together, creating a phased effect that pleased Dewey unless it got so far out of line that he took the needle off both records with a scrawk and announced that he was just going to have to start all over and try it again.

WDIA DJ and R&B singer Rufus Thomas referred to Dewey as "a man who just happened to be white," and he never lost his Negro audience, even after the white teen-age audience that Sam sensed out there made itself known. He went everywhere in Memphis, paraded proudly down Beale Street, greeted the same people who, the *Commercial Appeal* reported in 1950, had flocked to Grant's "just to see the man 'what gets hisself so messed up.' " He had several chances to go national but passed them—or allowed them to pass *him* up—by remaining himself. There were two kinds of people in Memphis, the *Press-Scimitar* declared in 1956, "those who are amused and fascinated by Dewey, and those who, when they accidentally tune in, jump as tho stung by a wasp and hurriedly switch to something nice and cultural, like Guy Lombardo." "He was a genius," said Sam Phillips, "and I don't call many people geniuses."

Dewey stopped by the recording studio after his show. It was well after midnight, but that was as good a time as any for Dewey. "Dewey [was] completely unpredictable," wrote *Press-Scimitar* reporter Bob Johnson, his (and Sam's) friend, in various celebrations of his spirit over the years. "He would call at three or four A.M. and insist I listen to something over the phone. I tried to tell him it was no time to be phoning anyone, but Dewey had no sense of time. Sometimes I wonder if there is a real

Dewey, or if he's just something that happens as he goes along." If he was a personality that just unfolded, though, it was because he cared so much about what he was doing. Whatever Dewey did, everyone agreed, it was from the heart. Ordinarily, when he stopped by the studio, all he could talk about at first was the show. "Oh God, he loved his show," Sam Phillips said. "He wasn't just playing records and cutting the monitor down. He was enjoying everything he said, every record that he played, every response he got from his listeners. Dewey could get more excited than anyone you ever saw." And he loved to argue with Sam. To Marion Keisker, Sam and Dewey were so close that she couldn't stand to be in the same room with the two of them—and it wasn't just that she saw Dewey as a bad influence (though she did). She was also, she admitted, jealous; she saw Dewey as a threat. "Dewey loved to argue with Sam, just for the sake of arguing," recalled the singer Dickey Lee. "Talking about how Sam can intimidate people, one night Sam was off on one of his tirades, and right in the middle Dewey had a rubber band and snapped it at Sam and hit him in the head. He thought it was the funniest thing. Sam would get so mad at Dewey, but he loved him. Dewey always referred to Sam as his half brother, even though they weren't related at all."

This particular night, though, there wasn't any arguing. Sam had something he wanted to play for Dewey, he said right off, and he was uncharacteristically nervous about it. Sam Phillips didn't like to ask a favor of anyone—and he didn't really consider that he was asking a favor now—but he was asking Dewey to listen to something, he was asking him to consider something that had never previously existed on this earth; this wasn't just a matter of sitting around and bullshitting and letting Dewey absorb whatever happened to come his way. "But, you know it was a funny thing," said Sam. "There was an element of Dewey that was a conservative, too. When he picked a damn record, he didn't want to be wrong. 'Cause he had that thing going, 'How much bullshit have you got in you, man, and when are you gonna deliver?' It so happened, by God, that people believed Dewey, and he delivered. 'Cause when he went on the air [he didn't have any scientific method], he just blabbed it right out, 'It's gonna be a hit, it's gonna be a hit, it's the biggest thing you ever heard. I tell you what, man, it's gonna knock you out.' And, you know, as much as he respected me and loved me, Dewey had some real hangups about what could be done locally—it was like if somebody was five hundred or a thousand miles away there was more intrigue about them. So it was an elongated education process, really, he wanted to make you prove it to him unequivocally. And he was so into the finished product he didn't care how it came about, it was just, what did you deliver for him to make his show great? I think he was just beginning to feel that by God, there was a legitimate record crusader in this town."

Dewey opened a Falstaff and sprinkled some salt in it, then sat back and listened intently as Sam played the tape of the single song over and over. Dewey knew the song, of course; he had played the Arthur "Big Boy" Crudup version many times on his own show. It was the sound that puzzled him. For once there was not much conversation as the two men listened, each wondering what exactly the other thought. "He was reticent, and I was glad that he was," said Sam. "If he hadn't been reticent, it would have scared me to death, if he had said, 'Hey, man, this is a hit, it's a hit,' I would have thought Dewey was just trying to make me feel good. What I was thinking was, where you going to go with this, it's not black, it's not white, it's not pop, it's not country, and I think Dewey was the same way. He was fascinated by it—there was no question about that—I mean, he loved the damn record, but it was a question of where do we go from here?"

They stayed up listening and talking in comparatively muted tones until 2 or 3 in the morning, when both men finally returned home to their respective families and beds. Then, what to Sam's surprise, the phone rang early the next morning, and it was Dewey. "I didn't sleep well last night, man," Dewey announced. Sam said, "Man, you should have slept pretty good, with all that Jack Daniel's and beer in you." No, Dewey said, he hadn't been able to sleep, because he kept thinking about that record, he wanted it for his show tonight, in fact he wanted two copies, and he said, "We ain't letting anybody know." His reticence, Sam said, was over on that day.

Sam cut the acetates that afternoon and brought them down to the station. He called Elvis after work to tell him that Dewey would most likely be playing the record on his show that night. Elvis' response was not uncharacteristic. "He fixed the radio and told us to leave it on that station," said Gladys, "and then he went to the movies. I guess he was just too nervous to listen." "I thought people would laugh at me," Elvis told C. Robert Jennings of the *Saturday Evening Post* in 1965. "Some did, and some are still laughing, I guess."

Vernon and Gladys did listen. They sat glued to the radio with Vernon's mother, Minnie, and the rest of the relatives listening in their nearby homes, until at last, at 9:30 or 10, Dewey announced that he had a new record, it wasn't even a record, actually, it was a dub of a new record that Sam was going to be putting out next week, and it was going to be a *hit,* dee-gaw, ain't that right, Myrtle ("Moo," went the cow), and he slapped the acetate—the acetates—on the turntables.

The response was instantaneous. Forty-seven phone calls, it was said, came in right away, along with fourteen telegrams—or was it 114 phone calls and forty-seven telegrams?—he played the record seven times in a row, eleven times, seven times over the course of the rest of the program. In retrospect it doesn't really matter; it seemed as if all of Memphis was listening as Dewey kept up his nonstop patter, egging his radio audience on, encouraging them to join him in the discovery of a new voice, proclaiming to the world that Daddy-O-Dewey played the hits, that we way uptown, about as far uptown as you can get, did anybody want to buy a fur-lined duck? And if that one didn't flat git it for you, you can go to. . . . And tell 'em Phillips sent you!

For Gladys the biggest shock was "hearing them say his name over the radio just before they put on that record. That shook me so it stayed with me right through the whole song—Elvis Presley—just my son's name. I couldn't rightly hear the record the first time round." She didn't have time to think about it for long anyway, because almost immediately the phone rang. It was Dewey for Elvis. When she told him Elvis was at the movies, he said, "Mrs. Presley, you just get that cotton-picking son of yours down here to the station. I played that record of his, and them bird-brain phones haven't stopped ringing since." Gladys went down one aisle of the Suzore No. 2, and Vernon went down the other—or at least so the story goes—and within minutes Elvis was at the station.

"I was scared to death," Elvis said. "I was shaking all over, I just couldn't believe it, but Dewey kept telling me to cool it, [this] was really happening."

"Sit down, I'm gone interview you" were his first words to the frightened nineteen-year-old, Dewey told writer Stanley Booth in 1967. "He said, 'Mr. Phillips, I don't know nothing about being interviewed.' 'Just don't say nothing dirty,' I told him. He sat down, and I said I'd let him know when we were ready to start. I had a couple of records cued up, and while they played we talked. I asked him where he went to high school, and he said, 'Humes.' I wanted to get that out, because a lot of people listening had thought he was colored. Finally I said, 'All right, Elvis, thank you very much.' 'Aren't you gone interview me?' he asked. 'I already have,' I said. 'The mike's been open the whole time.' He broke out in a cold sweat."

It was Thursday, July 8. Elvis escaped out in the hot night air. He walked back up Main to Third Street and then over to Alabama.

GOT TO BE ROCK AND ROLL MUSIC

When he did time for tax evasion in 1979, Chuck Berry spent his hours behind bars writing an autobiography. His distinctive voice makes it clear there was no as-told-to collaborator. Berry's song lyrics are among the best in the genre, bested only by the works of Bob Dylan.

Berry was the first black rock and roll superstar and was the target of persecution by the white establishment. He was convicted of a Mann Act violation that stymied his early career.

As John Lennon said, introducing Berry to a television audience, "If you tried to give 'rock and roll' another name, you might call it 'Chuck Berry.' "

IT WAS A HOT Friday typical of summer in the Gateway City. It was only May, but in Missouri the month doesn't matter. When it decides to be hot it just does it. Dad, Hank, and I had been disassembling an old frame bungalow in the suburbs of St. Louis but I'd asked for this day off because I had an urge to hit the road again in the new station wagon.

Ralph Burris, my high-school classmate and long-time friend, had agreed to take off with me to visit his mother in Chicago. We arrived at sundown in the equally hot but windy city and drove directly to Ralph's mother's home to pay our respects, ate a well-prepared supper, then hit the streets to paint Chicago's Southside. Starting on 47th Street at Calumet, we hit most of the blues joints, bar after bar, spending time only in those that had live music.

I saw Howlin' Wolf and Elmore James for the first time on 47th Street, a tour I'll never lose memory of. I didn't want to leave the place where Elmore James was performing but Ralph had seen these artists before and insisted that we try other places. At the Palladium on Wabash Avenue we looked up and found the marquee glowing with MUDDY WATERS TONIGHT. Ralph gave me the lead as we ran up the stairs to the club, knowing I sang Muddy's songs and that he was my favorite blues singer.

We paid our fifty-cents admission and scrimmaged forward to the bandstand, where in true living color I saw Muddy Waters.

He was playing "Mo Jo Working" at that moment and was closing the last set of the night. Once he'd finished, Ralph boldly called out from among the many people trying to get Muddy's autograph and created the opportunity for me to speak with my idol. It was the feeling I suppose one would get from having a word with the president or the pope. I quickly told him of my admiration for his compositions and asked him who I could see about making a record. Other fans of Muddy's were scuffing for a chance to just say hi to him, yet he chose to answer my question.

Those very famous words were, "Yeah, see Leonard Chess. Yeah, Chess Records over on Forty-seventh and Cottage." Muddy was the godfather of blues. He was perhaps the greatest inspiration in the launching of my career. I was a disciple in worship of a lord who had just granted me a lead that led to a never-ending love for music. It was truly the beginning as I continued to watch his most humble compliance in attempting to appease his enthused admirers. The way he communicated with those fans was recorded in my memory, and I've tried to respond in a similar way to fans of my own.

(Somewhere, somebody wrote in their column that on the occasion when I met Muddy he allowed me to play with his band. It has always hurt me when a writer replaces the truth with fictitious dramatic statements to increase interest in his story. I was a stranger to Muddy and in no way was I about to ask my godfather if I could sit in and play. He didn't know me from Adam on that eve and Satan himself could not have tempted me to contaminate the father's fruit of the blues, as pure as he picked it. Furthermore, I had wonders about my ability as a professional musician, singer, or anything else when in the presence of someone like the great Muddy Waters.)

I had planned to drive home to St. Louis that Sunday afternoon but, with anticipations of a chance at recording, I decided to stay over in Chicago until Monday. I couldn't believe I would be making connections with the Chess Record Company after being lucky enough to speak with Muddy, too.

Monday morning early I drove over to 4720 Cottage Grove Avenue to the Chess Record Company and watched from a store across the street for the first person to enter the door. After a lady entered, a man came in dressed in a business suit, so I ran across Cottage Grove to challenge my weekend dream. While I was posing just inside the office door, he looked up from scanning mail and said, "Hi, come on in," then left for a further office.

Before I started my well-rehearsed introduction, I saw a black girl receptionist (Adella, as I remember) and asked her if I could speak with Mr. Leonard Chess. I was getting more of the shivers as I glanced through the big window into the studio. She told me that the man I had followed in was himself Leonard Chess, and he reentered the outer office and beckoned me into his. He listened to my description of Muddy's advice and my plans and hopes, asking occasional questions regarding my expectations. Finally he asked if I had a tape of my band with me.

I had been taping at home on a seventy-nine-dollar, quarter-inch, reel-to-reel recorder that I'd purchased in contemplation of such an audition. I told him I was visiting from St. Louis, but could return with the tapes (which I hadn't truly made yet) whenever he could listen to them. He said he could hear them within a week and I left immediately for St. Louis. He had stood all the while I was talking to him with a look of amazement that he later told me was because of the businesslike way I'd talked to him.

After I traveled down from U.S. Highway 66, I contacted Johnnie Johnson and Ebby Hardy and began arranging rehearsals. Johnnie, Ebby, and I had been playing other people's music ever since we started at the Cosmo, but for this tape I did not want to cover other artist's tunes. Leonard Chess had explained that it would be better for me if I had original songs. I was very glad to hear this because I had created many extra verses for other people's songs and I was eager to do an entire creation of my own. The four that I wrote may have been influenced melodically by other songs, but, believe me, the lyrics were solely my own. Before the week had ended, I brought fresh recorded tapes to the ears of the Chess brothers in Chicago.

Chess was in the heart of the Southside of Chicago amid a cultural district I knew all too well. Leonard told me he had formerly had a bar in the neighborhood as well, which accounted for his easy relations with black people. When I carried the new tape up I immediately found out from a poster on the office wall that Muddy, Little Walter, Howlin' Wolf, and Bo Diddley were recording there. In fact Bo Diddley dropped by the studio that day.

Leonard listened to my tape and when he heard one hillbilly selection I'd included called "Ida May," played back on the one-mike, one-track home recorder, it struck him most as being commercial. He couldn't believe that a country tune (he called it a "hillbilly song") could be written and sung by a black guy. He said he wanted us to record that particular song, and he scheduled a recording session for May 21, 1955, promising me a contract at that time.

I went back to St. Louis to more carpenter work with Dad but also with a plan to cut a record with a company in Chicago. Each time I nailed a nail or sawed a board I was putting a part of a song together, preparing for the recording session to come. At the Cosmo Club I boasted of the records we were going to make soon and we took the lead in popularity over Ike Turner's band, our main rivals at the time in the East St. Louis music scene.

Muddy Waters was in the St. Louis area one night around this time and visited the Cosmopolitan Club. Enthralled to be so near one of my idols, I delegated myself to chaperone him around spots of entertainment in East St. Louis. Ike Turner was playing at the Manhattan Club and since he was my local rival for prestige I took Muddy there to show Ike how big I was and who I knew. When we got to the Manhattan Club, Muddy preceded Johnnie, Ebby, and myself up to the box office and announced, "I'm Muddy Waters." The cashier said, "A dollar fifty." Muddy just reached in his pocket and forked it out with no comment. That incident remains on my mind unto this very day. From that experience I swore never to announce myself in hopes of getting anything gratis, regardless of what height I might rise to in fame.

I took Muddy to my house that night, introduced him to Toddy, who was a devout lover of his music long before I came into her life with mine, and took a photo of him holding my guitar. May his music live forever, he will always be in first place at the academy of blues, my man, "McKinley Morganfield," Muddy Waters.

Finally the day came and I drove back to Chicago with my little band, on time, as I'd promised Leonard Chess. According to the way Dad did business, I was expecting Leonard to first take me into his office and execute the recording contracts. But instead he said he wanted to get "that tune" on tape right away. So we unloaded my seven-month-new red Ford station wagon and Phil Chess took the three of us into the studio and placed us around, telling us how we should set up for the session. I could see right away that Leonard was the brains of the company because he was busy making decisions and dictating to the five or six employees there. Phil ran around making friends and seeing that everybody was jockeyed into position for the flow of productions during the day.

I was familiar with moving in and away from the microphone to project or reduce the level of my voice but was not aware that in a studio that would be done by the engineer during the song. Having as much knowledge about recording as my homemade tapes afforded me was a big help, but I listened intently and learned much from the rehearsal of the tunes with Phil instructing us. I tried to act professional although I was as frightened and green as a cucumber most of the time.

The studio was about twenty feet wide and fifty feet long with one seven-foot baby-grand piano and about twelve microphones available. I had used only one for the tape I'd come to audition with and eight were used for our four-piece session. There was a stack of throw rugs, a giant slow-turning ceiling fan, and two long fluorescent lights over a linoleum tile floor. Leonard Chess was the engineer and operated the Ampex 403 quarter-inch monaural tape recorder. Through the three-by-four-foot studio control-room window we watched him, or sometimes his brother Phil, rolling the tape and instructing us with signs and hand waving to start or stop the music.

The first song we recorded was "Ida May." Leonard suggested that I should come up with a new name for the song, and on the spot I altered it to "Maybellene."

Leonard had arranged for a lyricist/musician, Willie Dixon, who'd written many of Muddy's tunes, to sit in on the session, playing a stand-up bass to fill out the sound of the music. Electric bass instruments were yet to come and Willie, stout as he was, was a sight to behold slapping his ax to the tempo of a country-western song he really seemed to have little confidence in.

Each musician had one mike, excepting the drummer, who had three. I had one for the guitar and one for my vocal, which I sat down to sing because a chair was there and I thought that was how it was supposed to be done. We struggled through the song, taking thirty-five tries before completing a track that proved satisfactory to Leonard. Several of the completions, in my opinion, were perfectly played. We all listened to the final playback and then went on to record the next song which was "Wee Wee Hours." By then it was midafternoon. Around eight-thirty that night we finished the recording session. "Maybellene," "Wee Wee Hours," "Thirty Days," and "You Can't Catch Me" were the songs completed. Leonard sent out for hamburgers and pop and we lingered an hour picnicking, an ordeal that became a ritual with Leonard bearing the tab.

It was nearly ten o'clock when we went into Leonard's office and sat down for the first time to execute the contract he'd promised. The recording contract he handed me seemed to be a standard form, having no company-name heading at the top. It was machine printed on one side of the single sheet of paper. The other paper he gave me was a publishing contract, a segment of the music business I was totally ignorant of. It was printed on a double sheet, but I didn't understand most of the terms and arrangements of publishing either. I did see the word *copyright* several times as I read through it and thus figured if it was connected with the United States government, it was legitimate and I was likely protected. I remembered when I was a child, Dad had talked about getting a patent for a perpetual-motion apparatus that he'd invented, telling us nobody could take your achievements from you when they're patented and copyrighted.

Anyway, I read it word for word. Some of the statements were beyond my knowledge of the record business, such as the "residuals from mechanical rights," the "writer and producer's percentages," and the "performance royalties and publisher fees," but I intentionally would frown at various sections to give the impression that a particular term (I actually knew nothing of) was rather unfavorable. From the white of my eyes I could detect Leonard watching my reaction closely all the while I was reading, which made me think I was being railroaded. In fact, the corner of my left eyeball was checking out his response to my reaction, yet still knowing full well I'd sign the darn thing anyway. I slowly read on, finally signing it at last. I took my single-page copy, shook hands, and bade happy farewells to what was now "my" record company, loaded up, and drove off into the night with Johnnie and Ebby to St. Louis.

As we drove home through the black night more songs were sprouting in my head.

Nelson George

THE GODFATHER OF SOUL

If you think rock and roll was just about music, then make sure you read this piece by Nelson George. Rock and roll symbolized the recognition of black America by white America, so it's no surprise the music arrived simultaneously with the great advances of the civil rights movement. Here, Nelson George underscores the musical and political importance of James Brown.

George, a former music critic for *Rolling Stone* and the *Village Voice*, is the author of *The Death of Rhythm and Blues, Where Did Our Love Go?*, and *Buppies, B-Boys, BAPs & Bohos.*

DURING THE 1960s James Brown single-handedly demonstrated the possibilities for artistic and economic freedom that black music could provide if one constantly struggled against its limitations. Brown was more than R&B's most dynamic performer. "J.B." used his prestige as a weapon to push through innovations in the sound and the marketing of black music. Though Berry Gordy's name tops the list of black music's great entrepreneurs, Brown's efforts—despite being directed in a single-minded celebration of self—are in some ways just as impressive. He was driven by an enormous ambition and unrelenting ego, making him a living symbol of black self-determination. White managers may have made all the business decisions for most black stars, but Brown maneuvered his white manager, Jack Bart, and later his son, Ben, into a comanaging situation, where no crucial decisions (and few minor ones) could be made without the singer's input. In the early sixties, when Brown's contemporaries (and rivals) Jackie Wilson and Sam Cooke traveled with, at best, a guitar and a bass player, Brown built a raucous revue backed by the preeminent big band of its era, one that performed with the flair of Louis Jordan's Tympany Five and the discipline of the Count Basie Orchestra. Where booking agents and arena managers often dictated appearances to even the biggest R&B acts, Brown's organization used their clout to demand the best dates and biggest dollars. Eschewing national promoters, Brown handled the chore himself, cutting out the middlemen, which allowed him to offer black retailers and deejays a piece of the action in exchange for special promotional "consideration." Motown may have been the sound of young America, but Brown was clearly the king of black America. How he managed his kingdom illustrates his impact and remains his enduring legacy.

Brown was rightfully dubbed "the hardest-working man in show business" because of a work load of five to six one-nighters a week from the mid-sixties through the early seventies. Until 1973 he worked anywhere from nine to eleven months a year. The only breaks in his nonstop touring came when he played a lengthy stand at the Apollo, Howard, Uptown, or elsewhere. What isn't generally known is that this rigorous schedule was very much of Brown's own making. Every two months or so Brown and his road managers (in the late 1960s it was Bob Patton and Alan Leeds) would pull out the Rand-McNally maps and decide the show's routing. A key city, "a money town" they called it, would be picked for the crucial Friday and Saturday night dates. Brown and company would then study the map and judge the next town they could reach comfortably by the next night. If they played Philadelphia's Uptown on Friday, maybe they'd hit Richmond, Virginia, Saturday, and Fayetteville, Arkansas, on Sunday. An ideal schedule would be laid out and then Brown's employees would call around the country to see if the show could be booked according to their plan. More often than not it was, since Brown was much loved by arena managers. For all the grit and earthiness of his music, Brown put on a clean show—no cursing, no gross sexuality—that brought in the entire family. Since arenas dealt directly with Brown's organization, instead of going through a local promoter, they never worried that Brown wouldn't show up or would be late—all consequences for such unprofessional conduct would fall directly on Brown. Brown's team was very sensitive to not overbooking a lucrative market and squeezing it dry. They tried to space dates in a "money town" between six to nine months apart and played slow markets once every year and a half.

Since Brown controlled his always lucrative shows, he was able to use them to reward and penalize deejays or retailers who had or had not cooperated in promoting his material. In smaller cities, Brown often awarded deejays, notoriously underpaid as we've seen, a piece of the date, ensuring both their loyalty and the play of Brown's current release in the weeks prior to his appearance. In many cases these deejays became known in the market as "Mr. Brown's representatives"—a prestigious title in the black community—and were expected to provide Brown's organization with firsthand feedback on his records and supervise distribution of posters promoting the show.

The local deejays, in conjunction with Brown's national office, coordinated radio time buys and the purchase of advertising space in the black press beginning two months before Brown came to town. Usually two weeks before the appearance, Brown's office would monitor ticket sales to see if additional promotional efforts (radio spots, ticket giveaways, etc.) were needed.

Unlike today's tours, where tons of equipment are carried from city to city by a convoy of trucks, the entire James Brown Revue—forty to fifty people and all the gear—traveled in one truck and one bus. In the mid- to late 1960s the show's equipment consisted of two Supertrooper spotlights, one microphone, and an amplifier for the saxophones. The drum and rhythm section (bass, guitars) weren't mixed at all except for their own on-stage amplifiers. Road manager Leeds remembers that in 1966, when Brown introduced a flickering strobe light into the act while dancing "the mashed potato, people in the audience were awestruck."

In 1985 it took the recording of "We Are the World" and the Live Aid concert to bring top stars and musicians together. In the R&B world twenty years before, it was customary for any other musicians in town to come around and say hello to the touring star. Backstage at a James Brown concert was a party, networking conference, and rehearsal studio all in one. Part of this was just professional camaraderie, though for many musicians these gatherings allowed them to bid for a spot in Brown's band. In the late 1960s, with Brown's low man making $400 a week and veteran players around $900, he was paying among the most generous rates in R&B.

Moreover, critics, deejays, and even other players generally acknowledged the band to be the best of its kind. Some thought Otis Redding's Bar-Kays were tough. So were the guys Sam and Dave used. Same for Joe Tex's band. But the JBs, as they came to be called, earned their reputation because they were as strong-willed and intense about their music as their boss. Under the guidance of Brown and superb mid-sixties bandleader Alfred (Pee Wee) Ellis, the JBs took the rhythm & blues basics laid down by Louis Jordan and his disciples and created a style, now known as funk, that inspired Sly Stone, George Clinton, and so many others to come.

Funk evolved while the JBs were on the road, on the tour bus, in hotels, backstage, and in hastily called recording sessions. A great many of

Brown's pioneering dance jams were cut following concerts, including the early funk experiment from 1967, "Cold Sweat," and the landmark 1970 single "Sex Machine." Often a rare off-day would suddenly become a work day when the musical mood struck Brown. He liked to record his music as soon as he got an idea. The spark often came on the road, as Ellis and the players strove to keep the show fresh. With these rearrangements, new songs emerged from old.

For example, in January 1967, Brown's "Let Yourself Go," a two-and-a-half minute dance track now little recalled, reached number five on *Billboard*'s soul chart. One reason it has faded from memory is that it was eventually overshadowed by a better song created from its chords. On the road that winter, "Let Yourself Go" became a ten-minute jam during which Brown displayed his mastery of several dances, including the camel walk and the mashed potato. While he was performing at the Apollo, someone pointed out that the jam was virtually a new tune. As a result, "There Was a Time," a song marked by one of the JBs' best horn lines, was recorded live and went on to become one of Brown's funkiest hits. As the melodies of Brown's songs became more rudimentary, and the interlocking rhythmic patterns grew more complex, the JBs began to use horns, guitar, and keyboards—usually melodic instruments—as tools of percussion. Short, bitter blasts of brass and reeds now punctuated the grooves and complemented Brown's harsh, declamatory vocals. Listening to recordings of the JBs from 1967 to 1969, the band's most innovative period, it is hard at times to distinguish the guitars from the congas because the band is so focused on rhythmic interplay.

As Robert Palmer wrote in the *Rolling Stone Illustrated History*, "Brown, his musicians, and his arrangers began to treat every instrument and voice in the group as if it were a drum. The horns played single-note bursts that were often sprung against downbeats. The bass lines were broken up into choppy two- and three-note patterns, a procedure common in Latin music since the forties but unusual in R&B." "Sheer energy" is what writer Al Young felt when he first heard Brown's classic "Cold Sweat." "James Brown was pushing and pulling and radiating in ultra-violet concentric circles of thermo-radiant funks," Young said. By the time of Brown's last great recording, "The Big Payback" in 1973, the JBs sounded as tense and sparse as a Hemingway short story, though admittedly a lot easier to dance to.

Brown's relentless flow of singles, many released in two parts, were products of an uncontrollable creative ferment. The grooves simply couldn't be contained by the three-minute 45 rpm format of the day.

Unfortunately, the twelve-inch single was not yet in vogue; it would have been the perfect format for Brown's propulsive music. But today Brown's output would be constrained by other marketing strategies and corporate-release patterns—the conventional wisdom that only so much product can be put out in any twelve-month period. At King Records, however, his recording home during his greatest years, Brown had carte blanche. It was a power he had fought for and won.

The sales of his 1962 *Live at the Apollo* were phenomenal. Even without wide white support, the record went gold at a time when most black studio albums sold only 200,000 copies; it stayed on *Billboard*'s album chart for sixty-six weeks, and reached number two. Despite this success, Brown felt his singles weren't being marketed properly. So in an ambitious stab at gaining more control of his career, in 1964 Brown formed Fair Deal Productions, and, instead of delivering his next set of recordings to King, he sent them to Smash, a subsidiary of Chicago's Mercury Records. One of the records was "Out of Sight," a brilliant cut that in its use of breaks—sections where voices, horns, or guitars are heard unaccompanied—anticipated the work of disco deejays of the next decade. With Mercury's greater clout, the song became one of Brown's first records to reach whites.

Syd Nathan, King's feisty president and a charter member of the R&B indie old school, didn't hesitate to sue, and for almost a year, Brown, Nathan, and Mercury battled. The outcome: Brown stayed with King, but Nathan promised more aggressive promotion and gave Brown broader artistic control—similar to what Ray Charles enjoyed at Atlantic and ABC and Sam Cooke had with SAR and later at RCA. It was this control that would allow Brown to make the most controversial and important records of his career.

Dr. Martin Luther King, Jr., was assassinated in Memphis on April 4, 1968. Brown was booked for that night at the Boston Garden. Initially city officials were going to cancel the show, in light of the riots shaking Boston's black neighborhoods. Then the idea of broadcasting the show live on public television stations was suggested as a way to keep angry blacks off the streets. And so it was. Today, tapes of that performance are bootlegged and still treasured by black-music fans. At the time, it served its purpose, keeping the historically tense relations between whites and blacks in that "liberal" city cool, at least for the evening.

For Brown, never one lacking in self-esteem, this confirmed his power in black America, a power that the previous summer had led vice president and presidential candidate Hubert Humphrey to give him an award for helping quell riots with public statements. A capitalist and a patriot (he played for troops in Vietnam and Korea), Brown was also genuinely moved by the black-pride movement. Seeking to fulfill his role as a leader, he cut "America Is My Home," and was branded an Uncle Tom by radical blacks. (His "Living in America" is the 1986 counterpart.) But he saw no contradiction, and shouldn't have, when he released "Say It Loud, I'm Black and I'm Proud" in the summer of 1968. Supported by the JBs' usual rhythmic intensity, Brown shouted out a testimonial to black pride that, like the phrase "Black Power," was viewed as a *call* to arms by many whites. For a time Brown's "safe" reputation with whites in the entertainment business suffered. In interviews, Brown has blamed resentful whites for his failure to enjoy another top-ten pop single until the 1980s. (In 1969 "Mother Popcorn" reached number eleven and "Give It Up or Turn It Loose" number fifteen.) Still, it didn't deter Brown from his newfound leadership role, and he went on to cut the message-oriented "I Don't Want Nobody to Give Me Nothing," the motivational "Get Up, Get Into It, Get Involved," the prideful "Soul Power," the cynical "Talking Loud and Saying Nothing," and the nondance rap record "King Heroin," a black jail-house rhyme put to music. The irony of Brown's musical statements and public posturing as "Soul Brother #1" was that he became an embarrassingly vocal supporter of that notoriously antiblack politician, Richard Milhous Nixon.

Much of Nixon's appeal for Brown was the president's advocacy of "black capitalism," a seemingly fine philosophy that saw an increase in black-owned businesses as the key to black advancement. At the time, Brown owned several radio stations, much property, and a growing organization. He identified with black capitalism's self-reliant tone. Nixon, who understood the desire for power, made Brown feel he was a key example of black capitalism at work, which appealed to the singer's gigantic ego. Brown didn't understand the nuances of Nixon's plan—reach out to showcase some black business efforts while dismantling Johnson's Great Society programs, which for all their reputed mismanagement had helped a generation of blacks begin the process of upward mobility.

But naive though he might have been about Nixon, Brown did choose this juncture in his long career to assume some kind of leadership role in black America. It wasn't enough for him to be an artist anymore; he saw himself as a spokesman with as much right to articulate his world view as H. Rap Brown, Stokely Carmichael, Eldridge Cleaver, or any of the other more obviously political figures who professed authority. The "Godfather of Soul" had decided that he, too, could aggressively project his vision.

Looking back I find it is simply impossible to resolve all the contradictions in James Brown. As a businessman with a long and lucrative career based on astute self-management, he was a sterling example, and advocate, of black self-sufficiency. He was also as happy as he could be within the white-dominated system, buying diamond rings for his fingers with the profits from his white fans. A stone-cold assimilationist in the general political realm, he carried himself with an arrogant, superconfident demeanor that in fact wasn't far removed from the street-corner polemical style of other, far more radical sixties black spokesmen. In a way, it is these very contradictions—and Brown's own unbothered attitude about them—that make him a consummate American.

There is another aspect of Brown, though, that causes some unease if we try to hold him up as a kind of model. Given the unbridled machismo that was part and parcel of the energy driving him (as well as Carmichael, Cleaver, and others), black women were simply attached as a postscript to a male-directed message. As Michelle Wallace, with some overstatement but a lot of truth, observed in *Black Macho and the Myth of the Superwoman,* these men thought of women as mothers, cooks, and servants of the revolution, not as its leaders. It didn't have to be that way. Black women were, of course, as capable of leadership as any male. Fallout from this political patriarchy would be felt in black literature in the future, but in the late 1960s, feminist issues weren't overtly part of the agendas of the nationalist or even civil-rights movements.

Philip Norman

A GOOD STOMPING BAND

George Harrison once said the Beatles had been a pretty good band before they became famous. When the band started out in the dives and strip clubs of Hamburg, Germany, they played six-hour, vocal-chord-shredding sets of American rock and roll. Norman's book *Shout!* recreates the grimy feel of the bawdy clubs. Back then the band included John, Paul, and George, along with doomed Stuart Sutcliffe (he died of a brain hemorrhage in 1962) and drummer Pete Best. Their manager was a local nightclub owner back home in Liverpool, Allan Williams, soon to be replaced by rich kid Brian Epstein, who would clean up the band and send them off to fame. Here they are, arriving in Hamburg.

THEY EXPECTED a city like Liverpool, and this, in a sense, they found. There was the same river, broad like the Mersey but unlike the Mersey crowded with ships and with shipyards, beyond, that seemed to grow out of lush forests. There was the same overhead railway that Liverpool had recently lost, although nothing resembling the same tired cityscape beneath. Not the bomb-sites and rubbish, but tree-lined boulevards, seamless with prosperity; chic shops and ships chandlers and cafés filled with well-dressed, unscarred, confident people. There was a glimpse of the dark-spired *Rathaus;* of the Alster lake, set about by glass-walled banks and press buildings, and traversed by elegant swans. What was said inside Allan William's minibus that August evening would be echoed many times afterwards in varying tones of disbelief. Wasn't this the country which had *lost* the war?

The journey from the West German frontier had been rich in incident. At one point, they were almost run down by a tram, in whose rails Lord Woodbine had accidentally engaged the minibus's front wheels. Allan Williams, taking over as driver on the outskirts of Hamburg, had immediately rammed a small saloon car.

They arrived on the Reeperbahn just as neon lights were beginning to eclipse the fairground palings of the night clubs and their painted, acrobatic nudes. Spotting the narrow road junction, where an *Imbiss* belched out fumes of *Frikadelli* and *Currywurst,* Allan Williams remembered where he was. They turned left onto Grosse Freiheit, welcomed by overarching illuminations and the stare of predatory eyes.

Even John Lennon, with his fondness for human curiosities, had not expected an employer quite like Bruno Koschmider. The figure which hopped out of the Kaiserkeller to greet them had begun life in a circus, working as a clown, fire-eater, acrobat and illusionist with fifty small cage birds hidden in his coat. His dwarfish stature, his large, elaborately coiffured head, his turned-up nose and quick stumping gait, all made even John not quite likely to laugh. Bruno, for his part, was unimpressed by the look of his new employees. "They were dressed in bad clothes—cheap shirts, trousers that were not clean. Their fingernails were dirty."

If Bruno was somewhat disconcerting, his Kaiserkeller Club brought much reassurance. The exterior portice bore, in large letters, the name DERRY AND THE SENIORS VON LIVERPOOL. A glimpse inside, on the way to Koschmider's office, showed what seemed a vast meadow of tables and side booths, shaped like lifeboats, around the stage and miniature dance floor. The Beatles, their spirits reviving, began to laugh and cuff one another, saying *this* was all right, wasn't it? Allan Williams reminded them they were not booked to play here but in Herr Koschmider's other club, the Indra.

Further along the Grosse Freiheit, beyond St. Joseph's Catholic Church, the illuminations dwindled into a region of plain-fronted bordellos interspersed with private houses where elderly *Hausfraus* still set pot plants on the upper window ledges. Here, under a neon sign shaped like an elephant, was to be found the Indra Club. Bruno Koschmider led the way downstairs into a small cellar cabaret, gloomy, shabby and at that moment occupied by only two customers. Down here for the next eight weeks, the Beatles would be expected to play for four-and-a-half hours each weeknight and six hours on Saturdays and Sundays.

Koschmider next conducted them to the living quarters provided under the terms of his contract with Allan Williams. Across the road from the Indra, he operated a small cinema, the Bambi Kino, which varied the general diet of flesh by showing corny old gangster movies and Westerns. The Beatles' lodgings were one filthy room and two windowless cubbyholes immediately behind—and in booming earshot of—the cinema screen. The only washing facilities were the cinema toilets, from the communal vestibule of which an old woman stared at them grimly over her saucer of *Pfennigs.*

It was some consolation to meet up with Derry and the Seniors and to learn that, despite munificent billing outside the Kaiserkeller, Liverpool's famous r & b group were also having to sleep rough. "Bruno gave us one little bed between five of us," Howie Casey, the sax-player, says. "I'd been sleeping on that, covered by a flag, and the other lads slept on chairs set two together. The waiters used to lock us inside the club each night."

The Bambi Kino was not a great deal worse than the cellar of Lord Woodbine's New Colony Club or the Gambier Terrace flat back home in Liverpool. Paul and Pete Best took a cubbyhole each while John, Stu and George flopped down in the larger room. All five were soon asleep, untroubled by sounds of gunfire and police sirens, wafted through the grimy wall from the cinema screen.

Their first night's playing at the Indra was a severe letdown. Half a dozen people sat and watched them indifferently from tables with red-shaded lamps. The clientele, mainly prostitutes and their customers, showed little enthusiasm for Carl Perkins's "Honey, Don't" or Chuck Berry's "Too Much Monkey Business." The club also bore a curse in the form of an old woman living upstairs who continually phoned Police Headquarters on the Reeperbahn to complain about the noise. Bruno Koschmider, not wishing for that kind of trouble, hissed at them to turn even their feeble amplifiers down.

Allan and Beryl Williams, Barry Chang and Lord Woodbine remained in Hamburg throughout that inaugural week. Williams, himself comfortably ensconced in a small hotel, did what he could to improve the Beatles' living quarters—it was at his urgent insistence that Bruno provided blankets for their beds. Beryl shopped in the city center with her brother, and Lord Woodbine, as usual, remained worried by nothing. He sang calypsos at the Kaiserkeller and, one night, grew so affected by its libations that he attempted to dive into the South Sea Islands mural.

Allan Williams, in his conscientious moments, worried about the club he had committed his charges to, and about their plainly evinced hatred of it. On their opening night, they had played the entire four-and-a-half-hour stretch mutinously still and huddled up. "Come on, boys!" Williams exhorted them from the bar. "Make it a show, boys!" Bruno Koschmider took up the phrase, clapping his large, flat hands. "Mak show, boys," he would cry. "Mak show, Beatles! Mak show!"

John Lennon's answer was to launch himself into writhings and shim-myings that were a grotesque parody of Gene Vincent on one crippled leg at the boxing stadium show. Down the street at the Kaiserkeller, word began to spread of this other group "Von Liverpool" who leaped around like monkeys and stamped their feet deafeningly on the stage. They were stamping out the rhythm to help their new drummer, Pete Best, and also to goad the old woman upstairs.

Before long, the rival groups from the Kaiserkeller had come up to the Indra to see them. Howie Casey was astonished at the improvement since their audition as the Silver Beatles in front of Larry Parnes. "That day, they'd seemed embarrassed about how bad they were," Howie says. "You could tell something had happened to them in the meantime. They'd turned into a good stomping band."

Derry and the Seniors brought with them a wide-eyed, curly-haired youth whom all the Beatles—George Harrison, especially—regarded with awe. Born Anthony Esmond Sheridan McGinnity, he was better known as Tony Sheridan, a singer and inspired solo guitarist with many appear-ances to his credit on the "Oh Boy!" television show. His talent, however, was accompanied by habits too blithely erratic to suit the rock and roll starmakers. When Bruno Koschmider hired him, he had been sacked from "Oh Boy!" and most other engagements, and was playing at the 2 I's cof-fee bar for £1 a night. Even now, the British police were hard on his trail in respect of various hire-purchase irregularities.

Anthony Esmond steered the Beatles, past beckoning doorway touts, for an insider's tour of the Reeperbahn's peculiar delights. They saw the women who grappled in mud, cheered on by an audience tied into a pro-tective bib. They visited the Roxy Bar and met ravishing "hostesses" with tinkling laughs and undisguisably male biceps and breastbones. Two streets away, where a wooden fence forbade entry to all under eighteen, their companions steered them through the Herbertstrasse, past red-lit shop windows containing whores in every type of fancy dress, all ages from nymphet to scolding granny, smiling or scowling forth, gossiping with one another, reading, knitting, listlessly examining their own frilly garters or spooning up bowls of soup.

The other initiation was into beer. For beer, damp-gold, foam-piling under thin metal bar taps, had never been more plentiful. Derry and the Seniors, when they first opened at the Kaiserkeller, had been allowed beer ad lib in breaks between performing. Though Koschmider had hastily withdrawn this privilege, the nightly allowance still seemed vast to five boys who, at home in Liverpool, had often been hard put to scrape up the price of a corporate half-pint. Then there were the drinks pressed on them by customers at the Indra; the drinks that would be sent up to them on stage while they played. It became nothing unusual for a whole crate of beer to be shoved at their feet by well-wishers whose size and potential truculence underlined the necessity of finishing every bottle.

Everything was free. Everything was easy. The sex was easy. Here you did not chase it, as in Liverpool, and clutch at it furtively in cold shop doorways. Here it came after you, putting strong arms around you, mincing no words; it was unabashed, expert—indeed, professional. For even the most cynical whores found it piquant to have an innocent boy from Liverpool: to lure and buy as a change from being, eternally, bait and merchandise.

The Freiheit provided an abundance of everything but sleep. Sheridan and the other musicians already knew a way to get by, as the barmaids and whores and bouncers and pickpockets did, without it. Someone in the early days had discovered Preludin, a brand of German slimming tablet which, while removing appetite, also roused the metabolism to goggle-eyed hyperactivity. Soon the Beatles—all but Pete Best—were gobbling "Prellys" by the tubeful each night. As the pills took effect, they dried up the saliva, increasing the desire for beer.

Now the Beatles needed no exhortation to "mak show." John, in particular, began to go berserk on stage, prancing and groveling in imitation of any rock and roller or cripple his dazzled mind could summon up. The fact that their audience could not understand a word they said provoked John into cries of *"Sieg Heil!"* and "Fucking Nazis!" to which the audience invariably responded by laughing and clapping. Bruno Koschmider, who had fought in a Panzer division, was not so amused.

At five or six A.M.—according to subsequent adventures—they would stagger back along the sunny Freiheit, past doorway touts unsleepingly active. Behind the Bambi Kino they would collapse into their squalid beds for the two or three hours' sleep that were possible before the day's first picture show. Sometimes it would be gunfire on the screen that jolted them awake, or the voice of George Raft or Edward G. Robinson.

Hounded into consciousness, they would dash to the cinema toilets while the basins were still clean. Rosa, the female custodian, for all her outward grimness, kept clean towels for them, and odds and ends of soap. "She thought we were all mad," Pete Best says. "She'd shout things at us—*verucht* and *beknaakt*—but she'd be laughing. We called her 'Mutti.' "

There were now five or six hours to be disposed of before they began playing and drinking again. At the Gretel and Alphons or Willi's Bar, the

Freiheit's two most tolerant cafés, they would breakfast on corn flakes or chicken soup, the only food which their dehydrated frames could endure. They would then drift around the corner, through the stench of *Frikadelli* and last night's vomit, to the shop on the main Reeperbahn which fascinated John Lennon especially with its display of flick knives, bayonets, coshes, swords, brass knuckledusters and tear gas pistols.

If not too devastatingly hung over, they might catch a tram into central Hamburg, and stroll on the elegant boulevards, looking at the clothes and the perfumes, the elaborate bakers and confectioners, the radios and tape recorders and occasional displays of imported American guitars, saxophones and drums. Since their wages, paid out by Bruno on a Thursday, seldom lasted more than twenty-four hours, such expeditions were usually limited to gazing and wishing. John, however, blew every *Pfennig* he had on a new guitar, an American Rickenbacker "short arm."

*   *   *

One bleary-eyed morning when they emerged from the Bambi Kino, a piece of good news awaited them. Bruno Koschmider, bowing at last to the complaints of his customers and the old woman upstairs, was moving them out of the Indra and into his larger, better club.

The Kaiserkeller, at first, threatened to eclipse even John Lennon in noise and spectacle. The noise came from an audience several hundred strong, frequently containing entire ships' companies from English and American Naval craft visiting the port. The spectacle was provided by Bruno Koschmider's white-aproned waiters, converging on any outbreak of trouble and quelling it with a high-speed ruthlessness that made Garston Blood Baths look like a game of patty-cake. If the troublemaker were alone, he might find himself propelled not to the exit but into the office of Willi, the undermanager, there to be worked over at leisure with coshes and brass knuckles. Finally, as the victim lay prostrate, Bruno himself would weigh in with the ebony nightstick from his desk drawer.

Bruno's chief bouncer, a tiny, swaggering youth named Horst Fascher, epitomized the breed. Horst had started life as a featherweight boxer and had represented both Hamburg and the West German national team before being banned from the ring for accidentally killing a sailor in a street fight. It was shortly after serving a prison sentence for manslaughter that he had entered Bruno Koschmider's employment. His squad, nicknamed locally "Hoddel's gang," recruited from his friends at the Hamburg Boxing Academy, were held among the Freiheit's other strongarm gangs in profound respect.

Horst took the Liverpool musicians—fortunately for them—to his heart. It became an unwritten rule at the Kaiserkeller that if a musician hit trouble, "Hoddel's gang" would swoop unquestioningly to his aid. Horst showed them the Reeperbahn's innermost haunts and its choicest pleasures; he also took them home to Neuestadt to meet his mother and brothers and taste Frau Fascher's bean soup. All he asked in return was the chance, sometimes after midnight, to get up with the group on stage and bellow out an Eddie Cochran song.

"The Beatles were not good musicians at the beginning," Horst Fascher says. "John Lennon was a very poor rhythm guitarist. I remember Sheridan telling me in amazement that John played chords with only three fingers. And always they are funny—never serious. But they steal from Sheridan, from the Seniors, all the time with their eyes. And all the time the bass drum is beating like your foot when you stamp.

"That John Lennon—I loved him, he was mad. A fighter. He is *zyniker.* You say to him, 'Hey, John . . .' He would say, 'Ah, so fuckin' what.' Paul was *lustig,* the clown. He gets out of trouble by making a laugh. George was *schuchtern,* the baby one. I could never get to know Stu. He was too strange. And Pete—he was *reserviert.* You had to pull words out through his nose."

Soon after the Beatles reached the Kaiserkeller, Derry and the Seniors finished their engagement there. The replacement group, brought out from Liverpool by Allan Williams, was Rory Storm and the Hurricanes. When Rory, blond and suntanned from Butlin's, saw the Hamburg living quarters, his stammer totally overcame him. Nor did his drummer, the little bearded one with rings on his fingers, show great delight at having to sleep on chairs covered with old flags. Ringo Starr, like all the Hurricanes, was used to a little more finesse. "You want to see what the Beatles have got to put up with," Allan Williams retorted.

Rory Storm's flashiness and acrobatic feats increased the wildness of the Kaiserkeller nights. A contest developed between the Beatles and Hurricanes to see which group first could stamp its way through the already old and half-rotten timbers of the stage. Rory did it at last, vanishing from sight in the middle of "Blue Suede Shoes." A case of junk champagne was the prize, washed down with more "Prellys" at their favorite bar, the Gretel and Alphons.

Bruno Koschmider fumed and fulminated—but they got away with it. They got away, somehow, with everything. John Lennon got away with standing out in the Freiheit in a pair of long woolen underpants, reading the *Daily Express.* George got away with it time after time in the *Polizei Stunde,* or midnight curfew hour when all under eighteen were supposed to have left the club. For their drinking, swearing, fighting, whoring, even vandalizing, Grosse Freiheit pardoned them all forms of retribution but one. Allan Williams, the self-styled "little pox doctor of Hamburg," received many a worried confidence in a back room at the Gretel and Alphons, and, like a connoisseur, held many a beer glass of urine speculatively up to the light.

Pete Best preferred not to take pills. When the others raced downstairs between spots to Rosa the WC attendant—now transferred from the Bambi Kino—when they clustered around the old woman in ankle socks, thrusting out Deutschmarks for Prellys from the sweet jar under her desk, Pete Best would not be with them. He had usually gone to sit and drink on his own, smiling the quirky smile that was addressed to no one, least of all the girls in surrounding booths who strove desperately to catch his eye.

Horst Fascher was not the only one to whom Pete Best seemed *reserviert*. Though perfectly amiable, and capable of drinking his share, he had showed himself to be devoid of the others' mad ebullience. He played drums well enough—or so it then seemed—hitting his bass pedal in the hard, stamping "mak show" beat. He seemed, even so, remote from the prancing frontal contest between John and Paul. He was, and knew it, the most handsome Beatle with his athlete's physique, his dark eyes, wry smile and neat, crisp Jeff Chandler hair. Like the girls back home in West Derby, the Kaiserkeller girls were mad about him. Craning their necks to see past John and George, past even Paul, they would scream at Pete Best in English and German to give them a smile.

Having the most German increased Pete's independence, and he was often away from the Freiheit in the daytime, sunbathing alone or buying new parts for his drums. His fellow Beatles grew accustomed to his absence. They had plenty afoot with Tony Sheridan and Rory Storm and the drummer from Rory's group, whom they were growing to like more and more. Ringo Starr in contrast with Pete Best, was friendly, simple, straightforward and, in his slow, big-eyed way, as funny as even John. They also liked the way he played the drums. They were happy with Pete Best's drumming until they began to notice Ringo's.

When Allan Williams next hit town, Paul and John met him, clamoring for his help to find a studio in which they could record. They wanted to try out some numbers with a member of Rory Storm's group, a boy named Wally, whose prodigious vocal range went from bass to falsetto. Pete Best would not be involved. They had already fixed up to use Rory Storm's drummer, Ringo Starr.

The studio Allan Williams found for them was a record-your-voice booth at the rear of Hamburg's main railway station. There, John, Paul and George, with Ringo on drums, backed the talented Wally through two numbers, "Fever" and "Summertime." The man who cut the acetate from their recording mistakenly handed back to Williams first an old-fashioned 78 rpm disc with a commercial message for a local handbag shop on its reverse. Eventually some 45 rpm discs were made, on the booth's Arnstik label, of "The Beatles mit Wally." Just for a few moments—subtracting Wally—the right four had found each other.

Tom Wolfe

WORDS TO THE WILD

Here, from the first flush of Beatlemania, is an account by
reporter Tom Wolfe of his car ride into Manhattan from the
newly renamed Kennedy airport, alongside Beatle George
Harrison.

BY 6:30 A.M. yesterday, half the kids from South Orange, N.J., to Seaford,
L.I., were already up with their translators plugged in their skulls. It was
like a Civil Defense network or something. You could turn anywhere on
the dial, WMCA, WCBS, WINS, almost any place, and get the bulletins:
"It's B-Day! 6:30 A.M.! The Beatles left London 30 minutes ago! They're 30
minutes out over the Atlantic Ocean! Heading for New York!"

By 1 P.M., about 4,000 kids had finessed school and come skipping and
screaming into the international terminal at Kennedy Airport. It took 110
police to herd them. At 1:20 P.M., the Beatles' jet arrived from London.

The Beatles left the plane and headed for customs inspection and
everybody got their first live look at the Beatles' hair style, which is a mop
effect that covers the forehead, some of the ears and most of the back of
the neck. To get a better look, the kids came plunging down the observation deck, and some of them already had their combs out, raking their hair
down over their foreheads as they ran.

Then they were crowding around the plate-glass windows overlook-
ing the customs section, stomping on the floor in unison, some of them
beating time by bouncing off the windows.

The Beatles—George Harrison, 20; John Lennon, 23; Ringo Starr, 23,
and Paul McCartney, 21—are all short, slight kids from Liverpool who
wear four-button coats, stovepipe pants, ankle-high black boots with
Cuban heels. And droll looks on their faces. Their name is a play on the
word "beat."

They went into a small room for a press conference, while some of
the girls tried to throw themselves over a retaining wall.

Somebody motioned to the screaming crowds outside. "Aren't you
embarrassed by all this lunacy?"

"No," said John Lennon. "It's crazy."

"What do you think of Beethoven?"

"He's crazy," said Lennon. "Especially the poems. Lovely writer."

In the two years in which they have risen from a Liverpool rock-and-roll dive group to the hottest performers in the record business, they had seen much of this wildness before. What really got them were the American teenage car sorties.

The Beatles left the airport in four Cadillac limousines, one Beatle to a limousine, heading for the Plaza Hotel in Manhattan. The first sortie came almost immediately. Five kids in a powder blue Ford overtook the caravan on the expressway, and as they passed each Beatle, one guy hung out the back window and waved a red blanket.

A white convertible came up second, with the word BEETLES scratched on both sides in the dust. A police car was close behind that one with the siren going and the alarm light rolling, but the kids, a girl at the wheel and two guys in the back seat, waved at each Beatle before pulling over to exit with the cops gesturing at them.

In the second limousine, Brian Sommerville, the Beatles' press agent, said to one of the Beatles, George Harrison: "Did you see that, George?"

Harrison looked at the convertible with its emblem in the dust and said, "They misspelled Beatles."

But the third sortie succeeded all the way. A good-looking brunette, who said her name was Caroline Reynolds, of New Canaan, Conn., and Wellesley College, had paid a cab driver $10 to follow the caravan all the way into town. She cruised by each Beatle, smiling faintly, and finally caught up with George Harrison's limousine at a light at Third Avenue and 63d St.

"How does one go about meeting a Beatle?" she said out the window.

"One says hello," Harrison said out the window.

"Hello!" she said. "Eight more will be down from Wellesley." Then the light changed and the caravan was off again.

At the Plaza Hotel, there were police everywhere. The Plaza, on Central Park South just off Fifth Ave., is one of the most sedate hotels in New York. The Plaza was petrified. The Plaza accepted the Beatles' reservations months ago, before knowing it was a rock-and-roll group that attracts teenage riots.

About 500 teen-agers, most of them girls, had shown up at the Plaza. The police had herded most of them behind barricades in the square between the hotel and the avenue. Every entrance to the hotel was guarded. The screams started as soon as the first limousine came into view.

The Beatles jumped out fast at the Fifth Avenue entrance. The teen-agers had all been kept at bay. Old ladies ran up and touched the Beatles on their arms and backs as they ran up the stairs.

After they got to the Plaza the Beatles rested up for a round of television appearances (the Ed Sullivan show Sunday), recordings (Capitol Records), concerts (Carnegie Hall, Wednesday) and a tour (Washington, Miami). The kids were still hanging around the Plaza hours after they went inside.

One group of girls asked everybody who came out, "Did you see the Beatles? Did you touch them?"

A policeman came up, and one of them yelled, "He touched a Beatle! I saw him!"

The girls jumped on the cops' arms and back, but it wasn't a mob assault. There were goony smiles all over their faces.

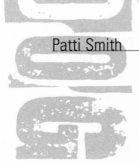

Patti Smith

Raised in New Jersey, daughter of a factory worker and a waitress, Patti Smith said her life was changed when she saw the Rolling Stones on *The Ed Sullivan Show*. Out of high school, working in a factory, her life was altered again when she discovered symbolist poet Arthur Rimbaud. With the Stones and Rimbaud rattling around in her head, she embarked on a career as a poet, her readings augmented by guitarist and critic Lenny Kaye. Kaye and Smith soon formed a band and the Patti Smith Group's albums, *Horses, Radio Ethiopia,* and *Easter* were critical successes. Her song, "Because the Night," was a late-1970s hit. After a retirement to raise a family, she returned to recording and touring in the 1990s, including a short tour with Bob Dylan.

have you seen
dylan's dog
it got wings
it can fly
if you speak
of it to him
its the only
time dylan
can't look you in the eye

have you held
dylan's snake
it rattles like a toy
it sleeps in the grass
it coils in his hand
it hums and it strikes out
when dylan cries out
when dylan cries out

have you pressed
to your face
dylan's bird
dylan's bird
it lies on dylan's hip
trembles inside of him
it drops upon the ground
it rolls with dylan round
it's the only one
who comes
when dylan comes

have you seen
dylan's dog
it got wings
it can fly
when it lands
like a clown
he's the only
thing allowed
to look dylan in the eye

Charles Shaar Murray

HENDRIX IN BLACK AND WHITE

Hendrix was rock and roll's most revolutionary musician. In the summer of 1967, Hendrix's first single, the unlike-anything-before-it "Purple Haze" was released, followed by his American debut ("re-debut" is more like it) at the Monterey Pop Festival. Following the Who's devastating performance (smashed guitar, smoke bombs . . . the usual), he played behind his back, smashed *his* guitar, then set fire to it. Critic John Morthland once wrote that Hendrix "created a branch on the pop tree that nobody else has ventured too far out on." This historical analysis by Charles Shaar Murray notes the strange, rumbling effect Hendrix had on both black and white rock and roll.

THE "CULTURAL DOWRY" Jimi Hendrix brought with him into the pop marketplace included not only his immense talent and the years of experience acquired in a particularly hard school of show business, but the accumulated weight of the fantasies and mythologies constructed around black music and black people by whites, hipsters and reactionaries alike. Both shared one common article of faith: that black people represent the personification of the untrammelled id—intrinsically wild, sensual, dangerous, "untamed" in every sense of the word. Within this fantasy, hipsters find everything to which they aspire, and their opposite numbers everything they fear, loathe and despise. The difference is that the hipster—in any of his succession of contemporary incarnations—is anxious to believe that his chosen favourite black entertainers are existential outlaws, while the conservative is willing only to accept reassuring images of blacks as non-threatening, mildly eccentric creatures, happy and willing to sing and dance for the amusement of their "betters." Ultimately, each stereotype is as fraudulent as the other: the black entertainer succeeds with the white audience either by embodying an aspect of blackness with which that audience feels comfortable, or else by appearing almost tangential to the black community: thus rendered unaffiliated, "universal."

* * *

Hendrix arrived in a London hipoisie which worshipped Americana—and black Americans in particular—from across a seemingly unbridgeable cultural abyss. They had sedulously studied and reproduced blues and soul music in an attempt to attain some degree of empathy with these transcendent outpourings of joy and pain, trying to crack the façade of true-Brit reserve by appropriating the persona of the blues singer or soul man. They knew more about Motown, Mingus and Muddy Waters than all but a few white Americans, but the cultural context from which these musics had sprung was a mystery to them. They understood the vocal tricks and guitar licks, and the best of them could reproduce them virtually at will, but actual contact with black Americans had left them puzzled and confused. For the most part, the black bluesmen they had met were twice or three times their age and decidedly cranky: the venerable reprobate Sonny Boy Williamson had used The Yardbirds, The Animals and others as backing groups, and had not been particularly impressed. "Those cats in England want to play the blues *so bad*," he told Robbie Robertson, later of The Band, "and they play 'em *so bad*." They, in turn, considered Williamson to be a fabulous monster, something along the lines of a centaur or a unicorn: a musician of awe-inspiring gifts, but chronically suspicious and secretive, almost perpetually drunk, either incapable of or unwilling to adhere to a set musical programme, and given to plucking chickens in his hosts' baths.

Sonny Boy Williamson, though, was a barely-literate sexagenarian from the Mississippi Delta, and it was scarcely surprising that he should find few points of contact with earnest young lower- middle- or working-class Englishmen; urban black Americans of the same age wouldn't necessarily have got much further with the old buzzard than The Yardbirds did. Nevertheless, British pop stars were just as likely to find themselves confused by encounters with their black American near-contemporaries. On their first sojourn in New York, The Beatles—doubtless in search of some sexual dalliance and general excitement—invited The Supremes (the Motown female vocal trio who were the Fab Moptops' only serious competition in the bestseller lists at the time) to visit them in their hotel suite. When Diana Ross and her colleagues arrived, both parties were utterly dumbfounded. The Supremes found a room clouded with marijuana smoke and four guys in jeans sprawled around completely hammered: The Beatles saw three girls in neat suits, complete with gloves, fur wraps and a chaperone. The Supremes couldn't believe that The Beatles were such doped-out slobs; The Beatles were shocked at how "prissy" and "square" black girls from Detroit could be. Each side's notions of what the other should be like were based on a fundamental misunderstanding, and the encounter soon collapsed under the weight of the participants' mutual embarrassment. The Detroit contingent expected English "class" and suavity à la David Niven from the Beatles, who in turn were convinced that The Supremes were raunchy, hell-raising party-timers—Bessie Smith songs come to life. The Fab Four failed completely to empathize with the aspirations of the upwardly mobile black proletariat; The Supremes utterly misread white rock and roll bohemia.

Jimi Hendrix, on the other hand, understood white bohemia quite instinctively, and white English rock and roll bohemia in particular; after all, he shared many of its tastes and obsessions, and for a while at least, he was perfectly happy to give them exactly what they wanted, to play the part of—to quote *Rolling Stone*'s John Morthland—"the flower generation's electric nigger dandy, its king stud and golden calf, its maker of mighty dope music, its most outrageously visible force." It was precisely this kind of role-playing which may have hindered acceptance by black audiences: he was enacting—in Summer of Love terms, admittedly—exactly the kind of stereotypes which many black Americans were so anxious to shake off. Even some of his new-found British buddies, like Eric Clapton, began to suspect the murderous irony with which he was pandering to those hoary old myths.

Hendrix was indeed flamboyant, exhibitionistic, obviously on drugs, fond of being photographed surrounded by blondes and almost totally lacking in the kind of dignity, discipline and restraint which black America had come to demand from its entertainers. It was the white critic Robert Christgau who saw Hendrix at Monterey and called him "a psychedelic Uncle Tom," but he undoubtedly echoed the feelings of a considerable number of black Americans who—initially, at least—considered Hendrix a stoned clown acting like a nigger for the amusement of white folks. Others, however, felt very differently. To a younger generation of black Americans, Hendrix's flamboyant self-assertion was a positive inspiration.

"You have to look at the society which makes us view ourselves a certain way," says Vernon Reid. "On one level, the idea of being flashy or outspoken is appealing because, from the time that you're small, if you're a black person, there is a social move to negate your existence. What is it like to be nothing? They don't come out and *say,* 'You're nothing!' but Band-Aid is flesh-coloured, even if it's not the colour of *your* flesh . . . it's a lot better now, but at the time Hendrix was coming up, that was the status quo. So when you see people who are black being outrageous, they are asserting themselves. There is a psychological need to assert themselves because there's a feeling that if you're black, you're not anything."

To say that Hendrix had no black constituency at all, though, is to pander to myth, and racist myth at that. "It had to be a new breed of blacks that would find him," said Bobby Womack, " 'cause the [record] companies didn't think [blacks] would relate to a nigger like him. I'd start seeing young black guys, fans, and they'd be dressin' just like him and I'd be thinkin' *'Damn, I never saw black hippies before.'* " Hendrix biographer David Henderson points out in *'Scuse Me While I Kiss the Sky* (1983) that blacks *did* attend his shows, even though the scale of Hendrix's white support rendered their presence less conspicuous; and that they *did* buy his records, though the fact that he'd gone straight to the pop charts rather than registering first on the R&B lists meant that all his sales counted as pop. What was incontestable was that he received little or no airplay on black radio stations, which felt that his music simply wouldn't fit into existing formats. The easy acceptance of the notion that he had no black following not only bound him closer to his white audience, but reinforced Mike Jeffery's belief that he should cater exclusively to it.

*   *   *

The day after Hendrix's triumph at Monterey, Pete Townshend wanted to make amends for the back-stage contretemps about who was going to follow who. He walked up to Hendrix at the airport and said, "Listen, no hard feelings. I'd love to get a bit of that guitar you smashed." Hendrix speared the gangling Townshend with an arctic stare and sneered, "Oh yeah? I'll autograph it for you, *honkie*." Townshend was devastated. "I just *crawled* away," he remembers ruefully. Such eruptions of overt racial hostility were exceedingly rare for Hendrix, even under intense provocation, but there was something about Townshend which must have gotten quite a distance up Hendrix's nose. Townshend was acutely jealous of Eric Clapton's friendship with Hendrix; he was desperate for Hendrix's acknowledgement and affection. And he didn't get it.

> *I thought, Eric's getting the big hugs, why aren't I? And I think the difference is that Eric feels perfectly natural with his adoption of blues music. He feels it inside; I don't. I don't even really feel comfortable with black musicians. It's always been a problem with me, and I think Jimi was so acutely sensitive in his blackness that he picked that up. [After Monterey] I felt a lot of hate, vengeance and frustration. Possibly because of my sensitivity, my uneasiness with black people, I felt I deserved it somehow.*

The differences between British and American racial politics were quite considerable in the mid-sixties. There is no living American who can remember a time when there were no blacks in the USA, but large-scale black immigration to the UK was a phenomenon of the fifties, and the vast majority of white Brits—to whom most blacks were still "foreign-ers"—were even less familiar with them than their American counter-parts. Sting, an adolescent when he first saw Hendrix playing a Newcastle club in late '66, had literally never seen an actual in-the-flesh black person in his life before. As a result, there was plenty of scope for mutual mis-understandings: Hendrix once refused to be interviewed by Caroline Coon, founder of the Release drug advisory centre, because when her name was mentioned he thought it was a tasteless racial jibe; and his first roadie, the late Howard "H" Parker, was fired in Sweden one morning when he told a hungover Hendrix that he resembled "a gorilla who's just lost his ba-nanas." Hendrix was insecure enough to think that H meant to insult him; H was insensitive enough to think that Hendrix could possibly interpret his "quip" in any other way.

Similarly in *'Scuse Me While I Kiss the Sky*—despite its flaws the best Hendrix biography published to date—David Henderson makes much of racial tensions within the Experience, citing Mitch Mitchell's "strange con-tempt" for Hendrix, and both Mitchell and Redding's use of terms like "nig-ger" and "coon" as part of their day-to-day banter. Both of them felt hurt by Henderson's implications, and many who knew the band confirmed that they did not, indeed, mean any harm. "Noel came from Folkestone, where there weren't any black people," said Robert Wyatt. "He doesn't have a malicious bone in his body, so it would have been unwitting." Stated simply, neither Noel nor Mitch had the faintest idea what black Americans did and didn't find offensive; or much awareness of how deeply words like that can cut. If they had, it is unlikely that they would have used those terms so casually. Whether or not he called them on it at the time, Hendrix would not have forgotten such utterances, and it would inevitably have contributed to his growing estrangement from them.

*   *   *

The Black Panther street-vending the party newspaper outside the Electric Lady studio knew that brother Jimi was generally good for a sale, but Hendrix withheld the public endorsement the Panthers sought from him. He was nevertheless aware of their attendance at his shows. "They come to the concerts, and I sort of feel them there—it's not a physical thing but a mental ray. It's a spiritual thing." It was often suspected that Hendrix's decision to record Ed Chaplin's pay-off album with Band of

Gypsys—Buddy Miles and Billy Cox, both black—was a conscious attempt to defuse black criticism of him, but it seems more likely that he simply wanted to recharge his batteries by playing with his oldest and most trusted friend and with his most entertaining new pal. Still, he did take more and more interest in "the community," and he was furious when Mike Jeffery booked him on to a TV talk show on a night when he had planned to play a benefit for The Young Lords, a Puerto Rican activist group. And when he appeared with blues singer Big Maybelle at a Harlem street party, David Henderson wrote, "a black nationalist type came up to Jimi and said, 'Hey, brother, you better come home.' Jimi quickly replied, 'You gotta do what you do and I gotta do what I got to do *now*.' "

'We was in America. We was in America. The stuff was over and startin' again . . . and it's time for another anthem, and that's what I'm writin' on now.'

Jimi Hendrix (1969)

Hendrix never quite got to write his anthem, though this author, at least, would argue that he said a great deal of what needed saying by remodelling the old one. He also never survived to realize just how unreachably utopian his vision turned out to be. America was indeed divided in terms of old and new, but the old ways included much racism, and the old ways won. A few concessions were necessary, but they were made—albeit somewhat grudgingly—and America moved, sullenly and anxiously, into the seventies. A significant number of blacks had made genuine inroads into the professions in the wake of the upheavals of the sixties; they were better represented than ever before in local government and the police, less condescendingly ignored and stereotyped on TV and in the movies. Nevertheless, this "progress" was resented by large numbers of whites, liberals as well as rednecks. The institution of "affirmative action" (or "positive discrimination") was regarded as discrimination against whites—as if "affirmative action" in favour of whites had not been operating in America ever since the first heisted African set foot on American soil. The kind of racial *rapprochement* which had put James Brown's "Say It Loud, I'm Black and I'm Proud" into the pop Top Five (it was, naturally, an R&B number one) was dead and gone.

THESE ARE THE GOOD OLD DAYS

Great music cities dominate rock and roll history—Memphis, New Orleans, and Chicago in the 1950s, Los Angeles in the early 1960s, and, by the mid-1960s, San Francisco emerged as the home to a new generation of rock and roll. The city's lifestyle was so intertwined with the music that the record business had to make attitude adjustments to deal with the new artists. Selvin recounts the first meetings between Warner Bros. executives and the Grateful Dead.

JOE SMITH and his wife were dining at Ernie's, the elegant San Francisco eatery where film director Alfred Hitchcock kept and regularly visited his wine collection. Smith, vice-president of Warner Brothers Records and a former disk jockey who always looked like the man who walked off the top of the wedding cake, wore a dark blue suit. His wife was in basic black and pearls. Tom Donahue reached him by phone at dinner. "The Dead want to talk with you now," Donahue told Smith. "They're at the Avalon."

"We're dressed up," Smith said.

"No one will notice," said Donahue.

The four-hundred-fifty-pound former Top Forty deejay whose nightly radio opening line was "I'm here to clean up your face and mess up your mind" had assumed a statesman-like role in the burgeoning scene after folding his Autumn Records label. He, in fact, sold his artist roster to Smith and Warner Brothers. Donahue and his partner, Bobby Mitchell, had also operated the city's first psychedelic nightclub, Mother's, on Broadway the previous year, where the Byrds and the Lovin' Spoonful, among others, appeared before that enterprise ran out of steam (and money). Now Donahue took a lot of acid and lunched daily at an outdoor table at Enrico's on Broadway and never, never picked up his own check.

When Smith and his wife climbed those stairs on Sutter Street leading to the ballroom, they might as well have been stepping into another world. At Warner's, Smith had built a successful record label on hits by acts like comedian Allan Sherman, sanitary folksingers Peter, Paul and Mary and chirpy pop vocalists like Petula Clark. The company forayed into current rock no more daringly than Dino, Desi and Billy, two teenage sons bearing the names of their famous Hollywood star fathers and a friend of theirs. What on earth could have prepared him for the sights and sounds of the Grateful Dead on the rampage and the Avalon Ballroom swimming in a tureen of colored, pulsing lights? The excitement made him tremble. Even the group's name bespoke some kind of new, slightly intimidating realm Smith had never imagined.

"Tom, I don't think Jack Warner will ever understand this," he told Donahue. "I don't know if I understand it myself, but I really feel like they're good."

Smith left his wife outside the dressing room and proceeded cautiously with Donahue, who introduced Smith to the Dead and the band's management. Smith recognized Rifkin and Scully as street-wise schemers. Garcia appeared the obvious leader but scrupulously refused to speak for the group. Phil Lesh was openly hostile. Pigpen barely acknowledged his presence. Smith was dazzled.

The Dead appointed attorney Brian Rohan to negotiate the contract for the band, for no reason other than they knew him from handling various criminal cases for Kesey. Rohan, who had no experience in such matters, found a local colleague who once represented jazz pianist Dave Brubeck. Other companies expressed interest in the group—Jerry Wexler of Atlantic Records came to see the band—but Smith made his case for Warner Brothers and it only remained to work out the details.

Rohan went to Burbank to begin contract talks and, on hearing what Warner's had to say, he simply got up and walked out of the office. The Warner's executives stood up and followed him. He shook his head and walked out of the bungalow, the Warner's people trailing, changing their tune as they went. By the time Rohan was done, the Grateful Dead had an unprecedented contract that allowed the band such historic concessions as unlimited studio time and a royalty rate calculated on the amount of time per album side, and not the number of cuts, since the Dead didn't plan filling up albums with two-minute tracks like Ricky Nelson or somebody. The group also retained complete control of song publishing, rare at the time.

Still that wasn't quite enough for Rifkin and Scully. When Joe Smith came up for the signing and met the two Dead managers at Donahue's apartment, they confided in Donahue there was one more thing they wanted. They wanted Joe Smith to drop acid. How could he really understand the band's music otherwise, they said. Smith made it clear he wouldn't be dropping any LSD and they signed the deal anyway.

Most of the band was now firmly ensconced in 710 Ashbury. When Garcia and Mountain Girl reconnected in December—Kesey left everybody behind, devoting his energies to quelling the legal maelstrom in which he was enmeshed—she moved into his upstairs room with him. She thought smoking the fragrant joints from the kilo of Acapulco gold kept in the kitchen pantry put golden halos around everywhere she looked. She would spend hours in the afternoon sitting on the front steps talking and carrying on until the chill of the evening fog drove everybody back inside.

Three band couples lived at the sprawling three-story Victorian two blocks up the hill front Haight Street—Scully and ladyfriend, Tangerine, Garcia and Mountain Girl, Pigpen and Veronica. Rifkin maintained the basement apartment that had been his original toehold on the building. Laird Grant, who handled equipment, and Bob Matthews, who worked on sound, lived there, as did guitarist Bob Weir, and Lady the Dog, a large black labrador. Jim and Annie Courson lived downstairs and ran the place. Bassist Phil Lesh lived around the corner on Belvedere Street with drummer Bill Kreutzman, still calling himself Bill Sommers, who had left a wife and young child living on the peninsula.

These were not idle times. The band practiced daily at the Sausalito Heliport. Most nights, everybody at 710 Ashbury was in bed by midnight except for Pigpen. He would often stay up drinking and softly singing blues. But Garcia customarily rose around six in the morning to begin his day by practicing guitar in his room. He played so much the calluses on his fingers were as hard as thumbtacks.

That Thanksgiving, after playing the night before at Bill Graham's Thanksgiving Eve party with Quicksilver, the band hosted a Thanksgiving dinner. All the sliding doors were pushed open and tables were placed end-to-end through the whole downstairs. The entire extended family, members of the Airplane, old Pranksters, broke bread and made merry. At one point, Lesh stood and offered a toast. "These are the good old days," he said. All nodded in agreement.

When the time came to actually record the Warner's album, the band traveled south in January and went to RCA Victor Studio A in Hollywood to work with producer Dave Hassinger, the same engineer the Airplane chose for *Jefferson Airplane Takes Off* because of his work with the Stones. The album went down in a three-day Dexamyl blitz that left the tempos eternally rushed and minor fixes forever unrepaired in the wake of the amphetamine tide. Essentially a distillation of the band's ballroom songbook, the recording repertoire concentrated on shorter pieces because that was as much of a studio mentality as the Dead could supply. At the Avalon or the Fillmore, the Dead would play songs as long as they felt good, as long as they made people dance, and when most of the audience is high on something, that can be a long time. The idea of reducing these numbers to three minutes simply provided the band another reason to approach the endeavor with a certain degree of disdain.

Richard Goldstein

NEXT YEAR IN SAN FRANCISCO

Here, a portrait of one of rock and roll's great voices, also one of its great tragedies.

TONIGHT'S crowd ambles languidly across the floor of Philadelphia's Electric Factory, a huge garage turned psychedelic playground. Mostly, they are straight kids come to gape at the hippies and fathom the Now. Ten years ago, they would have preened their pompadours before the cameras on American Bandstand. Today, they steal furtive drags on filter-tip cigarettes trying to look high. With coiled springs behind their eyes, they flash stiff South-Phillie grins at any chick who looks like she might go down. They've all had their palms read by the Wizard in the balcony, and their faces painted in the adjacent boutique. Now they stand like limp meringue, watching a local group called Edison's Electric Machine belt warm-up jive.

A real deathscene. Not a pleasant sight for Janis Joplin, who peers through a crack in the dressing room door, and scowls: "Oh shit. It's dead out there. We'll never be able to get into those kids. Want to see death? Take a look out there. You ever played Philadelphia? No, of course not. You don't *play* anywhere."

When Janis scowls, her whole face closes up around her mouth and even her eyelashes seem to frown. You could say she gets nervous before a set. The other members of Big Brother and the Holding Company sit guzzling beer, trying on beads, and hassling their road manager. But Janis stalks around the tiny room, her fingers drumming against a tabletop. She sips hot tea from a styrofoam cup. She talks in gasps, and between sentences, she belts a swig of Southern Comfort, her trademark. Tonight, a knowing admirer has graced her dressing room with a fifth, in lieu of flowers. "I don't drink anything on the rocks," she explains. "Cold is bad for my throat. So, it's always straight or in tea. Tastes like orange petals in tea. I usually get about a pint and a half down me, when I'm performing. Any more, I start to nod out."

Now the B-group files in, dripping sweat. The lead singer gingerly

172

places his guitar in its plush casket and peels off an imitation-brocade jacket, sweatshirt, pullover, and drenched undershirt. "Why do you wear all that clothing if it's so hot out there?" Janis asks.

"Because I'm freaky." And the door opens again to admit a fully-attired gorilla with rubber hands and feet. Janis glances briefly at the ground to make sure that it's still there, and then she offers the gorilla some booze and he lifts his mask to accept. His name is Gary the Gorilla, and Janis digs that, so she gives him her bottle to hold during the group's set and follows Peter the bassman through the door, while the crowd shouts for music. Gary unzips his belly and passes his feet around, and the lead singer of Edison's Electric Machine examines a rip in his brocade, consoling himself with the B-group's prayer: Next Year In San Francisco.

I first met them last year in San Francisco. In a ranch house with an unobstructed view of tickytack. They were assembled for an interview on Hippy-culture, and I began with a nervous question about turning on. In answer, somebody lit up and soon the floor was hugging-warm. I glanced down at my notes as though they had become hieroglyphics (which, it later turned out, they had). When it was time to split, and everyone had boarded a paisley hearse, I muttered something like: "We shouldn't be interviewed. We should be friends." And the car drove away laughing, with long hair flying from every window.

This summer, there will be 20,000 yelpers on Haight Street, hoping to get discovered, like Janis, in some psychedelic Schwab's. But I'm afraid Big Brother and the Holding Company is the last of the great San Francisco bands. With new groups trying on serious music like a training bra, they are a glorious throwback to a time when the primary aim in rock was "to get people moving"—nothing more or less. They were nurtured in the roots of the Hip renaissance (played the Trips Festival and the first productions of the Family Dog; jammed together in a big house at 1090 Page Street, a mecca for musicians back when the only interested talent scouts were cops). Now they are its most fragrant late-summer blossom.

In 1961, Janis and Chet Helms (proprietor of the Family Dog) hitch-hiked west. They were anonymous freaks then, newly plucked from Texas topsoil and still green.

"What were the two of you like then, Janis?"

"Oh—younger."

"How were you different from today?"

"We were . . . ummm . . . just interested in being beatniks then. Now, we've got responsibilities, and I guess you could say, ambition."

She was born in Port Arthur, Texas, in 1943. Dropped out of four or five schools. Sang in hillbilly bars with a local bluegrass band. For the beer. "We'd do country songs, and then the band'd shut up and I'd sing blues, 'cause that was my thing."

Her thing was no Patti Page regatta, no Connie Francis sob-along, but mangy backwoods blues, heavy with devotion to Bessie Smith. She still smears Bessie across everything she sings, making it possible for a whole generation of us to hear beyond the scratches in those old records. But she says she never really tried to sing until she joined Big Brother.

"See, Bessie, she sang big open notes, in very simple phrasing. But you can't fall back on that in front of a rock band. I mean, you can't sing loose and easy with a throbbing amplifier and drums behind you. The beat just pushes you on. So I started singing rhythmically, and now I'm learning from Otis Redding to push a song instead of just sliding over it."

It was Chet Helms who made Janis part of the Holding Company (before that, it had been an instrumental band, one of dozens formed during the merger of folk, jazz, and rock among Bay Area youth). From the start, their music began to clothe her voice. They taught her to blast, pound, and shatter a song. She returned the favor by directing her solos inward, toward the group's rhythmic heart. In fact, Janis has made her voice into a family. It shows. People think of Big Brother and the Holding Company as more of a commune than a group.

True, it's chic to deride the band as being unworthy of her magic, but they are certainly not lame companions. Her voice is vast enough to overwhelm any accompaniment less raucous than a bazooka, but with Big Brother behind her, freaking out like country cousins, there is no difference between voice and music—just Sound. Call that the sound of Janis Joplin and you might as well identify a fire by its smoke just because that's what hits you first.

"I have three voices," she explains. "The shouter; the husky, gutteral chick; and the high wailer. When I turn into a nightclub singer, I'll probably use my husky voice. That's the one my mother likes. She says, 'Janis, why do you scream like that when you've got such a pretty voice?' "

It's not a pretty sound she makes now. A better word for it would be "primal." She plants herself onstage like a firmly rooted tree, then whips more emotion out of her upper branches than most singers can wring out of their lower depths. She slinks like tar, scowls like sunburn, stings like war. And she does one other thing that makes it all so sexy. She needs. Needs to move. Needs to feel. Needs to be screamed at. Needs to touch—and be touched back.

" 'Ball and Chain' is the hardest thing I do. I have to really get inside my head, everytime I sing it. Because it's about feeling things. That means I can never sing it without really trying. See, there's this big hole in the song that's mine, and I've got to fill it with something. So, I do! And it really tires me out. But it's so groovy when you know the audience really wants you. I mean, whatever you give them, they'll believe in. And they yell back at you, call your name, and—like that."

It's always the same: at Monterey, where the nation discovered her; at the Avalon, where they know her best; at the Anderson, where the New York press corps took notes; and tonight at the Electric Factory, in Philadelphia. She begs and coaxes her audiences until they begin to holler, first in cliches like "do-it-to-it" and finally in wordless squeals. Suddenly, the room is filled with the agony in her voice. Kids surround the stage, shouting her name and spilling over with the joy of having been reached. Even the onlookers in neckties nod their heads and whisper "Shit . . . oh shit." Because to hear Janis sing "Ball and Chain" just once is to have been laid, lovingly and well.

Two sets later, they are back in the dressing room, flushed with sweat and applause. There is a tired hassle with the road manager. Dave the drummer changes into his third shirt that evening. And Janis is sitting on Gary the Gorilla's lap, fondling his furry knees and opening a second fifth of Southern Comfort.

"Why do I always hafta dance alone in these places?" she rasps, still recuperating from her solo. "I mean, you saw me dancing out there between sets. All those guys were standing around, panting in the corner. Finally, I had to say to one of 'em, 'Well, do you wanna dance, or not?' and he comes on waving his arms around like a fuckin' bat. Didn't even look at me. Now, why do things like that always happen?"

"Because you're so freaky looking," her road manager answers.

She nods slowly, and whispers, "Yeah."

She digs and detests her weirdness. She would like to be the freakiest chick in rock, and a gracious young lady as well. At a recent press party to celebrate the group's new contract with Columbia Records, Janis shook her hair only to confront a lady out of *Harper's Bazaar,* who covered up her drink and said, "Do you mind?" Janis answered in a tone out of *Evergreen,* "Fuck off, baby." But later she was seen pouting before a mirror, muttering, "Face it, baby, you've got ratty hair."

Now she moves out of the tiny room and surveys the remnants of this evening's scene: cigarette butts and a gaggle of local freaks. There are no pale young ladies searching for a seminal autograph in this crowd, but Peter the bassman is already making contact with a chick named Crafty. Gandalf, the wizard from the balcony, offers to read every palm in the house, whispering, "Hey—let's go up to your room and smoke."

Later, at a hamburger stand, Gandalf stops in the middle of a poem he is composing on a napkin and reflects: "Tomorrow, I'm gonna make it with Janis. I'm gonna just go up to her and say, 'Hey—let's make it.' 'Cause she's so groovy to watch. What a bod she must have under that voice." He pauses to consider it, and then asks a waitress for spare whipped-cream cans.

But Gandalf the Wizard may have to wait longer than tomorrow. For this very night (while Philadelphia sleeps), Janis is with Gary the Gorilla, and they are finishing off the second fifth together.

Peter Guralnick

RETURN OF THE KING

Elvis Presley in the late 1960s was still a rock and roll icon but also on the verge of becoming an artifact. His manager, Colonel Tom Parker, had kept Presley alive as a recording artist during the young man's two-year hitch in the military (1958–60), but on his return had swept him away to a career in Hollywood. Elvis accepted his fate and paychecks gamely, but the arrival of the Beatles and the changes in rock in the mid- and late-1960s frustrated him and he wanted to participate again. The venue chosen for his return was a Christmas-season television special in 1968.

In this passage from *Careless Love*, the second volume of Guralnick's Elvis biography, the king of rock and roll feels an unusual lack of confidence as he faces the late 1960s and in response stages one of the great comebacks in music history.

The cast of characters includes Elvis, of course, along with Colonel Parker. Other names to note: Steve Binder, mastermind of the "Elvis!" television special; executive producer Bob Finkel; rhythm and blues singer and Elvis movie stand-in Lance LeGault; Bones Howe, the show's music supervisor; Joe Esposito, foreman of the "Memphis Mafia"; another longtime member of the entourage, Alan Fortas; original bandmates Scotty Moore and D. J. Fontana; relation-by-marriage Gee Gee; and a couple of other pals named Charlie and Lamar.

ELVIS met with Binder and Howe that Friday at their offices on Sunset Boulevard. Joe and a couple of the guys waited in the reception room while they talked, and at first Steve didn't think he and Bones were getting through. He was so wound up by now, though, that nothing was going to stop his evangelical pitch. This was a chance to really say something to the world, he declared to Elvis; this was one of those rare opportunities to create something of genuine consequence; this was Elvis' chance to proclaim, through his music, *who he really was.* Bones, quieter, a little older and more reflective in manner than his partner, reminded Elvis of when they had worked together at Radio Recorders in the old days. They talked about the way that Elvis had made records back then—what had most impressed him about Elvis' sessions, Bones said, was that they were not dictated by the clock but by Elvis' own emotional commitment. That was how they would approach the special, Steve jumped back in—forget about the network, forget about the fancy trappings; they wanted to do a show that nobody else in the world could do but Elvis Presley. It would all stem from *his* life, *his* music, *his* experience, Steve said. How did he feel about that?

"Scared to death," Elvis replied, consciously deflecting the tension. Well, they'd have a show sketched out for him by the time he got back from Hawaii, Binder said, laughing. There'd be time for him to make his mind up about it then. For all that any of them knew, it could be the end of Elvis' career—but then again, it just might be the shot in the arm he so clearly needed at this juncture. It was Elvis' turn to laugh now, and they shook hands all around. He left their offices not really sure what he was letting himself in for but convinced that at least it was going to be *different.*

*　　*　　*

Elvis returned from his holiday thinner than he had been since he got out of the army, his sideburns longer, and, most significant, in a state of genuinely heightened anticipation about the show. Preproduction started on Monday, June 3, the day after his return. He reported to the Binder-Howe offices a little after 1:00 P.M., and, with the writers present, Steve ran through the approach that they had finally settled upon. At its heart was the Jerry Reed song "Guitar Man," which would be used as a kind of linking theme to tell a story that directly echoed Belgian playwright Maurice Maeterlinck's 1909 theater staple, *The Blue Bird.* In Maeterlinck's treatment a poor boy sets out to find fame and fortune and travels all over the world, only to discover in the end that happiness—in the form of the bluebird of the title—lies in his own backyard. Bones took a fairly dismissive view of the whole idea ("There was nothing original about it—television writers just look for a connection"), and Steve was not altogether convinced they had found the unlocking key, but when they presented it to Elvis for his reaction, to Steve's amazement Elvis simply bought the whole thing. "We told him, 'We don't want you to like it one hundred percent. We want to get your input. What you like. What you don't like.' He said, 'No, I like it all.' And the essence of the show never changed."

Preproduction continued at the Binder-Howe offices for the next couple of weeks, until they were scheduled to move to NBC for full-scale rehearsals. Every day Elvis showed up with at least one or two of the guys, meeting with Steve and Bones and the writers over Pepsi and cigars. He was practically beside himself on June 5, the day that Bobby Kennedy was killed, and could talk of nothing but the conspiracy against the Kennedys and the assassination of Martin Luther King two months earlier. It was all the more terrible that Dr. King should have been killed in Memphis, he said, thereby only confirming everyone's worst feelings about the South. To Steve this was more than just idle talk. "He had read a whole lot of books about the Kennedy assassination, and I just felt a real sense of compassion on his part." That was something that Binder wanted to get into the special. "I wanted to let the world know that here was a guy who was not prejudiced, who was raised in the heart of prejudice, but who was really above all that. Part of the strength that I wanted to bring to the show was [that sense of] compassion, that this was somebody to look up to and admire."

They talked about music, too. Would Elvis sing a new song simply if it said something to him, Binder asked, irrespective of politics or publishing? Absolutely, Elvis replied. Would he have done Jimmy Webb's "MacArthur Park" [a song of vaguely psychedelic, definitely pretentious lyrical obscurity], which had just topped the charts for actor Richard Harris after the Association, whom Bones was producing, turned it down for publishing reasons? Of course, Elvis said, as if nothing like that could ever happen to him. He *liked* "MacArthur Park," he said, acquiescing to Binder's enthusiasm. He definitely wanted to say something more with his music than a song like "Hound Dog" could express. One day they went out on Sunset and just stood there watching the hippies go by, too stoned to realize they were walking past Elvis Presley, or simply not caring. Steve saw it as a truly humbling experience for Elvis, a kind of "giant step in his psyche," though to Bones it was more like he just got a kick out of the experience. "We were just four guys standing out in front of this building, and after a while we got bored and went back upstairs."

* * *

The only substantive matter that the Colonel continued to bring up was the theme of the show itself: Elvis would end with a Christmas song. On that point he remained adamant, no matter how Binder tried to get around him on the subject. Steve continued to bring up the idea of Elvis delivering some loosely scripted closing remarks *after* he sang the Christmas song—but he was always short-circuited by the Colonel's matter-of-fact, implacable, almost irrational opposition, seemingly, to Elvis' saying anything at all.

That was the only real hitch, though, in the increasingly well calibrated feel of an operation that was finally coming together. Binder *believed* in his team; he knew what they were capable of. And he believed in himself. Now, at last, he was beginning to believe in Elvis. There was no question that the show had Elvis' full attention by this time—he wasn't simply present, he was *there,* just like the rest of them, twelve, fourteen, sixteen hours a day. Every night after rehearsals were over, he would unwind in his dressing room, laughing and joking with the guys as he and Charlie sang and played their guitars. One night Steve wandered into what had by now become a familiar scene and suddenly experienced a revelation. *This* was the way to go. *This* could be their way to make a statement—with a totally unscripted improv substituting for the stiff, somewhat arch "informal" segment specified in the script. In a burst of enthusiasm he suddenly thought: they could shoot it in the dressing room, cinema verité-style; for a moment he wanted to just throw out all the produced segments—this could become not simply the centerpiece but the whole show.

In the end, reality reasserted itself. After talking with Elvis, he settled on the idea of flying in original guitarist Scotty Moore and drummer D.J. Fontana to make Elvis feel more at home, then doing the best he could to re-create the informal atmosphere of the dressing room in the small boxing ring of a stage that had been designed for the more formal live concert at the heart of the show. Instead of scripting it, the director just ran down some of the topics that he would like Elvis to discuss—the bit about being shot from the waist up on *The Ed Sullivan Show,* the judge in Jacksonville in 1956 who wouldn't let him move around onstage, prompting Elvis to retaliate by crooking his little finger to suggest the banned movements. These things were essential, Steve said, to reestablish the rebel image. And when Elvis expressed concern that he might not be able to tell the stories very well without lines to deliver, Steve was quick to reassure him that all he had to do was wing it; the musicians would cue him, and he could always have a piece of paper nearby with the topic sentence for each anecdote written on it. It would be fine, Steve said soothingly; the moment would supply its own inspiration. And if he ran out of things to say, as a last resort he could always go back to that Jimmy Reed song he and Charlie were always fooling with; its lyrics—with their constant refrain about "Going up, going down, up down, down up, any way you want me"—might supply their own commentary.

Scotty and D.J. flew in on the weekend, five days before filming was scheduled to start. Although they had been told nothing other than that they were there to jam, things quickly fell into place, and before anyone knew it, it was almost like old times, with much of the easy give-and-take of the early days. D.J. offered some of the most uninhibited reminiscences, with Charlie egging him on, while Scotty contributed his own character- istically wry commentary, gently deflating some of the more exaggerated claims but then, with a wink, adding some of his own. One night they went out to Elvis' house for a post-rehearsal dinner and talked about the future. He wanted to do a European tour, Elvis told them. He wanted to record at Scotty's studio, just "woodshedding" like they were doing now. "He asked me if I thought that would be possible, just go in there for about a week and see what we could come up with, like we used to. I said, 'No problem—if you leave about half your guys at home.' He said, 'That's what I'm talking about.' But, of course, it never happened." Both Scotty and D.J. were impressed with Binder, they were excited by his enthusiasm and by what seemed like his total dedication to the task at hand. They worried, though, that maybe they weren't contributing enough—D.J. kept asking him what exactly he wanted them to do. "But he'd just say, 'Don't do noth- ing, just do what you're doing. That's all I want.' "

*　　*　　*

There was a press conference on Tuesday night, at which Elvis ac- quitted himself with his usual aplomb. He was doing the show, he said, be- cause "we figured it was about time. Besides, I figured I'd better do it before I got too old." "We also got a very good deal," the Colonel jumped in. "Besides the special, we're doing one picture, which NBC is producing. I would call that one very good deal." Elvis paid lip service to his ongoing Hollywood career, spoke almost reflexively of his unwavering commit- ment to someday becoming a serious actor and his constant search for better scripts, and skillfully deflected any serious questions about life, art, or career. "I loved his attitude," said Binder, who had one or two things to say himself about a show that was in his opinion "a matter of video- history significance." "Every time they'd ask a question, he'd have a funny way of tapping me on the leg, as if to say, 'Watch me put the guy on with this one.' And it was fun to watch the press just sitting there. I think he got satisfaction just out of being on top of it. He never, ever had to be pro- tected in that respect."

There was no disguising his jitteriness, though, as they began a com- plete run-through of the show the following day, and then on the twenty- seventh taped the midway sequence before getting ready for the "informal" show that evening. "I know you're nervous, man," he told Alan Fortas, who, with the ranch closed, had come out to the Coast earlier in the spring and had now been drafted to actually *appear* on camera in the informal sequence. "I know you're scared," he repeated, though Alan had little doubt he was really talking about himself.

There was a moment of panic on the producers' part as well. Bob Finkel had left it to the Colonel to give out tickets for the show. "The Colonel said to me, 'I'll take care of it. The demand will be unbelievable.' I said, 'Okay with me.' We start at six o'clock that night, whatever the hell it was, and I look out at four o'clock, and there's nobody there. *Nobody.* I went to the Colonel, and I said, 'Where the hell are these people that should be lined up all day?' He said, 'I don't know.' I said, 'What did you do with the tickets?' And he gave me some damn-fool answer." No one understood the Colonel's rationale. Evidently he had given out batches of tickets to gate guards and waitresses, along with the usual fan club presidents, and just assumed that the crowds would show. Finkel put it down to grandiose expectations—or perhaps to the one final put-on that he would never be able to top. Binder saw it as more intentional, stemming from the Colonel's simple desire to prove them all wrong. Whatever the reason, the Colonel never let on, he just went ahead and acted as if everything were normal, and in the end he and Finkel rounded up an audience. Which the Colonel then proceeded to arrange so that the most adoring female fans were at the front and the audience could be expected to replicate the kind of response that it had offered in 1956 and 1957.

Elvis told Steve Binder at the last minute that he didn't think he could go on. He'd changed his mind, he said, he had decided that this was not a good idea. What did he mean he'd changed his mind? the shocked director demanded, and even Joe was momentarily taken aback. He had never seen Elvis like this before. He had witnessed normal stage fright, of course, but he had always marked it down to entertainer's ego, to Elvis' simply wanting to be reassured and told that it was all right. Now he was not so sure, but together he and Binder managed to calm Elvis down. There was an *audience* out there, Steve said, he couldn't let down his fans. It didn't really matter what he did, they'd have two full run-throughs, and if they didn't like anything from either show, they could just throw the whole thing out. But what if he froze up? Elvis insisted. What if he couldn't think of anything to say? "Then you go out, sit down, look at everyone, get up, and walk off," Binder said firmly. "But you *are* going out there."

There is little evidence of this sense of panic in the show itself, unless it lies in the kind of awkward self-deprecation ("What do I do now, folks?"

are practically Elvis' first words to the audience) that has been an intrinsic part of his charm from the start. He appears calm but shy, modest but secure in his own beauty as the applause washes over him and he finds himself somehow, unexpectedly, at its center. The stage itself is a gaudily accoutered Hollywood version of a boxing ring (a small white square surrounded by a red border instead of ropes); there is barely enough room for the musicians, let alone their instruments, and D.J. sits expectantly, holding a pair of sticks poised not over a drum kit but an upside-down guitar case which Steve has seized upon wholeheartedly in the "improv" spirit of the occasion. There are five chairs arranged in a circle, with Elvis placed to command the attention of each, looking lean, lithe, and a little uncomfortable in his velvety black leather suit; even in repose, he appears ready to spring, with his long legs sprawled out casually in front of him. Almost as if to offset his sinuous charm, the three musicians—Scotty, D.J., and Charlie—are all dressed in a kind of burgundy velour, as is Alan Fortas, who looks a little bit like a designer fireplug and whose presence onstage is only meant to reinforce the overall sense of cinema verité that the director is aiming for. Alan has never played an instrument, but Binder from the beginning has viewed Elvis' interaction with the guys as part of the informal, dressing-room atmosphere, so Alan sits uncomfortably with his hands resting on the back of a guitar which will become one more element in this homemade "rhythm band." The only other onstage participant is Lance LeGault, who crouches directly behind Elvis holding a tambourine, while Joe and Lamar and Gee Gee hover watchfully in suits and ties, just a few feet from Elvis on the steps that lead up to the stage.

The small audience, no more than a couple of hundred, is strangely subdued—they seem more amazed that it is *Elvis* than at anything he might do, even as the object of their attention appears to be experiencing a similar sense of bewilderment, as he fumbles about for something to say, then glances down at the piece of paper with suggested subjects for discussion that sits on the glass tabletop in front of him. "This is supposed to be an informal section of the show," he jokes, "where we faint, or do whatever we want to do, especially me." He then makes a pass at returning to the script but gets no further than a few words about his first record and how "I first started out—in 1912," before pretending to lose the thread, casting his eyes down at the floor, and finally just trailing off, "And if I fall asleep here . . ." There are loud guffaws from the guys, as if to say, We don't really take any of this too seriously either.

And then, all of a sudden, everybody's feet are flying, as Elvis launches into a spirited, if not particularly tuneful, version of that first record, "That's All Right," and with "Heartbreak Hotel" breaks the tension once and for all not with a great performance but by forgetting the words to the song. One can't help but think that this is an instinctive ploy, because whether he actually remembers the words or not, he immediately enlists the audience's sympathy, declares his own vulnerability (while also rising above it), and sets the tone for the rest of the evening, an easygoing note of accidental inspiration. He also attempts to get up from his chair for the first time, a virtual impossibility given the chair's proximity to the edge of the stage and the absence of a guitar strap or boom mike—but that, too, sets a tone, as the audience comes to equate standing up with a kind of freedom, which Elvis struggles for the rest of the evening to achieve. This in turn lends further drama to the limited movement of which he is capable while seated, allowing him to elicit screams from the audience as his legs jackknife out from the chair in a variation on the gyrations for which he has always been known. By the time he begins the next song, the Leiber and Stoller ballad "Love Me," he is clearly in command, singing beautifully for the most part, frowning or pretending to belch when he doesn't, reaching out to the audience, as he always has, by mocking his own pretensions.

At this stage he must have run out of things to say, because, after switching guitars with Scotty, he takes Steve's advice and, for the first of three times in the course of this brief, hour-long set launches into the Jimmy Reed blues "Baby What You Want Me to Do?" "Are we on television?" he asks idly. "No, we're on a train bound for Tulsa," Charlie cackles. And from this point on, everything becomes slightly surreal—or, perhaps, it simply creates its own reality. For the rest of the show, Scotty never takes back his guitar; it is Elvis, who has never even played electric guitar on his own records, who now plays endearingly limited, bluesy, electric lead. The script might just as well be entirely forgotten by now, and yet its spirit is preserved in mockingly sardonic references to the topic suggestions. "It says here, 'Elvis will now talk about his first record and how things started happening after that,' " he woodenly intones, sharing the joke with the audience, as the guys' raucous response offers assent even before the joke is fully delivered.

It's hard to imagine what the producer and director must have been thinking—unless they were so caught up in the moment that there was no time to think. If they had suggested these ingredients from the outset as the formula for a network special, what would have been the Colonel's, the network's, the industry's response? And yet somehow it works. Elvis' inability to present himself as anything *but* himself, and the very amateurishness of that presentation; Charlie's wildly inappropriate behavior, the source of so much resentment within the group, and the "boys' night out" nature of his repartee; even the homemade, hit-or-miss quality of the music itself—all are strangely effective here. Each wildly unpredictable element seems only to encourage Elvis to forget himself all the more, encourages him, paradoxically, to *find* himself. It is 1955 and 1956 all over again, as, without rules, outside of all the normal guidelines of show business, of polite professional and social intercourse, with nothing in fact but a bemused instinct for his own charm, an innate belief in his ability to locate just what his audience is looking for, and a belief in that audience itself, Elvis explores uncharted territory, creates himself as he would like to be.

And then, for a moment, he disappears. He sings "Lawdy, Miss Clawdy" at Scotty's scripted request, repeating the verses over and over until he is, truly, lost in the music. He does charmingly melodic, almost crooning versions of "When My Blue Moon Turns to Gold Again" and "Blue Christmas," then launches into "Trying to Get to You," a number that he recorded at the end of his time at Sun and one which seems always to touch the deepest wellsprings of his emotions. The camera comes in for a tight focus shot as he plays once again with the notion of trying to stand. He is singing harder than he ever did, or ever had to, at the outset of his career, while playing with the audience, teasing it, miming emotion even as he feels it. He continues the process with Smiley Lewis' "One Night," where he does finally manage to stand and promptly pulls the guitar cord out of his amplifier. "I got to do it again, man," he says, and does—suspended between play and reality, unable at this point perhaps to tell the difference.

It seemed at first as if there would be little left for the eight o'clock performance. There was no attempt to turn the house for the second show, and perhaps out of a combination of the audience's familiarity with what was to come and Elvis' own sense of what he had accomplished, the second show was looser, louder, even more informal if possible. Jokes are delivered this time without the necessity of punch lines, lyrics are forgotten without even the artifice of conviction, and lines from the script are read out with even sharper sarcasm. "It's been a long time, jack," Elvis announces, as the guys whoop it up, repeating the lines that *they* have been given—"Aw, take it on home," "Tell it like it is," "Play it dirty"—like a mantra that has become an in-joke.

But then, just as you begin to think there is no way to reclaim the spell, Elvis once again finds what he is looking for at almost exactly the same point that it occurred in the earlier show. It starts, this time, with his rendition of "One Night," continues through a full-bodied version of "Love Me," and climaxes once again with "Trying to Get to You," as for a moment, at the end of the song, Elvis' eyes roll back in his head and he goes to another place, before moving on to a perfectly fine "Lawdy, Miss Clawdy," an explosive version of "Tiger Man" (the Joe Hill Louis blues he tried unsuccessfully to record while still at Sun), and "Memories," the syrupy Mac Davis-Billy Strange ballad that concludes both shows. It is, all in all, an astonishing triumph, even if you do not choose to overlook the panic-stricken start, but it really all comes down to that one moment in which not just self-consciousness, but consciousness itself, is lost, and it is little wonder that a number of those most closely associated with the production speculate that "after he finished singing, he was literally spent." After all, it is not so far from his own articulation in 1956 of what the sensation of being onstage was like for him. "It's like a surge of electricity going through you," he had said back then. "It's almost like making love, but it's even stronger than that. . . . Sometimes I think my heart is going to explode."

Terry Southern

RIDING THE LAPPING TONGUE

The Rolling Stones' American tour of 1972 was one of the first grown-up rock and roll tours—wall-to-wall media coverage, massive arena shows, all orgies all the time.

Barely a moment of the tour went unnoticed and it was chronicled in photojournalist Annie Leibovitz's stunning backstage portraits and in articles by everybody-who-was-anybody in the rock and roll world. Even Truman Capote was along for the ride—part of it, at least.

It was only natural that Terry Southern was there. The hippest of the hip, progenitor of New Journalism, co-author of *Candy,* screenwriter on *Dr. Strangelove* and *Easy Rider,* Southern had long been part of the rock and roll world. (That's him in the shades on the *Sgt. Pepper* cover.) Assigning him to cover the Stones' massive tour was a no-brainer for the *Saturday Review* editors.

Southern was born in Texas in 1924 and wrote the novels *The Magic Christian, Flash and Filigree, Texas Summer,* and *Blue Movie,* in addition to screenplays for *The Loved One* and *Barbarella,* among many others. He died in 1995.

WHETHER it's New York or Tuscaloosa, Norfolk or L.A., one factor is constant: The dressing room of the Rolling Stones is always Groove City— the juice flows, smoke rises, crystals crumble, poppers pop, teenies hang in, and Mick knifes through like a ballet-dancing matador . . . all to the funky wail of Keith's guitar tuning up, and sometimes the honking sax of a solid, downhome pickup sideman, like Texas Bobby Keys. And in Buddha repose, Charlie sits twirling his sticks Sid Catlett-style. Scene of good karma.

SLOW ZOOM IN ON MIRRORED FACE OF FALLEN ANGEL as Mick sits down at the lighted glass, and the make-up man leans in intensely to begin his magic ritual—transfiguration toward sympathy for the devil. I watch cautiously. It's a heavy number, a lot of head-stuff coming down.

Outside in the Washington, D.C., stadium, fifty thousand fans are stomping it up to the screams of Stevie Wonder . . . while they wait it out. Like the teenies, they've been hanging in—since two o'clock this afternoon, many since the night before. Now it's 10:30; they'll soon be impatient.

Just beyond the dressing-room entrance I squeeze through the gauntlet of cops, and one of them asks for my pass. I flash it: a small, white silk banner, lettered in red, glued to my sleeve:

ROLLING STONES ACCESS GUEST
Washington, D.C. July 4, 1972

It occurs to me he should be checking sleeves in the other direction. Without the pass, would I be forced to stay in the dressing room indefinitely?

But now I'm a part of the milling crowd, and almost at once a curious man lays a hand on my sleeve, his face like that of a red fox.

"I'd read this if I were you," he says in a voice with neither warmth nor accent, and he hands me the following mimeographed sheet:

THE STONES AND COCK ROCK

If you are male, this concert is yours. The music you will hear tonight is written for your head. It will talk to you about your woman, how good it is to have her under your thumb, so that she talks when she's spoken to. Men will play hard, driving music for you that will turn you on, hype you up get you ready for action . . . like the action at Altamont, San Diego, Vancouver. This is your night, if you are male. . . .

The Stones are tough men—hard and powerful. They're the kind of men we're supposed to imitate, never crying, always strong, keeping women in their place (under our thumbs). In Vietnam, to save honor (which means preserving our manhood), our brothers have killed and raped millions of people in the name of this ideal: the masculine man. Is this the kind of person you want to be? . . .

We resent the image the Stones present to males as examples we should imitate. . . .

If you are female, you don't need this leaflet to tell you where to fit in. You will get enough of that tonight. If you choose to be angry, to fight, to unite with other women to smash the sexist society that has been constructed to oppress you, tonight, here—and every day, throughout America—we the men who wrote this leaflet, will at-

tempt, to the extent we can successfully attack our own sexism, to support your struggle.

—*Men Struggling to Smash Sexism*

Later on the plane, I show this bit of weirdness to Keith. " 'Cock-rock,' " he muses with a wan smile. "So that's it. Right then, we'll use it," and he begins to beat out an eccentric tattoo on the glass holding his Tequila Sunrise, chanting Leadbelly style:

> Ah'm a cock-rockin' daddy,
> an' you oughtta see me bla-bla-bla. . . .

But the smile reflects the weariness of one too long and too profoundly misunderstood, and it doesn't sustain. "It's a drag, man, the way people dig evil—not evil itself, but the *idea* of it . . . grooving on the vicarious notion of it . . . it's *their* fascination with evil that locks us into this projection of it."

The Tequila Sunrise is a drink of exceptional excellence in every regard:

two parts tequila, three parts orange juice, one part gin, dash of grenadine.

Thus, your basic Tequila Sunrise is not merely one of those chic, absurdly yin, innocuously thirst-quenching drinks (so prized by dehydrated athletes, entertainers, and heavily dexed writers working against viciously unfair deadlines), it is also Bombsville-oh-roonie. Moreover (and here's another definite plus), the scarlet dash of grenadine into the orange, unstirred and allowed to seek its own cloudlike definition, lends the whole (in certain half-lights) an effect of advanced psychedelia.

In fact, some of our finest moments were aboard this plane, Sunrise in hand, hopping from one gig to the next—Fort Worth to Houston, Houston to Nashville, Nashville to New Orleans—short flights, and, like the dressing rooms, a boss groove and comfort to us all. The craft itself was a regular four-engine passenger plane, refurbished somewhat toward the concept of comfort and groove. A few seats had been replaced with a large buffet, always laden with endsville goodies, mostly to eat. The fuselage was emblazoned with the Stones' symbol, fashioned by Warhol, a giant, red extended tongue, not outthrust so much as lolling or lapping.

Hence the craft's name, unofficially, *The Lapping Tongue* . . . or, more familiarly, *Tongue.*

The stewardesses—two fabulous teenies nicknamed Ruby T. and Brown Sugar—would begin mixing the Tequila Sunrises as soon as we started up the ramp. On most planes, of course, you can't get a drink until you're in the air—aboard *The Lapping Tongue* you usually had a drink in hand before reaching your seat.

By way of indicating the scope of the operation, the roster of Tour Personnel as it appeared on the cockpit door of the *Tongue* numbered forty-nine, though only about half this number were actually on the plane—the logistics of tour travel (advance PR men, security arrangements, property trucks, etc.) requiring otherwise—so that at any given moment the plane was no more than a quarter full . . . leaving ample room for "dancing in the aisles," so to speak.

The fantastic T. Capote joined the tour in New Orleans, and together we were soon contriving a few chuckles by way of fantasizing a nifty skyjack action and subsequent media coverage:

CAPOTE SKYJACKS ROLLING STONES
Writer's Demands for Return of Group
Described as "Extremely Bizarre"

NEW ORLEANS (AP) June 30—Well-known author Truman Capote, in what authorities termed "a curiously worded document," made known today the "conditions" under which he will release the English rock group, "The Rolling Stones," after having commandeered their private DC-7 by claiming to have "a laser beam concealed on my person." His first demand was that the plane and its passengers ("kit and caboodle") be flown at once to Peking "for immediate acupuncture treatment of the eardrums." Subsequent demands were of a more complex nature, though often quite general. "Grotesquerie in high places," stated one such condition, "to cease tout de suite." Another demand concerned "authors Vidal and Mailer" and referred to "an unnatural act," though it was not specific, saying merely "as shall become them." . . .

et cetera, et cetera, building, gathering momentum, reaching out, even into areas of possibly questionable taste—certainly beyond the purview of a quality-lit mag of *SR* stamp and kidney. Suffice to say we grooved in this odd manner until the real thing came along—namely, the fabulous Brennen's restaurant where the great Tru used to dwell, and it was red-carpet time for the prodigal's return. *Gumboville!* Louisiana gumbo. Surely the supreme funkiness of *haute cuisine* the world over. HOLD ON GUMBO, SHIMMERING DISC OF AROMATIC DELIGHT, MOVE IN ON SLOW WAVERING DISSOLVE, back through time and space to the Coliseum in Vancouver, on Saturday, June 3, where the tour began, as the announcer says to a hushed and darkened house: "Ladies and gentlemen, the greatest rock-and-roll band in the world—The Rolling Stones," while from the top balcony someone drops a long string of exploding firecrackers, and Mick leaps into the purple pool of light. *"Dig it!"* he screams, and Jumping Jack Flash is on.

With the American tour completed, it has become apparent to certain persons who did not previously recognize it—critics and the like—that Mick Jagger has perhaps the single greatest talent for "putting a song across" of anyone in the history of the performing arts. In his movements he has somehow combined the most dramatic qualities of James Brown, Rudolf Nureyev, and Marcel Marceau. He makes all previous "movers"—Elvis, Sammy Davis, Janis Joplin, and even (saints protect me from sacrilege) the great James B. himself—appear to be waist deep in the grimpenmire. This tradition (of movin' and groovin') had its modest beginning with Cab Calloway at the Cotton Club in Harlem where he would occasionally strut or slink about in front of the bandstand by way of "illustrating" a number. After each he would take his bow, mopping his forehead, beaming up his gratitude for the applause as he reverted to his "normal" self for the next downbeat (and invariably a change of pace). This tradition, where the performer presents a series of alternating masks—each separated by a glimpse of (presumably) his own actual face (smiling while he readjusts the mike, wipes his brow, waits for the applause to die, etc.)—has been sustained right up through the present, with Elvis and Sammy Davis being its ultimate personifications. The phenomenal thing Jagger has accomplished is to have projected an image so overwhelmingly intense and so incredibly comprehensive that it embraces the totality of his work—so that there is virtually no distinction between the person and the song. This is all the more remarkable when it is realized that there is also virtually *no connection* between the public midnight-rambler image of Jagger and the man himself. On the contrary, he is its antithesis—quiet, generous, and sensitive. What this suggests; then, is an extraordinary potential for *acting;* and this is, in fact, his future—a future that began with his superb

characterization in *Performance,* and that would have included the role of
Alex in *A Clockwork Orange,* for which he was ideal, had it not been for
Kubrick's aversion to big guns.

While his movements are the synthesis and distillation of all that has
gone before or all that appears to be possible in and around a song on a
stage, his *sound* is uniquely his own. Its roots, of course, are in the music
of the black South—and, with the exception of Elvis Presley, he has done
more than anyone else to liberate it from the "race record" category of limited pressings on obscure labels distributed solely in the black ghettos of
America.

SLOW PULL BACK REVEALING MICK NOT ALONE ON STAGE BUT WITH SEVERAL OTH-
ERS. PAN LEFT, IN ON KEITH. Keith creates the music to which Mick moves, and
while the heaviest impact of the group is undeniably audiovisual, the
sound alone has made the Stones the only white band played on a number of otherwise exclusively "black music" disc-jockey programs around
the country. "I usually do it," says Keith, "with the idea of its being moved
to." Yet when you hear the sheer, drifting lyricism of things like "Ruby
Tuesday," "Dandelion," "She's a Rainbow," or the intricately haunting
beauty of "2,000 Light Years" and "Paint It Black," one is amazed that
Keith's body of work hasn't received more considered critical attention. It
is certainly as deserving of such as Paul McCartney's or that of any other
contemporary composer.

QUICK SLAM CUT to backstage in the heart of Dixie. A short, fat man in a
business suit, face perspiring, big white handkerchief in hand, trying to get
into the dressing-room area and being circumvented, in a coolly muscular way, by our two black security chiefs, Stan (The Man) Moore and Big
Leroy Leonard. Ever ready, I switch on my Sony cassette and move right in.

Stan (to Leroy): "Well now, he *say* he the *mayor.*"
Leroy: "Shee-it."
Stan: "He *say* he want to present them the *keys to the city.*"
Leroy: "Shee-it."

Turns out it *is* the mayor. So the lads dutifully assemble, and somehow
(*noblesse oblige*) manage to keep a straight face while he addresses them
(verbatim transcript):

Wal, ah tell you one *thing—them boys you got there [referring to
Stan and Leroy] sho do look after you, and that's a fact . . . [winks]*

. . . wouldn't mind havin' a few like that mahself, hee-hee . . . wal, now then, ah got to tell you all when it comes to music, *Law'ance Welk is moah to* mah *taste, not to say* undahstandin', *hee hee . . . but mah daughtah, Thelma Jean, says you awright, an' ah reckon anything good enuf foah Thelma Jean, wal now, er, uh, is good enuf foah me . . . so ah want to present you boys with the* keys *to this heah city!! Now y'all enjoy yourselves, ya' heah?*

CLOSE UP MAYOR'S GRINNING FACE, CURIOUSLY MALEVOLENT. DISSOLVE THROUGH TO MATCH WITH SIMILAR PERSPIRING ROUND WHITE FACE, GRIM: This time it's a policeman. He's got an armlock on a young man, hustling him up the exit ramp with what appears to be undue urgency. It put me in mind of a Perelman satire on Kipling, and I wondered what the cop would think if I began jumping with glee and yelling: "Frog's march him! For God's sake, frog's march him!"

Stan looked on sadly. "Man," he sighed, "that's the hardest part of my job—trying to cool out the cops."

"Overreacting?"

"I used to call it that, but that doesn't tell the story. You see, if a man is *aware* that he's overreacting but he does it anyway, then you're into something else. The other day a police chief told me he wanted to have fifteen officers, in riot helmets, standing shoulder to shoulder in front of the stage facing the audience. Can you dig it? *They* become part of the spectacle, like if you're playing inside a prison, or at a Hitler rally. I ask him: " 'Will they have their guns drawn?' I don't think he knew I was kidding. 'They can get 'em out quick enough,' he said. You see, he was probably hoping they'd *charge the bandstand.* I mean, why should the Hell's Angels get all the publicity? That's where he was at."

MONTAGE, SERIES OF QUICK CUTS: TOP SHOT, 2,500 screamers storming the backstage area (Vancouver) after being told the concert is sold out, sending thirty-one police to the hospital. Crowd and fighting dissolve when opening chords of "Brown Sugar" are heard. CLOSE UP, Botticelli face upturned at the edge of the stage (Seattle), radiantly ecstatic as she screams at Bill Wyman: "Bill, Bill! Oh my God, you are so *stone beautiful* I can't believe it!" MEDIUM SHOT, sea of astonishment as audience stares up in narcissistic enchantment (San Francisco) at Chip Monck's fantastic forty-foot mirror slowly turning above the stage, affirming existence and placing them, for a fleeting moment at least, in the same glittering picture as the Stones. LONG SHOT from top balcony (Los Angeles) Mick Jagger quells fifth-row disturbance by taking a drink from his water jug, then dispensing contents, benediction-style, over the fray, calming them wondrously. CLOSE UP, face in twisted anguish (San Diego), screaming like a character out of Burroughs: *"I got the fear!"* while being forcibly subdued by three big cops. A red-haired girl tries to help him, is dragged away by the hair. Others join in; fighting begins. LONG SHOT, Keith swooping in and out of purple-haze spot (Tucson) with extraordinary birdlike movements. MEDIUM SHOT, young man clutching harmonica hurls himself on stage (Albuquerque) and practically into the arms of Stan the Man. The young man's eyes are wildly alight. "I gotta blow with Mick," he's yelling. "You gotta let me do the gig with Mick!" Stan firmly escorts him away, murmuring, "Hey, baby, this isn't cool—let the cat do his thing, you do yours." A giant harness bull rushes over, truncheon at the ready and eager to use it. "No, it's cool, it's cool," says Stan and leads the boy off the stage. EXTREME CLOSE UP, slender fingers racing back and forth, Paderewski-style, on edge of stage (Denver), belonging to young mystery man who follows Stones everywhere, manages to get practically *under* Nicky Hopkins's piano at each concert. Has never tried to meet him. MATCH CUT to other fingers, dealing . . . bad scorpio vibes from out of place (Minneapolis); tripping hustler tries to rip off locals with weirdly cut coke, New Jersey grass, and other indigestibles. MEDIUM SHOT, young girl crying uncontrollably as her boy friend holds her hands and keeps saying, "You mustn't rub it in," and the tear gas continues to slowly filter in from the outside, where they decided to lob a few canisters (better safe than sorry, eh?) into the crowd, just to show they meant business. MEDIUM SHOT, Mick burying his face in an urn of rose petals, then flinging them over the crowd (Kansas City), floating down through the blue smoke slow-motion time, and the darling frenzied teenies, leaping gazellelike, grasping at each tiny dream. LONG SHOT AND SLOW ZOOM IN TO CLOSE on the great Charlie Watts (Fort Worth), arms rising alternately, slowly, but in each upraised hand sticks twirling with strobe-effect speed over his head. CLOSE UP, heeled boot rapping out crack-crack-crack flamenco tempo, as Keith surges into "Midnight Rambler" (Nashville) and turns it every way but loose. MEDIUM GOING TO CLOSE, full-on weirdness (Washington, D.C.) as paraplegic is hoisted from band-side wheelchair and onto the shoulders of his buddy. Buñuel City. SLOW SWEEP PAN of four enchanted front-row (Norfolk, Va.) teenies in T-shirts (braless though pert) lettered:

Mick Taylor—We Love You!

And when he gave them his smile (boss charm, boss humility), they squirmed and squealed, and (or so it seemed) tingled all over. CLOSE UP, rich golden glow of the Selmer bell as Bobby Keys brings it all back home (Charlotte, N.C.) in an extended magic line of "Sweet Virginia." CLOSE UP, the groove and gas craglike features of the great Chip Monck—now in gnarled concern, as he points to a jagged opening in the concrete foundation of the bandstand, where a bomb had been planted earlier in the day and had gone off prematurely. Don't tell Mick. CLOSE UP, thermometer reading 115° (Toronto), heat prostration rampant, people falling like proverbial flies. Mick zooms in, does his fantastic thing, and off. In the dressing room it was *exhaustionville extremis,* everyone falling down, apart, lying on the floor; forget it. Seemed impossible that anyone could do a second show, especially Mick. SLAM CUT to Mick leaping into "Jumping Jack Flash"—a satyr possessed, mad dervish, speed beyond the point of no return. . . .

"One thing about Mick," someone muttered, "he goes all out—every time."

That seemed to say exactly where it was at. None of the grand old clichés, like "great showmanship" . . . "kid's gotta lotta heart" . . . "the show must go on" . . . nothing like that, just a straightforward *"he goes all out . . .* [and the pause was like *bop-bop-bop*] *. . . every time."*

Later, over a big Teq Sun on the *Tongue,* in the extreme rear of the plane (banquetted for boss comf and conviv), I gave it certain thought. True enough, I decided, there's not been one like him, nor is there apt to be. I was quaffing off the last of the T.S. in a silent toast, one hand raised toward our fabulous nifties for the old refill, when who should fall by but the great Keith himself—snarling he was, and out of sorts by bloody weirdo half.

"Have a look at this then, mate," he said, affecting a curious accent, and tossed a copy of a pop-Sun-mag-sup (*NYTimes Mag,* July 16). It was one of those stories written by someone so far removed from the scene as to be remarkable for *any* truth at all. The author was described in the square below as "the rock-music critic for the *Times."*

"What's that then, 'rock-music, critic for the *Times'?"*

"Well, that's pretty heavy," I said. "It's something like being football critic for *Women's Wear Daily."*

Then I read with some amazement that the Stones (especially as represented by Mick) have copped out, have joined the genteel elite, indeed *"have used their radicalism to gain admittance to the easy good life of wealthy members of the entertainment world's establishment."*

I laid the rag aside and went for another Teq Sun. While standing there at the bar, I became aware of a foot-tapping melody nearby.

"What's that then?" I asked.

"Oh well, that's the Mick's new thing," was the answer. "You know, like the successful young poet asked the old poet, 'What shall I do now? and the old poet said, 'Etonnes-moi!' "

I listened more carefully. It was a full-on studio-type recording, quite impressive—as indeed were the lyrics, 'It was the title song of an album in progress, to be called The ———— Blues. For those readers who are into literary anagrams and the like, the omitted is a ten-letter word beginning with a "c" and ending with an "r." And it isn't "contractor."

Jaan Uhelszki

I DREAMED I WAS ONSTAGE WITH KISS IN MY MAIDENFORM BRA

Published in a Detroit-area near-commune by the most exciting gaggle of rock and roll writers of the time (Lester Bangs, Dave Marsh, Ben Edmonds . . . and the list goes on) *Creem* magazine called itself "America's only rock'n'roll magazine," a throwing-down-of-the-gauntlet to *Rolling Stone,* which even in the early 1970s was seen as heavily corporate. This charming article by one of the magazine's founders shows the *Creem* kids-are-all-right approach to rock and roll writing. Just because they took the music seriously didn't mean that they couldn't have fun.

WELL, not exactly my idea of the perfect fantasy, but I was curious about life on the other side of the footlights. Armed with an abundance of determination and a tight pair of Danskins (Danskins aren't only for dancing), I approached Larry Harris, the vice president of Casablanca Records, with my plan: "How about if I join Kiss for a night?"

No answer, and then nervous laughter. Obviously, Larry thought I just wanted to know what it was like to mouth kiss a vampire. Sure, they were eager for a feature on the band but this scheme was just a little bizarre. I pushed the point and they told me disturbing tales of other fresh faced females who were transformed into raging teenage nymphs after attending a Kiss concert. "But I don't want to *see* the show, I want to be in it!" I persisted. Reluctantly the Casablanca crowd conceded (only after making me promise not to call Kiss a glitter band), assuring me I could join these contorted Kewpie dolls on stage for one number or four minutes, whichever came first, on the following Saturday.

* * *

Thursday: I decided to drop in on the Detroit rehearsal to see what kind of atrocities I'd be in for. Soon after I arrived I found some of the band lounging on the side of the stage so I walked up and asked what they thought of the idea of me being a Kiss (Kissette?) for one night. They all

197

looked at me vacantly, and I realized that NO ONE HAD TOLD THEM! I felt like a Rockette who gets told thanks at the open call before she's had a chance to do her dance; but undaunted I fumed at the executive-in-residence, and demanded he explain the plan.

I returned to an empty seat in the vacant hall and continued to watch the band rehearse, to "pick up some tips." A stagehand divulged that bassist Gene Simmons had accidentally set his hair on fire while practicing the fire breathing segment of the show, which I admit made me squirm and fear for my own charred remains. My visions of stardom were quickly evaporating like warm Jell-O. During their break, Simmons came over and pulled out the few strands of his singed curls, assuring me, "It was nothing," but I couldn't prevent myself from biting the Lilac Frost off my nails. I was beginning to have misgivings. I think Ace Frehley did, too, because he just stared over my left shoulder, but Peter raised a comradely drumstick when Paul Stanley stated as he pointed to the empty stage: "Saturday Night, that's you up there!"

*   *   *

The next afternoon, Kiss comanager Joyce Biawitz called the office and reminded me to gather together all my baubles, spangles, and feathers for my big debut.

"But, but, Joyce," I sputtered, thinking of the promise Larry'd extracted. "I threw all my rhinestones away. Everybody knows glitter died last season."

*   *   *

Kiss is indisputably Detroit's favorite new band and tonight they are playing to a sellout crowd of 13,000. Maybe they represent some surrogate MC5 that made it with the same subversive tendencies and the wild excesses and brutalism. Maybe it's the 110 decibels. Kiss's Street Rock (which has been dubbed "Thunder Rock") is no more than a bastardization of heavy metal. Its fanatical drive and strong basic rhythm slug you in the gut. I mean, have you ever seen a girl dance in her wheelchair before?

Kiss is a package deal, allowing both the audience and themselves to let out their pent-up frustrations and feelings. When Kiss flaunt and strut across the stage, they are stand-ins for all those underage punks with their rebel hearted outlaw fantasies that are only realized through rock-'n'roll.

What am I going to pack to become a Kiss? I ponder over breakfast, wincing at the memory of last night's show. What if that geekish bass player bites my neck, oozing red blood-goo on my unsuspecting shoulder?

Anxiety knots my stomach so much that I can't even force a single Sugar Crisp down my throat, so I return upstairs to case my closet. One leotard—black, one pair tights—black, and one pair six-inch platforms—also black. I zipped up my Samsonite and hurried out the door, Junior's warning still ringing in my ears.

Stage manager Junior Smalling is a frightening and humorless man, who wears an oversized pair of blue plastic glasses and posses the self-given nickname, "Black Oak." Last night he demanded my presence at the Eastern Airlines desk at 10:45 A.M. (for an 11:20 flight), and although it was now after eleven and my ticket was in order, I still dared not move until Junior arrived. At eleven-ten he strode in, lugging a battered briefcase and an ugly scowl. He didn't acknowledge me, but instead barked at the airline clerk. Finished, he whirled on the band like an angry parent. "What the fuck is wrong with you guys? We get you watches, and you still can't get here on time. We coulda missed the plane and the gig, so hustle them asses to the plane!" Finally he looks down at me and spits: "What are *you* waiting for? Get to gate thirty-four!" Then almost kindly he adds, "Didn't anybody ever tell you to wear tall shoes around these guys?"

Seated in 8A my fear of flying is mixing badly with my apprehension. After a round of Hail Marys I look up to see Gene Simmons seated next to me, sans makeup of course although he still makes a scene in his seven-inch platforms, cheese colored scarf, and black polish that he is presently chipping off his stubby nails. Of all the members of the band, his appearance is the most obscured by the paint; he might just as easily be Omar Sharif or Joe Namath for that matter. Instead he was a former lifeguard, then a Boy-Friday at *Vogue,* has a B.A. in Education but secretly confesses a desire to be Bela Lugosi (and is lovingly dubbed Mr. Monster by his fellow inmates). Circulating around the plane is the current issue of one of *Creem*'s competitors, which has done a full feature on Kiss. Eventually the copy drifts to our seat and Gene insists on reading the story aloud to me.

"How come after everything I say, they always add 'Gene expounds'?" he pouts.

"Probably because you went to college," I explain.

We exit the plane without incident, except that most of us are over six-foot-something. Me, I feel a lot like Lewis Carroll's Alice after drinking the small potion, until I notice that Paul Stanley isn't that much loftier than me. As I remember, yesterday I came about eye level to his Keith Richard button.

"What'd you do, shrink overnight?" I ask.

"No, didn't you know I gave up platforms? I wanted a new look," he says coquettishly, tossing back his head of perfect curls, but he blows the cool by dropping screaming yellow zonker sunglasses.

"Hollywood?" I venture.

"No, I wear 'em because I don't like to see people looking at me all the time," he confesses. Stanley is a confident young man, bordering almost on arrogant. With or without his makeup he possesses an intense magnetism; Paul is the throb of the teenage heart, luring them away from their Barbie dolls into the backroom.

"What do you do about all those oversexed preteen glitter queens that are after you?"

"When a thirteen-year-old groupie comes on to you, what is that? That holds nothing for me, I'd feel more like a lecher, or a baby-sitter," he admits.

Believe it or not, the Gorgeous George of the group was once an ugly duckling, never getting any of the girls he wanted. "You know, I was an ugly kid. I looked like I was put together with spare parts. 'Okay, Mac, here's a set of legs, stick 'em on Stanley.' I used to be fat and had the funkiest hair. In fact I even used to iron it, or use this Puerto Rican product called Perma Straight that had directions in both English and Spanish. Back in 1966, the only thing I wanted to be was John Sebastian."

Yesterday an ugly duckling, today a superstar stud. When he shed his skin, and eighteen pounds, Paul became the pretty boy, a rock'n'roll rake in tight jeans. "I know I can have any girl I want now, they are the ones that come after me; but I'm real together about it. They're not after my mind," he says. "You know, the sad part about it is, if you're ugly people hate you."

Across the table Ace Frehley pulls out a package of Sweet 'n Low and trickles it onto his iced tea. "Gotta get rid of my beer belly, you know," he explains.

"You don't drink beer anymore?" I ask, remembering a once drunken Ace doing Rodney Dangerfield impressions that were so hilarious, I feared for my bladder.

"No, I drink wine now."

"But Ace, you won't be funny anymore," I implore.

"Well, wine isn't as jolly, but I'm still funny," he brags. "Hey, what's a specimen?"

"I don't know."

"An Italian astronaut."

*   *   *

Kiss are essentially street snots yanked from their gangs and plugged into an amp. They were brash JD's, tattooed and tough, who knew exactly what and who they were. Today, they still proudly display their tattoos (except Gene) but now their "colors" are a little more obvious—the paint they wear onstage. Kiss's identities seem to be the result of some concurrent conception by Eric Van Daniken, Walt Disney, Stan Lee, and Russ Meyer. Although they wear makeup, the classic stereotype of a flit, Kiss emerge as four macho lugs. "Hey, Uhelszki, you put out?" somebody asked.

*　　*　　*

We enter Johnstown, Pa., in a rented limo driven by a freckle-faced strawberry blonde. "You know, whenever we have a female limo driver I just feel like saying, 'You get in the backseat, and let me drive,' " says Paul. "Or just get in the backseat . . ." he jokes. The driver titters, throws Paul a toothpaste smile, and continuously sneaks glances at him in her rearview mirror.

"Is this your regular job?" he asks her.

"Yes."

"Well what's your irregular job?" he jives. As we get out of the car she anxiously waits for Paul to beckon her, and when he doesn't she reluctantly pulls away.

"Paul, you're just a tease," I admonish.

"Yeah, I know, that's all the fun. Getting it is nothing."

*　　*　　*

"Room 421, miss." Key in hand, I rejoin the gang and anxiously ask, like an old hand, "When's the sound check?"

"What sound check?" Gene blankly answers.

"You mean I don't get to rehearse?" I ask nervously.

"Nah, you'll catch on, just follow us," says Paul.

"Yeah, but I've got nothing to wear . . ." I say with a trace of panic.

"Don't worry, we'll take care of you kid, your name in lights," jokes Bill Aucoin, their manager.

It's 4:00 P.M. and all I have between me and showtime is Saturday afternoon TV. I'm watching *Soul Train* without having the slightest idea what I'm seeing, when the phone rings.

"Uhelszki?" (By this time I am one of the boys, and either called Uhelszki or kid.)

"Yeah?"

"What size shoe do you wear?"

"Eight and a half. Why?"

"Too bad. I thought we could snazz you up in a pair of silver boots."

"Well, maybe I could stuff 'em with Kleenex."

"Nah, wouldn't work. Don't worry, I'll rummage around some more."

I felt like I was getting ready for that Big Date—you know, the prom or Homecoming—when actually I was going to be onstage for a total of four minutes in an Ice Arena in Nowhere, Pennsylvania. But still fidgety, I kept trying on my leotard over and over, checking the image in the mirror, and feeling a lot like the motorcycle moll in *Naked Under Leather*. Drawing the drapes, I practiced a few classic Kiss kicks in the bathroom mirror without much success. My practice was cut short by a knock at the door, and an ominous voice: "Be in the lobby in one hour!" The Voice commanded; mine, as a mere member of the shock troops, was but to obey.

Room service came, and I left it untouched, which was probably for the better. I didn't want my thighs glaring out at all America . . . well, at Johnstown, Pa.

This is it, light the lights
This is it, your night of nights. . . .

Absurdly, this song kept threading its way through my brain like some hold on sanity. It was too late to back off.

The dressing room in all of its filthy linoleum splendor wasn't the worst of its lot. Once inside, I'm afflicted with a bad case of modesty, and become obsessed, like a cat searching for a spot to drop her kitten, with finding a secluded corner to change into my clothes. Would a phone booth do? Clutching my costume, I spot an empty stall and dart in relieved, bolting the door. Like a quick-change artist, I tear off my T-shirt, tug at my Landlubbers, and don my basic black, feeling more like a naked seal than part of Kiss. Timidly, I sneak out of the stall and approach Ace: "Hey, do you have another pair of tights I can wear? I'm freezing," I lie.

"Yeah, but they're size D," says Ace.

"That's okay."

"But, Jaan, yours look better. They're much hotter, because you can see your skin through them. Doncha wanna look good in pictures?"

"That's what I was afraid of."

"Hey, hey, if you don't watch those legs they're gonna get grabbed," leers Simmons.

Embarrassed, I turn on Junior and shout: "Hey, how long until we go on!"

"Lookit her, give her a black outfit, and make her a Kiss, and already she's hardcore," he laughs.

*　　*　　*

The first band is done and the crowd is a stiff. No encore. Bill Aucoin sticks his head into the dressing room, shoves five backstage passes toward us, and tells us we've got 45 minutes until showtime. My palms have started to sweat so much that they're beginning to obliterate the lettering on my pass, so I stick it on my right shoe, figuring the local goon squad would never believe that I was "Kiss for a Night" and give me the shove, figuring me to be just another fanatical Kiss groupie who had painted her face like her heroes, which seems to be the current fashion among the fans. In keeping with the code of concealing the real identity of Kiss, my photographer can't start shooting until the guys have sufficiently obscured their features. Tired of pacing, I take a spin around the backstage area, which is littered with underage glitter queens of varying age and brilliance. A 14-year-old Patty Play Pal accosts me.

"You know Gene Simmons?" she drools.

"Yeah," I reply matter-of-factly.

"Does he really do those *things* with his tongue?" she asks excitedly.

"I guess so," I reply.

"Gee, I wish he'd use that tongue on me," she says wistfully.

*　　*　　*

I return, and Kiss are in the final stages of completion, and ready to give me tips on cosmetology. I'm hesitant to let them know that the last time I put on face makeup was in the tenth grade, in the girls' john at Southfield High School, and all my technique consisted of was to smear Touch-and-Glow over my adolescent visage.

"I always wear a shower cap to keep the grease outta my hair," explains Peter as he smears some goop on his face.

"Yeah, Uhelszki, you gotta get rid of those bangs!" barks Simmons, yanking two clumps of my hair and wrapping elastic bands around them, so my carefully fully blow-dried hair is imprisoned in two sprouts on top of my head.

"Ouch!" I complain.

"Shuddup kid!" kids Simmons. "You're the one who asked for this." Suddenly Paul looks at Gene, and the two of them grin, nod their heads, and attack my hair with a rattail comb and a can of hairspray. "Ah, perfect," sighs Paul, as he admires my new fright-wig concoction.

Ace, oblivious to what happened, shoves a bottle of cocoa butter toward me. "Here, use this. It'll seal your pores." I guess I looked confused because Ace asked me, "How come you don't know anything about putting on makeup, and you're a chick?"

I ignore the remark and furiously pat the butter all over my naked face. "Broadway Red?" I ask, picking up a worn tube of lipstick.

"Yeah, I love it," says Peter. "In fact, if the day ever comes and I do a solo album, I'm going to call it *Broadway Red*."

By general consensus, Kiss have decided to make me up as a composite of all of them, just like the back cover of the *Hotter than Hell* album. Now for the actual transformation: sidestraddling the bench, I face Simmons in his black satin prize fighter's robe with OTTO HEINDEL emblazoned on the back, trying not to giggle as English comes out of this Halloween-monster thing. "It's time to make a little monster. Now watch, so you can do this," he instructs as if he were a counselor for the Elizabeth Arden School of Beauty. "First rub Stein's clown white all over your face. Smooth it very lightly, only using a little around the eyes."

I dip my fingers in the jar, and start smearing the stuff on my face.

"No, Uhelszki, like this!" he admonishes, losing patience and doing it himself. "Okay, now sprinkle baby powder all over your face, so the base will set." I look at Paul in the mirror and start to laugh.

"Don't you know we're the clowns of rock'n'roll?" Paul jokes. Ace scowls at his reflection, muttering that he made "the goddamn lines too thick." Unsatisfied, he storms out the door. Peter dabs on his last whisker, and preens in front of the mirror, caressing his lean leather thighs: "Tony Curtis, eat your heart out!"

Gene etches Maybelline black on my dry to normal skin, sketching in his bat insignia. "Hey! Don't make her up just like you," yells Stanley.

"I'm not, I told you, we each get a crack at her." Ace splotches a silver dot on my nose, and Peter adds his own feline touch in messy black crayon. Paul pauses over the conglomeration, and draws a smaller version of his star. Funny, somehow, I feel some kind of immunity behind the paint, a little more confidence. Maybe this rock'n'roll business won't be so bad after all. Gene holds up a mirror and stands back, telling me to look at my reflection. "Don't you feel special?" he inquires.

"No, silly," I admit.

"Come on, you look very groupie."

"I do not!" I argue.

"No, that's great! Get off on it tonight, while you got it," he says.

"So then you think I look okay?" I ask.

"Yeah, but I look better!" He laughs.

Now the presentation of my plugless wonder. Junior shoves a red guitar in my hands and I fumble with it. "You mean you don't even know how to hold a guitar?" he asks incredulously.

"No, do you know how to change a typewriter ribbon?" I retort. Paul comes to my rescue and shows me how to handle the Fender. "Here, hold it like this, off to one side. Now wear it low and slinky, so it looks sexy."

My last touch is the freak paraphernalia, and I go from person to person collecting their junk jewelry and brutish decorations. Finally I was outfitted in a studded collar, a menagerie of plastic eyeball (and other unidentified organs) rings, a metal cuff, and a studded belt whose buckle encased a tarantula named Freddy. Unfortunately Freddy kept slipping off my thirty-five inch hips, and finally had to be taped to my tights with gaffer's tape. Readying for a gig with Kiss fell short of my expectations and their reputation. I expected some gruesome ordeal, but instead we took turns mugging in the mirrors, exchanging gossip ("Did you see the set of tits on that fifteen-year-old broad?") and advice. I felt more like I was at a Tupperware party than in a rock'n'roll dressing room, but then the "worst" was yet to come. "I've got a run in my tights," I whined.

"Don't worry," comforted Bill, "who's going to notice 50 rows back?" Like a rock'n'roll Casey Stengel, Bill gave me an impromptu pep talk, about standing up straight, not watching the audience, and looking "like you belong there." As he finished we were out the door, and believe it or not I was raring to go, running down the hallway. Without realizing it, I was halfway up the stairs to the stage when Junior grabbed me. "Hey, sweetheart, where you going?" he laughed.

What he didn't realize was that I was getting a little trigger happy, and maybe even stagestruck, but just in case I motioned him over to me. "I have every intent of going through with this, but when it's time for me to go onstage, don't give me a hand sign, just shove."

The set seemed to take forever; I felt like I was sitting through the rock version of *Gone With the Wind*. I had already shredded four Kleenexes, I had to go to the bathroom, and the makeup was beginning to itch unbearably. As I raised a lone fingernail to scratch, Bill Aucoin was at my side, like a trained pro, grabbing my hand. "That's a no-no," he said and fanned my face to relieve the irritation. "Did you know you're on next?" he inquired.

I didn't. Visions of graduation day floated through my head, that fear of slipping before the entire school before you got your hands on the diploma. Only difference was that if I slipped onstage, Kiss would use it as part of the act. So in this sense I *couldn't* make a mistake. Just a damn fool of myself.

From stage left I peeked at the greedy crowd, and was horrified that the stage was only inches off the floor—well, 24 inches. This struck me as odd, since this is a Kiss concert and everybody knows their reputation for riling up an audience, whether it be amorous ladies intent on wrapping their arms around Ace's mike stand, or just uncounted masses of genderless groupies who want to cop a feel.

Countdown. Then the shove, and I'm onstage, moving like I'm unremotely controlled. Forgetting completely that I am in front of five thousand people participating as one fifth of this sadistic cheerleading squad, bobbing and gyrating instinctively, I no longer hear the music, just a noise and a beat. On cue I strut over to Simmons's mike and lean into it and sing. Singing loud without hearing myself, oblivious to everything but those four other beings onstage. Gene whispers for me to "shake it" and I loosen up a little more, until I feel like a Vegas showgirl going to a go-go. Suddenly it strikes me: I like this. And I venture a look at the crowd, that clamoring, hungry throng of bodies below me. All I can think at that moment is how much all those kids resemble an unleashed pit of snakes, their outstretched arms bobbing and nodding, as if charmed by the music. I wonder if they will pick up on the hoax? But they keep screaming and cheering, so I might just as well be Peter Criss, unleashed from his drum kit, as anyone. The only difference is, I am the only Kiss with tits.

I slide over to Stanley's mike, sneaking up behind him, and mimic his calisthenics. He whirls around and catches me, emitting a huge red crimson laugh from his painted lips. I push my unplugged guitar to one side and do an aborted version of the bump and the bossa nova, singing into Paul's mike this time.

I wanna rock and roll all night, and party every day!

. . .

And right on cue, to add that dash of drama, Junior's beefy arms ceremoniously lift me and the guitar three feet off the stage, and I look like a furious fan who almost managed to fulfill her fantasy, but was foiled in the end. But you know something? I feel foiled; *I wanted to finish the song. My song!*

*　　*　　*

We trekked back to the dressing room and now, after the ordeal, my legs went marshmallow. Wanting to appear blasé after my big debut, I grabbed a wooden chair and draped myself over it.

"It was hysterical!" laughed Paul. "I knew you were gonna be on-stage, but then I forgot about you, then all of a sudden I look and see you dancing, looking like Minnie Mouse."

"You're a perfect stage personality," said Gene. "All of a sudden you were hogging the mike. You took over, stealing scenes like a pro. You know, the kids thought you were a part of the show."

Junior walked over, and I was afraid of his verdict but he liked it, he liked it! "You did it! You got out there like a trouper. I gave you the sign and away you went. That must have been very, very heavy for you."

"I didn't think they noticed . . ." I sputtered.

"I was watching people in the front row, and they were saying, 'Who is this chick. What *is* she doing up there? What's going on?" Junior continued.

*　　*　　*

The party was over, the fans dispersed, but the five of us were armed with five boxes of Kleenex and four bottles of cold cream. "You know, if we don't get rich, I'm gonna need a padded cell," confessed Peter.

"Didn't you hear, Peter, we're the next Beatles!" laughed Paul.

The next morning, as we sleepily wandered to the coffee shop to await the limousines, each member of the group greeted me, not with "Good morning," but with a mimic of my stage shimmy. "You deserve it, Jaan, you told us you were shy. I never thought you could be such a ham," explained Bill.

As we said our good-byes, Gene Simmons said over his shoulder: "Whenever you feel like putting on that makeup again, give us a call."

Bob Marley and Timothy White

WORTH DYING FOR

No popular musician has ever been such a combination of political and musical figure. Robert Nesta Marley not only affected rock and roll with the reggae music he made with the Wailers and his Rasta lifestyle—he played a part in the social changes in his homeland of Jamaica. Timothy White wrote the book on Marley, *Catch a Fire*.

[T]HEM higher people in the government should clean up the dumps and slums and feed my people, our children! . . . I read the paper and I am ashamed. . . .

. . . What is righteousness rule the earth. It goes that there are two things on the earth: good and bad. You have the Devil and you have God. Well, if you live right, yar Rasta, and if you live wrong you're the Devil. . . .

Is it possible to be both righteous and rich?

The thing is, your mind is the whole thing, because we are the richest people upon the earth. Richer than rich, our father Creator. . . .

. . . My richness is to live, and walk on the earth and bear fruit. And you can grow. That is what richness is. Richness is when your mind can tell you, "Get up and do something" when you want to do it, 'cause you no want to do something your mind can't tell you for do it.

Your music is full of images of struggle, calls for equal rights and revolution. How do Rastas feel about armed struggle?

Armed struggle? I don't want to fight, but when I move to go to Africa, if they say no, then me personally will have to fight. Me don't love fighting, but me don't love wickedness either. My father was a captain in the army; I guess I have a kinda war thing in me, but is better to die fighting for yar freedom than to be a prisoner all the days of your life.

Anthony DeCurtis

A LIFE AT THE CROSSROADS

Discovering Robert Johnson was the key moment in Eric Clapton's life as a musician. When he first heard *King of the Delta Blues Singers* as a teenager, Clapton said, it came as a shock that there could exist feeling so powerful on record. "It seemed like he wasn't playing for an audience at all," Clapton said, "he was just playing for himself."

Like Johnson, Clapton was always independent, always changing. First he was a pop star with the Yardbirds, then, after working construction, he became Johnson's most fervent disciple in his stint with John Mayall's Bluesbreakers. Then followed the spoiled-rock-star period of Cream and Blind Faith, followed by the redemption of rhythm and blues with Delaney and Bonnie. Finally, a true solo career and the singing voice he'd been so shy about with some of his earlier groups. He might have started with a Robert Johnson infatuation and a strong desire to imitate him, but he ended up absorbing that influence and marrying it with his own experience.

Anthony DeCurtis tells Clapton's life story in this essay, which appeared as the booklet notes to Clapton's four-disc career retrospective, *Crossroads.* DeCurtis won a Grammy Award for this piece. He has served as senior features writer at *Rolling Stone,* where he was in charge of the music section. He has served as a critic for National Public Radio and as a host for VH-1 programming. He is the editor of *Present Tense: Rock & Roll and Culture* and *The Rolling Stone Illustrated History of Rock & Roll.*

OVER THE past twenty-five years Eric Clapton's extraordinary career has traced a dramatic progression marked by musical pioneering, restless shifts of direction, spiritual awakenings, backsliding and, at one point, a total retreat into isolation. Clapton's mysterious, internally determined moves from budding pop star to purist blues man to rock guitar hero to laid-back troubadour have challenged the faithful and won new converts at every turn.

Through all the personal and artistic upheavals, part of Eric Clapton has consistently remained detached and calm, as if he accepted in his heart that he was destined for such shocks—and that acceptance brought a certain peace. At the same time he has maintained a fierce, private idealism about his playing. "My driving philosophy about making music," he told *Rolling Stone* in 1974, "is that you can reduce it all down to one note if that note is played with the right kind of feeling and with the right kind of sincerity."

It makes sense, then, that Robert Johnson's tough, transcendent masterpiece, "Crossroads," has become Clapton's signature song. On the path of life, crossroads are where the breakdowns and breakthroughs come, where danger and adventure lie. As he has forged and disbanded musical alliances, altered his sound and his look, pursued and dodged fame, Eric Clapton has brought himself to the crossroads and proven himself time and time again.

Clapton's bold search for his own identity is the source both of his enormous artistic achievement and his inner strife. That search acquired its momentum in the earliest years of his life. Clapton was born on March 30th, 1945 in Ripley, a small village about thirty miles outside—and a universe away from—London. His mother raised him until he was two years old, at which point she moved abroad, leaving him in the loving hands of her mother and stepfather.

The elderly couple was indulgent of Eric—they bought him his first guitar on an installment plan when he was in his teens—but the stigma of being born out of wedlock in a small town made a forceful impression on him. The "secret" of Clapton's illegitimacy was a secret only from him. "I was raised by my grandparents, thinking that they were my parents, up until I was nine years old," Clapton explained to J.D. Considine in *Musician* in 1986. "That's when the shock came up, when I found out—from outside sources—that they weren't my parents, they were my grandparents. I went into a kind of . . . shock, which lasted through my teens, really, and started to turn me into the kind of person I am now."

Clapton was more pointed in Ray Coleman's authorized biography, *Clapton!,* published in 1985, about how hard it was to learn the truth about his background. "My feeling of a lack of identity started to rear its head then," he told Coleman. "And it explains a lot of my behavior throughout my life; it changed my outlook and my physical appearance so much. Because I still don't know who I am."

Like so many rockers, Clapton did a brief stint in art school—the Kingston College of Art, in his case. His formal education got derailed, however, when he was about sixteen and began to make the bohemian scene in London, where he discovered folk-blues. Eventually he would go on to play acoustic gigs in coffee-houses and pubs, accompanied by a vocalist and doing tunes by Big Bill Broonzy, Ramblin' Jack Elliott and Blind Boy Fuller.

Another revelation struck around that time, as well. "Every Friday night, there would be a meeting at someone's house, and people would turn up with the latest imported records from the States," Clapton recalled in a 1985 *Rolling Stone* interview with Robert Palmer. "And shortly, someone showed up with that Chess album, *The Best of Muddy Waters,* and something by Howlin' Wolf. And that was it for me. Then I sort of took a step back, discovered Robert Johnson and made the connection to Muddy." In later days, Clapton would come to refer to Muddy Waters as his "father." And Johnson's haunted country blues affected Clapton so deeply that he would tell Dan Forte in *Guitar Player* more than two decades later, "Both of the Robert Johnson albums (*King of the Delta Blues Singers,* Volumes 1 and 2) actually cover all of my desires musically. Every angle of expression and every emotion is expressed on both of those albums."

The first band Clapton joined was the fledgling R&B outfit, the Roosters. The Roosters would last only a few months, from March to October of 1963, according to rock historian Pete Frame. But during that period the band's bassist, Tom McGinness, who later played with Manfred Mann and McGuinness Flint, turned Clapton on to blues guitarist Freddie King's instrumental "Hideaway," and another influential figure entered Clapton's pantheon. Playing John Lee Hooker and Muddy Waters' tunes with the Roosters sharpened Clapton's playing, according to the band's pianist Ben Palmer, one of the guitarist's oldest friends. "It was immediately obvious that he was something that none of the rest of us were," Palmer says in *Clapton!* "And he had a fluency and command that seemed endless. The telling point was that he didn't mind taking solos, which people of our standard often did because we weren't up to it."

Following an extremely short stay with the pop band Casey Jones and the Engineers—headed by Liverpool singer Brian Cassar, who was trying to cash in on the record-company signing spree in the wake of the Beatles' success—Clapton joined the seminal Sixties band, the Yardbirds, in October of 1963. In their early days the Yardbirds—who, in addition to Clapton, consisted of vocalist Keith Relf, guitarist Chris Dreja, bassist Paul Samwell-Smith and drummer Jim McCarty—were an exuberant London

R&B band that covered tunes like John Lee Hooker's "Boom Boom" and Billy Boy Arnold's "I Wish You Would."

On "I Ain't Got You"—and in his brief solo on the catchy New Orleans novelty, "A Certain Girl"—Clapton flashes the biting, fiercely articulate phrasing characteristic of his best playing. But in general Clapton was inhibited by the Yardbirds' harmonica-driven rave-up style. Despite his youth, Clapton was sufficiently confident of his musical tastes to become disgruntled when the Yardbirds, at the urging of manager Giorgio Gomelsky, edged away from the blues in order to pursue pop success. Clapton left the group by mutual agreement shortly after they recorded Graham Gouldman's "For Your Love" in quest of a hit.

Splitting from the Yardbirds on the brink of their commercial breakthrough was the first time Clapton displayed his willingness to pursue his own musical vision at whatever the cost—and it was far from the last. However high-minded and necessary such decisions were, Clapton is not beyond questioning them to a degree, in retrospect. "I took it all far too seriously," he states in *Clapton!* "Perhaps if I'd been able to temper it, I might not have been so frustrated. . . . I still take it too seriously, in terms of relationships and being able to get on with other musicians. I'm far too judgemental, and in those days I was a complete purist. If it wasn't black music, it was rubbish."

Of course, seriousness about black music was hardly a problem during Clapton's tenure with John Mayall's Bluesbreakers in 1965 and 1966. A keyboardist with a vocal style derived from Mose Allison and Freddie King, Mayall was twelve years Clapton's senior and the father of the British blues scene. Mayall's Bluesbreakers were the proving ground for a host of ambitious young musicians in the mid to late Sixties, including Jack Bruce, Mick Taylor, Peter Green, Aynsley Dunbar, John McVie and Mick Fleetwood.

Clapton raided Mayall's vast collection of singles, and the two men thrived on each other's enthusiasm, as is evidenced by the raw Chicago blues power of their duet on "Lonely Years" and the spry assurance of their instrumental jam, "Bernard Jenkins." Though barely into his twenties, Clapton shaped an agressive, tonally rich playing style with the Bluesbreakers. Drawing on Freddie King, Otis Rush and Buddy Guy in a way that blended respect with his own precocious mastery, Clapton unleashed some of the finest blues guitar playing of his generation on the 1966 *Bluesbreakers—John Mayall with Eric Clapton* LP. In addition, Clapton sang his first lead vocal on that record, a spare, eloquent reading of Robert

Johnson's "Ramblin' On My Mind" that captures all that song's edgy amalgam of anguish and submerged threat.

Clapton's scorching club performances in London during his time with Mayall—represented in this collection by his ignition of Billy Myles' "Have You Ever Loved a Woman," with Jack Bruce on bass—quickly established a cult following for the young guitarist. "Clapton Is God" graffiti began appearing around the city, defining a central tenet of the Clapton mythology to this day. And though the comparisons with God would prove to be a hellhound on Clapton's trail, he understandably received the adulation more positively at first.

"My vanity was incredibly boosted by that 'God' thing," Clapton says in Coleman's biography. "I didn't think there was anyone around at that time doing what I was doing, playing the blues as straight as me. I was trying to do it absolutely according to its rules. Oh yeah, I was very confident. I didn't think there was anybody as good."

However appealing, the adulation did not prevent Clapton from taking a three-month break from the Bluesbreakers in 1965, and it was during that period that Jack Bruce joined the band. Playing with Bruce upon his return spun Clapton's head around. Bruce's jazz background gave his playing an improvisational flair, and Clapton, who, despite his own purist impulses, had been feeling somewhat constrained in Mayall's strict blues format, felt a new sense of freedom. "Most of what we were doing with Mayall was imitating the records we got, but Jack had something else," Clapton told *Rolling Stone,* "he had no reverence for what we were doing, and so he was composing new parts as he went along playing. I literally had never heard that before, and it took me someplace else. I thought, well, if he could do that, and I could, and we could get a drummer . . . I could be Buddy Guy with a composing bass player. And that's how Cream came about."

Formed in 1966, Cream's impact on the world of pop music was immense. Rock bands to that point had played almost exclusively before crowds of screaming teeny-boppers—a major reason why live performance was beginning to seem pointless to bands whose music and ideas were becoming more sophisticated. Discussing rock and roll in musical terms was a joke to the mainstream media, and alternative media had not yet sprung up. Cream was a primary catalyst in transforming rock and roll into music that could be performed in concert before adults and analyzed with the same rigor that blues or jazz could be. The declaration implicit in the band's name was itself a demand to be taken seriously. In

Coleman's terse summary, "They made musicianship hip." Clapton forever defined the role of guitar hero at this point, and with Bruce on bass and the redoubtable Ginger Baker on drums, Cream defined the power trio.

In their range and power, Cream forced a dichotomy between the studio and the stage. In the studio, the band was something like a later evolution of the Yardbirds. They could contain hip innovations within pop-song structures, as on "I Feel Free"; rework the blues, as on Willie Dixon's "Spoonful" and the Albert King-derived "Strange Brew"; journey into psychedelic wonderland, as on "Tales of Brave Ulysses" and "White Room"; or simply cut a radio-perfect, guitar-charged hit like "Sunshine of Your Love."

Live, however, Cream was essentially a rock-and-roll jazz band. Songs became thematic statements that provided the occasion for lengthy improvisational jams, with Baker and Bruce muscling each other into unexplored territory as Clapton wailed and roared above them. The propulsive live version of "Crossroads" included here is a Cream classic, and a masterpiece of concision—edited, as it was, by engineer Tom Dowd for the *Wheels of Fire* album—compared to the much longer renditions the band typically fired up.

The hero-worship Clapton had inspired when he was with the Bluesbreakers reached a fever pitch with Cream. The pressures of the inordinate praise heaped upon him, the wild improvisational competitiveness of Cream's gigs, and the fighting that resulted from Bruce and Baker's inability to get along gradually took their toll on Clapton.

"All during Cream I was riding high on the 'Clapton is God' myth that had been started up," Clapton told Robert Palmer. "Then we got our first kind of bad review, which, funnily enough, was in *Rolling Stone.* The magazine ran an interview with us in which we were really praising ourselves, and it was followed by a review that said how boring and repetitious our performance had been. And it was true! . . . I immediately decided that that was the end of the band."

Cream split up in November of 1968, about six months after that review appeared, and Clapton began jamming with Steve Winwood, the keyboardist and sterling R&B vocalist who had made his own youthful mark with the Spencer Davis Group and Traffic. The two men had played and recorded together two years earlier, and Clapton admired Winwood's tunefulness as a singer and songwriter—qualities that stood in sharp relief after the jazz-rock experimentalism of Cream.

But, given their musical pedigrees, Clapton and Winwood were hot commercial commodities. Because all three of its members had been eminent figures on the British scene, Cream had begun a trend toward supergroups, and the prospect of Winwood and Clapton teaming up was too hot a proposition for the business people to resist. What began idyllically with Clapton and Winwood jamming together at their homes in the country and searching for new musical directions quickly became a cash cow. Ginger Baker and Rick Grech, bassist of the English folk-rock band Family, were recruited as the rhythm section, and Blind Faith was born.

Formed in early 1969, Blind Faith debuted at a huge outdoor concert in London's Hyde Park in June of that year, recorded one album and then launched an arena tour in America. The band broke up in late 1969, and Clapton offered this bluntly honest obituary in *Rolling Stone* shortly afterwards: "We didn't rehearse enough, we didn't get to know each other enough, we didn't go through enough trials and tribulations before the big time came."

Still, the *Blind Faith* album, recorded in February, May and June of 1969 had a number of splendid moments. Steve Winwood's searching "Can't Find My Way Home," with Clapton on acoustic guitar, is a fine example of the kind of melodic, song-centered work Clapton was becoming more interested in after Cream. Among the earliest tunes Blind Faith laid down in the studio, Clapton's "Presence of the Lord" was the first non-instrumental song he ever recorded that he wrote fully on his own. It was also the first of the hymn-like spiritual songs of faith that would become a staple of his work in years to come.

The opening act on the Blind Faith tour of America in 1969 was a rocking R&B band led by Delaney and Bonnie Bramlett. Delaney and Bonnie played a loose, engaging blend of the full range of American soul music, and their unassuming, good-hearted shows seemed to Clapton a sharp contrast to Blind Faith's headline gigs. Clapton began spending more and more time with Delaney and his band, traveling from gig to gig on their tour bus and popping up on stage during their sets. In a 1970 interview in *Rolling Stone,* Clapton recalled that "on certain nights I'd get up there and play tambourine with Delaney's group and enjoy it more than playing with Blind Faith. . . . And by then I kind of got this crusade going for Delaney's group. I wanted to bring them over to England."

Blind Faith splintered once their blitz of America ended. At that point, Clapton not only sponsored a tour of England for Delaney and Bonnie, he played guitar with the band and recorded the infectiously upbeat single, "Comin' Home," with them. A live album from the tour was released later. More important, however, Delaney was the agent of a significant emotional breakthrough for Clapton.

Since about 1968, Clapton had been growing bored with virtuoso musicianship and more interested in songs that had clearly delineated structures and put across a pleasing groove. The Band's *Music from Big Pink,* which came out that year, made a striking impression on him and fueled his dissatisfaction with Cream. Discussing Cream's break-up in *Rolling Stone* in 1974, Clapton said "another interesting factor was that I got the tapes of *Music from Big Pink* and I thought, well, this is what I want to play—not extended solos and maestro bullshit but just good funky songs." The concise, melodic "Badge," which Clapton co-wrote for Cream's *Goodbye* album with George Harrison, who also plays guitar on the song, was one product of this interest. Forming a band with Steve Winwood and serving as a guitar-slinger side-man to Delaney and Bonnie were other manifestations of it.

Yet despite his strong performances on "Ramblin' on My Mind," "Crossroads" and other tracks, Clapton was still extremely shy about his singing. Clapton told Robert Palmer that on the night he and Delaney met, "Delaney looked straight into my eyes and told me I had a gift to sing and that if I didn't sing, God would take it away. I said, 'No, man, I can't sing.' But he said, 'Yes, you can.' . . . That night we started talking about me making a solo album, with his band."

When Delaney and Bonnie's tour of England ended, the two men went into the studio in Los Angeles and began work on Clapton's first solo album, *Eric Clapton.* Delaney's influence on the record was considerable. He produced the album—which includes the joyful "Blues Power" and the fiery "Let It Rain"—and supplied most of the players from his own band. His hand is especially evident on the alternative version of J.J. Cale's "After Midnight"—which Delaney mixed and which features a horn section that does not appear on the LP track. With Delaney's encouragement, Clapton emerged as a front man for the first time since he had been propelled into superstardom with Cream. Clapton wrote or co-wrote eight of the eleven tunes on the record, sang all the lead vocals and played crisply and spiritedly. He was now ready to put together a band of his own.

When Clapton learned that three members of Delaney's band—keyboardist Bobby Whitlock, bassist Carl Radle and drummer Jim Gordon—had had a falling out with their boss and were available, he scooped them up. The band came together and did their first recording while they were all working on the sessions for George Harrison's *All Things Must Pass* album, which Phil Spector was producing. They recorded a blistering version of "Tell the Truth"—backed with the salacious "Roll It Over," featuring Harrison and Dave Mason on guitars—as a single, with Spector at the board. But, at the band's insistence, the track was recalled within days of its release.

Still ambivalent about his rock-star status, Clapton avoided using his own name and debuted his new band at a benefit concert in London as Derek and the Dominos. And rather than play large halls, he booked a club tour of England for their first trip out. As undisputed leader of the Dominos, Clapton was able both to play songs he felt comfortable with and to stretch out in solos when he desired. "It wasn't until I formed Derek and the Dominos and we played live that I was aware of being able to do exactly what I wanted and was happy with it," Clapton told Dan Forte in 1985. But Clapton's musical satisfaction contrasted with the emotional pain he was experiencing. He had fallen in love with Pattie Boyd Harrison, who at the time was married to his best friend, George Harrison. With the turmoil of a classic blues triangle worthy of Robert Johnson exploding inside him, Clapton left for Miami with the Dominos to make *Layla*.

Layla was recorded with legendary producer Tom Dowd under the most extreme conditions. Critic Robert Palmer visited the sessions and later recalled, "There was a lot of dope around, especially heroin, and when I showed up, everyone was just spread out on the carpet, nodded out." Shortly after the band arrived in Miami, Dowd took them to see the Allman Brothers, and Duane Allman was invited to play slide guitar on the album. Allman also teamed up with Clapton for a duet on Little Walter's "Mean Old World," which was not included on the LP.

Driven creatively by his new band, the formidable playing of Allman and his own romantic agony, Clapton poured all he had into *Layla*'s title track, which was inspired by a Persian love story he had read, *The Story of Layla and Majnun* by Nizami. The song's extended lyrical coda was composed independently by drummer Jim Gordon on piano, and Gordon had to be convinced to allow the piece to be tacked onto "Layla."

After completing *Layla,* Derek and the Dominos launched a tour of America, from which the previously unreleased live versions of "Key to the Highway" and "Crossroads"—in a more churning, exploratory rendition than the one recorded with Cream—included in this collection are taken. The band then returned to England, and in April and May of 1971 attempted to record a second studio album—five tracks of which are presented in this collection for the first time: "One More Chance," Arthur Crudup's "Mean Old Frisco," the instrumental "Snake Lake Blues," a cover of Willie Dixon's "Evil," and an uncompleted studio version of "Got to Get Better in a Little While," which the band performed live on the album, *Derek and the Dominos in Concert.* In his 1985 interview in *Rolling Stone*

Clapton told Robert Palmer that the sessions for a follow-up LP to *Layla* "broke down halfway through because of the paranoia and the tension. And the band just. . . . dissolved."

Once the Dominos broke up, Clapton's drug dependence worsened and kept him virtually a prisoner in his home for the rest of 1971—though he did emerge to play at George Harrison's Concert for Bangladesh that summer—and much of the following year. During this period he felt both personally and emotionally adrift, and the long-standing identity issues arose once again. "The end of the Dominos came too soon, and that left me very high and dry as to what I was supposed to be," he told *Guitar Player* in 1985. "I'd been this anonymous person up until that time. It was difficult for me to come to terms with the fact that it was *me,* that I was on my own again."

Part of that difficulty may have resulted from the origins of Derek and the Dominos in Clapton's own psychic need. Despite the enormous satisfactions the band brought him, Clapton told *Musician* that Derek and the Dominos were "a make-believe band. We were all hiding inside it. Derek & the Dominos—the whole thing was . . . assumed. So it couldn't last. I had to come out and admit that I was being me. I mean, being Derek was a cover for the fact that I was trying to steal someone else's wife. That was one of the reasons for doing it, so that I could write the song, and even use another name for Pattie. So Derek and Layla—it wasn't real at all."

Clapton's good friend Pete Townshend of the Who organized a concert at London's Rainbow Theatre in January of 1973 to create some momentum for the guitarist's return to action. Clapton played at the highly emotional show with Townshend, Ron Wood and Steve Winwood, and later that year took an acupuncture cure to end his drug addiction. Once that problem was behind him, Clapton contacted Tom Dowd and returned to Miami to record *461 Ocean Boulevard.*

Featuring a band of American musicians, including Carl Radle, brought together by Dowd, *461 Ocean Boulevard* is Clapton's great comeback LP. Appropriately, it opens with "Motherless Children," a traditional tune whose rollicking energy in Clapton's slide-guitar version counterpoints its relevance to the circumstances of his early life. The deeply felt "Let It Grow" finds Clapton once again "standing at the crossroads," and this time making a choice to affirm life, love and, by extension, his ability to reach within himself and create art. And *461 Ocean Boulevard* contained Clapton's cover of Bob Marley's "I Shot the Sheriff"—represented here in a tougher, more expansive live rendition from the band's December 5th, 1974 concert at the Hammersmith Odeon in London—

which exposed millions of Americans to reggae music for the first time when it became a Number One hit. During the *461 Ocean Boulevard* sessions at Criteria Studios in Miami, Clapton also recorded Jimmy Reed's insinuatingly seductive "Ain't That Lovin' You" with Dave Mason on guitar—a previously unreleased track included in this collection.

461 Ocean Boulevard re-established Clapton in both critical and commercial terms, but it also ushered in the phase of his career that engendered concern in many of his longest-standing followers. In their concentration on songwriting, vocals and melody, *461 Ocean Boulevard* and the nine studio LPs that have followed it de-emphasize the pyrotechnic guitar work that characterized Clapton's tracks with the Bluesbreakers, Cream and Derek and the Dominos—though there's certainly no shortage of excellent playing. Working with a variety of producers—including Dowd, Glyn Johns and Phil Collins—Clapton alternated between American and British bands, experimenting with a wide variety of sounds and styles. Conventional pop songs and laid-back ballads of broad appeal appeared on those records and jarred the sensibilities of some fans.

A number of issues are important for understanding Clapton's music since 1974. One is that, while Clapton is still gripped by the blues and inclined to explore his favorite standards at length in live performance (note his probing reading of Otis Rush's "Double Trouble" in this collection), that impulse is no longer single and all-consuming. Since the latter days of Cream, the thrust of Clapton's music has been towards melody, and the artists that have interested him—the Band, Bob Dylan, Bob Marley, J.J. Cale, country singer Don Williams—are often more subtle than they are explosive. Taken together those artists and Clapton's blues idols are the influences behind his most notable work of the late Seventies and Eighties.

In 1985 Clapton spoke of a desire he felt during the Seventies "to be more of a composer of melodic tunes rather than just a player, which was very unpopular with a lot of people." The remark echoes something he said eleven years earlier, in expressing admiration for Stevie Wonder: "I think when it comes down to it, I always go for singers. I don't buy an album because I like the lead guitar. I always like the human voice most of all." The greatest blues guitar playing, after all, is modeled on the sound of the human voice.

Blues, country, folk, rock and pop have come to share a place in Clapton's music. He offered a sensitive reading of Elmore James' "The Sky Is Crying" on *There's One in Every Crowd* (in addition to recording James' "(When Things Go Wrong) It Hurts Me Too" during the sessions for that album), and, in a live cut from 1977 included here, did an upbeat take on "Further On Up the Road," which over the years has become one of his signature tunes. Members of the Band were a prominent presence on the gently rolling *No Reason to Cry* album, which featured Clapton's optimistic "Hello Old Friend." Bob Dylan appeared on that record as well, sharing the vocal on his enigmatic song, "Sign Language."

Clapton also turned in fine versions of Dylan's "Knockin' on Heaven's Door"—another expression of the guitarist's spiritual side—and his swinging "If I Don't Be There By Morning." J.J. Cale's ominously enticing "Cocaine," included on Clapton's 1978 multi-platinum LP, *Slowhand,* has proven to be one of Clapton's most popular tunes, and Clapton's own catchy hit, "Lay Down Sally," from that same album, owes a clear debt to Cale. The affectionate "Wonderful Tonight," also from *Slowhand,* was simply born of Clapton's wish to write a love song.

Clapton's popularity as a live performer has consistently grown over the past ten years, and his videos and the pop-oriented LPs he has made with producer Phil Collins—*Behind the Sun* and *August* (which was co-produced by Tom Dowd)—have brought his music to a younger audience eager to learn about his past. He composed soundtracks for the BBC television series *Edge of Darkness,* which won prestigious BAFTA and Ivor Novello awards in Great Britain, and for the film *Lethal Weapon.* He contributed songs to films, including "Heaven Is One Step Away" for *Back to the Future* and two tracks for *The Color of Money,* directed by Martin Scorsese.

As a blues prodigy, Clapton built a commanding reputation very early in his twenties. By the time he was thirty he had, like many masters, become intrigued by simplicity—the one-note philosophy. The calm that he felt at his core—through the times of revolutionary innovation, through the drugs and the cure, through heartbreak and happiness, at the crossroads and further on up the road—finally entered his music.

In *Musician* in 1986 Clapton said, "I think that the ultimate guitar hero should be a dispenser of wisdom, as well as anything else. . . . that's the one thing I will say that I'm still striving after, outside of perfection as a musician: the attainment of wisdom, in any amount."

If wisdom can be reflected in the creation of a superbly accomplished body of work and in the defeat of personal adversity, ERic Clapton has already achieved the major portion of his goal. And the remainder has not escaped him. It awaits him—and us, his audience—at the spectacular series of crossroads to come.

Dave Marsh
I WANNA KNOW IF LOVE IS REAL

With *Biograph* in 1985, Bob Dylan had helped send rock into the boxed-set era. But the real kick in the pants came next with the hype surrounding Bruce Springsteen's *Live/1975–1985*. Unlike Dylan's full-career retrospective, much of Springsteen's set was from his recent live tours. Springsteen was at that point the latest Mr. Rock and Roll and one of his fervent admirers, Dave Marsh, here takes us through the massive collection.

WHAT MADE the live set a distinctive part of Bruce Springsteen's album series was its continuity and its narrative quality. "I guess what I was always interested in was doing a *body* of work—albums that would relate to and play off of each other," Bruce had told Kurt Loder in his *Rolling Stone* interview. "And I was always concerned with doin' *albums* instead of, like, collections of songs . . . I was very concerned about gettin' a group of characters and followin' them through their lives a little bit."

Like its brethren, the live album told a tale—not a simple or necessarily obvious one, but a story nevertheless. The album had no title until very late, and the name eventually selected was the most neutral possible: *Bruce Springsteen and the E Street Band Live/1975–1985*. But that was just a feint. At heart this album was the latest in a series through which a rock star and his cast of characters struggled from innocence to maturity.

How do you get from the innocent glory of "Thunder Road," as performed at the Roxy in 1975 before an audience of perhaps 500, to the harrowing rampage that runs from "Born in the U.S.A." to "War," sung in the same city ten years later before an audience of 100,000? Posing that question, with all its internal and external implications, unlocks *Bruce Springsteen and the E Street Band Live,* adding dimensions that few rock albums—let alone live albums or retrospectives—have ever possessed.

Because the live album was a five-record boxed set, it was frequently compared to Dylan's *Biograph,* whose five discs spanned the length of a twenty-five year career. That album had sold relatively well—more than

221

200,000 copies—and it probably did help inspire Springsteen and manager/producer Jon Landau. But the album that *Live* really resembles most is Neil Young's *Decade,* a three-record set from 1976 programmed and annotated by Young himself with an eye toward making a case for his artistic development and achievements. (*Biograph* was put together without Dylan, and it includes many minor rarities at the expense of some of his core material and greatest performances.)

As Bruce looked over the music he'd made in the previous decade, he found himself, like Young, recapitulating his passage from childhood dreams of rock and roll glory to grappling with the real thing as an adult. It was an intensely personal story but, at its broadest, it was also the rock and roll archetype come to life and brought up to date. The album did *not* conform to rock and roll mythology; these descendants of Johnny B. Goode grew up, and the ending of their story was collected, not chaotic, open rather than closed, nurturing rather than wasteful.

By the time he released each of his preceding albums, Bruce had invariably come to understand the implications of what he'd done, but he'd rarely understood it much before then. This time, the music's secrets revealed themselves to him more rapidly; that was one reason the assembly could proceed so swiftly. That only made sense: he was gathering up old friends, not creating new ones. But as these familiar faces shifted themselves into position, Bruce found them telling a new version of their stories.

"The record opens with 'Thunder Road,' and as I've said before, when the *Born to Run* album came out, the record was so tied in with who I was. I felt like, hey, I felt like I was born," Springsteen said in early 1987. "I felt like it was a birthday. I know that's why those words are in the title. *Born*— what is that word there? That's there because it's real. And"—he began to laugh at his own presumption—"that's probably why the word *run* is there—that's real, too.

"And that "Thunder Road' is the birth song; it's the panorama, the scene and the characters, setting the situation. So that was why, from the very beginning, we knew that that was gonna start the live album.

"Then you get 'Adam Raised a Cain'; we wanted a gut punch right after that, just so you'd be ready for what was gonna happen. And then you get to 'Spirit in the Night,' which is kinda the cast of characters— friends. It's a real localized situation. Then you get 'Sandy.' That's the guy and he's on the boardwalk, and I guess that was me then, when I was still around Asbury. And there's the girl.

"That first side, that's the whole idea: Here it is. This is the beginning of the whole trip that's about to take place. All those people. Some of 'em are gonna go, some of 'em are gonna stay, some of 'em are gonna make that trip, some of 'em aren't gonna make it. And let's see what happens.

"And then you flip the thing over. 'Paradise by the "C"'—the Clarence instrumental—that's bar-band music, that's who we are. And that's real important. That sets the tone. That's what we were doing in those clubs—we were blowin' the roof off with that kinda stuff. People were dancin' and goin' crazy and havin' a great time.

"And then you get that 'Growin Up.' That sort of a little bit of a statement of purpose. Sort of. And then there's the rest of that—'Saint in the City,' 'Backstreets,' 'Rosalita,' and 'Raise Your Hand.' 'Rosalita' was funny because, even though it came before 'Born to Run,' the guy gets the girl—or he's trying to get the girl. And he's got the record deal, and he's trying to get away. And if he gets all these things, he thinks everything gonna be *great*. And I guess that was kind of . . . *That happened,* I guess.

"Then the 'Hungry Heart' side with all those songs from *The River*, which is funny, because that side felt right there even if it was a little out of chronological order . . . and I think it felt right because the next thing you hear, you hear that big crowd. Right after 'Rosalita,' you get 'Raise Your Hand,' and that's the idea: You want it and then, Bang! You got it.

"And the rest of that side is kind of 'Two Hearts' and 'Cadillac Ranch' and 'You Can Look But You Better Not Touch.' And now the underside starts to kinda sneak in there; you start to pick up a little undercurrent there."

That undercurrent motivated Bruce's best songs from *Darkness on the Edge of Town* to *Born in the U.S.A.*, from "Badlands" to "Reason to Believe" to "Dancing in the Dark"—that is, from the confidence of youth to a crisis of faith to the realization that you overcome only when you keep moving. Like all journeys to experience, it began with questions that seem simple: Why me? What about everybody else? What next?

"At some point I said to myself—and I know this is one of the things that caused me a lot of distress—I said, Well, okay, what if I am the guy in 'Born to Run,' with the bike and the girl, shooting down the road," Bruce said. "But when you get out there a little way, there's not that much traffic. And you can't see the people in the cars next to you; all the windows are tinted. And all of a sudden you're out there, but where is everybody? So I guess I kinda thought, Well, all right, you know; so maybe I get to do these things, but what about everybody else?

"And that didn't come from a real selfless motivation or some idea to do good. Because I understood that it was a simple self-preservation. I realized that you will *die* out there, simple as that. I understood that underneath this illusion of freedom was an oppressiveness that would kill me. And that where maybe I was different was that I knew it.

"So when I got in that situation, I felt tremendously threatened and I didn't know why. It was totally instinctive. Matter of fact, I don't think I really knew why until not that long ago. But initially, when I was 25, it was just instinctive—I felt threatened, I felt in danger. And it was funny because those were the exact opposite responses that people generally have. But I didn't know why I'm havin' 'em; I was just havin' 'em.

"So initially, I wanted to just reject the whole thing—'This is bad; all this is bad'—as people have done before. I think you look at some of the older rock and rollers, they've chosen to reject it and their opposite choice was to move to religious fundamentalism. But I got so alienated from religion when I was younger that there was no way that that was ever gonna be an alternative, in that sense, for me. I just could never see it.

"I think when I got in that spot, I really did feel—and not in a paranoid fashion—attacked on the essence of who I felt that I was. So at that point I realized that, unattached from community, it was impossible to find any meaning. And if you can't find any meaning, you will go insane and you will either kill yourself or somebody will do the job for you, either by doping you or one thing or another.

"I began to question from that moment on the values and the ideas that I set out and believed in on that *Born to Run* record: friendship, hope, belief in a better day. I questioned all of those things. And so *Darkness on the Edge of Town* was basically saying, You get out there and you turn around and you come back because that's just the beginning. That's the real beginning.

"I got out there—hey, the wind's whipping through your hair, you feel real good, you're the guy with the gold guitar or whatever, and all of a sudden you feel that sense of *dread* that is overwhelming everything you do. It's like that great scene in *The Last Picture Show* where the guy hits the brakes and turns around. The *Darkness* record was a confrontation record: 'Badlands,' 'Adam Raised a Cain,' 'Racing in the Street'—all those people, all those faces, you gotta look at 'em all. Right through to 'Darkness on the Edge of Town'—that was a whole other beginning.

"Now, you strip a whole bunch of things away from the thing, and you lose a lot of your illusions and a lot of, I suppose, your romantic dreams. And you decide . . . you make a particular decision. And that is a decision, I believe, that saves your life—your real life, your internal life, your emotional life, your essential life. Because you can live on, you know. But I knew that the reason I began to do what I did was for connection. I desperately needed connection. I couldn't get it; I wanted it.

"And that's why my guitar was my lifeline. That was my connection to other people, more than anything else. Because other things will not sustain you. Maybe for a while you'll be distracted and have some fun, but in the end, your real life, you'll die, you will really die. And then once that happens, I believe there's only a certain amount of time before the physical thing catches up to you.

"So you've got that situation, where I turn around—on the live record, that's where 'Badlands' fits. Then you're there—from 'Badlands' through to 'War' really. But from 'Badlands' through to 'Reason to Believe,' that's kind of an investigation of that place."

Springsteen began to question not only the values he'd found in rock and roll but whether rock and roll itself, which offered the most romantic illusion of Yankee individualism imaginable, was worth the effort. It all came back to the questions he'd asked himself as he put together *Born in the U.S.A.*

"Is making the Loud Noise worth it?" is how he put it in the winter of '87. "That's a question that I feel like I'm constantly asking myself, and the only answer I come up with is, Well, you don't know unless you try.

"I think that when I did the *Nebraska* record, obviously I was in a deepening process of questioning those values that were set out in *Born to Run*. I did the *Darkness on the Edge of Town* thing, and with *The River* thing I allowed some light to come in, part of the time. I had to—had to. In a funny way, I felt that I didn't have the center, so what I had to do was I had to get left and right, in hope that it would create some sort of center—or some sense of center. That probably wasn't embodied in any one given song or something, and that was the juggling that I had to do on that record."

So the same Bruce Springsteen who had sung "I'm pullin' outta here to win" at the beginning of *Born to Run* found himself opening *Nebraska* by imagining someone being hurled into a "great void." But that wasn't all.

"That void that you feel in that situation is the same one you can feel breathin' down your neck when you got that sun behind you, drivin' down the road: you got the girl, got that guitar. It's the same for some reason. Because of that isolation. There are guys who come home from the factory, sit in front of that TV with a sixpack of beer, that are as isolated as the *Nebraska* record, if not more so."

It's the spectre of that void that sends men down to the river when their dreams fall through or their marriages crumble or the plant closes and leaves them not just without a paycheck but empty of purpose. And rich men or poor, when they've stared long enough into that void, they make a leap. The may jump into the abyss of doubt or across a chasm of faith, but they leap.

Having reached that desperate place himself, Bruce Springsteen pushed forward, not because he rejected the hopelessness he found, but because he accepted it. "That was the subject of the *Nebraska* record," he said. "And it's the central thing at this moment in our band; we're kinda locked in with this thing. That was just the idea of the band, from the very beginning, from the minute when I touched the guitar for the first time. That was what moved me. And that's why as you follow the way the whole thing has developed, the moment after *Nebraska* and before *Born in the U.S.A.* is where I'm having this exact conversation with Jon . . . about these things. These are what the records are about.

"When you're in the live record, you run up to 'Reason to Believe' and at that point—well, that was the bottom. I would hope not to be in that particular place ever again. It was a thing where all my ideas might have been musically but they were failing me personally.

"I always feel like I was lucky. I got to a point where all my answers— rock and roll answers—were running out. All the old things stoped work- ing—as they should've and as they have to, and as time and the world and the way it is demands and dictates, in order for you to go on. They run dry, not as a joyous thing in and of itself, but as some sort of shelter for your inability to take your place in the world, whatever that may be. That's when either you recognize that that's happening or you don't and you continue with your trappings and your ceremony, whatever *that* may be, and slowly you just get strangled to death and you die. You just die."

It was at this point that Bruce Springsteen did a remarkable thing. Rather than surrendering to the "trappings and ceremony" of showbiz rite or retreating into a cocoon of protective "artistic independence" (as Young and Dylan had done), he reached out, opening himself in a way that very few public figures have ever done. He found a response as powerful as any public figure has ever known and learned to live with it. Was he another Elvis? Of course not. He didn't start something; he helped put it on the road to completion. But Bruce Springsteen had finally become like Elvis in another way. He used popular music to change himself and the slice of history he could affect. And rather than dying, he lived more whole than before.

Bruce had finally circumvented—or rather, defused—the trap depicted by the Band's Robbie Robertson:

See the man with the stage fright
Just standin' up there with all his might
And he got caught in the spotlight
But when we get to the end, you wanna start all
over again

Springsteen escaped this Sisyphean fate by ignoring the advice given in "Stage Fright": "You can make it in your disguise / Just never show the fear that's in your eyes." On the contrary, he'd taken the risk of turning the glare of his personal terrors full upon his audience and, what was most startling, found that many recognized them as their own.

When they did, Bruce Springsteen crossed the line between idol and hero as defined by the art critic John Berger: "The function of the hero in art is to inspire the reader or spectator to continue in the same spirit from where he, the hero, leaves off. He must release the spectator's potentiality, for potentiality is the historical force behind nobility. And to do this the hero must be typical of the characters and class who at that time only need to be made aware of their heroic potentiality in order to be able to make their society juster and nobler. . . . The function of the idol is the exact opposite to that of the hero. The idol is self-sufficient; the hero never is. The idol is so superficially desirable, spectacular, witty, happy, that he or she merely supplies a context for fantasy and therefore, instead of inspiring, lulls. The idol is based on the *appearance* of perfection, but never on the striving towards it."

But what Springsteen achieved also confounded Berger, because he'd done it through the mechanism of popular culture, mediated by one of the country's largest corporations. Like most good leftists, Berger believes that culture to be bankrupt; like any pragmatic member of the working class, Bruce Springsteen worked with the tools that came to hand.

If Springsteen proved able to restore a sense of center to rock and roll without entirely dulling that idiom's status as the cutting edge of popular culture, it was not only because he'd dared expose to a mass audience what seemed to be his least conventional thoughts and feelings but also because he'd done that while risking the inconveniences and dangers of genuine mass popularity. It would have profited him not at all to gain the pink Cadillac and lose his own soul, but it would have served him equally poorly to have hardened his heart against the public from which he sprang. In that regard, his success was genuinely antibohemian, because it sprang not from a refusal to participate in social conventions, but from a refusal to be excluded from them.

For its first five sides, then, *Bruce Springsteen and the E Street Band Live/1975–1985* defines a dream and chronicles its dissolution and the ways that dawning realizations transform the dreamer. Its final four are concerned with how you live with what's left. The transition is expressed on Side Six, which runs from "This Land is Your Land" to "Reason to Believe," a leap every bit as long as it looks. Introducing Woody Guthrie's greatest hit, Springsteen acknowledges that Guthrie wrote in anger, but when Bruce sings the song it's about dreams and vision. What's emphasized isn't the grandeur of the landscapes or the mockery society makes of them, it's the voices that call out at the end of each verse, promising something better.

"Nebraska" and "Johnny 99" are songs about people who cannot hear those voices, the consequence of which is a death sentence. But "Reason to Believe" is something worse: a requiem for those who have heard the voices, pursued them to the end, and then discovered that they were lying. It's about the greatest menace that lurks in the darkness on the edge of town, about the compulsion to leap into the river and be swept downstream, about the temptation to run and keep on running, not toward freedom but away from the facts. Springsteen defines the song precisely: "That was the bottom."

"But at the end of *Nebraska,* I wrote another song with the word *born* in it, which is really weird," Springsteen observed. "And from that point on, the answer to 'Reason to Believe' was 'Born in the U.S.A.'—I guess either record, but particularly the live version. That's the answer to it. That's the only answer that I can perceive. And that connects back to 'Badlands,' you know. And that was the moment that I felt I'd gotten things in a little healthier perspective, and that I stopped—I didn't stop using my job; I stopped abusing my job, which I felt part of me had been doing. In the end, I just understood a lot more about what it takes to get by.

"No, it ain't gonna save you; you gotta save yourself. And you're gonna need a lotta help."

The rest of the record—and, it is not entirely unreasonable to imagine, the rest of Bruce Springsteen's work—is about giving that help, and, just as important, receiving it. It begins with "Born in the U.S.A.," with that singer "born down in a dead man's town." But at the end, standing in the shadows of a prison, the singer has made a choice: He will run, and keep on running, but he will never *fail* to look back. He will always remember what's been done to him—and to his friend at Khe Sanh, that woman he loved in Saigon, and the Viet Cong—and those memories will shape his future, no matter where it leads. In order to be a "cool rockin' daddy in the

U.S.A.," you have to go beyond hearing the voices Woody Guthrie wrote about; you have to try to answer them back—you have to join them. And that is exactly what "Seeds," "The River" and "War" do.

"The 'Born in the U.S.A.' side, that's everything I know—at the moment, or at that time," Springsteen said with a short laugh. "And I know Jon felt that the opening section of 'The River' as the real center of the record. It moves out in all directions. The band on that night, the thirtieth of September 1985, they were great that night. They just played better than other nights. And it was a thing where just intensity and the forward thrust of the music was the best it's ever been."

Springsteen knew exactly what he was doing in the live show when he didn't stop for a reaction after "War." He compared his sense of what to do with Alfred Hitchcock's *Vertigo*—the entire film leads up to James Stewart stepping out onto a ledge, a shot that lasts less than ten seconds and is almost immediately followed by the picture's end. Springsteen calls what he learned from watching this "the integrity of the moment," which, he adds, "is a lesson I can use, because I'll be excessive. I've got the energy and I'll crank on forever. But you get to a point, you gotta have the confidence not to do that. You need confidence to do less and let it be more."

At the end of the album version of "War," the cheers are quickly faded out and the record moves with barely a pause into "Darlington County" and "Working on the Highway," the most modest of the *Born in the U.S.A.* songs and the most embedded in the workaday world. But as life goes on, what might be missed is that it doesn't end with the "Born in the U.S.A." to "War" sequence. It carries the story onward, forward, and since that means eschewing melodrama, what's left is a finish that's as oddly muted as the start. Even when anthems like "The Promised Land" and "No Surrender" crop up in the aftermath of "War," they are cooled down, taken in stride, without a hint of finality.

Ending the album proved one of the most difficult aspects of making it. Bruce knew that he didn't want to finish with the rock and roll medleys that always concluded his shows. But knowing what he didn't want only emphasized the magnitude of the question: So how do you end the first ten years of your career as a star?

"The first time we played it through the way it was, I wasn't sure. And then we played it again and it started to really sync in—'cause 'Born to Run' tops the tenth side and you go all the way back to 'Thunder Road.' And it restates the central question.

"And the central question of 'Born to Run' is really 'I wanna know if love is real.' That's the question of that song. We go from there; we go to 'No Surrender,' a reaffirmation and restatement of all those things in the present tense. Then we get to 'Tenth Avenue'; believe it or not, that kinda connects back up to 'Spirit in the Night.' That's the cast of characters and friends; it's the band. And hey, that's what we did, you know."

At one point the plan was to end the album right there. The song told the band's story and it was modest. "We didn't want to end it with something big," Bruce said. It was Jon Landau, arguing for the smaller noise for once, who suggested that a love song would be more appropriate. And although "Jersey Girl" had already been issued (as the B side of the "Cover Me" single in 1984), although it was one of only three songs in the set that Bruce didn't write, although it was obscure and quiet and ended the record somewhat mysteriously, it still felt like the right ending.

"That's the same guy that's on the boardwalk in 'Sandy,' back in the same place," Bruce said. "The same guy in 'Rosalita'—you know, he got that Jersey girl. I guess I wanted the record to feel like the middle of summer—real soft moonlight, you're taking a real slow ride in that convertible, and you're back in that place where you began. You got somebody beside you and you feel good, and you've been through all those things.

"When I listened to that song, I'd always see myself ridin' through Asbury. There'd be people I know a little bit on the corner, and we'd just drive by. I guess that you feel in some way you're changed forever. But you also have all these connections, so you really feel at home.

"The most important thing, though, is that the question gets thrown back at 'Born to Run.' 'I wanna know if love is real.' And the answer is yes."

Joyce Millman

PRIMADONNA

**Producer Phil Spector and Motown mogul Berry Gordy had
made millions masterminding the girl group sound of the
1960s. Here Joyce Millman makes the case that Madonna
Louise Ciccone was the one-woman girl group of the 1980s
and her own best mastermind.**

MOST GIRLS who grew up during the sixties and early seventies learned
more about their place in society from Barbie than they did from their
mothers. Barbie was the madonna/whore complex molded into shapely
plastic, a mute ideal of wholesome yet suggestive beauty emphasized in
sexy/adorable clothes designed to turn Ken's head its full 360 degrees.
She could be outfitted for a range of glamorous fantasy careers or re-
warding helpmate ones. And, having no genitals, she was an archetype of
chastity. Of course, the most coveted item in the Barbie wardrobe was a
voluminous white lace wedding gown. So in 1984, when Madonna Louise
Ciccone, Barbie's most apt pupil, posed in a (punky) white wedding gown
for the laughably literal madonna/whore cover of her second album, *Like
a Virgin,* the little girls—and a lot of us big girls—understood. Madonna
was not out to attack traditional institutions or soil traditional daydreams
(how could the glowing romantic-rebirth imagery of "Like a Virgin" have
been so seriously misread?). No, she was as staunchly middle-class as the
most loyal of her fans; like them, she was shaped by the pop culture that
Barbie reflected—parents' Fab Fifties stability mixed with the fallout of the
sixties social change and the trickle-down of seventies permissiveness.
For the young girls who bought *Like a Virgin* in droves and made her the
most popular (and notorious) white female singer of her time, Madonna
is the last word in attitude and fashion, the epitome of cool. Madonna is
the video generation's Barbie.

And those girls couldn't have a smarter or spunkier role model.
Madonna injects middle-class ideas of femininity with examples of what
feminism means to her, and it means simply "equal opportunity." Instead
of Barbie's teasing aloofness, she offers an aggressive sexuality that im-

plies it's acceptable for women not only to initiate relationships (and she does in "Physical Attraction," "Borderline," "Crazy for You," "Into the Groove," etc.), but also enjoy them. Barbie had the land-of-make-believe carte blanche (not to mention the costumes) to be all things at once, but Madonna does it for real. A singer, songwriter, actress, comedienne, and now—on her latest, nerviest, and most assured album, *True Blue*—a record producer, Madonna exemplifies the women's-movement slogan that any girl can grow up to be whatever she wants to be (though, not surprisingly, *Ms.* magazine didn't have the guts to make her its token rocker in its 1985 Women of the Year roundup, favoring instead the nearly presexual and less explicitly feminist Cyndi Lauper); in songs like "Over and Over" ("You try to criticize my drive") and, of course, "Material Girl," she asserts that nice girls no longer have to sublimate ambition. Most tantalizing (and controversial) is her insistence that a woman—even a professional woman—ought to be able to act flirty, sexy, or sentimental without being written off as an airhead. Like (the more buttoned-up) Chrissie Hynde, Madonna refuses to suppress her female sensibilities and urges to make it in a man's world.

Director Susan Seidelman knew what she was doing when she cast Madonna as the woman Everywoman wanted to be in *Desperately Seeking Susan;* with her independence, earthy good humor, and the-hell-with-fashion sense of style, Madonna has always suggested the brave bohemian that all the other girls admired, emulated, and whispered about in high school. Maybe that's why she's made such a persuasive pied piper. Her legion of wannabes demonstrate that things haven't really changed—girls and women are still slaves to fad and fashion, they still wait to be told what to do. But Madonna isn't merely this year's girl, like a Farrah, or a Princess Diana (whom she impersonated with such girls-play-dress-up glee on *Saturday Night Live*). She's an idol with clout, and every public move shows that she's considering her power carefully. The message she delivers in her warm, lowbrow way—the balloons that fell on the audience during her *Like A Virgin* concerts read "Dreams Come True"—is no Cinderella story of passivity; it's an illustration that, yes, dreams come true *if* you work for them.

Part of Madonna's appeal is the way she sounds so carefree. Her unabashedly disco-derived singles (a string that *True Blue* continues) are tailored for maximum fun and the top ten. Madonna may have worked with a succession of (male) songwriting partners and producers for her three albums (on *True Blue,* she gets her first production credit, as an equal with Pat Leonard and Stephen Bray), but her sound is her own; her voluptuous voice, sometimes sugary and high, sometimes steamy and low, delivers a vitality, a *humanness,* that's more bewitching than any of her glamour-girl poses and more luminous than her fame. She has the flair for finding outside material that meshes with her own sentiments, and the instinct for zooming in on the pitch of a song with some of the most evocative fadeouts this side of Smokey Robinson. Many of her original lyrics may be little more than romantic clichés ("You must be my lucky star," "You must be an angel"), but like girl-group divas Ronnie Spector, Darlene Love, and Mary Weiss (the Shangri-Las), Madonna uses her wholehearted singing to enrich her words. She always sounds as if she has absolute faith in her fairy tales—a faith, she understands, that binds her to her fans. Indeed, in the video for her new single "Papa Don't Preach," wearing faded jeans, a bottle-blond gamin hairdo, and "Italians Do It Better" t-shirt, Madonna looks like your average teenage girl from Medford or Chelsea; she looks at home walking through an aging neighborhood of cramped two-family houses, opening an ornately grilled screen door, entering a family room filled with plain furniture and her own baby pictures.

Yes, Madonna is the girl group of the eighties, sympathetically articulating the turbulent teenage emotions sparked by awakening sexuality, class consciousness, and individuality (not to mention peer pressure and parental clampdown), with bubble-gum dance trappings adding an unmistakably urban working-class ambiance. (As Regina's "Baby Love," E. G. Daily's "Say It" and Alisha's "Baby Talk," among others, attest, she's even inspired a Madonna Sound.) And the big-hearted *True Blue* is her most girl-groupish album yet, from its front-stoop view of love, work, dreams, and disappointments, to its chiming bells and female backing harmonies, to its cast of lovingly rendered Ordinary Joes. The insouciant "Where's the Party" depicts a working girl blowing off the day-to-day grind on the dance floor. In the black-leather-jacket bop "Jimmy Jimmy" (with nods to "Uptown" and "Leader of the Pack"), Madonna admires a neighborhood wiseguy's ambition all the more because she knows he's "just a boy who comes from bad places." And the tranquil "La Isla Bonita" and the Feed-the-World fiesta "Love Makes the World Go Round" are "Up on the Roof"-type imaginary escapes from the city snarl, the kind of Latin-flavored sweets that Blondie could never resist. (Madonna is what Debbie Harry might've become had Blondie not diluted their love of disco and pop with punk-intellectual irony.)

Throughout *True Blue,* Madonna transforms her own marital bliss ("This is dedicated to my husband, the coolest guy in the universe," writes Mrs. Sean Penn on the inner sleeve) into high-school-accessible motherly-tender firmness. "I don't want to live out your fantasy / . . . This time you're gonna have to play my way," she chirps in "White Heat," a scrappy valentine to James Cagney that blows kisses to the Leader of the Brat Pack as well. "Don't try to resist me," she warns in her sultriest lower register on "Open Your Heart." And in the endearing title track, Madonna finally goes to the chapel with the guy as bells ring like crazy and a trio of backing Madonnas falls into a "Johnny Angel" swoon.

But on *True Blue*'s boldest number, Madonna ventures into territory no girl group was allowed to explore. "Papa Don't Preach" (written by Brian Elliott, with additional lyrics by Madonna) is the first song she's recorded in which she takes off from her image (and accepts her role) as the voice of girlhood. In the guise of a teenager who's worked up the courage to tell her father about her unplanned pregnancy, Madonna forces her wannabes to consider the risks and responsibilities of their sexuality. She makes them agonize with her over the choice a girl "in trouble" (as the song so girls'-bathroomishly puts it) faces: she can "give it up," as her friends urge (and "give it up" is a term ambiguous enough to suggest adoption and abortion), or, as she wails with frighteningly childish stubbornness, "I made up my mind / I'm keeping my baby." Although the melody is as insistently chugging as "Into the Groove" or "Dress You Up," the mood of "Papa Don't Preach" is tense and claustrophobic, from the melodramatic slashes of strings to the way Madonna's voice wavers between brassy determination and husky uncertainty; there's only the faintest hope of happily-ever-after in her shaky "He says that he's gonna marry me / We can raise a little family / Maybe we'll be all right." And when Madonna unfurls the heartrending cry, "What I need right now is some good advice / *Please* / Papa don't preach," she expresses all the pain of growing up too fast.

On the radio during the last two months, the sparse, sirenic number-one ballad "Live to Tell" (the theme for Sean Penn's film about terror in the bosom of the family, *At Close Range*) was a chilling riddle, Madonna's hushed singing overwhelming everything else on the top forty with its nameless sadness. What's the lesson she's learned? What's the secret she hides? On *True Blue*, "Live to Tell" makes a provocative companion to "Papa Don't Preach." With Madonna measuring the safety of silence against the urge to unburden herself, "Live to Tell" captures the utter loneliness of those times during adolescence when the world crashes down on you with each new problem, but fear of rejection, punishment, condemnation, of inflicting pain—prevents you from confiding in your parents. And that fear encircles "Papa Don't Preach." The most haunting line of the song isn't "I'm keeping my baby," but the whimper, deep into the fadeout, "Don't you stop loving me daddy." A call for parent-child communication as tortured as the Shangri-Las' "I Can Never Go Home Anymore," "Papa Don't Preach" is Madonna's finest three minutes, not merely because it addresses teen pregnancy but because it suggests that a portion of the blame rests on parents' reluctance to discuss, not lecture about, sex. At a time when pregnancy among American teens is epidemic, "Papa Don't Preach" makes parental insensitivity and unreality seem like the greater evil.

Still, despite its message that parents can no longer afford to ignore their teenagers' sexuality, "Papa Don't Preach" may well be misappropriated by the forces of repression the song scorns, the way "Born in the U.S.A." backfired on Bruce Springsteen. How long will it be before some Right-to-Life organization twists the song ("I'm keeping my baby," indeed) into an anthem? Or before Madonna is attacked by the literal-minded—or misunderstood by some of her fans—as glamorizing teen pregnancy? But, like Springsteen, Madonna trusts her listeners to get the point. Most important, "Papa Don't Preach" opens a long overdue and desperately needed discussion on a topic that, as far as pop-single queens go, has begun and ended with the Supremes' "Love Child" (and, sung from the point of view of the out-of-wedlock child, that song is just an old-fashioned scare story about the dangers of premarital sex). "Papa Don't Preach" (and all of *True Blue*) shows that Madonna has figured a way to get tough while remaining ravishingly faithful to her fans' concerns, to pop simplicity, and to herself. At last, Barbie has a voice. Female adolescence will never be the same.

Jon Pareles

PRECIOUS ODDBALL

Rock Ages Gracefully, Part I. Kurt Cobain's fondness for Neil Young's line, "It's better to burn out than to fade away," might have blinded him to other options. In his review of a 1994 Bob Dylan concert, Pareles celebrates a performer who still finds meaning and pleasure in live performance. Far from fading away, Dylan's heavy touring schedule finds him nightly raging against the dying of the light—if we may borrow a line from that other Dylan—Dylan Thomas.

BOB DYLAN doesn't act as if his songs are classics. He is a throwback to an era when a musician's job was to perform live, not to perfect a studio arrangement. His music stays in the present tense. Mr. Dylan won't recreate his old recordings; with every new band, and sometimes with each performance, he toys with tempos, rhythms and melodies, rarely content to sing a line the same way twice. Over a three-decade career, some of his live efforts have been garbled, even perverse. But with his current band Mr. Dylan has reclaimed his place as a great American musician: an improviser with deep, broad roots.

At Roseland on Tuesday night, opening a three-night stand, Mr. Dylan was dressed as a country preacher, or a Western gunslinger, in a black frock coat. He sang as if savoring every word, still finding new shadings in his own lyrics: a touch of cocky threat in "I'll Be Your Baby Tonight," a slow-building ardency in "Tears of Rage." A new song, "God Knows," mixed a lover's declarations of fidelity with portents of apocalypse.

John Jackson on guitar and Tony Garnier on bass bobbed and weaved beside Mr. Dylan onstage, both wearing hats; Winston Watson on drums and Bucky Baxter on steel guitar worked behind their instruments. It's a nonchalantly brilliant band, as good as any of Mr. Dylan's past groups, including The Band; Mr. Dylan's fans deserve a live album from this lineup. Mr. Dylan doesn't simply sing with the group; he is meshed with it as lead guitarist, playing plucky, insistent phrases and riffs. His harmonica solos were tautly focused, too, with terse lines and syncopated choral wheezes.

Together, Mr. Dylan and the group make the songs seem as if they're just falling together, perfectly. The band's only mannerism is to end too many songs by dropping to half speed, a touch of grandiosity.

The band rocked like Creedence Clearwater Revival in "If You See Her, Say Hello," howled through "All Along the Watchtower," then switched to jaunty western swing for "I'll Be Your Baby Tonight." Playing acoustic instruments, the band moved toward bluegrass ("Don't Think Twice, It's All Right") and mountain folk songs, including a version of "Mr. Tambourine Man" that still, three decades later, conveyed wide-eyed anticipation.

"Me, I'm still on the road / headin' for another joint," Mr. Dylan sang (at a playful double speed) in "Tangled Up in Blue," and he still treats his music that way. In an era when most big-time rockers shun spontaneity, Mr. Dylan is an oddball, and a precious one.

Gavin Martin

ARTICULATE SPEECH OF THE HEART

Rock Ages Gracefully, Part II. This brief piece is a reflection on the ability of singers as diverse as Frank Sinatra and Van Morrison to transcend generations with the common themes of loneliness and despair. Morrison, the Irish R&B singer, is in his fourth decade as a performer.

GOING TO a Van Morrison show has become a neo-religious event for me, sometimes as much for what happens offstage as on. On a recent pilgrimage I asked my friend Stan if he'd ever suspected, twenty-five years ago when he first heard "Gloria," that in 1989 he'd still be listening to Van, going to see him and getting the same kind of thrill.

"No," he said, "but then we were always taught to believe that the sort of things we liked wouldn't last very long." That was a lie when they said it about Van Morrison and Them, a lie when they said it about Elvis, Chuck Berry, or the Beatles. And it was a lie when they trotted it out for a previous generation about the skinny kid from Hoboken, New Jersey who made the bobbysoxers scream and swoon.

Frank Sinatra fits into this story and here's how I know. Years before I was born my parents had a severely mentally handicapped son. After a few years what they dreaded became obvious—they could no longer care for him at home and they had to make the very painful decision to put him in an institution. My older sister will never forget the day they had to deliver my brother into care. The traumatic event was heightened because her kid brother cried long and loud when my mother and father left him in the clutches of the hospital doctors.

She remembers the evening that followed because she felt a fear and isolation in the family home she'd never known before. My mother disappeared on a long walk around the neighborhood and my father locked himself in a room with the record player. Over and over the same record was played on the Dansette: Frank Sinatra's *Only the Lonely*, perhaps the most mournful, aching white blues album I know.

I've only learned about all this recently. I knew nothing about it when

I gave my dad a copy of Kitty Kelley's scurrilous Sinatra biography *His Way* a couple of Christmases ago. My dad's not the sort of man to be up-front or always say exactly what's on his mind, so he told me it was a good read "but it didn't tell you anything about the music." Since I've come to know *Only the Lonely* I realize what my old man was really saying, that Kitty Kelley had actually told him less than bugger about the Frank Sinatra he knew, the voice that called out to him in his darkest hour. That was a voice that caressed the very lineaments of grief and despair as, accompanied by Nelson Riddle's muted horns and crying strings, Frank sang about the pain that will not be conquered. "It's a lonesome old town . . ."

My dad's pretty sick now and I don't know if I'll ever be able to sit down and talk about this with him and I'm not sure if it matters too much either. The Frank Sinatra Kitty Kelley never told us about is what matters here. Because somewhere in there lies a whole side to my father's experience that I'd otherwise never be able to feel or know.

And Van, who knows more than a thing or two about all this, was in great form this particular night, too. Just as well, because after *Only the Lonely* I need all the ammunition I can muster for the next time my dad and I start up the old argument about the relative merits of our favorite singers. Big kids that we are, there's a part of both of us that wants to play out the old generation gap lie about who's better, who's best, and who'll last longer. But inside, we both know what we're talking about is something much deeper than our bickering could ever fathom.

"Fame requires every kind of excess."

Here are some of the weirder, sadder, meaner chapters in rock and roll history. In this section, we offer you death and destruction and ravenous groupies and inflatable record producers. It's amazing rock and roll has survived its many knockouts, but it has, always coming back out of the corner with some new crazed, adrenaline energy. If rock and roll could survive J. Edgar Hoover, then Danny and the Juniors were right—it *is* here to stay.

TESTIMONY IN THE PAYOLA HEARINGS

Mae Axton was a Jacksonville, Florida, schoolteacher and part-time songwriter when her path crossed Elvis Presley's. She had music-industry connections and so she signed on to do publicity for the Florida leg of Elvis's breakthrough 1955 tour of the South. Axton and Elvis hit it off and a few months later, Axton offered Presley a song on the condition that he make it the first release under his brand-new RCA recording contract. After reading about a young man's suicide in the local newspaper (the note said, "I walk a lonely street"), Axton was inspired. When Elvis heard "Heartbreak Hotel," he loved it and met Axton's first-release condition.

A couple of years later, when Congress began its investigation of the payola scandal, Axton took umbrage at comments ASCAP officials had made about their company's chief rival, BMI, which represented Mae Axton and tons of other rock and roll songwriters. Here are excerpts from her testimony.

Mrs. Axton: I am Mae Boren Axton. I am a schoolteacher and have been for 16 years. Currently, I am employed at Ribault High School in Jacksonville, Fla.

During the time I have taught school I have done other things to supplement my salary, including writing, working in radio and television, doing advertising work, and in recent years as a professional songwriter.

I asked for the privilege of appearing before this committee because some of the statements made by the proponents of this bill have aroused me to what I consider justified indignation. You see, I am a songwriter who is affiliated with BMI, and I am also a writer of compositions popularly termed "rock and roll."

Among them, perhaps the most successful being, Heartbreak Hotel, recorded by Elvis Presley.

Senator Pastore: You wrote Heartbreak Hotel?

Mrs. Axton: Yes, sir.

A few weeks ago I sat in this very room and I heard proponents of the bill very callously slander, in my opinion, writers of BMI. I heard, too, with a great deal of horror, accusations that BMI and its writers, through the medium of rock and roll music particularly, had deliberately and callously either caused or contributed to juvenile delinquency.

* * *

Mrs. Axton: Well, I want to say here if it is true that writers of BMI, writers of rock-and-roll affiliated with BMI, like Mae Axton, have contributed deliberately and viciously to juvenile delinquency, I certainly would be a modern Dr. Jekyll and Mr. Hyde. And I know that it is not true, because I am a very respected member of my community, I am the wife of a schoolteacher, coach, athletic director who deals all the time with teen-agers, even for more years than I have. I am the mother of two children, and I teach these young people because I like to teach them. I find that they need people who care about them to help guide them.

I have turned down, incidentally, many more lucrative jobs so I could teach, because I sincerely believe and have felt a sort of commission, a compulsion, I believe that the good Lord endowed me with some sort of love and some sort of understanding of the teen-agers that makes it necessary for me to be a part of developing and guiding these boys and girls who are going to lead the destinies of our world.

Senator Pastore: How old are your children?

Mrs. Axton: One just turned 21, the other is 17.

Senator Pastore: You are a very young mother.

Mrs. Axton: Thank you, sir.

I, for many years, have been active in church and civic activities, and of course school, PTA, and all the affiliated organization of school work, and yet, the proponents of this bill would have you believe that as a BMI writer and particularly as a writer of rock-and-roll music, that I personally have contributed to this juvenile delinquency, as I have mentioned earlier, and the foundation to the reason why I wanted to appear before this committee was because I felt that these charges needed to be answered, and because I would also like to tell you what Broadcast Music, Inc., has meant to me, and I am sure to many other writers like me, who perhaps would not have had the chance to have their tunes heard had it not been for the open door policy of BMI.

First, I would like to tell you how I happened to become a song writer, being a schoolteacher and then how I happened to become affiliated with BMI.

Since I was a kid in school, I started writing things for programs. Then when I started teaching, I would write songs to fit particular occasions for civic clubs, community, school, and church affairs, and finally, at the urging of my friends I submitted some for possible remuneration to compensate for the notoriously small income of the schoolteacher. I can go back to the time when I received $70 a month for teaching school. My first song was accepted by a publisher in Tennessee, Count Me In, and was recorded by Capitol Records.

I can't describe the delight, perhaps excitability in my own heart as the typical teen-ager of the rock-and-roll of today, when that record was first played, and I heard a diskjockey call me and say: Listen to something. I was excited and happy. Following this, this initial release, I was advised by some people to join an organization called ASCAP.

I was given an address to write, and I made not only 1 but 2 inquiries, and to this date have never received an answer, even.

I sometime later—I didn't stop songwriting, I went on. It was a challenge, and it was fun, and I continued songwriting, and sometime later someone suggested that—it was a BMI affiliate suggested that I join an organization called Broadcast Music, Inc., and so I wrote them and within a matter of a few days, I got an application for membership, so I filled it out and sent it in, and almost immediately got a contract with BMI.

* * *

Senator Pastore: At the time you wrote to ASCAP were you then a member of BMI?

Mrs. Axton: No. I didn't know what either organization was. Schoolteachers don't know a lot of things.

* * *

Senator Pastore: Now, what is your agreement with BMI? Do they subsidize you in any way?

Mrs. Axton: No, sir, I get royalties.

Senator Pastore: Let's get that on the record from one who has the experience. What is your association or your contractual relationship with BMI?

Mrs. Axton: Well, I have a contract, I don't know the details of it, I am perhaps too much of an idealist to pay as much attention as I should to every detail of a contract, and the technical areas of songwriting, or anything—perhaps I do not know as much as I should.

* * *

I am sure had I been born in a different age, I would have written whatever songs the teen-agers liked at that time, whether during the stone ages or whatever it might be.

* * *

I want to add here, too, that I believe it is because people like a song, and that is why it advanced to the status it did, in national lime-light, and not because any recording company, or any broadcaster, gave it any special breaks.

We who are engaged in any kind of education, and I say my mind, because I am just common, ordinary run-of-mill type of school-teacher.

Senator Potter: What do you teach?

Mrs. Axton: Speech and journalism.

Senator Potter: You should teach a little songwriting on the side.

Mrs. Axton: Well, we have some good jam sessions with the teen-agers and they love it.

Senator Pastore: What instrument do you play?

Mrs. Axton: I play the piano. I wish I could play the guitar, but I can't. My son does.

Senator Pastore: Was that your inspiration for writing?

Mrs. Axton: Yes; I taught first-year music. And I am actually more a poet, I suppose, and a true lyricist. I have written poetry since I was 6 or 7 years old. I started my first efforts and got started having them pub-lished when I was a pre-teen-ager, and I liked the rhythmic flow of po-etry, and I think it expresses something that perhaps prose could never quite reach, so from that, as I say, I started writing lyrics, and sometimes little tunes to go with the lyrics, sometimes lyrics to put with something else, someone else would do.

Senator Pastore: How about Heartbreak Hotel? Was the tune yours?

Mrs. Axton: Yes; the idea actually came from a friend of mine whose name is on that, Tommy Dirden. He came over to my house that evening and asked if I read the paper. I was busy writing a story for a maga-zine and I said, "No; I haven't had time."

He said, "There is something in this that distresses me." He said he read where a man had committed suicide and he left one sen-tence: "I walk a lonely street." If you know the song, that is a part of the song, so that is Tommy's, or the newspaper's, I don't know whose—perhaps the man who died. He said, "It worries me to death."

I said, "It is a tragic thing," and of course it impressed me terribly, things of that sort do, but I said, "Think of the heartbreak he must have left behind him, so there ought to be a Heartbreak Hotel at the end of that lonely street."

He said, "That is a terrific idea."

And I said, "You know, I think I would rather stop the story and write a song." He dubbed it off for me on tape 20 minutes later. It was one of those things that came as a result of a tragic experience that in a vicarious manner I had participated in, you see.

*   *   *

I try to write the kind of songs that may assuage grief, may inspire someone, make the lonely a little less lonely, may give an opportunity, an outlet, we might say, for the excess energy of these youngsters who I sincerely believe are trying to keep pace with the fastest moving age the world has ever known.

In all humility, I think that I have accomplished this to some degree, with some of my tunes, in the case of at least some people.

From a purely personal viewpoint, I might add that my son, my youngest son, a senior in high school, will go to college next year because of the supplemental money that I have been able to earn from songwriting to add to the schoolteachers' salary that my husband and I make, because we are both schoolteachers, and so we have the limited income of schoolteachers.

We are very happy that Johnny will be in college next year, because of the open-door policy in our sincere opinion, of BMI and the encouragement that they have given me. I want to say this, that anything, anything at all that would tend to make BMI another ASCAP, or even, much worse, to eliminate BMI as a competitive organization would certainly be a fatal blow to songwriters like me, and in the long run would do a tremendous disservice to the American people, and I would like to add here that writers of music everywhere give hope to the eager and the weary alike, and I think it is most important that we keep it so that any song by any writer in any day and age has its chance, its rightful chance to be heard, and it is my firm conviction that the best way to preserve the situation is to keep BMI intact and keep Broadcast Music, Inc., open door and open door ever and always.

Senator Pastore: Thank you very much, Mrs. Axton.

Senator Potter: You have been an outstanding witness, and if I have any bills I would like to have pushed, I would like to have you testify in behalf of them.

Senator Pastore: Senator Thurmond.

Senator Thurmond: I have enjoyed your testimony, and you are very impressive.

Mrs. Axton: Thank you, sir.

Senator Pastore: Thank you very much.

THE PLANE CRASH

Johnny Ace killed himself—or was killed—over a game of cards just as his career was taking off in 1955. After that, this 1959 disaster was rock and roll's first big tragedy. Here's a radio bulletin announcing the deaths. Don McLean didn't call it "the day the music died" for nothing.

FOR THE PAST few hours, we've been furiously trying to put together this story, the story of a happy success for three young singers that ended in a very sad death this morning early in the cornfield near Mason City and Clear Lake, Iowa.

If you're one of those that loves rock and roll (and there are many) or if you're one of those that hates rock and roll (and there are many) you'll realize that this is a very big day in the lives of many of those in our generation because this is a day that ended in tragedy for three of the biggest names in the music business.

The names, in order of bigness, probably would be Ritchie Valens, Buddy Holly of the Crickets and also the Big Bopper.

A FOOL IN LOVE

She was Anna Mae Bullock of Nut Bush, Tennessee, and life was on a simple, if unexceptional course. But then she saw the Kings of Rhythm, and bandleader Ike Turner fell in love with her voice. He rechristened Anna Mae and pushed her onstage, where she emerged as one of the great voices of rock and roll history.

Ike was a founding father of rock (under the name Jackie Brenston and His Delta Cats, the Kings of Rhythm recorded "Rocket 88") and saw the young girl with the spectacular voice as the ticket to the fame that had so skillfully eluded him. Ann, as the first Ike and Tina hit implied, was a fool in love. Eventually, after years of cult fame, a near-miss at mega-celebrity with Phil Spector (he crafted his magnum opus, "River Deep, Mountain High," for her voice), the Ike & Tina Turner Revue became a major attraction . . . and then Tina left, with only her name, tired of Ike's abuse. She told her life story to her eternally youthful collaborator, MTV personality Kurt Loder, author of Bat Chain Puller.

Tina: In the very beginning, Ike and I really were just like brother and sister. I wasn't his type of woman, and he wasn't my type of man, either. But we communicated through music. I loved what he played. I didn't like the songs he had me sing, necessarily, but I liked singing. And I could sing his ideas.

*   *   *

Ike: The first time I went with her, I felt like I'd screwed my sister or somethin'. I mean, I hope to die—we really had been like brother and sister. It wasn't just her voice. I had another girl in St. Louis that sang better than she did, girl named Pat—I don't know her last name, but I got a baby by her, too. Anyway, Ann and me was tight.

Tina: Yes, I fell in love. Became addicted to it, you might say. Well, everybody liked Ike then, pretty much, and some loved him a lot. He was a different person at that time—kind of shy, in a way; didn't drink or take drugs or anything. I would have been lost in my life at that point without him. I mean, I could do two things: work in a hospital or sing with Ike's band. I didn't know anything else. Or anybody else. And I wanted to sing.

Ann remained loyal to her mentor, but was often appalled by his violent life-style. A popular tale told around St. Louis, to which Ike's name is generally attached (and in connection with which he later appeared in court), concerns the unauthorized acquisition of twenty thousand dollars from a local bank, allegedly to obtain new uniforms for the Kings of Rhythm. Ike doesn't deny the story, exactly, but he's vague about details.

But during the end of January 1960, Ann became pregnant again, this time by Ike. At the same time, Ike decided to get back together with Lorraine Taylor, by whom he'd since fathered a second son, Michael, born February 23, 1959. He maintained Ann, however, as his number-one-girl-on-the-side. Depressed, and uncomfortable with Lorraine back on the scene, Ann moved out of the house on Virginia Place and back over to St. Louis, where she rented a small house of her own and found a woman nearby who would keep Craig while she was at work. Maybe, she kept telling herself, she wasn't really pregnant.

Amid the usual blur of unending club and college gigs, Ike began preparing to cut "A Fool in Love" as his next single. The session would be conducted at Technisonic, with the lead vocal assigned to Art Lassiter, late of the Trojans, now with Ike and, on his own, doing Ray Charles covers around the area backed by a female vocal quartet called the Artettes. Ike liked the all-girl backup idea, and asked Lassiter to bring along three of the Artettes—Frances Hodges, Sandra Harding, and Robbie Montgomery (the last pregnant by Lassiter at the time)—to the "Fool in Love" session. The resulting record would be farmed out to whatever label would have it. All went well right up to the day of the session, in the early spring of 1960, when Lassiter, unhappy with his financial arrangement, failed to show.

*   *   *

Ike: Man, I sat there and wrote that song for Art Lassiter, and then he was gonna beat me outta some money. So I had Ann do it. This was out at Technisonic, and the guy that owned the place, all he ever cut out there was TV commercials. When she started singin', "Hey-hey-heyyy-hey-heyyyy"—boy, he turned red. "Goddam it," he said, "don't you scream on my mike!"

*   *   *

Tina: I don't know what Art Lassiter's argument with Ike was. They fought a lot. Ike was always losing singers—he was very hard to work for. Well, I had been there at the house when they were rehearsing the song, so I knew it. And Ike had already booked the studio time, so he said, "Little Ann, I want you to come and do this demo for Art." I didn't really want to sing it—I didn't care for all that "hey-hey-hey" stuff. But I did it. It was a demo. I think Ike planned to record it again with Art Lassiter's voice if he could get him back. But it didn't work out that way.

Ike sent tapes of "A Fool in Love" to a St. Louis disc jockey, who in turn sent them out to several record companies, including Sue in New York City. Sue was that rarest of record-biz phenomena, a label owned and operated by a black man. Its proprietor, Henry "Juggy" Murray, had grown up on the streets of Hell's Kitchen dancing for nickels on street corners. He acquired his unusual nickname from a liquor-loving but near-blind grandfather who, in reaching for his favorite jug, more often than not wound up latching on to little Henry.

*   *   *

Juggy Murray signed up Ike and his song for a twenty-five-thousand-dollar advance. He told Ike to forget about recutting the tune with a male vocal—it was Ann's voice that made the track. Maybe, Juggy suggested, Ike should concentrate on making her the star of his stage show—not just have her up there singing background with the other singers, but save her for the "star time" segment that wound up each set. Ike, after a frustrated decade of striving, could almost feel his grasp closing around the brass ring of the big time. One day he announced to Ann that "A Fool in Love," her lead-vocal debut, would be released under a new name. Not the Kings of Rhythm this time; "A Fool in Love" would be credited to Ike and Tina Turner.

Tina?

Turner?

Ike explained: As a kid back in Clarksdale, he'd become fixated on the white-jungle goddesses who romped through Saturday-matinee movie serials—revealingly rag-clad women with long flowing hair and names like Sheena, Queen of the Jungle, and Nyoka—particularly Nyoka. He still remembered *The Perils of Nyoka,* a fifteen-part Republic Pictures serial from 1941, starring Kay Aldridge in the title role and featuring a villainess named Vultura, an ape named Satan, and Clayton Moore (later to be TV's

Lone Ranger) as the love interest. Nyoka, Sheena—Tina! Tina Turner—Ike's own personal Wild Woman. He loved it.

Ann, however, had reservations—about this name change, about her whole relationship with Ike. At first they had been just friends—fine. But now here she was pregnant by the guy, and getting in deeper every day. She wanted to sing, and—yes—she wanted to be a star. But what about love, and marriage? She wanted them too. But Ike—with his compulsive womanizing and violent temper—seemed an unlikely candidate for either. When she had become pregnant, he had left her and gone back to Lorraine. Could he ever change? She doubted it. She did love him, it was true—he was her guide, her show-biz teacher. Whatever she—a twenty-year-old country nobody from Nut Bush, Tennessee—had achieved so far in her young life was due to him. She knew how long he'd lusted after a hit record, and she vowed that if he finally got that hit with her, she wouldn't desert him. But . . . maybe she and Ike could go back to being just friends, fellow professionals.

Tina: I loved Ike—as much as I knew about love then—but I didn't want our relationship to go any farther. He had already told me that if the record was a hit, he wanted to leave St. Louis and go to California, and he wanted me to come with him. I'd said I didn't know about that—I didn't even know what California looked like. He described a place where there were lots of pink houses and palm trees, and I closed my eyes and tried to visualize that. After a while, it started to seem like a little paradise.

But we were two totally different people. I knew it could never work out between us. So when he got the record deal, I went to talk to him. First, he told me how it was going to be from then on: He would pay my rent, but basically keep all the money for himself. I told him I didn't want to get involved any further with him. And that was the first time he beat me up. With a shoe stretcher—one of those men's shoe trees with the metal rods in the middle? Just grabbed one of those and started beating me with it. And after that he made me go to bed, and he had sex with me. My eye was all swollen—God, it was awful. And that was the beginning, the beginning of Ike instilling fear in me. He kept control of me with *fear.*

Why didn't I leave him? It's easy now to say I should've. But look at my situation then: I already had one child, and I was pregnant with another by him. Singing with Ike was how I made my living. And I was living better than I ever had in my life. What was I going to do—run back to Barnes Hospital and try to get my job back as a nurse's aide? No. I was hurt and I was scared, but I couldn't think about going back. I had to keep going forward. So I decided to stay with Ike. Because I really did care about him. And I knew the story of how he had tried to get his career going for so long, and how every time he'd get a foothold, people would walk out on him. And I swore I would not do that to him. So I said to myself: "I'll stay right here, and I'll just try to make things better." I wasn't as smart then as I am now. But who ever is?

*　　*　　*

"A Fool in Love" started making noise the minute it was released. At last, Ike was going to have a hit with his name on it—a hit that he controlled. If, that was, he could get the newly christened Tina Turner out of the hospital. Because his lead singer, inarguably pregnant at this point, had come down with hepatitis after cutting the record—an advanced case by the time she tore herself away from Ike's endless gigging to see a doctor, who speculated that she'd probably been bitten by infectious mosquitoes at an outdoor show that summer. Ike's patience dwindled in direct proportion to the length of her confinement, which, as "Fool" hit the airwaves, had lasted six weeks. And still the doctors wouldn't let her go. Ike became frantic. Because with the release of "A Fool in Love," Tina, unlike Ike's interchangeable array of other vocalists, could not be replaced.

Tina: I had taken Craig to the doctor with a cold or something, and the doctor looked at me and said, "Mother, you have jaundice, we can't release you." And zip—right into the hospital. I couldn't believe it. But it was really serious. I was turning yellow—my eyes were totally yellow, and real glassy. I couldn't eat anything, but I had to go to the bathroom all the time. I had fever, and I was real tired. I mean, my bloodstream was infested. It was killing me, and I hadn't realized it.

Well, I was pregnant, too, of course. Not showing yet, though—I walked into that hospital in a tight dress and high heels, honey. But after two weeks in there, my stomach went boof! So there I was, lying in bed with the big stomach, and yellow jaundice. Not feeling too glamorous, you know? And then Lorraine was wanting to know who this baby was by, right? Oh, God. So after about six weeks I'm lying there, and what starts coming on the radio?

"You're just a fool, you know you're in love . . ."

The record is getting played! And this is St. Louis, so it's getting played a lot. And boy, I got to hate that goddamn song. I'd have to lie there, all sick and swollen up, and listen to "A Fool in Love" every day, and I'd be thinking—it sounds funny now, but it's the truth—I'd be thinking: "What's love got to do with it?" You know? Because here I was, pregnant by Ike Turner, who's gone back to his wife, and now she's getting suspicious. . . . I mean, this was not my idea of love at all.

Then the record started getting really hot. Ike was ready to travel. One day he came to see me and he said, "You gotta get out of this damn hospital." He said, "These doctors are crazy if they think they're gonna keep you in here forever." Well, I was getting better by then, but the doctors still didn't want me out on the street yet, because I might've still been contagious. Ike said, "The record is hitting, I've got some dates booked, and you've gotta sneak outta here." I said, "All right."

So Ike found out the best way to get out, and he had somebody bring me some clothes to wear, and one night after dinner—"TV out, radio off, goodnight, Mother"—I got up and snuck out of the hospital in an orange maternity suit. Bright orange, Lord. Ike sent somebody to pick me up—he always had somebody else do his dirty work—and I walked out the exit he'd told me about and got right into the car and went back to the little house I was renting. The next night, Ike came over and told me what was happening. The record had hit, and we were going on tour. We had an engagement the following day at a theater in Cincinnati, Ohio, with Jackie Wilson. Well, I could not imagine myself being onstage pregnant. But Ike . . . Ike was from the underworld, you know? Totally. And you'd do what he said. So I had to get myself ready. For a costume, I designed a kind of sack dress and put chiffon over the top—people didn't realize I was pregnant for a long time. And the next day we left, the musicians first, packed into a station wagon with all their gear, and then Ike in his Cadillac an hour or two behind them. Fortunately, I always rode with Ike, because on the way to Cincinnati there was an accident; the station wagon turned over. None of the guys got really hurt, but they were all skinned and bruised. We finally got to Cincinnati, though, and that's where we played the first Ike and Tina Turner show. Some of the band guys weren't too clear about this new billing—they thought I'd changed my name to "Ockateena" or something. They played the date in their wrinkled clothes, all torn and beaten—and the people loved us. Our record was way up in the charts by then. We were riding high.

The Ike and Tina Turner Revue was thus launched on its first tour. An immediate requirement was female backup singers to replicate the new "Fool in Love" sound.

* * *

But what to call this new trio? Clearly they required a distinctive designation within Ike's carefully structured Revue. Many people are willing to take credit for supplying the famous name. . . . Ike himself dismisses all such claims, contending he came up with the name—and quickly had it copyrighted—all by himself. In any case, with Ray Charles and his Raelettes all the rage in R & B circles at the time, Ike's choice of a handle for his female backup group was hardly original: He decided to call them the Ikettes.

In August 1960, "A Fool in Love" climbed to number two on the R & B charts. Propelled by its success, the Revue had begun playing bigger clubs, and finally made it to the theaters too: At the Apollo in New York City, on a typically star-studded bill with Hank Ballard and the Midnighters, Ernie K-Doe, Joe Jones, Lee Dorsey, and comic Flip Wilson, Tina—eight months pregnant—wowed the crowd by jumping off the stage and down into the audience. In Philadelphia on October 3—the week "A Fool in Love" peaked on the pop charts at number twenty-seven—Ike and Tina appeared on Dick Clark's *American Bandstand,* the eight-year-old local dance show that had gone national three years earlier. This was it: the big time. And then, more wondrous yet, the Revue was off to fabled Las Vegas.

Tina: I thought, "Oh, Las Vegas! Will we have one of those rooms with the star on the door?" But the place we played was across the tracks, in another Hole. It was a big club, but predominantly black—not like those places on the Strip where Diahann Carroll and those kinds of people played. We were always kind of second fiddle, you know? Anyway, I had been wearing a maternity girdle to hold me in place, and Ike wasn't looking at me that much—I mean, Ike didn't like kids, he never wanted kids, and he never paid any attention to a woman *with* kids. But we got to this hotel in Las Vegas, and I started undressing to take a shower, and that's when Ike got a good look at my stomach. I was really blown up by then. And he said, "Girl, when're you supposed to have that baby?" I said, "Well, sometime this month." I'd only had one child before, and my mother wasn't around this time, so what did I know? But Ike got all scared. He canceled the date we were supposed to play and he told Jimmy Thomas, "Get the car, we're goin' to Los Angeles." You see, he wanted me to have the baby there because he could work in L.A. So we took off, and Jimmy would hit a bump in the road every now and then, and Ike would curse him out, scared to death I was going to go into labor out there in the desert between Las Vegas and Los Angeles.

We arrived in L.A. around seven in the evening, checked into a hotel, ordered dinner—and I started feeling pressures. At one in the morning, I woke up and I was in labor. Of course, Ike was no help, so I got up and went into the living room. After a while, I was tossing and turning so much that Ike got up and called Annie Mae Wilson. By about seven o'clock in the morning, Ike had found out about this shot I could get to freeze my muscles and hold off the labor until I could make it to the hospital, which was pretty far away. Well, this involved going to a doctor nearby. So Annie Mae arrived and took me in the car and we headed off onto the freeway; I got the shot, we got back on the freeway, and then the labor started again anyway—I began dilating right there in the middle of the midmorning traffic. We finally arrived at the hospital, and I made it up all these steps and got inside, and Annie Mae said, "She's fixin' to have this baby," and they took me right away. Ike was nowhere around, of course.

In the early morning hours of October 27, Tina gave birth to her second son, Ronald Renelle. The baby, as Lorraine, among others, was not slow to notice, had a very familiar look about him.

Tina: That was a shameful period for me. Up till then, Lorraine never really knew what was going on, because Ike and I had kept our relationship sort of low-key—everyone thought we were still just friends. But out on the road, the fans all thought Ike was my husband—because I was pregnant, and I was out there with him, right? And that was a dilemma for Lorraine. But she hardly ever traveled with us, so she thought the fans just misunderstood the situation. Sometimes she would come out, and then I felt really bad, because everybody knew by then and they would all be mumbling about it. And then in the car, I would have to ride in the front seat because Lorraine would be in the back with Ike, and the fans would see us and go, "Oh, we thought you two were husband and wife." And I'd have to say, "No, no . . ." I became very unhappy with that setup. I mean, here I was having a baby for this man, and here was the common-law wife that I was replacing. And when she left to go back home again, I really was like Ike's wife—which was where the fans had got the idea in the first place. Or maybe he'd be carrying on with one of the Ikettes—although in the beginning he kept that sort of thing kind of hidden from me. Anyway, it was awful. Then the baby was born, and he came out looking just like Ike. That's when Lorraine finally got fed up and decided to leave him. So eventually we got all the kids, and we just started living together. But the whole thing was a public scandal, really embarrassing.

I had other things to worry about, though, when I got out of the hospital three days later. Because Ike had this important date up in Oakland, I think it was. It was just two days away, and he said I had to make it. Well, I was real weak, but I rested those two days and then I went to do the show. Now, Ike didn't miss a trick: While I had been in the hospital, he had found this other girl that looked like me and he used her on some dates, telling the people she was Tina. Actually, she was a prostitute, and she had been turning tricks, too—and of course the men she pulled had thought they were making love to me. Can you believe it? And so these guys started calling my room, saying like, "You were with me last night and you promised me a date"—and I was going, "What are you talking about?" Ike wasn't around, so I called this girl up to my room and told her, you know, "You can't do this." She started cursing—and I don't know where I got the strength from, but I picked her up and threw her in the bathtub! I wanted to kill her. I thought I'd never be able to clear my name after that.

So then I got dressed and went onstage and did the show. It wasn't too bad. I only did two songs, and I sat down to sing them. Bled a lot when I hit the high notes, though. After that, I got two weeks to completely recover.

Dave Marsh

MERCHANTS OF FILTH

You can tell the history of rock and roll by telling the story of just one song. Here we have the whole spectacle represented: the unappreciated composer and original artist Richard Berry; white performers exploiting black artists; FBI investigations of subversive kids' music; and the eventual reward for the innovator. "Louie Louie" has it all. In this excerpt from his excellent book about the song, Dave Marsh talks about the supposed dirty lyrics that propelled the tune into urban-legend status.

BACK IN 1963, everybody who knew anything about rock'n'roll knew that the Kingsmen's "Louie Louie" concealed dirty words that could be unveiled only by playing the 45 rpm single at 33⅓. (In a later version, they were audible to anybody who really paid attention, a cultic/conspiratorial touch worthy of Foucault's Pendulum.) This preposterous fable bore no scrutiny even at the time, but kids used to pretend that it did, in order to panic parents, teachers, and other authority figures. Eventually those ultimate authoritarians, the FBI, got involved, conducting a thirty-month investigation that led to "Louie"'s undying—indeed un-killable—reputation as a dirty song.

So "Louie Louie" leaped up the chart on the basis of a myth about its lyrics so contagious that it swept cross country quicker than bad weather. Nobody—not you, not me, not the G-men ultimately assigned to the case—knows where the story started. That's part of the proof that it was a myth, because no folk tales ever have a verifiable origin. Instead society creates them through cultural spontaneous combustion. The time and conditions become propitious and, suddenly, puppies are microwaved, innocent tourists return from Mexican vacations with a stray dog that's really a rat, hooks dangle from the door handles of cars parked on Lover's Lane late Friday night, Procter & Gamble suffers under the sign of Satan, and truck drivers pick up hitch-hiking ghosts, some of them reincarnations of Jesus. The fable of "Louie Louie" 's dirty lyrics is akin to those, although J. Edgar

Hoover never sent his legions of over-scrubbed cementheads to investigate the illegal importation of Mexican rats as household pets.

*   *   *

The FBI files on "Louie Louie" detail an investigation for a violation of what it dubs "ITOM," the Federal law against Interstate Transportation of Obscene Material. Because of ITOM, copies of "Louie Louie" sent from an FBI office travelled under special "obscene cover" (which probably means festooned with warning labels, like the ones identifying nuclear waste and rap records), lest the Bureau itself be criminalized.

Such strictures against violating the obscenity laws applied to stuff that today's *Hustler* reader happily brings home to the kiddies. America locked down tight against the porno fiends. Max Feirtag claimed in 1964 that he'd never seen a copy of the dirty words because no one would risk mailing him one. The FBI actually destroyed the first few "Louie" specimens it analyzed. Contact with pornography, even if the porno in question could not be discerned, represented a contagion that could infect the mental and moral hygiene of Bureau-crat and civilian alike.

The feds' two-and-a-half-year pursuit of "Louie Louie" consumed the energy and attentions of agents in six major cities. Yet the vaunted G-men, for all their moral hygiene and ideological integrity, couldn't figure out the joke—let alone the lyrics—even though they had access to the most modern criminological tools, state-of-the-art surveillance techniques, and a Limax music crib sheet. The agents sat befuddled, staring at poorly typed copies of the "real" (that is, the spurious) words passed along by eager snitches. And they did this for twenty-one months, until November 1965, before they even figured out that it might be helpful to talk to Paul Revere and Raiders.

The FBI never talked to Jack Ely, the actual singer on the Kingsmen's actual "Louie." In fact, given the Lynn Easton-led Kingsmen's vested interest in steering everybody away from the fact that Lynn hadn't been the lead singer (viz., the liner notes to their first album), Jack believes that the FBI may not know to this day that he was ever involved in the record.

Even a competent FBI would have been hard-pressed to figure out who originated the scam. But at least the Bureau might have spent some time trying to locate him or her, rather than deciding at the outset that the absurd rumor must be true and setting out to investigate the song, instead of the story.

Through its bumbling of elementary investigative principle, the FBI blew whatever slim chance there was of ever identifying the source of the original dirty "Louie Louie" fable. And this person (or persons) unknown is one of the true geniuses of the "Louie" legend, for it is this cock-and-bull story that ensured the song's eternal perpetuation.

Since we'll never know for sure, we're reduced to theories. One says that the whole thing started as a collegiate prank, dreamed up and spread around either by a cabal in a Midwest frat house or by a lone-wolf, Pacific Northwest college student. Richard Berry tried explaining it to the *Indianapolis News* in 1986: "What happened is that a bunch of college kids back in Indiana got hold of a printing press and started printing up and distributing their own ideas of what they thought they heard.

Over the years, some of the lyrics have been changed by various people, which adds to the mystique of the song." This doesn't sound much like Richard Berry speaking, but there's no reason to suppose that the interview was done by an imposter. Is there?

The tradition of the covertly risque lyric forms the essence of some notable rhythm and blues careers, for instance, those of Hank Ballard and Rufus Thomas. Heavy sexual innuendo informed everything from the El-Chords' merely dirty "Peppermint Stick" to Little Richard's "Miss Molly, who sure like[d] to ball," to Ballard's notorious "Work with Me, Annie" series. Among the adult black people who were their intended listeners, such records represented a realistic ribaldry. This was true from the earliest classic blues records (you want to hear dirty records, check out such blessed geniuses as Bessie Smith and Ma Rainey, on such items as "I'm Wild About That Thing" and the original "See See Rider," all of them made between 1920 and 1940 when Ronald Reagan's innocent America supposedly prevailed) right up through the "Annie" series. By the time Fats Domino added the leer to "I found my thrill on Blueberry Hill," though, teenage titillation rather than frank, adult sexual humor was at work. For R&B's new audience of young white outsiders, the early rock'n'rollers' unfamiliarity with the patterns of black speech coupled with poor recording fidelity spiced even innocent tunes. As R&B historian Peter Grendysa put it, "Getting there was half the fun, and sometimes what we thought we heard was much better than the real thing."

"Louie Louie," from Richard Berry's version to the Kingsmen's, had nothing to do with any of this. That poor half-in-the-bag Jamaican sailor can't even get into the same country as his girl. But the rumor that "Louie Louie" was a dirty record captured the American imagination, not just because teenagers need to know, right now and for sure, things that adults will never figure out in a decade, but because the Dirty "Louie" fable fundamentally reflected the country's infantile sexuality. An adolescent fixation would have run its course far more quickly.

The idea that "Louie Louie" might be "dirty" sustains itself to this day because it hit adults as hard as it does kids—and if you take a cold, hard look at the real America, no wonder. We're dealing with the concept of someone actually (well, possibly) singing about sex (sort of) in a nation that still goes into a giggling spasm when someone makes a fart joke, a society that tried to put a TV star in jail for jacking off at an adult film. America needs to foster panics like the ones over "Louie" and Pee Wee from time to time in order to have a way of releasing the tensions caused by so many self-consciously tightened sphincters, artificially dehydrated vulvas, and willfully suppressed erections. In a culture that interprets puberty as a tragedy of lost innocence rather than as a triumphal entry into adulthood, the possibility of someone actually giving vent to sexual feeling remains deliriously scandalous. Sex is bad, and somebody singing about it would be really bad.

So the story circulated that if you listened to "Louie Louie" with a knowing ear, you'd hear the Kingsmen describe debauchery and bliss. And if you couldn't hear those dirty words even after all that toil, you might be handed—as I was sometime in 1964 or 1965—a copy of the real lyrics at the back of the school bus. A copy that you then went home and tried to hide from your mother's prying eyes and then proceeded to lose, so that years later you couldn't remember more than a fragment or two: "She had a rag on, I moved above," "I stuck my boner in her hair."

Indeed, it may be fairly said that the only genuinely useful purpose to which the FBI put America's tax dollars in the "Louie Louie" investigation was in accumulating variant versions of these supposed dirty words. The most common set, collected by the FBI in Tampa, Florida, in 1964, went like this:

> *CHORUS:* Oh, Louie, Louie, oh, no
> Get her way down low
> Oh, Louie, Louie, oh, baby
> Get her down low
> A fine little girl a-waiting for me
> She's just a girl across the way
> Well I'll take her and park all alone
> She's never a girl I'd lay at home.
> *(CHORUS REPEAT)*

At night at ten I lay her again
Fuck you, girl, Oh, all the way
Oh, my bed and I lay her there
I meet a rose in her hair
(CHORUS REPEAT)
Okay, let's give it to them, right now
She's got a rag on I'll move above
It won't be long she'll slip it off
I'll take her in my arms again
I'll tell her I'll never leave again
(CHORUS REPEAT)
Get that broad out of here!

Like the folk song collectors who prided themselves on compiling variant texts of the ancient Appalachian ballads, the Bureau also dug up a couple of variant Dirty "Louie"s. The crudest wasn't even set out in the style of verse, just slammed down, word-after-word with all the dispassion of the most perfunctory porn. Or maybe it had been scribbled furtively in some junior high hallway, with the thought that the authorities were hot on the trail:

Fine little girl waits for me get your thrills across
 the way girl I dream about is all alone she
 never could get away from home
Every night and day I play with my thing I fuck
 your girl all kinds of ways. In all night now
 meet me there I feel her low I give her hell
Hey youth bitch. Hey lovemaker now hold my
 bone, it won't take long so leave it alone. Hey
 Senorita I'm hot as hell I told her I'd never lay
 her again.

Then there's the one the circulated in Detroit during the song's 1965–66 revival there (the one I got on the bus, I think):

CHORUS: Lou-ii Lou-ii Oh, no. Grab her way down
 low.
(REPEAT)
There is a fine little girl waiting for me
She is just a girl across the way

When I take her all alone
She's never the girl I lay at home.
(CHORUS)
Tonight at ten I'll lay her agam
We'll fuck your girl and by the way
And . . . on that chair I'll lay her there.
I felt my bone . . . ah . . . in her hair.
(CHORUS)
She had a rag on, I moved above.
It won't be long she'll slip it off.
I held her in my arms and then
And I told her I'd rather lay her again.
(CHORUS)

"Louie Louie" survived despite as much as because of the spell cast by the "dirty lyrics" legend. Exactly why either song or rumor persisted remains indecipherable. Surely no one—not Richard Berry nor Rene Touzet, not Max Feirtag nor Lynn Easton, not Buck Orrnsby nor Ron Holden nor Mark Lindsay nor Rockin' Robin Roberts (God rest his rockin soul), nor any man whose lips have ever shaped a "Let's give it to 'em, right now!" or fingers pounded out a *duh duh duh, duh duh,* and certainly not poor Jack Ely—could resolve any of "Louie" 's central mysteries, even if chained to a radiator and grilled for bread-and-water weeks with rubber truncheons and 300-watt bulbs angled square in the eyes, while a tape loop of Amy Grant singing the best of 2 Live Crew played ceaselessly in the background.

What *can* be deciphered are some facts: For instance, the approximate date when all this furor started. That would be about November 1963, when the Kingsmen's record began treating the Billboard charts the way King Kong dealt with the Empire State Building. The G-men learned of it belatedly. The earliest reference to "Louie" in the FBI file is contained in a March 27, 1964, memo from Indianapolis. This memo reports an unnamed local woman saying that "about November, 1963, she purchased a record under Wand label at Blanchard's, a record shop in Crown Point, Indiana. . . . Record was publicly displayed, was routinely priced, and was not suspected of being obscene when purchased.

"Sometime after buying the record, [blacked out] heard from various acquaintances the record had obscene lyrics if the 'Louie Louie' side were played at a speed of 33⅓ instead of the normal 45 rpm. About 1/29/64, a co-worker gave [blacked out] a typed sheet of lyrics, which were allegedly transcribed from the record when played in this manner, and which appear obscene.

"She said the record was widely played in the area and was once ranked first on the WLS Radio (Chicago) record survey.

"She said she played the record in the manner described above and the lyrics seem to follow very closely to the words on the typewritten sheet. She said the typed page was a transcription by some unknown person in Crown Point area and was not furnished with the record." The SAC also sent along her transcript of the dirty lyrics (the first set above) and asked the FBI lab to determine their authenticity by comparing them with the disc. The memo further reported that on March 25, Assistant U.S. Attorney (AUSA) Lester R. Irvin of Hammond, Indiana, asked the FBI to see if the record violated U.S. Code Section 1465, Title 18, the ITOM law. Irvin said that if Hoover's boys found the obscenity, he'd jail the perpetrators.

So the FBI lab made its initial "unintelligible" analysis. What did not follow, at least as far as can be determined from the released files, was what you'd expect: an interrogation of the woman who made the complaint, the co-worker who gave her the dirty lyrics, whoever gave them to the co-worker and on back to the source of the story. Instead of investigating the story, the Bureau took the tale at face value and set about investigating the music, with the object of making it criminal.

The Kingsmen's "Louie" held in the *Billboard* Top 10 from December 7 (when it made its virtually unprecedented jump from No. 23 to No. 4) into January, when it peaked at No. 2. (Although the record did make No. 1 in the industry's other trade paper, *Cash Box,* it's the *Billboard* ranking that's definitive.) Along the way, "Louie" outstripped such enduring wonders of the recording arts such as Rufus Thomas's "Walking the Dog," "I'm Leaving It Up to You" by Dale and Grace, and the Beach Boys' so-jive-it's-cool "Be True to Your School." But our boy "Louie" was kept out of *Billboard's* top spot by—ring in another offbeat chorus of *duh duh duh, duh duh* 'cause there ain't a writer in the world with the guts to make this up—"Dominique" by the Singing Nun Soeur Sourire a/k/a Sister Luc-Gabrielle), singing, in French, the praises of her Dominican order.

Now, nobody operating in their right mind, the record business or even *Billboard's* employ, ever believed that "Dominique" was more popular than "Louie Louie." In both the short and long run, "Louie" far outsold "Dominique" or any other record on the chart at the end of 1963. But "Dominique," quintessential elephant trash, was a No. 1 record, and "Louie Louie," archetype of termite trash, wasn't—because *Billboard's* Hot

100 chart measured not popularity or record sales but a combination of sales, airplay and proper decorum (and perhaps the amount of any given record label's advertising budget devoted to *Billboard*) as determined by a mystical formula comprehended by fewer mortals than grasp the essence of "Do wah diddy." So "Louie" and such Top 10 cohorts as the Murmaids' "Popsicles and Icicles" were cast into outer darkness while Soeur Sourire reigned.

Even if "Louie" was cheated without a glimmer of Christian conscience out of its rightful rank at the top of a chart that everybody outside the music business believed reflected record sales and not mumbo-jumbo, the Kingsmen enjoyed a good long run in the Top 10. Whether that run was stimulated or deterred by the dirty lyrics rumors is hard to figure out. Although "Louie Louie" fell to No. 3 on the year-end chart, by January 4 it was back to No. 2, probably because the rumors began to pick up speed. But such innuendo impedes radio airplay and demolishes decorum, the most intangible elements in the Hot 100 formula (ad lineage can be counted). Anyway, when "Dominique" finally faded on January 11, the record that cashed in the chips for the top was Bobby Vinton's cornball "There, I've Said It Again."

Vinton remained at No. 1 through January 25, with the Kingsmen breathing down his Mr. B collar, but slamming into third place was another foreign disc: the Beatles' "I Want to Hold Your Hand." (At No. 4, curiously enough, was the venerated termite classic, "Surfing Bird" by the Trashmen, a record that makes "I Want to Hold Your Hand" sound like "Dominique.") By February 1, 1964, the Beatles had conquered *Billboard*'s top slot and that was it for your basic American termite for a good, long spell.

Maureen Cleave

MORE POPULAR THAN JESUS

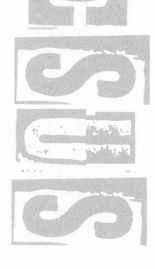

In the summer of 1966, on the eve of the Beatles' last tour of America, the group was criticized in the press, churchgoers in the Deep South burned Beatles albums, and Beatles concerts were picketed throughout the country. A comment John Lennon made to a British journalist months before had just been reprinted in the American teen magazine *Datebook,* and all hell broke loose. Lennon said, "Christianity will go. It will vanish and shrink. . . . I don't know which will go first— rock and roll or Christianity." Lennon also noted that his band was now "more popular than Jesus."

Lennon's statements on religion and comparative values were taken in context by English readers. But lifted from a serious discussion and put into a fan mag, they caused a furor. There were album bonfires, Ku Klux Klan demonstrations, and denouncements from pulpits. The story broke as the band was preparing to begin its American tour. Manager Brian Epstein considered cancelling the tour for fear of violence against the group. "If anything were to happen to any of them," Epstein said, "I'd never forgive myself." Epstein ended up providing this spin to the press: Lennon's remark was only his way of commenting on the decline of spiritual values. Lennon eventually apologized at a press conference during a stop on the tour: "I'm sorry I opened my mouth. I'm not anti-God, anti-Christ or anti-religion. I wouldn't knock it. I didn't mean we were greater or better."

The interviewer was Maureen Cleave, a *London Evening Standard* reporter who had covered the Beatles from the days of their first success in England and was, one of their confidantes. Here, then, is that famous "Jesus quote"—in context.

IT WAS this time three years ago that The Beatles first grew famous. Ever since then, observers have anxiously tried to gauge whether their fame was on the wax or on the wane; they foretold the fall of the old

Beatles, they searched diligently for the new Beatles (which was as pointless as looking for the new Big Ben).

At last they have given up; The Beatles' fame is beyond question. It has nothing to do with whether they are rude or polite, married or unmarried, 25 or 45; whether they appear on *Top of the Pops* or do not appear on *Top of the Pops*. They are well above any position even a Rolling Stone might jostle for. They are famous in the way the Queen is famous. When John Lennon's Rolls-Royce, with its black wheels and its black windows, goes past, people say: "It's the Queen," or "It's The Beatles." With her they share the security of a stable life at the top. They all tick over in the public esteem—she in Buckingham Palace, they in the Weybridge-Esher area. Only Paul remains in London.

The Weybridge community consists of the three married Beatles; they live there among the wooded hills and the stockbrokers. They have not worked since Christmas and their existence is secluded and curiously timeless. "What day is it?" John Lennon asks with interest when you ring up with news from outside. The fans are still at the gates but The Beatles see only each other. They are better friends than ever before.

Ringo and his wife, Maureen, may drop in on John and Cyn; John may drop in on Ringo; George and Pattie may drop in on John and Cyn and they might all go round to Ringo's, by car of course. Outdoors is for holidays.

They watch films, they play rowdy games of Buccaneer; they watch television till it goes off, often playing records at the same time. They while away the small hours of the morning making mad tapes. Bedtimes and mealtimes have no meaning as such. "We've never had time before to do anything but just be Beatles," John Lennon said.

He is much the same as he was before. He still peers down his nose, arrogant as an eagle, although contact lenses have righted the short sight that originally caused the expression. He looks more like Henry VIII than ever now that his face has filled out—he is just as imperious, just as unpredictable, indolent, disorganised, childish, vague, charming and quick-witted. He is still easy-going, still tough as hell. "You never asked after Fred Lennon," he said, disappointed. (Fred is his father; he emerged after they got famous.) "He was here a few weeks ago. It was only the second time in my life I'd seen him—I showed him the door." He went on cheerfully: "I wasn't having *him* in the house."

His enthusiasm is undiminished and he insists on its being shared. George has put him on to this Indian music. "You're not listening, are you?" he shouts after 20 minutes of the record. "It's amazing this—so cool. Don't the Indians appear cool to you? Are you listening? This music is thousands of years old; it makes me laugh, the British going over there and telling them what to do. Quite amazing." And he switched on the television set.

Experience has sown few seeds of doubt in him: not that his mind is closed, but it's closed round whatever he believes at the time. "Christianity will go," he said. "It will vanish and shrink. I needn't argue about that; I'm right and I will be proved right. We're more popular than Jesus now; I don't know which will go first—rock 'n' roll or Christianity. Jesus was all right but his disciples were thick and ordinary. It's them twisting it that ruins it for me." He is reading extensively about religion.

He shops in lightning swoops on Asprey's these days and there is some fine wine in his cellar, but he is still quite unselfconscious. He is far too lazy to keep up appearances, even if he had worked out what the appearances should be—which he has not.

He is now 25. He lives in a large, heavily panelled, heavily carpeted, mock Tudor house set on a hill with his wife Cynthia and his son Julian. There is a cat called after his aunt Mimi, and a purple dining room. Julian is three; he may be sent to the Lycée in London. "Seems the only place for him in his position," said his father, surveying him dispassionately. "I feel sorry for him, though. I couldn't stand ugly people even when I was five. Lots of the ugly ones are foreign, aren't they?"

We did a speedy tour of the house, Julian panting along behind, clutching a large porcelain Siamese cat. John swept past the objects in which he had lost interest: "That's Sidney" (a suit of armour); "That's a hobby I had for a week" (a room full of model racing cars); "Cyn won't let me get rid of that" (a fruit machine). In the sitting room are eight little green boxes with winking red lights; he bought them as Christmas presents but never got round to giving them away. They wink for a year; one imagines him sitting there till next Christmas, surrounded by the little winking boxes.

He paused over objects he still fancies; a huge altar crucifix of a Roman Catholic nature with IHS on it; a pair of crutches, a present from George; an enormous Bible he bought in Chester; his gorilla suit.

"I thought I might need a gorilla suit," he said; he seemed sad about it. "I've only worn it twice. I thought I might pop it on in the summer and drive round in the Ferrari. We were all going to get them and drive round in them but I was the only one who did. I've been thinking about it and if I didn't wear the head it would make an amazing fur coat—with legs, you see. I would like a fur coat but I've never run into any."

One feels that his possessions—to which he adds daily—have got the upper hand; all the tape recorders, the five television sets, the cars, the telephones of which he knows not a single number. The moment he approaches a switch it fuses; six of the winking boxes, guaranteed to last till next Christmas, have gone funny already. His cars—the Rolls, the Mini-Cooper (black wheels, black windows), the Ferrari (being painted black)— puzzle him. Then there's the swimming pool, the trees sloping away beneath it. "Nothing like what I ordered," he said resignedly. He wanted the bottom to be a mirror. "It's an amazing household," he said. "None of my gadgets really work except the gorilla suit—that's the only suit that fits me."

He is very keen on books, will always ask what is good to read. He buys quantities of books and these are kept tidily in a special room. He has Swift, Tennyson, Huxley, Orwell, costly leather-bound editions of Tolstoy, Oscar Wilde. Then there's *Little Women,* all the *William* books from his childhood; and some unexpected volumes such as *Forty-One Years in India,* by Field Marshal Lord Roberts, and *Curiosities of Natural History,* by Francis T. Buckland. This last—with its chapter headings "Ear-less Cats," "Wooden-Legged People," "The Immortal Harvey's Mother"—is right up his street.

He approaches reading with a lively interest untempered by too much formal education. "I've read millions of books," he said, "that's why I seem to know things." He is obsessed by Celts. "I have decided I am a Celt," he said. "I am on Boadicea's side—all those bloody blue-eyed blondes chopping people up. I have an awful feeling wishing I was there—not there with scabs and sores but there through *reading* about it. The books don't give you more than a paragraph about how they *lived;* I have to imagine that."

He can sleep almost indefinitely, is probably the laziest person in England. *"Physically* lazy," he said. "I don't mind writing or reading or watching or speaking, but sex is the only physical thing I can be bothered with any more." Occasionally he is driven to London in the Rolls by an ex-Welsh guardsman called Anthony; Anthony has a moustache that intrigues him.

The day I visited him he had been invited to lunch in London, about which he was rather excited. "Do you know how long lunch lasts?" he asked. "I've never been to lunch before. I went to a Lyons the other day and had egg and chips and a cup of tea. The waiters kept looking and saying: 'No, it *isn't* him, it *can't* be him'."

He settled himself into the car and demonstrated the television, the folding bed, the refrigerator, the writing desk, the telephone. He has spent many fruitless hours on that telephone. "I only once got through to a person," he said, "and they were out."

Anthony had spent the weekend in Wales. John asked if they'd kept a welcome for him in the hillside and Anthony said they had. They discussed the possibility of an extension for the telephone. We had to call at the doctor's because John had a bit of sea urchin in his toe. "Don't want to be like Dorothy Dandridge," he said, "dying of a splinter 50 years later." He added reassuringly that he had washed the foot in question.

We bowled along in a costly fashion through the countryside. "Famous and loaded" is how he describes himself now. "They keep telling me I'm all right for money but then I think I may have spent it all by the time I'm 40 so I keep going. That's why I started selling my cars; then I changed my mind and got them all back and a new one too.

"I want the money just to *be* rich: The only other way of getting it is to be born rich. If you have money, that's power without having to be powerful. I often think that it's all a big conspiracy, that the winners are the Government and people like us who've got the money. That joke about keeping the workers ignorant is still true; that's what they said about the Tories and the landowners and that; then Labour were meant to educate the workers but they don't seem to be doing that any more."

He has a morbid horror of stupid people: "Famous and loaded as I am, I still have to meet soft people. It often comes into my mind that I'm not really rich. There are *really* rich people but I don't know where they are."

He finds being famous quite easy, confirming one's suspicion that The Beatles had been leading up to this all their lives. "Everybody thinks they *would* have been famous if only they'd had the Latin and that. So when it happens it comes naturally. You remember your old grannie saying soft things like: 'You'll make it with that voice.' " Not, he added, that he had any old grannies.

He got to the doctor 2¾ hours early and to lunch on time but in the wrong place. He bought a giant compendium of games from Asprey's but having opened it he could not, of course, shut it again. He wondered what else he should buy. He went to Brian Epstein's office. "Any presents?" he asked eagerly; he observed that there was nothing like getting things free. He tried on the attractive Miss Hanson's spectacles.

The rumour came through that a Beatle had been sighted walking down Oxford Street! He brightened. "One of the others must be out," he said, as though speaking of an escaped bear. "We only let them out one at a time," said the attractive Miss Hanson firmly.

He said that to live and have a laugh were the things to do; but was that enough for the restless spirit?

"Weybridge," he said, "won't do at all. I'm just stopping at it, like a bus stop. Bankers and stockbrokers live there; they can add figures and Weybridge is what they live in and they think it's the end, they really do. I think of it every day—me in my Hansel and Gretel house. I'll take my time; I'll get my *real* house when I know what I want.

"You see, there's something else I'm going to do, something I must do—only I don't know what it is. That's why I go round painting and tap-ing and drawing and writing and that, because it may be one of them. All I know is, this isn't *it* for me."

Anthony got him and the compendium into the car and drove him home with the television flickering in the soothing darkness while the Londoners outside rushed home from work.

Ronnie Spector with Vince Waldron

INFLATABLE PHIL

Here's one of those weird scenes inside the gold mine that Jim Morrison warned us about. Producer-wünderkind Phil Spector plucked Veronica Bennett off the streets of New York and turned her into the leader of the sonic assault known as the Ronettes. When the girl-group sound waned in the late 1960s, Spector married Ronnie Bennett and carried her off to his Hollywood castle and made her share air space with plastic products. Read on.

THE MORNING after my wedding night, I woke up to the sound of a pile driver in the front yard. It was like coming back from a bad dream. I was lying on my mother's bathroom floor, my back felt like a pretzel, and I couldn't even remember why I was there. That's when I heard the construction crew banging away outside the window. I looked around for my mother, but she was already up.

The clanging outside was getting louder and louder, so I walked over to the window and peeked through the curtains. That's when I saw about a half dozen men putting up these big ten-foot poles all around the edges of the yard. I couldn't figure out what they were doing—I was so groggy I thought maybe they were putting up basketball hoops.

Then I glanced over to their truck, were I saw six other guys unrolling about a hundred yards of barbed wire and chain link. They were obviously building some kind of fence, but I didn't know why.

I was still trying to figure it out when I noticed that some of the guys had caught sight of me standing in the window, still wearing my skimpy negligee from the night before. I jumped back and closed the curtain. Then I grabbed my mother's robe and headed upstairs to my bedroom, praying that Phil wouldn't be in there.

I didn't have to worry—no one was in the room. But there were a dozen red roses on my pillow. I picked up the card and read an apology written in Phil's scratchy handwriting.

Forever yours,

Okay?—Phil

I sat down on the edge of the bed and breathed a sigh of relief. "Thank God, the nightmare's over." I guess I should have still been mad, but I wasn't.

By the time I got down to the kitchen, George Johnson was already fixing breakfast for Phil and my mom. Phil got up and pulled my chair out for me, like I was his little queen. It was crazy. Here he was acting like a perfect gentleman, when only a few hours earlier he had been raving like a maniac. But what's even crazier is how willing I was to forgive and forget.

The truth is, I didn't hold it against Phil when he went nuts like that. And I still don't. I knew that he only flipped out because of his insecurities, and I figured he hated himself enough without me adding to his troubles. If I could remain his loving and patient wife, I thought, Phil would eventually come around to being a kind and loving husband. At least that was my fantasy. And I was determined to make it come true. I was going to have my Ozzie and Harriet life, even if I had to go through hell to get it.

I had high hopes for my marriage, but I soon discovered that life as a millionaire's wife wasn't all that different from just being shacked up with a millionaire. At least not if that millionaire was Phil Spector.

After the wedding, Phil seemed no more eager to get back to the studio than before. But by that time it almost didn't matter—I'd been away from recording for so long that my confidence was almost completely drained away. I'd always been a little insecure that I didn't have a gospel-trained voice like Patti LaBelle, but after my own husband turned his back on me, I began to wonder if I was ever any good to begin with. Finally, I just grew to accept that I was all washed up.

"Forget about singing," I told myself. "Your voice is not happening. That's done with. Just try to be a good wife. That's your life now."

The trouble was, I didn't know how to be a good wife when there was nothing wifely for me to do. I'd get up in the morning and there'd be a maid there to do up the beds. Then I'd go downstairs and find another maid vacuuming my rugs. There was even a guy who came in twice a week to do the dusting.

I wasn't even welcome in my own kitchen. I found that out the hard way, after I snuck down there late one night to fix myself an egg salad sandwich. George couldn't find his measuring cup the next day, and I caught hell for it. No matter how much I denied touching that measuring cup, Phil wouldn't let up.

"It doesn't matter!" he shouted. "You were in the kitchen, and you shouldn't have been there. I pay George good money to cook for us, so stay the hell out of there and let him do his job."

I looked over at George, hoping he might come to my defense. But he kept right on chopping onions. After Phil left, he looked up and said, "This isn't my argument, Miss Veronica. You know that."

My only household duty was to get up in the morning and discuss with George what Phil and I wanted for dinner. After that, I'd go out to the pool and watch Phil do his laps. I never learned how to swim, so I'd just splash around in the shallow end. Then I'd go back into the house and watch other people do my housework. I felt so bored and useless that after a while I'd just go into the TV room and watch old Bette Davis movies. And those didn't exactly cheer me up.

Bette always seemed to be crying about something. Or getting drunk. After I saw a few of these films, I started to notice that whenever Bette Davis or Joan Crawford got depressed, they always went to the bar and got a drink. After a while I started doing the same thing.

Phil had a liquor cabinet in his downstairs game room. It was hidden away in the wall behind the fireplace, but I discovered it by accident one night while he was out at the pool hall. I was poking around the game room, bored as usual, when I saw this little button hidden away in the back of a thick wooden pillar. Naturally, I pushed it. Out of nowhere this antique bar swung down like something out of an old mystery movie. And suddenly I'm standing there looking at a half dozen bottles of vodka, scotch, and rye whiskey.

I poured myself a full glass of scotch in a big beaker. No one ever taught me how to drink, so I just treated alcohol like it was soda pop. Of course, it was a lot harder going down than pop, and it didn't taste as good. In fact, I hated the taste of liquor. But I knew that if I drank enough of it I would begin to feel a little light-headed, so I'd hold my nose and down it went.

After I discovered Phil's magic bar, I'd sneak down there and make myself a drink whenever he left me alone at night. Then I'd take it back up to the TV room and sit there, my drink in one hand and a cigarette in the other, just like Bette Davis. If the movie was sad—and they always seemed sad to me, even the comedies—I'd run into the bathroom and cry. Pretty soon I'd pass out and go to sleep. And that was always the best thing about alcohol, that it made me sleep.

*   *   *

Of all the things that seemed to go wrong during that first year of marriage, I think the thing that depressed me worst of all was that I couldn't get pregnant. And I wanted kids more than anything. My fantasy of marriage had always been to have kids, a loving husband, and a great career. After six months of marriage to Phil, I would have been willing to settle for just the kids. But I couldn't even have that. No matter what we did, I just couldn't get pregnant. And we tried everything.

We kept a thermometer near the bed and tried to have sex when my body was at just the right temperature to make a baby. We had sex in all different positions, and at all different times of the day. I even had artificial insemination. I'd take Phil's sperm to the doctor's office and have it injected. But that didn't work either.

I went to ten different doctors. I saw specialists in England and America and Europe, too. And every one said the same thing: "Your body's fine. Just relax and let nature take its course." But when nature didn't take its course, I blamed myself completely. And once I decided it was all my fault, I started putting myself down worse than ever. I couldn't make it as a singer, I was a flop as a wife, and now I find out I'm a failure at being a woman, too! It wasn't long before I began to seriously wonder if maybe I wasn't just a bad person all around.

It never even occurred to me that the problem might have been with Phil. Of course, he never considered going in for an examination himself. The most he ever did was go into the bathroom and jerk off into a jar so I could take it to the doctor for artificial insemination. But none of the doctors ever suggested that it might be a low sperm count on Phil's part. "Just relax," they told me. "You'll have your baby." But I convinced myself they were lying.

The worst part about not being able to have kids was that this was the one area where Phil and I agreed completely. He wanted children as badly as I did. That was all we talked about. I guess we both wanted to start building a family because our careers just weren't happening.

Our lovemaking got a little strained under the pressure to get results, but we kept at it. Up until then we'd always had a pretty good sex life. He sometimes wore a hat to bed because of his hangup about being bald, but other than that, I had no complaints. Even so, good sex or bad, we still couldn't make any babies.

Phil still spent a lot of time alone in his study. There, or downstairs playing pool in his game room. Phil's pool craze began around the time he went into retirement in 1966, but after we got married it turned into a real obsession. He actually started paying big-time pool hustlers like Minnesota Fats and Willie Moscone to come over to the house and play with him. And whenever those big shots came over for one of Phil's all-night tournaments, I'd have to go downstairs so he could show me off.

"This is my wife, Veronica," he'd announce. And then there would be the pictures. "Hey, Fats," Phil would say. "You want to take a picture with my wife? Come on, Veronica, stand over there with Fats." From the way they looked at me, it was obvious that most of these guys thought I was pretty hot stuff. Phil noticed this, too, so he always made sure to pack me up and send me back upstairs as soon as the cameras stopped clicking.

Then he'd follow me upstairs to give me a good-night kiss before he went down to be with his pool friends. I'd just have time to get snuggled up in bed when he'd come walking in with a tray of grilled cheese sandwiches in one hand and my favorite doll in the other. Then he'd set the tray on my bedside table and place the doll gently in my arms. "Good night, darling," he'd say, stroking my cheek with the back of his fingers. "I'll see you in the morning." He'd put on a Tony Bennett or Frank Sinatra record and turn off the lights. Then he'd be gone. Even when he was abandoning me to play pool with a bunch of fat guys, Phil still made me feel like I was the only girl in the world.

The fact is, for Phil I *was* the only girl in the world. And he never let me forget it. I thought he'd be less jealous after we got married, but he actually got worse. I came down to the swimming pool in a bikini once, and Phil practically fell off the diving board.

"Are you crazy?" he asked. "Get back in the house before somebody sees you."

"Oh, Phil," I said, trying not to take him too seriously. "Who's gonna see me in my own yard?"

"The *manservants,*" he whispered, as if I was an idiot for not realizing it sooner. So back I went to change my suit.

I never could get used to the life of a recluse. I grew up in New York, where you could always run out to the corner store in rain or sleet or snow. But there are no corner stores in Beverly Hills. Where I lived, you were lucky if you could find a corner. The only time I got out was when Phil let George Brand or one of the other servants drive me over to my friend Bobbie Golson's house, and even then he would have them wait outside in the car so they could bring me back after an hour. I was starting to feel like a prisoner in my own house, and it was beginning to get to me.

Phil must have sensed I was going a little nuts under the strain, because he finally surprised me with a car of my own for my twenty-fifth birthday in 1968. It was a Camaro, orange and white, and I was blown away when I first saw it in the driveway, all wrapped in a huge white ribbon.

A brand-new car! All shiny and new. And it was mine, all mine. And there certainly wasn't any doubt about that, because Phil had it monogrammed in about twenty-three places. No matter where you looked—on the doors, on the top of the trunk, even on the glove compartment—you couldn't miss the initials *V.S.* for Veronica Spector.

Looking back, it's interesting that he chose those particular initials. Veronica was Phil's name for me. He never called me Ronnie anymore. It was like he saw me as two different people—Ronnie, the happy, sexy rock and roller that I was before the marriage; and Veronica, the obedient Beverly Hills wife that he wanted now.

After Phil went into his early retirement, my rock and roll past became a painful reminder of the accomplishments he could no longer live up to. So he erased Ronnie from his mind. And now, in her place, he was trying to create Veronica, a loyal and quiet wife who would be perfectly happy to waste away with him in the dark corners of his musty old mansion. He may not even have been completely aware of it himself, but Phil was trying to brainwash me every single day of our marriage.

And he was a born expert at mind control. His giving me a monogrammed car is a perfect example. He knew that the only time I would ever really be alone was when I was driving, so he made sure that the car I drove was loaded with little initials that sent a message loud and clear: "You may be alone in your car, but you're not free. You're 'V.S.' now—Mrs. Veronica Spector—and don't you forget it. Little Ronnie Bennett is dead."

It might seem farfetched that anyone would put that much energy into controlling someone else's life, but that was Phil. You've got to remember, the man was a genius. And he had nothing better to do with his life after he retired from rock and roll. So turning me into the perfect wife became his major project, just as making me into a number-one singer had been his goal five years earlier.

Monogramming my car was just the beginning. That was nothing compared to my custom-made inflatable Phil. I got him the same night Phil gave me the car. In fact, I was still gushing over my new Camaro when Phil walked back and popped open the trunk. "There's more," he said. "Wait'll you see this." And in all the years I knew Phil, I don't think I was ever quite as amazed as when he reached into the trunk of my brand-new car and pulled out that life-sized inflatable plastic mannequin.

"What do you think?" he asked, holding it in the air like a giant trophy. I didn't know what to say. The thing was as big as he was, and it was dressed in a pair of his best pants and a freshly ironed shirt. In fact, the thing looked exactly like Phil in every way, except that its knees were bent in a permanent sitting position.

"Well," I said. "It's you, right?" He nodded his head.

"C'mon," he said. "Is it perfect or what?"

"Yeah. It's . . . really . . ." I paused, wracking my brain for the right word. "Perfect. But, Phil. What is it supposed to do?"

"I'll show you," he said. I watched in utter amazement as he walked to the passenger door, opened it, and carefully placed the inflatable Phil in the bucket seat. Then he fastened a seat belt across the guy's lap, straightened its shirt collar, and adjusted the cloth hat that sat on top of the thing's pink plastic head. "There," he said, stepping back. "Oh, wait," he added. "Almost forgot the finishing touch."

Then he ran back over to the inflatable man, pulled out a cigarette, and fitted it into the thing's mouth. Finally, he slammed the door and stood back. "Tah-*daah!*" he said, turning to me with a crooked little smile. "What do you think?"

"It's great, Phil," I said, and I wasn't lying. Sitting there like that, this plastic guy really did look almost real. "But I still don't get it," I said. "Why do I want it to look like there's somebody in the car with me when there isn't?"

"Don't you get it?" he asked in a tone of voice that made me feel like I must've missed something. "It's for when you're driving alone." I still looked completely confused, so he spelled it out for me. "Now nobody will fuck with you when you're driving alone."

So that was it. Phil had actually gone to the trouble of making a dummy of himself to watch over me when he wasn't around. I was wondering if he'd gone insane as I watched him make a few last-minute adjustments in the tilt of the guy's hat. He really was proud of his little masterpiece.

"Phil," I said, giving him a great big kiss. "Sometimes you really are too much."

ALTAMONT

It was supposed to be a Woodstock West. Approximately 300,000 fans descended on the Altamont Speedway outside of San Francisco in December 1969 to hear a free concert by the Rolling Stones, the Grateful Dead, Jefferson Airplane, Santana, and the Flying Burrito Brothers. Instead of the "peace, love and flowers" promised—and, mostly, delivered—at Woodstock, Altamont offered paranoia, hate, and murder.

Stage security was managed by the Hell's Angels, the outlaw motorcycle gang. The Rolling Stones and the Grateful Dead, co-sponsors of the concert, thought they got a bargain: for $500 worth of beer, they got the bad-ass Angels to patrol the stage. What the musicians probably didn't consider was that the Angels would turn on the audience and, in one case, the performers. (Marty Balin of Jefferson Airplane was punched by an Angel.)

The concert had started as a logistical nightmare, and then things got worse. In addition to the Stones (Mick Jagger, Keith Richards, Charlie Watts, Bill Wyman, and Mick Taylor), the cast included stage announcer Sam Cutler, filmmakers Albert and David Maysles (whose cameras recorded the murder of a fan at Altamont), a lot of burly Hell's Angels, thousands of drunken fans, writer Stanley Booth, and, possibly, the ghost of Robert Johnson. There were four deaths, total, at the concert. The Maysles brothers couldn't find a better title for their documentary than the name of a new Stones song: "Gimme Shelter."

ON THE PA system Sam was saying, "The reason we can't start is that the stage is loaded with people. I've done all I can do. The stage must be cleared or we can't start." His voice sounded dead tired and flat and beyond caring.

An Angel—President Sonny Barger of the Oakland chapter, I believe—

took the mike and said, in a voice not unlike Howlin' Wolf's, "All right, everybody off the stage including the Hell's Angels," and people started to move. Angels were on top of the trucks, behind the stage, on the side of the stage, on the steps to the stage. I was holding my notebook, thinking, God, where to begin, when I was wheeled around—All *right, off the stage.* Looking to see what had me, I found his body to my left, dressed in greasy denim, but no head. Still, he picked me up by the biceps so quickly and brought me with such dispatch to his eye level that I couldn't complain about losing lots of time. His eyes were hidden under the lank rat-blond hair that fell over his grime-blackened face. There they were, glints in the gloom, but they were not looking at me or at anything, he was so high he was blind, eyeless in Gaza.

Eyeballs rolling like porcelain marbles in their sockets, jaws grinding, teeth gnashing saliva in anger, "Off the *stage,"* he repeated in mild admonition, gentle reproof. It was that ever fresh, ever new, ever magic moment when you are about to be beaten to a pulp or to whatever your assailant can manage. This one, unlike the old last of the Confederates cop at the Ed Sullivan show, could, at least with his comrades, pound me into tapioca. I was in midair, still holding my notebook, thinking that I could reach up and thumb his eyes, I could put my hands behind his head and bring my knee up fast, depriving him of his teeth, or I could shove two fingers into his nostrils and rip his face off, but a little bird on the hillside was telling me that the moment I did any of these things, hundreds of Angels would start stomping. I don't remember what I told him. My next clear memory is of being alone again behind the amps. I wasn't even wearing any badges. Earlier today, on the way to the helicopter, Ronnie had been talking about newspapermen calling for press passes, not believing there weren't any. It's free, he told them, just come. Free at last. Well, not exactly. . . .

The Stones were coming up the four steps between the trucks onto the stage, a brightly lit center in the black fold of hills. The crowd, estimated by the news media at between two and five hundred thousand, had been tightly packed when we struggled through them about five hours ago. Now they were one solid mass jammed against the stage. There were eager-eyed boys and girls down front, Angels all around, tour guards trying to maintain positions between the Angels and the Stones. A New York City detective at Altamont was a long way off his beat. The expressions on the cops' faces said they didn't like this scene at all, but they're not scared, just sorrowful-eyed like men who know trouble and know that they are in the midst of a lot of people who are asking for it. Against the stage, in the center of the crowd, a black cop with a mustache watched, his expression mournful, his white canvas golf-hat brim pulled down as if he were in a downpour.

Sam came to the singer's mike and in an infinitely weary voice said, "One, two, testing," then with a glimmer of enthusiasm, "I'd like to introduce to everybody—from Britain—the Rolling Stones."

There was a small cheer from the crowd—they seemed numb, not vibrant like the audiences in the basketball gyms after Tina Turner—whoops and yells and shrieks but not one great roar. Bass-thumps, guitars tuning, drum diddles, Mick: "All right! Whooooh!"—rising note—"Oww babe! Aw yeah! Aww, so good to see ya all! Whoo!" Last tuning notes, then the opening chords of "Jumpin' Jack Flash." . . .

Some people were dancing, Angels dancing with their dirty bouffant women. A pall of wariness and fear seemed to be upon the people who were not too stoned to be aware, but the music was pounding on and though the drums were not properly miked and the guitars seemed to separate and disappear in places and you couldn't really hear Wyman's bass, it was hanging together.

"Ooh, yah," Mick said as the song ended. He stopped dancing, looked into the distance, and his voice, which had been subdued, now began to sound pacific, as he glimpsed for the first time the enormity of what he had created. One surge forward and people would be crushed. Half a million people together, with neither rules nor regulations as to how they must conduct themselves, can through sheer physical weight create terrible destruction. "Oooh, babies—" low motherly tone "—there are so many of you—just be cool down front now, don't push around—just keep still." He laughed as if he were talking to a child, looking down at the pretty stoned faces before him. "Keep together—oh yah."

Keith tested the first three notes of "Carol," unleashed the riff, and Mick leaned back to sing

> Oh, Carol! Don't ever steal your heart away
> I'm gonna learn to dance if it takes me all night
> and day

The sound was better, drums and bass clearer, guitars stronger. At the end Mick said, "Whoo! Whoo! Aw, yes!" He hoisted a bottle of Jack Daniel's that was sitting in front of the drums. "I'd like to drink, ah, drink one to you all."

Keith set out on "Sympathy for the Devil." As Mick sang, "I was around when Jesus Christ had his moment of doubt and pain," there was a low explosive *thump!* in the crowd to the right of the stage, and oily blue-white smoke swirled up as if someone had thrown a toad into a witches' cauldron. People were pushing, falling, a great hole opening as they moved instantly away from the center of the trouble. I had no idea people in a crowd could move so fast. Mick stopped singing but the music chugged on, four bars, eight, then Mick shouted: "Hey! Heeey! Hey! Keith-Keith-Keith!" By now only Keith was playing, but he was playing as loud and hard as ever, the way the band is supposed to do until the audience tears down the chicken wire and comes onstage with chairs and broken bottles. "Will you cool it and I'll try and stop it," Mick said, so Keith stopped.

"Hey—hey, peo-ple," Mick said. "Sisters—brothers and sisters—*brothers and sisters—come on* now." He was offering the social contract to a twister of flailing dark shapes. "That means everybody just cool out—will ya cool out, everybody—"

"Somebody's bike blew-up, man," Keith said.

"I know," Mick said. "I'm hip. Everybody be cool now, come on all right? Can we still make it down in the front? Can we still collect ourselves, everybody? Can everybody just—I don't know what happened, I couldn't see, but I hope ya all right—are ya all right?" The trouble spot seemed still. Charlie was making eager drum flutters, Keith playing stray notes.

"Okay," Mick said. "Let's just give ourselves—we'll give ourselves another half a minute before we get our breath back, everyone just cool down and easy—is there anyone there who's hurt—huh?—everyone all right—okay—all right." The music was starting again. "Good, we can groove—summin' very funny happens when we start that numbah-ah, ha!"

Keith and Charlie had the rhythm pattern going, tight and expert, and Mick asked again to be allowed to introduce himself, a man of wealth and taste, but not about to lay anybody's soul to waste. Keith's solo cut like a scream into the brain, as Mick chanted, "Everybody got to cool out—everybody has got to cool right out—yeah! Aw right!"

Sounding like one instrument, a wild whirling bagpipe, the Stones chugged to a halt. But the crowd didn't stop, we could see Hell's Angels spinning like madmen, swinging at people. By stage right a tall white boy with a black cloud of electric hair was dancing, shaking, infuriating the Angels by having too good a time. He was beside an Angel when I first saw him, and I wondered how he could be so loose, nearly touching one of those monsters. He went on dancing and the Angel pushed him and another Angel started laying into the crowd with a pool cue and then a number of

Angels were grabbing people, hitting and kicking, the crowd falling back from the fury with fantastic speed, the dancer running away from the stage, the crowd parting before him like the Red Sea, the Angels catching him from behind, the heavy end of a pool cue in one long arc crashing into the side of his head, felling him like a sapling so that he lay straight and didn't move and I thought, My God, they've killed him. But they weren't through. When he went down they were all over him, pounding with fists and cues, and when he was just lying there they stood for a while kicking him like kicking the dead carcass of an animal, the meat shaking on the bones.

The song was over and Mick was saying, "Who—who—I mean like people, who's fighting and what for? Hey, peo-ple—I mean, who's fighting and what for? Why are we fighting? Why are we fighting?" His voice was strong, emphasizing each word. "We don't want to fight. Come on—do we want, who wants to fight? Hey—I—you know, I mean like—every other scene has been cool. Like we've gotta stop right now. We've gotta stop them right now. You know, we can't, there's no point."

Sam took the microphone. "Could I suggest a compromise, please." He was a bit more awake now and the soul of peace and reason. "Can I ask please to speak to the—" He stopped then because the logical conclusion was, "—to the Hell's Angels and ask them please to stop performing mayhem on people."

"Either those cats cool it," Keith said, "or we don't play. I mean, there's not that many of 'em."

It was a fine brave thing to say, but I had made up my mind about fighting the Hell's Angels while one of them had me in the air, and probably the rest of the people present had concluded some time ago that the first man who touched an Angel would surely die. Even as Keith spoke an Angel was ripping into someone in front of stage left. "That guy there," Keith said, "if he doesn't stop it—"

There was a pause while another Angel did slowly stop him. Still another Angel yelled to ask Keith what he wanted. "I just want him to stop pushin' people around," Keith said.

An Angel came to the mike and bellowed into it. "Hey, if you don't cool it you ain't gonna hear no more music! Now, you wanta all go home, or what?" It was like blaming the pigs in a slaughterhouse for bleeding on the floor.

*   *   *

You felt that in the next seconds or minutes you could die, and there was nothing you could do to prevent it, to improve the odds for survival. A bad dream, but we were all in it.

I looked around, checking my position, which if not the worst was not good, and saw David Maysles on top of a truck behind the stage. Ethan Russell and Al Maysles were up there with their cameras, and more people, including a couple of Hell's Angels sitting in front dangling their legs over the side like little boys fishing at a creek in the nineteenth century.

"Hey! David!" I said.

"You want to get up here?"

"Sure." I stuck my notebook behind my belt and swung aboard, being careful not to jostle the Angels. At least now I would be behind them, instead of having it the other way round, which had given me worse chills than the wind did up here. It was cold away from the warm amps but this was, I hoped, a safer place and better to see from.

Hunkered behind the Angels, I noticed that only one wore colors, the other one in his cowboy hat and motorcycle boots was just a sympathizer. Sam was saying, "The doctor is going through in a green jumper and he's just here—" pointing in front "wavin' his hand in the air, look" The mass, like a dumb aquatic beast, had closed up again except for a little space around the body. (The boy didn't die, to my and probably his—surprise.) "Can you let the doctor go through please and let him get to the person who's hurt?" Someone in front spoke to Sam, who added wearily, "We have also—lost in the front here—a little girl who's five years old."

Charlie was playing soft rolls, Keith was playing a slow blues riff. "Let's play cool-out music," Keith said to Mick.

They played a repeating twelve-bar pattern that stopped in half a minute. "Keep going," Mick said, and it started again, a meditative walking-bass line, the Stones trying to orient themselves by playing an Elmore James/Jimmy Reed song they had played in damp London caverns. "The sun is shining on both sides of the street," Mick sang. "I got a smile on my face for every little girl I meet." The slow blues did seem to help things, a little. A huge Angel with long blond hair, brown suede vest, no shirt, blue jeans, was standing behind gentle Charlie, patting his foot, one giant hand resting on Charlie's white pullover. The song ended without event and Mick said, "We all dressed up, we got no place to go," which was all too true.

"Stray Cat," Keith said, but there was another flurry of fighting stage right, partly hidden from us by the PA scaffold, a tower of speakers.

"Hey—heyheyhey look," Mick said. Then to Keith or to no one he said, "Those *scenes* down there."

I leaned forward and spoke to the cowboy hat. "What's happening, man," I asked. "Why are they fighting?"

Over his shoulder, out of the corner of his mouth, he said, "Some smart asshole, man, some wise guy wants to start trouble—and these guys are tired, man, they been here all night, some wise guy starts something they don't like it—arhh, I can't tell you what happened." Taking a jug of acid-apple juice from his Angel friend, he drank till his eyes looked, as Wynonie Harris used to say, like two cherries in a glass of buttermilk. Me, I lay low.

"Stray Cat" started, Mick sounding perfunctory, forgetting the words here and there, Keith playing madly.

A girl down front was shaking with the music and crying as if her dream of life had ended. In the backstage aisle between the trucks, the Angels and their women were doing their stiff jerking dance. Most of the women were hard-looking tattooed types with shellacked hairdos, but one of them, no more than fourteen, with a dirty, pretty-baby face, wearing a black leather jacket, was moving the seat of her greasy jeans wildly, and I thought of the little guerrilla in Fort Collins and was glad she wasn't in this crowd.

The Angel standing with his hand on Charlie's shoulder was being asked to step down off the stage by one of the New York heavies, a red-faced, red-haired, beefy man dressed in the light golf-jacket uniform. You could follow what they were saying by their gestures. The cop told the Angel to step down, the Angel shook his head, the cop told him again and pushed him a little. The cop had a cigarette in his mouth and the Angel took it out, just plucked it from between the cop's lips like taking a rose from the mouth of the fair Carmen, causing the cop to regard the Angel with a sorrowful countenance. It was only when two more men in golf jackets turned around and faced the Angel with expressions equally dolorous that he went down the steps. He came back a minute later but stayed at the rear of the stage, dancing, twitching like a frog attached to electrodes.

As "Stray Cat" ended, Mick said, "Ooh baby," looking up as if for deliverance and finding a shapeless human mass reaching into the darkness as far as be could see. "Baby—all along a hillside—hey, everybody, ah—we gone do, we gone do, ah—what are we gonna do?"

"Love in Vain," Keith said. The slow elegant Robert Johnson line began, building slowly. "I followed her to the station with my suitcase in my hand—oh, it's hard to tell, when all your love's in vain." The Stones had not forgotten how to play, but nobody seemed to be enjoying the music, at least nobody who could be seen in the lights that made the stage the glowing center of a world of night. Too many people were still too close together and the Angels were still surly. At stage right an Angel with a skinful of acid was writhing and wringing his hands in a pantomime of twisting Mick's neck. At stage left Timothy Leary huddled with his wife and daughter, looking as if he'd taken better trips. The stage skirts were so crowded that Mick had only a limited area to work. He looked cramped, smaller than ever and cowed, frightened, but he kept on singing.

Things were quiet during "Love in Vain" except for some heavy jostling down front, the prevailing mood of impending death, and the fear and anguish you could see in the faces. "Aw yeah," Mick said as the song ended. "Hey, I think—I think, I think, that there was one good idea came out of that number, which was, that I really think the only way you're gonna keep yourselves cool is to *sit down.* If you can make it I think you'll find it's better. So when you're sitting comfortably—now, boys and girls—" withdrawing the social contract "—Are you sitting, comfortably? When, when we get to really like the end and we all want to go absolutely crazy and like jump on each other then we'll stand up again, d'you know what I mean—but we can't seem to keep it together, standing up—okay?"

In the background Keith was tooling up the opening chords of "Under My Thumb." A few people in front of the stage were sitting, going along with Mick, who for the first time in his life had asked an audience to sit down. The anarchist was telling people what to do. Then, just before he began to sing, he said, "But it ain't a rule."

"Under My Thumb" started—"Hey! Hey! Under my thumb is a girl who once had me down—" and Mick had sung only the first line of the song when there was a sudden movement in the crowd at stage left. I looked away from Mick and saw, with that now-familiar instant space around him, bordered with falling bodies, a Beale Street nigger in a black hat, black shirt, iridescent blue-green suit, arms and legs stuck out at crazy angles, a nickle-plated revolver in his hand. The gun waved in the lights for a second, two, then he was hit, so hard, by so many Angels, that I didn't see the first one—short, Mexican-looking, the one who led me onstage?— as he jumped. I saw him as he came down, burying a long knife in the black man's back. Angels covered the black man like flies on a stinking carcass. The attack carried the victim behind the stack of speakers, and I never saw him again.

The black man, Meredith Hunter, nicknamed Murdock, was eighteen years old. He had come to Altamont with his girlfriend, Patty Bredehoft, a blond Berkeley High School student, and another couple. They had arrived in Hunter's car at about two o'clock in the afternoon, parked on the highway and walked over to hear the bands. Near the end of the day Patty

Bredehoft and the other couple were back at the car when Hunter, who had been hanging around the stage area, came to get her to go hear the Rolling Stones. Later she told the Alameda County Grand Jury, "When we finally worked our way up to the front of the crowd and the Rolling Stones started playing, there was a lot of pushing and there were Angels on the stage. And Murdock kept trying to go farther up toward the front. I couldn't keep up with him because I wasn't strong so I sort of waited back, didn't try to get as far as he did. He was as close as he could get, where there were some boxes with people standing on the boxes. I'd say there was about five people in between me and him, estimating, because the crowd was moving around, but I could see the upper part of his body.

"I was getting pushed around, and as I glanced up there, I saw either he had hit Murdock or pushed him or something, but this Hell's Angel who was standing, pushed him or knocked him back. It didn't knock him down, but knocked him back over the stage, and as he started to come back forward towards the Hell's Angel, another Hell's Angel who was on the stage grabbed him around the neck. They were scuffling around. I'm not sure which Hell's Angel it was, but I just remember he was scuffling around and there was a couple of people blocking my view of him because he was down on the ground. I couldn't really see him. As the people backed away, Murdock came around by my side and pulled a gun out. Then they came toward—well, a group of Hell's Angels—I'm not sure they were all Hell's Angels, but I know most of them were—they came toward him and they reached for his arm and then they were all kicking and fighting and stuff, Murdock and the Hell's Angels, and the fight more or less moved around towards where the scaffold was on the edge of the stage.

"I followed them around and then I was standing there watching them fight, or watching whatever—I couldn't really tell what was going on underneath the scaffold, and the Hell's Angel—I thought he was, was a Hell's Angel, but I wasn't quite sure because he had the jeans jacket on, but I couldn't see the back to see if it had colors on. He was holding the gun in his hand, laying in the palm of his hand, to show it to me, and he said something like, 'This is what we took from him. He was going to kill innocent people, so he deserved to be dead.' "

A young man named Paul Cox, who had been standing beside Meredith Hunter before the violence started, talked to the grand jury and to *Rolling Stone*. "An Angel kept looking over at me and I tried to keep ignoring him and I didn't want to look at him at all, because I was very scared of them and seeing what they were doing all day and because he kept trying to cause a fight or something and kept staring at us. He kept on looking over, and the next thing I know he's hassling this Negro boy on the side of me. And I was trying not to look at him, and then he reached over and shook this boy by the side of the head, thinking it was fun, laughing, and I noticed something was going to happen so I kind of backed off.

"The boy yanked away, and when he yanked away, next thing I know he was flying in the air, right on the ground, just like all the other people it happened to. He scrambled to his feet, and he's backing up and he's trying to run from the Angels, and all these Angels are—a couple jumped off the stage and a couple was running alongside the stage, and his girlfriend was screaming to him not to shoot, because be pulled out his gun. And when he pulled it out, he held it in the air and his girlfriend is like climbing on him and pushing him back and he's trying to get away and these Angels are coming at him and he turns around and starts running. And then some Angel snuck up from right out of the crowd and leaped up and brought this knife down in his back. And then I saw him stab him again, and while he's stabbing him, he's running. This Negro boy is running into the crowd, and you could see him stiffen up when he's being stabbed.

"He came running toward me. I grabbed onto the scaffold, and he came running kind of toward me and fell down on his knees, and the Hell's Angel grabbed onto both of his shoulders and started kicking him in the face about five times or so and then he fell down on his face. He let go and he fell down on his face. And then one of them kicked him on the side and he rolled over, and he muttered some words. He said, 'I wasn't going to shoot you.' That was the last words he muttered.

"If some other people would have jumped in I would have jumped in. But nobody jumped in and after he said, 'I wasn't going to shoot you,' one of the Hell's Angels said, 'Why did you have a gun?' He didn't give him time to say anything. He grabbed one of those garbage cans, the cardboard ones with the metal rimming, and he smashed him over the head with it, and then he kicked the garbage can out of the way and started kicking his head in. Five of them started kicking his head in. Kicked him all over the place. And then the guy that started the whole thing stood on his head for a minute or so and then walked off. And then the one I was talking about, he wouldn't let us touch him for about two or three minutes. Like, 'Don't touch him, he's going to die anyway, let him die, he's going to die.'

"Chicks were just screaming. It was all confusion. I jumped down anyway to grab him and some other dude jumped down and grabbed him, and then the Hell's Angel just stood over him for a little bit and then walked away. We turned him over and ripped off his shirt. We rubbed his back up and down to get the blood off so we could see, and there was a big hole in his spine and a big hole on the side and there was a big hole in his temple. A big open slice. You could see all the way in. You could see inside. You could see at least an inch down. And then there was a big hole right where there's no ribs on his back—and then the side of his head was just sliced open—you couldn't see so far in—it was bleeding quite heavily—but his back wasn't bleeding too heavy after that—there—all of us were drenched in blood."

*　　*　　*

When the trouble with the boy in the green suit started, the Stones had stopped playing. "Okay, man," Keith said, "look, we're splitting, if those cats, if you can't—we're splitting, if those people don't stop beating everybody up in sight—I want 'em *out of the way.*"

An Angel in front of the stage was trying to tell Keith something, but Keith wouldn't listen. "I don't like *you* to tell me—" he went on, but another Angel, onstage, stopped him. "Look, man," the Angel said, "a guy's got a gun out there, and he's shootin' at the stage—"

"Got a gun," someone else yelled.

*　　*　　*

After another pause during which no one onstage did anything but look anxiously around, Mick said, "It seems to be stuck down to me will you listen to me for a minute—please listen to me just for one second a'right? First of all, everyone is gonna get to the side of the stage who's on it now except for the Stones who are playing. Please, everyone—everyone, please, can you get to the side of the stage who's not playing. Right? That's a start. Now, the thing is, I can't see what's going on, who is doing wot, it's just a scuffle. All I can ask you, San Francisco, is like the whole thing—this could be the most beautiful evening we've had this winter. We really—y'know, why, why—don't let's fuck it up, man, come on—let's get it together—everyone—come on now—I can't see you up on the hillsides, you're probably very cool. Down here we're not so cool, we've got a lot of hassles goin' on. I just—every cat. . . ."

There were shouts from the darkness. Mick peered out blindly past the stage lights and answered, "Yeah, I know, we can't even see you but I know you're where—you're cool. We're just trying to keep it together. I can't do any more than ask you—beg you, just to keep it together. You can do it, it's within your power—everyone—Hell's Angels, everybody. Let's just keep ourselves together.

"You know," Mick said with a sudden burst of passion, "if we *are* all one, let's fucking well *show* we're all one. Now there's one thing we need—Sam, we need an ambulance—we need a doctor by that scaffold there, if there's a doctor can he get to there. Okay, we're gonna, we gonna do—I don't know what the fuck we gonna do. Everyone just sit down. Keep cool. Let's just *relax,* let's get into a groove. Come on, we can get it together. Come on."

"Under My Thumb" was starting to churn again. The band sounded amazingly sharp. The crowd was more still. Without knowing exactly what, we all felt that something bad had happened. I assumed, and I was not given to flights of horrible imaginings, that the Angels had killed several people. Gram [Parsons] told me later that he saw Meredith Hunter lifted up, with a great spreading ketchup-colored stain on the back of his suit. Ronnie was running to the First Aid tent, outdistancing the Hell's Angel who had been leading him. Hunter was there when Ronnie came up, calling for a doctor. A cop said, "You don't have to scream for a doctor for this guy, he's dead."

Over the last notes of "Under My Thumb," Mick sang, "It's all right—I pray that it's all right—"

*　　*　　*

Around the stage people were dancing, but in front of the stage, staring at Mick, one curly-haired boy in a watch cap was saying, Mick, Mick, no—I could read his lips. Behind the boy a fat black-haired girl, naked to the waist, was dancing, squeezing her enormous breasts, mouth open, eyes focused on a point somewhere north of her forehead. As the song ended, the girl, her skin rose-florid, blinking off and on like a pinball machine in orgasmic acid flashes, tried to take the stage like Grant took Richmond. Completely naked now, she was trying to climb over the crowd to get a foot onstage, where five Angels were at once between her and the Stones, kicking and punching her back, her smothering weight falling on the people behind her.

*　　*　　*

"Hey, come on, fellows," Mick was saying, getting a bit frantic, "like one of you can control one little girl—come on now, like—like—like—just sit down, honey," he said to the girl, who was still on her back, flashing her black-pelted pelvis, her eyes black whirlpools staring at the sky as if she were trying to get above the stage, above the lights. If she could come up to there and keep coming into the night, above the world, she would shed her grossness like a chrysalis and be reborn, airborne, an angel of God. The Hell's Angels leaned out over the stage to stop her, to grab her, to slap her teeth out and smash her goddamn gums, thumb her crazy eyes out, pop her eardrums, snatch her bald-headed, scalp the cheap cunt.

"Fellows," Mick said, trying gently to move the Angels away, "can you clear—uh—and she'll—let—let—let them deal with her—they can deal with her." The people down front were managing to crawl out from under the girl, the Angels wanting to stay and get their hands on her. "Fellows, come on, fellows," Mick said, "they're all right."

Keith started playing and Wyman and Charlie and Mick Taylor joined in, as the Angels slunk bloodlusty to the side.

* * *

The Angels were cracking their knuckles, looking around red-eyed for flesh to rip. How are we gonna get out of here? I wondered. Will we get out, or will we die here, is it going to snap and the Angels like dinosaurs kill themselves and all of us in a savage rage of nihilism, the plain to be found in the morning a bloody soup littered with teeth and bones, one last mad Angel, blinded by a comrade's boots and brass knuckles, gut sliced asunder by his partner's frogsticker, growling, tearing at the yawning slit under his filthy T-shirt, chomping on his own bloody blue-white entrails.

"Rape-murder—it's just a shot away," Mick sang over and over. In the crowd by stage left, where the trouble with the black boy in the green suit had taken place, an Angel was punching someone, but the victim went down fast and it was over. Standing close by, looking on, was a girl with phosphorescent white hair, a chemical miracle. It was impossible to tell whether she was with the Angel or the victim. "Love, sister, it's just a kiss away," Mick sang as the song thundered to a stop.

"Yuhh," Mick said, very low, then "Yuhhh," again, lower, like a man making a terrible discovery. "Okay . . . are we okay, I know we are." He was looking into the crowd. As if he had waked up once again, he shouted, "Are y'havin' a good ti-i-ime? OOH—yeah!"

* * *

"Justliketosaaaayyy," Mick said, then paused and seemed to lose himself once more, wondering what it was he'd like to say. After a moment he went on briskly: "Well there's been a few hangups you know but I mean generally I mean ah you've been beautiful—" in a lower tone—"you have been so groovy—aw!" (brisk again) "All the loose women may stand and put their hands up—all the loose women put their hands up!" But the loose women were tired like everybody else. A few girls stood up, a few hands were raised into the murk. On this night no one would think of playing "I'm Free," though that had been the whole idea of the concert, to give some free glimmer to Ralph Gleason's rock-and-roll-starved proletariat and to get away from the violence of the system, the cops' clubs, Klein's mop handle. The biggest group of playmates in history was having recess, with no teachers to protect them from the bad boys, the bullies, who may have been mistreated children and worthy of understanding but would nevertheless kill you. The Stones' music was strong but it could not stop the terror. There was a look of disbelief on the people's faces, wondering how the Stones could go on playing and singing in the bowels of madness and violent death. Not many hands were in the air, and Mick said, "That's not enough, we haven't got many loose women, what're ya gonna do?"

The band started "Honky Tonk Women," playing as well as if they were in a studio, Keith's lovely horrible harmonies sailing out into the cool night air. Nobody, not even the guardians of public morality at *Rolling Stone* who pronounced that "Altamont was the product of diabolical egotism, hype, ineptitude, money manipulation, and, at base, a fundamental lack of concern for humanity," could say that the Rolling Stones couldn't play like the devil when the chips were down.

You know what they say: rock and roll is all about attitude.

TOO EARLY to get up, especially on Saturday. The sun peeks over his windowsill. Isolated footsteps from the street. Guys who have to work on Saturday. Boy! That's what they'll call you all your life if you don't stay in school. Forty-five definitions, two chapters in *Silas Marner,* and three chem labs. On Sunday night, he will sit in his room with the radio on, bobbing back and forth on his bed, opening the window wide and then closing it, taking a break to eat, to comb his hair, to dance, to hear the Stones—anything. Finally, cursing wildly and making ugly faces at himself in the mirror, he will throw *Silas Marner* under the bed and spend an hour watching his tortoise eat lettuce.

In the bathroom he breaks three screaming pimples. With a toothpick he removes four specks of food from his braces, skirting barbed wires and week-old rubber bands. Brooklyn Bridge, railroad tracks, they call him. Metal mouth. They said he smiled like someone was forcing him to. Bent fingers with filthy nails. Caved-in chest with eight dangling hairs. A face that looks like the end of a watermelon, and curly hair—not like the Stones, not at all like Brian Jones—but muddy curls running down his forehead and over his ears. A bump. Smashed by a bat thrown wildly. When he was eight. Hunchback Quasimodo—Igor—Rodan on his head. A bump. Nobody hip has a bump or braces. Or hair like a fucking Frankenstein movie. He licks his braces clean and practices smiling.

Hair straight and heavy. Nose full. Lips bulging like boiling frankfurters. Hung. Bell bottoms and boss black boots. He practices his Brian Jones expressions. Fist held close to the jaw. Ready to spring, ready to spit. Evil. His upper brace catches on a lip.

He walks past his parents' room, where his mother sleeps in a gauzy hairnet, the covers pulled over her chin, her baby feet swathed in yellow calluses. Her hand reaches over to the night table where her eyedrops and glasses lie. He mutters silently at her. The night before there had been a fight—the usual fight, with Mommy shouting "I'll give you money! Sure, you rotten kid! I'll give you clothing so you can throw it all over the floor—that's blood money in those pants of yours!" And him answering the usual "geh-awf-mah-bak" and her: "Don't you yell at me, don't you—did you hear that (to no one). Did you hear how that kid . . . ?" and him slamming the door—the gray barrier—and above the muffled ". . . disrespects his mother . . . He treats me like dirt under his feet! . . . and he wants me to buy him . . . he'll spit on my grave" . . . and finally dad's groaning shuffle and a murmured "Ronnie, you better shut your mouth to your mother," and him whispering silently, the climatic, the utter: "Fucking bitch. Cunt. Cunt."

Now she smiles. So do crocodiles. He loves her. He doesn't know why he cursed, except that she hates it. It was easy to make her cry and though he shivers at the thought of her lying across the bed sobbing into a pillow, her housedress pulled slightly over a varicose thigh, he has to admit doing it was easy.

On the table he sees the pants she bought him yesterday. Her money lining his pocket, he had taken the bus to Fordham Road and in Alexander's he had cased out the Mod rack. Hands shaking, dying for a cigarette, he found the pants—a size small but still a fit. He bought them, carried them home clutched in his armpit, and desposited them before her during prime "Star Trek" TV time.

"Get away. I can't see. Whatsamaddah, your father a glazier or something?" and when he unveiled the pants and asked for the usual cuff-making ritual (when he would stand on the ladder and she, holding a barrage of pins in her mouth, would run the tailor's chalk along his shoe line and make him drag out the old black sewing machine), the fight began—and ended within the hour. The pants, hemmed during "The Merv Griffin Show" as the last labor of the night, now lay exposed and sunlit on the table. $8.95 pants.

They shimmer. The houndstooth design glows against the formica. Brown and green squares are suddenly visible within the gray design. He brushes the fabric carefully so the wool bristles. He tries them on, zipping up the two-inch fly, thinking at first that he has broken the zipper until he realizes that hip-huggers have no fly to speak of. They buckle tightly around his hips, hug his thighs, and flare suddenly at his knees. He races to the mirror and grins.

His hips are suddenly tight and muscular. His waist is sleek and his ass round and bulging. Most important, the pants make him look hung. Like the kids in the park. The odor of stale cigarettes over their clothing, medallions dangling out of their shirts. Their belt buckles ajar. They are hip. They say "Check out that bike." Get bent on Gypsy. Write the numbers of cruising police cars all over the walls. ROT, they call themselves. Reign of Terror. In the park they buzz out on glue, filling paper bags and breathing deeply, then sitting on the grass slopes, watching the cars. Giggling. Grooving. High.

Sometimes they let him keep the models that come with the glue. Or he grubs around their spot until, among the torn bags and oozing tubes, he finds a Messerschmitt or Convair spread across the grass ruins as though it had crashed there.

He unzips his pants and lets them hang on the door where he can watch them from the living room. He takes a box of Oreos from the kitchen, stacking the cookies in loose columns on the rug. He pours a cup of milk and turns on the TV. Farmer Gray runs nervously up and down the screen while a pig squats at ease by his side. His pants are filled with hornets. He runs in a cloud of dust toward a pond which appears and disappears teasingly, leaving Farmer Gray grubbing in the sand. Outasight!

He fills his mouth with three Oreos and wraps his feet around the screen so he can watch Farmer Gray between his legs. Baby habit. Eating cookies on the floor and watching cartoons on Saturday morning. Like thumbsucking. They teased him about it until he threw imaginary furniture into their faces. A soft bulge on his left thumb from years of sucking—cost them a fortune in braces. Always busting his hump.

He kills the TV picture and puts the radio on softly, because he doesn't want to wake Daddy who is asleep on his cot in the middle of the living room, bunched up around the blanket, his face creased in a dream, hands gripping his stomach in mock tension. Daddy snores in soft growls.

He brushes a flock of Oreo crumbs under the TV and rubs a milk stain into the rug. Thrown out of your own bed for snoring. You feel cheap, like Little Bo Peep; beep beep beep beep.

There is nothing to stop him from going downstairs. The guys are out already, slung over cars and around lampposts. The girls are trickling out of the project. It's cloudy, but until it actually rains he knows they will be around the lamppost, spitting out into the street, horsing around, grubbing for hooks, singing. He finishes four more cookies and stuffs half an apple onto his chocolate-lined tongue.

Marie Giovanni put him down bad for his braces. When she laughs her tits shake. Her face is pink; her hair rises in a billowing bouffant. In the hallway, she let Tony get his fingers wet. Yesterday she cut on him; called him metal mouth.

He flicks the radio off, grabs the pants from the hanger, and slides into them. He digs out a brown turtleneck from under a rubble of twisted clothing (they dress him like a ragpicker) and shines his boots with spit. They are chipping and the heels are worn on one side, but they make him look an inch taller, so he wears them whenever he can.

He combs his hair in the mirror. Back on the sides, over the ears, so the curl doesn't show. Over the eyes in the front to cover up his bump. Straight down the back of his neck, so it rests on his collar. He checks his bald spot for progress and counts the hairs that come out in his brush. In two years he knows he will be bald in front and his bump will look like a boulder on his forehead.

He sits on his bed and turns the radio on. From under the phonograph he lifts a worn fan magazine—*Pop* in bright fuchsia lettering—with Zal Yanovsky hunched over one P, Paul McCartney contorted over the other, and Nancy Sinatra touching her toes around the O. He turns to the spread on the Stones and flips the pages until he sees The Picture. Mick Jagger and Marianne Faithfull. Mick scowling, waving his fingers in the air. Marianne watching the camera. Marianne, waiting for the photographer to shoot. Marianne. Marianne, eyes fading brown circles, lips slightly parted in flashbulb surprise, miniskirt spread apart, tits like two perfect cones under her sweater. He had to stop looking at Marianne Faithfull a week ago.

He turns the page and glances at the shots of Brian Jones and then his eyes open wide because a picture in the corner shows Brian in Ronnie's pants. The same check. The same rise and flare. Brian leaning against a wall, his hands on the top of his magic hiphuggers. Wick-ked!

He flips the magazine away and stands in a curved profile against the mirror. He watches the pants move as he does. From a nearby flowerpot he gathers a fingerful of dirt and rubs it over his upper lip. He checks hair, nose, braces, nails, and pants. He likes the pants. They make him look hung. He reaches into his top drawer and pulls out a white handkerchief. He opens his fly and inserts the rolled cloth, patting it in place, and closing the zipper over it. He looks boss. Unfuckinbelievable.

In the elevator Ronnie takes a cigarette from his three-day-old pack and keeps it unlit in his mouth. Marie Giovanni will look at his pants and giggle. Tony will bellow "Check out them pants," and everyone will groove on them. In the afternoon, they will take him down to the park and turn him on, and he will feel the buzz they are always talking about and the cars will speed by like sparks.

Brian Jones thoughts in his head. Tuff thoughts. He will slouch low over the car and smoke with his thumb over the cigarette—the hip way. And when he comes back upstairs they will finally get off his back. Even on Fordham Road, where the Irish kids crack up when he walks by, even in chemistry and gym, they will know who he is and nod a soft "hey" when he comes by. He'll get laid.

Because clothing IS important. Especially if you've got braces and bony fingers and a bump the size of a goddam coconut on your head.

And especially if you're fourteen. Because—ask anyone. Fourteen is shit.

Pamela Des Barres

EVERY INCH OF MY LOVE

Celebrated groupie Miss Pamela here recounts the beginning of her long relationship with Jimmy Page, guitar wizard of Led Zeppelin.

THE NEXT night my dear Mercy accompanied me to the Whiskey to see Led Zeppelin, having served her very hard time. I got sticky thighs over the very naughty Jimmy Page while I watched him reinvent guitar playing. He was wearing a pink-velvet suit and his long black curls stuck damply to his pink-velvet cheeks. At the end of the set he collapsed to the floor, and was carried up the stairs by two roadies, one of them stopping to retrieve Jimmy's cherry-red patent-leather slipper. After this thrilling display, we made our way to Thee Charming Experience, where I peered through the sticky din at Zeppelin carousing at the darkest table in the back, and was very proud not to know them. One of the guys in the entourage was carrying a young girl around upside down, her high heels flailing in the air, panties spinning around one ankle. He had his face buried in her crotch and she was hanging on to his knees for dear life, her red mouth open wide in a scream that no one could hear. It was impossible to tell if she was enjoying herself or living a nightmare.

Someone else was getting it right on the table. Horrible things were going on, but I was finding it difficult to keep my eyes from straying to the salacious display. Jimmy Page sat apart from it all, observing the scene as if he had imagined it; overseer, creator, impeccably gorgeous perfect pop star, and he was staring right at me. I turned away, and luckily he couldn't see me blushing in the dark. Mercy leaned over and whispered, "Dangerous man."

*　　*　　*

When Led Zeppelin was due to hit town, the groupie section went into the highest gear imaginable; you could hear garter belts sliding up young thighs all over Hollywood. LZ was a formidable bunch, disguised in velvets and satins, epitomizing The Glorious English Pop Star to perfection; underneath the flowing curls and ruffles lurked slippery, threatening thrill bumps. The two sides of me were fighting it out, and the sinning side I hoped to squelch in Kentucky was about to score a major knockout.

Thee Experience was reeling as Bo Diddley took over the dance floor, duck-walking back and forth with his big boxy guitar. I was all in white, trying to prove my purity in this dodgy den of iniquity, sipping red wine through a straw, waiting nonchalantly for Led Zeppelin to arrive. I was feeling haughty one minute and petrified the next, trying to get a little tipsy before the demonic darling darkened the seedy doorstep. Robert Plant was the first to walk in, tossing his gorgeous lion's mane into the faces of enslaved sycophants. He walked like royalty, his shoulders thrown back, declaring his mighty status in this lowly little club. He was followed by the king of rowdy glaring roadies, Richard Cole, who seemed to be scanning the room for likely-looking jailbait. They were surrounded in seconds by seductive ready-willing-and-able girls, who piled up at their table like clusters of grapes going bad. I was noticing that the whole group was there except for Mr. Page, when Richard Cole stumbled over and handed me a scrap of paper with Jimmy's number at the Continental Hyatt House scribbled on it. He leaned into me and mumbled thickly in my ear, "He's waiting for you."

The Continental Riot House was just a few blocks down Sunset Boulevard, but I didn't leap out of my seat to dash out the door. I hadn't fully decided to make myself readily available for him anyway. I was intrigued, and wanted to be intriguing. So I sat there on my ass, watching Bo Diddley repeat history, tingling all over, thinking about Jimmy Page waiting waiting in his lair.

*　　*　　*

Led Zeppelin live in 1969 was an event unparalleled in musical history. They played longer and harder than any group ever had, totally changing the concept of rock concerts. They flailed around like dervishes, making so much sound that the air was heavy with metal. Two hours after the lights went out, as the band sauntered offstage, the audience was a delirious, raving, parched mass, crawling through the rock and roll desert thirsting for an encore. Twenty long minutes later, mighty Zeppelin returned to satiate their famished followers.

The long ride from Santa Barbara was one of those dream experiences that leave you glowing in the dark. From the moment Jimmy slid his small velvet-clad ass across the seat of the limo, right next to mine, until the door was thrown open in front of Thee Experience, we cooed and giggled like doves in heat. It was a hundred-mile drive, which gave him plenty of time to come out with *"all the lines."* He told me he had gotten my number the last time he was in town but was too nervous to use it until the last day, and he called and called but the line was constantly busy. Mmm-hmm. He said he wanted to spend time with me MORE THAN ANYTHING IN THE WORLD. Tell me more. I kissed and slobbered all over the inside crease of his slim white arm until he rolled his head back against the plush seat, gasping, "Oh, Pamela, yes, yes, yes." Yeah yeah yeah. He warned me that his previous L.A. girlfriend would probably be in the club and that I would have to give him the chance to "explain" to her about me. Uh-oh.

I climbed out of the warm, dark backseat womb, full of wet kisses and flaming glazed eyes, and found myself in the precarious position of sharing this splendid divinity with Catherine James, the most gorgeous rock courtesan alive. She and I hissed at each other from a dark distance, and I beat the old hasty retreat back to my cozy pad, where I tossed around in the sheets with the vision of Jimmy's backyard peacocks strutting across my latticed brain. I was turned inside out, pulsating with creamy pink desire for this most coveted hunk of drool material, but I was too thin-skinned to take the chance of being scorned this soon.

*   *   *

I knew he had gone to Texas, and I couldn't hang around the house waiting for his call—I'd go mad. So I went to a friend's pool and lolled in the sun, perspiring over my brief but pungent memories of Jimmy Page. When I arrived home I saw the phone was off the hook, and I thought, "Oh no, even if he tried to call, he'd say, 'Your phone was busybusybusy again.' As soon as I set it down in the cradle, it rang. "Long distance, Mr. Page calling." The first thing he said was, "Oh, the elusive Miss Pamela, you took your phone off the hook because you knew I was calling."

He knew what to say all right; he could have given a Master's course in how to turn a fairly sane girl into a twittering ninny. No one had ever gushed over me, or given me all the lines before, and I could feel myself falling apart and turning into one of those gooey unrecognizable substances. He told me he was going to come to my door, sweep me off my feet, and take me away in his white chariot; he told me he was my knight in shining armor; he told me he didn't know what was coming over him, he had never felt like this before. He taunted me with those freaking peacocks that walked by his bedroom window, as if someday in the near future I might be able to lift my head from the pillow and see them for myself. He acted like he couldn't believe I ever gave him a second glance. When I told him I missed him, he came out with, "Oh Miss P. Really? Are you telling me the truth?" My melting heart wasn't ready for this guy. I swallowed it all whole, and it was fucking delicious.

*　　*　　*

Well, he came to my door with his roadie Clive, and swept me into his white limo, and took me to see the Everly Brothers at the Palamino. We got all caught up in those glorious harmonies. Jimmy's eyes misted up and he squeezed my hand on certain meaningful lyrics: "Mmmmmm, I never knew what I missed until I kissed you . . ." He looked hard at me with a tiny smile on his rosebud lips, making me sweat with suspense about the long night to come. He put something into my hand, and it turned out to be a silver ring with twenty little pieces of turquoise embedded in it, and I wondered if I was going steady with the best guitar player in the world. He always messed with his black curls, poofing and fluffing them around his flawless face; he wore emerald velvet and white chiffon, thin little socks, and the most perfect brooch on his lapel. I couldn't wait to get back to the hotel and take it all off.

*　　*　　*

I saw Jimmy's whips curled up in his suitcase like they were taking a nap and pretended I didn't, looking quickly away as if I had seen someone's personal private peep show. He came up behind me and put his hands gently around my throat and said, "Don't worry Miss P., I'll never use those on you. I'll never hurt you like that." Then he sucked on my neck, and when I could feel the bruise being called up out of my bloodstream, he tossed me down on the bed and told me he would throw the whips away to show how much I meant to him. After ripping into my antique-lace dress and making raging, blinding love to me, he wrapped the whips round and round his forearm and slid the leather coils into the plastic flowered wastebasket, where they remained until he left for Somewhere U.S.A. a week later.

We talked about how much better it would have been had we met before all the pop-star-groupie business started and got in the way of a meaningful and honest relationship. He vowed not to let it get in our way, but inserted a clause that allowed him to "do things" on the road because he got so "bloody bored." I shuddered at what those "things" might have been, and inwardly craved impossible monogamy with my precious Mr. Page.

When he picked me up late one night, I opened the door and our gaze locked for many entrancing moments before I collapsed in his arms at the sheer relief of seeing him. This unpremeditated display prompted him to say, "Your insides are so sensitive, I knew you were different." Clutching me to his thin, trembling chest, shaking with the outrage of our positions in life, he moaned, "Oh Miss P., how are we going to get rid of them all?"

He had been in my life a mere few days and was already driving me wild-wildwild. We only saw the rest of the group ("Percy," "Bonzo," and "Jonesy") at gigs because he wanted to hole up and be alone with me. He invited me into his private world, and I was hope hope hoping that the glass slipper would fit my size-seven foot.

On his day off, we stayed in my bedroom, listening to the test pressing of *Led Zeppelin II* over and over again while he took reams of notes. I had to comment on every solo, and even though I believed the drum solo in "Moby Dick" went on endlessly, I held my tongue and went on pressing his velvet trousers and sewing buttons onto his satin jacket. I told him about Nudie, "the rodeo tailor," and the whole team, including their massive manager, Peter Grant, got fitted out in cowboy clothes. We went to the Glass Farmhouse, where Jimmy got a long antique coat embroidered with a dragon and a silly velvet hat with a feather in it. I was holding his hand, and in my ultimate glory by his side. The roadies, even Robert and Bonzo, began to tease us about how long our fling was lasting, how Jimmy never spent so much time with a girl on the road before. All the other guys were married, so they watched Jimmy's love life with envious glee.

*   *   *

We stayed in this elegant suite with a king-sized bed up on a platform, and sat right in the front row to see the King reclaim his throne. He was wearing black leather and looked like ten greek Gods as he tore through "Love Me Tender," "Don't Be Cruel," and "Jailhouse Rock." He was sweating, he was in the flesh, he was alive, inhaling and exhaling. And there I was in Las Vegas, breathing the same air as Elvis Presley, sitting between Jimmy Page and Robert Plant, completely and entirely beside myself. Some sideburned grease monkey appeared after the show, asking Jimmy if he would like to meet Elvis. He said, "No, thank you," and I never quite got over it.

*   *   *

I had taken some very intense mescaline, and Jimmy watched over me, making sure I was having a good time. He liked to be in control, and didn't take many drugs or drink much alcohol. I think he believed his beauty was too important to tamper with. He was always in the mirror, primping on his splendid image, and putting perfect waves in his long black hair with a little crimping machine. He used Pantene products, and whenever I smelled them, for years afterward, I remembered being buried in his hair.

I was a fool for him, and prayed to anyone who might possibly be holy that I wasn't just a one-tour wonder. I could be true-blue to his image forever if I had a hinting hope of another healthy slug of him. More than anything, I ached to meet him somewhere on the road, which would be a miraculous accomplishment indeed.

*   *   *

I was pacing around the apartment in a numb fog, so when the phone finally rang, Michele answered it. "Pamela, it's Jimmy, it's Jimmy!!" I was like Sleeping Beauty waking up after a hundred years of death sleep as his sweet voice told me how "the scenes" he was having were like "eating hamburger," and how he really "needed" to see me. While my tears of relief dribbled into the receiver, he told me, "The boys really like you, they usually hate the girls I see." He promised to send me a plane ticket the next morning and I said a silent prayer that he would. As I started to pack my suitcase to go on the road with Led Zeppelin, I felt strong because I had called to Jimmy like a cavewoman deep down inside myself, and it had worked.

I waited all morning for my airline ticket to arrive, and when it didn't, I started shivering and couldn't stop. Michele was trying to hold me up, because I was a quivering heap curled up on the floor in a fetal position. I asked her to hand me my journal, and with shaking hand I wrote: "Why did he even bother to call me? At least I wouldn't have heard his sweet voice, and the hurt would be healing instead of fresh blood still flowing . . . where is the white chariot, Mr. Page?" Michele made me a cup of tea, and I stood in the doorframe to steady myself. After two sips, I dropped the cup of steaming Earl Gray, grasped the doorframe with one hand, clutched at my heart with the other, and slid dramatically down to the floor as the doorbell rang. Suddenly I could run, and standing at my front door was a messenger boy holding my TWA ticket to New York. "Miss Pamela Miller?" he asked, and I kissed him like Blanche DuBois kissed the "young, young, young man" in *Streetcar,* then whirled around until I got dizzy, and fell down again. The sun was shining; I was a twenty-year-old blonde with blue eyes and a ticket to New York sent to me by Jimmy Page, the most beautiful Englishman alive.

The next three days on the road with Led Zeppelin were classic rock and roll heaven; I was exactly what I had always aspired to be: the girlfriend of the lead guitar player in the world's biggest and best rock and roll band. I was the only girl allowed backstage, and while the band went over the set list and got all dolled up, I sat on the ample lap of the world's greatest and most monumental rock and roll manager, Peter Grant. I had heard horrendous tales of Mr. Grant's kneecap-breaking escapades; his reputation as being a teeming Goliath preceded his paunch, but he and I developed a special relationship, and I was bounced on his knee on many occasions. He was always *right there* for "his boys," and nothing, not even his family, took precedence. Peter and the whole group called me "P," and I accepted the endearment with slavish gratitude.

I was on the left side of the stage where Jimmy entranced eighty thousand Led Zeppelin maniacs with his magic guitar fingers and black-satin suit emblazoned with gold dragons climbing up his long legs. The audience was in a frenzy, and from my vantage point, sitting up on Jimmy's amp, I almost felt like one of the group; I could see what they saw, and feel what they felt pouring from the frenzied fanatics. The wild-eyed girls looked up at me and wondered which member of the group I was sleeping with, and I was so proud. I wore four huge, clunky turquoise-and-silver bracelets all the way up my right arm that each member of Zeppelin had given me to take care of during the show. Turquoise was very big in 1969, and these particular bracelets were the heaviest, gaudiest pieces ever made by American Indians in the entire state of Arizona. I gazed out at Jimmy under the bright lights with his violin bow, tears filling my eyes at the thought of being able to take off his soaking-wet chiffon shirt after the show, tell him how magnificent he had been onstage, and climb into the long black limo with him and head for the hotel.

Don DeLillo

FREE OF OLD SAINTS AND MARTYRS

Used to be you got into rock and roll to meet girls. Then it became like a political statement or something. As the sixties limped to a close, the rock-star job description got revised. Suddenly, it got a little harder to be a plain, old-fashioned hedonist.

FAME REQUIRES every kind of excess. I mean true fame, a devouring neon, not the somber renown of waning statesmen or chinless kings. I mean long journeys across gray space. I mean danger, the edge of every void, the circumstance of one man imparting an erotic terror to the dreams of the republic. Understand the man who must inhabit these extreme regions, monstrous and vulval, damp with memories of violation. Even if half-mad he is absorbed into the public's total madness; even if fully rational, a bureaucrat in hell, a secret genius of survival, he is sure to be destroyed by the public's contempt for survivors. Fame, this special kind, feeds itself on outrage, on what the counselors of lesser men would consider bad publicity—hysteria in limousines, knife fights in the audience, bizarre litigation, treachery, pandemonium and drugs. Perhaps the only natural law attaching to true fame is that the famous man is compelled, eventually, to commit suicide.

(Is it clear I was a hero of rock'n'roll?)

Toward the end of the final tour it became apparent that our audience wanted more than music, more even than its own reduplicated noise. It's possible the culture had reached its limit, a point of severe tension. There was less sense of simple visceral abandon at our concerts during these last weeks. Few cases of arson and vandalism. Fewer still of rape. No smoke bombs or threats of worse explosives. Our followers, in their isolation, were not concerned with precedent now. They were free of old saints and martyrs, but fearfully so, left with their own unlabeled flesh. Those without tickets didn't storm the barricades, and during a performance the boys and girls directly below us, scratching at the stage, were less murderous in their love of me, as if realizing finally that my death, to be authentic, must be self-willed—a successful piece of instruction only if it occurred by my own hand, preferably in a foreign city. I began to think their education would not be complete until they outdid me as teacher, until one day they merely pantomimed the kind of massive response the group was used to getting. As we performed they would jump, dance, collapse, clutch each other, wave their arms, all the while making absolutely no sound. We would stand in the incandescent pit of a huge stadium filled with wildly rippling bodies, all totally silent. Our recent music, deprived of people's screams, was next to meaningless, and there would have been no choice but to stop playing. A profound joke it would have been. A lesson in something or other.

In Houston I left the group, saying nothing, and boarded a plane for New York City, that contaminated shrine, place of my birth. I knew Azarian would assume leadership of the band, his body being prettiest. As to the rest, I left them to their respective uproars—news media, promotion people, agents, accountants, various members of the managerial peerage. The public would come closer to understanding my disappearance than anyone else. It was not quite as total as the act they needed and nobody could be sure whether I was gone for good. For my closest followers, all it foreshadowed was a period of waiting. Either I'd return with a new language for them to speak or they'd seek a divine silence attendant to my own.

I took a taxi past the cemeteries toward Manhattan, tides of ash-light breaking across the spires. New York seemed older than the cities of Europe, a sadistic gift of the sixteenth century, ever on the verge of plague. The cab driver was young, however, a freckled kid with a moderate orange Afro. I told him to take the tunnel.

"Is there a tunnel?" he said.

The night before, at the Astrodome, the group had appeared without me. Azarian's stature was vast but nothing on that first night could have broken the crowd's bleak mood. They turned against the structure itself, smashing whatever was smashable, trying to rip up the artificial turf, attacking the very plumbing. The gates were opened and the police entered, blank-looking, hiding the feast in their minds behind metered eyes. They made their patented charges, cracking arms and legs in an effort to protect the concept of regulated temperature. In one of the worst public statements of the year, by anyone, my manager Globke referred to the police operation as an example of mini-genocide.

"The tunnel goes under the river. It's a nice tunnel with white tile walls and men in glass cages counting the cars going by. One two three four. One two three."

I was interested in endings, in how to survive a dead idea. What came next for the wounded of Houston might very well depend on what I was able to learn beyond certain personal limits, in endland, far from the tropics of fame.

*   *   *

I had a visitor, four days into unbroken solitude, a reporter this time, flamboyantly bald and somewhat dwarfish, dressed in sagging khaki, drifts of hair from outlying parts of his head adorning the frames of his silver-tinted glasses, an emblem on the sleeve of his battle jacket—RUNNING DOG NEWS SERVICE.

"Where do you want to sit?"

"Your manager told us you were approachable," he said. "We've known for seventy-two hours where you were located but we didn't want to make a move until we got ahold of Globke. We don't operate mass-media-crash-style. We wanted Globke's version of your frame of mind in terms of were you or were you not approachable. I'll take this chair and we can put the tape recorder right here."

"No tape," I said.

"That's what we anticipated."

"No notes either."

"No notes?"

"Note-taking's out."

"You want some kind of accuracy, don't you?"

"No," I said.

"Then what do you want?"

"Make it all up. Go home and write whatever you want and then send it out on the wires. Make it up. Whatever you write will be true."

"We know it's asking a lot to expect an interview, even a brief one, which is what we assure you is what we want, but maybe a statement will have to do. Will you give us a statement?"

"A statement about what?"

"Anything at all," he said. "Just absolutely anything. For instance the rumors. What about the rumors?"

"They're all true."

"Okay, but what about authorities in Belgium?"

"Does Globke have Belgium under contract? If Globke doesn't have it under contract, whatever it is, I'd be guilty of malfeasance in discussing it publicly."

"Authorities in Belgium want to question you about your alleged financial involvement in a planeload of arms confiscated in Brussels that was supposedly on its way to either this or that trouble-spot, depending on which rumor you believe."

"Do you know what the word malfeasance means? This is a word that carries tremendous weight in a court of law. Much more weight than misfeasance or nonfeasance."

"Okay, but what about the damage to your vocal chords from the continuous strain and the story that you'll never perform in public again?"

"You decide," I said. "Whatever you write will be true. I'll confirm every word."

"Okay, but what about Azarian? Azarian says he's reorganizing the group along less radical musical lines. Will you make a statement about that?"

"Yes," I said.

"What's your statement?"

"Azarian has been horribly disfigured in a gruesome accident. His face is being reconstructed with skin and bone taken from the faces of volunteers. His voice is not his voice. It belongs to a donor. What Azarian seems to be saying is really being said by another person's vocal chords."

"That's the other thing. An accident. You were in an accident and you're hidden away in some rich private clinic in south central Maryland. The accident thing was interesting to us, ideologically. An accident for somebody like you is the equivalent of prison for a revolutionary. We were kind of rooting for an accident. Which is, wow, really weird. But that's what happens. You get into guerrilla ideology, you find yourself trying to handle some pretty unwholesome thoughts."

"There's no such region as south central Maryland."

"Okay, but listen to this on the subject of accidents. We got a tip from I won't say what source that your manager was about to leak word of an accident. We figure he wanted to co-opt all the other accidents. He wanted exclusive rights to your accident. Anyway his story had you half-dead when a schooner piled into some rocks during a storm off the coast of Peru. First you're missing and presumed drowned. Then you're half-dead aboard a rescue vessel. And Peru does have a coast because I was there two years ago Christmas. But he dropped the idea for whatever reason. This is pretty sophisticated stuff, Bucky. I mean there's rumor, there's counter-rumor, there's manipulation, and there's, you know, this ultra-morbid promotional activity. What's it all mean?"

"The plain man of business is gone from the earth."

"Before I forget," he said, "we'd like to add your name to a list of sponsors that we use on all correspondence pertaining to the black captive insurrection fund. The other names are on this sheet. Should I leave it and you can get back to us or do you want to look at it now? It's up to you, whatever you want me to do with it."

"Tear it in four equal pieces," I said.

"Okay, can we get on to some more statements now?"

"I don't think so, no."

"We'd like a short statement about your present whereabouts."

"I'm wherever you want me to be."

"We know where you are at this point. We want to know what you're doing here."

"Nothing."

"But why here?" he said. "Will you make a statement about that?"

"You know where you are in New York. You're in New York. It's New York. This fact is inescapable. In other places I didn't always know where I was. What is this, Ohio or Japan? I wanted to be in one place. An identifiable place."

"Okay, but you've got a studio-equipped house in the mountains and it's almost inaccessible to anybody who doesn't have a detailed map. We still don't see why you're here rather than there. You've lived there. It must be identifiable."

"How tall are you?" I said.

"Six feet even."

"Incredible."

"It's the way I hunch."

"You're a six-foot dwarf."

"I hunch. I can't help it. I've always hunched."

"It's really a studio-equipped mountain," I said. "There is no house as such. There's the facsimile of a house. There's the pictorial mode of a house. Exactly what my house in the mountains would look like if I had a house and there were mountains. My present state of mind doesn't accommodate the existence of mountains. I am in a plains mood."

"Can we discuss your personal life?" he said.

"Sure we can. I won't be here while we're discussing it because I'm going out now. But you go right ahead. Everything you report will be true. I'll personally vouch for every syllable."

"Your manager told us you were approachable."

"That wasn't Globke you talked to. That was the facsimile of Globke. Transparanoia markets facsimiles. Everybody under contract has his or her facsimile. It's one of the terms in the standard contract. Once you sign the contract, you're obliged to live up to the terms. This is basic to a sound contractual relationship. At this precise moment in duplicate time, Bucky Wunderlick is having his toenails clipped in the Waldorf Towers. You've been conducting an interview with his facsimile."

I could see myself reflected in his glasses as I rose from my bowl-shaped chair and moved slowly backward toward the door. He raised an arm in shaggy homage.

"Peace."

"War."

John Lennon

THE BALLAD OF JOHN AND YOKO

At the end of the 1960s, sick of being a Beatle and in love with Japanese musician/conceptual artist Yoko Ono, John Lennon decided he wanted out of the greatest rock and roll show on earth and just wanted some peace.

I'D ALWAYS had a fantasy about a woman who would be a beautiful, intelligent, dark-haired, high-cheek-boned, free-spirited artist (à la Juliette Greco).

My soul mate.

Someone that I had already known, but somehow had lost.

After a short visit to India on my way home from Australia, the image changed slightly—she had to be a dark-eyed *Oriental*. Naturally, the dream couldn't come true until I had completed the picture.

Now it was complete.

Of course as a teenager, my sexual fantasies were full of Anita Ekberg and the usual giant Nordic goddesses. That is, until Brigitte Bardot became the "love of my life" in the late Fifties. All my girlfriends who weren't dark-haired suffered under my constant pressure to become Brigitte. By the time I married my first wife (who was, I think, a natural auburn), she too had become a long-haired blonde with the obligatory bangs.

Met the real Brigitte a few years later. I was on acid and she was on her way out.

I finally met Yoko and the dream became a reality.

The only woman I'd ever met who was my equal in every way imaginable. My better, actually. Although I'd had numerous interesting "affairs" in my previous incarnation, I'd never met anyone worth breaking up a happily-married state of boredom for.

Escape, at last! Someone to leave home for! *Somewhere to go.* I'd waited an eternity.

* * *

Since I was extraordinarily shy (especially around beautiful women), my daydreams necessitated that she be aggressive enough to "save me," i.e., "take me away from all this." Yoko, although shy herself, picked up my spirits enough to give me the courage to get the hell out, just in time for me to avoid having to live with my ex-wife's new nose. She also had had side-interests, much to the surprise of my pre-liberated male ego.

They got the new nose. And I got my dream woman. Yoko.

Having been brought up in the genteel poverty of a lower-middle-class environment, I should not have been surprised by the outpouring of race-hatred and anti-female malice to which we were subjected in that bastion of democracy. Great Britain (including the now-reformed Michael Caine, who said something through his cute Cockney lisp to the effect that "I can't see why 'ee don't find a nice English girl"). What a riot! One of "our boys" leaving his Anglo-Saxon (whatever that is) hearth and home and taking up with a bloody Jap to boot! Doesn't he know about *The Bridge on the River Kwai?* Doesn't he remember Pearl Harbour!

The English press had a field day venting all their pent-up hatred of foreigners on Yoko. It must have been hard for them: what with the Common Market and all, they'd had to lay off hating frogs, wogs, clogs, krauts, and eye-ties (in print, that is), not to mention the jungle bunnies. It was humiliating and painful for both of us to have her described as ugly and yellow and other derogatory garbage, especially by a bunch of beer-bellied, red-necked "aging" hacks: you are what you eat and think. We know what they eat and are told what to think: their masters' leftovers.

It was hard for Yoko to understand, having been recognized all her life as one of the most beautiful and intelligent women in Japan. The racism and sexism were overt. I was ashamed of Britain. Even though I was full of race and anti-female prejudice myself (buried deep where it had been planted), I still bought that English fairy story about the Yanks being the racists: "Not us, old boy, it just wouldn't be cricket." The "Gentleman's Agreement" runs from top to bottom. But I must say I've found on my travels that every race thinks it's superior to every other; the same with class (the American myth being they have no class system).

It was a horrifying experience. I thought of asking Johnny Dankworth and Cleo Lane for advice, but never did (they were the only other biracial couple I'd heard of in Britain). The press led the howling mob, and the foul-mouthed Silent Majority followed suit. The hate mail from the cranks was particularly inspiring; I tried to publish it at Jonathan Cape but they thought . . . Still, it made a change from the begging letters which always coincided with whatever well-publicized particular problems we were facing at the moment, e.g.,

> I'm sorry to hear of your wife's recent miscarriage. We, too, have suffered the same tragedy as you, sir, but unlike your good selves do not have the wherewithal to purchase a nice semidetached in the south of France, and as you have so much money, you would be making a 100-year-old spastic and his deaf wife and little crippled children very happy. Sir, it's not too much to ask, . . . etc.

Or:

> I, too, was planted and wrongfully arrested by the world-renowned British police [another myth down the drain], and also recently narrowly escaped death in a car crash in Scotland, and wondered if you could see your way to helping a blind priest and his invalid mother get to church on Sundays . . . etc., etc., etc.

And was Jerusalem builded there? I doubt it.

Apart from giving me the courage to break out of the Stockbroker Belt . . . Yoko also gave me the inner strength to look more closely at my other marriage. *My real marriage.* To the Beatles, which was more stifling than my domestic life. Although I had thought of it often enough, I lacked the guts to make the break earlier.

My life with the Beatles had become a trap. A tape loop. I had made previous short excursions on my own, writing books, helping convert them into a play for the National Theatre. I'd even made a movie without the others (a lousy one at that, directed by that zany man in search of power, Dick Lester). But I had made the movie more in reaction to the fact that the Beatles had decided to stop touring than with real independence in mind. Although even then (1965) my eye was already on freedom.

Basically, I was panicked by the idea of having "nothing to do." What is life, without touring? Life, that's what. I always remember to thank Jesus for the end of my touring days; if I hadn't said that the Beatles were "bigger than Jesus" and upset the very Christian Ku Klux Klan, well, Lord, I might still be up there with all the other performing fleas! God bless America. Thank you, Jesus.

When I finally had the guts to tell the other three that I, quote, wanted a divorce, unquote, they knew it was for real, unlike Ringo and George's previous threats to leave. I must say I felt guilty for springing it on them at such short notice. After all, I had Yoko—they only had each other. I was guilty enough to give McCartney credit as a co-writer on my first independent single instead of giving it to Yoko, who had actually co-authored it ("Give Peace a Chance").

I started the band. I disbanded it. It's as simple as that. Yoko and I instinctively decided that the best form of defense was attack—but in our own sweet way: *Two Virgins,* our first LP, in which the sight of two slightly overweight ex-junkies in the nude gave John and Yoko a damned good laugh and apoplexy to the Philistines of the so-called civilized world! Including those famous avant-garde revolutionary thinkers, Paul, George and It's Only Ringo. I bear them no ill will. In retrospect, the Beatles were no more an important part of my life than any other (and less than some).

It's irrelevant to me whether I ever record again. I started with rock and roll and ended with pure rock and roll (my *Rock and Roll* album). If the urge ever comes over me and it is irresistible, then I will do it for fun. But otherwise I'd just as soon leave well enough alone. I have never subscribed to the view that artists "owe a debt to the public" any more than youth owes its life to king and country. I made myself what I am today. Good and bad. The responsibility is mine alone.

All roads lead to Rome. I opened a shop; the public bought the goods at fair market value. No big deal. And as for show biz, it was never my life. I often wish, knowing it's futile, that Yoko and I weren't famous and we could have a really private life. But it's spilt milk, or rather blood, and I try not to have regrets and don't intend to waste energy and time in an effort to become anonymous. That's as dumb as becoming famous in the first place.

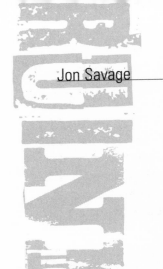

RUINED FOR LIFE

The first and even the second generation of rock and rollers must have been a little frightened by the punk rockers who emerged in the mid-1970s. Now they knew how their parents had felt in the 1950s. Like the rock of the 1960s, punk energized itself with trans-Atlantic inspirations, as the Ramones begat the Sex Pistols, and the Pistols spit their inspiration back in American faces, birthing the next generation in rock and roll. It's a beautiful thing, really.

I got you in my camera
I got you in my camera
A second of your life, ruined for life
You wanna ruin me in your magazine
You wanna cover us in margarine
Now is the time, you got the time
To realize, to have real eyes.
—*John Lydon for the Sex Pistols: "I Wanna Be Me"*
(1976)

Punk was out of the starting blocks, and, just as the Ramones' first album accelerated a generation of English musicians, the competition to form Punk Rock groups intensified. During the spring of 1976, McLaren and Bernie Rhodes were actively trying to fashion groups out of the musicians that had ebbed in and out of London SS. Understanding that the Sex Pistols would be more impressive if they could appear as the spearhead of a new generation, McLaren embarked on a policy of nurturing an environment where people make things happen.

"The 101'ers were doing well," says Joe Strummer about his first group, named after their squat at 101 Walterton Terrace. Nurtured by a resident spot at their local pub, the Chippenham, and the surrounding squat community, the 101'ers had just released their first single, a fast, intense Pub Rocker called "Keys to your Heart." "We were working very hard: we did twelve gigs in fourteen days in places like Sheffield, and it was up and down every day, but we were invisible. In April the Sex Pistols played the Nashville for the first time, supporting us. I walked out onstage while they were doing their soundcheck and I heard Malcolm going to John, 'Do you want those kind of shoes that Steve's got or the kind that Paul's got? What sort of sweater do you want?' And I thought, 'Blimey they've got a manager, and he's offering them clothes!' The rest of my group didn't think much of all this, but I sat out in the audience. Lydon was really thin: he pulled out his snot rag and blew into it and he went, 'If you hadn't guessed already, we're the Sex Pistols,' and they blasted into 'Substitute.'

"They did 'Steppin' Stone' which we did but they were light years ahead of us. The difference was, we played 'Route 66' to the drunks at the bar, going 'Please like us.' But here was this quartet who were standing there going, 'We don't give a toss what you think, you pricks, this is what we like to play and this is the way we're gonna play it.' They were from another century, it took my head off. They honestly didn't give a shit. The audience were shocked.

"After that I started going down to Tuesday nights at the 100 Club. That's when Bernie Rhodes came up to me and said, 'Give me your number, I want to call you about something.' We had some dates supporting Kilburn and the High Roads but I split the group up. They thought I was mad. They were probably right, but it was a case of jump that side of the fence or you're on the other side. Remember the T-shirt that Bernie and Malcolm designed, 'Which side of the bed'? It was so clear."

"Strummer came rushing up to me in the Red Cow: 'Have I done the right thing?'," says Roger Armstrong. " 'What?' 'I've left the 101'ers.' He was in tow with Mick Jones and Bernie, and he started on a whole rant about how this was the future. I knew Bernie from the great King's Road triumvirate. Malcolm, Bernie and Andy Czezowski: the tailor, the rabbi and the accountant. It was a funny alliance: they all got their band out of it."

Solidarity, however, was not the main spur. Both the Ramones and the Sex Pistols had already shown the way: it was possible to make a loud noise, express hostility, learn in public and get attention. This temporary advantage had to be exploited quickly: the result was a frantic jockeying for position, like a game of musical chairs.

"I saw Bernie and Malcolm as competitors," says Chrissie Hynde, "when they could have been working together. Everything that Bernie did seemed like a pale version of what Malcolm was doing with the Sex

Pistols. For instance, when I finally came back from France, I was going to do something with Mick Jones. Mick phoned me up one day and said, 'I want you to talk to Bernie who's going to manage us.' 'I'm in a band with *you,* I don't want to talk to this other guy.' He goes, 'Alright, I'll try to explain. You won't sing at all, you'll just play the guitar and be in the background. The band's going to be called School Girls Underwear.' I thought, 'I'm going to be in a band called School Girls Underwear, I'm *sure.'*

"I had a meeting with Malcolm over some won ton soup. The Sex Pistols were going and he wanted another band. What Malcolm did at this point was he would meet people at parties who were personalities and put them together. He said he'd met this great kid drummer called Chris Miller, who was Rat Scabies by now, and he had these other people. So we went to meet this guy coming off the train from Hemel Hempstead, and it was David Zero, who later changed his name to Dave Vanian: he looked like Alice Cooper.

"Later on we went to some retro clothing store in Covent Garden and there was another David who they'd tried out for the Sex Pistols. He didn't want to be in a band at all, but Malcolm dragged him into it because he thought he had the right personality. That was very Malcolm: he didn't care about the music at all, he was just interested in personalities. So we had the black David and the white one: they were the singers. I was supposed to play guitar, not sing at all. We were to be called the Masters of the Backside."

London SS had finally split two ways: guitarist Bryan James teamed up with drummer Chris Miller, now named Rat Scabies after a bout of the disease. Miller's old Croydon friend Ray Burns was brought in on guitar. He was a working-class drop-out whose manic behaviour masked real sensitivity. "Tony James was the bass player," says Burns, "they gave him the elbow because he was too interested in his clothes, so I got the job. Then they chopped my hair off. I didn't mind: I was like a hippy with teeth. That was London SS: when Chrissie Hynde joined it became Mike Hunt's Honourable Discharge.

"Malcolm came and put us in rehearsal for two days and then came down with Helen and Rotten and all those people, and they sat down watching us, laughing, and told us to fuck off. No commercial possibilities. Malcolm was good to us: he gave us money and talked sense. Chrissie left: we started playing ourselves. Brian and Rat had met Vanian at the Nashville—they thought he looked good. The name 'The Damned' was Brian's idea. We were damned really: everything that could go wrong did."

Within weeks of forming, the Damned were given rehearsal space by John Krivine and Andy Czezowski and were being groomed as Sex competitors. Meanwhile, Bernard Rhodes was working on the other half of London SS. "One morning I was signing on," says Joe Strummer, "and there were these people staring at me on the bench. I was thinking there was going to be a ruck. It was Paul Simonon, Mick Jones and Viv Albertine: these were the weeks that Bernie had pulled Mick and Paul out of London SS and put them together. If they'd have come up to me, I'd probably have swung at one of them. Get it in first: Lisson Grove was the worst place on earth.

"By that time Bernie had fallen out with Malcolm over the swastika, because Bernie's mother was a refugee from Europe. Bernie called me and I agreed to meet him and Keith Levene. We drove over to Shepherd's Bush to the squat where Paul and Mick and Viv had been staying—that's why they'd been staring at me—and we put the group together there and then. For about a week we were the Psychotic Negatives, then we were the Weak Heartdrops, after a Big Youth lyric, then Paul thought of the name the Clash."

The Sex Pistols had had great publicity but it worked both ways. After the reports of violence, doors were closing in their faces: they were banned now from the Marquee and the Nashville, and El Paradise had proved too unstable as a regular venue. The day that the *NME* piece about the Nashville fight came out, the group played a club called the Babalu halfway up the Finchley Road: "That was the best concert we ever did," says Glen Matlock: "there were about thirteen people there, including us."

McLaren and Helen Mininberg collected what press material the group had and wrapped it with an A3 poster, two photos printed at the Labour Party Press at Peckham Rye by McLaren's old friend Jamie Reid, who had been brought into the fold for his printing expertise. Armed with this pack, McLaren approached booking agencies, but without success. McLaren then decided to ask John Curd, a bearish man who promoted concerts at the Roundhouse, if the Sex Pistols could be added to the forthcoming Ramones bill. Malcolm and Nils went to Curd's home, where they were thrown bodily down the stairs.

"That was the incident that made McLaren want to go totally outside the music industry," says Jonh Ingham. "His idea was to create your own, total alternative to what was going on in the business at that time. Malcolm was trying to get his band into situations. One of his things was, 'You have to pay to see them, because then you're making an active effort.' That was the opposite to what the Pub Rockers were thinking, which was get your band in front of any audience: what he was doing was creating an audience that was specifically *for* the band."

During May, the group were set a new challenge: a tour of the north of England. "That was ridiculous," says Nils Stevenson. "Malcolm would give us just about enough money to get there, then you have to fend for yourself. Steve would steal chocolate bars to eat. You had to make sure you got your money as most people didn't want to pay after seeing the group. Frightening times playing these really straight places. I'm totally non-aggressive, but my adrenalin was so whacked up that I'd be up on stage kicking punters off.

"In Barnsley, we played this awful place out in the sticks, just this pub in the middle of nowhere. The place filled up and things got a bit hairy, so I made the landlord call the police, who escorted us out. In Hull things got very nasty, we had to high-tail it out of there. Rotten would get very lippy and put the crowd down, but it wasn't too bad. It was just that the look of the band and their lack of professionalism used to incense these people. They wanted a hippy group with long hair but these kids really pissed them off.

"We'd have the cheapest, cheapest vans: we had one to go to Scarborough that wouldn't go up hills, so we had to look at the Ordnance Survey map. Glen worked out this ridiculous route, all the way round everywhere, but it was flat so we could get to the venue. You'd tell Malcolm about all these problems when you got home and he'd be very apologetic, but the same thing would happen again the next week.

"There were ridiculous arguments going on in the van. You can imagine how petty John could be, depending on his mood. Rotten would always insist on going in the comfy seat: 'I'm the star, fuck off.' It could be quite uncomfortable with all four of them together, but it was all superficial: as soon as they were on their own everyone would be as sweet as a nut. Rotten would generally want the company of everybody but would be too insecure and would put on this weird front all the time and wander off by himself, watching people to see if they had noticed."

"It was vile, horrible, a nightmare," says John Lydon. "No chance to relax, nothing, nylon sheets. What you can never get in your book is the utter, total boredom of being in a band."

"It was like little boys," says Glen Matlock. "Imagine being in a van with Rotten. And the places! We were playing in Whitby and they kept telling us to turn it down. In the end we were just larking about pretending to mime. This bloke comes up and says: 'It's no good lads. Look we'll

ELVIS PRESLEY. At the end of the 1960s, the once and future King of Rock and Roll was unrecognized on a Los Angeles Street. Then he began a magnificent comeback, with a 1968 television special and a series of early 1969 recording sessions back home in Memphis. He then embraced the audience he had largely avoided for a decade and spent his last years jumpsuiting his way across the arenas of the American Heartland.

CHUCK BERRY.
He said he wanted to write about things both black and white kids could understand, so that he could help bridge the races.

LITTLE RICHARD.
When producer Bumps Blackwell met him, he saw "this cat in a loud shirt, with hair waved up six inches above his head. He was talking wild, thinking up stuff just to be different."

THE BEATLES. For most of the 1960s, Ringo, Paul, George, and John could look down upon a rock and roll world that had nearly deified them, making them—for a time at least, in John's words—"more popular than Jesus."

THE SUPREMES. Unstoppable hit machine in the onslaught of Beatlemania, they were Motown's preeminent ambassadors to the world.

THE ROLLING STONES. Founded 1962, the band continues to conquer nations with corporate megatours at least once every other fiscal year. Here in the mid-1970s, Keith Richards holds the fort while Mick Jagger communes with his muse.

JAMES BROWN. His big breakthrough to a mass audience came in 1964 when he taped "The T.A.M.I. Show" for television. The Rolling Stones were scheduled to follow Brown, but after watching him rehearse, Mick Jagger asked to go on earlier so as not to suffer by comparison.

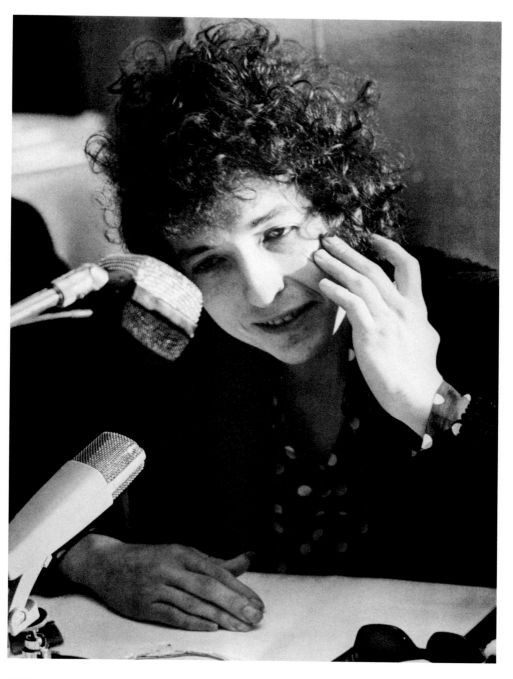

BOB DYLAN. Here's His Bobness, resplendent in polka dots and trademark smirk, toying with reporters at a press conference during his brief season as the king of rock and roll in the mid-1960s.

OTIS REDDING. Jon Landau called 1965 the year that modern soul music began to take shape. No surprise then that Redding released *The Dictionary of Soul* that year.

ARETHA FRANKLIN. She continued what Ray Charles had begun—the secularization of gospel. After years of overlooked recordings on Columbia, she was signed to Atlantic, and executive Jerry Wexler had the smarts to take her south, to Muscle Shoals, Alabama, to record.

TINA TURNER. One of rock and roll's greatest voices, she spent a decade living the unglamorous road life with the Ike and Tina Turner Revue until they finally found a mass audience.

JIMI HENDRIX. Critic Paul Williams said there were two Hendrixes: "one personified as the most animate guitar that ever deigned to talk to you or me, and the other, equally powerful but so simple we sometimes fail to notice its impact, his human voice."

THE DOORS. Lester Bangs wrote, "The Stones were dirty but the Doors were dread, and the difference is crucial, because dread is the great fact of our time." Left to right, at Morrison Hotel: Ray Manzarek, Jim Morrison, Robbie Kreiger, and John Densmore.

JANIS JOPLIN. She mattered as much for herself as for her music, critic Ellen Willis said. "Among American rock performers she was second only to Bob Dylan in importance as a creator/recorder/embodiment of her generation's history and mythology."

ERIC CLAPTON. He survived heroin, being called God, and loving his best friend's wife to shake off the residue of 1960s superstardom and emerge as a mature singer and pop star in the 1970s and onward. Here he is post-smack, onstage in the middle of the 1970s.

BRUCE SPRINGSTEEN. Leading the charge in the 1980s, he was backed by the magnificent E Street Band, which punctuated his street anthems with superlative evocations of early rock and roll excitement.

PATTI SMITH. Seeing the Rolling Stones on "The Ed Sullivan Show" changed her life. If not for that racket, she might be an English professor talking about poetry to eighteen-year-olds today. Instead, she is a poet and rock and roll star.

MADONNA. She was a one-woman girl group in the early 1980s, dancing through videos with disco-derived music that sounded so carefree. But that was several lifetimes ago.

NIRVANA. Record executives lunged toward Seattle in the early 1990s in the same way that they had swooped down on San Francisco in the late 1960s. Krist Novaselic, Kurt Cobain, and Dave Grohl went from independent-label obscurity to major label popularity overnight.

pay you what you're due, but you can't hear the bingo in the other room.' We'd played for about 15 minutes."

The pattern was the same in or outside London: rejection by most people and instant identification on the part of a tiny but significant minority. "My boyfriend then, Peter Lloyd and I lived in Ferryhill just outside Durham," says Pauline Murray of Penetration, "but we'd go to see everything in Newcastle. We'd seen pictures of the Sex Pistols looking great. We were real provincial fans. When we eventually got to London, and saw Johnny Rotten on a bus, we followed him into this shop: the jukebox had songs like 'Little Johnny Jewel' and Jonathan Richman, which we hadn't heard.

"In Newcastle, you could watch things as they came along, track it all through—T. Rex and Roxy Music, Mott the Hoople, Hawkwind, Cockney Rebel and then nothing for a long time. We started to go and see Doctors of Madness, who were a real record-company type band: then we saw the Sex Pistols in Northallerton, in this tiny club. A short while later they played with the Doctors of Madness in Middlesbrough and they wiped them out. They wiped a lot of bands out. It sounds a cliché now but I saw it happen. All those bands lost their confidence when the Sex Pistols came along."

"My life changed the moment that I saw the Sex Pistols," says Howard Devoto. "I immediately got caught up in trying to make things happen. Suddenly there was a direction, something I passionately wanted to be involved in. It was amazingly heady. I'd said to Malcolm, 'Do you want to come and play at my college?' and he said, 'If you can set it up, we'll do it.' I tried to persuade the Students' Union to put them on, but they wouldn't go for it. Not because of their reputation, just that they had never heard of them. There was still very little in the press."

Howard and Peter had already formed their own Sex-Pistols type group and had changed their identities to seal this pact of transformation. Instead of McNeish, there was Shelley, the name Peter would have had if he was a girl. Howard Trafford became Devoto. The group name, the Buzzcocks, came from a February *Time Out* review of *Rock Follies* which ends, "get a buzz, cock." The next thing was to play out, and promoting a Sex Pistols' concert was the easiest way: "Someone told me about this little hall above the Free Trade Hall," says Devoto, "I got it for the fourth of June, and meanwhile we were planning to play ourselves."

"The other two bottled out," says Shelley, "so we got this band, the Mandala Band, to play with the Pistols. We were organizing this thing and we put an ad in the *New Manchester Review* for a drummer and bass player. On the Friday afternoon we arrived at the Lesser Free Trade Hall and Howard said to me, within earshot of Malcolm, that a bass guitarist had called him, and they were calling back. As the doors were getting ready to open, I was in the box office taking the money: Malcolm was in the street saying to people, 'Come on in, there's a great band from London, you know, they're going to be famous. Roll up! Roll up!'

"There was this guy standing on the steps, saying he was waiting for somebody, he probably said he was waiting for a guitarist. So Malcolm said: 'Oh, you're a bass guitarist?' 'Yeah.' Malcolm said: 'Oh, they're in here,' and brought him inside to the box office and said to me, 'Here's your bass guitarist.' And there was the bemused Steve Diggle, with collar-length hair. It was a real Brian Rix farce. So I said, 'Now you're here, come and see this group.' And he liked it, and so we said, 'We've got a band, we're not too dissimilar,' and we made arrangements."

Advertised by a four-side, folded A_4 leaflet, the Manchester concert was a good opportunity to establish the Sex Pistols outside London, since Manchester is England's third largest city and the gateway to the North and North West. The concert was poorly attended but, again, the seventy or so people there included future performers and media names—such as Peter Hook and Bernard Sumner of Joy Division/New Order, Morrissey, Factory's Tony Wilson—who would lay the foundations for Manchester's future musical preeminence.

"That first appearance was quite difficult," says Morrissey; "There weren't any instructions. Being northern, we didn't know how to react: people were very rigid. There was a support group from Blackburn, and their hair swept off the stage. People were unwilling to respond to the Sex Pistols; the audience was very slim. It was a front-parlour affair. The Sex Pistols still had slightly capped sleeves and flares were not entirely taboo at that point: their jeans were somewhere in the middle. I liked them, but they seemed like a clued-in singer and three patched musicians."

"At that time, I'd never known what a good audience was," says John Lydon, "but when an audience behaves badly to you, it does tend to make your work better." Bolstered by their rejections, the Sex Pistols were building up speed. "There was a sudden point when I realized how good they were," says Ray Stevenson. "It was at the 100 Club: that telepathy and tension, where John would be slagging off the audience, Steve and Paul would be doing something, and they would just go into a number at the perfect moment. John's control. I was seeing them as amateurs, and to imagine this bozo kid from Finsbury Park with no schooling was phenomenal."

"They were having such fun," says Caroline Coon; "Steve told me he wanted to play guitar like Jimi Hendrix. Chris Spedding gave them a confidence they hadn't had: after he produced their first demo tape he said they had the most expressive guitar lines he'd heard in two decades of working in Rock'n'Roll. Steve was a typically underprivileged child, but he was the musician in the Sex Pistols. Johnny was like a young Rimbaud: thoughtful, angry, beautiful. I don't think he ever realized how beautiful he was."

Tapes exist of both the Manchester concert and a performance at the 100 Club on the 29th of the month. Manchester is a quantum leap from the Nashville in April, but the 100 Club tape is something else. Here the Sex Pistols are wound up to a pitch of impossible tautness: they swoop and drive through their set of fifteen songs (more than half of all they would ever play in their brief life). They begin with an improvisation, "Flowers of Romance," loosely based on Mud's "Dynamite," over which Lydon chants and rants. Phrases leap out of the aural streetfight: "True love and peace," "Jah Rastafari."

The songs are a series of musical manifestos: each sets up a statement which is only partially resolved at the song's end. They pass in a strip of rough harmonies from Glen, sounds of aerial battle from Steve Jones's guitar, and a rhythm section that never lets up. Lydon is mesmerizing: taunting both McLaren—"you always hide when I want money from you"—and his audience of peers. Just after "Flowers of Romance," Jones breaks a string but Lydon keeps the crowd entertained with a non-stop stream of squeals, sarcasm and invective, delivered in a bewildering variety of voices.

In the intimate setting of the 100 Club, the group could relax enough to take risks with their material and their performances. There they began to master their environment, using the acoustics of the small club to experiment with overload, feedback and distortion. Electric amplification had provided much of the excitement of early Rock'n'Roll: pushing their equipment to the limit—even further than the early Who—the Sex Pistols twisted their limited repertoire into a noise as futuristic as their rhetoric.

"Electricity come from other planets," quipped Lou Reed in a song released that summer. In return, the audience took the electricity of the group's performances to develop a sympathetic new style. Apart from the gelled, spiky, electric-shock hairstyle, there was "gobbing," the habit of spitting which began as a response to Lydon's constant expulsion of phlegm over the audience, and pogoing, the frozen leap, as though on a pogo stick, to gain a view: an action born out of necessity in the club's packed space.

But, just as the Sex Pistols inspired loyalty, then they deliberately fostered division. There were still fathers to be killed, people to be forcibly alienated. New material like "I Wanna Be Me" was a diatribe against a "typewriter god" suspiciously like Nick Kent. The lyric was quickly accompanied by a physical attack. "It was a week after seeing the Rolling Stones in Paris," says Kent, "where somebody pulled a gun on Mick Jagger backstage. There was a lot of violence in the air. I went over to Malcolm and for the first time ever he was quite cold. I just thought: 'Well, he's in a bad mood,' and sloped off to the very back of the 100 Club where I waited for the group to perform. I was sitting there, fairly drugged-out: my reactions to what did occur were very slow. I started noticing that this guy would, whenever he walked past, kick me in the shins. At first it seemed like a clumsy mistake: the second time, this was on purpose.

"I knew his name was Sid, because at the final night of the Stones at Earl's Court, all the future hierarchy were gathered in their Sunday best to get in and were unable to. He was obviously wearing his father's old clothes, he had the bog-brush hair and he looked really lairy. It was quite interesting to see that guy with the Richard Hell hair: Bryan James and Chrissie pointed Sid out to me. They'd tried him out as a singer. So he was starting to harass me and then he disappeared for a while. Then I noticed he was following Lydon around: everywhere Lydon went, he would go.

"Lydon by that point was the Don: he was top cat. In the classic star tradition, he didn't take the stage with the other three members: he would wait until they had turned up. I remember seeing Malcolm, Lydon and Sid, and Lydon was pointing my way. My mind was like a stranger: I remember this really malevolent look on all three. It all happens very quickly: Lydon goes on stage, and Sid decides to stand directly in front of me. I tapped him on the shoulder and I said, very careful: 'Could you move over?'

"Sid immediately pulled this chain out. He made some remark which he thought was insulting like: 'I don't like your trousers.' The guy next to me immediately makes a motion towards Vicious and then pulls his knife out and he really wants to cut my face. Years later I find his name is Wobble. This was a real speed freak, and this is when it got very unhealthy. I remember putting my hands up and not moving a muscle, and then Vicious tapped him on the shoulder and he disappeared immediately. It was all set up: Vicious then had a clear aim and got me with the bike chain."

"I used to get violent on a few occasions," says Wobble. "The one with Nick Kent was not one of those. Kent was with some geezer who demanded that we step aside, they couldn't see the band. I said 'Fuck off,' which was pretty standard. Sid wasn't a rucker, but he lashed him with a chain and then I had a go, but we were just mucking about. What I didn't know then was if you set yourself up as a hard man someone will come looking for you who's harder than you are."

"It wasn't painful," says Nick Kent: "The main thing was that it drew a lot of blood, which was just pouring down my face and my chest. Ron Watts grabbed Sid off me. All those guys there like Mick Jones didn't do a fucking thing. I was just trying to get the hell out of there—it had been years since I had been involved in any violence—and Vivienne comes up and says: 'Oh God, that guy's a psychopath. He'll never be at one of our concerts again, I promise that. It's not our fault, we're so sorry.'

"I saw Vivienne a month after that; the Ramones were playing and guess who she was with? With Sid, pogoing around. She came up to me and started to give me this: 'You can't handle violence; you're just a weed.' I was completely dazed: what is this macho shit? Lydon then came up to me and said: 'What's all this shit you're saying about us? You're trying to get us banned, aren't you?' 'The people that were telling you this aren't telling you the truth,' I replied; he just turned round to me and said: 'I know the truth.'

"I just thought, what have I done to bring this on? It was like a shower of abuse. It was really like that T-shirt, going from one side to the other side. I think for that gig Malcolm worked out a thing that a fight was going to occur, because it made the publicity. Having seen the three of them work it out, it was quite clear. Malcolm is one of those people who gets an idea and he is going to see that idea through hell and high water."

Another new song was "New York," a diatribe aimed this time at David JoHansen and Syl Sylvain. Lydon's lyrics are fluently vituperative, but they originate from McLaren. "Malcolm was real disappointed in me when I went with David JoHansen to Japan," says Syl Sylvain, "he wrote me this letter where he got really mad. But if the song says anything bad about New York, it has to do with Malcolm as much as with us: he was so in love that he got bitter."

But then it suited everybody to slag off New York: in the competition to patent Punk, London was coming up fast. On 4 July, there was the first chance to see "New York" live, when the Ramones played the

Roundhouse. "They had never played a larger venue than a club," says Nick Kent, "and all of a sudden they are on a much larger stage. Culture shock. They plugged into this huge PA stack and started playing—and it just went off. Kaput. It was a damp squib. Then they came back on and just did it. It was good, but there was a lot of violence. It got very territorial."

The same night, the Sex Pistols played at the Black Swan in Sheffield with the future Clash. "It was a Sunday," says Joe Strummer, "but two hundred people turned up: they were very receptive." Two days later, the Damned played their first concert supporting the Sex Pistols at the 100 Club. "They were so bizarre," says Jonh Ingham. "They never rehearsed. They were all playing this white-light speed, and just by chance things would mesh and fall apart and mesh again. It was like this phasing up and down: very odd, but funny."

On the 9th of the month, the Sex Pistols played their first concert on a large stage, at a Lyceum all-nighter. "They were absolutely petrified backstage," says Ingham. "They were taking it as very important: it had never occurred to me that they really wanted to win people over. That was the night that John stubbed out cigarettes on the back of his hand when he was singing: that frightened me. He was the most maniacal thing alive: it was back to Iggy, that unpredictability. He already had cigarette burns on his wrists: it was one of the games Sid and he played in their Hampstead bedsit.

"At the Lyceum, there was suddenly this major step up in musical ability. Glen was phenomenal, Paul was right on the beat. It was in one night: they were all just there. Suddenly you knew this was a great band. By now everyone was being very serious about making this happen, it was quite clear that this was the only thing that was going to break through and create a new generation of music."

Robert McG. Thomas, Jr.

ROCK AND ROLL TRAGEDY

Drummer Keith Moon had died in 1978, but the remaining members of the Who decided to carry on. So Pete Townshend, Roger Daltrey, and John Entwistle hired Kenney Jones and the Who set off on its first U.S. tour with the new lineup in 1979. When they played Riverfront Coliseum in Cincinnati, eleven concertgoers were killed—some were trampled and some were asphyxiated in a rush to get into the coliseum.

Robert McG. Thomas, Jr., covered the story for the *New York Times*.

DEC. 4, 1979. Eleven persons were killed and at least eight others were severely injured last night when thousands of young people waiting to attend a rock concert suddenly rushed the doors of the Riverfront Coliseum in Cincinnati.

"It was mayhem—bodies were all over," said Norman Wells, Assistant Fire Chief, one of scores of rescue workers summoned to the white concrete arena on the banks of the Ohio River, where an estimated 20,000 fans had gathered for a concert by The Who.

According to Chief Wells and other officials, the incident began just before the 8 P.M. scheduled start of the concert, when some of the fans managed to open one of the arena's doors, touching off a stampede.

Victims Crushed to Death

Officials at the Hamilton County Morgue said that those who died apparently had been crushed to death.

"We have all sorts of life-saving devices," said a paramedic who asked not to be identified. "We have drugs, we have highly trained people, and none of it did a bit of good. They just died."

Despite the deaths and injuries, the concert proceeded as scheduled.

"We figured it would be better to let it go than create another panic situation," Chief Wells said.

Neither the fans inside nor the performers were told of the deaths. When the concert was over about 10 P.M., many of those leaving the arena told television interviewers that they had been unaware of the deaths and injuries.

Officials said that seven young men and four young women, all in their teens and early 20's, had died. The police did not immediately release names of the victims and said some had no identification.

It was not immediately known how many were injured, although officials said that eight had been hospitalized with severe internal and other injuries.

The victims were among thousands of fans who had purchased general admission tickets and begun lining up as early as 1:30 P.M. in an effort to be assured a good seat.

At the time of the incident, eight of the coliseum's many doors had reportedly been opened, creating consternation among the fans lined up outside one door at the southwest corner, which remained shut.

The police later said coliseum officials failed to open enough doors to handle the crowd.

As the doors sprang open and the fans rushed forward, many fell and were trampled.

It Was No Use

"First, they threw a bottle through a window in the door," said Ray Schwertman, an usher. "Then they pushed through the hole, making it bigger. Three or four of us tried to hold them back, but it was no use. We couldn't hold them back.

"They carried in one boy and laid him on a table and he died. Others were laying out on the plaza."

"I was in the middle," said one fan, 17-year-old Michael Jordan. "It was crazy. You had to fight to save your life."

Another fan, Suzanne Sudrack, 15, said, "You could see people getting hurt. People were flailing elbows and smashing noses. You could see people going down."

Within minutes, the downtown area around the arena was filled with ambulances, fire engines and police and rescue units as the Hamilton County Disaster Group was activated. The alert directed doctors to nearby hospitals.

Although there have been larger disturbances at other rock concerts, and incidents involving more injuries, none has resulted in so many deaths.

Seventy-five people were hospitalized and 650 were treated for injuries at the site of a rock concert last year in Ontario, Calif.

The most notorious of the rock concert disturbances occurred in Altamont, Calif., in 1969, when a performance by the Rolling Stones was broken up by members of a motorcycle gang and a member of the audience was killed.

FED BY THINGS WE HATE

The jaded 1970s begat New Wave by decade's end and few bands ranged as high on the Satire Meter as Devo, the rubber-wigged minimalist Akron rock band. Whereas other New Wavers affected skinny ties, clipped vocals, and rooster hair, Devo offered a mechanized, nearly robotic version of the future.

Here two members of Devo meet beat guru William S. Burroughs, author of *Naked Lunch* and *Cities of the Red Night*. *Trouser Press* put Burroughs together with the band's Jerry Casale and Mark Mothersbaugh (who went on to be the house composer for the "Rugrats" enterprise) to discuss liberalism and conservatism, audiences and performers, and cabbages and kings.

William S. Burroughs: One thing that's been very encouraging in the past 30 years is the worldwide cultural revolution and the fact that the generation gap is getting wider. A lot of pressure to decriminalize marijuana is coming from congressman and judges whose sons were getting busted. That apparently is all over the world, even in the Far East, which is usually so conservative, and the Moslem world. One of the big factors in that has been pop music. It's everywhere: it gets behind the Iron Curtain and all through the Orient and makes these changes.

Jerry Casale: [Devo chose rock as a medium for its message] because it's the most hideous area there is. It's exciting because it's filthy—nauseous yet erect.

WSB: Wait a minute. You chose it because you like music.

Mark Mothersbaugh: That's not true.

WSB: No? You don't feel some aptitude for music? The reason I write is because I have always had some natural aptitude for words.

MM: Well, the equipment was just inexpensive. We couldn't be filmmakers because we couldn't afford the equipment.

JC: On an immediate, unguarded level, there's no doubt about it: There's some drive to do it because you can do it. But then when you add to that the consciousness, the willful use of this innate ability, that's where it gets into "you do it because you hate it," because you hate what's being done.

The arena is so complex and vulgar, it's filled with the worst con artists, the most bizarre people, the biggest amount of bucks, the most mass dissemination. It deals with electronic innovations, it deals with TV, theater and dance, it deals with the immediacy of performance itself, so it's packed full of nuances. The limitations are what you place on it. You could certainly go into that area and twist it, do anything you want with it, and your success or failure is largely on your own lack of or inclusion of vision over a sustained period. As soon as you forget what you want to do, it's over. But what most of 'em want to do is exactly what the zombies who run everything want 'em to do, because there are plenty of lackeys out there that are happy to be voluntary robots and get paid for it. Their particular hack imaginations synch up with those who want to give 'em bucks to do it.

So Devo enters the scene knowing all that, but knowing also there's no choice but the basement or that. Now what do we do? We let all the demons come out. All the horrible supermarket themes and elevator music and TV theme songs and MOR ballads on radio that filled us up while we were growing up become twisted. If anything, Devo is on a performance level the enactment of a mutation aesthetic.

William, you and David Bowie had a discussion in *Rolling Stone* in 1974 about whether to use sonic warfare onstage. Bowie said he was not interested in doing that to people. He said he would never turn it on a crowd and make them shit their pants. I suppose we would. I think to send a whole crowd in, give 'em Kimbies at the door and inform them as part of Devo's performance they're gonna get to shit their pants *en masse* at the end of the night—that we probably have that tendency to do it, whatever you want to decide about that.

WSB: In a sense, if any artist is successful he would do exactly that. If you wrote about death completely convincingly you'd kill all your readers.

JC: What's going too far though? Making them shit their pants?

WSB: Would it be going too far to kill them? I'll ask that question.

JC: Well, I suppose there's still some liberalism left in Devo; we'd say yes. We'd want 'em to come back and shit again.

WSB: If your music or your novel isn't fun, nobody's gonna read it or listen to it. Showbiz!

JC: We base our aesthetic on self-deprecating humor. We include ourselves in it. But obviously there's something behind it. We have that sense—maybe that's the midwestern part—that sense of shame about being human.

WSB: Everybody does. That's part of being human.

JC: But dealing with it and admitting it is rare. The masses are bad spuds who resort to defense mechanisms like fundamentalist religion and other psychotic values, far-rightists who deny it because they cannot deal with it. They've worked themselves into a constipated corner where to admit it is threatening to the rigid order they created. Good spuds have the ability to make fun of themselves.

JC: There's no question in our minds that humans are Devo. We've stated our case. I don't even see how you can disagree with it.

WSB: I feel there are too many of them.

JC: Too many humans.

WSB: It's intolerable.

JC: It seems like humans have always taken care of themselves like any other organism; there's a self-defeating gene that makes sure they wipe themselves out in the right numbers. Possibly that's all going on again. In other words, the artificial manifestations of that basic urge would be Reagan's politics and the far right; environmental manifestation would be the very strong death wish to allow pollution to take over—like, fuck it, here we go. Maybe this stuff is all perfectly in keeping with human existence on the planet. Maybe we shouldn't bitch about anything or be appalled. Maybe we've got some erroneous ideas about enlightened human beings that could live in a different manner.

WSB: There's no way that things are. Things are changing with such rapidity.

JC: We wish!

WSB: They are.

JC: Well, changing but staying right the same.

WSB: Not really. Remember, 40 years ago the word "fuck" couldn't appear on printed paper. It was a whole different world then. No one questioned the Depression. No one questioned the right of a cop to beat up a nigger. All that is gone in the last 40 years. The only way it could come back would be with an out-and-out fascist takeover—a real police state. We talk about fascism here but we don't know what we're talking about.

JC: I know that, but there are different forms of it.

MM: There are new ways to do the same things they used to do. They aren't beating them over the head with clubs, they aren't stopping you with gunfire. But there are new, more subversive, nastier ways to control people.

WSB: Yeah, but just compare that with living in Argentina, where 4,000 people are dragged out of their beds and shot every year just for nothing, just for any liberal association. I've talked to people who've just gotten out of that. I'd rather have this than that, wouldn't you?

JC: That's a more mature attitude. [Laughter]

WSB: You don't want to starve to death, either . . .

JC: No.

WSB: Well, that's what I mean. Some things are a hell of a lot worse than others.

JC: More immediate and more crude, maybe.

MM: There's a good chance 4,000 people are gonna get dragged out of their houses in New York and shot each year. It just won't be by cops.

JC: Those things are all on the continuum; there's no dichotomy there.

WSB: None whatsoever. And the reason we aren't dragged out and shot is probably because other people are. We pay the price of other people starving. We buy our relative freedom. That's the whole CIA policy: Let it happen somewhere else. Everything is political in a sense. You can't say "politics stops here."

JC: We think everything is political anyway. . . . It's like an inverted aesthetic 'cause we're dealing in subversive sickness—taking what you know about society and people and what we agree with and applying it to an aesthetic to make the very sick people buy it.

WSB: It's always been my feeling the very sick are *not* going to buy it. They're not gonna buy anything—except more sickness. You can't tell anybody anything they don't know already. It's only people that are in your areas of synchronicity that are going to respond.

JC: But what do people know?

WSB: You make people aware of what they know and don't know.

JC: We're just trying to put out information. You can't tell people what they don't know; that's why mass education is a joke. We know the world's upside-down.

WSB: It's obviously completely ill-intentioned so far as our species is concerned. There's something behind the whole scene—any scene, if you see chaos, ask yourself who profits in this. Somebody does. Of course, in a situation of chaos one group who's going to profit are the very rich. Not the fairly rich—I'm talking about a very, very select club. They can weather anything. Inflation's to their advantage because they can buy things nobody else can buy.

"Pessimistic" is a meaningless word. The captain says the ship is sinking; Is he a pessimist? If the ship actually is sinking, no!

JC: That's exactly it. We're accused all the time of pessimism; we're maligned for being cynical and it's frankly disgusting because all we're doing is reporting the facts. Because we question popular mythologies about progress and the value structure it's all based on as being absolutely rancid, then of course we're accused of having sour grapes. It's ridiculous; all you have to do is look at Jerry Falwell and Ronald McDonald and Ronald Reagan and start putting it all together. What we see, then, are born-again Christians dressed in double-knit pilgrim suits with particle guns that look like blunderbusses gettin' in station wagons and searching out people who aren't Christian enough to eat Thanksgiving turkey.

WSB: The born-again Christian thing is advantageous to the very rich, to keep people in line. It isn't an accident at all.

JC: Possibly we're even as popular as we are because we're misperceived as sickness. We didn't put things together quite the same way somebody else would, being from the midwest and being raised in mindless eclectic filth. We responded to it and received all the information, but what we chose to do about it was kind of aggressive in a malign way. Not really malign; we can see how it's perceived that way. Because we're pissed-off spuds with a plan; we aggressively take the case to those who make life hideous.

We'd like to make Devo a Church of De-evolution—legally, seriously, a cable franchise same as Oral Roberts, Garner Ted Armstrong, all those evil fuckers. Not pay taxes, like them. Not be presented in the rock 'n' roll arena as labor for a corporate record company but rather the Church of De-evolution. Then, whatever you're presenting is suddenly appearing in a whole new context. We'd probably be assassinated.

JC: De-evolution is basically an extended joke that was as valid an explanation of anything as the Bible is, a mythology for people to believe in. We were just attacking the ideas humans have that they're at the center of the universe—that they're important, that they must be immortal, that there must be a Guide. The whole (what we think of as inverted) valued system that precipitates every cultural/political form follows from it.

WSB: Essentially monotheism—Christ and Muhammad. Incidentally, Muhammadan fundamentalists are fully as bad as Bible-belters; in fact, I think they're worse.

JC (to Mark): See, we've been leaving them out.

WSB: They're more used to killing, for one thing; it comes more naturally to them. In Egypt they have seen these people as a political mass, and the same thing could happen here. Fundamentalists are seen in Egypt as subversive, as a political danger to the regime. They're the ones who killed Sadat. It's as if Jerry Falwell's boys had assassinated President Reagan.

JC: If there's anything important about history, it's that stupidity wins. We're paranoid for good reasons: hundreds of years where assholes take over, knowledge is lost and things go backwards. We question the whole theory concerning progress, and the middle-class idea of a "better life."

WSB: You must remember this is a modern idea. While it completely permeates America and a good deal of Western Europe now, progress is a new concept; it came in with the industrial revolution. Another idea that came in there that we are really suffering from now is "the more the merrier"—more producers, more consumers, more people and therefore more pollution, depletion of resources, etc. Inflation's a direct result of overpopulation: less and less for more and more.

I think the concept of progress is pretty much devaluated in respectable intellectual circles. I mean, it's a pretty primitive person—although god knows there are millions and millions of those—who really believe in progress at this time. We've seen where it goes; we've seen places like Hawaii stopping progress saying "We don't *want* any more hotels built here. The ocean's gonna be so polluted you can't go in, so what do they come to Waikiki for?" That's a very simple illustration of how the whole idea of progress is breaking down.

JC: We really agree. We're attacking the idea that there is progress, the whole mythology of the last 300 years, the industrial revolution, which we feel has gone nowhere. We're at the end of it. You see exactly what consumerism has done, you see exactly what sin, guilt, work and disease have wrought as cornerstones of culture, and it's still operating. That's why we thought "Working in the Coal Mine" was so funny. "Lord, I'm so tired; how long can this go on?" The answer is it can go on as long as there's one guy to swing a pick ax.

WSB: Most of the trouble we have now was quite predictable at the beginning of the industrial revolution because nothing was done to control it—the same way they don't do anything about pollution until it's too late. Many scientists say that the cumulative effect of the radiation level already is lethal. We can go so far as to say we don't have more than 100 years.

JC: When you consider how this happens, it becomes obvious to us that it's inherent in human design—that humans are unfortunately very predictable in their response patterns.

WSB: It's not an either/or position. There's no doubt that there isn't a damn thing you can do about a lot of what's happening. It's like the fall of the Roman empire: people knew that the currency was going and the barbarians were moving in from the north, but life went on: people wrote poetry, played music. It almost becomes like the weather: there isn't anything you can do about it, so why keep yourself in a state?

JC: Devo deals with people who eat McDonald's hamburgers and wear Jordache jeans; that's our dilemma. I guess we're almost fed by the things we hate.

WSB: Everybody is. Can man exist without enemies? Well, the answer is he never has.

JC: We're looking at the planet, pretending we're hovering in the starship Enterprise, observing the planet for a month. You can tune in anywhere.

WSB: I would say, "I want to see the manager. Who is responsible for this mess?"

STATEMENT TO THE SENATE COMMERCE COMMITTEE

The Parents Music Resource Center drew the usually aloof Frank Zappa from hiding in 1985, when Tipper Gore—not yet the Second Lady, but the wife of an influential senator—bought her daughter Prince's *Purple Rain* album and was disgusted by references to masturbation in the lyrics. After comparing notes with her pals, the PMRC was born. Gore and the other "Washington Wives" (so dubbed by the press) wanted the recording industry to label albums with stickers that described songs with offensive content. Urging record-industry regulation, the PMRC took its case to the Senate Commerce Committee. Zappa, John Denver, and Twisted Sister lead singer Dee Snider testified before the committee.

Zappa had already had a run-in over the content of one of his albums. MCA backed out of a deal to distribute Zappa's Barking Pumpkin Records in 1984 because an employee at the pressing plant objected to Zappa's material. After he found another distributor, Zappa produced a warning label for his albums: "This album contains material which a truly free society would neither fear nor repress. In some socially retarded areas, religious fanatics and ultra-conservative political organizations violate your First Amendment Rights by attempting to censor rock & roll albums. We feel that this is un-Constitutional and un-American."

THESE ARE my personal observations and opinions. I speak on behalf of no group or professional organization. My full statement has been supplied to you in advance. I wish it entered into the *Congressional Record.* Since my speaking time has been limited to ten minutes, I will read only part of it. I address my comments to the PMRC and the public, as well as this committee.

The PMRC proposal is an ill-conceived piece of nonsense which fails to deliver any real benefits to children, infringes the civil liberties of people who are not children and promises to keep the courts busy for years, dealing with the interpretational and enforcemental problems inherent in the proposal's design.

It is my understanding that, in law, First Amendment issues are decided with a preference for the least restrictive alternative. In this context, the PMRC's demands are the equivalent of treating dandruff by decapitation.

No one has forced Mrs. Baker or Mrs. Gore to bring Prince or Sheena Easton into their homes. Thanks to the Constitution, they are free to buy other forms of music for their children. Apparently they insist on purchasing the works of contemporary recording artists in order to support a personal illusion of aerobic sophistication. Ladies, please be advised: the $8.98 purchase price does not entitle you to a kiss on the foot from the composer or performer in exchange for a spin on the family Victrola. Taken as a whole, the complete list of PMRC demands reads like an instruction manual for some sinister kind of "toilet training program" to housebreak ALL composers and performers because of the lyrics of a few. Ladies, how dare you?

The ladies' shame must be shared by the bosses at the major labels who, through the RIAA, chose to bargain away the rights of composers, performers, and retailers in order to pass H. R. 2911, the blank tape tax: A PRIVATE TAX, LEVIED BY AN INDUSTRY ON CONSUMERS, FOR THE BENEFIT OF A SELECT GROUP WITHIN THAT INDUSTRY.

Is this a "consumer issue"? You bet it is. PMRC spokesperson Kandy Stroud announced to millions of fascinated viewers on last Friday's ABC *Nightline* debate that Senator Gore, a man she described as "a friend of the music industry," is co-sponsor of something she referred to as "anti-piracy legislation." Is this the same tax bill with a nicer name?

The major record labels need to have H. R. 2911 whiz through a few committees before anybody smells a rat. One of them is chaired by Senator Thurmond. Is it a coincidence that Mrs. Thurmond is affiliated with the PMRC? I can't say she's a member, because the PMRC HAS NO MEMBERS. Their secretary told me on the phone last Friday that the PMRC has NO MEMBERS . . . only FOUNDERS. I asked how many other D.C. wives are NONMEMBERS of an organization that raises money by mail, has a tax-exempt status, and seems intent on running the Constitution of the United States through the family paper-shredder. I asked her if it was a cult. Finally, she said she couldn't give me an answer and that she had to call their lawyer.

While the wife of the Secretary of the Treasury recites *"Gonna drive my love inside you . . . ,"* and Senator Gore's wife talks about "BONDAGE!" and

"Oral sex at gunpoint" on *The CBS Evening News*, people in high places work on a tax bill that is so ridiculous, the only way to sneak it through is to keep the public's mind on something else: "PORN ROCK."

The PMRC practices a curious double standard with these fervent recitations. Thanks to them, helpless young children all over America get to hear about oral sex at gunpoint on network TV several nights a week. Is there a secret FCC dispensation here? What sort of end justifies THESE means? PTA parents should keep an eye on these ladies if that's their idea of "good taste."

Is the basic issue morality? Is it mental health? Is it an issue at all? The PMRC has created a lot of confusion with improper comparisons between song lyrics, videos, record packaging, radio broadcasting and live performances. These are all different mediums, and the people who work in them have a right to conduct their business without trade-restraining legislation, whipped up like an instant pudding by The Wives Of Big Brother.

Is it proper that the husband of a PMRC NON-MEMBER/FOUNDER/PERSON sits on any committee considering business pertaining to the blank tape tax or his wife's lobbying organization? Can any committee thus constituted "find facts" in a fair and unbiased manner? This committee has three. A minor conflict of interest?

The PMRC promotes their program as a harmless type of consumer information service, providing "guidelines" which will assist baffled parents in the determination of the "suitability" of records listened to by "very young children." The methods they propose have several unfortunate side effects, not the least of which is the reduction of all American music, recorded and live, to the intellectual level of a Saturday morning cartoon show.

Teenagers with $8.98 in their pocket might go into a record store alone, but "very young children" do not. Usually there is a parent in attendance. The $8.98 is in the parent's pocket. The parent can always suggest that the $8.98 be spent on a book.

If the parent is afraid to let the child read a book, perhaps the $8.98 can be spent on recordings of instrumental music. Why not bring jazz or classical music into your home instead of Blackie Lawless or Madonna? Great music with NO WORDS AT ALL is available to anyone with sense enough to look beyond this week's platinum-selling fashion plate.

Children in the "vulnerable" age bracket have a natural love for music. If, as a parent, you believe they should be exposed to something more uplifting than "SUGAR WALLS," support Music Appreciation programs in schools. Why haven't you considered YOUR CHILD'S NEED FOR CON-

SUMER INFORMATION? Music Appreciation costs very little compared to sports expenditures. Your children have a right to know that something besides pop music exists.

It is unfortunate that the PMRC would rather dispense governmentally sanitized heavy metal music than something more "uplifting." Is this an indication of PMRC's personal taste, or just another manifestation of the low priority this administration has placed on education for the arts in America? The answer, of course, is NEITHER. You can't distract people from thinking about an unfair tax by talking about Music Appreciation. For that you need SEX . . . and LOTS OF IT.

Because of the subjective nature of the PMRC ratings, it is impossible to guarantee that some sort of "despised concept" won't sneak through, tucked away in new slang or the overstressed pronunciation of an otherwise innocent word. If the goal here is TOTAL VERBAL/MORAL SAFETY, there is only one way to achieve it: watch no TV, read no books, see no movies, listen to only instrumental music or buy no music at all.

The establishment of a rating system, voluntary or otherwise, opens the door to an endless parade of Moral Quality Control Programs based on "Things Certain Christians Don't Like." What if the next bunch of Washington Wives demands a large yellow "J" on all material written or performed by Jews, in order to save helpless children from exposure to "concealed Zionist doctrine"?

Record ratings are frequently compared to film ratings. Apart from the quantitative difference, there is another that is more important: People who act in films are hired to "pretend." No matter how the film is rated, it won't hurt them personally. Since many musicians write and perform their own material and stand by it as their art (whether you like it or not), an imposed rating will stigmatize them as INDIVIDUALS. How long before composers and performers are told to wear a festive little PMRC ARMBAND with their Scarlet Letter on it?

The PMRC rating system restrains trade in one specific musical field: rock. No ratings have been requested for comedy records or country music. Is there anyone in the PMRC who can differentiate INFALLIBLY between rock and country music? Artists in both fields cross stylistic lines. Some artists include comedy material. If an album is part rock, part country, part comedy, what sort of label would it get? Shouldn't the ladies be warning everyone that inside those country albums with the American flags, the big trucks and the atomic pompadours there lurks a fascinating variety of songs about sex, violence, alcohol and THE DEVIL, recorded in a way that lets you hear EVERY WORD, sung for you by people who have been to prison and are PROUD OF IT?

If enacted, the PMRC program would have the effect of protectionist legislation for the country music industry, providing more security for cowboys than it does for children. One major retail outlet has already informed the Capitol Records sales staff that it would not purchase or display an album with ANY KIND OF STICKER ON IT.

Another chain with outlets in shopping malls has been told by the landlord that if it racked "hard-rated albums" they would lose their lease. That opens up an awful lot of shelf space for somebody. Could it be that a certain Senatorial husband-and-wife team from Tennessee sees this as an "affirmative action program" to benefit the suffering multitudes in Nashville?

Is the PMRC attempting to save future generations from SEX ITSELF? The type, the amount and the timing of sexual information given to a child should be determined by parents, not by people who are involved in a tax scheme cover-up.

The PMRC has concocted a Mythical Beast, and compounds the chicanery by demanding "consumer guidelines" to keep it from inviting your children inside its SUGAR WALLS. Is the next step the adoption of a "PMRC National Legal Age For COMPREHENSION Of Vaginal Arousal"? Many people in this room would gladly support such legislation, but, before they start drafting their bill, I urge them to consider these facts:

1. There is no conclusive scientific evidence to support the claim that exposure to any form of music will cause the listener to commit a crime or damn his soul to hell.
2. Masturbation is not illegal. If it is not illegal to do it, why should it be illegal to sing about it?
3. No medical evidence of hairy palms, warts, or blindness has been linked to masturbation or vaginal arousal, nor has it been proven that hearing references to either topic automatically turns the listener into a social liability.
4. Enforcement of antimasturbatory legislation could prove costly and time-consuming.
5. There is not enough prison space to hold all the children who do it.

The PMRC's proposal is most offensive in its "moral tone." It seeks to enforce a set of implied religious values on its victims. Iran has a religious government. Good for them. I like having the capitol of the United States in Washington, D.C., in spite of recent efforts to move it to Lynchburg, Virginia.

Fundamentalism is not a state religion. The PMRC's request for labels regarding sexually explicit lyrics, violence, drugs, alcohol, and especially OCCULT CONTENT reads like a catalog of phenomena abhorrent to practitioners of that faith. How a person worships is a private matter, and should not be INFLICTED UPON OR EXPLOITED by others. Understanding the fundamentalist leanings of this organization, I think it is fair to wonder if their rating system will eventually be extended to inform parents as to whether a musical group has homosexuals in it. Will the PMRC permit musical groups to exist, but only if gay members don't sing, and are not depicted on the album cover?

The PMRC has demanded that record companies "reevaluate" the contracts of those groups who do things on stage that THEY find offensive. I remind the PMRC that GROUPS are comprised of INDIVIDUALS. If one guy wiggles too much, does the whole band get an "X"? If the group gets dropped from the label as a result of this "reevaluation" process, do the other guys in the group who weren't wiggling get to sue the guy who wiggled because he ruined their careers? Do the FOUNDERS of this TAX-EXEMPT ORGANIZATION WITH NO MEMBERS plan to indemnify record companies for any losses incurred from unfavorably decided breach-of-contract suits, or is there a PMRC secret agent in the Justice Department?

Should individual musicians be rated? If so, who is qualified to determine if the GUITAR PLAYER is an "X," the VOCALIST is a "D/A," or the DRUMMER is a "V"? If the BASS PLAYER (or his senator) belongs to a religious group that dances around with poisonous snakes, does he get an "O"? What if he has an earring in one ear, wears an Italian horn around his neck, sings about his astrological sign, practices yoga, reads the Quaballah or owns a rosary? Will his "occult content" rating go into an old ColntelPro computer, emerging later as a "FACT," to determine if he qualifies for a homeowner loan? Will they tell you this is necessary to protect the folks next door from the possibility of "devil-worship" lyrics creeping through the wall?

What hazards await the unfortunate retailer who accidentally sells an "O" rated record to somebody's little Johnny? Nobody in Washington seemed to care when Christian terrorists bombed abortion clinics in the name of Jesus. Will you care when the "FRIENDS OF THE WIVES OF BIG BROTHER" blow up the shopping mall?

The PMRC wants ratings to start as of the date of their enactment.

That leaves the current crop of "objectionable material" untouched. What will be the status of recordings from the Golden Era prior to censorship? Do they become collector's items . . . or will another "fair and unbiased committee" order them destroyed in a public ceremony?

Bad facts make bad law, and people who write bad laws are, in my opinion, more dangerous than songwriters who celebrate sexuality. Freedom of speech, freedom of religious thought, and the right to due process for composers, performers and retailers are imperiled if the PMRC and the major labels consummate this nasty bargain. Are we expected to give up Article One so the big guys can collect an extra dollar on every blank tape and ten to twenty-five percent on tape recorders? What's going on here? Do WE get to vote on this tax? There's an awful lot of smoke pouring out of the legislative machinery used by the PMRC to inflate this issue. Try not to inhale it. Those responsible for the vandalism should pay for the damage by VOLUNTARILY RATING THEMSELVES. If they refuse, perhaps the voters could assist in awarding the Congressional "X," the Congressional "D/A," the Congressional "V," and the Congressional "O." Just like the ladies say: these ratings are necessary to protect our children. I hope it's not too late to put them where they REALLY belong.

Lynn Hirschberg

STRANGELOVE

Here's Courtney Love of Hole, profiled moments before her great fame as rock star, wife-then-widow of another rock star, and respected film actress. She survived the days of his'n'her syringes to earn acclaim as an artist in music and film.

COURTNEY LOVE is late. She's nearly always late, and not just ten, fifteen minutes late, but usually more than an hour past the time she's said she'll be someplace. She's late for band rehearsals, she was late when she used to strip, she was even an hour late for a meeting with a record company executive who wanted to sign her band, Hole. Courtney assumes that people will wait. She assumes that people will forgive her as they stare at the clock and stare at the door and wonder where the hell she is. And they do forgive her. Until they can't stand it anymore and then they get mad, fed up, and move on. But by that time Courtney is gone, she's off keeping someone else waiting.

When she does show up, she *shows* up. When you're an hour late, you can really make an entrance. She's tall and big-boned and her shoulder-length hair is cut like a mop and dyed yellow-blonde. The dark roots show on purpose—nothing about Courtney is an accident—and today she's attached a plastic hair-clip in the shape of a bow to a few strands. She's wearing black stockings with runs in them, a vintage dress that's a size too small, and a pair of black clogs. Her skin, which has been heavily Pancaked and powdered to cover an outbreak of acne, is pasty-white, and her lips are painted bright red. She has beautiful round blue-green eyes, which she has carefully made up, but the focus in on her mouth. She's all lipstick.

And talk. From the moment Courtney sits down at a table in City, her favorite restaurant near her home in Los Angeles, the verbal pyrotechnics begin. You get the sense that she has a monologue going twenty-four hours a day and that sometimes she includes others. When she's not talking, she doesn't seem to be listening exactly but, rather, *absorbing*: Who is this person? What is his context? What can I learn/get from him? are the thoughts coursing through her brain. With Courtney, it's not so much scheming as it is focus. She has known what she wanted and what she wanted was to be a star. More precisely, Courtney always thought she *was* a star. She was just waiting for everyone else to wake up.

It looks as if, after a few false starts—an acting career that didn't quite take, some stints in other bands that didn't work out—Courtney is having her moment. She and Hole were just signed to a million-dollar record deal; she is married to Kurt Cobain, the lead singer of Nirvana, and within the realm of the alternative-music scene, Courtney is now regarded as a train-wreck personality: she may be awful, but you can't take your eyes off her.

Her timing is excellent: in the wake of the huge success of Nirvana, an extremely talented rock band from Seattle that surprised everyone in the industry by selling (so far) seven million records worldwide, there has been a frenzy to sign other bands in the punk-grunge-underground mode. The music ranges from almost pop to loud thrashing—the only real unifying link is that most of the bands are on independent labels and appeal to college audiences. "No one can get a seat on a plane to Seattle or Portland now," says Ed Rosenblatt, president of Geffen Records, Nirvana's label. "Every flight is booked by A&R people out to find the next Nirvana."

Last August, Hole, which is much more extreme and less melodic than Nirvana, released *Pretty on the Inside* on Caroline Records, an independent label that is a subsidiary of Virgin. The record is intensely difficult to listen to—Courtney's singing is a mix of shouting, screeching, and rasping—but her songwriting, which has been compared to Joni Mitchell's, is powerful. *"Pretty on the Inside,"* writes Elizabeth Wurtzel in *The New Yorker,* "is such a cacophony—full of such grating, abrasive, and unpleasant sludges of noise—that very few people are likely to get through it once, let alone give it the repeated listenings it needs for you to discover that it's probably the most compelling album to have been released in 1991."

Courtney's postfeminist stance (she has the power—she just wants to be loved) echos throughout her songs. Her chosen topics—rape and abortion, to name two—are extremely provocative. "Slit me open and suck my scars," she sings about sex. "Don't worry baby, you will never stink so bad again," she intones about a botched abortion. In her strongest song, "Doll Parts," she turns introspective: "I want to be the girl with the most cake / He only loves those things because he loves to see them break. . . ."

Even before Nirvana's massive success, Hole was lumped with Babes in Toyland, L7, the Nymphs, and other female-led underground groups.

Although these bands were quite different from one another, and wildly competitive, they were dubbed "foxcore." And when Nirvana's album *Nevermind* started to sell like mad, the so-called foxcore bands suddenly seemed commercially viable. "There's a pre-Nirvana record-industry perception of this kind of music," says Gary Gersh, the Geffen Records A&R person who signed Nirvana. "And there's a post-Nirvana record-industry perspective. But if you're out there and trying to sign the next Nirvana, you're chasing your tail. The game is not finding the next Nirvana, because there won't be a next Nirvana."

It is somehow appropriate that Madonna's new company, Maverick, was the first to be interested in signing Courtney Love to a major record deal. In mid-1991, Guy Oseary, an enthusiastic nineteen-year-old who was working for Madonna and her manager, Freddy De Mann, at their then unnamed company, told his bosses about Hole. He also contacted Courtney's lawyer, Rosemary Carroll, and Hole-mania began. "Courtney has been orchestrating this game plan from the beginning," says Carroll. "She was always very aware of the business, of her place in the business."

Courtney claims she never wanted to sign with Maverick. "Freddy would have me riding elephants," she says. "They don't know what I am. For them, I'm a visual, *period*." Madonna's presence worried her even more: she did not want to share the spotlight with the premier blonde goddess of the last decade. "Madonna's interest in me was kind of like Dracula's interest in his latest victim."

But Courtney, who is nothing if not shrewd, knew that one offer could spur others. Besides, she had another ace to play: by late '91 she was dating Kurt Cobain. When Hole went to England, she wasn't shy about either Madonna's interest or her new boyfriend. She gave lots of interviews and the notoriously fickle British music magazines, who adored her grunge-rock sound and her torn thirties tea dresses, proclaimed her their new genius. "The British tabloids called me 'leggy' and 'stunning'," she recalls. "The best article was about Madonna. It had a really big picture of me as a blonde and a really small picture of her as a brunette. I cut that one out."

For his part, Oseary, who saw Courtney and Hole as his private find, was shocked. "The stories in the English press went, 'Madonna doesn't have AIDS and she wants to sign Hole'," he recalls, sounding rather exasperated. "From then on, it was 'Madonna's Hole,' 'Madonna's Hole.' Suddenly, we were just *one* of the bidders. At Hole's next show, thirteen A&R people were there!"

So it began—the first ever bidding war over an unsigned female band. (In the record business, independent labels are not considered contenders—until you're on a major label, you're unsigned.) It wasn't clear whether or not most of the bidders liked, or even knew, Hole's music—it was the magic combination of Madonna's interest, Kurt Cobain's interest, and the strength of Courtney's personality. In any case, Clive Davis, president of Arista Records, reportedly offered a million dollars to sign the band. Rick Rubin, head of Def American, was interested, but he and Courtney clashed when they met. She had similar difficulties with Jeff Ayeroff at Virgin. "Now Kurt," she exclaims, "is able to go into Capitol, go into a meeting, decide he doesn't like it halfway through, walk out on the guys mid-sentence, and everyone goes 'There goes Kurt. He's moody. Nirvana's great.' But I go in and spend three hours with Jeff Ayeroff and tell him more about punk rock than he ever knew. I give him quality time, but I'm sorry, I don't want to be on his label and he gets a boner about it and calls me a bitch."

In the end, she signed with Gary Gersh at Geffen, the same label as Nirvana. "We didn't make the deal because she is married to Kurt Cobain," says Ed Rosenblatt. "But it is weird. Hole is a band who we happen to believe in, and, oh, by the way, she's married to . . ."

Courtney's deal, worth a million dollars, is bigger and better than her husband's. She and Carroll insisted on that. "I got excellent, excellent contractual things," she boasts. "I made them pull out Nirvana's contract, and everything on there, I wanted more." She pauses. "No matter what label I'm on, I'm going to be his wife," she says. "I'm enough of a person to transcend that."

Probably. But in the circles she travels in, Kurt Cobain is regarded as a holy man. Courtney, meanwhile, is viewed by many as a charismatic opportunist. There have been rampant reports about the couple's drug problems, and many believe she introduced Cobain to heroin. They are expecting a baby this month, and even the most tolerant industry insiders feel for the health of the child. "It is appalling to think that she would be taking drugs when she knew she was pregnant," says one close friend. "We're all worried about that baby."

"Courtney and Kurt are the nineties, just more talented version of Sid and Nancy," says one executive. "She's going to be famous and he already is, but unless something happens, they're going to self-destruct. I know they're both going to be big stars. I just don't want to be a part of it."

Courtney has heard all this before and, in a perverse way, she thrives on it. "I heard a rumor that Madonna and I were doing heroin together," she says rather gleefully, lighting up a cigarette. "I've heard I have live sex onstage and that I'm H.I.V. positive."

Courtney laughs. None of these statements is true, although the live sex thing is a very persistent rumor. "Now," she continues, balancing a cigarette on the edge of the ashtray, "I get a chance to prove myself. And if I do, I do. If I don't—*hey,* I married a rich man!"

She drags for dramatic effect. She's joking, and, then again, she isn't. Audacity is one of the keys to her charm. "You know, I just can't find makeup that stays on in the summer," she says, abruptly changing the subject. Courtney stamps out her cigarette, rummages through her purse, and heads off to the bathroom.

"Only about a quarter of what Courtney says is true," says Kat Bjelland, the leader of Babes in Toyland. "But nobody usually bothers to decipher which are the lies. She's all about image. And that's interesting. Irritating, but interesting."

When it comes to biographical information, Courtney is hard to track. She says she was born in San Francisco in 1966 (that date seems off—she is probably older than twenty-six, although not much), her father was involved in the Grateful Dead, and her mother, who was married several times since, is closer to Courtney's four half-siblings, one of whom is a Rhodes scholar. Courtney hated school and moved around quite a lot: from boarding school in New Zealand to a Quaker school in Australia to where she ended up—Oregon. At twelve, she stole a Kiss T-shirt from Woolworth's and was sent to a juvenile detention center. "To be quite honest," she recalls, "I got into it. I was very semiotic about my delinquency. I studied it. I learned a lot. I'd grown up with no discipline and I learned a lot about denial. It did not have an adverse affect on me."

After three years, around 1981, she was out and living on a small trust fund. She pretty much decided that music would be her world. She also began stripping—an occupation that has, on and off, supported her for most of her adult life. "I didn't want to sell drugs," she explains. "I didn't want to steal cars. I didn't want to be a prostitute. So I stripped.

"And I was fat then," she continues. "You can be fat and strip. I'd strip at Jumbo's Clown Room. Or I'd work in the day at the Seventh Veil. I didn't have a gimmick. I see girls now who are trying to be alternative. They won't make a dime. You've got to have the white pumps, pink bikini, fuckin' hairpiece, pink lipstick. Gold and tan and white. If you even try and slip a little of yourself in there you won't make any money."

Through the classifieds in a punk fanzine called *Maximum Rock N Roll,* Courtney had begun corresponding with Jennifer Finch, a kindred spirit who was living in L.A. "I came up and visited her," Courtney says, "and entered the glamorous world of 'extra' work."

Jennifer had been working part time as punk-rock color on such TV shows like *Quincy* and *CHiPs,* and she brought Courtney along. "I met a lot of people through that," she says. One of those people was Alex Cox, who was about to direct *Sid and Nancy.* "All the punk-rock extras went up for parts in *Sid and Nancy,*" Courtney recalls. "He met me and he put his arm around me and said the most subversive thing he could think of was foisting me on the world. That was back when I was really overweight, too. But I wasn't scared. I wanted to act ever since Tatum O'Neal won the Oscar."

She was cast as Nancy Spungeon's best friend, and then Cox wrote *Straight To Hell,* an incomprehensible spaghetti Western, for her. There were rumors that the two were lovers, but Courtney vehemently denies any romantic involvement. "I was sexless," she says. "People say we were a couple because that's how they explain his interest in me. During that time, I did not sleep with anybody. I was fat, and when you're fat you can't call the shots. It's not you with the power."

Following *Straight To Hell,* Courtney decided to (briefly) abandon her musical aspirations and concentrate on acting. She took the $20,000 that she was paid, moved out of Jennifer's house, rented an apartment, and bought a pink Chanel suit. She was taking the bus—she still doesn't know how to drive, despite having lived in L.A. for ten years—but she was well dressed.

"I didn't quite pull it off," she says. "A friend went to a party and told Jennifer, 'Courtney was wearing Chanel and she had a glass of champagne in her hand, but her makeup was exactly the same.' It wasn't quite right. I had this publicist who was obsessed with Madonna and obsessed with me and she decided to make me into a star. I just couldn't pull it off. I'd get zits."

It occurred to Courtney that you could have acne and still be a rock star, so she moved back to Portland, slimmed down, and started singing in bands, including Faith No More, which has gone on tour with Guns 'N Roses and Metallica. She met Kat Bjelland, and in '84 or '85, Courtney and Jennifer and Kat moved to San Francisco and started a band called Sugar Baby Doll. "We wore pinafores, and played twelve-string Rickenbackers," she says. "It was a disaster." It wasn't a punk band—Sugar Baby Doll was softer, sweeter. "Jennifer and I were not into it," recalls Kat. "We wanted to play punk-rock. Courtney thought we were crazy. She hated punk then."

In the alternative world, integrity and credentials are everything—and Courtney is viewed by most as a late convert to the world of punk. "I was New Wave more than hardcore," she admits. "I thought the whole punk scene was really ugly and unglamorous and I needed it to be glamorous. I'm into it now, but back then I'd go to Black Flag (a seminal L.A. punk band) shows and refuse to go in. It was just all these boys killing each other."

After the San Francisco debacle, she moved to Minneapolis and played briefly with Kat's new band, Babes in Toyland. (Jennifer was back in L.A. forming her band, L7.) She and Kat clashed, and she went to Alaska to strip. Then she moved to Portland briefly, and by 1989 she was back in L.A. "I just couldn't take it anywhere else." she explains. "Minneapolis was so fucking un-pretentious. Everyone has a flannel collection and is in a band named after a welding instrument."

She put an ad in the *Recycler* ("I want to start a band. My influences are Big Black, Stooges, Sonic Youth and Fleetwood Mac") and stripped to pay the rent. "I worked at Star Strip," she says. "The girls in the place are superconstructed. They're a little classy. Three of them had fucked Axl Rose." Soon she had put together Hole, and started to rehearse in earnest.

"The first time I saw her onstage she was dressed like a soiled debutante," says Rosemary Carroll, Courtney's lawyer. "Her dress was ripped and she was a mess, except for a perfectly pressed huge pink bow on the back of her dress. She was riveting to watch. Courtney had a presence and a power that was fascinating."

Hole played around L.A., but they weren't discovered until they went to England in late 1991. Courtney may have been jumping on the fox-core/alternative bandwagon in America (although she would claim otherwise), but in England she was perceived as an original. With her dirty baby-doll dresses and dark kinky songs, she was the U.K. music-press pinup choice. "I thought they'd be terrified of me," she says. "This loud American woman. But it *worked*! We sold a lot of records."

And they came back to a buzz in the States. By then, she was together with Kurt and the Madonna thing happened and everything was falling into place. "It wasn't surprising," Courtney says. "I mean, I wasn't surprised. I always knew."

It's about seven P.M. on a balmy night in early summer and Courtney is knocking on the door of her apartment. She lost her key or forgot her key or she can't find her key. Whatever. *"KU-RT,"* she singsongs. "Come to the door."

After a short wait, he opens it. "Where's your key?" he asks, looking as if he's just woken up. Kurt is wearing pajama bottoms, is bare-chested, and has a sparkly beaded bracelet on his wrist. He is small and very thin and has pale-white skin. His hair, which he's dyed red and purple in the past, is now blonde, and his eyes are very blue. His face is quite beautiful, almost delicate. Where Courtney projects strength, Kurt seems fragile. He looks as if he might break.

"God, it's hot in here," Courtney says, marching into the apartment. Kurt explains that he's turned the heat on—it feels around a hundred degrees in the living room. "I'm still cold," he says, slumping into an overstuffed armchair. He looks exhausted.

Their home, in the Fairfax area of L.A., is sparsely furnished. There are guitars in their open cases on the floor, and a Buddhist altar has been set up against one wall. Dead flowers sit in a vase next to a pair of those see-through body-anatomy dolls. In fact, there are dolls everywhere: infant dolls with china heads that Kurt is using in the next Nirvana video, a plastic doll that he found while on tour, and many, many toy monkeys. Painted on the fireplace, which is covered with candy hearts and heart-shaped candy boxes, are the scrawled words MY BEST FRIEND. "We had a fight last night," explains Courtney. "So I wrote that to remind him."

She continues the apartment tour, showing off a drawing that Kurt's sister did, a photo of him at six with a drum, another doll, whose head is cracked open. In the kitchen, Courtney has taped lists all over the cabinets. "Kurt's ex-girlfriend made these," she says. "I found them when I went through his stuff." She reads aloud from one: "1. Good Morning! 2. Will you fill up my car with unleaded gas? 3. Sweep kitchen floor. 4. Clean tub. 5. Go to Kmart. 6. Get one dollar in quarters." This last one seems to crack her up. "He never did any of that stuff."

The phone rings. Kurt has disappeared into the bedroom, and Courtney goes to answer it. "Hi, Dave," she says. It is Dave Grohl, the drummer of Nirvana. The band has been on hiatus for a few months and Dave is calling from Washington D.C. "I'll go get him," Courtney says, sounding more than slightly perturbed. She puts down the receiver. "Just call me Yoko Love," she says. "Everyone just fucking hates my guts."

This may be true. Since Courtney and Kurt's courtship began last year, she has reportedly antagonized Grohl and Krist Novoselic, the other two members of Nirvana. "Courtney always has a hidden agenda," says someone close to the band. "And Kurt doesn't. He's definitely being led."

While it's difficult to determine Courtney's ulterior motive with regard to Kurt, she does have mini-feuds galore. Her major complaint in terms of Nirvana seems to be with Novosolic's wife, Shelli. Courtney's gripe is vague—something about Shelli making Kurt sleep in the hallway of their house. "I wouldn't let her come to my wedding," Courtney says.

She definitely relishes her position as Mrs. Kurt Cobain. It was one of her goals, not something she left up to fate. The couple first met eight or so years ago in Portland. "Back then," she recalls, "we didn't have an emotion towards each other. It was, like, 'Are you coming over to my house?' 'Fuck you.' That sort of thing."

By the time they met again, Kurt was a star and Courtney was much less casual in her approach. She realized that, when it comes to romance, aggressive behavior can be very appealing. "People say, 'How did she get Kurt?'" says one friend. "Well, she *asked*. And she wouldn't take no for an answer."

Courtney pursued him for months—got his number, called him, told interviewers that she had a crush on him. She even resorted to religion. "Courtney chanted for the coolest guy in rock 'n' roll—which, to her mind, was Kurt—to be her boyfriend," says Jimmy Boyle, a friend who works for Def American. Finally, she persuaded an eager-to-please prospective manager to give her tickets (plane and concert) to a Nirvana show in Chicago.

"I was there in Chicago when they consummated their relationship," says Danny Goldberg, senior V.P. at Polygram, and Nirvana's (and now Hole's) manager. "We chatted for a while and Courtney worked her way into the other room, where Kurt was. I didn't see sparks, but they did go home together. That was in early October. They were married in February."

It wasn't really quite that simple. Initially, Kurt had his doubts. Reportedly, he had been too busy recording and then touring with Nirvana to focus much on romance. "Kurt is very smart," says one friend, "but he's shy. A lot of people mistake that shyness for lack of confidence, but he does know his own mind. When Courtney showed up, I think he was attracted to her flamboyance. She was very sexual and I think she just took him over. He went on TV and said she was the best fuck in the world."

Still, there were problems. "He thought I was too demanding, attention-wise," Courtney says matter-of-factly. "He thought I was obnoxious. I had to go out of my way to impress him."

By the time he proposed ("I just knew he should ask me if he had brains at all."), she was pregnant. The wedding was in Hawaii: Kurt, who once planned to wear a dress, wore pajamas, and Courtney wore "a white diaphanous item that had dry rot. It had been Frances Farmer's in a movie." She signed a pre-nuptial agreement (her idea) and they did not go on a honeymoon. "Life is a perennial honeymoon right now," she says. "I get to go to the bank machine every day."

All this would be perfect, except for the drugs. Twenty different sources throughout the record industry maintain that the Cobains have been heavily into heroin. Earlier this year, Kurt told *Rolling Stone* that he was not taking heroin, but Courtney presents another, extremely disturbing picture. "We went on a binge," she says, referring to a period in January when Nirvana was in New York to appear on *Saturday Night Live.* "We did a lot of drugs. We got pills and then went down to Alphabet City and Kurt wore a hat, I wore a hat, and we copped some dope. Then we got high and we went to *S.N.L.* After that, I did heroin for a couple of months."

"It was horrible," recalls a business associate who was traveling with them at the time. "Courtney was pregnant and she was shooting up. Kurt was throwing up on people in the cab. They were both out of it."

Courtney has a long history with drugs. She loves Percodans ("They make me vacuum."), and has dabbled with heroin off and on since she was eighteen, once even snorting it in Room 101 of the Chelsea Hotel, where Nancy Spungeon died. Reportedly, Kurt didn't do much more that drink until he met Courtney. "He tried to be an alcoholic for a long time," she says. "But it didn't sit right with him."

After their New York binge, it was suggested to Courtney that she have an abortion. She refused and, reportedly, had a battery of tests that indicated the fetus was fine. "She wanted to get off drugs," says Boyle. "I brought her herbs to ease the kick, so she wouldn't freak out so badly. I was bringing stuff over to her house every day because it's a whacked-out thing to do to a kid."

According to several sources, Courtney and Kurt went to separate detox hospitals in March. "After a few days, she left and went and got him," says one insider. "They never went back." Whether or not they are using now is not clear. "It's a sick scene in that apartment," says a close friend. "But, lately, Courtney's been asking for help."

"Kurt's the right person to have a baby with," Courtney continues. "We have money. I can have a nanny. The whole feminine experience of pregnancy and birth—I'm not into it on that level. But it was a bad time to get pregnant and that appealed to me." She smiles. "Besides, we need new friends."

This is a sly reference to Kurt's phone call, which is winding down. "Dave is upset," Kurt says after hanging up. "So," Courtney says, "what do you want to do? Why don't you start a new band without Krist?" Kurt pauses. He looks upset. "But I want Dave," he says. "He's the best fucking drummer I know."

They are both silent a few minutes. Kurt looks so tired he seems to be asleep with his eyes open. Courtney suggests they go out to buy cigarettes. "Will I get hassled?" says Kurt, who, due to the popularity of Nirvana videos, is recognized everywhere. "Get used to it!" says Courtney. He shrugs—it doesn't look as if he wants to move an inch, much less miles into the world. "You're such a grump," she says. It's frustrating—you marry a millionaire rock god and all he wants to do is stay home and mope. "We never do anything," Courtney whines. "We never do anything fun." Kurt is silent. "O.K.," he says finally. "Where are the car keys?" As Courtney searches for them, Kurt heads off to the bedroom to put on a shirt. "You know, he drives really well," she says as he hunts through a pile of stuff. "He likes safety."

There's just been an earthquake—6.1 on the Richter scale—but Courtney and Kurt don't notice. They are too busy shopping. Kurt is excited—this store, American Rag, which is huge and specializes in authentic vintage clothes mixed with clothes that are new but appear to be vintage, has an enormous collection of used jeans in very small sizes. He is making his way through the rack very, very slowly. "I got him to wear boxers," Courtney says, helping him to find his size. "You can't believe how tacky he was. He wore bikinis. Colored. Just a tacky thing."

She gets impatient and heads off to inspect a rack of dresses. She is very specific about style. She tries to achieve what she terms a *"Kinderwhore look,"* which seems to mean either ripped dresses from the thirties or one-size-too-small velvet dresses from the sixties. Her hair and makeup remain consistent: white skin, red lips, blond hair with black roots. "It's a good look," she explains. "It's sexy, but you can sit down and say 'I read Camille Paglia.' "

Courtney is extremely possessive of this style statement—she is currently in a war with her erstwhile friend Kat Bjelland because of a borrowed velvet dress. Or, at least, that's what started it.

"Kat has stolen a lot from me," she says, hitting on one of her very favorite themes. "Dresses. Lyrics. Riffs. Guitars. Shoes. She ever went out after Kurt. That was the last straw. Because I put up with the lyric stealing. And I put up with her going to England first in a dress that I loaned her. Now I can't wear those fucking dresses in England anymore."

Kat isn't Courtney's only target—she's convinced that nearly everyone in the music scene today is either plundering her shtick or is just plain worthless. She hates Inger Lorre, lead singer of the Nymphs ("Fucking despicable"); despises Pearl Jam, another terrific Seattle band ("They're careerist and they go out with models"); is angry with Faith No More ("The new record is called *Angel Dust*—they stole that from me"); has quarreled with Jennifer Finch of L7 (more stolen lyrics); and is convinced that Axl Rose is "an ass—and he also goes out with models."

And so on. Not surprisingly, she also has a few concerns about Madonna. "I didn't want to get involved with her, because she's a bad enemy to have," Courtney says, giving a navy dress a closer inspection. "I don't want her to know anything about me because she'll steal what she can. What I have is mine and she can't fucking have it. She's not going to be able to write lyrics like me, and even if she does get up onstage with a guitar, it's not going to last. I don't care how vain and arrogant this sounds, but just watch: in her next video, Madonna's going to have roots. She's going to have smeared eyeliner. And that's me." Courtney pauses, pressing the dress against her body to check the size. "In some pictures I come across as a fourteen-year-old battered rape victim," she continues. "And she wants that image." Madonna's response to this outburst? "Who," she asks, "is Courtney Love?"

Nevertheless, Courtney is very serious about her vendettas. They have an equalizing effect: by trashing the likes of Madonna she becomes, in some twisted way, her peer. "Courtney's delusional," says Bjelland, who hasn't spoken to her in a year. "I called her a while ago because I was worried about her baby and her sanity, but I never heard back from her. In the past, I always forgave her, but I can't anymore. Last night I had a dream that I killed her. I was really happy."

None of this fazes Courtney—she isn't particularly interested in the consequences of her actions. She is, instead, after a certain acknowledgement. Courtney wants her power known, and aside from the fact that everyone is stealing from her, she feels one of the main obstacles on this quest in the whole beauty thing. She has written a fanzine for Hole devotees called *And She's Not Even Pretty* because, she explains, "a lot of anti-Courtney factions say 'And she's not even pretty.' Here's this new rock star—Kurt—and he's supposed to be married to a model and he's married to *me.*"

This delights her, and she takes her stack of dresses over to Kurt, who is carefully looking at each pair of jeans. He seems in a trancelike state, and the salespeople, who all recognize him, keep their distance. "Isn't he pretty?" she says. Kurt doesn't seem to hear her. "We go out once in a while and women look at him like they're starving," she goes on. Kurt continues to move through the rack in slow motion. "A lot of people want a piece of that new fame thing," she says. "I can understand that."

It's later the same evening and Kurt is sitting in the parking lot of a 7-Eleven, waiting for Courtney to buy dinner, which consists of cookies, fruit juice, and cigarettes. As he stares out the window, a large van pulls up and a guy in full heavy-metal gear gets out. He is wearing a Nirvana T-shirt.

"That guy has on a Nirvana T-shirt," Kurt says rather sadly. The heavy-metal audience was not what he had in mind when he wrote "Smells Like Teen Spirit." "I'm used to it now, I guess," he says softly. "I've seen it a lot."

Commercial success in the alternative world ruins your credibility, and Kurt is deeply concerned with staying true to his vision. He wouldn't perform at Axl Rose's thirtieth-birthday bash (Rose is a big Nirvana fan) and turned down a spot on this summer's Metallica-Guns 'N' Roses tour. Still and all, "the general consensus is that Nirvana should quit," says Bjelland. "They've reached *nirvana*. What are you going to do after that?"

This is ridiculous logic, but it is the conventional wisdom within the community. "Courtney," Kurt says when she returns, "that heavy-metal guy was wearing a Nirvana T-shirt." "I know," she says, munching on a cookie. "I saw him." There is a long pause while they ponder this reality.

"I'm neurotic about credibility," Courtney says finally, "And Kurt is neurotic about it, too. He's dealing with people who like his band who he despises. For instance, a girl was raped in Reno. When they were raping her, they were singing 'Polly,' a Nirvana song." Courtney pauses. "These are the people who listen to him."

"But there are all kinds of fame," she continues. "Like The Replacements had a Respect fame. *Big Respect Fame.* And that kind of fame can really mess with your head. Rather than, say, Paula Abdul fame. That is Valley Fame."

Kurt laughs. Courtney has a basic, commonsense approach to business matters that clearly appeals to him. "Credibility is credibility. They think they can market it. And I say, let them try." Kurt turns the key in the ignition. "Why do *I* want what I want?" she says, although no one's asked the question. "You have to give yourself some bogus-sincere nineties little reason about what it is that's making you go. And mine is influence." Kurt smiles. He knows what she's talking about.

"Hi!" It's a month later and Kurt sounds like a new man. Cheerful! Alert! He's talking on the phone from their hotel room in Seattle, where he and Courtney are rehearsing with their respective bands. "It's great to play with the boys again," he says. He chatters on about his car (an old Plymouth Valiant) and the recent riots in L.A. "Courtney is out at the sauna," he says. "She's really pregnant now, but she's not that big. I think we'll have a little elf baby."

Four hours later, Courtney is on the line. She, too, sounds happy and less manic. She's full of news: there are rumblings that Gus Van Sant (*Drugstore Cowboy, My Own Private Idaho*) wants to put her in his next movie, she's found a new bassist for Hole, and she and Kurt have bought a house in Seattle. "Nothing is better that being landed gentry," she says. "You must own property. That's what I told Kurt."

Nirvana is going to be on a mini-tour in Scandinavia, and the baby is due in early September. "It's the same day as the MTV Video Awards." Courtney says. "I think it's very important that Kurt play that, but he doesn't think like I do. If I was him, I'd have to play the video awards. I appreciate money. Kurt doesn't see it the same way."

This is typical Courtney—eyes always on the prize. "I heard a couple new rumors about me," she says gleefully. "That I'm Nike and Kurt married me for Nike money. That's why he's attracted to me."

She laughs. There's still talk about the drugs and she knows it. Throughout the industry, there is increased worry about little Frances Bean. "The worst thing," she says, avoiding mention of the persistent drug rumors, "is when people say Kurt's helping me to make it." She pauses. "If anything, Kurt has hurt me." That's going too far, and Courtney stops herself. "No," she says, back pedaling. "Things are really good. It's all coming true." Courtney laughs. "Although it could fuck up at any time. You never know."

Jeffrey Rotter

OUR LITTLE SATAN

Here's a dispatch about another one of rock and roll's crossdressing devil worshippers.

HELL MIGHT be for children, but on this particular Halloween, Asbury Park, New Jersey, is running a close second. A derelict seaside resort an hour's drive from New York City, this string of boarded-up corn dog stands and wasted art-nouveau theaters is as good a setting as any to wait out the end of a millennium.

It's 2 P.M., a scant 27,754 hours before the turn of the century, and I'm idling behind a convoy of soccer moms in Volvo station wagons, their kids anxious to shed the 'rents and greet their fellow Marilyn Manson fanatics. The band's legion of Goth-come-latelies, a.k.a. "Spooky Kids," are dressed to impress, attired, Trekkie-style, after a favorite band member. In line in front of me, a carload of little Twiggys, dressed in the bassist's soiled tartan skirt and pigtails, bid Mom a grudging farewell and rush to the box office. On the curb beside them, a wee Pogo strokes his peach-fuzz Fu Manchu. A pair of Marilyn Mansons lean against the tour bus.

If Asbury Park is the picture of an old leisure establishment in decay, then Marilyn Manson—Manson, bassist Twiggy Ramirez, keyboardist Madonna Wayne Gacy (alias Pogo), drummer Ginger Fish, and new guitarist Zim Zume—are just the opposite, decay turned into leisure. Manson's mad concoction of shock theater, Nine Inch Nails-derived techno-Goth, and Satan-inspired daily affirmations have found their mark in the vast, bepimpled ear of adolescent America. Spooky shit in the ignoble tradition of Alice Cooper, Glenn Danzig, and Chitty Chitty Bang Bang, the band's second full-length release, *Antichrist Superstar,* arrived on the *Billboard* Top 200 at No. 3. MTV loves Manson, as does director David Lynch, who cast him as a seedy porno star in his new film, *Lost Highway.* Conservative watchdogs Bill Bennett and C. DeLores Tucker despise Manson, accusing *Antichrist*'s distributor, MCA, of "peddling filth for profits." As for Manson himself, he's pleased to be of service: "There's so many

358

people who wouldn't even have a job if they didn't have a bad guy to fool around with."

Like many kids, Marilyn Manson, *née* Brian Warner, discovered the escapism of rock at a Sunday-school backmasking lecture. He found all his future idols there: Kiss, Alice Cooper, the Beatles, David Bowie. "When they said, 'You shouldn't listen to this,'" recalls Manson, "I wanted to know why."

Born to a working-class family in Canton, Ohio, Manson suffered a typically awkward Christian-school youth. "I didn't have a good time," he winces. "I had bad acne. I was really skinny. The jock kids loved to beat the shit out of me. I didn't have a clique to fit into. That's probably why I relate to my fans so much."

Sunday school also skewed Manson against Christian authority. Still, for a would-be Satan, Manson can be downright righteous. "People are very surprised to hear me say that a lot of my values are Christian values," says the Bible-quoting Manson, whose own twist on "love thy neighbor" adds the conditional "unless they deserve to be destroyed." "I think that's part of my shock. I just don't like the way that Christianity combined with the influence of television has bred a nation of weakness."

The standard-bearer of moral "weakness" for Manson was his own grandfather, whose taste for enemas, bestial porn, and toy trains left deep scars. "He had this train set in his basement," remembers Manson, "and whenever he turned it on, it was to mask the sound of his masturbating. I would tell my parents, but nobody believed me. He was the one who convinced me that things that were supposed to be pure and American were not."

Manson split the hypocrisy of home for Fort Lauderdale, Florida, at 18, for a college track in journalism. In 1990, he met guitarist Daisy Berkowitz, and the two founded Marilyn Manson and the Spooky Kids, a drum machine-driven four-piece performance-art group. When Nine Inch Nails was on a club tour of Florida, Manson interviewed Trent Reznor for his college newspaper and they exchanged phone numbers. A few slots opening for NIN followed. Later that year, Manson got a call from Reznor: "Trent called me just after his *Broken* album was finished and asked if I wanted to be in a NIN video," Manson says, still relishing his stroke of good fortune. "We went to the Sharon Tate house for the shoot, and while I was there, he told me he wanted us to be the first band on his new label."

The band's first album, *Portrait of an American Family,* and breakthrough EP, *Smells Like Children,* had aspirations about as low as Grandpa Manson's: a little shock schmaltz, a few coy jabs at tabloid culture, and a cheesy Eurythmics cover. Manson had grander, nastier ideas, but they needed more stately mansions than the band alone could build. With Reznor (a coproducer of all the band's material) taking a more active role, *Antichrist Superstar* is the fulfillment of the band's operatic promise.

On *Antichrist,* Reznor bigs up the Manson like he's remixing the *Nibelungenlied,* downspiraling dense horror-rock through a riotous digital din. "I wanted to show that the band had some scope, that it wasn't all guitar-bass-drums," Reznor says. "If you make a whole album of 200 b.p.m. songs, after about three minutes, it's not scary anymore." The result is a well-paced, organic, and yes, scary concept album that casts Manson as a lowly worm who becomes a rock'n'roll Antichrist and destroys the world. For Manson, the album appeals to "the element of everybody's personality that is nihilistic and hopeless, and decides that, rather than come to a solution [to the world's problems], things should be brought to an end."

But the Antichrist isn't such a Gloomy Gus after all. The "up" side to Manson is a downright sunny call for kids to reject Christianity and "be their own gods." It's a philosophy that, unfortunately, takes its cues from Satanism and Nietzsche. "Satanism," says Manson, "if it was packaged differently. . . ." It would be Scientology? "Yeah, exactly." Manson believes his fans are "selling their souls to themselves. They're forming their own values and their own morals based on what makes them happy, not on what makes their parents happy." Which makes him—what?—*Kids Are People Too* in a bodice and jackboots?

It's nearly 11 P.M. at the Asbury Park Theater and the crowd is so wound-up, they could mosh to *Charlie and the Chocolate Factory.* And that's just what they do. When the familiar balloon of the *Oompa-Loompa* theme springs from the P.A., signaling the Reverend's arrival, the joint erupts. Manson still looks a little ill at ease from a bomb threat that delayed the show some two hours, but makes no reference to it until late in the set. As the band bashes out the last measures of "Tourniquet"—one of the keenest measures of teen worthlessness since Alice Cooper's "I'm Eighteen"—Manson's mind is on the bomb: "How many of you came here to see me die tonight?" The crowd, not quite getting it, responds in the affirmative. Manson looks bummed, but all this ties in nicely with his messiah trip. "No matter how much they love you, they want a tragedy," he says later.

Marilyn Manson, philosopher? No, worse. Try preacher. The scariest moment of the night—scarier, in some ways, than the bomb threat—is the church revival/Nazi rally that accompanies "Antichrist Superstar," the fist-pumper that signals the Antichrist's ascension. The lights come up to a nervous martial beat, and illuminate a massive pulpit draped in the Antichrist's emblem, a swastika-fied variation on the electric-shock warning symbol. Dressed in a Swaggart-cut leisure suit, twitching like an Eva Peron marionette, Manson leads his band through a totalitarian slapstick routine that's equal parts tele-evangelist, statesman, and rock star. His reich'n'roll is a little *Kampf* and a little camp, recycling agit-props from Pink Floyd's bong classic *The Wall,* Charlie Chaplin's *The Great Dictator,* and Leni Riefenstahl's *Triumph of the Will.*

The routine is a scathing parody and a sincere scare, both. Regrettably, Manson is ill-equipped or unwilling to resolve the contradiction. "It's the study of how people make rock'n'roll totalitarian," says Manson, waxing academic. "But it's also a call to arms. It's a pep rally for the apocalypse." This is the scary part of Manson, and of rock at large: For all its promise of individual rebellion, "think for yourself" is not a message that goes platinum. But try telling that that to the little Mansons camped out by the tour bus.

Early the next morning the bomb still hasn't exploded, and, despite radio broadcasts to the contrary, Manson is still ticking. We're sitting in the suite atop the Berkeley Carteret Hotel, in the same room that Johnny Cash used decades ago, and Manson is looking more like Brian Warner than I've ever seen him. "There's days when I'd love for everybody to realize that things have gone too far, and that we need to be born again so that we can appreciate the little things." Manson pauses to look at the television that is always on, even when he sleeps. "Then there's other days when I think the world deserves to be destroyed. Why should I help anybody? Everybody's stepped on me my whole life. I've put on this crown," he sighs, "but I'm not sure if I want it."

5. PRESENT AT THE CREATION

"The tape is going and that is *Bob fucking Dylan* over there singing, so this had better be me sitting here playing *something*."

There's a bootleg of the Bob Dylan "Like a Rolling Stone" session. After *that* take, the one eventually released, the song goes on majestically for a minute more, past the point where the record fades. Suddenly, the band stops and there's a stunned silence, a *what-in-the-hell-did-we-just-do* serenity. You can sense in the stillness the feeling that everyone there knew something great had been birthed. But we don't have to imagine what it was like to be there, because Al Kooper, terrified, was at the organ, and he has a good memory. Here he tells his tale. And Nik Cohn at the dawn of disco, the creators of punk rock looking back, and Jackson Browne, standing alone onstage after a show, looking out at an empty coliseum. This is rock and roll history in the first person.

Doc Pomus

TREATISE ON THE BLUES

During the early years of rock and roll, Doc Pomus (real name Jerome Felder) wrote (alone or in collaboration) "Save the Last Dance for Me," "This Magic Moment," "Teenager in Love," "A Mess of Blues," "Little Sister," "Lonely Avenue," "I Count the Tears," and "Boogie Woogie Country Girl." These selections from his journals come from the last years of his life.

I ALWAYS believed in magic and flying and that one morning I would wake up and all the bad things were bad dreams and Daddy would be alive and heroic and Mama would understand and be proud of me only because she understood me and my kid brother was a kid again and I would sing to him and he would have that 10-year-old-I-worship-you look in his eyes. And I would get out of the wheelchair and walk and not with braces and crutches. And I would walk down all streets and no one would stare at me and young girls in see-through dresses would smile at me, dazzled by my appearance and glow, and men would listen to my words carefully and I could wander around all night without fear in my soul and I could sit by a lonely stoop at 1:00 A.M. with friends and have a convertible top open at 2:00 A.M. and walk or park in Prospect Park or Central Park. I would always sing and everybody would love to hear me sing and my children were little children in my arms and the woman or women in my life would stay young forever and love me in a young way forever.

*   *   *

Every night I dream
when I wake up I'll fly
but when the morning comes
I still can't reach the sky

I just can't grow no wings
and do those kinds of things
cause since you left you see
the magic's died in me

Once I burned the sky
the mountains and the sea
the whole damn crazy world
the mountains and the sea
that all belong to me.

*   *   *

I used to get up and sing the blues—not thinking I was black or white—just closing my eyes and leaning back on the crutches. I got to the point where I sensed audiences learned show business tricks—pacing—openers, closers. Little mannerisms that became identifiable—swinging the mike from hand to hand, swaggering the body in rhythm. Eventually developed a style. And learned how to introduce numbers and in an emergency could emcee in a passable but professional way.

And all the time I was writing blues—mostly for myself—but occasionally I'd go around to the record companies and they would take a song for Joe Turner or Laverne Baker, or Gatemouth Moore or Lil Green and then I started recording myself. I always had a record going on the jukebox—no hits—but there was always one out.—

I was beginning to get a reputation but underneath—I was always trembling and screaming. My hotel room was always the scene of endless trips in and out of the bed.—In and out of the bathroom—Constantly changing clothes always on the phone—anything to keep me from quietly living with myself and thinking about what was going to happen.—Always trying to maneuver a girl in the room—talk to her—make love to her—or write a song—or write an article—or write a story or listen to the blues—on the radio on records—and listen and lose myself.

*   *   *

I'm boring, I'm boring, boring
It's a natural fact
I'm an opening act.

*   *   *

I quote Robert Palmer—from his book *Deep Blues* page 103 (discussing Muddy Waters slide techniques) "Musicians trained in say the classical music of India which puts the premium on the ability to hear and execute 5 microtonal shadings, would recognize in the astonishing precision and emotional richness of the variously flattened thirds and fifths sprinkled through the solo something close to his own tradition. Literacy, which trains one to focus on the linear continuity of words and phrases rather than on their intonational subtleties, tends to obliterate such minutely detailed and essentially non-linear modes of expression. Perhaps this explains why many of the young city-bred blacks who have taken up the blues in recent years have had almost as much trouble playing music as subtle as Muddy's as the legions of blues-smitten whites."

Hmmmmmm

I do declare—

I think I'll read this to Joe [Big Joe Turner] and get his academic reaction and find out if there's any validity or reality or maybe he'll write a treatise for Robert Palmer, Jerry Wexler, and Muddy Waters—or Gary Giddins or Robert Christgau or Dave Marsh or Lightnin' Hopkins or John Lee Hooker or Dr. Clayton—oops he's dead and anyway Palmer never heard of him. At least he never mentioned him in his book *Deep Blues*.

*   *   *

Bob Dylan once said he's like an antenna that takes songs from the ozone.

When I'm in between songs, most of the time, I have no idea where they come from—how I invented them—and whether they'll come again.

I know what he means—I have similar feelings. Though I don't feel like an antenna—I think that at the times of productivity a chemical combination or chemical or metaphysical or physical combination or some strange reality or unreality becomes grounded enough to come from my body to my voice or pen or pencil.

James Brown with Bruce Tucker

THE T.A.M.I. SHOW

James Brown is the hardest-working man in show business, the man with the plan, Soul Brother No. 1, Mr. Sex Machine, able to stop revolutions with a single UNHH! He's the Godfather of Soul, he's Super Bad, he's Mr. Dynamite, he's on the good foot now.

Bruce Tucker is a music journalist.

I SAW the Rolling Stones the first time when we were on *The T.A.M.I. Show* together. It was a TV film with a whole lot of acts that were popular then: Chuck Berry, Bo Diddley, the Supremes, Smokey Robinson and the Miracles, Marvin Gaye, Lesley Gore, Jan and Dean, Gerry and the Pacemakers. We taped it at the Santa Monica Auditorium in November 1964, and I think it came out early the next year. It was directed by Steve Binder, the cat who directed Elvis's television special in 1968.

My group and I got to the auditorium to rehearse about eight in the morning. I think we did our segment three times all the way through in rehearsal. The production crew was taping all the rehearsals and blocking the show out, and then later in the day we were going to do the actual performance in front of an audience made up of mostly white teenagers. Motown had gotten very hot by then, and there were a lot of young white kids hanging all over the Motown stars. When Byrd and some of the other fellas saw what was happening, they started worrying. "Man," they said, "it doesn't look like we're going to get such a good reception." I said, "Don't even worry about it. Once we get through, we aren't going to be able to get out of this place." I think the other acts knew it, too, even if the audience didn't. They made it plainly understood they didn't want to come anywhere after us. They knew what we could do. So the Stones, who were really big already, were scheduled to follow us.

They came in around one in the afternoon, with a bunch of guards, went straight to their dressing room, and didn't let anybody get near 'em. Meantime, we were out there doing another rehearsal. When we did, a lot of people came out of their dressing rooms to watch, Mick included. I think he'd heard about us already, but when he saw what we did, he couldn't believe it. After he saw me, he didn't even want to rehearse. Some discussion started then about them going on sooner. I heard that Mick smoked a whole pack of cigarettes, he was so nervous. We thought that was a good sign, but we knew we still had to deal with the audience of young, young kids.

A funny thing happened when the actual show went on. Lesley Gore went out and did two songs. When she came off, a bunch of people crowded around asking for her autograph. Then this older lady—I don't know if it was her mother, her keeper, or whoever—said, "Oh, no, don't bother her, don't bother her. She's tired now. Wait until she rests." We had already been out there and nearly killed ourselves twice already, and she hadn't even done any rehearsals. When the lady said that, we all looked at each other and said, "There must be something we don't know."

We went on, a little nervous because we didn't think this audience really knew us, but when we went into "Out of Sight," they went straight up out of their seats. We did a bunch of songs, nonstop, like always. For our finale we did "Night Train." I don't think I ever danced so hard in my life, and I don't think they'd ever seen a man move that fast. When I was through, the audience kept calling me back for encores. It was one of those performances when you don't even know how you're doing it. At one point during the encores I sat down underneath a monitor and just kind of hung my head, then looked up and smiled. For a second I didn't really know where I was.

The Stones had come out in the wings by then, standing between all those guards. Every time they got ready to start out on the stage, the audience called us back. They couldn't get on—it was too hot out there. By that time I don't think Mick wanted to go on the stage at all. Mick had been watching me do that thing where I shimmy on one leg and when the Stones finally got out there, he tried it a couple of times. He danced a lot that day. Until then I think he used to stand still when he sang, but after that he really started moving around. Anyway, after they were finally able to get on the stage, they got over real good. At the end, all of the people on the show came out and danced for the finale. Later on, Mick used to come up to the stage, and he became a good friend of mine. I like Mick, Keith Richards, and all the guys. I don't think of them as competition; I think of them as brothers.

*   *   *

I was keeping busy on the road, recording a lot of the acts, doing instrumentals, and doing some television like *The Lloyd Thaxton Show* and

Where the Action Is. The Flames and I did a cameo in a Frankie Avalon movie, *Ski Party,* dressed up in ski outfits. I was a little surprised at how much work it is to make a movie, but Frankie was a very easy person to work with. I never had any burning desire to be a movie star the way a lot of singers have—Elvis, Sinatra, or Frankie Avalon, for that matter. It wasn't something that was open to people of my origin at that time anyway. Louis made a lot of movies, but he always played himself and was never really the star of them.

Meantime, it was a standoff between King Records and Mercury. I started to think there was something funny about it; Mercury seemed more interested in putting Mr. Nathan out of business than in recording me on vocals. The doors at King were all but closed; they had beat him, he had nothing to fight with. I felt bad about it, so I went to Arthur Smith's studio in Charlotte, North Carolina, cut "Papa's Got a Brand New Bag," and sent the tape to Mr. Nathan. It was done underground—I had to sneak the tape to him.

The song started out as a vamp we did during the stage show. There was a little instrumental riff and I hollered: "Papa's got a bag of his own!" I decided to expand it into a song and cut it pretty quick to help Mr. Nathan, so when we went into the studio I was holding a lyric sheet in my hand while I recorded it. We were still going for that live-in-the-studio sound, so we cranked up and did the first take.

It's hard to describe what it was I was going for; the song has gospel feel, but it's put together out of jazz licks. And it has a different sound—a snappy, fast-hitting thing from the bass and the guitars. You can hear Jimmy Nolen, my guitar player at the time, starting to play scratch guitar, where you squeeze the strings tight and quick against the frets so the sound is hard and fast without any sustain. He was what we called a chanker; instead of playing the whole chord and using all the strings, he hit his chords on just three strings. And Maceo played a fantastic sax solo on the break. We had been doing the vamp on the show for a while, so most of it was fine, but the lyrics were so new I think I might have gotten some of them mixed up on the take. We stopped to listen to the playback to see what we needed to do on the next take. While we were listening, I looked around the studio. Everybody—the band, the studio people, *me*— was dancing. Nobody was standing still.

Pop said, "If I'm paying for this, I don't want to cut any more. This is it."

And that *was* it. That's the way it went out. I had an acetate made and took it to Frankie Crocker, a deejay in New York. He thought it was terrible, but he put it on the air and the phones lit up. Then he admitted I was right about it.

"Papa's Bag" was years ahead of its time. In 1965 soul was just really getting popular. Aretha and Otis and Wilson Pickett were out there and getting big. I was still called a soul singer—I still call myself that—but musically I had already gone off in a different direction. I had discovered that my strength was not in the horns, it was in the rhythm. I was hearing everything, even the guitars, like they were drums. I had found out how to make it happen. On playbacks, when I saw the speakers jumping, vibrating a certain way, I knew that was it: deliverance. I could tell from looking at the speakers that the rhythm was right. What I'd started on "Out of Sight" I took all the way on "Papa's Bag." Later on they said it was the beginning of funk. I just thought of it as where my music was going. The title told it all: I had a new bag.

Patti Smith

RISE OF THE SACRED MONSTERS

Here's one of those sun-also-rises-sun-also-sets kind of moments as we witness again the spectacle of generations changing hands. In this case, the black-and-white radiation-spewing Stones on TV inspired a young girl in New Jersey to make rock and roll poetry into her life's work.

LOOK BACK, it was 1965. Pa was shouting from the tv room, "jesus christ! jesus christ!" I flew up those stairs pumping in 3.D. Bad black widows . . . water moccasins . . . red snake long as a fire hose. See our house was built on a long swamp. on easter a boy died. he sank in the quick mud and the next morning he floated up like ivory soap. Mama made me go to the wake. the afternoon was hell hot. mosquitoes and steam were rising from the swamp. the world series was on. the women sat around the casket. all the men sat around the tv.

Which brings me back to pa. I ran in panting. I was scared silly. there was pa glued to the tv screen cussing his brains out. A rock'n'roll band was doing it right on the ed sullivan show. pa was frothing like a dog. I never seen him so mad. but I lost contact with him quick. that band was as relentless as murder. I was trapped in a field of hot dots. the guitar player had pimples. the blonde kneeling down had circles ringing his eyes. one had greasy hair. the other didn't care. and the singer was showing his second layer of skin and more than a little milk. I felt thru his pants with optic x-ray. this was some hard meat. this was a bitch. five white boys sexy as any spade. their nerves were wired and their third leg was rising. in six minutes five lusty images gave me my first glob of gooie in my virgin panties.

That was my introduction to the Rolling Stones. they did Time is on my side, my brain froze. I was doing all my thinking between my legs. I got shook. light broke. they were gone and I cliff-hanging. like jerking off without coming.

Pa snapped off the tv. but he was too late. they put the touch on me. I was blushing jelly. this was no mamas boy music. it was alchemical. I couldn't fathom the recipe but I was ready. blind love for my father was the first thing I sacrificed to Mick Jagger.

Time passed. I offered up everything I didn't have. every little lamb. I can tie the Stones in with every sexual release of my late blooming adolescence. The Stones were sexually freeing confused american children, a girl could feel power. lady glory, a guy could reveal his feminine side without being called a fag. masculinity was no longer measured on the football field.

Ya never think of the Stones as fags. In full make-up and frills they still get it across. they know just how to ram a woman. they made me real proud to be female. the other half of male. they aroused in me both a feline sense of power and a longing to be held under the thumb.

The Aftermath album was the real move. two faced woman. doncha bother me. the singer displays contempt for his lady. he's on top and that's what I like. then he raises her as queen. his obsession is her. "goin home." What a song. so wild so pump pumping. do it down in the basement. don't come til the last second. cockpit. cover you like an airplane. stones music is screwing music.

They rechanneled hot rivers at 78 speed. they were a guide for every shifty white kid. who could get behind the sun tanned soul of Jan and Dean? look back on the T.A.M.I. show. Leslie Gore was auntie mama. the spastic moves of Gerry and the Pacemakers. god bless the marvelous majorette precision of Motown. the T.A.M.I. shows saving grace was pure spade. until the last precious moments with the Rolling Stones. They radiated from that silver screen. my head spun my pussy dripped my pants were wet and the Rolling Stones redeemed the white man forever.

No wonder the Christian god banned the image. jealous bastard. he must have foreseen the black and white movie. who can reject the power of that image? real or 3-D the magic leaks thru. if you got it, and they had it.

I seen them live in 1966. In the heart of the february freeze. Frank Stefanko picked me up in a towtruck. we cruised thru every redlight in south phillie.

It was my first white concert. Now at the Roxy the spades danced on the ceiling. But this was different. These blonde screamers were after more than a party.

Mick ripped off his flowered shirt and did a fandango. satisfaction, tambourine on head he strutted like some stud. virgin fell off her folding chair and broke her leg. I sussed it all out. this was not tv this was real. I could enter the action. I got set to out stoneface Bill Wyman. the cornerstone of the stones. relentless as Stonehenge as a pyramid. any hard edged kid took to him. He was on stage right to catch some spit from Mick. Then hell broke. handkerchiefs folded like flowers. a million girls busting my spleen. oh baudelaire. I grabbed Brian's ankle and held on like a drowning child. It seemed like hours. I was getting bored. I looked up. I yawned. Bill Wyman cracked up. Brian grinned. I got scared. I squeezed out and ran. like the altar boy who busts his nut to peek in the sacred chalice. once achieved what next? I left without my hat. I was soaking wet. sweat was freezing on my face.

The politics of speed. Between the Buttons came out. That's when I zoomed in on Brian. I got obsessed with him. Focused on him like some sick kodak. Brian between the what? Look at that cover. look at him. he's exposed, he's cold as ice. his powdery skin. his shadow eyes. a doomed albino raccoon. I seen them do Ruby Tuesday on tv. Mick was on top he was the prince. decked in a mirrored shirt and shingled hair. he made his first public ballet bow. Brian was crouched down. he seemed covered with a translucent dust. mr. amanda jones.

And around and around we went. We were all shaking with the nervous glitter of the Rolling Stones. They affected our every move. Look back. They stole the boatneck from the beatnik and stole it from them. Ethnic sleaze. We chopped our hair like our favorite Stone. What blonde didn't scissor after Brian. Me I inspect no less than forty Keith Richards head shots for my coif guide. We donned long scarves, striped pants, elegant rags. Anything stoned. You are what you dance to. Fashioned after them we opened our movements, our walks, our eyes and our flys. Yeah the Stones styled on. Everything about them was cool. They were like spades that way. Backstreet pimps. Cool from their shades to their shoes. Their classic is the soft white low heeled leather dancing shoe. That shoe is showcased on the cover and inside of High Tide and Green Grass. A shoe designed for comfort and agility on stage. Mick still flashes the white shoe. Jumping Jack Fancy Footwork.

By 1967 they all but eliminated the word guilt from our vocabulary. Lets Spend the Night Together was the big hit. Its impossible to suffer guilt when you're moving to that song. The Flowers album was for loners and lovers only. It provided a tight backdrop for a lot of decadent fantasy. And by 67 fantasy had already got the best of me.

I was a little loose in the attic. When I was a kid I tied do-rags around my head tight. I was scared my sound would fly out at night. Scared my vital breath would make the big slip. some ventriloquist. So I steered from drugs and threw myself in full frenzied dance.

I never considered the Stones drug music. They were the drug itself. They took up where Martha and the Vandellas left off. Real heatwave dancing music. thru demon genius they hit that chord. basic as Charlie's drum beat. as primitive as a western man could stand. find the beat and you dance all night. dive into Gimme Shelter full volume. Its always been easy to let it loose to the Stones, cause they're so cool. so worthy.

Plenty of body shot. they had their brain shot too. Remember "We Love You?" the beat was hidden. it was far from western but when it needled ya you were shot up but good. madly intoxicating. erotic and extending. Like the Satanic Majesty. Real search party music. hang your lantern high. Brain operation. Then they backed it up with Beggars Banquet. Pure hump hump. Get that trojan.

Body and brain. They spell cocaine, the inner search light. speed and slow motion. perfect show job. the results are alchemical. and if you can't afford it the Stones are it. Sticky Fingers. Exile on Mainstreet. Stick your nose in the speakers and get frostbite.

But in 1969 you know cocaine was not the national drug. Flower power was wilting and there was no sign of a great snow drift. Me, I was out of synch with life. I had to get out. I piled my Stones pix in a Bob Dylan Tarantula shopping bag and ran to paris. There I was anonymous. Off season. Americans were rare as radium. I teamed up with a fire-eater called Andrillias. He had a crooked arm and a way with women. A face as sculptured and as non-committal as Charlie Watts. His cloak was strictly civil war. He taught me how to light a cigarette in the wind and the way to an American's fat wallet. He would strip to the waist. The fire would jump and the crowd would shout. I'd sashay within and out. jingle jangle. pickpocket a guy who looks just like a daddy.

Things changed hands. A fire eater needs to move. I stayed in Paris looking for bulges in American trousers. Soon after it hit the papers. Brian was leaving the Stones. That got me shook. I kept reading the news over and over. As if to uncover some invisible print. I was so sure there was more to the story. Then Godards One Plus One was released. It showcased the Stones. I went sniffing for clues. Christ I hated that movie. It exposed Mick. made him look like an ass. Being a true American I don't like people rocking my idol. So I wore blinders and zoomed in on Brian. He wasn't human and not super human. rather transparent. The bruised and vulnerable soul of the Stones.

I tried to touch. I made this chant:

Brian Brian/I'm not crying/I'm just trying/to reach you.

My own mantra. Hard contact. Mix and melt and warn a sacred stranger. A weakling.

The fire eater reappeared. We withdrew to a town called the "wishing well." I tried to can my obsession. I was getting wall-eyed. I made Lizzie Borden look like a seamstress. I breathed deeper. forget Brian. ya don't even know him. Relax. Dig a hole and shit like a cat. like Voltaire.

So I slept it off like a good drunk. Snails crawled up the walls. Albino chickens and a big black dog circled the hut. One night of peace. Then I fell so fast. No longer tense I was a perfect trance target. When sleep covered me I'd dream a death dream of Brian. By the fourth night I wished I was dead. My body erupted. I was covered with an unknown rash. I could hardly breathe. I dropped a pot of boiling water on my legs. They bubbled up like jelly fish.

He'd drown in his own tears. mock turtle.

He'd swell up from swallowing too much rain.

*   *   *

dressed in victorian lace he'd choke

Mick would cover his eyes. Keith would cry like the warrior.

Night after night. Until my eyes burned like a leg.

It was July 2. The doctor thought I was bats. He gave me morphine for the pain. He whispered sweet dreams.

That night stretched like a cloud. A hypnotic. I was aware of the droning of bees. In the garden the blonde woman was preparing a mixture of pollen and pure honey. Keith was twisting her arm. He had a leather erection. Mick was writhing. some dizzy ritual. The pollen made me wheeze. I laid in the grass and puked. The dew was cooling my hot leg. Someone grabbed my ankle. bruising it. I was saved. I was suffocating in my own warm vomit. I gulped sweet oxygen and turned. Brian was still holding on. I wanted to speak to him but I got caught up in the lace border of his cuff. I traced the delicate embroidery until it stretched across my field of vision like queen anne's lace.

It was morning. It was dazzling. It was July 3rd. By night fall the whole world knew that Brian Jones was dead.

I went home to America and threw up on my fathers bed.

I was antique. He had returned to light and I was holding baby hair.

Brian was a length ahead. He was gonna dig up the great African root and pump it like gas in every Stones hit. But it wasn't time yet. Unlucky horoscope. Imagination and realization were ticking on separate time-pieces.

But Brian was in a hurry. Running neck and neck with his vision was his demon. He would soon as stick his dick up the baby dolls ass. Shove pins in the heads of innocents. Torn between evil energy and pure spirit. Bad seed with a golden spleen. The Stones were moving toward a mortal merging of the unspoken monument and the hot dance of life. But they were moving too slow for Brian. So slow he split. In two.

*   *   *

377

Death by water. Just a shot away from the heart of Ethiopia. Rising to original heights. Up and over Adams apple sauce. There are blonde hairs raveling in the Stones vital breath. ha ha. Brian got the last laugh.

And the sacrifices continue. moving toward the perfect moment. the miracle of Altamont. The death of the lime green spade. Not shocking. Necessary. The most graceful complete moment. Compare his dance of death with Mick's frenzied movement. Mick's spastic magic. Unlucky motor.

Give history a chance. St. Meredith. his image in pure copper rising over the speedway. Our jesus of Brazil.

Look back Altamont. Our Rome. water babies. no flow. no one. gimme gimme. a private piece of the action. some footage. some tail. hold it to the ego like gold plate. no collective act.

And Mick was no flashing priest. A pretty sailor thrown in a cell of sissy athletes. All panting into anarchy. They pluck up Mick like the old fairy tale. Split the goose that lays the slow golden eggs. shake that magic maker. extract that diamond tooth.

I pray that its alright. well it wasn't. Not until that flash of silver. that very silent knife. skin pop. Washed in the blood of the lamb any villain comes out clean as Niagara falls.

That's the western movement. That's the way of rock n roll. At my first school dance Jo-Jo Rose got stabbed. U.S. Bonds was lip-synching "Quarter to Three." Nobody is erecting monuments to Jo-Jo Rose. Nobody's blaming U.S. Bonds neither.

Blame Mick Jagger? For what? for performing thru theory not grace. The alchemy was not there. The performer and the audience have got to be as intimate as the killer and his victim. Like in Performance. Takes two to make the radio. Contact pill. If you can see it you can get it. Brian dreamed of it. Mick failed at it.

But you know he's redeemed. Mick did it. This is no stylistic trick. Tuesday night July 25 1972 at Madison Square Garden. A sacred peep show. Pope don't bless my flashlight. I found my own way.

* * *

Born to be. Born to be me. Got my ticket for free. What would I wear? Keith Richards gear? bone in the ear? Naaa. Lay the flash aside. Dress like Don't Look Back. Just the right dark glasses. Blow my last buck to be cool. grab that taxi. adjust my shades and light a Kool. Pat my flask of Jack Daniel's. I get there. Completely solitaire.

My seat juts out. Overlook the ground floor. Left handed stage view. Nobody can get in my way. Nothing but ramp and space. A box seat. Tuesday was the off night. The double show day. Rock stars make their own labor laws. Inhuman work load. No party. No hip chicks. Just fans. Everyone a stranger. Good. I could play at being a cool and perfect stranger myself. I sat there feeling incognito hot shit. Then my stomach started feeling funny. Detached jello. Regulate my breath. Be a breathing camera. The hungry eye.

My eye rolled down the stream of light. Stevie Wonder was on. Funny bone. He sniffed out his territory. More suspicious than a tom cat. He wasn't singing he was breathing. That amazing thick veined neck. Motown was moving. Wall to wall production. A full blown track with no vocal. He was laughing. He could give a shit. He was great. He hit the drums. He just don't make mistakes. He makes it all up. As Judy Linn said: "I would not like to be Stevie Wonder's drummer. It would be like directing Orson Welles in a movie." A real visual performer. When he's behind his putney he deals in nouns. Look Stevie. Roll on. 20,000 eyes are watching you. Your eyes are turned in. When you sing you really sing. He set me up for the Stones. Pulling my vision in. Inverted flashlight.

I was sorry to see him go. In fact. Panic struck. It was too quick. The equipment men moved like magnets. Cleared the stage. Room to dance to breathe. The lights went out and the crowd rose up. Someone rested a birthday cake on an amp. The first hint of ritual. What are you doing on your birthday?

Then something snapped. I'm no screamer. I swear. When the roller coaster crashes. I hold my breath. I refuse to let loose. It's a matter of pride. But I cracked. My tear ducts burst. They were there in 4-D. Fell on one knee. Couldn't see. My brain cracked like an egg. The gold liquid spurted all over the stage. Mick bathed in it. Keith got his feet wet. Then I calmed quick. It was like coming without jerking off. They hadn't even finished brown sugar and I was cool as a snake. Physically for me the concert was over. Like hearing the punchline then sitting thru the long drawn out joke.

The rest was pure head motion. Like viewing any ancient ceremony. Pass the sacred wafer. Transfixed my open laughter. My brain was open as a loft. No mere image. I was ashamed. They were just men. Charlie raised over like King Drum. Bill in red velvet. His bass way up. His classic dignity. Mick Taylor completing the triangle. The maypole.

Mick and Keith wove their magic round. Keith a drunken kid. He was moving so good. Thin raunchy glitter. I don't care what anyone says. He's the real rolling stone. He got the silver. Basic black guitar. Like a convertible. Like heartbreak hotel. His plexiglass one got stolen.

Stealing stealing I feel so good when I'm stealing. Keith from Charlie. Mick from the crowd. It was plain to see their mercury was frozen. But it was Mick who seemed affected most. It got me shook. To hear him talk. As if we were to blame.

His frothing mouth. His skeleton chest. No longer a boy with soft flesh. His nipples weren't hard. He wasn't erect. The warrior class gone fag. The dying Mayan. Infections on his fingers. He was decked out like a tacky harlequin. Were they holes or were they rhinestones on that white flight suit? Spangled satin open to the stomach. Covered in sentimental airplane leather. The leather was soon discarded. It was tougher than he was. He never raised his arm that high. Rather he twisted his fragile frame like the mime. The fluid monkey. Then more fluid. then water. then piss.

Mick you devil dog you. He was on the verge of collapse. But not in the way you gossip about. But the way that transcends into light. This was the off night. The night he really did it. The night he never dared to do. He got too much money riding on his act. The other concerts were fantastic polished sideshows. Mick spitting glitter. 40 carat dandruff. The flash of these premeditated concerts was only temporarily blinding. The one I seen was different. I'll hold forever. The one barely documented. The least starstudded. The magic accident. The hallmark of a ten year project. Mick do you know you really did it?

*   *   *

Redemption don't come easy. ringo. Mick needed help and we knew it. He tried to speak. He slurred jagged poetry:

You're very warm. warm warm warm.

here in new york. new york new york new york.

tired tired. bang bang bang.

It made some uncomfortable. Some threw rotten apples. Keith swept over. Magic mafia. He put his life in front of Mick. The Stones thru a field of protection over as relentless as barbed wire.

Some were afraid he'd drop. We can't let another human god collapse. There's a shortage. Crowd sent him energy. in waves. Invisible friction. A collective shot of speed and desire. "I'm a little hoarse," he begged. Wooooo. The crowd gave him what they had. Proud to offer a sliver of their vocal to Mick Jagger. So he breathed "Love in Vain." I swear in slow motion. The way a morphine man whirls. Clockless abandon. So slushy. The kind of confidence in death that cocaine produces. If he lost the beat a new one was invented. The true language of ritual. Not remote but in the moment. What a beautiful bird what a beautiful burst.

To Midnight Rambler he worked hard. Calisthenics. Frenzied push-ups. Mad shadow box. Anything to keep him up. No one dared rush the stage. Might break the current. Death of holy Frankenstein. It was less a rock concert than a battle for survival.

Completely protected by the Rolling Stones. In return he extended them. Their cosmic monkey. Their ballet flower girl. He was no strutting cock. Not now. He fluttered like a swan; a holy ghost.

Not without sacrifice. He was loosing his grip. He introduced the band. A long silence before Keith. Death rattle. Did he introduce Brian Jones? Freeze that moment. I got no Maysley video to look back on. What was he saying? The silence was anything but golden. Does the lion drown underwater? Or does he swallow the golden fish? Brian swimming thru the crowd. I looked down. They were modulating. Jagger was apologizing. Incoherent. drooling. the heat. the drink. I was in shock. My heart stopped this short. from stopping.

*   *   *

Now get this. The performer is given a character. The masked millionaire. A man of wealth and taste. One night he loses it. Lifts the veil and reveals. He moves outside his own choreography.

Mick did it. He whirled round and round. Spun all over the stage. Senile Magi. Identical to his true and original chemistry. Not childlike but the child itself. Not drugged but the uncut crystal. He had sacrificed the image of Mick Jagger. He had gone so far he could do no wrong. Or right. Just beyond judgement.

On stage there was a huge mirror. The amateur alchemists' trick. To blend the Stones and Mick and spectators as one. Two way X-ray. The stones have stolen from everyone and spit it back again. this is what you were. This is what we've become. The only surviving mirror of every great move in the sixties. They were playing as good as a record. That's rare for them. Not a false move and not perfect either.

The concert was ending. Mick passed the test. Proved he was a human god. He saw that death-light was just a shot away. He went berserk. Wild adrenalin. He went for broke. And captured the whole casino.

The goodie-goodie medicine man. Back up the sacred monsters. Rise up angel. You made it Mick. We could have chomped you up like raw meat. But you won. You drained our brain.

Some last minute flashes. Mick shook out olympic energy. He was a ring-a-ding baptist. Water water everywhere. On the skull and in the face. Good as spit. He hugged his hornplayer. He was popping like a weasel. His head bobbing like a drowning man. His face was full of silly grace. The sky was racing toward a full moon. He blew out his candles and the lights went up. At last we were revealed. The art of the spectator frozen forever. Got nothing live without audience.

We rose without shame. This was our show too. Raised our arm to jumping jack flash. Our Savior is a white nazi. Jesus . . . Hitler . . . Dylan . . . Jagger. Give it all to the total performer. The millionaire martyr. Light broke. Brian Jones. It was over. I ran home.

*   *   *

For the first time completely satisfied. Like a good cinderella I was home before midnight. A perfect stranger stopped me:

Did you ever see a concert like that?

Only in my head.

I tied a do-rag round it. My brain oiled. A texas gusher. Sick with the tropical heat I slept deep. and I dreamed this dream:

Mick Jagger lying down. I lay down. We fall asleep. We dream the same dream. Breathe the same air. In a circle. That widens encircles the room. the house. the universe.

and I dreamed this dream:

I steal the genet skin of my sleeping lover. With my new full blown cock I fuck every blonde in the world.

and I dreamed this dream:

Sick with white logic. I ride the roller coaster. higher and higher. thru cloud matter. Take the big plunge. My mouth a big white O. Everything explodes. Pure light. Undulating form. Contracting within a prism. Which widens like a pure white loft. Waiting for someone to come out of somewhere. Brian Jones enters. Very formal. Very aware. He explains his brain. and brain waves. and halo light.

I can't help it. I cry out. How are you? Have you been all right? He smiles. He turns away and says: "I have everything under control."

> "In this life there is no pleasure greater
> than coming back to life again
> after having been torn to shreds."
> —*The Popul Vuh*

HOW DOES IT FEEL?

In 1965 Al Kooper was a young New York songwriter, turning out pop tunes for the youth market. He had been aware of Bob Dylan, like everyone else, since the release of his early acoustic albums with the finger-pointing songs on them. Kooper got to know Tom Wilson, Dylan's producer, and when Wilson played "Subterranean Homesick Blues," Dylan's first rock and roll single, Kooper was electrified. He wanted to be part of whatever it was Dylan was doing, and so he capitalized on his friendship with Wilson and got into the session for "Like a Rolling Stone" on June 15, 1965. Kooper picks up the story from there.

THERE WAS no way in hell that I was going to visit a Bob Dylan session and just sit there like some reporter from *Sing Out!* magazine. I resolved that not only was I going to go to that session, I was going to *play* on it. I stayed up through the night preceding the session, running down all seven of my guitar licks over and over again. Despite my doodling at the piano, I was primarily a guitar player and, having gotten a fair amount of session work under my belt, had developed quite an inflated opinion of my dexterity on said instrument.

The session was called for two o'clock the next afternoon. Taking no chances, I arrived an hour early and well enough ahead of the crowd to establish my cover. I slipped into the studio with my guitar case, unpacked, tuned up, plugged in, and sat there trying my hardest to look like I belonged. The other musicians, all people I knew from other sessions around town, slowly filtered in and gave no indication that anything was amiss. For all they knew, I could have received the same phone call they'd gotten. Tom Wilson hadn't arrived as yet, and he was the only one who could really blow the whistle on my little ego drama. I was prepared to tell him I had misunderstood him and thought he had asked me to play on the session. All bases covered.

Suddenly Dylan exploded through the doorway, and in tow was this bizarre-looking guy carrying a Fender Telecaster guitar *without* a case. Which was weird, because it was the dead of winter and the guitar was all wet from the rain and snow. But he just shuffled over into the corner, wiped it off, plugged in and commenced to play some of the most incredible guitar I'd ever heard. That's all the Seven Lick Kid had to hear; I was in over my head, I anonymously unplugged, packed up, and did my best to look like a reporter from *Sing Out!* magazine.

Tom Wilson made his entrance, too late, thank God, to catch my one-act abortion. I asked him who the guitar player was. "Oh, some friend of Dylan's from Chicago, named Mike Bloomfield. I never heard of him but Bloomfield says he can play the tunes, and Dylan says he's the best." That's how I made my introduction to a man who can still make me smile whenever he picks up a guitar.

The band quickly got down to business. They weren't too far into this long song Dylan had written before it was decided that the organ part would be better suited to piano. The sight of an empty seat stirred my ambitions once again; didn't matter that I knew next to nothing about playing a goddamn organ. In a flash I was on Tom Wilson, telling him that I had a great part for the song and *please* (oh God please) could I have a shot at it.

"Hey," he said, "you don't play the organ."

Yeah, I do, and I got a good part, all the while racing my mind in overdrive to find anything that I could play at all.

Already adept at wading through my bullshit, Tom says, "I don't want to embarrass you, Al, I mean . . ." and was then distracted by some other studio obligation. Claiming victory by virtue of not having received a direct "no," I'm off to the organ.

Me and the organ. If the other guy hadn't left the damn thing turned on, my career as an organ player would have ended right there. I figured out as best I could how to bluff my way through while the rest of the band rehearsed one little section of the song. Then Wilson is saying, "Okay, let's try it again, roll the tape," and I'm on my own.

Check this out: There is no music to read. The song is over five minutes long. The band is so loud that I can't even *hear* the organ, and I'm not familiar with the instrument to begin with. But the tape is going, and that is *Bob fucking Dylan* over there singing, so this had better be me sitting here playing *something.* The best I could manage was to play kind of hesitantly by sight, feeling my way through the changes like a little kid fumbling in the dark for a light switch. After six minutes they'd gotten the first complete take of the day down, and all adjourned to the booth to hear it played back.

Thirty seconds into the second verse, Dylan motions towards Tom Wilson. "Turn the organ up," he orders.

"Hey, man," Tom says, "that cat's not an organ player." *Thanks, Tom.*

But Dylan isn't buying it. "Hey, now don't tell me who's an organ player and who's not. Just turn the organ up."

He actually liked what he heard!

At the conclusion of the playback, the entire booth applauded the soon-to-be-a-classic "Like a Rolling Stone," and Dylan acknowledged the tribute by turning his back and wandering into the studio for a go at another tune. I sat, still dazed, at my new instrument and filled in a straight chord every now and again. No other songs were gotten that day, but as everyone was filing out Dylan asked for my phone number—which was like Brigitte Bardot asking for the key to your hotel room—and invited me back the next day. I walked out of that studio realizing that I had actually *lived* my fantasy of the night before, but not *exactly* as I had planned it.

Jules Siegel

A TEEN-AGE HYMN TO GOD

When Fitzgerald said there are no second acts in American lives, he might have been reading Brian Wilson's mail. After a spectacular first act of superb American rock and roll ("I Get Around," "Don't Worry Baby," "Little Deuce Coupe," "California Girls"), composer-producer Wilson and his band, the Beach Boys, neatly packaged up that era with a coming-of-age album, *Pet Sounds,* and a stunning single, "Good Vibrations," in 1966 and prepared for a second act. They never really came back from intermission. Here's a cautionary tale about what happened when Wilson tried to fuck with the Beach Boys formula. This was written for the *Saturday Evening Post,* which aggressively rejected it, despite Siegel's excellent track record with the magazine.

IT WAS just another day of greatness at Gold Star Recording Studios on Santa Monica Boulevard in Hollywood. In the morning four long-haired kids had knocked out two hours of sound for a record plugger who was trying to curry favor with a disc jockey friend of theirs in San José. Nobody knew it at that moment, but out of that two hours there were about three minutes that would hit the top of the charts in a few weeks, and the record plugger, the disc jockey and the kids would all be hailed as geniuses, but geniuses with a very small g.

Now, however, in the very same studio, a Genius with a very large capital G was going to produce a hit. There was no doubt it would be a hit because this Genius was Brian Wilson. In four years of recording for Capitol Records, he and his group the Beach Boys, had made surfing music a national craze, sold 16 million singles and earned gold records for ten of their twelve albums.

Not only was Brian going to produce a hit, but also, one gathered, he was going to show everybody in the music business exactly where it was at; and where it was at, it seemed, was that Brian Wilson was not merely a Genius—which is to say a steady commercial success—but rather, like

Bob Dylan and John Lennon, a GENIUS—which is to say a steady commercial success and hip besides.

Until now, though, there were not too many hip people who would have considered Brian Wilson and the Beach Boys hip, even though he had produced one very hip record, "Good Vibrations," which had sold more than a million copies, and a super-hip album, *Pet Sounds,* which didn't do very well at all—by previous Beach Boy sales standards. Among the hip people he was still on trial, and the question discussed earnestly among the recognized authorities on what is and what is not hip was whether or not Brian Wilson was hip, semi-hip or square.

But walking into the control room with the answers to all questions such as this was Brian Wilson himself, wearing a competition-stripe surfer's t-shirt, tight white duck pants, pale green bowling shoes and a red plastic toy fireman's helmet.

Everybody was wearing identical red plastic toy fireman's helmets. Brian's cousin and production assistant, Steve Korthoff, was wearing one; his wife, Marilyn, and her sister, Diane Rovell—Brian's secretary—were also wearing them, and so was a once dignified writer from the *Saturday Evening Post* who had been following Brian around for two months trying to figure out whether or not this 24-year-old oversized tribute to Southern California who carried some 250 pounds of baby fat on a 6 foot 4 inch frame, was a genius, Genius or GENIUS, hip, semi-hip or square—concepts the writer himself was just learning to handle.

Out in the studio, the musicians for the session were unpacking their instruments. In sport shirts and slacks, they looked like insurance salesmen and used-car dealers, except for one blonde female percussionist who might have been stamped out by a special machine that supplied plastic mannequin housewives for detergent commercials.

Controlled, a little bored after twenty years or so of nicely paid anonymity, these were the professionals of the popular music business, hired guns who did their job expertly and efficiently and then went home to the suburbs. If you wanted swing, they gave you swing. A little movie-track lushness? Fine, here comes movie-track lushness. Now it's rock & roll? Perfect rock & roll, down the chute.

"Steve," Brian called out, "where are the rest of those fire hats? I want everybody to wear fire hats. We've really got to get into this thing." Out to the Rolls-Royce went Steve and within a few minutes all of the musicians were wearing fire hats, silly grins beginning to crack their professional dignity.

"All right, let's go," said Brian. Then, using a variety of techniques ranging from local demonstration to actually playing the instruments, he taught each musician his part. A gigantic fire howled out of the massive studio speakers in a pounding crush of pictorial music that summoned up visions of roaring, windstorm flames, falling timbers, mournful sirens and sweating firemen, building into a peak and crackling off into fading embers as a single drum turned into a collapsing wall and the fire engine cellos dissolved and disappeared.

"When did he write this?" asked an astonished pop music producer who had wandered into the studio. "This is really fantastic! Man, this is unbelievable! How long has he been working on it?"

"About an hour," answered one of Brian's friends.

"I don't believe it. I just can't believe what I'm hearing," said the producer and fell into a stone silence as the fire music began again.

For the next three hours Brian Wilson recorded and re-recorded, take after take, changing the sound balance, adding echo, experimenting with a sound-effects track of a real fire.

"Let me hear that again." "Drums, I think you're a little slow in that last part. Let's get on it." "That was really good. Now, one more time, the whole thing." "All right, let me hear the cellos alone." "Great. Really great. Now let's do it!"

With twenty-three takes on tape and the entire operation responding to his touch like the black knobs on the control board, sweat glistening down his long, reddish hair on to his freckled face, the control room a litter of dead cigarette butts, Chicken Delight boxes, crumpled napkins, Coke bottles and all the accumulated trash of the physical end of the creative process, Brian stood at the board as the four speakers blasted the music into the room.

For the twenty-fourth time, the drums crashed and the sound-effects crackle faded and stopped.

"Thank you," said Brian, into the control-room mike. "Let me hear that back." Feet shifting, his body still, eyes closed, head moving seal-like to his music, he stood under the speakers and listened. "Let me hear that one more time." Again the fire roared. "Everybody come out and listen to this," Brian said to the musicians. They came into the control room and listened to what they had made.

"What do you think?" Brian asked.

"It's incredible. Incredible," whispered one of the musicians, a man in his fifties, wearing a Hawaiian shirt and iridescent trousers and pointed black Italian shoes. "Absolutely incredible."

"Yeah," said Brian on the way home, an acetate trial copy or "dub" of the tape in his hands, the red plastic fire helmet still on his head. "Yeah, I'm going to call this "Mrs O'Leary's Fire" and I think it might just scare a whole lot of people."

As it turns out, however, Brian Wilson's magic fire music is not going to scare anybody—because nobody other than the few people who heard it in the studio will ever get to listen to it. A few days after the record was finished, a building across the street from the studio burned down and, according to Brian, there was also an unusually large number of fires in Los Angeles. Afraid that his music might in fact turn out to be magic fire music, Wilson destroyed the master.

"I don't have to do a big scary fire like that," he later said, "I can do a candle and it's still fire. That would have been a really bad vibration to let out on the world, that Chicago fire. The next one is going to be a candle."

A person who thinks of himself as understanding would probably interpret this episode as an example of perhaps too-excessive artistic perfectionism. One with psychiatric inclinations would hear all this stuff about someone who actually believed music would cause fires and start using words such as neurosis and maybe even psychosis. A true student of spoken hip, however, would say hang-up, which covers all of the above.

As far as Brian's pretensions toward hipness are concerned, no label could do him worse harm. In the hip world, there is a widespread idea that really hip people don't have hang-ups, which gives rise to the unspoken rule (unspoken because there is also the widespread idea that really hip people don't make any rules) that no one who wants to be thought of as hip ever reveals his hang-ups, except maybe to his guru, and in the strictest of privacy.

In any case, whatever his talent, Brian Wilson's attempt to win a hip following and reputation foundered for many months in an obsessive cycle of creation and destruction that threatened not only his career and his future but also his marriage, his friendships, his relationship with the Beach Boys and, some of his closest friends worried, his mind.

For a boy who used to be known in adolescence as a lover of sweets, the whole thing must have begun to taste very sour; yet, this particular phase of Brian's drive toward whatever his goal of supreme success might be began on a rising tide that at first looked as if it would carry him and the Beach Boys beyond the Beatles, who had started just about the same time they did, into the number-one position in the international pop music fame-and-power competition.

"About a year ago I had what I considered a very religious experience," Wilson told Los Angeles writer Tom Nolan in 1966. "I took LSD, a full dose of LSD, and later, another time, I took a smaller dose. And I learned a lot of things, like patience, understanding. I can't teach you or tell you what I learned from taking it, but I consider it a very religious experience."

A short time after his LSD experience, Wilson began work on the record that was to establish him right along with the Beatles as one of the most important innovators in modern popular music. It was called "Good Vibrations," and it took more than six months, ninety hours of tape and eleven complete versions before a 3-minute 35-second final master tape satisfied him. Among the instruments on "Good Vibrations" was an electronic device called a theramin, which had its debut in the soundtrack of the movie *Spellbound,* back in the forties. To some people "Good Vibrations" was considerably crazier than Gregory Peck had been in the movie, but to others, Brian Wilson's new record, along with his somewhat earlier release, *Pet Sounds,* marked the beginning of a new era in pop music.

"THEY'VE FOUND THE NEW SOUND AT LAST!" shrieked the headline over a London *Sunday Express* review as "Good Vibrations" hit the English charts at number six and leaped to number one the following week. Within a few weeks, the Beach Boys had pushed the Beatles out of first place in England's *New Musical Express's* annual poll. In America, "Good Vibrations" sold nearly 400,000 copies in four days before reaching number one several weeks later and earning a gold record within another month when it hit the one-million sale mark.

It was an arrival, certainly, but in America, where there is none of the Beach Boys' California-mystique that adds a special touch of romance to their records and appearances in Europe and England, the news had not yet really reached all of the people whose opinion can turn popularity into fashionability. With the exception of a professor of show business (right, professor of show business; in California such a thing is not considered unusual) who turned up one night to interview Brian, and a few young writers (such as the *Village Voice's* Richard Goldstein, Paul Williams of *Crawdaddy,* and Lawrence Dietz of *New York Magazine*), not too many opinion-makers were prepared to accept the Beach Boys into the mainstream of the culture industry.

What all this meant, of course, was that everybody agreed that Brian Wilson and the Beach Boys were still too square. It would take more than "Good Vibrations" and *Pet Sounds* to erase three and a half years of "Little Deuce Coupe"—a lot more if you counted in those J. C. Penney-style custom-tailored, kandy-striped short shirts they insisted on wearing on stage.

Brian, however, had not yet heard the news, it appeared, and was steadily going about the business of trying to become hip. The Beach Boys, who have toured without him ever since he broke down during one particularly wearing trip, were now in England and Europe, phoning back daily reports of enthusiastic fan hysteria—screaming little girls tearing at their flesh, wild press conferences, private chats with the Rolling Stones. Washed in the heat of a kind of attention they had never received in the United States even at the height of their commercial success, three Beach Boys—Brian's brothers, Dennis and Carl, and his cousin, Mike Love—walked into a London Rolls-Royce showroom and bought four Phantom VII limousines, one for each of them and a fourth for Brian. Al Jardine and Bruce Johnston, the Beach Boys who are not corporate members of the Beach Boys enterprises, sent their best regards and bought themselves some new clothing.

In the closing months of 1966, with the Beach Boys home in Los Angeles, Brian rode the "Good Vibrations" high, driving forward in bursts of enormous energy that seemed destined before long to earn him the throne of the international empire of pop music still ruled by John Lennon and the Beatles.

At the time, it looked as if the Beatles were ready to step down. Their summer concerts in America had been only moderately successful at best, compared to earlier years. There were ten thousand empty seats at Shea Stadium in New York and eleven lonely fans at the airport in Seattle. Mass media, underground press, music industry trade papers and the fan magazines were filled with fears that the Beatles were finished, that the group was breaking up. Lennon was off acting in a movie; McCartney was walking around London alone, said to be carrying a giant torch for his sometime girlfriend Jane Asher; George Harrison was getting deeper and deeper into a mystical Indian thing under the instruction of sitar-master Ravi Shankar; and Ringo was collecting material for a Beatles museum.

In Los Angeles, Brian Wilson was riding around in the Rolls-Royce that had once belonged to John Lennon, pouring a deluge of new sounds onto miles of stereo tape in three different recording studios booked day and night for him in month-solid blocks, holding court nightly at his $240,000 Beverly Hills Babylonian-modern home, and, after guests left, sitting at his grand piano until dawn, writing new material.

The work in progress was an album called *Smile*. "I'm writing a teenage symphony to God," Brian told dinner guests on an October evening. He then played for them the collection of black acetate trial records which lay piled on the floor of his red imitation-velvet wallpapered bedroom with its leopard-print bedspread. In the bathroom, above the wash basin, there was a plastic color picture of Jesus Christ with trick effect eyes that appeared to open and close when you moved your head. Sophisticate newcomers pointed it out to each other and laughed slyly, almost hoping to find a Keane painting among decorations ranging from Lava Lamps to a department-store rack of dozens of dolls, each still in its plastic bubble container, the whole display trembling like a space-age Christmas tree to the music flowing out into the living-room.

Brian shuffled through the acetates, most of which were unlabelled, identifying each by subtle differences in the patterns of the grooves. He had played them so often he knew the special look of each record the way you know the key to your front door by the shape of its teeth. Most were instrumental tracks, cut while the Beach Boys were in Europe, and for these Brian supplied the vocal in a high sound that seemed to come out of his head rather than his throat as he somehow managed to create complicated four and five part harmonies with only his own voice.

"Bicycle rider, see what you done done to the church of the native American Indian . . ." [Brian sang]. A panorama of American history filled the room as the music shifted from theme to theme; the tinkling harpsichord sounds of the bicycle rider pushed sad Indian sounds across the continent; the Iron Horse pounded across the plains in a wide open rolling rhythm that summoned up visions of the old West; civilized chickens bobbed up and down in a tiny ballet of comic barnyard melody; the inexorable bicycle music, cold and charming as an infinitely talented music box, reappeared and faded away.

Like medieval choirboys, the voices of the Beach Boys pealed out in wordless prayer from the last acetate, thirty seconds of chorale that reached upward to the vaulted stone ceilings of an empty cathedral lit by thousands of tiny votive candles melting at last into one small, pure pool that whispered a universal amen in a sigh without words.

Brian's private radio show was finished. In the dining-room a candle-lit table with a dark blue cloth was set for ten persons. In the kitchen, Marilyn Wilson was trying to get the meal organized and served, aided and hindered by the chattering suggestions of the guests' wives and girl-friends. When everyone was seated and waiting for the food, Brian tapped his knife idly on a white china plate.

"Listen to that," he said. "That's really great!" Everybody listened as Brian played the plate. "Come on, let's get something going here," he ordered. "Michael—do this. David—you do this." A plate-and-spoon musicale began to develop as each guest played a distinctly different technique, rhythm and melody under Brian's enthusiastic direction.

"That's absolutely unbelievable!" said Brian. "Isn't that unbelievable? That's so unbelievable I'm going to put it on the album. Michael, I want you to get a sound system up here tomorrow and I want everyone to be here tomorrow night. We're going to get this on tape."

Brian Wilson's plate-and-spoon musicale never did reach the public, but only because he forgot about it. Other sounds equally strange have found their way on to his records. On *Pet Sounds,* for example, on some tracks there is an odd, soft, hollow percussion effect that most musicians assume is some kind of electronically transmuted drum sound—a conga drum played with a stick perhaps, or an Indian tom-tom. Actually, it's drummer Hal Blaine playing the bottom of a plastic jug that once contained Sparklettes spring water. And, of course, at the end of the record there is the strangely affecting track of a train roaring through a lonely railroad crossing as a bell clangs and Brian's dogs, Banana, a beagle, and Louie, a dark brown Weimaraner, bark after it.

More significant, perhaps, to those who that night heard the original instrumental tracks for both *Smile* and the Beach Boys' new single, "Heroes And Villains," is that entire sequences of extraordinary power and beauty are missing in the finished version of the single, and will undoubtedly be missing as well from *Smile*—victims of Brian's obsessive tinkering and, more importantly, sacrifices to the same strange combination of superstitious fear and God-like conviction of his own power he displayed when he destroyed the fire music.

The night of the dining-table concerto, it was the God-like confidence Brian must have been feeling as he put his guests on his trip, but the fear was soon to take over. At his house that night, he had assembled a new set of players to introduce into his life game, each of whom was to perform a specific role in the grander game he was playing with the world.

Earlier in the summer, Brian had hired Van Dyke Parks, a supersophisticated young songwriter and composer, to collaborate with him on the lyrics for *Smile.* With Van Dyke working for him, he had a fighting chance against John Lennon, whose literary skill and Liverpudlian wit had been one of the most important factors in making the Beatles the darlings of the hip intelligentsia.

With that flank covered, Brian was ready to deal with some of the other problems of trying to become hip, the most important of which was how was he going to get in touch with some really hip people. In effect, the dinner party at the house was his first hip social event, and the star of the evening, so far as Brian was concerned, was Van Dyke Parks's manager, David Anderle, who showed up with a whole group of very hip people.

Elegant, cool and impossibly cunning, Anderle was an artist who had somehow found himself in the record business as an executive for MGM Records, where he had earned himself a reputation as a genius by purportedly thinking up the million-dollar movie-TV-record offer that briefly lured Bob Dylan to MGM from Columbia until everybody had a change of heart and Dylan decided to go back home to Columbia.

Anderle had skipped back and forth between painting and the record business, with mixed results in both. Right now he was doing a little personal management and thinking about painting a lot. His appeal to Brian was simple; everybody recognized David Anderle as one of the hippest people in Los Angeles. In fact, he was something like the mayor of hipness as far as some people were concerned. And not only that, he was a genius.

Within six weeks, he was working for the Beach Boys; everything that Brian wanted seemed at last to be in reach. Like a magic genie, David Anderle produced miracles for him. A new Beach Boys record company was set up, Brother Records, with David Anderle at its head and, simultaneously, the Beach Boys sued Capitol Records in a move designed to force a renegotiation of their contract with the company.

The house was full of underground press writers; Anderle's friend Michael Vosse was on the Brother Records payroll out scouting TV contracts and performing other odd jobs. Another of Anderle's friends was writing the story on Brian for the *Saturday Evening Post* and a film crew from CBS-TV was up at the house filming for a documentary to be narrated by Leonard Bernstein. The Beach Boys were having meetings once or twice a week with teams of experts, briefing them on corporate policy, drawing complicated chalk patterns as they described the millions of dollars everyone was going to earn out of all this.

As 1967 opened it seemed as though Brian and the Beach Boys were assured of a new world of success; yet something was going wrong. As the corporate activity reached a peak of intensity, Brian was becoming less and less productive and more and more erratic. *Smile,* which was to have been released for the Christmas season, remained unfinished. "Heroes And Villains," which was virtually complete, remained in the can, as Brian kept working out new little pieces and then scrapping them.

Van Dyke Parks had left and come back and would leave again, tired of being constantly dominated by Brian. Marilyn Wilson was having headaches and Dennis Wilson was leaving his wife. Session after session was cancelled. One night a studio full of violinists waited while Brian tried to decide whether or not the vibrations were friendly or hostile. The answer was hostile and the session was cancelled, at a cost of some $3,000. Everything seemed to be going wrong. Even the *Post* story fell through.

Brian seemed to be filled with secret fear. One night at the house, it began to surface. Marilyn sat nervously painting her fingernails as Brian stalked up and down, his face tight and his eyes small and red.

"What's the matter, Brian? You're really strung out," a friend asked.

"Yeah, I'm really strung out. Look, I mean I really feel strange. A really strange thing happened to me tonight. Did you see this picture, *Seconds*?"

"No, but I know what it's about; I read the book."

"Look, come into the kitchen; I really have to talk about this." In the kitchen they sat down in the black and white hound's-tooth check wall-papered dinette area. A striped window shade clashed with the checks and the whole room vibrated like some kind of pop art painting. Ordinarily, Brian wouldn't sit for more than a minute in it, but now he seemed to be unaware of anything except what he wanted to say.

"I walked into that movie," he said in a tense, high-pitched voice, "and the first thing that happened was a voice from the screen said 'Hello, Mr Wilson.' It completely blew my mind. You've got to admit that's pretty spooky, right?"

"Maybe."

"That's not all. Then the whole thing was there. I mean my whole life. Birth and death and rebirth. The whole thing. Even the beach was in it, a whole thing about the beach. It was my whole life right there on the screen."

"It's just a coincidence, man. What are you getting all excited about?"

"Well, what if it isn't a coincidence? What if it's real? You know there's mind gangsters these days. There could be mind gangsters, couldn't there? I mean, look at Spector, he could be involved in it, couldn't he? He's going into films. How hard would it be for him to set up something like that?"

"Brian, Phil Spector is not about to make a million-dollar movie just to scare you. Come on, stop trying to be so dramatic."

"All right, all right. I was just a little bit nervous about it," Brian said, after some more back and forth about the possibility that Phil Spector, the record producer, had somehow influenced the making of *Seconds* to disturb Brian Wilson's tranquillity. "I just had to get it out of my system. You can see where something like that could scare someone, can't you?"

They went into Brian's den, a small room papered in psychedelic orange, blue, yellow and red wall fabric with rounded corners. At the end of the room there was a jukebox filled with Beach Boys singles and Phil Spector hits. Brian punched a button and Spector's "Be My Baby" began to pour out at top volume.

"Spector has always been a big thing with me, you know. I mean I heard that song three and a half years ago and I knew that it was between him and me. I knew exactly where he was at and now I've gone beyond him. You can understand how that movie might get someone upset under those circumstances, can't you?"

Brian sat down at his desk and began to draw a little diagram on a piece of printed stationery with his name at the top in the kind of large fat script printers of charitable dinner journals use when the customer asks for a hand-lettered look. With a felt-tipped pen, Brian drew a close approximation of a growth curve. "Spector started the whole thing," he said, dividing the curve into periods. "He was the first one to use the studio. But I've gone beyond him now. I'm doing the spiritual sound, a white spiritual sound. Religious music. Did you hear the Beatles album? Religious, right? That's the whole movement. That's where I'm going. It's going to scare a lot of people."

"Yeah," Brian said, hitting his fist on the desk with a large slap that sent the parakeets in a large cage facing him squalling and whistling. "Yeah," he said and smiled for the first time all evening. "That's where I'm going and it's going to scare a lot of people when I get there."

As the year drew deeper into winter, Brian's rate of activity grew more and more frantic, but nothing seemed to be accomplished. He tore the house apart and half redecorated it. One section of the living-room was filled with a full-sized Arabian tent and the dining-room, where the grand piano stood, was filled with sand to a depth of a foot or so and draped with nursery curtains. He had had his windows stained gray and put a sauna bath in the bedroom. He battled with his father and complained that his brothers weren't trying hard enough. He accused Mike Love of making too much money.

One by one, he cancelled out the friends he had collected, sometimes for the strangest of reasons. An acquaintance of several months who had become extremely close with Brian showed up at a record session and found a guard barring the door. Michael Vosse came out to explain.

"Hey man, this is really terrible," said Vosse, smiling under a broad-brimmed straw hat. "It's not you, it's your chick. Brian says she's a witch and she's messing with his brain so bad by ESP that he can't work. It's like the Spector thing. You know how he is. Say, I'm really sorry." A couple of months later, Vosse was gone. Then, in the late spring, Anderle left. The game was over.

Several months later, the last move in Brian's attempt to win the hip community was played out. On 15 July, the Beach Boys were scheduled to appear at the Monterey International Pop Music Festival, a kind of summit of rock music with the emphasis on love, flowers and youth. Although Brian was a member of the Board of this non-profit event, the Beach Boys cancelled their commitment to perform. The official reason was that their negotiations with Capitol Records were at a crucial stage and they had to get "Heroes And Villains" out right away. The second official reason was that Carl, who had been arrested for refusing to report for induction into the army (he was later cleared in court), was so upset that he wouldn't be able to sing.

Whatever the merit in these reasons, the real one may have been closer to something another Monterey board member suggested: "Brian was afraid that the hippies from San Francisco would think the Beach Boys were square and boo them."

Whatever the case, at the end of the summer, "Heroes And Villains" was released in sharply edited form and *Smile* was reported to be on its way. In the meantime, however, the Beatles had released *Sgt Pepper's Lonely Hearts Club Band* and John Lennon was riding about London in a bright yellow Phantom VII Rolls-Royce painted with flowers on the sides and his zodiac symbol on the top. In *Life* magazine, Paul McCartney came out openly for LSD and in the Haight-Ashbury district of San Francisco George Harrison walked through the streets blessing the hippies. Ringo was still collecting material for a Beatles museum. However good *Smile* might turn out to be, it seemed somehow that once more the Beatles had outdistanced the Beach Boys.

Back during that wonderful period in the fall of 1966 when everybody seemed to be his friend and plans were being laid for Brother Records and all kinds of fine things, Brian had gone on a brief visit to Michigan to hear a Beach Boys concert. The evening of his return, each of his friends and important acquaintances received a call asking everyone to please come to the airport to meet Brian, it was very important. When they gathered at the airport, Brian had a photographer on hand to take a series of group pictures. For a long time, a huge mounted blow-up of the best of the photographs hung on the living-room wall, with some thirty people staring out—everyone from Van Dyke Parks and David Anderle to Michael Vosse and Terry Sachen. In the foreground was the *Saturday Evening Post* writer looking sourly out at the world.

The picture is no longer on Brian's wall and most of the people in it are no longer his friends. One by one each of them had either stepped out of the picture or been forced out of it. The whole cycle has returned to its beginning. Brian, who started out in Hawthorne, California, with his two brothers and a cousin, once more has surrounded himself with relatives. The house in Beverly Hills is empty. Brian and Marilyn are living in their new Spanish Mission estate in Bel-Air, cheek by jowl with the Mamas and the Papas' Cass Elliott.

What remains is "Heroes And Villains," a record some people think is better than anything the Beatles ever wrote.

Joan Didion

WAITING FOR MORRISON

The Doors mixed blues and baroque music behind the sometimes-stolid pronouncements of lead singer and aspiring poet Jim Morrison. Lester Bangs once wrote, "Jim Morrison is one of the fathers of contemporary rock. The Stones were dirty, but the Doors were *dread,* and the difference is crucial, because dread is the great fact of our time." *Saturday Evening Post* columnist—and soon-to-be-novelist—Joan Didion visited a session for the Doors' third album, *Waiting for the Sun,* to report on this rock and roll star/symbolist poet.

IT WAS SIX, seven o'clock of an early spring evening in 1968 and I was sitting on the cold vinyl floor of a sound studio on Sunset Boulevard, watching a band called The Doors record a rhythm track. On the whole my attention was only minimally engaged by the preoccupations of rock-and-roll bands (I had already heard about acid as a transitional stage and also about the Maharishi and even about Universal Love, and after a while it all sounded like marmalade skies to me), but The Doors were different, The Doors interested me. The Doors seemed unconvinced that love was brotherhood and the Kama Sutra. The Doors' music insisted that love was sex and sex was death and therein lay salvation. The Doors were the Norman Mailers of the Top Forty, missionaries of apocalyptic sex. *Break on through,* their lyrics urged, and *Light my fire. . . .*

On this evening in 1968 they were gathered together in uneasy symbiosis to make their third album, and the studio was too cold and the lights were too bright and there were masses of wires and banks of the ominous blinking electronic circuitry with which musicians live so easily. There were three of the four Doors. There was a bass player borrowed from a band called Clear Light. There were the producer and the engineer and the road manager and a couple of girls and a Siberian husky named Nikki with one gray eye and one gold. There were paper bags half filled with hard-boiled eggs and chicken livers and cheeseburgers and empty bottles of apple juice and California rosé. There was everything and every-body The Doors needed to cut the rest of this third album except one thing, the fourth Door, the lead singer, Jim Morrison, a 24-year-old grad-uate of U.C.L.A. who wore black vinyl pants and no underwear and tended to suggest some range of the possible just beyond a suicide pact. It was Morrison who had described The Doors as "erotic politi-cians." It was Morrison who had defined the group's interests as "anything about revolt, disorder, chaos, about activity that appears to have no meaning." It was Morrison who got arrested in Miami in December of 1967 for giving an "indecent" performance. It was Morrison who wrote most of The Doors' lyrics, the peculiar character of which was to reflect either an ambiguous paranoia or a quite unambiguous insistence upon the love-death as the ultimate high. And it was Morrison who was miss-ing. It was Ray Manzarek and Robby Krieger and John Densmore who made The Doors sound the way they sounded, and maybe it was Manzarek and Krieger and Densmore who made seventeen out of twenty interviewees on *American Bandstand* prefer The Doors over all other bands, but it was Morrison who got up there in his black vinyl pants with no underwear and projected the idea, and it was Morrison they were waiting for now.

"Hey listen," the engineer said. "I was listening to an FM station on the way over here, they played three Doors songs, first they played 'Back Door Man' and then 'Love Me Two Times' and 'Light My Fire.' "

"I heard it," Densmore muttered. "I heard it."

"So what's wrong with somebody playing three of your songs?"

"This cat dedicates it to his family."

"Yeah? To his family?"

"To his family. Really crass."

Ray Manzarek was hunched over a Gibson keyboard. "You think *Morrison*'s going to come back?" he asked to no one in particular.

No one answered.

"So we can do some *vocals*?" Manzarek said.

The producer was working with the tape of the rhythm track they had just recorded. "I hope so," he said without looking up.

"Yeah," Manzarek said. "So do I."

My leg had gone to sleep, but I did not stand up; unspecific tensions seemed to be rendering everyone in the room catatonic. The producer played back the rhythm track. The engineer said that he wanted to do his deep-breathing exercises. Manzarek ate a hard-boiled egg. "Tennyson made a mantra out of his own name," he said to the engineer. "I don't know if he said 'Tennyson Tennyson Tennyson' or 'Alfred Alfred Alfred' or 'Alfred Lord Tennyson,' but anyway, he did it. Maybe he just said 'Lord Lord Lord.' "

"Groovy," the Clear Light bass player said. He was an amiable enthusiast, not at all a Door in spirit.

"I wonder what Blake said," Manzarek mused. "Too bad *Morrison's* not here. *Morrison* would know."

It was a long while later. Morrison arrived. He had on his black vinyl pants and he sat down on a leather couch in front of the four big blank speakers and he closed his eyes. The curious aspect of Morrison's arrival was this: no one acknowledged it. Robby Krieger continued working out a guitar passage. John Densmore tuned his drums. Manzarek sat at the control console and twirled a corkscrew and let a girl rub his shoulders. The girl did not look at Morrison, although he was in her direct line of sight. An hour or so passed, and still no one had spoken to Morrison. Then Morrison spoke to Manzarek. He spoke almost in a whisper, as if he were wresting the words from behind some disabling aphasia.

"It's an hour to West Covina," he said. "I was thinking maybe we should spend the night out there after we play."

Manzarek put down the corkscrew. "Why?" he said.

"Instead of coming back."

Manzarek shrugged. "We were planning to come back."

"Well, I was thinking, we could rehearse out there."

Manzarek said nothing.

"We could get in a rehearsal, there's a Holiday Inn next door."

"We could do that," Manzarek said. "Or we could rehearse Sunday, in town."

"I guess so." Morrison paused. "Will the place be ready to rehearse Sunday?"

Manzarek looked at him for a while. "No," he said then.

I counted the control knobs on the electronic console. There were seventy-six. I was unsure in whose favor the dialogue had been resolved, or if it had been resolved at all. Robby Krieger picked at his guitar, and said that he needed a fuzz box. The producer suggested that he borrow one from the Buffalo Springfield, who were recording in the next studio. Krieger shrugged. Morrison sat down again on the leather couch and leaned back. He lit a match. He studied the flame awhile and then very slowly, very deliberately, lowered it to the fly of his black vinyl pants. Manzarek watched him. The girl who was rubbing Manzarek's shoulders did not look at anyone. There was a sense that no one was going to leave the room, ever. It would be some weeks before The Doors finished recording this album. I did not see it through.

WOODSTOCK NATION

Nearly a half-million kids showed up on a farm near Bethel, New York, for the Woodstock Music and Arts Fair of August 1969. Promoters hadn't counted on that many and at first it looked like they would take a titanic bath—$1.3 million down the drain. Later, however, because of the film and recordings of the events, they made a ton of money.

Bill Graham was rock and roll's leading impresario, owner of the best rock venues of the 1960s, the Fillmore in San Francisco and the Fillmore East in New York. Woodstock's organizers realized they were ill equipped for what was about to happen, and turned to Graham for help. Graham had a condition—a prime spot for the new band Santana, which he managed—but he was also generous with advice, helped convince wary rock bands that it was OK to play this gig, and offered the assistance and expertise of his Fillmore East staff.

When Graham died in a 1991 helicopter accident, he had been working with journalist Robert Greenfield to assemble an oral-history biography. The characters in this selection include Fillmore East director Kip Cohen; filmmaker Jon Davison; Fillmore East controller Jane Geraghty; filmmaker Jonathan Kaplan; Woodstock promoter Michael Lang; Barry Melton of Country Joe and the Fish; rock light-show designer Chip Monck; John Morris, first director of the Fillmore East; Fillmore house manager Jerry Pompili; band leader Carlos Santana; Jefferson Airplane manager Bill Thompson; Pete Townshend of the Who; and communal leader Wavy Gravy (once known as Hugh Romney).

KIP COHEN: Woodstock capitalized on the smarts that our staff had created for themselves in running the Fillmore. John Morris, Chip Monck, and Chris Langhart were the nucleus of people who staged the festival.

JERRY POMPILI: Two days before the festival, the sheriff's department, which was providing security for the gig, walked off. All right? So guess who was left doing the security for Woodstock? Sixty-four people from the Fillmore East who for three fucking days didn't sleep, barely got fed, and lived in fucking mud. *Right? Wonderful.*

At the end of this, John Morris made this wonderful speech to them, telling them what a wonderful job they had done. But he couldn't pay them. All right? *John Morris.* All right? When he got back into town, I almost *killed* him. I said, "These fucking people better get paid in like forty-eight hours or you will leave this town in *pieces,* you know?" He paid them. But they were the people who really held it together.

JANE GERAGHTY: Bill was *not* for Woodstock. He hated it and he didn't want it to happen. He was *virulently* opposed to it. In one sense, he was probably right, in terms of what happened there. Some bands got paid, some didn't. It was a disaster in the sense that they *didn't* sell a lot of tickets. And in the sense that it was *very* poorly run. But Bill went up there. He wanted to see it. So did Frank Barsalona.

I think people made money *before* the event and then not after. They paid themselves nice salaries to organize it for months. That's my impression. They didn't get rich but you could have had a nice job with them for weeks, and then it didn't matter whether the festival happened or not.

BILL: Michael Lang called me and he said, "Bill, we're doing this and we've got this place upstate and a lot of bands are reluctant to come in." The extent of my involvement with Woodstock before the festival happened was on the phone. I was telling them who they should book and on the other end, I was telling agents and managers that this was okay to do. That it *could* work. But I was never involved in any of the negotiations that went on.

It was obvious to me that they were rank amateurs who were in way over their heads. But anybody who would've tried what they were doing would've been a rank amateur. Because it had never been done before. These people however had very little or no experience in either public assemblage or presenting music. They had no reason to be nervous about me or what I might do to their festival but they did come to me. We talked on the phone and then there was a meeting in a loft somewhere in New York.

It was very clear what our relationship would be. I would tell them the bands that I thought would help them whom they hadn't yet thought of themselves. If there were bands they had chosen that they wanted me to comment on, I would. They were having trouble with some bands and they wanted to use my name and say that I was involved.

I said, "Up to the point in the area that I am helping you with you can." I knew they had Chip Monck doing the staging so I could vouch for their personnel. I was not running the operation so I could not guarantee what would happen but I said they could use my name. In return for Santana being put on the show on Saturday night. During *prime time.* Which was difficult. What I wanted was no seven in the morning or three in the afternoon. Because Santana still had no album. People on the East Coast had heard of them. But never really *seen* them before.

In terms of the Fillmore East staff, they didn't take them. I gave them to them. I didn't want to stop the idea. I just always related to the person who bought a ticket. What were they going to get for their money? I went up there a week before to look at the site. The site looked good. I thought at the time that it couldn't come off smoothly because it was such a huge thing and there were no blueprints. It was a first. I knew there were going to be some faults, namely traffic. Ninety thousand mice trying to get to one hole, there had to be *some* problems.

They expected a hundred thousand. I thought there would be a quarter of a million. I came back to the city and then I went back up the day before. I didn't work the festival. I walked around constantly and it was a sight to behold. Because the previous festival I had been to where there was an attempt by nonprofessional entrepreneurs to put on something like this was Monterey. Monterey in 1967 was the egg for Woodstock in 1969.

But it was very East Coast, Woodstock. In the sense that there is a way that West Coast people greet each other and say, *"Hello, how are you?"* On the East Coast, it was peace and love but also, "Hey, how you doing?" There was a system of checking someone out that did not exist in California. On the East Coast, it was like they were all adversaries calling time-out for the day. Whereas on the West Coast, they were all like angels flying around who decided, "Oh, let's land *here* for a while." It was an entirely different feel.

*　　*　　*

WAVY GRAVY: I remember when they still had only about fifty thousand people on the field. One of the promoters said to me and Tom Law, "You want to clear these people off? We want to start taking tickets."

And I said, "Do you want a good movie or a bad movie?" Because I knew they had sold the movie rights. So they had a conference and Mel Lawrence got on the walkie-talkie and the next thing we knew it was a free festival. Which I thought was very perceptive of them. To see that this was the way to go. If not for the movie, though, they would have cleared that field and tried to collect tickets. They would have *had* to.

CHIP MONCK: Michael Lang turned around and told me at about six in the morning as people were waking up in the field, "Oh, by the way, you are *also* the emcee." I was standing there and my knees were knocking together and I was absolutely scared shitless. We were all knee-deep in the mud, therefore it was all, "Please. Do me a favor. Do the best performances that you can under the circumstances. Everyone is here to support you. We would like you *not* to perform over an hour. As far as a blue backing or a white so-and-so, or anything that you are used to, or anything that you would usually think is necessary, that isn't even in the cards. So don't bother me about it. But please. Anything else I can do for you? I would be delighted."

I've got a wonderful picture. A slide of Graham at Woodstock. A beautiful color shot of him. He was the most respected of all the systems in that chaos. He was there to help. But he never stepped in and made any criticism or anything. All he did was assist. Which I thought was very gracious of him.

JOHN MORRIS: The reason Bill came to Woodstock was that I was still in love with the man. I still had it in there for him. I called Bill and I said, "Bill, I'd like you to come to the Woodstock Festival."

He said, "Nah, you know. I *hate* festivals."

I said, "Bill, I've booked you into the Concord."

I booked him there and I sent a ticket for him and a ticket for Bonnie, and I flew them both out. On stage the first day, Bonnie was cold. I had a very favored yellow cotton Dunhill turtleneck that I gave to Bonnie to put on and all hell was breaking loose. I turned to Bill and I said, "I need your help. I need you to help me. I need you to work on this thing. You've got to stay and work with me."

He looked me in the face and said, "Get me a helicopter and get me out of here."

I said, "Bill, I need your help. You know what to do. You're calm and cool, you don't do drugs. You're one of the major people in this business. There are hundreds of thousands of people out there. This is like a war and we're in it. I need your help."

And he said, "Get me a helicopter and get me out of here."

Bonnie stood there with her mouth open as he walked off the stage. She put her arms around me and said, "I'm sorry, John." I said, "It's okay." And I never ever saw that yellow sweater she had on again. He let me down. It was the only time. He just couldn't deal with it. At all.

BILL: What came out at Woodstock was that they expected the audience to accept whatever shortcomings they had. Oops, I'm sorry. Ooops, sorry. Sorry, sorry, sorry. It was sloppy in the sense of time. Half hours and forty-five minutes between sets. If one guy in a band was late, they had to wait for him.

Hundreds if not thousands of kids pitched their tent somewhere down the road five miles away. So what were they blessed with? The experience of breathing the same air? They had come from somewhere and paid good money to get there and then what did they get? Look at those roads. Look at that access and egress. Once you got past the main area, even with the delay towers, the sound was *awful.*

When Santana went on, I went into the crowd and I talked to some of the movie people about it. My remark is somewhere in the outtakes of the movie which they never used. They asked me what I thought about how Santana was playing and I said, "It sounds like background music in a Tarzan movie." In other words, only the congas carried. All you could hear was a faint buddda-buddda-boom-boom-boom.

CARLOS SANTANA: I remember having a meeting with Bill Graham in Sausalito because he really liked us and he said, "I'm helping the guy putting together this concert at Woodstock. Only on the condition that you guys get on the show."

He did that with Michael Lang. He told him, "I'll help you. *If* you put Santana on here." This was without us having an album out. People didn't know us from Adam. We had done one festival in Texas and then one in Atlanta. We opened for Janis Joplin in Chicago. By the time we played Woodstock, we were pretty much ready as far as seeing how other musicians did their thing. It was kind of scary going out in front of that much of a crowd. But I felt that if Bill believed we could do it, we could do it, man.

It was funny because every time we had some big part in our lives that gave us more latitude, it seemed like Jerry Garcia was always there. We got to Woodstock at like eleven in the morning. It was a disaster area, first of all. They flew us in on a helicopter. We hung around with Jerry Garcia and we found out that we didn't have to go on until eight at night. They told us to just cool out and take it easy.

One thing led to another. I wanted to take some mescaline. Just at the point that I was coming on to it, this guy came over and said, "Look, if you don't go on right *now,* you guys are not going to play."

I went out there and I saw this ocean as far as I could see. An ocean of flesh and hair and teeth and hands. I just played. I just prayed that the Lord would keep me in tune and in time. I went, "You just keep me in tune and in time." I had played loaded before but not to that big of a crowd. Because it was like plugging into a whole bunch of hearts and all those people at the same time. But we managed, you know.

When we got to New York later on, the ladies were already there, ladies who knew Miles, who knew Jimi Hendrix, the cosmic family they called it at the time, they all started hanging around with us, and they said, "Man, Jimi Hendrix *liked* you. He really *loved* your band."

JONATHAN KAPLAN: Marty Scorsese directed the movie. Not to take anything away from Michael Wadleigh, but basically he had the center camera at the stage. Marty was the one saying, "Hey, here, *this.* Get that. I hear this guy's going to do a meditation session. Somebody go shoot that."

JON DAVISON: Of course, the great moment in the movie is when Bill talks about digging trenches and pouring in gasoline and lighting it. Burning trenches to keep them back. Everybody else is talking about peace and love and what a beautiful experience it is and how it's going to change the world and there is Bill explaining it in terms of a military conflict.

Woodstock *the Movie:*
QUESTION: From a practical point of view, how could they limit the crowd? Because they didn't want this many people here really, I don't think.
BILL: So you find a control point at the beginning of the highways

and those with tickets are allowed in and those without tickets are not. And you have to have some control. You *have* to have some.

You know, when you have those man-eating *marabunta* ants coming over the hill in South America, if they want to cut 'em off and stop them from coming, they make a ditch. They put oil in the ditch, they make a flame. I'm not saying they should put up flame to stop the people. There has to be *some* way to stop the influx of humanity.

BILL: Once the movie came out, over the next few years that story got me more hatred from people than anything else. Kids would come up to me at shows and say, *"Hey! How could you want to boil me in oil?"* But I said it. So I didn't really object when they left it in. Even if they did so in order to make me look bad. Like I was the enemy opposed to all the wonderful kids coming there to have fun for *free*.

JOHN MORRIS: I think the movie is really close to what happened at the event. It is the most amazing documentary I think I've ever seen. I remember standing with Bill at the opening. The thing with Bill is that for some reason I always sort of forgive him in hopes that he will forgive me. Like God will let you off in the end. We were standing at the back of the theater and Bill was taking notes on the movie. And they got to the sequence where he's in it with the ants and pouring gasoline to keep them out. Because there's Bill Graham on film in his most down, negative way. He saw it and he snapped a pen in half and it shot right into the audience. This was at the premiere.

BILL: About a week before the festival, the word went out that they had finally made a deal with Michael Wadleigh to make a film with Warner Brothers. The deal they were offering to everybody was that whatever the act was paid to perform, they would get half of that amount again when they gave away their film rights. I said, "You mean Santana is going to sign away their film rights for seven hundred and fifty dollars? *No.*"

They said, "Anybody who doesn't sign doesn't play."

Whoever I spoke to, I said, "We'll be there. We're going to play. Don't put anything in front of me to sign."

Finally, they said, "Bill, you've *got* to sign this." But I never did.

Santana played and there was a lot of bitching and a lot of bickering. It was ugly the way that it went down. Warner Brothers was going to make *millions* on the movie. Eventually, I went to them and negotiated. I got a rather large figure for Santana. More than thirty-five thousand dollars. But the price was fair because Santana was so good that day. To the best of my knowledge, everyone that played there other than Santana got half of what their earnings were that night.

The footage they had on Santana was *magic.* I said, "You want to use this, there's a price. You know it's going to be a hit. You don't want to pay the price. Don't use it." Eventually it got to a point where I said, "Look, the word out on the street is that I'm mad. You want to believe that I'm going to blow up your building? Fine. But this is not right. I represent only *this* band. Not the others."

Three hundred thousand people had seen Santana at Woodstock. I said to them, "There's only one thing the audience didn't seem that day when Santana was on, and that was *bored.*"

CARLOS SANTANA: You got to understand one thing. Those artists who were not in the movie, they weren't in the movie because they *sucked* that day. I was there and I witnessed it. A lot of people played *really* bad. They got pretty wasted before they got out there and they didn't sound very professional. If you had put them in the movie, they wouldn't be very proud to watch it today. The main peak for me was Sly Stone. Bar none. He took over that night. By the time Jimi Hendrix went on, it was too late. He paid the price for being the big thing and closing the show.

BILL THOMPSON: I was talking to this guy, Michael Lang, and Artie Kornfeld. And they were walking around with their shoes off, talking about love and beauty and peace. I was a little suspicious. In fact, I organized all the managers of the Saturday show along with Wiggy, the road manager of The Who, the guy from Creedence Clearwater, Stan Markham from Santana, and Rock Scully from The Dead. I organized everybody and we said, "Hey, we want to get our money. Because there ain't going to be any money here." And they started talking about peace and love and all that stuff.

We said, "Hey, we got everybody in the motel here. And we're not going to play unless we get the money."

So they opened up a bank on Saturday to pay everybody. *Cash.*

We got it *all* in cash. The Airplane got the second highest money there. Which was fifteen thousand dollars. Jimi Hendrix got seventeen-five.

JOHN MORRIS: It was John Roberts and Joel Rosenman who went and got the money out of the bank. The bands were figuring they weren't going to get paid and realized it was no fun. The kids were having a great time. But there was a tremendous difference in what was going on up on the stage.

BILL: The Who were brilliant. I'm just a big Townshend fan and a big Who fan. Townshend is like a locomotive when he gets going. He's like a naked black stallion. When he starts, look out. Sly Stone kicked *ass.* He really did. But there weren't too many others that I liked. Not live. Hendrix was okay. I had heard him better. "The Star-Spangled Banner" was unreal. As creative a two minutes as you can probably find in rock and roll.

PETE TOWNSHEND: Woodstock was horrible. Woodstock was only horrible because it went so wrong. It *could* have been extraordinary. I suppose with the carefully edited view that the public got through Michael Wadleigh's film, it was a great event. But for those involved in it, it was a terrible shambles. Full of the most naive, childlike people. We have a word for them in England. *Twits.*

I imagine some people managed to go through it completely unscathed and have a really good time. I had taken my wife there with our new baby, who was about six months old or something. At university, her favorite thing now is to go up to people and say, "You know, I was at Woodstock."

I was nervous because we didn't go there by helicopter. We went by road. We got as far as the car could go in the mud and it got stuck. It became the hundred and ninety-fifth limo to get stuck. We got out and landed in mud and that was it. There was nowhere to go. There were no dressing rooms because they had all been turned into hospitals. There was nowhere to eat. Somebody came out of the canteen, which was where we had been naturally gravitating toward in order to sit down and eat because we were told that we wouldn't be on for fifteen hours.

To get us there in the first place, the production assistant in the limo had told us we were on in fifteen minutes. Then when we got there, they said, "Oh, sorry. We meant fifteen *hours."* As we were going toward the canteen, somebody came out saying that the tea and coffee had got acid in them and all the water was polluted with acid. I spent a bit of time on the stage but everybody was very freaked. I would find a nice place to sit and listen to somebody like Jefferson Airplane and then some lunatic would come up to me like Abbie Hoffman or some stagehand and go, *"Ahhhhhhh! Aaaaaaah! Buuuuuuuupw!"*

It was very very frightening. Somebody else would come up to me and go, "Isn't this just *fantastic!* Isn't it *wonderful!"* They would go over the hump of their cheap acid and into *dreamland.* People kept talking about America. It was most unfortunate. They kept talking about the American Dream and the New Albion. All kind of hippie-esque stuff was coming out and I kept thinking to myself, "This *can't* be true. This *can't* be what's happening to America. We're just arriving here. We're just about to break big and the whole thing's turning into Raspberry Jell-O. I don't *believe* it."

BILL: By the third day, it had become a survival camp. It was like, "I live in Poland. It's miserable in Poland? I *live* here. It's *my* country." This was their country. Their space. But it wasn't all that pleasant all the time. Sometimes, there were great highs. But by the third day with the mud and the food running out and the discomfort, it became like a camp of people who were in retreat from something. *Another* kind of war.

BARRY MELTON: I can always tell who was *really* there. When they tell me it was great, I know they saw the movie and they weren't at the gig. It really wasn't all that great to be there and it wasn't really all that great to perform there. Except that everyone had an overriding sense that they were taking part in some momentous and historical event. There had never been that many people together to do anything before. Our equipment got rained on. We only got half our money.

We played right after Joe Cocker and in the time we were setting up our equipment, it started raining cats and dogs. That sequence in the movie when somebody's screaming, *"No rain! No rain! No rain!"* *I'm* doing the screaming. Definitely induced. In the altered state. I tried to convince the audience that if they all put their thoughts together, they could stop the rain. There were enough people there to psychically achieve the result. It *did* stop raining. *Eventually.*

BILL: The single most significant thing about Woodstock was that relative to most countries, if you got four or five hundred thousand people together, you would have had some major problems. There were some deaths at Woodstock. But that there were so few is a miracle. In light of what people did to themselves, and the amounts they used. I don't think there was any malicious attempt on anybody's part on the production side, in terms of lying to the public about who would play, and who wouldn't. There was no false advertising. Did anybody make money at Woodstock? The movie people.

There was the Woodstock gig followed by the Woodstock film followed by the Woodstock album, which was a monster. Woodstock *made* Joe Cocker, Ten Years After, Mountain, Sly Stone, and Santana. Woodstock also triggered the managers of groups to realize, "Why play five gigs for ten dollars a piece? Let's play one gig in a canyon for *fifty thousand dollars.*"

By helicopter, the Concord was ten miles and a couple of minutes away from Woodstock. In every other way, it was three thousand miles. The guests and the staff knew what was going on over there but it was like a big Chinese wedding in the heart of Chinatown, or the seventy-fifth anniversary of the most powerful guy down there. Outside of Chinatown, what more does anyone know about it but that? It was like another planet to them. The only point of connection was, "Hey, my grandson *could* be there. I bet he is. My God, he could get killed with all those kids in one spot."

The people from the festival should've tied in a little more with the community up there. If nothing else, it would've been funnier. The new world of Woodstock and the old world of the mountains.

Michael Lindsay-Hogg

Lindsay-Hogg delivered some great moments in British rock history as director of the Beatles' "Hey Jude" and "Revolution" promotional films and the coming-apart documentary, *Let It Be*. He also directed *The Rolling Stones Rock'n'Roll Circus*, which went unreleased for thirty years.

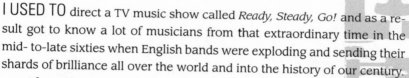

I USED TO direct a TV music show called *Ready, Steady, Go!* and as a result got to know a lot of musicians from that extraordinary time in the mid- to-late sixties when English bands were exploding and sending their shards of brilliance all over the world and into the history of our century.

After a time some of the bands didn't like appearing on the TV shows (*RSG!* off the air by now) and also wanted more influence over the way they were presented, so we did a few of what are now called videos and were then called promos, some of the early ones being "Jumping Jack Flash," "Hey Jude," "Revolution," "Happy Jack." And then the prime bands, the Rolling Stones and the Beatles, became interested in longer-form presentations.

Beggars Banquet: Not necessarily to promote this album but around the time of its release, the Rolling Stones, the original ones, with Brian Jones, decided they wanted to do their own TV special which we called *The Rolling Stones Rock'n'Roll Circus. . . .* To celebrate the release of *Beggars Banquet,* the Rolling Stones gave a lunch in a large dark restaurant in Kensington. "Don't wear good clothes," they said to me. Cream cakes was the why. At the end of lunch, large cakes with whipped cream topping were put in front of the band members who picked up gobs of aerated froth and, laughing and snickering like the naughty children of tabloid dreams, pressed it into the face of whoever they were next to: girlfriends, Lord Harlech, anxious press agents, drunken journalists, whoever. The photos in the paper the next day made it look like a very festive occasion, with Brian enjoying it the most.

We shot the *Circus* in a converted warehouse near Wembley the week before Christmas. After the Who, Jethro Tull, Marianne Faithfull, and a

Lennon-Clapton-Richard-Ono band, the Rolling Stones went on stage to do their part in their own show.

It was 2 A.M., and they had been hanging around since noon, when we'd shot their entrance into the Big Top. They were tired and irritable and, in one or two cases, a little unsteady. But think of it this way—if a group of nuns had been sitting around for fourteen hours, with only their guitars for company, and drinking nothing stronger than tea, they too might be in a fractious mood.

"You Can't Always Get What You Want" went okay after many takes, then lots more of the album, take after ragged take, and then it was 5 A.M. and time for "Sympathy for the Devil," the one we'd all looked forward to, when we were fresher and clearer earlier in the day/night. We did a take which was a shambles, for Mick, for them, for me, for the cameras. Pissed off and tired, Mick went to talk to his troops, a little touch of "Harry in the night," and then when the music started again, he forced himself into a performance, teasing, innocent, jaded, electric, the like of which I'd never seen before. Then, the song over, the twenty-five-year-old boy, half-naked, stood up, his sharpshooter's mind relaxed, the marathoner's body drooped. He looked at the others, smiled and yawned. Brian smiled back. It was the last time he played with the Rolling Stones.

Less than a month after shooting *The Rolling Stones Rock'n'Roll Circus,* I started working on *Let it Be.*

I'd worked with the Beatles before, first "Paperback Writer," then "Revolution" and "Hey Jude." When we were doing "Revolution," I remember two things. One is when going into the studio before we started shooting, I fell into step with John Lennon. He didn't look his best, a late night or something. I asked him if he wanted make-up so he'd look a little "healthier." He said no. "Why?" I asked. "Because I'm John Lennon." What's important to make clear is that he didn't mean he was too grand to be made up, but, instead, he was going to perform as himself, not as an actor pretending to be someone. If he looked a little ropey, that was the way he looked that day. The next thing I remember was that John wanted a big close-up on the lyric "If you go talking about Chairman Mao, you ain't gonna make it with anyone anyhow," because he thought that was the key lyric of the song.

For "Hey Jude," we had a crowd as part of the production, for the chorus, meant to represent all different sorts. So for the last four minutes of the song, take after take, the Beatles were surrounded by a mix of male and female, young and old, students, businessmen, housewives, kids, the postman, and the Beatles found they were more or less enjoying playing again with live bodies around them. Remember they hadn't worked in front of any kind of audience since they'd stopped touring in 1966 and so, because of the "Hey Jude" experience (perhaps not unconnected with the massive record sales and the acknowledged aid the video had given), they thought that they wanted to do some sort of show which would be recorded as a TV special, and that there would also be a documentary of the making of the show.

So, early in January 1969, the Beatles, myself, a couple of cameramen and other technicians met at Twickenham Studios, where we'd shot "Hey Jude." The first thing I realized was, and this may seem dopily obvious, that they were musicians first, not actors. And what they wanted to get right were their songs, their music. And that at this early stage of their work, the cameras were intruders more so now probably than they would have been before. There had been a major change in the way they worked since they had stopped touring. During coming into the studio and then touring again and then recording the songwriters writing together back at the Rolling type years later). But because the Beatles, principally Lennon weren't constantly with each other they had slowly d so there'd be a song writ-ten by one of them like sidemen, instructed and rehearsed and re- e. Also, during this time, John had met Yoko closeness, there were now five people in the

whatever, take on their own life and perhaps was curdled. Different, usually un-agreeing participants in conflicting directions. An in-tended lackadaisical ones, no-shows, rows should be (shoot it in the Cavern or an am-having, John wanting immediately to get in with the proviso that there be no TV show, o. our small film crew was an accepted nui-sa. er's day. We left Twickenham and all moved to t. studio at Apple in London. Things seemed to impr hermetic studio again the tensions simmered, didn't men, in their mid-to-late twenties, tested to-gether their differences, were entering a different stage of their lives, and not only one. Jealousies about credit and acknowledgment, in-equalities to do with songwriting percentages, vastly different personal lives and desires, money worries (uncollectable royalties and a cash-haemorrhaging Apple Co.), were forces ulcerating what had seemed eternal friendships—or maybe that's just what we'd hoped they'd be.

We in the film crew felt we were actors in an updated version of Sartre's *No Exit,* where people meet in hell and can't get out. What was going to become of all this stuff we were grinding out, two cameras for eight hours every day?

One Saturday, the Beatles and I and a few others were having lunch in the boardroom—which was also the dining-room—discussing what we were going to do, whether it would just be another unrealized and junked rock'n'roll project. My version of what happened is that I said we needed some sort of resolution to the film, a sense we were going somewhere, a sort of conclusion. "You wouldn't do it at the Cavern, or in the amphitheatre in Tunisia. Why don't we just do it on the roof?" The reason I say "my version" is, in light of events, there are several claimants for this suggestion including, I think, the cook who'd made the apple crumble.

So, after lunch, while the others went off to different pursuits, Paul, the late Mal Evans (later shot, like John, in America) and I went up on the roof and had a look, and the idea started to take on a life. The rest is part of rock'n'roll history.

We had decided to start playing around 12:30, to get the lunchtime crowds. The Beatles were, typically, still arguing at 12:20 if they'd really do it and then, enthusiastically or reluctantly, according to character, they finally went up the narrow staircase onto the roof. It was the last time they, as a performing group, as the Fab Four, as the repository of a generation's dreams and happiness, ever played together. The final words of the film were John's: "I hope we passed the audition."

Jackson Browne

THE LOAD-OUT

**Life on the road, as viewed by one of the recognized
Shakespeares of the Southern California sound.**

Now the seats are all empty
Let the roadies take the stage
Pick it up and tear it down
They're the first to come and the last to leave
Working for that minimum wage
They'll set it up in another town

Tonight the people were so fine
They waited there in line
When they got up on their feet
They made the show and that was sweet
But I can hear the sounds
Of slamming doors and folding chairs
That's a sound they'll never know

Roll them cases and lift them amps
Haul them trusses down and get 'em up those
    ramps
'Cause when it comes to moving me,
You know you guys are the champs
But when that last guitar's been packed away
You know that I still want to play
So just make sure you got it all set to go
Before you come for my piano

But the band's on the bus
And they're waiting to go
Got to drive all night
And do a show in Chicago

Or Detroit. I don't know.
We do so many shows in a row.
And these towns all look the same

We just pass the time in the hotel rooms
And wander around backstage
'Til those lights come up
And we hear that crowd
And we remember why we came

Now we got country and western on the bus,
R and B, we got disco, 8-tracks and cassettes and
    stereo
We got rural scenes and magazines
And we got truckers on CB
We got Richard Pryor on the video

We got time to think of the ones we love
While the miles roll away
But the only time that seems too short
Is the time that we get to play

You've got the power of what we do
You can sit there and wait or you can pull us
    through
Come along and sing this song
You know that you can't go wrong
When that morning sun comes beating down
You're going to wake up in your town
But we'll be scheduled to appear
A thousand miles away from here

Nik Cohn
TRIBAL RITES OF THE NEW SATURDAY NIGHT

Recorded music began replacing live bands in many clubs in the mid-1970s and it was a sign that the organic nature of rock and roll was being overpowered by the more machinistic, disk-jockey-driven seamless sound of disco. Nik Cohn's 1976 *New York* magazine article looked at the emerging club scene growing up around the new music. If the story sounds a little familiar, it's because it was the basis for the film *Saturday Night Fever*, which made John Travolta a film star.

WITHIN the closed circuits of rock & roll fashion, it is assumed that New York means Manhattan. The center is everything, all the rest irrelevant. If the other boroughs exist at all, it is merely as a camp joke—Bronx-Brooklyn-Queens, monstrous urban limbo, filled with everyone who is no one.

In reality, however, almost the reverse is true. While Manhattan remains firmly rooted in the sixties, still caught up in faction and fad and the dreary games of decadence, a whole new generation has been growing up around it, virtually unrecognized. Kids of sixteen to twenty, full of energy, urgency, hunger. All the things, in fact, that the Manhattan circuit, in its smugness, has lost.

They are not so chic, these kids. They don't haunt press receptions or opening nights; they don't pose as street punks in the style of Bruce Springsteen, or prate of rock & Rimbaud. Indeed, the cults of recent years seem to have passed them by entirely. They know nothing of flower power or meditation, pansexuality, or mind expansion. No waterbeds or Moroccan cushions, no hand-thrown pottery, for them. No hep jargon either, and no Pepsi revolutions. In many cases, they genuinely can't remember who Bob Dylan was, let alone Ken Kesey or Timothy Leary. Haight-Ashbury, Woodstock, Altamont—all of them draw a blank. Instead, this generation's real roots lie further back, in the fifties, the golden age of Saturday nights.

The cause of this reversion is not hard to spot. The sixties, unlike previous decades, seemed full of teenage money. No recession, no sense of danger. The young could run free, indulge themselves in whatever treats they wished. But now there is shortage once more, just as there was in the fifties. Attrition, continual pressure. So the new generation takes few risks. It goes through high school, obedient; graduates, looks for a job, saves and plans. Endures. And once a week, on Saturday night, its one great moment of release, it explodes.

Vincent was the very best dancer in Bay Ridge—the ultimate Face. He owned fourteen floral shirts, five suits, eight pairs of shoes, three overcoats, and had appeared on *American Bandstand.* Sometimes music people came out from Manhattan to watch him, and one man who owned a club on the East Side had even offered him a contract. A hundred dollars a week. Just to dance.

Everybody knew him. When Saturday night came around and he walked into 2001 Odyssey, all the other Faces automatically fell back before him, cleared a space for him to float in, right at the very center of the dance floor. Gracious as a medieval seigneur accepting tributes, Vincent waved and nodded at random. Then his face grew stern, his body turned to the music. Solemn, he danced, and all the Faces followed.

In this sphere his rule was absolute. Only one thing bothered him, and that was the passing of time. Already he was eighteen, almost eighteen and a half. Soon enough he would be nineteen, twenty. Then this golden age would pass. By natural law someone new would arise to replace him. Then everything would be over.

The knowledge nagged him, poisoned his pleasure. One night in January, right in the middle of the Bus Stop, he suddenly broke off, stalked from the floor without a word, and went outside into the cold darkness, to be alone.

He slouched against a wall. He stuck his hands deep into his overcoat pockets. He sucked on an unlit cigarette. A few minutes passed. Then he was approached by a man in a tweed suit, a journalist from Manhattan.

They stood close together, side by side. The man in the tweed suit looked at Vincent, and Vincent stared at the ground or at the tips of his platform shoes. "What's wrong?" said the man in the suit, at last.

And Vincent said; "I'm old."

Before Saturday night began, to clear his brain of cobwebs and get himself sharp, fired up, he liked to think about killing.

During the week Vincent sold paint in a housewares store. All day, every day he stood behind a counter and grinned. He climbed up and down ladders, he made the coffee, he obeyed. Then came the weekend and he was cut loose.

The ritual never varied. Promptly at five the manager reversed the "Open" sign and Vincent would turn away, take off his grin. When the last of the customers had gone, he went out through the back, down the corridor, directly into the bathroom. He locked the door and took a deep breath. Here he was safe. So he turned toward the mirror and began to study his image.

Black hair and black eyes, olive skin, a slightly crooked mouth, and teeth so white, so dazzling, that they always seemed fake. Third-generation Brooklyn Italian, five-foot-nine in platform shoes. Small purplish birthmark beside the right eye. Thin white scar, about two inches long, underneath the chin, caused by a childhood fall from a bicycle. Otherwise, no distinguishing marks.

That was the flesh; but there was something else, much more important. One night two years before, he had traveled into Queens with some friends and they had ended up in some club, this real cheap scumhole; he couldn't remember the name. But he danced anyhow and did his numbers, all his latest routines, and everyone was just amazed. And then he danced with this girl. He'd never seen her before and he never saw her again. But her name was Petulia, Pet for short, and she was all right, nice hair, a good mover. And she kept staring right into his eyes. Staring and staring, as though she were hypnotized. He asked her why. "Kiss me," said the girl. So he kissed her, and she went limp in his arms. "Oooh," said the girl, sighing, almost swooning, "I just kissed Al Pacino."

In his first surprise, assuming that she must be teasing, Vincent had only laughed and blushed. But later, thinking it over, he knew she had really meant it. Somehow or other she had seen beneath the surface, had cut through to bedrock, to his very soul. That was something incredible. It blew his mind. In fact, if anyone ever asked him and he tried to answer honestly, looking back, he would say that was the happiest, the very best, moment of his life.

Since then, whenever he gazed into the mirror, it was always Pacino who gazed back. A killer, and a star. Heroic in reflection. Then Vincent would take another breath, the deepest he could manage; would make his face, his whole body, go still; would blink three times to free his imagination, and he would start to count.

Silently, as slowly as possible, he would go from one to a hundred. It was now, while he counted, that he thought about death.

Mostly he thought about guns. On certain occasions, if he felt that he was getting stale, he might also dwell on knives, on karate chops and flying kung fu kicks, even on laser beams. But always, in the last resort, he came back to bullets.

It felt just like a movie. For instance, he would see himself at the top of a high flight of stairs, back against a wall, while a swarm of attackers came surging up toward him to knock him down, destroy him. But Vincent stood his ground. Unflinching, he took aim and fired. One by one they went crashing backward, down into the pit.

When the battle ended and he had won, he stood alone. Far beneath him, he knew, there was blood and smoke, a chaotic heap of bodies, dead and dying. But that did not enter the physical vision. On the screen there was only Vincent, impassive, ice cold in triumph, who put his gun back into its holster, wiped away the sweat that blinded him, straightened his collar, and, finally, in close-up, smiled.

At one hundred, he let out his breath in a rush. The strain of holding back had turned him purple, and veins were popping all over his neck and arms. For some moments all he could do was gasp. But even as he suffered, his body felt weightless, free, almost as if he were floating. And when he got his breath back, and the roaring in his temples went away, it was true that he felt content.

That was the end; the movie was complete. Turning away from the glass, and away from Pacino, he would flush the toilet, wash his hands. He combed his hair. He checked his watch. Then he went out into the corridor, back into the store. The week behind the counter had been obliterated. No drudgery existed. He was released; Saturday night had begun.

Lisa was in love with Billy, and Billy was in love with Lisa. John James was in love with Lorraine. Lorraine loved Gus. Gus loved Donna. And Donna loved Vincent. But Vincent loved only his mother, and the way it felt to dance. When he left the store he went home and prepared for 2001 Odyssey. He bathed, he shaved, he dressed. That took him four hours, and by the time he emerged, shortly after nine, he felt reborn.

He lived on the eleventh floor of a high-rise on Fourth Avenue and 66th Street, close beside the subway tracks, with the remnants of his family. He loved them, was proud that he supported them. But when he tried to describe their existence, he would begin to stammer and stumble, embarrassed, because everything came out so corny: "Just like a soap," he said, "only true."

His father, a thief, was in jail, and his oldest brother had been killed in Vietnam. His second brother was in the hospital, had been there almost a year, recovering from a car crash that had crushed his legs. His third brother had moved away to Manhattan, into the Village, because he said he needed to be free and find himself. So that left only Vincent, his mother, and his two younger sisters, Maria and Bea (short for Beata), who were still in school.

Between them they shared three rooms, high up in a block of buildings like a barracks. His windows looked out on nothing but walls, and there was the strangest, most disturbing smell, which no amount of cleaning could ever quite destroy.

Hard to describe it, this smell; hard to pin it down. Sometimes it seemed like drains, sometimes like a lack of oxygen, and sometimes just like death, the corpse of some decaying animal buried deep in the walls. Whichever, Vincent wanted out. He would have given anything. But there was no chance. How could there be? He could never abandon his mother. "You must understand," he said. "I am the man."

Here he paused. "I am her soul," he said. Then he paused again, pursing his lips, and he cast down his eyes. He looked grave. "Understand," he said, "my mother is me."

It was the guts of winter, bitter cold. But he would not protect himself. Not on Saturday night, not on display at Odyssey. When he kissed his mother good-bye and came down onto Fourth, strutting loose, he wore an open-necked shirt, ablaze with reds and golds, and he moved through the night with shoulders hunched tight, his neck rammed deep between his shoulder blades in the manner of a miniature bull. A bull in Gucci-style loafers, complete with gilded buckle, and high black pants tight as sausage skins. Shuffling, gliding, stepping out. On the corner, outside Najmy Bros. grocery, he passed a Puerto Rican, some dude in a floppy velour hat, and the dude laughed out loud. So Vincent stopped still, and he stared, a gaze like a harpoon, right between the eyes. "Later," he said.

"Later what?" said the dude, lolling slack, sneaking his hand back in his pants pocket, just in case, with a big dumb grin slapped clean across his face. "Later who? Later where? Later how?"

"Hombre," said Vincent, expressionless, "you will die."

It was not quite his own. To be perfectly truthful, he had borrowed the line from Lee Van Cleef, some Italian Western that he'd seen on late-night TV. But he drawled it out just right. A hint of slur, the slightest taste of spit. "Hombre, you will die." Just like that. And moved away. So slick and so sly, that the dude never knew what hit him.

Two blocks farther on, Joey was waiting in the car. Joey and Gus in the front, Eugene and John James and now Vincent in the back, trundling through the icy streets in a collapsing '65 Dodge. Nobody talked and nobody smiled. Each scrunched into his own private space; they all held their distance, conserved their strength, like prizefighters before a crucial bout. The Dodge groaned and rattled. The radio played Harold Melvin and the Blue Notes. Everything else was silence, and waiting.

John James and Eugene worked in a record store; Gus was a house painter. As for Joey, no one could be sure. In any case, it didn't matter. Not now. All that counted was the moment. And for the moment, riding out toward 2001 Odyssey, they existed only as Faces.

Faces. According to Vincent himself, they were simply the elite. All over Brooklyn, Queens, and the Bronx, even as far away as New Jersey, spread clear across America, there were millions and millions of kids who were nothing special. Just kids. Zombies. Professional dummies, going through the motions, following like sheep. School, jobs, routines. A vast faceless blob. And then there were the Faces. The Vincents and Eugenes and Joeys. A tiny minority, maybe two in every hundred, who knew how to dress and how to move, how to float, how to fly. Sharpness, grace, a certain distinction in every gesture. And some strange instinct for rightness, beyond words, deep down in their blood: "The way I feel," Vincent said, "it's like we have been chosen."

Odyssey was their home, their haven. It was *the* place, the only disco in all Bay Ridge that truly counted. Months ago there had been Revelation; six weeks, maybe two months, on, there would be somewhere else. Right now there was only Odyssey.

It was a true sanctuary. Once inside, the Faces were unreachable. Nothing could molest them. They were no longer the oppressed, wretched teen menials who must take orders, toe the line. Here they took command, they reigned.

The basic commandments were simple. To qualify as an Odyssey Face, an aspirant need only be Italian, between the ages of eighteen and twenty-one, with a minimum stock of six floral shirts, four pairs of tight trousers, two pairs of Gucci-style loafers, two pairs of platforms, either a pendant or a ring, and one item in gold. In addition, he must know how to dance, how to drive, how to handle himself in a fight. He must have respect, even reverence, for Facehood, and contempt for everything else. He must also be fluent in obscenity, offhand in sex. Most important of all, he must play tough.

There was no overlapping. Italians were Italian, Latins were greaseballs, Jews were different, and blacks were born to lose. Each group had its own ideal, its own style of Face. But they never touched. If one member erred, ventured beyond his own allotted territory, he was beaten up. That was the law. There was no alternative.

Then there were girls. But they were not Faces, not truly. Sometimes, if a girl got lucky, a Face might choose her from the crowd and raise her to be his steady, whom he might one day even marry. But that was rare. In general, the female function was simply to be available. To decorate the doorways and booths, to fill up the dance floor. Speak when spoken to, put out as required, and then go away. In short, to obey, and not to fuss.

Fuss, in fact, was the one thing in life that Faces loathed most of all. Vincent, for example. The moment that anyone started to argue, to flush and wave his hands, he would simply turn his back and start walking. No matter what the circumstance, there could be no excuse for whining. It was not clean. It made him sick at his stomach.

That was why he loved to dance, not talk. In conversation, everything always came out wrong, confused. But out on the floor it all somehow fell into place. There was no muddle, nothing that could not be conveyed. Just so long as your feet made the right moves, kept hitting the right angles, you were foolproof. There were certain rules, watertight. Only obey them, and nothing could go wrong.

Sometimes, it was true, people did not understand that. Some outsider would stumble in, blundering. A complete un-Face, who wore the wrong clothes and made the wrong moves, who danced last month's routines. And that could be ruinous. Absolutely disastrous. Because the whole magic of the night, and of Odyssey, was that everything, everyone, was immaculate. No detail was botched, not one motion unconsidered.

Purity. A sacrament. In their own style, the Faces were true ascetics: stern, devoted, incorruptible. "We may be hard. But we're fair," said Vincent. So they gathered in strict formation, each in his appointed place, his slot upon the floor. And they danced.

On the first night when the man in the tweed suit arrived from Manhattan, it was only nine o'clock and Odyssey was still half empty. He had come on the Brooklyn-Queens Expressway and when he descended into Bay Ridge itself, he found himself in a dead land. There were auto shops, locked and barred; transmission specialists, alignment centers. Then the Homestead Bar and Grill, and the Crazy Country Club, advertising "warm beer and lousy food." But there were no people. Only railroads and junkyards, abandoned car seats, hubcaps, tires, scattered by the side of the road. A wasteland.

It was another frozen night and, when he climbed out of the car, the sidewalks were so icy that he slithered at every step. Guard dogs snapped and leaped in the darkness, and sleet whipped at his eyes. So he huddled deeper, tighter, into his overcoat, and set off toward a small red light at the farthest end of the street.

This was 2001 Odyssey. On the step outside, Vincent stood waiting, smoking, and did not seem to feel the cold at all. His hair was blow-waved just so, his toe caps gleaming. Brut behind his ears, Brut beneath his armpits. And a crucifix at his throat.

Inside, Odyssey was as vast and still as a Saturday-night cathedral. Music blared from the speakers, colored lights swirled back and forth across the dance floor. But no one answered their call. Perhaps a dozen girls sat waiting, on plastic seats, in scalloped booths. Four Faces in shiny suits stood at the bar, backs turned to the floor. The manager standing by the door scratched himself. That was all.

Then the music changed to *Baby Face,* and a boy in a red-patterned shirt began to dance alone. He came out of nowhere, down from the tiers of seats at the very back of the hall, the bleachers, which were completely shrouded in darkness. Skinny, shrimpish, he stood out in the very center of the floor, caught by the swirling lights, and did one half of the Rope Hustle. Only half, of course, because the Rope Hustle cannot really be performed without a partner. So he twirled in irregular circles, his arms twining and unfurling about his neck, vaguely as if he were trying to strangle himself. And the Faces at the bar, without even seeming to look, began to snigger.

Hearing mockery, the boy flushed and lowered his eyes, but he did not back down. For twenty minutes, half an hour, he kept on spinning, wheeling, in total isolation. "Later on, he'll have to leave," said Vincent. "Now it doesn't matter. Not yet."

"Who is he?" asked the man in the suit.

"His born name is Paul. But he calls himself Dean. A very weird guy."

"How come?"

"He cries."

When at last the boy came off the floor, he sat down at the bar and stared directly ahead, towards the mirror. His face was pale and pinched, his Adam's apple kept leaping in his throat, and he ordered lemonade. Over his heart there was a small tin button printed with black letters that said: "I believe." He drank his lemonade in three clean gulps. Then he wiped his lips and went straight back on the floor, still all alone, as if to resume a vigil.

When the music turned to *Wake Up Everybody,* he spun too fast, lost control, stumbled. Then Vincent sighed and shook his head. "Funny guy," he said. "When I was five, my father broke my arm. Twisted it until it snapped. Because he was drunk, and he hated me. But I didn't cry. Not one tear."

Gradually, the floor began to fill; the night embarked in earnest. The girls emerged from their booths, formed ranks, and began to do the Bus Stop. A band appeared in blue denim suits embossed with silver studding. Blacks from Crown Heights, who played as loudly and as badly as anyone possibly could, grinning, sweating, stomping, while the dancers paraded beneath them, impassive.

One after another the stock favorites came churning out. *Bad Luck* and *Supernatural Thing, What a Difference a Day Made, Track of the Cat,* each reduced to the same automaton chugging, interchangeable. Nobody looked and no one ever applauded. Still, the band kept pounding away, kept right on grinning. "These guys. Those shines," said Vincent. "We wind them up like clockwork. We pay, and they perform."

Outside, his companions sat in the car, Joey and Gus in the front, Eugene and John James in the back, drinking whiskey from a bottle in a paper bag. They still made no conversation, did not relax. But as the alcohol hit, they started to mumble.

"Mother," said Eugene.

"Eff," said Gus.

"Mothereffing right," said Joey.

Sometime after ten, feeling ready, they stepped out on the sidewalk and moved toward Odyssey in a line, shoulder to shoulder, like gunslingers. Heads lowered, hands thrust deep in their pockets, they turned into the doorway. They paused for just an instant, right on the brink. Entered.

Vincent was already at work on the floor. By now the Faces had gathered in force, his troops, and he worked them like a quarterback, calling out plays. He set the formations, dictated every move. If a pattern grew ragged and disorder threatened, it was he who set things straight.

Under his command, they unfurled the Odyssey Walk, their own style of massed Hustle, for which they formed strict ranks. Sweeping back and forth across the floor in perfect unity, 50 bodies made one, while Vincent barked out orders, crying One, and Two, and One, and Tap. And Turn, and One, and Tap. And Turn. And Tap. And One.

They were like so many guardsmen on parade; a small battalion, uniformed in floral shirts and tight flared pants. No one smiled or showed the least expression. Above their heads, the black musicians honked and thrashed. But the Faces never wavered. Number after number, hour after hour, they carried out their routines, their drill. Absolute discipline, the most impeccable balance. On this one night, even Vincent, who was notoriously hard to please, could find no cause for complaint.

At last, content in a job well done, he took a break and went up into the bleachers, where he sat on a small terrace littered with empty tables and studied the scene at leisure, like a general reviewing a battlefield. From this distance, the action on the floor seemed oddly unreal, as though it had been staged. A young girl in green, with ash-blond hair to her shoulders, stood silhouetted in a half-darkened doorway, posed precisely in left profile, and blew a smoke ring. Two Faces started arguing at the bar, fists raised. The dancers chugged about the floor relentlessly, and the band played *Philadelphia Freedom*.

"How do you feel?" asked the man in the tweed suit.

"I'm thinking about my mother," said Vincent.

"What of her?"

"She's getting old. Sometimes she feels so bad. If I was rich, I could buy her a house, somewhere on the Island, and she could take it easy."

"What kind of house?"

"Big windows. Lots of light," Vincent said, and he spread his hands, describing a shape like a globe. "Space. Chickens in the yard. A grand piano. Grass," he said. "My mother likes grass. And blue sky."

Down below, without his presence to keep control, the order was beginning to fall apart. Around the fringes, some of the dancers had broken away from the mainstream and were dabbling in experiments, the Hustle Cha, the Renaissance Bump, even the Merengue. Vincent looked pained. But he did not intervene. "Chickens," he said. "They lay their own eggs."

A fight broke out. From outside, it was not possible to guess exactly how it started. But suddenly Gus was on his back, bleeding, and a Face in a bright-blue polka-dot shirt was banging his head against the floor. So Joey jumped on the Face's back. Then someone else jumped in, and someone else. After that there was no way to make out anything beyond a mass of bodies, littered halfway across the floor.

Vincent made no move; it was all too far away. Remote in his darkness, he sipped at a Coca-Cola and watched. The band played *You Sexy Thing* and one girl kept screaming, only one.

"Is this the custom?" asked the man in the suit.

"It depends."

"On what?"

"Sometimes people don't feel in the mood. Sometimes they do," said Vincent. "It just depends."

In time, the commotion subsided, the main participants were ushered outside to complete their negotiations in private. Those left behind went back to dancing as if nothing had happened, and the band played *Fly, Robin, Fly.*

John James, the Double J, appeared on the terrace, lean and gangling, with a chalky white face and many pimples. There was blood beneath his nose, blood on his purple crepe shirt. "Mother," he said, sitting down at the table. "Eff," said Vincent.

So the night moved on. The Double J talked about basketball, records, dances. Then he talked about other nights, other brawls. The music kept playing and the dancers kept on parading. From time to time a girl would stop and look up at the terrace, hoping to catch Vincent's eye. But he did not respond. He was still thinking about his mother.

Somebody threw a glass which shattered on the floor. But the Faces just went One, and Two, and Tap, and Turn. And Tap, and Turn, and Tap.

"I was in love once. At least I thought I was," said Vincent. "I was going to get engaged."

"What happened?"

"My sister got sick and I had to stay home, waiting for the doctor. So I didn't get to the club until midnight. Bojangles, I think it was. And by then I was too late."

"How come?"

"She danced with someone else."

"Only danced?"

"Of course," said Vincent, "and after that, I could never feel the same. I couldn't even go near her. I didn't hate her, you understand. Maybe I still loved her. But I couldn't stand to touch her. Not when I knew the truth."

Around two, the band stopped playing, the Faces grew weary, and the night broke up. Outside the door, as Vincent made his exit, trailed by his lieutenants, a boy and a girl were embracing, framed in the neon glow. And Vincent stopped; he stared. No more than two yards distant, he stood quite still and studied the kiss in closest detail, dispassionate, as though observing guinea pigs.

The couple did not look up and Vincent made no comment. Down the street, Joey was honking the car horn. "God gave his only son," said John James.

"What for?" said Vincent, absent-mindedly.

"Rent," replied the Double J.

It was then that something strange occurred. Across the street, in the darkness beyond a steel-mesh gate, the guard dogs still snarled and waited. Gus and Eugene stood on the curb directly outside the gate, laughing, stomping their feet. They were drunk and it was late. They felt flat, somehow dissatisfied. And suddenly they threw themselves at the steel wires, yelling.

The guard dogs went berserk. Howling, they reared back on their hind legs, and then they hurled themselves at their assailants, smashing full force into the gate. Gus and Eugene sprang backwards, safely out of reach. So the dogs caught only air. And the Faces hooted, hollered. They made barking noises, they whistled, they beckoned the dogs toward them. "Here, boys, here," they said, and the dogs hurled forward again and again, in great surging waves, half maddened with frustration.

Even from across the street, the man in the suit could hear the thud of their bodies, the clash of their teeth on the wires. Gus sat down on the sidewalk, and he laughed so much it hurt. He clasped his sides, he wiped away tears. And Eugene charged once more. He taunted, he leered, he stuck out his tongue. Then he smacked right into the fence itself, and this time the dogs flung back with such frenzy, such total demonic fury, that even the steel bonds were shaken and the whole gate seemed to buckle and give.

That was enough. Somewhat chastened, though they continued to giggle and snicker, the Faces moved on. Behind them, the dogs still howled, still hurled themselves at the wires. But the Faces did not look back.

When they reached the car, they found Vincent already waiting, combing his hair. "Where were you?" asked Gus.

"Watching," said Vincent, and he climbed into the back, out of sight. Inside 2001 Odyssey, there was no more music or movement, the dance floor was deserted. Saturday night had ended, and Vincent slouched far back in his corner. His eyes were closed, his hands hung limp. He felt complete.

Another Saturday night. Easing down on Fifth and Ovington, Joey parked the car and went into the pizza parlor, the Elegante. Vincent and Eugene were already waiting. So was Gus. But John James was missing. Two nights before he had been beaten up and knifed, and now he was in the hospital.

It was an old story. When the Double J got home from work on

Thursday evening, his mother had sent him out for groceries, down to Marinello's Deli. He had bought pasta and salad, toilet paper, a six-pack of Bud, a package of frozen corn, gum, detergent, tomato sauce, and four TV dinners. Paid up. Combed his hair in the window. Then went out into the street, cradling his purchases in both arms.

As he emerged, three Latins—Puerto Ricans—moved across the sidewalk toward him and one of them walked straight through him. Caught unawares, he lost his balance and his bag was knocked out of his arms, splattering on the curb.

Produce scattered everywhere, rolling in the puddles and filth. The frozen corn spilled into the gutter, straight into some dog mess, and the Latins laughed. "Greaseballs," said John James, not thinking. All that was on his mind was his groceries, the need to rescue what he'd lost. So he bent down and began to pick up the remnants. And the moment he did, of course, the Latins jumped all over him.

The rest was hazy. He could remember being beaten around the head, kicked in the sides and stomach, and he remembered a sudden sharp burn in his arm, almost as though he had been stung by an electric wasp. Then lots of shouting and scuffling, bodies tumbling all anyhow, enormous smothering weights on his face, a knee in the teeth. Then nothing.

In the final count, the damage was three cracked ribs, a splintered cheekbone, black eyes, four teeth lost, and a deep knife cut, right in the meat of his arm, just missing his left bicep.

"Three greaseballs at once," said Gus. "He could have run. But he wouldn't."

"He stuck," said Vincent. "He hung tight."

Judgment passed, the Faces finished their pizzas, wiped their lips, departed. Later on, of course, there would have to be vengeance, the Latins must be punished. For the moment, however, the feeling was of excitement, euphoria. As Eugene hit the street, he let out a whoop, one yelp of absolute glee. Saturday night, and everything was beginning, everything lay ahead of them once more.

But Vincent hung back, looked serious. Once again he had remembered a line, another gem from the screen. "Hung tight," he said, gazing up along the bleak street. "He could have got away clean, no sweat. But he had his pride. And his pride was his law."

Donna loved Vincent, had loved him for almost four months. Week after week she came to Odyssey just for him, to watch him dance, to wait. She sat in a booth by herself and didn't drink, didn't smile, didn't tap her foot or nod her head to the music. Though Vincent never danced with her, she would not dance with anyone else.

Her patience was infinite. Hands folded in her lap, knees pressed together, she watched from outside, and she did not pine. In her own style she was satisfied, for she knew she was in love, really, truly, once and for all, and that was the thing she had always dreamed of.

Donna was nineteen, and she worked as a cashier in a supermarket over toward Flatbush. As a child she had been much too fat. For years she was ashamed. But now she felt much better. If she held her breath, she stood five-foot-six and only weighed 140 pounds.

Secure in her love, she lived in the background. Vincent danced, and she took notes. He laughed, and she was glad. Other girls might chase him, touch him, swarm all over him. Still she endured, and she trusted.

And one Saturday, without any warning, Vincent suddenly turned toward her and beckoned her onto the floor, right in the middle of the Odyssey Walk where she took her place in the line, three rows behind him, one rank to the left.

She was not a natural dancer, never had been. Big-boned, soft-fleshed, her body just wasn't right. She had good breasts, good hips, the most beautiful gray-green eyes. But her feet, her legs, were hopeless. Movement embarrassed her. There was no flow. Even in the dark, when she made love, or some boy used her for pleasure, she always wanted to hide.

Nonetheless, on this one night she went through the motions and nobody laughed. She kept her eyes on the floor; she hummed along with the songs. Three numbers went by without disaster. Then the dancers changed, moved from the Walk to something else, something she didn't know, and Donna went back to her booth.

Obscurity. Safety. She sipped Fresca through a straw and fiddled with her hair. But just as she was feeling stronger, almost calm again, Vincent appeared above her, his shadow fell across her just like in the movies, and he put his hand on her arm.

His shirt was pink and scarlet and yellow; her dress was pastel green. His boots were purple, and so were her painted lips. "I'm leaving," Vincent said, and she followed him outside.

His coat was creased at the back. He didn't know that, but Donna did; she could see it clearly as they walked out. And the thought of it, his secret weakness, made her dizzy with tenderness, the strangest sense of ownership.

"What's your name?" Vincent asked.

"Maria," said Donna. "Maria Elena."

They sat in the back of Joey's car and Vincent pulled down her tights. There was no space, everything hurt. But Donna managed to separate her legs, and Vincent kissed her. "Are you all right?" he asked.

"I love you," said Donna.

"No, not that," said Vincent. "I mean, are you fixed?"

She wasn't, of course. She wasn't on the pill, or the coil, or anything. Somehow or other, she'd never got around to it. So Vincent went away. He simply took his body from hers, climbed out of the car. "Vincent," said Donna. But he was gone.

She didn't feel much, did not react in any way. For the next few minutes, she sat very still and tried not to breathe. Then she went home and she slept until noon the next day, a sleep of absolute immersion, so deep and so silent that, she said later on, it felt like Mass.

Another week went by; another Saturday night arrived. But this time it was different. On Thursday afternoon she had bought her first packet of condoms. Now they nestled in her purse, snug upon her lap. She was prepared.

Everything seemed changed in her, resolved. Tonight she didn't sit alone, felt no need to hide. She danced every number whether anyone asked her or not. She drank Bacardi and Coke, she laughed a lot, she flapped her false eyelashes. She wore a blue crepe blouse without any bra, and underneath her long black skirt, cut in the style of the forties, her legs were bare.

Even when Vincent danced near her, she hardly seemed to notice. It was as if she were weightless, floating free. But when the man in the tweed suit sat down beside her in her plastic booth, in between dances, and asked her how she felt, she could not speak, could only place her hand above her heart, to keep it from exploding.

Finally, shortly after one o'clock, Vincent decided to leave. He disappeared toward the cloakroom to retrieve his coat, and while his back was turned, Donna slipped by, out onto the street, where she waited.

It was raining hard, had been raining all night. Turning up her collar, tightening the belt on her coat, which had once belonged to her older sister, Donna pressed back into the angle of the wall, right underneath the neon sign. And she began to talk. Normally she was cautious, very quiet. But now the words came out in a torrent, an uncontrollable flood, as though some dam had burst deep within her.

She talked about dances she had been to, clothes that her friends had bought, boys who had left her, a dog she had once owned. She talked about home and work, and the rain came down in a steady stream. Ten minutes passed. She said she wanted three children.

At last the door opened and Vincent came out, ducking his head against the downpour. The light fell full on Donna's face; she tried to smile. Her hair was slicked flat against her skull and Vincent looked her over with a look of vague surprise, as if he couldn't quite place her. Her makeup was smudged; the tip of her nose was red. She was fat. Vincent walked straight past her.

He went off down the street, moved out of sight, and Donna remained behind, still standing on the sidewalk. "Oh," she said, and she brought her hand up out of her left coat pocket, loosely holding the packet of unused condoms.

She opened it. Gently, methodically, she took out the sheaths and dangled them, squeezed between her forefinger and thumb. One by one, not looking, she dropped them in the wet by her feet. Then she went home again, back to sleep.

Another Saturday night. The man in the tweed suit was sitting in the bleachers, around one o'clock, when Eugene approached him and sat down at his table. "Are you really going to write a story?" Eugene asked.

"I think so," replied the man.

"There are some things I want you to put in. As a favor," Eugene said. "Things I'd like to say."

He was lean and wiry, vaguely furtive, in the style of a human stoat, and his yellow shirt was emblazoned with scarlet fleurs-de-lis. His voice was high-pitched, squeaky; his left eye was forever squinting, half shut, as if warding off an invisible waft of cigarette smoke. At first glance he might have passed for an overgrown jockey. But his real ambition was to become a disk jockey, or possibly a TV quizmaster: "Something daring. Anything. It doesn't matter what," he said.

Now he wanted to declare himself, to make a statement, his testament.

"Go ahead," the man said. "Tell me."

"First," said Eugene, "I want to mention my mother and father, my brothers, my uncle Tony, my grandmother. Also, Roy and Butch at Jones Beach, and Charlie D. in Paterson. And Alice, she knows why."

"Anyone else?"

"And everyone, as well."

The way he spoke, measured, remote, it was as though he addressed them from a very great distance, an alien world. From prison, perhaps, or an army camp. Or some secret underground, a Saturday-night cabal, known only to initiates. "Is that all?" asked the man in the suit.

"Just tell them hello," said Eugene, "and you can say I get by."

On Wednesday evening, to help time pass, Vincent went to see *The Man Who Would Be King,* and rather to his surprise, he liked it very much. On his own admission, he did not understand it, not entirely, for India and the Raj were too far away, much too unreal to make any practical sense. Still, he enjoyed the color and flash, the danger, the sense of everything being possible, all dreams of adventure coming true.

Afterwards, he sat on a low wall outside a basketball court, across the street from the high rise, and considered. The man in the suit was there again, asking more questions. So Vincent talked about living on the eleventh floor, his windows that looked out on nothing, the smell. And working in a housewares store, selling paint and climbing ladders, grinning for his living. "Stuck," he said. "They've got me by the balls."

"How about the future?" asked the man in the suit.

"What future?" Vincent said, and he looked askance, as though the man must be retarded to ask such a question. This was not the Raj; he was not floating in a film. There were dues to pay, people to support. That took money. And money, in this place, meant imprisonment.

Still the man persisted, asked him to imagine. Just conceive that he was set free, that every obstacle was suddenly removed and he could be whatever he pleased. What would he do then? What would give him the greatest pleasure of all, the ultimate fulfillment?

Vincent took his time. This was another dumb question, he knew that. Yet the vision intrigued him, sucked him in almost despite himself. So he let his mind roam loose. Sitting on the wall, he bent his head, contemplated the cracks in the sidewalk. Pondered. Made up his mind. "I want to be a star," he said.

"Such as?" asked the man in the suit.

"Well," said Vincent, "someone like a hero."

Six weeks passed. Six more weeks of drudgery, six more Saturdays. The Odyssey began to wind down, lose its novelty. It was time to move on. But no replacement had been found, not as yet. So there was a hiatus. The Faces kept in training, waiting for the next step. A fresh sensation, another explosion. Meanwhile, they marked time.

Sure enough, their patience paid off. Outside the pizza parlor, on another Saturday night, Joey, Vincent, the Double J, and Eugene sat waiting in the Dodge, raring to go. But Gus did not show up.

Twenty minutes passed, then 30, 40. They were almost ready to go on without him. Then suddenly he came out of the shadows, running, burning. His face was flushed; he was all out of breath. Too wild to make sense, he could only spew out obscenities, kick at the curb, pound his fists, impotent, on the body of the car.

At last he simmered down, choked out his explanations. And the news was indeed enormous. That afternoon, just three hours earlier, his younger sister, Gina, had been molested, debauched, as she crossed a children's playground in the park.

Gus poured out the story. After his sister had finished her lunch, she went to the apartment of her best friend Arlene, who lived about ten blocks away. Both of them were eleven years old and together they spent the afternoon nibbling chocolate candies, trying out different makeups, sighing over photographs of Donny Osmond. Then Gina walked home in the dusk, alone, wrapped in her imitation-leather coat, which was short and showed off her legs. Soon she came to McKinley Park. To make a shortcut, she turned off the street and headed across the park playground.

It was getting dark and the playground was empty, spooky. Gina hastened. Halfway across, however, a man appeared, coming from the opposite direction. He had wispy hair and a wispy beard, and he was talking to himself. When Gina came level with him, he stopped and stared. "Pretty. Pretty. Pretty," he said. Just like that. And he looked at her legs, straight at her kneecaps, with a strange smile, a smile that made her want to run. So she did. She sped out of the playground, into the street, down the block.

Just as she reached the sanctuary of her own hallway, Gus was coming down the stairs. So she bumped straight into him, jumped into his arms. "What's wrong?" he said. But she couldn't say. She just dug her nails into his arms, and she sort of sighed. Then she burst into tears.

He carried her upstairs, cradled like an infant. In time, she was comforted, she calmed down. Finally she told her story, was put to bed, and soon fell asleep. Now all that remained was revenge.

Vengeance. When Gus completed his story, he laid his forehead against the roof of the Dodge in order to feel something cold against his skull, which seemed as though it were burning. There he rested for a moment, recovering. Then he straightened up, and he banged his clenched fist into the meat of his left palm, once, twice, three times, just like on TV. "Mother," he said. "I'll kill him."

"Tear his heart out," said Joey. "Eff him in the place he lives."

"Cut off both his legs," said Vincent. "Kill him. Yes."

They all knew who it was. They didn't even have to ask. In Vincent's own building there was a man called Benny, a wimp who had wispy hair and a wispy beard, who shuffled, and he was really weird. He had these crazy staring eyes, this horrible fixed stare. Everyone steered clear of him. Nobody would talk to him or go close to him. Children threw stones to make him go away. Still he hung around, staring.

No question, he was diseased. One day a bunch of kids had waited for him in the park, jumped him, and tried to teach him a lesson. But he would not learn. The more they abused him, beat on him, the stranger he became. He talked to himself, he mumbled stuff that no one could understand. And often, late at night, blind drunk, he would stand outside people's windows, yell and carry on and keep them from their sleep.

And now this. The final outrage. So the Faces drove back toward the highrise, piled out of the car, descended on the building in a wedge.

Enforcers. Vigilantes. In silence, they came to Benny's door and Gus rang the bell, banged on the door. A minute passed and there was no answer. Gus banged again. Still no reply. Inside the apartment, everything seemed quiet, absolutely still. Gus banged a third time, a fourth, and then he lost patience. He started raging, kicking the door, barging into it with his shoulder. But nobody moved inside or made a sound, and the door would not give way.

Defeated, the Faces stood around in the hallway, feeling vaguely foolish. At first their instinct was simply to wait it out, keep a vigil till Benny came home. But within a few minutes, hanging about, doing nothing, that plan lost its attraction. The hall was deserted, there was no sign of action. Just standing there grew boring, and they started to fret.

Loitering outside the front doorway, aimless, it was Eugene who came up with the solution. "I don't care. No sweat," he said. "Somebody's going to pay."

"Mothereffing right," said Gus, and he slammed his fist into his palm again; he threw a right cross into space. "Those greaseball bastards."

"Mothers," said the Double J.

"Those mothereffing freaks," said Gus. "We're going to rip them apart." And the man in the tweed suit, who had been watching, was forgotten. The Faces looked past him, hardly seemed to recognize his shape. "We're going," said the Double J.

"Where to? Odyssey?" asked the man.

"Hunting," said Gus.

They moved back to the car, they clambered inside. Of course, the man in the suit wanted to go along, wanted to watch, but they wouldn't let him. They said that he didn't belong, that this was no night for tourists, spectators. He tried to argue but they would not hear him. So he was left behind on the sidewalk, and they traveled alone.

But just before the Dodge moved off, Vincent rolled down his window, looked out into the dark. His face was immobile, frozen, in the best style of Al Pacino. "What is it?" asked the man in the suit.

Vincent laughed, exulted. "Hombre, you will die," he said, to no one in particular. And the Faces drove away, off into Saturday night. Horsemen. A posse seeking retribution, which was their due, their right.

Legs McNeil and Gillian McCain

PUNK APOSTLES

It's strange, but here we are feeling all warm, nostalgic, and oogly about gobs of spit, green hair, and safety pins jammed through ear lobes. Studs Terkel was busy so McNeil and McCain wrote the oral history of punk music.

Nancy Spungen: Punk started in the sixties with garage bands like the Seeds and Question Mark and the Mysterians. Punk is just real good basic rock & roll, with really good riffs—it's not like boogie rock. It's not very embellished, intricate music—it's not with the synthesizers, it's just real basic fifties and early sixties rock.

Eliot Kidd: The only thing that made the music different was that we were taking lyrics to places they had never been before. The thing that makes art interesting is when an artist has incredible pain or incredible rage. The New York bands were much more into their pain, while the English bands were much more into their rage.

*   *   *

Sterling Morrison: Lou Reed's parents hated the fact that Lou was making music and hanging around with undesirables. I was always afraid of Lou's parents—the only dealing I'd had with them was that there was this constant threat of them seizing Lou and having him thrown in the nuthouse. That was always over our heads. Every time Lou got hepatitis his parents were waiting to seize him and lock him up.

John Cale: That's where all Lou's best work came from. His mother was some sort of ex-beauty queen and I think his father was a wealthy accountant. Anyway, they put him in a hospital where he received shock treatment as a kid. Apparently he was at Syracuse University and was given this compulsory choice to either do gym or the Reserve Officers Training Corps. He claimed he couldn't do gym because he'd break his neck and when he did ROTC he threatened to kill the instructor. Then he put his fist through a window or something, and so he was put in a mental hospital. I don't know the full story. Every time Lou told me about it he'd change it slightly.

*   *   *

Al Aronowitz: I gave the Velvet Underground their first gig. I put them on as the opening act at the Summit High School in New Jersey and they stole my wallet-size tape recorder first thing. They were just junkies, crooks, hustlers. Most of the musicians at that time came with all these high-minded ideals, but the Velvets were all full of shit. They were just hustlers.

And their music was inaccessible. That's what Albert Grossman, Bob Dylan's manager, always used to ask—whether music's accessible or inaccessible—and the Velvets' music was totally inaccessible.

But I'd committed myself. So I put them into the Café Bizarre and I said, "You work here and you'll get some exposure, build up your chops, and get it together."

*   *   *

Lou Reed: Andy Warhol told me that what we were doing with the music was the same thing he was doing with painting and movies and writing—i.e., not kidding around. To my mind nobody in music was doing anything that even approximated the real thing, with the exception of us. We were doing a specific thing that was very, very real. It wasn't slick or a lie in any conceivable way, which was the only way we could work with him. Because the very first thing I liked about Andy was that he was very real.

*   *   *

Danny Fields: Everybody was in love with everybody. We were all kids, and it was like high school. I mean it was like when I was sixteen, this one likes this one this week, and this one doesn't like that one this week, but likes this one, and there are all these triangles, I mean it wasn't terribly serious. It just happened to be people who later on became very famous because they were so sexy and beautiful, but we didn't realize it at the time, we just all were falling in and out of love—who could even fucking keep track?

Everybody was in and out of love with Andy, of course, and Andy was in and out of love with everybody. But people that were most "in-loved-with" were the people, I think, who fucked the least—like Andy. I mean the people who you really know went to bed with Andy, you could count on the fingers of one hand. The people who really went to bed with Edie or Lou or Nico were very, very few. There really wasn't that much sex, there were more crushes than sex. Sex was so messy. It still is.

* * *

Lou Reed: The old sound was alcoholic. The tradition was finally broken. The music is sex and drugs and happy. And happy is the joke the music understands best. Ultrasonic sounds on records to cause frontal lobotomies. Hey, don't be afraid. You'd better take drugs and learn to love PLASTIC. All different kinds of plastic—pliable, rigid, colored, colorful, nonattached plastic.

Ronnie Cutrone: The sixties have a reputation for being open and free and cool, but the reality was that everybody was straight. Everybody was totally straight and then there was us—this pocketful of nuts. We had long hair, and we'd get chased down the block. People would chase you for ten blocks, screaming, "Beatle!" They were out of their fucking minds—that was the reality of the sixties. Nobody had long hair—you were a fucking freak, you were a fruit, you were not like the rest of the world.

So for me, there was a strong pull toward the dark side. Lou and Billy Name would go to this Vaseline bar called Ernie's—there would be jars of Vaseline on the bar and there was a back room where the guys would go to fuck each other. While I was never gay, I was into sex, and when you're thirteen or fourteen, sex is not that available from women. So I figured, Gee, wouldn't it be great to be gay?

So I tried it, but I was a miserable failure. I remember I was actually sucking this guy off once, and he said, "Man, you're not into this." I went, "Yeah, I know. I'm sorry."

Lou Reed: Honey, I'm a cocksucker. What are you?

* * *

Iggy Pop: The first time I heard the Velvet Underground and Nico record was at a party on the University of Michigan campus. I just hated the sound. You know, "HOW COULD ANYBODY MAKE A RECORD THAT SOUNDS LIKE SUCH A PIECE OF SHIT? THIS IS DISGUSTING! ALL THESE PEOPLE MAKE ME FUCKING SICK! FUCKING DISGUSTING HIPPIE VERMIN! FUCKING BEATNIKS, I WANNA KILL THEM ALL! THIS JUST SOUNDS LIKE TRASH!"

Then about six months later it hit me. "Oh my god! WOW! This is just a fucking great record!" That record became very key for me, not just for what it said, and for how great it was, but also because I heard other people who could make good music—without being any good at music. It gave me hope. It was the same thing the first time I heard Mick Jagger sing. He can only sing one note, there's no tone, and he just goes, "Hey, well baby, baby, I can be oeweowww . . ." Every song is the same monotone, and it's just this kid rapping. It was the same with the Velvets. The sound was so cheap and yet so good.

*   *   *

Kathy Asheton: The first time I saw Iggy's band, the Prime Movers, was at a club in Ann Arbor called Mother's. I was fourteen, still in my innocent, virginal days, and the very next night the MC5 played. They were from Detroit and no one knew who they were.

The MC5 were Detroit hoods. Greasers. Wayne Kramer was completely greased out, but Fred had long hair, which was rare at that time. So I instantly got a crush on Fred. He actually came offstage and asked me if I wanted to slow dance, while the rest of the band played on. I told him, "NO!"

Fred was sort of taken aback by that, like he thought I was just going to leap at him. Anyway, he convinced me to dance—a slow dance.

Wayne Kramer: We had existed in a couple of forms before we were known as the MC5. Me and Fred Smith had been in rival neighborhood bands in Lincoln Park, a suburb of Detroit. Fred's band had been called the Vibratones and mine was the Bounty Hunters, named after Conrad Colletta's dragster of the same name.

We all shared a love of hot rods and big-assed engines. I even took a job at the drag strip selling ice cream—"ICE COLD, ICE COLD ICE CREAM!"—just so I could be there every week. Drag racing was in our blood. I mean, it was loud and fast, just like the music.

*   *   *

Iggy Pop: Once I heard the Paul Butterfield Blues Band and John Lee Hooker and Muddy Waters, and even Chuck Berry playing his own tune, I couldn't go back and listen to the British Invasion, you know, a band like the Kinks. I'm sorry, the Kinks are great, but when you're a young guy and you're trying to find out where your balls are, you go, "Those guys sound like pussies!"

I had tried to go to college, but I couldn't do it. I had met Paul Butterfield's guitarist, Mike Bloomfield, who said, "If you really want to play, you've got to go to Chicago." So I went to Chicago with nineteen cents.

I got a ride with some girls that worked at Discount Records. They dumped me off at a guy named Bob Koester's house. Bob was white and ran the Jazz Record Mart there. I crashed with him and then I went out to Sam's neighborhood. I really was the only white guy there. It was scary, but it was also a travel adventure—all these little record stores, and Mojos hanging, and people wearing colorful clothes. I went to Sam's place and his wife was very surprised that I was looking for him. She said, "Well, he's not here, but would you like some fried chicken?"

So I hooked up with Sam Lay. He was playing with Jimmy Cotton and I'd go see them play and learned what I could. And very occasionally, I would get to sit in, I'd get a cheap gig for five or ten bucks. I played for Johnny Young once—he was hired to play for a white church group, and I could play cheap, so he let me play.

It was a thrill, you know? It was a thrill to be really close to some of those guys—they all had an attitude, like jive motherfuckers, you know? What I noticed about these black guys was that their music was like honey off their fingers. Real childlike and charming in its simplicity. It was just a very natural mode of expression and life-style. They were drunk all the time and it was all sexy-sexy and dudey-dudey, and it was just a bunch of guys that didn't want to work and who played good.

I realized that these guys were way over my head, and that what they were doing was so natural to them that it was ridiculous for me to make a studious copy of it, which is what most white blues bands did.

Then one night, I smoked a joint. I'd always wanted to take drugs, but I'd never been able to because the only drug I knew about was marijuana and I was a really bad asthmatic. Before that, I wasn't interested in drugs, or getting drunk, either. I just wanted to play and get something going, that was all I cared about. But this girl, Vivian, who had given me the ride to Chicago, left me with a little grass.

So one night I went down by the sewage treatment plant by the Loop, where the river is entirely industrialized. It's all concrete banks and effluvia by the Marina Towers. So I smoked this joint and then it hit me.

I thought, What you gotta do is play your own simple blues. I could describe my experience based on the way those guys are describing theirs . . .

So that's what I did. I appropriated a lot of their vocal forms, and also their turns of phrase—either heard or misheard or twisted from blues songs. So "I Wanna Be Your Dog" is probably my mishearing of "Baby Please Don't Go."

Ron Asheton: Iggy called me up from Chicago and said, "Hey, how about you guys coming to pick me up?" That was the beginning of Iggy deciding, "Hey, why don't we start a band?"

*   *   *

Iggy Pop: On my twenty-first birthday we opened for Cream. I had spent the day transporting a two-hundred-gallon oil drum from Ann Arbor to Detroit so that we could put a contact mike on it and Jimmy Silver would hit it on the one beat of our best song. I got it up the three flights of stairs into the Grande Ballroom, by myself, and then we discovered that our amps didn't work. And when we went out onstage everybody yelled, "We want Cream! We want Cream! Get off, we want Cream!"

I'm standing there, having taken two hits of orange acid, going, "Fuck you!" It was one of our worst gigs ever.

I went back to Dave Alexander's house with him. I was heartbroken. I thought, My god, this is twenty-one. This is it. Things are just not going well.

Dave's mom served me a cheeseburger with a candle in the middle of it. The idea was to keep going and things would get better. Don't give up.

*   *   *

Danny Fields: The night the MC5 played at the Fillmore East was a historic night in the history of rock & roll and alternative culture. It was just after *Kick out the Jams* was released.

The background is that the Motherfuckers were a radical East Village group who had been demanding that Bill Graham turn the Fillmore East over to them one night a week because it was in the "Community." My favorite word, the "Community." They wanted to cook meals in there and have their babies make doody on the seats. These were really disgusting people. They were bearded and fat and Earth motherish and angry and belligerent and old and ugly and losers. And they were hard.

So Bill Graham and the Fillmore were under pressure from the Community and the radical elements of the Lower East Side to turn the theater over to them. Meanwhile, the MC5 album came out and Jac Holzman thought, Wouldn't it be a great idea if we present the band at the Fillmore and give all the tickets away free! The "people's band"! This way the Fillmore gets a lot of publicity and we can promote the show on the radio and everyone will be happy!

So they booked a Thursday night, and to placate the Community five hundred tickets were given to the Motherfuckers to distribute to their fat, smelly, ugly people. Then we found out later the tickets were locked in Kip Cohen's desk. The tickets never left his desk! The time for the show approached and the Community was getting more and more angry about what happened to their entrée into the show. And since the MC5 were legendary as the band of the Movement, the only band to have played Chicago in 1968, the audience was composed of the leaders of the antiwar movement in America, people like Abbie Hoffman and Jerry Rubin. This was very high level underground stuff.

And then I did perhaps the stupidest thing in my life. There I was, sitting up at the Elektra offices, smoking cigarettes, sucking acid, smoking pot, saying, "Aaww, I have to get this band downtown? What do I do?"

So I called ABC Limo Company. We arrived downtown in the midst of the Motherfuckers banging on the doors of the Fillmore to be let in free. And right at that moment comes this big symbol of capitalist pigism, a huge stretch limo, and the MC5 get out. The Motherfuckers start screaming, "TRAITORS! BETRAYAL! YOU'RE ONE OF THEM, NOT ONE OF US!"

And the MC5 are going, "What did we do wrong?" Maybe I should have sent them in a jeep or a psychedelic van. It didn't occur to me. I didn't anticipate how the image of a limo was going to affect these loathsome people. You can imagine, a bunch of people that would call themselves the "Motherfuckers," what they would be like.

*   *   *

Iggy Pop: When we came to New York to play Ungano's, I went up to see Bill Harvey, the general manager of Elektra, and said, "I can't possibly do four gigs in a row without drugs—hard drugs. Now it's gonna cost this much money, and then we'll pay you back . . ."

It was like a business proposition, right? And he's looking at me like, "I do not believe this!"

But to me it was very official, and very logical, you know, "What's wrong with that?"

*   *   *

Danny Fields: By 1971, the Stooges were getting ready to do a third album. Jim Silver left as the Stooges' manager because he was dabbling in health foods and it started being a lot more profitable than managing the Stooges, who were like an oven that burned money. So he just started backing away from the Stooges, and I became the Stooges' de facto manager.

I worked with them long-distance since I was working for Atlantic Records in New York. The Stooges had their songs ready for their next album—what was to become *Raw Power*—and I loved it. I was just thrilled.

So I called Bill Harvey, the executive from Elektra who had fired me—we still hated each other, but I still had to have a relationship with him since the Stooges were still signed to his label—and I said, "It's time to pick up the option."

I think he had determined beforehand that he wasn't going to pick up the option. He just went through the motions.

*   *   *

It was hell managing Iggy. We were all in New York, and they were out in Detroit and no one understood anything about money. Actually, there was no money. The record company didn't support them and they didn't sell any records.

And Iggy had a drug problem. The Alice Cooper band and the Stooges would play the same show and they'd get paid $1,500 a night. It would come showtime and there would be the guys in Alice's band looking for the mirror to put on eye makeup—you know, being real professional—and then we'd have to go look for Iggy.

And I'd find him lying there, down around the toilet bowl with a spike in his arm, and I'd have to pull it out, with blood spurting all over the place, and I'd be slapping his face, saying, "It's showtime!"

Was that fun? Yeah, right.

Dee Dee Ramone: The first time I saw Iggy was at the Stooges' show at the Electric Circus on St. Marks Place in June of 1971. They went on real late because Iggy couldn't find any veins to shoot dope into anymore because his arms were so fucked-up. He was pissed off and wouldn't come out of the bathroom, so we had to wait.

Iggy Pop: I was backstage looking for a vein and screaming, "Get out! Get out!" to everybody, even my friends—and they were all thinking, God, he's going to die, blah, blah, blah.

Finally, I'm up there on the stage, and as soon as I walked on that stage, I could feel it. I knew I just had to puke. I wasn't going to leave the stage, though, because I felt that would have been considered deserting one's audience.

Dee Dee Ramone: The band finally came out and Iggy seemed very upset. He was all painted in silver paint and all he had on was a pair of underwear. The silver paint was smeared all over him, even in his hair. But his hair and fingernails were gold. And someone had also sparkled him up with glitter. They went on and played the same song over and over. It only had three chords. And the only words to it were "I want your name, I want your number."

Then Iggy just looked at everybody and said, "You people make me sick!" Then he threw up.

Leee Childers: Geri Miller was down front again. She had this horrible little voice and she was right down front screaming, "Throw up! Throw up! When are you gonna throw up?" And he did! He threw up. Iggy always satisfied his audience.

Iggy Pop: It was very professional. I don't think I hit anyone.

*   *   *

Patti Smith: If I didn't think so much of myself, I'd think I was a name dropper. You can read my book, *Seventh Heaven,* and who do you get out of it?

Edie Sedgwick, Marianne Faithful, Joan of Arc, Frank Sinatra; all people I really like. But I'm not doing it to drop names. I'm doing it to say this is another piece of who I am. I'm shrouded in the lives of my heroes.

Bebe Buell: Todd Rundgren introduced me to Patti. She was his girlfriend before me. I liked her immediately. She told me I looked like Anita Pallenberg, Nico, and Marianne Faithfull all rolled into one cream puff. Those were her exact words to me. Then she said, "You gotta cut your hair into bangs." At the time I had long hair and Patti told me to cut it with the bangs and stuff, so I did. Then she tried to talk me into dyeing it white, but I wouldn't.

I used to drive Patti crazy. I'd go visit her every day. I would just show up on Twenty-third Street where she was living with Allen Lanier, you know, right after they'd just fucked or she was fixing one of her shrines or she was writing, but she'd always let me come in.

We'd sit and talk and she told me, "I really want to sing." I'd told her, "So do I." This is way before she started singing. So we'd put on records and sing to them at the top of our lungs. We'd put on "Gimme Danger" and try to imitate the attitude on the vocals, trying to get it right in our throats. Patti would say, "Yeah, this is how you learn how to sing." We'd use hairbrushes for microphones and stand in front of the mirror and sing. I had great times with her like that—she was really fun. Sometimes I would bring pot and Patti could not smoke a lot because she's just so smart and crazy that after two hits, she'd be like off, man—in the stratosphere, with philosophy and telling me stories about Sam Shepard.

I was so young and crazy—I would always go running to Patti every time I had a problem with Todd. Patti still loved Todd a little, so it was hard for her to have this little brat coming over, asking her for advice about Todd when she still had a lot of feeling for him, even though she was living with Allen. Sometimes I would catch Todd and Patti hugging or something, and I would get very teenage about it. I'd go over to Patti and say, "Why you hugging my boyfriend?" She'd say, "Relax. It's okay, just cool out, little girl."

*   *   *

David Johansen: There wasn't a lot of intellectualizing going on when we started the New York Dolls. It was just a bunch of guys practicing in a storefront who started playing together. The Dolls consisted of myself on lead vocals, Johnny Thunders on lead guitar, Syl Sylvain on rhythm guitar, Arthur Kane on bass, and Billy Murcia on drums. None of us said to each other, "You wear this or you do that."

I don't know where the glitter thing came from. We were just very ecological about clothes. It was just about taking old clothes and wearing them again. I think they called it glitter rock because some of the kids who used to come to see us put glitter in their hair or on their faces. The press figured it was glitter rock—the term itself came from some writer, but it was just classical rock & roll. We used to do Otis Redding songs, Sonny Boy Williamson songs, Archie Bell and the Drells songs, so we didn't consider ourselves glitter rock, we were just rock & roll.

And we thought that's the way you were supposed to be if you were in a rock & roll band. Flamboyant.

*   *   *

Jerry Nolan: The Dolls started playing around, mostly at a place called the Mercer Arts Center, every Tuesday, and the Diplomat Hotel. I fell in love with them right away. I said, "Holy shit! These kids are doing what nobody else is doing. They're bringing back the three-minute song!" These were the days of the ten-minute drum solo, the twenty-minute guitar solo. A song might take up a whole side of an album. I was fed up with that shit. Who could outplay who? It was really boring. It had nothing to do with rock & roll. Then there was Top Forty, which was steady work and you made a few bucks, but I just hated playing Top Forty.

The Dolls not only appealed to the kids, they were drawing the young art crowd: Andy Warhol, actors and actresses, other musicians.

*   *   *

David Johansen: The audiences there were pretty depraved, so we had to be in there with them. We couldn't come out in three-piece suits and entertain that bunch. They wanted something more for their money. And we were very confrontational. We were very raw. We were really into confronting the audience: "HEY YOU STUPID BASTARDS, GET UP AND DANCE!" We were not polite.

Leee Childers: The Dolls created a huge scene and it became extremely fashionable to go see them. You didn't just go see the Dolls—you had to be seen seeing the Dolls.

It was an actual participatory thing. And the people not onstage were just as much a part of the show as the people onstage. Everybody in the audience was just as outlandish as the Dolls were. There was Wayne County, the Harlots of 42nd Street, Sylvia Miles, Don Johnson, Patti D'Arbanville, all that kind of gang, were all in the audience, dancing.

Then of course there was David Bowie and Lou Reed, watching and learning. David Bowie came to see the New York Dolls a lot. Lou came to see them a few times.

So when the Dolls played the Mercer Arts Center, it was one of those rare times when the fashionable place to be was actually the right place to be, because it was the best rock & roll in a long time. Real rock & roll.

David Johansen: People who saw the Dolls said, "Hell, anybody can do this." I think what the Dolls did as far as being an influence on punk was that we showed that anybody could do it.

It used to be when we were kids, man, rock & roll stars were like,

"Wow, I got my satin jacket and I'm really cool and I live in this gilded cage and I drive a pink Cadillac." Or some crap like that. The Dolls debunked that whole myth and that whole sexuality.

Because basically we were these kids from New York City who spit and fart in public, were raunchy and just debunked everything. It was just so obvious what we were doing to rock & roll—we were bringing it back to the street.

Richard Hell: Music had just become so bloated. It was all these leftover sixties guys playing stadiums, you know, being treated like they were very important people, and acting like they were very important people. It wasn't rock & roll, it was like some kind of stage act. It was all about the lights and the poses. With the Dolls, it was just like the street put onstage, you know? That was another cool thing about them, they were exactly the same offstage as they were on.

David Johansen: It was real easy to take over because there was nothing happening. There weren't any bands around so we just came in and everybody said the Dolls are the greatest thing since Bosco. But we were the only band around, really, so we didn't have to be that good.

*   *   *

Bebe Buell: I always liked Sable Starr and Laurie Maddox—the two big groupies in L.A. They got completely trashed by Pamela Des Barres in her book *I'm with the Band.* God, who does Miss Pamela think she is, Queen of the Pussies? Miss Pamela took down everyone she thought was competition. Laurie and Sable didn't give a fuck. They weren't competitive. They didn't have to be. Every rock star that came to L.A. wanted to meet them, it wasn't the other way around. It was like, "We've got to meet this Sable Starr and Laurie Maddox, and we got to meet Rodney Bingenheimer and Kim Fowley." There was a certain crowd you had to meet when you were in L.A.

Sable Starr: David Bowie came into town and wanted to meet me, so it wasn't a thing where I had to go running after him. Those days were crazy, every day I was on the go, from one hotel to another, cause Silverhead were staying at the Hyatt House and Bowie was staying at the Hilton, and it was just back and forth all the time. So I went up to meet David Bowie. It's funny, cause he's bisexual, and he had this guy traveling with him, Freddy. Freddy was really pretty.

I sat on David's lap and said, "It is true, you've got different-colored eyes." Just the whole trip, and I was very good at that. Most girls are really shy, they just sit down and wait. But I'd jump right on their laps.

David said, "Oh, you're very cute. Freddy, isn't she cute?" I said, "Are we gonna fuck tonight?" I just came out and said it. And David started laughing and I said, "Really." He goes, "I'd like to, but I don't like Queenie. But I like Laurie." I said, "Well, we'll get rid of Queenie and we'll meet you at the Rainbow later." So he said okay. So me and Laurie went back to the Hyatt House and were just screaming, "We're gonna fuck David Bowie!" We were so excited. And so we went to the Rainbow, and that was another neat thing about being a groupie. Upstairs at the Rainbow they have like just one table. Me and David were sitting there, with a couple of other people. And to have all your friends look up and see you—that was cool. That was really cool.

Then this guy came up and said, "David Bowie, I'm going to kill you." Some hippie was freaking out and started like trying to punch him. So David's bodyguard was throwing the guy down the stairs and David was really freaking because he's very paranoid about that—he had voodoo dolls and stuff—"Oh, I'd better go home and chant, he's trying to kill me!" So he's dragging me down the stairs and all these girls came up to him saying, "David, do you want to take me home?" And he said, "No, I'm with her tonight." So we get out to the car and this guy's going, "I'm coming to your show tomorrow night and I'm going to fucking kill you! I've got a gun." It was very heavy.

Back at the hotel we were sitting around. I had to go to the bathroom, and David came in and had a cigarette in his hand and a glass of wine. And he started kissing me—and I couldn't believe it was happening to me, because there'd been Roxy Music and J. Geils, but David Bowie was the first heavy.

So we went to the bedroom and fucked for hours, and he was great. I don't know where Laurie was. She was always there, but she never was, you know? So I woke up that morning and he said I had to go because his wife Angie was coming. I kept saying I wanted to meet her and stuff. He said he had a surprise for me and gave me tickets for that night's show in Long Beach. He really liked me a lot, David Bowie. I became very famous and popular after that, because it was established that I was cool. I had been accepted by a real rock star.

* * *

Danny Fields: I don't think Dee Dee was a full-time hustler and I know he wanted girls more than he wanted boys. I thought that was very modern. I think everybody should be able to fuck everybody and that gender should be of little consideration. In that way, Dee Dee was very modern. I don't think he was ashamed of having done it.

I mean, I hustled. I hustled people for money. You know, a young poor guy needs a richer older guy to help him get through some difficult moments and if you gotta go to bed with them, so what?

Jim Carroll: A lot of times it would be in a car, but that made me really uncomfortable, so I'd try to convince the guy to take me to this hotel off Second Avenue that was right across from the synagogue. The other guys thought I was asking too much because it was asking them to put out another fifteen or twenty bucks for a room. But I convinced the guy that it'd be much more comfortable than a car, and then we wouldn't have to worry about the law.

There was also the nighttime scene during the summer—on Central Park West, right across from the Museum of Natural History. That was pretty good. I mean, the park was much better than a car, I always thought.

Dee Dee Ramone: When I was fifteen I started buying dope at the fountain in Central Park and bringing it back to my neighborhood in Queens and selling it. I would buy a half load from my dealer, which was fifteen two-dollar bags. I could get three dollars a bag for them in Queens, so if I sold ten of them, I'd make my money and still have five left over.

You could snort one two-dollar bag and get loaded. Three two-dollar bags would keep me nice for the day. That was when the dope in New York was coming from France and it was strong stuff that would make you itch and nod. Real dope.

I was making out pretty good selling dope in Queens, until one day I got caught short and started withdrawing. I went back to my mom's apartment and was shaking and in a lot of pain. My mom was so pissed off she picked a pot off the stove and threw it at me. Then she broke my records and threw my guitar out the window. Since my dad wasn't around, I wasn't afraid of her anymore, so I started screaming, "Get the fuck out of here, you fucking whore cunt!"

And she did.

After my mom found me withdrawing from dope, and we'd had our fight, I couldn't live in the house anymore. And I had nowhere to live in Forest Hills. But I had to go somewhere, so I decided to hitchhike to California.

Some guys from Flint, Michigan, picked me up somewhere in

Illinois in their junk car. I don't know much about cars, but it was really a piece of junk. They would drive the car real slow up the hills, then speed down them like a maniac. These guys were like really demented, they were talking all this sick stuff. They kept saying how they wanted to cut someone's head off. They wanted to strangle somebody. They had a thin wire and two hoops, and they wanted to garrote somebody.

Finally they pulled over to a gas station in South Bend, Indiana, and robbed the place and we all got arrested for armed robbery.

No one got away with nuthin. The police caught us because the driver tried to step on the gas in the junk car and it stalled. The cop who caught us tried to give me a break. He gave me ten phone calls to try and get the bail money. He was really nice. So I called everybody. I called my father, my grandmother in Missouri, and everybody said, "Fuck you."

That was the first time I ever asked my father for anything. I was desperate. I was really scared. It was a rough place. My father said, "Fuck you! Rot there, you deserve it!" and hung up. So I was stuck there and sentenced to ninety days because I had a weapon on me. The other guys got off because their parents came and got them.

I was fifteen and locked up. The jail was a bullpen. They had about ten little cells, and then they would open it up in the day and keep us all in one big room. I was in jail for three months and then they let me out.

I had nowhere to go, so after I got back from being in jail and going to California, I went back to Queens. I went back to living with my mom and there was this guy, John Cummings, who became Johnny Ramone, that lived across the street, and who was friendly to me.

He worked for a dry cleaners and I would usually see him around, making deliveries. I thought he was cool because he dressed like he wanted to, even when he was working. He wore his hair long, down to his waist, a tie-dyed headband, jeans, a Levi jacket, and cheap Keds. So we were checking each other out. I didn't know him that well, but one day I met him on the sidewalk by my house—Tommy, Joey, Johnny, and I all lived right next to each other, in those nice apartment buildings in Forest Hills—and Johnny and I spoke to each other and both kind of blurted out that we liked the Stooges.

I couldn't believe it, because at that time, no one was into the Stooges. I was raised in Germany and didn't like the United States. It was too weird. There was just all this awful music around. In the early seventies rock & roll was like America and Yes—and I hated it. That's when I started getting into the New York Dolls.

Then I discovered the Stooges and that all seemed to go together and the Stooges became my ultimate favorite group. I would just die to go see them, but they only came to New York every nine months or so. But anytime they ever played New York, I'd see them.

*   *   *

Bob Gruen: The first time I went to England the only phone number I had was for Malcolm McLaren. I'd met him in New York when he was hanging out with the New York Dolls. So I called him up and he took me down to the Club Louise.

There were all these kids hanging out, wearing weird clothes and starting to cut their hair in that weird spiky way. There was one band that had formed on the scene and that was the Sex Pistols. They came into the club and they were posturing, ridiculous—like they were the big stars. All the kids were standing around like, "Oooh, it's them, they're so great."

The Sex Pistols were the complete center of attention in this group of kids that included Joe Strummer and Mick Jones and Billy Idol and Adam Ant and Siouxsie Sioux. All of them were saying, "I wish I could have a band."

So I said, "Just do it. It doesn't seem to be too hard." You know, "Too cool for school and too dumb to get a job."

Malcolm McLaren: As a child, whenever they used to tell me to write "I will not be bad" I just changed the "not" to "I will be so bad." And that amused me no end—but in art school, it was somewhat of a loss. To me, the establishment's notion of bad needed to be redefined. And the notion of good meant to me things that I felt absolutely needed to be destroyed.

At the beginning of the seventies, when I had left art school, that meant to me Brian Ferry. It meant to me green velvet loomed pants. It meant to me hippies, bright young things, social realism, the American flag, television, and PG ratings. The first T-shirt I designed was purely about trying to determine that if you were to wake up one morning and find which side of the bed you'd been lying on, you'd know that there would be a list of either "good" names or "bad" names, and that list was the beginning of me deciding how to use "bad" and make it work in a way that ultimately might change popular culture itself.

In that list there was a name—the Sex Pistols, which meant to me all sorts of things. It came about by the idea of a pistol, a pinup, a young thing, a better-looking assassin—a sex pistol. And to launch that idea in the form of a band of kids who could be deduced as being bad was perfect, especially when I discovered those kids had the same anger as I did. And they could possibly help me to keep dreaming, and make me refuse to ever return to what I was terrified of—normality.

Mary Harron: You could really feel the world moving and shaking that autumn of 1976 in London. I felt that what we had done as a joke in New York had been taken for real in England by a younger and more violent audience. And that somehow in the translation, it had changed, it had sparked something different.

What to me had been a much more adult and intellectual bohemian rock culture in New York had become this crazy teenage thing in England. I remember going to see the Damned play that summer, who I thought were really terrible. I was wearing my *Punk* magazine T-shirt and I got mobbed. I mean I can't tell you the reception I got. Everyone was so excited that I was wearing this T-shirt that said *"Punk."*

I was just speechless.

There I was backstage, and there were hundreds of little kids, like nightmares, you know, like little ghouls with bright red dyed hair and white faces. They were all wearing chains and swastikas and things stuck in their head, and I was like, "Oh my god, what have we done? What have we created?"

I felt like we had been doing this thing—and now that we had created something else that we never intended, or expected. I think English punk was much more volatile and edgy and more dangerous.

* * *

Malcolm McLaren: The Sex Pistols were identical to the New York Dolls. David Johansen was like Johnny Rotten, Johnny Thunders was exactly like Steve Jones, Arthur Kane was exactly like Sid Vicious, and in a way, Paul Cook was like Jerry Nolan, except he wasn't a drug taker.

So after Johnny Thunders, I knew exactly where Steve Jones stood, and after David Johansen I knew exactly where Johnny Rotten was gonna stand, and they *were absolutely identical* in terms of their actions.

Johnny Rotten was the person who, if anybody offered him anything he'd be over there, but if there was somebody who'd love him more than the person next to him, he'd be over *there.* He would suffer less criticism than everybody else, same as David Johansen.

Tom McGrath

INTEGRATING MTV

In the early 1980s people who should know better were calling rock videos a new art form. Really . . . and with a straight face. Journalist McGrath tells the story of MTV's early years and here focuses on the significance of Michael Jackson's video-friendly *Thriller* album.

BY THE time he was twenty-three, Michael Jackson was already a legend in the music business. As part of the Jackson Five and as a solo artist, Jackson had proved himself to be one of the most popular—not to mention most exciting—performers in pop music. In 1979, Jackson's first solo album, *Off the Wall,* had spawned four hit singles and sold more than eight million copies.

Could he top it? Jackson, his management, and the executives at CBS Records all hoped so. And by the time his next solo album, *Thriller,* was ready for release in the fall of 1982, it was clear that everyone involved was out to make the record a mega-success. They wanted to get as much radio air play on as many different radio formats as possible. In October, six weeks before the album itself came out, Epic released a single from *Thriller* called "The Girl Is Mine," a duet with Paul McCartney. Just as they'd hoped, Top-40 radio ate it up, and by December the song had risen to No. 2 on *Billboard*'s Hot 100. Then in January, with "The Girl Is Mine" sliding back down the charts and *Thriller* having just hit the stores, Epic released two singles simultaneously, hoping to get both in the top ten at the same time. One was "Billie Jean," a dance track aimed at urban and Top-40 radio; the other was "Beat It," a rock-flavored song featuring heavy-metal guitarist Eddie Van Halen that was targeted at album rock radio.

Radio was only one part of the strategy that Epic and the Jackson camp had plotted out for turning *Thriller* into a mega-hit. The other was music video. In many ways video was a natural for Jackson. While offstage Michael might have been painfully shy, the instant he stepped in front of an audience or a camera his every move demanded that you watch him, as he danced and spun and slid and darted and dipped to the music. He was a truly visual performer, the kind you needed to see in order to fully appreciate, and the kind for whom music video was ideally suited.

Nevertheless, all involved with *Thriller* knew that getting MTV to play Michael Jackson videos was anything but a sure thing. The reason was simple: In the channel's first eighteen months, as it had become a cult hit among white suburban teenagers all over America, it had played only a handful of clips by black artists. From Bob Pittman's and everyone else at MTV's point of view, it was simply a matter of format. Ever since the MTV flag was planted in the moon during the summer of 1981, the channel had positioned itself as a rock and roll station. And because only a few black acts—Tina Turner, Prince, Joan Armatrading, the Bus Boys—played what most people called rock and roll anymore, only a few had their clips played on the network. For Pittman, programming head Les Garland, and the rest of them, the situation was no different from radio, where few album rock stations played many black artists.

But that argument didn't fly with everyone. MTV's original head of talent and artist relations, Carolyn Baker, who was black, had questioned why the definition of music had to be so narrow, as had a few others. What's more, as MTV received more and more press attention, a growing number of journalists and music critics and black artists really began to slam the network for its segregated view of music. True, the critics said, album rock stations didn't play many black acts, either. But other radio formats did, and black music was still widely available on the radio. MTV, on the other hand, was still the only music video channel on television, and therefore, according to the critics, it had an obligation to expose blacks acts and to educate its viewers as to what else was out there.

Probably the most vocal critic of MTV was black musician Rick James. Despite the fact that his most recent album, *Street Songs,* had sold more than three million copies in 1982, MTV had passed on clips for his songs "Super Freak" and "Give It to Me Baby." The funk star clearly wasn't pleased by what he considered a snub, so in early 1983 he took every opportunity to publicly call MTV a racist network.

Despite the inability of Rick James and other black artists to get their clips on the air, and despite the fact that the music on *Thriller* was no more "rock and roll" than anything on *Street Songs,* in January Michael Jackson and Epic went ahead and made videos for the two singles they had just released. Steve Barron, a twenty-seven-year-old British director who'd done clips for the likes of Human League, Rod Stewart, and Adam and the Ants, shot the video for "Billie Jean." Bob Giraldi, a forty-four-year-old American commercial director best known for his Miller Lite "Tastes Great, Less Filling" ads, shot "Beat It."

"Billie Jean" was finished first, and in the middle of February Epic delivered the clip to MTV—at which point Bob Pittman and Les Garland and everyone else involved with programming MTV found themselves facing a dilemma. On the one hand, "Billie Jean," with its thumping beat and bass line and heavy use of synthesizers, was clearly not a rock and roll song—at least not the way MTV was defining it. But by the time the video itself was delivered to them, there were some equally compelling reasons why the channel should play it. "Billie Jean" was as hot a song as the music industry had seen in years. After only a handful of weeks on the charts, it was already in the Top 10, and it looked as if it was headed for No. 1. Moreover, CBS and Epic had a great deal invested financially, strategically, and emotionally in Michael Jackson, and they desperately wanted the clip played.

Finally, and maybe most compelling of all, the video itself was irresistible, the best a number at MTV had ever seen. Though the concept itself was enticing enough—in it Michael played a sort of mystical healer, one whose powers allowed him to appear and disappear at will—what really made the clip work was Michael's performance. Dressed in a glittering black jacket and wearing one white glove, he jumped and spun and slid all over the clip's surrealistic city street set. You couldn't take your eyes off of him.

It was a tough call to make, and years later there would be some disagreement about what exactly happened. The way Les Garland would remember it, the day he first saw "Billie Jean," he called Bob Pittman, who was in Los Angeles on business, and said that despite "Billie Jean" not being a perfect fit musically, he and the others in programming really thought they had to play it. Pittman agreed to look at it, so Garland sent it to him in California via overnight mail. The next day, Pittman, looked at it, called Garland back, and, after the two of them discussed it for a few minutes, told him to go ahead and put it on the air.

Others would claim the decision wasn't that simple. That spring, a story began circulating that CBS Records boss Walter Yetnikoff and some others at the company had threatened to pull all of the label's videos off the air if MTV didn't play "Billie Jean." Years later Pittman and Garland would deny that any such threat was made, pointing out that such a stunt would have been ridiculous. How would Yetnikoff ever explain to Billy

Joel or Journey or any other CBS act that their clips were going to be sacrificed for the good of Michael Jackson's career?

Either way, on March 2, one week after the song hit No. 1 on *Billboard*'s Hot 100, the "Billie Jean" video debuted on MTV.

"Beat It" arrived a couple of weeks later, and if they were all impressed by "Billie Jean," they were absolutely floored by "Beat It." This second clip was even better than the first. Costing more than $150,000 and directed by Broadway choreographer Michael Peters, the video looked like an updated, inner-city version of *West Side Story.* They even got members of real Los Angeles street gangs to appear in it. But what made it great was the dancing. Michael, dressed in a red leather jacket, snapped and stepped and shrieked to the music, this time with more than a hundred talented extras moving along with him.

Never before had there been a video like this one. Almost single-handedly, this shy former child star had taken the entire field of music video and lifted it up a notch artistically. The reaction to both clips once they'd been aired—and to the songs, and to the album, and to Michael himself—made that clear. All across the country, in bars and basements and breakfast nooks and anywhere else that the MTV pipeline reached, people were watching the two clips and nodding that, yes, these were the best they'd ever seen, these were what video had the potential to become. Certainly record sales reflected people's excitement. *Thriller* had already sold more than two million copies by the time MTV first played "Billie Jean," but after the video went on the air, the album began to sell at a remarkable eight hundred thousand copies per week.

And as that spring went by, Michael seemed only to get hotter. In early May, forty-five million people tuned in to watch him perform a version of "Billie Jean" on an NBC-TV special called *Motown 25.* By June, "Billie Jean" had racked up an incredible thirteen weeks at No. 1, "Beat It" had spent several weeks in the Top 10, and *Thriller* had sold more than seven million copies.

Michael Jackson was the hottest pop star on the planet in nearly twenty years—and you could see him almost hourly on your favorite music video channel. While Michael and MTV were both absolutely on fire, the two weren't competing with each other; they were helping each other. Some would turn on their televisions merely to catch "Billie Jean" and "Beat It," and then find themselves mesmerized by the rest of what they were seeing on MTV. Others would tune in merely to watch MTV, and then find their jaws dropping at Michael's videos. The synergy was phenomenal. It was as if a couple of supercharged rockets had somehow hooked up in midair, and now the two of them were hurtling toward the heavens, linked together and moving faster than anyone could ever have imagined.

After "Billie Jean" and "Beat It," everything changed. Everything. With MTV spreading like never before and Michael demonstrating how mesmerizing these promo clips could be, music video was suddenly everywhere. It was as though, after eighteen months of methodically infecting a select audience in American cities, the video virus just said, the hell with it, and began infecting everyone. The entire culture had been exposed.

Music video was everywhere that summer. Only four years earlier, Michael Nesmith had been forced to create *Popclips* just so he'd have a venue for showing his own videos—now there were pop clips all over the tube. All across the country, in big cities and small towns, at large network-owned-and-operated stations and tiny UHF outfits, local TV outlets were producing their own video clip programs or signing up for one of the dozen or so syndicated video shows that were coming down the pike. The record labels gave out the clips for free, and the ratings were usually terrific, so they couldn't help but make money. A few bigger players had started getting in on things, too. Cable's Playboy Channel announced it was launching a show (developed by none other than Fred Seibert and his partner Alan Goodman) that would feature R-rated videos like Duran Duran's "Girls on Film." Ted Turner's superstation, WTBS, debuted its own weekend-night clip show called *Night Tracks.* Even the broadcast networks, which years ago had decided there was little money in rock and roll, got involved. In July, NBC premiered a weekly ninety-minute program called *Friday Night Videos.*

But video's ubiquitous presence wasn't limited to television. Someone had developed—or rather redeveloped—a video jukebox (long live the Scopitone!) and was installing it in restaurants and bars all over America, while every dance club worth its plastic and chrome had now put in a video screen. RockAmerica, a company that supplied clips to clubs, reported that it was serving three hundred clients that summer, a substantial increase from the year before.

No one had a bigger case of video fever than the record companies themselves. While just twenty-four months earlier, Bob Pittman and Carolyn Baker had practically had to beg the industry to let MTV use their clips, now, having finally seen the channel for themselves and witnessed just what video had done for acts like Michael Jackson and Duran Duran, executives in both New York and Los Angeles were taking to the form like kids to a new toy. They couldn't get enough. At almost every record company, video departments were expanding, and video itself was suddenly being viewed as a serious promotional tool. Executives had finally caught on to the tremendous potential video had when it came to marketing artists. Consequently, the number of clips being made skyrocketed, as did the money labels were willing to put into each one. Probably the best place to see the change was in MTV's weekly music meeting. While a year earlier programming head Les Garland and his team had been looking at four or five new videos each week, these days they found themselves screening up to thirty-five new clips per meeting.

That spring the music industry finally broke out of its three-and-a-half-year slump—sales in the first half of 1983 were up 10 percent. And most people weren't shy about giving music video the credit for the turnaround—rightfully so. Michael Jackson and Duran Duran were the best examples of the effect the channel could have, but they certainly weren't the only ones. A slew of new acts on the charts had broken through commercially because of video, and they were a pretty diverse bunch. Some, like the British band Culture Club, who hit it big with "Do You Really Want to Hurt Me," were brand-new acts. Others, like heavy-metal act Def Leppard, whose *Pyromania* album was now flying out of record stores, had been around the block a time or two without much luck. Still others, like Texas blues band ZZ Top, whose videos for "Gimme All Your Lovin' " and "Legs" were among the most popular on MTV, had scored hits before, but now found themselves catapulted to an entirely new level by music video. Another success story wasn't even a band; it was a movie. Back in the spring, MTV had started playing a video pulled from the film *Flashdance*. The result was that the movie, which owed much of its own visual style to music video, was tops at the box office for weeks, and just a month after its release the *Flashdance* soundtrack had sold 1.5 million copies.

Most infected by the video fever were the people in the creative communities in New York and Los Angeles. Following the lead of commercial director Bob Giraldi, who'd made such a splash with Michael Jackson's "Beat It," directors from other media were suddenly on the phone with their agents trying to line up video work. Filmmaker Tobe Hooper, who'd directed the movie *Poltergeist,* shot Billy Idol's clip "Dancing with Myself," while commercial director Tim Newman did ZZ Top's videos, and another commercial director named Jay Dubin was doing Billy Joel's newest clips. They all loved doing them, because video gave them a chance to be experimental and creative.

The artists themselves were also beginning to take video seriously. In the wake of Michael Jackson's amazing clips, the feeling that had been bubbling below the surface for several years suddenly came rushing up: namely, music video could be art. Most of the clips hadn't yet achieved that status. As performance artist Laurie Anderson put it that summer, "Much of it is just boys playing guitar on the roof, boys playing guitar in the shower." But things were changing. Singer Kim Carnes, who'd had a hit a couple of years earlier with the song "Bette Davis Eyes," announced that video was transforming the way she made albums: As she was recording, she was already thinking of what was going on visually. Singer/song-writer Rickie Lee Jones did her one better: She said she was actually writing the videos as she was writing the songs.

Not surprisingly, the obsession with music video did wonders for MTV. In recent months, the press—through shows like *Nightline* and *20/20* and publications like the *New York Times Magazine*—had all but officially upgraded the channel's societal status. MTV was no longer just a rising star; the channel that had started in a basement in Fort Lee, New Jersey, was now a full-fledged cultural phenomenon.

Jason Gross

LICENSED TO DOWNLOAD

Some of the first sound recordings came on things that looked like toilet-paper rolls. From those goofy-looking cylinders to things like bulletproof 78 rpms, then LPs and cassettes and, for the last two decades, CDs, rock and roll in all of its variations has always embraced emerging technologies. The Internet became the new frontier of music technology at the end of the last century.

When the Beastie Boys released a two-disc retrospective in 1999, ads promoting the set challenged readers to go to the group's website, download additional songs, and make their own damn anthology if they didn't like this one. The Beasties' embrace of online music, captured in this interview in an Internet magazine, is another one of their who'd-a-thunk-it surprises—like their endurance, their growing eclecticism, and their social consciousness. Not bad for some white suburban rappers who delivered a new variation on frat-boy rock with their mid-1980s arrival.

BORN OF humble white-dopes-on-punk beginnings, the Beastie Boys have spent the past 17 years evolving into one of the pop world's strongest forces. The group's debut LP, 1986's *Licensed to Ill,* sold more than 5 million copies and helped erase the color line in rap. Subsequent albums, including the classic *Paul's Boutique,* found the trio stretching lyrically and musically. After becoming entrepreneurs—the Beasties' label, Grand Royal Records, inked a deal with Capitol in 1993—the group developed a more mature attitude, not just in its music but in its sense of social responsibility. Since 1996, the Beastie Boys have organized the yearly Tibetan Freedom Concerts to raise awareness of the Chinese-occupied nation's plight. The Beastie's latest release, the multiplatinum *Hello Nasty,* debuted at No. 1, setting a 1998 record for first-week sales.

The Internet has proved to be both an ideal and a tricky place for the band. Last summer, the Beasties started posting MP3 tracks on their site along with their new single. At the end of the year, Capitol persuaded them to remove the tracks, only to relent when the Beasties' online fans revolted. In March, the group launched an online radio station, Grand Royal Radio [www.grandroyal.com/grRadio]. And May brought another online initiative: exclusive remixes, available for free download, that doubled as Kosovar-refugee relief fund-raisers (for each download, both the band and Microsoft donated $1 to various charities).

With ceaseless globe-trotting since July 1998, the Beasties were difficult to pin down. Schedules exploded without any advance notice, sometimes for no reason, sometimes for good reason. MCA, aka Adam Yauch, postponed an interview after he scored an audience with the Dalai Lama. The Beasties finally checked in en route to Italy and agreed to talk about the Net despite screaming roadside fans and a temperamental cell phone. MCA and Mike D (aka Michael Diamond) were obliging. Ad-Rock (aka Adam Horovitz) opted to supervise the group's sound check instead, in part because he's the least computer-literate of the three.

Y-LIFE: Let's start simply. Why is the Internet important to the Beastie Boys?

MIKE D: At first, it was this completely new forum where all of a sudden we could put together what we've done. As it evolved, it became clear to us that it was an amazing means of communicating directly to our fans and to people in general. So instead of us putting our stuff out there and, say, it having to go through a media format, what we're putting out is going directly to the people out there who are interested.

MCA: I wouldn't necessarily say that the Net is important to the band, but I think it's a great format for the discussion of ideas. I think that in many ways, it can take the better aspects of television and magazines and combine them in an open way. I like the anarchy of it. I hope there aren't too many regulations put on the whole thing. I kind of like the way that anybody can communicate with anybody.

Y-LIFE: Why did the band decide to start its own online radio station?

MIKE D: A lot of times, like with the way we make records, technology will come along and we'll end up using that technology to make something new. The Net radio station came about after we were shown the SHOUTcast technology. Suddenly, we were able to have streaming audio on our site, working like a radio station. Right now, we can branch out and have all kinds of music that we're interested in that maybe goes beyond the music that we're making.

MCA: It sounded like a really cool thing, the way that anybody could put stuff out there. The important thing about it is how many people can be involved in broadcasting. A lot of this stuff, like radio stations and record labels, has been so exclusive for so long.

Y-LIFE: Why did you choose to use the MP3 format for your music online?

MIKE D: Again, that was just a technology that came along, and all of a sudden we were able to put up some live songs that we'd been doing on tour. For all we knew, kids probably had their own bootleg versions of it anyway, 'cause we'd been on tour for a while. We thought that if people were going to check it out, at least let it come from *our* Web site.

Y-LIFE: How do you see the whole controversy that happened with your record company when the group originally put the MP3 files online?

MIKE D: I think it actually got a little blown out of proportion. We had the files up there, and it had been drawing a lot of attention. All of a sudden, Capitol decided, "There's all these kids downloading music, and our biggest-selling artist is doing this? We can't have this happening!" They called us up and said, "Please take them off. We're getting all this pressure from other labels. We shouldn't have artists doing this right now." We told them that if we took them down, there would be a huge outcry. Sure enough, we had piles of e-mails and responses saying, "What's going on here?" It got pretty far, and they couldn't stop it. So the files went back up.

When we switched from vinyl to CD, it changed how people listen to music. The same thing could happen here, but I don't know. You could go from CDs to digital downloading to digital streaming. Is that going to change the way that everything functions? Maybe, maybe not.

MCA: To the best of my understanding, the whole controversy is over how record labels are going to be able to charge money for music. I think that's a fear that's come up before, when cassette tapes first came out. They thought that everyone would tape records, and the record labels wouldn't be able to sell them anymore. I personally don't think it'll be much of a problem.

MIKE D: I definitely think it's going to change things. It's just a matter of how and in what ways. Anyone who says they know exactly how it's going to happen is either a real genius or is lying.

MCA: I guess in some ways, you could say that the Internet changed the way the music business operates. I think record stores are a good thing, though. When we first started out as a hard-core band, we spent a lot of time hanging out at Rat Cage Records, which ended up starting a label. There's something fun about being in a record store, looking at different albums, and sharing ideas with people.

There was a really interesting quote from Chuck D. He was thinking about music differently: People shouldn't be looking at selling 100,000 records; people should be looking at selling 30,000. People have been very spoiled that way. Maybe more people will be playing music and putting music on the Web. There might be more styles and niches, rather than just a few mainstream artists.

Y-LIFE: Have your Web site and the Net in general helped spread the word about the Tibetan Freedom Concerts?

MCA: Yeah, I think it's been a good forum for people who are into that type of communication. It's been good not just for sharing information but also for discussion. That's an important aspect of what's going on with the Tibetan shows.

Y-LIFE: What do you like to check out when you go online?

MIKE D: I'm on tour, so I really don't have much time. I'm strictly an e-mail kind of person. When I do have time beyond the e-mail realm, it's probably for the most part checking out different types of music and getting information about it that I can't read about necessarily in a popular magazine.

Y-LIFE: As musicians and label heads, what kinds of things do you hope will happen with the Internet?

MIKE D: A record label will listen to someone's demo now and say, "I think it's great, but I don't think we can put it out, 'cause it's not going to reach enough people." I think those days are over now. If someone thinks it's creative and it's great, they can put it out there. And if it reaches two people or 200,000 people, it can work on all those different levels.

"Unless my body reaches a certain temperature, starts to liquefy, I just don't feel right."

Think of soul music as the greatest achievement in rock and roll. After all, if rock came from the blending of white and black cultures, soul signified that the mass audience was ready for the real, undiluted thing: James Brown, Otis Redding, Aretha Franklin, Sam and Dave, and others. It came from the black church, but it's also the work of white guys like Dan Penn, Spooner Oldham, Steve Cropper, and "Duck" Dunn working with black singers like Wilson Pickett, Eddie Floyd, and Joe Tex to make beautiful music that saw no color. Soul music is the earthiness of Stax/Volt and the Muscle Shoals sound and the high gloss of Motown. It's the struggle between the sacred and the profane, between the eternal soul and the neverending groove.

Lucy O'Brien

GIRL GROUPS

For much of its first decade rock and roll was a boys' club, but the girl groups of the early 1960s provided a reversal of fortune for rock and roll women. Producer Phil Spector used female singers as essential elements in his wall of sound production technique. Likewise, Berry Gordy's Motown Records moved the Supremes and other female groups to the forefront.

Yet women performers were often still treated as second-class citizens or mere decorations. One of Spector's groups, the Crystals, was unavailable when he wanted them, so he made records with Darlene Love and backing singers and released them under the Crystals' name. They were just more bricks in the wall of sound.

THE GIRL-GROUP sound was clearly identifiable: like punk, it blasted the market for a short period before mutating, maturing and becoming assimilated into mainstream pop. Like punk or house music, its impact was considerable. It articulated the *Zeitgeist,* the fresh ebullient hope of the early '60s; it feminized rock and provided the basis for the '60s beat groups of the famed "British Invasion," particularly The Beatles. The demise of the girl-group era is often blamed on The Fab Four; it's ironic that in appropriating the girl-group sound a male band inadvertently destroyed it through their own success. In the same way that a white person (Elvis) made millions out of the previously segregated blues, so it took a male band to capitalize on the female-group sound, and when they moved on to rock, their teen muses were left behind. Male beat groups from The Beatles to Manfred Mann drew on the girl-group sound to achieve a kind of permanency, while the women, apart from Diana Ross and Ronnie Spector (who were stars), were considered throwaway.

$$* \qquad * \qquad *$$

Small record labels often form a cluster, a buzz and an identity around which things happen. No matter how tiny the original group of enthusiasts, entrepreneurs and artists—from the stars and then a myth can be built. The luminous girl sound was centered around the independents Red Bird, Dimension, Philles, Scepter, Laurie and, of course, Motown. Not all their product was exclusively girl group, but it was an area in which each specialized. Major labels such as Columbia, Mercury, Brunswick, RCA and Liberty tried to launch their own girl groups—RCA in particular, with Reparata and The Delrons—but few of them had major hits. As with any street craze, the majors were too large to react quickly enough to the taste and demand of a fickle, volatile market.

Girl groups had most success with the songwriters, labels and producers who focused completely on their sound. Feeding the small labels were three main husband-and-wife songwriting teams: Gerry Goffin and Carole King, Ellie Greenwich and Jeff Barry, along with Barry Mann and Cynthia Weil, all based in New York's centre of song publishing, the Brill Building. Although other writers figured on the scene, until Motown these three partnerships were the nucleus of the girl-group industry.

*   *   *

The Shangri-Las' story was almost as dramatic and seedy as their songs. Their svengali was a cult, eccentric producer from Long Island called George "Shadow" Morton (so-called because he would disappear for spells of time), who masterminded the pathos of their first hit "Remember (Walkin' In The Sand)," complete with crying seagulls. Leased to Red Bird Records via Ellie Greenwich, who was a schoolfriend of Morton's, the song went to No. 5 in 1964. This brought a whole new dimension to the girl-group sound, the concept of girl-talk as pop opera. Inspired by its success, Red Bird teamed Morton with Greenwich and Barry for the follow-up "Leader Of The Pack," a motorbike tragedy where the heroine's rebel boyfriend is killed in a high-speed crash. A song featuring the technique of call and response, it is one of the most heart-wrenching classics in girl-pop history. For me and my friends, who encountered it second time around when it shot into the UK charts in the early '70s, this was our pre-teen drama, the one we learned the words to—right down to every tear and every rev of that deadly motorbike.

"That was a little soap opera," says Greenwich. "I hear people singing it now, and it makes me feel proud." The Shangri-Las were lead singer Betty Weiss, her sister Mary, and twins Marge and Mary Ann Ganser, streetwise kids from Queens who epitomized the white girl-group sound— slightly nasal, crystal clear, talking tough. Although obedient during the flush of their early career, once it peaked after their last Top Ten hit "I Can

Never Go Home Anymore" in 1965, The Shangri-Las lost their direction. Betty had left the group, while the remaining three aimlessly toured the country without management or adequate record company support. Despite eleven hits, they never realized their potential—maybe because their use of pop banter and serious girl-talk was too ahead of its time. A fitting epitaph, their last single, "Past, Present And Future," a spoken-word song that "bubbled under" in 1966, was described by critic Richard Williams as "one of the most inventive and moving tracks in all of pop."

Altogether more wholesome, Lesley Gore presented an image of white suburban Jewish Americanism that slotted more comfortably in the pages of teen magazines. Ironically, she delivered a message that was far more feminist than the helpless-girlfriend status of The Shangri-Las. "You Don't Own Me," one girl's determined caution to a possessive boyfriend delivered by Gore with an air of self-contained independence, hit the Top Five in 1963. This followed three huge hits, the first of which, the gloriously spoilt teen queen anthem "It's My Party," went straight to No. 1 earlier that year. Discovered by producer Quincy Jones while still at high school in New Jersey, Gore marked the transition of white female solo artists from the over-sugared, careful tones of the '50s to fully fledged '60s soul/pop. She was one of the few women in the girl-group era to be marketed as a magazine personality and role model.

Such success was much easier for white women in an industry where black performers were considered to be "minority" interest—vocal vehicles for girl-group songs rather than their main exponents. It took an all-black, independent company to tip the balance—Berry Gordy's Motown. Even when his label was a baby Detroit office, Gordy nursed the ambition of launching a black female diva on a par with such white mainstream stars of his era as Debbie Reynolds or Doris Day.

The experiment began with Mary Wells, Motown's first female star, and the first artist to give them an international profile when "My Guy" went to No. 1 in the UK in 1964. Wells had the intelligence and sense of class that Gordy was looking for, but she was lured away from the label and signed to Twentieth Century Fox on the (unfulfilled) promise of a film contract. A stylized '60s "sharp girl" with her huge eyes, tight mohair skirts and a walk, Wells left Motown in 1964 when she refused to renew the contract she had signed at the age of seventeen. Without Smokey Robinson's focused attention as producer and writer her career foundered, with unremarkable stints on various labels throughout the '60s and '70s. She died of throat cancer in 1992 after decades of litigation with Motown. Although bitter for a long time, she recognized the importance of the label, once saying: "Until Motown, in Detroit, there were three big careers for a black girl. Babies, factories or daywork. Period."

Even though Gordy was an enabler, he did not encourage solidarity or independence among his female artists. "I guess people at Motown figured, if we can disunite The Marvelettes, we can fight them," said Gladys Horton, founder member of the group. She was the one to take the girls' reconstructed blues song "Please Mr Postman" to Berry Gordy, which after some treatment by Motown producers became a No. 1 hit in 1961. The Marvelettes went on to have several Top Ten hits, including "Beechwood 4–5789," but within eighteen months of their initial success, Gordy lost interest and the group dropped from the charts. Although they were able vocalists and arrangers, Horton felt that Motown looked down on them as naïve "hicks from the sticks." Coming from the dirt-track town Inkster, Michigan, they lacked the sophistication of the other female acts. "We weren't pretty city girls from the projects like The Supremes, with nice clothes and make-up on and long nails," she said. "We had no experience of life at all."

Motown became a conduit for upward mobility with the establishment of its famed charm school under the tutelage of Maxine Powell, a dignified lady whose task it was to smooth out the "street" from her girls. For artists like Martha Reeves, this was a challenge. "I had been captain of my cheering team and a tomboy. I had very little grace, and no idea how to be charming—I just knew I could sing," Reeves said in 1994. Sitting in a London hotel suite smoking roll-ups and dressed in a brightly coloured jacket and gold chains, she may not have been the epitome of taste, yet she still exuded grace and poise, giving everyone full attention and courteously greeting the waitress.

*   *   *

Reeves hasn't always been so sanguine. For many years she was locked in disputes with Motown over royalties, and once said, according to writer Gerri Hirshey, "I think I was the first person at Motown to ask where the money was going. And that made me an enemy. Did I find out? Honey, I found my way to the door." Reeves now denies she said that. Feeling her views have been misrepresented, she is usually reluctant to give interviews, but decided to speak out on this occasion partly as a way of laying the battles to rest and partly to get due acknowledgement as one of the key female players in the driving force of Motown. Starting there as a secretary, Reeves had a practical, working knowledge of the company that made her less content to just sing and look decorative.

My relationship was with the producers and musicians. I wasn't an artist or a groupie. I became the A&R secretary: there were sixteen guys in the department and no women. I started keeping records because they weren't. Not only did I love the music, I had compassion for the musicians. I knew how to handle the producers. I think it helped my tracks—I had some of the hottest tracks that came out of Motown, "Nowhere To Run" and "Dancing In The Street" speak for themselves. That was only because I got to know the guys writing them, they looked out for me real good.

Martha and The Vandellas certainly had some of Motown's "blackest" tracks. Reeves's earthy soul voice took girl-group music into a darker, more funky vein—released amid the mid-'60s turmoil of US race riots and civic unrest, Vandellas songs encapsulated the frenzied upheaval of the time. Although she says that the No. 1 worldwide hit "Dancing In The Street" was only about "dancing, getting people united as one again," against the backdrop of the Detroit riots, many took its message to be radical. That radical essence was still there when she performed live in the early '90s. She and two sisters Lois and Delphine were in a Brixton club doing what amounted to a nostalgia show, and when they launched into "Nowhere To Run" the crowd roared. Thirty years dropped before our eyes, as we felt the heat of that intense '60s soul maelstrom. A song she must have sung a thousand times before lived anew.

Though she had a talent Gordy respected—the run of Vandellas hits continued until 1967—Reeves was not the glitzy superstar material he had in mind. Too pushy and outspoken, she defended her Vandellas at every turn and fought for session musicians to be properly paid. It grieved her that even while her group were at the peak of their success, Gordy focused his attention on the "no hit" Supremes.

Nobody was competing at first. We were all hopefuls, all wannabes. We were sisters, and the early Motown Revues were like camping tours or girl scouts. We ate together, we grew together, we learned together . . . you can't take that away. The rivalry started when the groups were separated off, and Berry selected Diana Ross and The Supremes as his favorite pet group. I guess we were all trying to contend for his affection.

Gordy has been condemned for his treatment of The Vandellas, The Marvelettes, and indeed The Velvelettes, another Motown girl group who scored a classic hit in 1964 with "Needle In A Haystack," but he had a clear idea of the girl group he wanted to take "uptown," and these acts did not have the finesse needed to get there. He didn't waste time, and went straight for it when he saw it. Was that cold ruthlessness, or professional instinct? Snobbery within Motown meant the country gals, those with the rougher edges, didn't fit—but if that was the criterion, maybe they were on the wrong label. It wasn't just the rawness that mattered. Although she was one of the finest soul singers of her generation, scoring hits with The Pips like the original "I Heard It Through The Grapevine" and "Help Me Make It Through The Night," Motown act Gladys Knight was too experienced, her delivery almost too mature. It wasn't until she left Motown in 1973 (amid legal difficulties over royalties) for Buddah Records that her career fully flourished. Songs such as "Midnight Train To Georgia" and "The Best Thing That Ever Happened To Me" showed an adult range and depth. In contrast, Gordy's glittering female icon had to have a girlish innocence that would slot perfectly into the young, aspiring pop market. Impossible hopes and expectations were projected on to Motown, and in its search for prestige those who couldn't be groomed into compliance inevitably would remain in the background.

The hunch he had about Miss Ross proved to be correct—even though it took three years to get there. In 1964 The Supremes' second single "Where Did Our Love Go" went straight to No. 1, starting a record run of thirty hit singles up to 1972, twelve of which reached No. 1. One of the first black acts to play New York's Copacabana, they were soul divas who sold massively to the white mainstream, and did more to sustain the girl-group myth than all their forerunners and rivals combined.

"We were our own Disney World," Mary Wilson said, thirty years after that first No. 1. "The Supremes, The Four Tops, The Temptations—we were the rides, we touched the world." The Supremes were the fairy-tale ideal, role models for the aspiring female fans who made up a large proportion of their record buyers. Ross in particular was adept at ladies' talk, exuding the appeal of the girl in the class who dressed the best, knew the best make-up tips, how to get your man, how to get the best man. She appeared open and vulnerable without laying herself on the line, a role that she still performs today.

Although chat-show host Oprah Winfrey tried to pin Ross down during an interview in 1993 on the eve of publication of her unrevealing autobiography *Secrets of a Sparrow,* Ross would not be drawn, protesting, "The girls ignored me in the dressing room and that hurt . . . but, hey, let's not get negative!" Over the years Ross has made several attempts to rehabilitate her reputation, mainly since 1986 when Mary Wilson published her memoirs *Dreamgirl: My Life as a Supreme,* in which she claimed Ross was manipulative, selfish and duplicitous. She also said that Ross was unmoved when Florence Ballard, the third original member of The Supremes, who had the strongest soul voice, was sacked from the group. Ballard resented the fact that she was pushed into the background, while Ross was brought into the limelight. Although nasal and peculiar, Ross's voice was distinctive, and it became the Supremes' trademark, at the expense of Ballard. As blunt and upfront as Ross was tactical, Ballard didn't endear herself to the Motown godfathers early on when she loudly remarked about Gordy: "Ain't that the man who rips his artists off?"

Overweight and drinking to numb her depression, Ballard was forced to leave in 1967. The name of the group was then changed to Diana Ross and The Supremes, emphasizing Motown's decision to single out Ross as the star artist. Her solo career came to fruition when she quit the group in 1970 and went solo, while The Supremes went on to have a few more hits like "Floy Joy" and "Automatically Sunshine" with Jean Terrell at the helm. Meanwhile Ballard's career and health deteriorated. She lived alone on welfare, memories and drink until 1976 when she died of a heart attack at the age of thirty-two. Her death punctured the myth of the three Detroit princesses from the projects, highlighting a grittier story of female friendship and rivalry. Wilson told me:

> I have a huge portrait of Flo near my bed. I wake up every morning and her eyes stare at me. Our friendship never changes, it's very spiritual. She's as alive as ever. I felt the loss when Flo left—that was the end. The connection between the three of us had been broken. It was a very hard time because I was still in the group trying to keep my head above water. I was just sorting out where I wanted to go.

She remained through line-up changes to the bitter end of The Supremes, touring under the name long after the group had been officially disbanded by Motown, having to get accustomed to a lower profile after a decade at the top of the charts. Ross by comparison kept up the superstar momentum, working diligently to fulfil the promise that Gordy saw in her. She employed an expensive, supportive team around her, averaged a major hit a year throughout the '70s and '80s, appeared on Broadway and starred in movies, notably the 1972 biopic *Lady Sings the Blues,* where her portrayal of Billie Holiday was highly acclaimed. One of the main lessons Wilson learned was how divisive and unfair the industry could be:

If you work with friends you have to try and communicate even when it's not the easiest thing to do, especially in business matters. Business gets in the way and you lose a friendship that shouldn't have been lost. That was true with Diana, but money has nothing to do with what we feel inside for each other. The business happened so fast it got out of our hands. But I know in my heart she loves me and I love her.

On the subject Ross is curt and clear. "Mary's book seemed to say that if her life didn't work, it was because I left The Supremes. If Florence Ballard left the group because she was unhappy, I didn't know about it," she said in 1993. "If a person's life isn't working, they want to blame someone else. I'd rather take responsibility for my own life. I no longer see Mary."

Like many women who were stars in the girl-group era, Wilson is still searching for that elusive record deal. She plays corporate dates and gala events for nostalgia fans, and wrote a second book, *Supreme Faith: Someday We'll Be Together,* about her experience as a woman coping with the '60s legacy. "It's a comeback book, about the woman's plight—what happens after women have been major stars. I also do a lecture called 'Dare to Dream,' which is inspirational and motivational, a lesson in what you should and shouldn't do."

She finds it frustrating when "people see you one way and want to keep you that way," and it hurts when record companies say she is a has-been. Maybe Wilson lacked Ross's audacity; she didn't make enough noise. But then, she smiles to herself, "Berry always said I was a quiet rebel. A classy lady rebel."

Daniel Wolff

A CHANGE IS GONNA COME

Sam Cooke was an artist with his feet in two worlds. With hits such as "You Send Me," "Only Sixteen," and "Wonderful World," he is recognized as one of the architects of soul music. Yet his desire for success led him to make compromises to the world of popular music and all of the tuxes and supper club appearances that path entailed. Because of his early death—on December 11, 1964, of a shooting in a sleazy L.A. motel—Cooke has been the subject of a lot of *what ifs*. His posthumously released song, "A Change Is Gonna Come," seemed to point in a new direction. He certainly would have been at the forefront of the soul music movement that he inspired.

ON SUNDAY, September, 15, 1963, Birmingham's 16th Street Church was bombed; fifteen people were injured, four Negro schoolgirls were killed. Protests across the country were immediate and immense. In New Orleans, at a memorial service for the children, police beat the president of the Shreveport NAACP. When Sam Cooke, Bobby Bland, Dion, and Little Willie John played that city's New Orleans Municipal Auditorium on Thursday, September 26, the local Negro paper took the occasion to mention that, among rock & roll fans, anyway, integration seemed to work: "white girls and Negro girls, white boys and Negro boys seated side by side and together whopping it up."

But five days after Cooke's concert, ten thousand people marched on the New Orleans city hall chanting "Freedom!" and accusing Mayor Shiro of not living up to his promises of integration. That night, the mayor appeared on TV to say he was unimpressed by the demonstration and felt Negro ministers "should devote their time to make useful citizens of 'their people.' "

Sam, still touring the area, pulled into Shreveport early on the morning of October 8. As usual, most of the package stayed at the Negro hotel, the Royal, on Marlin Street, but Cooke had asked S. R. Crain to book four rooms at Shreveport's Holiday Inn, and S. R. had gotten a telegram back confirming the reservations. They arrived at around six in the morning, his brother Charles driving a Maserati that Sam had recently picked up secondhand from singer Eddie Fisher. The car was in fine condition except that it had a short somewhere in the electrical system that made the horn go off when you took a sharp turn. So, as Charles pulled into the Holiday Inn driveway, there was a quick beep, and then Sam went to register.

The motel clerk took one look at Mr. Cooke and said the rooms weren't ready. "Look," Sam replied, "I wired. Why *aren't* the rooms ready?" The only answer was they wouldn't be ready till twelve o'clock. At that, Sam went off. "Well, man, what am I supposed to do? Sit around your lobby till noon?"

After a few choice words for the clerk, Sam decided to leave: he was tired and it wasn't worth arguing with the man. He told Barbara and the others, they put their bags back in the car, and the group drove back down to the Royal Hotel to get some sleep. The Maserati's horn went off briefly again when Charles pulled out. They had barely unloaded at the Royal when five squad cars came squealing up and arrested Sam, Barbara, Charles, and S. R.

The headline in the *New York Times* read, "Negro Band Leader Held in Shreveport." The paper reported that Sam and his associates were arrested for disturbing the peace "after they tried to register at a white motel." The police description was that Sam "repeatedly blew the horn, yelled and woke guests . . ." although, in Cliff White's words, "From the parking lot through the front of the hotel to the lobby, there was hardly a disturbance."

Never mind why they were there, the inside of a Southern jail was no place any of them wanted to be—especially with all this talk about Northern agitators. Sam explained who he was, but none of the white cops seemed very impressed. The patrolman on duty duly noted their names and ages. When he got to Crain, he said "You with this show, boy?" S. R., fiercely proud, stood clutching his tour briefcase. "Yes, I'm with them." Okay, then he was under arrest, too, for attempting to stay at a white motel. Crain—somewhere between angry and ingratiating—remembers mentioning how, actually, it was a red motel. The cop didn't laugh. "Throw that grip over here, and you go around there."

Crain asked him not to throw the grip; his money was in there. With that, the officer decided to have a little fun with the old Negro. "How much money you got in there?" he said, smiling.

"I guess I got about, uh, fifteen thousand dollars."

The cop just laughed and signaled to have the case opened. In it lay Sam's share of the profit from a couple of weeks of touring. The cops were bug-eyed. After a series of calls, they let the group off, Crain paying the bond from his briefcase full of $100 and $500 bills. Because of what was happening in Birmingham, the national press jumped on the incident, and it helped make Sam's reputation as a civil rights crusader. Meanwhile, the important work he'd been doing all along—in the music and at his shows—went largely unnoticed.

Sam and Barbara returned to Los Angeles long enough for Sam to stick his head into the SAR offices and check how the latest singles by Johnnie Taylor, the Valentinos, and Mel Carter were doing. Then he flew to New York for what had become his annual week at the Apollo. His last appearance had set a new attendance record; this time, he was headlining with Motown's Mary Wells, working on her eighth Top Forty hit. Sam's picture was all over the city; he and the band were in an ad for L&M cigarettes and getting some teasing for it from the likes of Cassius Clay, who was also staying at the Hotel Teresa. Clay was in town to plug a record he'd cut, "I Am the Greatest," and to appear on Jack Paar's show to hype his upcoming title fight against Sonny Liston. Nobody, recalls fight fan Curtis Womack, thought he had a chance of winning; he looked too young and pretty for one thing. Womack remembers Clay hanging around the hotel, always on the prowl for the girls that found their way to Cooke. The only celebrities that impressed the boxer, according to his friend the photographer Howard Bingham, were R&B stars. Clay "loved Fats Domino, Little Richard, Jackie Wilson, Sam Cooke . . . all those guys . . . It's like he's still a kid, looking up, and they're the ones on the pedestal."

The opening show at the Apollo was at twelve-thirty; Bobby Schiffman arrived to find lines around the block. Soon the theater was jammed to the walls, and Schiffman remembers thinking gleefully, "This is going to be the biggest week in the history of this theater! We are going to plow people in here every day to capacity!" At two o'clock, news reached New York that President Kennedy had been shot in Dallas. Frank Schiffman announced it from the Apollo stage, and the crowd was stunned. Some shouted, several women got hysterical. Like the rest of America, Harlem stayed home and watched television that weekend. Sam canceled his shows and flew back to Los Angeles. There you could drive down Western Avenue's nightclub row for six or eight blocks without seeing another car. The *Los Angeles Sentinel* reported that the "tan population" hadn't wept so unashamedly since Medgar Evers died.

But not all the "tans" felt that way. Clay's friend and adviser Malcolm

X would soon be disciplined by his fellow Muslims, ostensibly for commenting that Kennedy's death was "chickens coming home to roost." Sam and Malcolm were friends by now; Alex remembers the Muslim leader coming down to New York's Warwick Hotel to see Cooke, and Jess Rand recalls a dinner at a seafood restaurant in Harlem. Malcolm "absolutely shined me off," says Rand, till the white man finally asked, "Do you really hate me that much?" "No," Malcolm replied, "I don't hate you as you. I hate you—what the Caucasian people stand for in this country."

Now, the week of Kennedy's death, Malcolm wrote an open letter to Jackie Robinson: ". . . you Negro leaders whose bread and butter depend on your ability to make your white boss think you have all these Negroes 'under control,' better be thankful that I wasn't in Mississippi after Medgar Evers was murdered, nor in Birmingham after the murder of those four innocent little Negro girls." It surprised some of his friends that Sam had begun to hang out with people who talked this way. Two weeks after Kennedy's assassination, Clay and Cooke appeared together on the nationally televised *Jerry Lewis Show*. Afterward, Clay invited him down to Miami for the Liston fight at the end of February. Malcolm would be there. Sam accepted happily.

*　　*　　*

Sam was now determined to spend less time on the road. He wanted to finally make good on his promise to concentrate on the business end of his career, and he also had a new project in mind that combined his ideas on civil rights and music.

The project centered around Harold Battiste. Battiste had been at that first Dale Cook session in New Orleans. He'd helped transcribe "You Send Me" over at Specialty, and for a while after Bumps Blackwell left he'd worked as Art Rupe's A&R man. After arranging and playing on a number of New Orleans indy hits, Battiste—a man of considerable pride and energy—got tired of the setup whereby outside, mostly white-owned labels profited off the crack local musicians. In 1961, he decided to try to organize the Crescent City's music scene and formed the All for One (A.F.O.) Executives: a corporation of the best of New Orleans musicians. Battiste brought together saxophonist Red Tyler (the same who'd written "Forever" for Dale Cook), Chuck Badie on bass, John Boudreaux on drums, and Melvin Lastie on cornet.

The theory behind the A.F.O., as he told author John Broven, was that instead of getting a flat fee, "musicians who play on the session should own the session." Battiste knew full well how much the A.F.O. threatened the music industry. Far beyond black-owned companies like SAR or Detroit's Motown, this was the equivalent of automobile workers claiming to own the cars that came off their assembly lines. For a brief time, it worked. At the end of 1961, the A.F.O. had a giant #3 hit with Barbara George's "I Know" (one of the songs Sam called for in "Havin' a Party"). Then the A.F.O.'s distribution deal fell apart, and other local musicians began to resent its musical monopoly. By the fall of 1963, they arrived in Los Angeles, having essentially been run out of New Orleans.

If anything California proved tougher, and they were on the verge of giving up altogether when Battiste and Lastie happened to drop by the SAR offices on a day Zelda needed somebody to write lead sheets. The working relationship soon grew. Sam, a longtime admirer of the band, knew the A.F.O. could help both his music and his label. "I hate to see you guys break up," he told Tyler. "I'm going to have each of you guys on a hundred-dollar retainer a week." It saved the group, but Battiste hadn't come West just to be part of a studio band again. He had an idea.

"I wanted to set up something in southeast or South-Central Los Angeles to facilitate a lot of the black talent. I developed a thing—we called it the Soul Stations. The concept was a series of small offices in the black community that would allow the talent in the community to have a place to come and present themselves, present their material, in an atmosphere where they felt nonthreatened." As a kid, Sam had seen all the groups that had come out of Bronzeville; he knew the deep well of singers in gospel; but, even more, the Soul Stations appealed to his growing sense of pride. As Battiste remembers it, the whole project was based on a single question about black music: "Man, if this is really ours, why don't we own it?"

Sam decided to bankroll not just the band, but Battiste's concept. The A.F.O. found a little storefront on Vermont and 37th, near USC, and Sam paid the rent as well as buying some inexpensive recording equipment. He called it Soul Station #1: the first in a series. It was little more than an audition studio at first, but it held the germs of larger concepts. "I remember, vividly, sitting at the house [on Ames Street]," Battiste recounts, "and we got to talking about the racial things. . . . We were talking almost in the realm of the Black Muslim kind of thing. About trying to find solutions for the tremendous problems our people were having. Sam was really concerned about that."

Cassius and Malcolm were having their influence, but Sam's concern also came from his own background of pride and independence. More and more, his friends saw him reading books on black and African history; Cliff White in his unassuming way turned him on to W. E. B. DuBois and Booker T. Washington. "Sam," says Cliff, "was deep, deep into that business."

Battiste's concept also meshed with Sam's anger at the injustices of the music industry. White can remember Cooke walking in on some of the early Hugo and Luigi sessions and stopping in his tracks to ask: "Well, you mean to tell me out of all the musicians in this city, there are only two black musicians who can play?"—then refusing to record till they changed the band. Curtis Womack recalls a knock-down, drag-out Sam had with some union guys at the Apollo. "Nigger, we gonna squash you like a roach!" they yelled, and Sam responded in a rage, "All they got is a charter. They're taking people's money." According to Curtis, Sam was talking about forming a black equivalent with performers like James Brown and Ray Charles: something like R. H. Harris's Quartet Union.

Now, the A.F.O. became Sam's recording band. First he brought them in to fill out the *Good News* LP. On songs like his remake of the country tune "Tennessee Waltz," their dance-smart soul horns, Badie's heavy bass line, and the second-line drumming added an edge to Cooke's modified supper-club sound. The same holds true for Sam's remake of Johnnie Morisette's "Twisting Place" (with changed lyrics, a slowed beat, and a new title, "Meet Me at Mary's Place"). The *Good News* session also got an enormous boost from its backup singers, the Soul Stirrers. Sam gloried in their familiar harmonies. Then, blurring distinctions further, he brought the A.F.O. to the Stirrers' session, where they cut "Oh, Mary Don't You Weep" and "Lookin' Back" for SAR.

Sam finished up the *Ain't That Good News* LP with a ballad session that included Earl Palmer and a big string section. On tunes like Battiste's "Falling in Love" and Irving Berlin's "Sitting in the Sun," he doesn't try to jazz up the melody or even "interpret" in any discernible way. Instead, his voice aches over the heartbreak as Rene Hall's string arrangement swells in perfect accompaniment. He sounds like a man released—and that's particularly clear in the one Cooke original done that night, a tune he'd been telling his friends "scared him."

"Blowin' in the Wind" had continued to bother Sam. "Geez," he told Alex, "a white boy writing a song like that?" It was a challenge to Sam—as a black man and as a songwriter—and he began working on an answer. Crain can remember him humming the tune on the road through Louisiana and Texas before he finally got back to Los Angeles and finished it. "If you ever listen to a Soul Stirrer song," says the old manager of the group, "you'd recognize it." Of course, if you ever heard "Blowin' in the

Wind," you'd recognize it, too. Or Sam's earlier hit, "Nothing Can Change This Love." Or any number of old country blues. Part of what's extraordinary about the song—which Sam called "A Change Is Gonna Come"—is how it combines forms, and in the process, combines meanings.

"Change" opens in a wash of strings with a French horn calling, then Palmer finds an easy beat, and Sam comes in testifying—his voice up high in its range and urgent. He was born by the river in a little tent. If that sounds like gospel—born again in some tent-revival baptism—when he adds that he's been running ever since, we're into the blues. Badie's heartbeat of a bass line gives an undertone of sadness as Sam hits the chorus for the first time: a change is gonna come. Next, he borrows a line from "Ol' Man River"—afraid of living, scared of dying—and, in one phrase, the Reverend's son passes out of the realm of gospel, announcing that he doesn't know what's up there "beyond the sky." Still, a change is gonna come.

These first two verses, general enough to be from some old spiritual, call up the whole scarred history of his people. Then Sam brings us to the present. he goes downtown to the movies and gets told he can't hang around. "This was him talking about these kids going to the sit-ins," said Alex, and many have taken this song to be a musical equivalent of Dr. King's philosophy. Up to this point, it might be, but if you look at "Change" as a sermon, the song's bridge is where we head toward the lesson. In Dr. King's speeches, it was often the "moral curve of the universe" that guaranteed God would eventually bring freedom to His people. But Cooke's already declared he doesn't know what's up there, and in the bridge, when he goes and asks his brother for help, he gets knocked back to his knees. It's a brutally realistic observation of what had gone down during the past summer of 1963. Nevertheless, "Change" ends with a statement of faith: there've been times, Sam admits, he didn't think he could make it; now he thinks he can. A change is gonna come. What sort of faith—what kind of change? We aren't given that, only the rising ache of his voice over the final sweep of sound.

After Sam's death, many of his friends concluded that he'd been scared of "Change" because it was an omen of his own passing. But it's equally possible that he was scared by the song's emotional and artistic leap. "A Change Is Gonna Come" is Sam Cooke taking the chance of commenting on current events—a risk all his hardheaded careerism argued against. When Battiste heard it, it seemed like the culmination of all their talk about race: "one way to express how he was feeling about what he needed to do." While "Change" can be taken as pure observation—as general as some ancient slave chant—it can also read as the story of one man's life: the tent by Clarksdale's Sunflower River, the sorrow too personal to name. It may have scared Sam because the Ivy League crooner, the sexy soul man, had chosen to reveal himself.

Finally, what pushes it beyond a song like Dylan's "Blowin' in the Wind" is how it tries to unite its audience. "Change" crosses musical barriers, combining gospel, blues, the nightclub ballad, and the protest song. It wants to be speaking at the same time to Sister Flute, to the drunk on the corner, to the white ladies in their gowns and the kids at the sit-ins. It implies they all have something in common. All the divisions come together here—in his voice—and it carries us over. No wonder the song scared him.

Patricia Smith

LIFE ACCORDING TO MOTOWN

No comment necessary.

A THIN layer of Vaseline and a thick pair of sweatsocks made your legs look bigger, made the muscles of your calves bulge. So when you jumped rope or when you just WALKED, the boys all came around, they sniffed at you like hot, hungry dogs, their pelvises just wouldn't sit still.

And you always had to make your hair look like more hair than it was. First you crammed the pores of your scalp with grease, then you flattened your hair with a pressing comb until it lay flat and black upside your head like ink. I was always trying to work a couple of rubberbands up on my little bit of hair, and the result could have been called pigtails—until the rubberbands popped off, that is.

If you lived on the west side of Chicago in the '60s and your hair was long and wavy and your skin was cream and your legs shone like glass, your ticket was as good as written.

But if you were truly bone black and your hair practically choked on its kinks, you waited for the music to give you a shape.

The Marvelettes made me pretty, Smokey wailed for just a little bit of me, and the Temptations taught me to wait, wait, wait, for that perfect love.

Every two weeks, a new 45 hit the streets, but I already knew it, crying in my room under the weight of an imaginary lover, breathing steam onto mirrors, pretend slow dancing in the arms of a seriously fine young thang who rubbed at the small of my back with a sweet tenor.

In the real world the boys avoided me like creamed corn—but I was the supreme mistress of Motown, wise in the ways of love, pretending I knew why my blue jeans had begun to burn.

Those devils from Detroit were broiling my blood with the beat. They were teaching me that wanting meant waiting. They were teaching me what it meant to be a black girl.

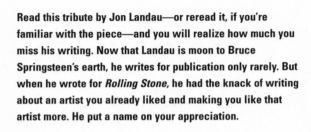

<u>Jon Landau</u>

OTIS REDDING, KING OF THEM ALL

Read this tribute by Jon Landau—or reread it, if you're familiar with the piece—and you will realize how much you miss his writing. Now that Landau is moon to Bruce Springsteen's earth, he writes for publication only rarely. But when he wrote for *Rolling Stone,* he had the knack of writing about an artist you already liked and making you like that artist more. He put a name on your appreciation.

MUSICIANS see themselves in different ways. Some, the rarest, are artists prepared to make any sacrifice to preserve the integrity of their art. Others are poseurs who adopt the artist's stance without the art, who therefore appeal to the segment of the audience that likes to think of itself as being serious but isn't. And then there are those performers who are neither of these, but see themselves as entertainers. They make no pretense of aiming at any particular artistic standard, but are openly and honestly concerned with pleasing crowds and being successful. Such a man was Otis Redding.

Redding deeply desired success and he deeply desired security, the title of one of his earliest hits. To acquire them he became an entertainer, which is what he knew how to do best. He saw it as his way out of a dreary lower-class existence in Macon, Georgia. And, until his death in an airplane crash last December, he devoted all his energy to achieving his goal.

However, given these motivations, it is still not at all strange to find that Redding developed a style that was deeply personal, intimate, and not nearly as commercial as it might have been. And that indicates that Redding did not commit himself to doing only that which would make him popular. He couldn't. He didn't have the ability that would have allowed him to see which way the wind was blowing, and to head in that direction. His understanding of music was not something that he could put on or take off, depending on chart trends. He was truly a "folk" artist and he couldn't escape the musical climate which surrounded him all his life, and out of which he created his own music.

Wanting to make good is characteristic of all soul artists, for they all have similar backgrounds, James Brown as much as Wilson Pickett as much as Redding himself. All are from rural parts of the south. Their musical influences are limited to folk, country and western, blues, gospel, and some pop. And they have to fasten together their own styles from this limited background. The limitations of their adolescent encounters with music often preclude the possibility of true flexibility. They have no choice but to put all they know into the one form of music they have found to express themselves in. The lack of intellectuality and detachment which is necessarily a part of this expression is responsible for the resultant intimacy of the music. Soul music approaches folk music in its lack of self-consciousness. And it is art, even though the artist may not seek to do anything beyond entertain.

Otis Redding was the most recent, most influential, and most talented of a long line of such musicians. He based a good deal of his style on two of his really important predecessors: Little Richard, one of his boyhood idols, and Sam Cooke. During Redding's childhood years, which he spent in Dawson and Macon, Georgia, Little Richard was creating his dynamic, shouting kind of R&B and putting it high on the pop charts. Because Richard was also a native of Macon, he made a deep impression on Otis. This influence can be heard most directly on his first album, *Pain in My Heart,* recorded in 1962 and 1963. On it there are several cuts which sound so much like Little Richard it is hard to tell the difference.

It didn't take long for Redding to outgrow his reliance on Little Richard, but he never outgrew his love for Sam Cooke or the influence Cooke's music had on him. Cooke was the top star in his field from 1957, when he had the number one hit of "You Send Me," until his tragic death in 1964. There is no soul star who would not credit him with being a major stylistic influence; most, in fact, would say he was *the* important influence. He had a soft, mellow voice which could be unbearably personal even singing the most mediocre tunes. Redding included Cooke's songs on all but one of his albums, and one of his most popular numbers in performance was always Cooke's "Shake."

Redding's entrance into show business is a straightforward story. He paid his dues early with a group called Johnny Jenkins and the Pinetoppers. In his late teens, he became vocalist of the group and he got a lot of experience playing for demanding audiences along the Southern college fraternity circuit. In 1962, Jenkins was to record a number for Atlantic Records without Redding, but he asked Otis to drive him to Memphis, where the sessions were scheduled. When Jenkins got through recording, there were still 40 minutes of studio time remaining. Otis got permission to record a tune he had written called "These Arms of Mine." This became Otis' first release, and it launched him as a solo artist. Memphis became his recording home and he made all his records with the wonderful musicians who played on "These Arms of Mine," namely Booker T. Jones and the MG's and the horns of the Mar-Keys.

Between 1962 and 1964 Redding recorded a series of soul ballads. These songs were characterized by unabashedly sentimental lyrics begging forgiveness or asking a girl friend to come home. The titles are revealing: "Pain in My Heart," "Mr. Pitiful," and "That's How Strong My Love Is," the last, one of Otis' finest recordings. He soon became known as "Mr. Pitiful" from the hit song, and earned a reputation as the leading performer of soul ballads.

Otis' big leap, both as an artist and as a star, came in 1965, a crucial year in pop music marked by the advent of the Rolling Stones. It was also the year that modern soul began to take shape. In the summer of '65, Wilson Pickett's "Midnight Hour" was climbing the charts (recorded with the same musicians that Redding used) and James and the Flames hit with "Papa's Got a Brand New Bag." In addition, the Stones acknowledged the importance of soul music as a basis for the new rock by releasing *Out Of Our Heads,* which included their versions of hits by Solomon Burke, Don Covay, Marvin Gaye, and Otis. And, finally, the summer of 1965 was when Otis released his own beautiful composition, "Respect."

"Respect" was a smash on the soul charts. Artistically, it was a driving, pounding record which showed off the unrepressed quality of the Memphis sound at its very best. Otis' singing was frantic, powerful and charming. It got him out of the cul-de-sac of pure soul ballads and, along with "I've Been Loving You Too Long" (his finest soul ballad), was the highest state of artistic development he had attained. It was the first record which was pure Redding.

He was now self-reliant and no longer leaned on anyone else's style.

Unfortunately for Redding, white America waited for Aretha Franklin and 1967 to dig "Respect." But the sizable success of Redding's recording in the Negro market indicated that his greatest hope for making it with pop audiences would be with the faster songs. The slow, eloquent, majestic ballads he sang so well simply required too much patience from a car-radio audience. Otis followed "Respect" with his super-hyped-up version of "Satisfaction," repaying the Stones the admiration they had shown him. The Stones soon pronounced Redding's version the best they had heard. It became his best-selling single, and if the white DJs who control suburban radio had given it more airplay, the record could have been a giant hit.

But here Redding encountered a final hindrance on the road to complete success, as have Chuck Berry and James Brown. None of these artists make nice music. In fact, some people might even think it vulgar. The mass white audience was not ready for him.

In spite of this, Otis Redding was a fantastically popular performer. He had the ghetto circuit—Harlem and Watts—locked up. He was successful financially and owned a huge ranch home in Macon. Still, I would guess that fame was as important to him as financial reward, as he made clear in his rewrite of the Temptations' "My Girl," where he sings, "I don't need no money, all I need is my fame."

He continued to release soul ballads even though he knew that fast tunes were the key to success in the pop market (as his good friends at Stax, Sam and Dave, recently proved with their gold record of "Soul Man"). Redding loved his music, and when he talked about it in interviews he revealed a deep understanding of what it was all about. The main feature of modern soul, according to Redding, was the stomp beat. The old-fashioned shuffle was an anachronism; only one of his important records had it—"Shake." But beyond any musical understanding of the imperatives of his own style, Redding never was confused about his purpose as an entertainer. He believed in communication. Every device and technique he created was designed to further his communicative potentiality. At the root of Redding's conception of communication was simplicity. Redding's music was always deliberately simple. Direct, unintellectual, honest, and concise.

In 1965, Redding's style reached artistic fruition. Early in that year, his album, *Dictionary of Soul,* was released. The cover was a typically tasteless Stax-Volt cover, but the record inside was the finest ever to come out of Memphis, truly one of the finest pop recordings of the decade, and certainly it is the best example of modern soul ever recorded.

Dictionary of Soul indicated finally that if Otis were to make it outside of the regular soul audience, it would have to be because soul music was making it with the pop audience. Redding was not going to change his music. He knew how to do his thing, loved it, had already received recognition for it, and was confident that his turn would come. It's doubtful the idea of altering his style to boost record sales ever occurred to him. He had perfected his own thing: his vocal syntax, his rapport with his sidemen, and his linear, totally committed music. In *Dictionary*, the result of this perfection is evident throughout. Religious in its emotional intensity, it expresses a way of life. Particularly awesome is the consummate skill with which the soul ballads were performed, notably "You're Still My Baby" and "Try a Little Tenderness." He sang the blues like no one else on "Hawg For You," and he breathed new life into the Beatles' "Day Tripper." Here is Redding's blood and guts, and anyone who hears *Dictionary* recognizes its greatness instantly.

While Redding continued to tour Negro stops and consolidate his status in the soul hierarchy (second only to James Brown in terms of personal popularity), an unusual train of events took place. Soul music, largely through the efforts of Aretha Franklin, began to take over the pop charts. It soon became clear the new wave would be the earthy Memphis soul that Redding had been practicing for the preceding five years. "Soul Man" was a success. Redding was next in line. A throat operation, however, postponed Redding's chance to cut a single at the most opportune moment. In spite of this minor setback, the likelihood of Redding's imminent success was recognized by one of the prime movers in the modern soul movement, Jerry Wexler.

Redding's friend, guitarist and sometime-collaborator Steve Cropper best expresses why those who knew Redding felt he was verging on superstardom. In an interview some months before Redding's death, he said: "Otis is the only one I can think of now who does it [sings soul] best. He gets over to the people what he's talking about, and he does it in so few words that if you read them on paper they might not make any sense. But when you hear the way he sings them, you know exactly what he is talking about." Here is the key again: communication. Just how good Redding was at it is hard to describe. I only saw him perform once, at a revue in Boston. The audience was overwhelmingly black and sat through two and a half hours of soul music before Redding made his appearance. The crowd was growing restless and had heard too many singers say "Let me see you clap your hands" and all that. Then Redding came on. The first thing he did was say "Let me see you clap your hands." You immediately forgot the preceding two and a half hours and clapped your hands. You knew instantly you were in the presence of an absolute master. Then he said "Shake" and kept on repeating it until everybody said it. The band still had not played a single note. At last he started to sing, and then he danced, joked and performed until you finally understood.

Otis Redding's music had the power to make you dig yourself. The people who were really close to Redding's music, the people whose way of life Redding expressed, those people will tell you that is what soul is all about. They will tell you that Wilson Pickett has style and that James Brown has sex. But Otis Redding had soul. He was truly the king of them all.

Robert Gordon

DAN AND SPOONER

Most of the great soul recordings came from either Memphis or Muscle Shoals, Alabama, and at its root, soul music was America fully integrated. While the singers might be black, a lot of the musicians, producers and writers, were pure Deep-South white. Dan Penn and Spooner Oldham were major parts of the soul music universe and here they reminisce about those days, their memories bouncing up and down the highway between Memphis and the Shoals. Penn and Oldham wrote a number of great songs together, but Penn's greatest collaborations were probably with Chips Moman, including "The Dark End of the Street," the all-time greatest cheating song, recorded memorably by such great singers as Gram Parsons, Percy Sledge, Aretha Franklin, the Rev. Clarence Carter, and Penn himself. Sometimes called "the white Ray Charles," Penn is the Memphis *griot* who starts off the story. After years of lurking behind the scenes with only intermittent recordings, Penn decided to make a solo album in the early 1990s, and Robert Gordon was there.

DAN PENN speaks in the softest of southern drawls. His manner today is sagelike, a fine whiskey that's mellowed in a fine oak barrel. The wiry speed demon of yore has been replaced by a ruminator with a trucker's gut. The fire still crackles when his poker face breaks and the corners of a grin creep around the toothpick he chews. Once the wildest of them all, or perhaps the most driven, Penn today spends time in his garden and working on vintage cars. "Me and [Chips] Moman had tried to produce some records together, but I was having a pretty hard time getting my ideas across," he continues. "So I told him, 'I want to produce a record and I want to do it my way and I want to do it by myself.' It didn't make no difference to me who it was, I would have cut anybody. I was twenty-six years old, I was ready to cut a hit. Chips was big friends with this disc jockey, Roy Mack, and Chips had him bring this band in. Their little singer was acting kind of smart-aleck, so I told Roy to bring me another singer and

I'd cut 'em. I handed them a tape with some Wayne Carson songs on there, and told them to pick anything they wanted from this tape, but make sure that we do 'The Letter.' They came Saturday morning about ten o'clock and they had Alex Chilton with them, who I'd never seen. We started running 'The Letter' down, and he sounded pretty good. I coached him a little, not much, told him to say 'aer-o-plane,' told him to get a little gruff, and I didn't have to say anything else to him, he was hooking 'em, a natural singer."

This natural singer, at sixteen, had come up a natural artist. His father's day gig was commercial lighting, but in the glow of the moon he was a well-respected jazz pianist. His mother ran an art gallery out of their expansive home, and the couple's fondness for hospitality created a salon atmosphere in the early 1960s, attracting artists like William Eggleston and Burton Callicott. In a time when hi-fi was rare and record collections more so, Sidney Chilton, Alex's father, had both. From his bedroom at night, Alex heard the sounds of blues and jazz, Chet Baker, Ray Charles, Dave Brubeck, Mingus wafting up the stairs and into his bedroom.

*   *   *

The Box Tops' John Evans remembers picking up the Wayne Carson demo tape the night before the session. "We were going to rehearse and we played the tape. I think there were three songs. I've forgotten one altogether. There was one called either 'White Velvet Cat' or 'Pink Velvet Cat' that was unbelievably bad. Imagine a small-town, country-influenced songwriter growing up on fifties rock and roll and trying to write a sophisticated slightly jazzy song based on his experiences at a local bar seeing a beautiful woman. On the other hand, imagine him trying to do something like the Everly Brothers, and that's 'The Letter.' " The band played the demo at their rehearsal on Friday night. Everyone laughed at the cat song and agreed that "The Letter" was the one to cut. While Evans began mapping out the chord changes, one member went off to meet his girlfriend, Alex and another went to get some beer; rehearsal never really happened.

They showed up at the studio promptly at ten A.M. on Saturday. Evans describes Dan Penn's arrival, shortly behind them: "He was wearing this polyester narrow-brimmed fishing hat thing on the back of his head, a white T-shirt with a pack of Lucky Strikes rolled up in his sleeve. We didn't see Lucky Strikes much back then, so that put him on another planet. Also, we came from schools where you had to wear the right brands of the right clothing. One thing you would never do was wear false copies of madras handwoven cloth from India. But he was wearing madras that looked like it came from Kmart. He was wearing Bermuda shorts down to his kneecaps, and sports socks with different colored stripes. And hi-top tennis shoes. He walked in, drawling his talk, and Danny, our drummer, in his white button-down-collar Gant shirt, said, 'Where's Chips?' Dan said, 'Chips won't be in today, I'll be cutting you.' We get introduced all around, and Danny, who'd cut with Chips before, is behind this guy's back, rolling his eyes like, What's wrong with this weirdo and why did Chips do this to us?"

John Evans says "The Letter" took over thirty takes. Penn was twisting knobs and making studio adjustments for about half of them. The rest were working up the song, getting a single take all the way through, the lead vocals becoming slightly more gruff each time. The studio was still moaning: Penn had to get on his knees to change the routing of cords through a patch bay; Chilton remembers that the recording console had big dials for faders, like a radio station board. There was no Leslie speaker for the Hammond organ; instead it was miked from the little built-in cone near the player's feet, giving it a funeral parlor sound. By three o'clock, the band was done.

Penn: "And we cut 'The Letter.' One Saturday morning. Put some strings and horns on it with Mike Leach and then me and this black fellow that used to hang around the studio, we took the jet sound off a record in the office next to the control room. He put the needle on the acetate for me, and I went inside and I was working to get it in the right spot. We got lucky and I mixed it down, and I thought it was okay. 'I'm a Believer' was happening then, little organ going *chink chink chink*. You'll hear a little of that in 'The Letter.' I thought I got my licks in on a little rock and roll record. I didn't think, 'This is a million seller.' But it was."

*   *   *

"I was coming back through Memphis around 1990, been down in Alabama, and I thought I'd slip over to the old American and see where we'd made all the records." Dan Penn is speaking. "I drove up there and I couldn't find it. The building was nowhere to be seen. I pulled my car up there and sat for a little bit and said, Yeah, there was the control room and here's where he was when we were putting the jet plane on 'The Letter.' Here's where it all happened. It was real strange to see that place gone— as much as had gone down over there. I felt kind of empty, useless, kind of sad. And glad, too, like, this is where we done it, thank God for this little place. But that's Memphis. I'm sure the Stax people, when they pull up over where their building used to be, they must feel the same way. Memphis scraped them away."

Dan Penn's drawl is soft as cotton, slow and thick as mud. Where he's from in Vernon, Alabama, there must be plenty of people who sound just like him, but somehow the forces of life cloverleafed around Dan Penn, creativity intersecting with calculation, poetry getting tangled up in daily language, the passions of black and white culture twining themselves around a country boy, allowing him to effortlessly capture human emotions. His songs sound as truthful today as they did two and three decades ago: "Do Right Woman," "At the Dark End of the Street," "Cry Like a Baby." He began on the fraternity circuit with the soulful Mark V and later with the grittier Pallbearers, who carried him onto the stage in a casket. His vocals, gruff like Chilton's Box Tops era, can be heard on his 1972 debut album, *Nobody's Fool.* His second album, with the working title *Emmett the Singing Ranger Live in the Woods,* was produced by Jim Dickinson, mixed by Penn, and is now languishing in an unknown corner of the Arista vaults (probably near the same forgotten crevice where the Goldwax masters lay). In 1982, he released a gospel album about which he says, "I wouldn't call it great." In late 1993 I was present while Penn recorded a new album in Muscle Shoals for Sire Records, released in 1994 as *Do Right Man.*

The Alabama musical environment was even more insulated from national trends than Memphis's. The story is told of one musician accidentally walking in on a prominent Muscle Shoals producer while he was using the toilet. This producer, involved in bringing the world many hits of the 1960s and 1970s which remain staples of oldies radio—this producer was discovered not to be seated on the toilet bowl, but rather crouching on it, his feet on the rim and his knees around his chin, the technique acquired in the outhouses of his youth which kept his toes from being nibbled on.

Radio was their link with the outer world. "When I first heard Presley I was as enthralled as anybody," Penn says. "Sun was knockout. But it didn't last all that long, because as soon as he started making those slick movies and those funny little teenybopper records, well I slid away real fast and I never did go back. Here comes Ray Charles and then I don't have to worry about it no more because I know which way I'm going." Ray Charles led to Bobby Bland, whose singing was so gutsy that Penn puts him in a pantheon high and separate. In 1993, when Penn was recording his Sire album, he insisted that the photographer shoot him in front of the

Muscle Shoals Sound Studio, where he posed in a hat and sunglasses, a coat thrown over his shoulder in direct imitation of and adulation for Bobby Bland's *Two Steps from the Blues*.

Rock and roll didn't get it for Dan Penn, two steps from Bobby Bland. "Chuck Berry didn't register on my little funk meter. He was cute and he was smart, but he never went to church. I never heard that in his voice. And if I can't hear that in your voice, I don't want to listen very long. It's gotta have that soul. Bobby Bland, Ray Charles, Aretha Franklin—Chuck Berry's over there, *'chinkalinkaching,'* and these guys are *serious*." Penn got serious early on, selling a country song to Conway Twitty, "Is a Bluebird Blue." (Not a man of means, Penn was spotted shortly thereafter eating a large steak. "Man with a Conway Twitty song," he said, "can eat what he wants.") When he was interviewed on the radio, the disc jockey said, "Tell us something about yourself, Dan," and teenaged Dan gave his height and weight. And that was it. He'd told 'em something. He's always stood out as someone who knows a little more, shows a little less, and probably has a really good idea if it can be drawn out of him.

In 1967, in the aftermath of the British Invasion, Penn turned out "At the Dark End of the Street," a collaboration with his friend Chips Moman. Pilled up at a music convention in Nashville, they took a break from a poker game, went to a piano, and hammered out the song in less than an hour, returning to play another hand. "We were always wanting to come up with the best cheatin' song. Ever. Me and Rick Hall began looking for the *best* cheatin' song years before 'Steal Away.' I don't know why 'Dark End' is so great. I guess it's the word 'street.' Everybody's interested in that word. The sounds that we were getting back then was the sounds of the street. And streets change. Now we've got *boomboompa boom chichichi,* and that's what the street is now, but in 1967, 'At the Dark End of the Street,' that had the street. I like to collaborate because two heads are better than one. It's easier to perform the miracle. And the miracle is, Can we jerk it out of the air or can't we. There are all kind of ideas always floating around. Other than Spooner Oldham, I guess Moman would be the closest person I ever come to breathing together with. All writers, music people, they can be playing poker, they can be swimming, whatever they're doing, and all they really want is another great song."

Spooner Oldham is a boyhood friend of Penn's who followed shortly behind him to American Sound from Muscle Shoals. Oldham joined the studio staff as a songwriter and also played keyboards on some sessions; this was when two keyboardists were as common as two guitarists. "Dan was living in Vernon, Alabama, when I met him," says the gentle Oldham, one of the few who speak slower than Penn, whose voice is even thicker and softer. "He'd come up to Muscle Shoals occasionally, to a little piano room over the drugstore. I'd written a couple of songs that I'd never showed anybody. I didn't really know any songwriters and there was no market here at the time. So we decided to get together one night and we wrote three or four songs. I can't attest to the quality or integrity, but we did realize that we could sit down and sing and play our instruments and write together. And we've just continued."

I learned all about Spooner Oldham's keyboard playing while watching him smoke a cigarette. After years of admiring his keyboard playing—on soul records, on Bob Dylan records, Ry Cooder, Neil Young, the Box Tops—I spent a few days with him in Muscle Shoals at Penn's recent recording sessions. Pictures of Spooner show a man impossibly thin. Even when you look right at him, you almost can't see him. He's never at the center of a crowd, nor is he far enough outside the edge to draw attention. He's like a distant star made visible only by looking away; if you look too closely at him—or listen too closely to what he's playing—he vanishes. His visage is beautiful, all lines and texture. When he smiles, it involves his whole face.

Spooner keeps a pack of filter cigarettes along with his nonfilters, for variety. He is always smoking, which does not mean that he always has a lit cigarette. The process is such a part of him that when he is empty-handed, he has just finished one or is preparing to light another. He rubs his hand across some pocket and like magic, a cigarette appears between his fingers. Once there, plenty of time will pass before it meets a match. Spooner coddles his cigarette, holds it now by the filter, now by the tip. If he were to do something as direct as point, he might use it for emphasis. But emphasis from "ol' Spoon," as Penn refers to his lifelong friend, comes not directly but indirectly.

On the final day of Dan Penn's 1993 sessions, they were scheduled to record three songs. The album was a mix of old material and new, and while some of the best had already been cut, Penn had saved three doozies for the end: "Dark End of the Street," "You Left the Water Running," and "Do Right Woman." When the Hammond B3 broke down at the start of the day, everybody poured more coffee and continued to schmooze. The delay may have postponed the actual recording, but rehearsal began when the coffee was brewed, when one player entered the studio and encountered another. The way that southern musicians play together is just an extension of the way they interact; their style is evident when they lace their shoes, when they play ping-pong, when they smoke a cigarette.

That last day, they got "Dark End" after five takes but recorded a dozen of the upbeat "You Left the Water Running." They didn't need that many, but playing the song was fun. Each take told the story differently. It was after ten P.M. when they began running down "Do Right Woman," the song that Aretha Franklin and William Bell and Gram Parsons have made a fundamental part of life. Players wandered on and off the studio floor, greeting old friends who dropped by to say hello, who stuck around once ensnared in the magic. Penn grabbed an acoustic guitar and began trying to remember the song's changes. Bassist David Hood was across the room, apparently in a world of his own though he was actually encoding on paper the chord sequence that Penn was remembering. Spooner was at the organ, following Dan's lead, playing his part slow and full like blood from a deep wound.

No one told the others when to join in, and in the control room, they didn't need to be told when to roll tape. It all happened as naturally as sunset. Suddenly the first take was done, and there was discussion about what to do differently, and by the third take, they had it. "Should we go listen?" someone asked, and Penn paused, because he knew he had a take he could use, but he knew that if they got up, they'd never come back—magic time would be gone—so he said, "Let's do one more," and they did, and it was as if they had turned the first line of the song into credo, dogma, religion: "Take me to heart/and I'll always love you." No one said it but everyone felt that if they walked outside at that moment, the world would have been a different place; what they'd done in this little room a few feet from the Tennessee River seemed to have affected the course of mankind. And when they finished, drained by the intensity, Penn said, "One more."

There were three guitarists on the floor, three keyboardists, bass, and drums. But the space in the song was so wide that a history, a human, a life could get lost in it. From my seat on the sofa in the control room, I looked out at the dimmed room where the musicians' souls were naked as God and they were no longer breathing air but breathing this song, no longer humans but entirely musicians, part of a tribe whose numbers were no greater than those within earshot at that moment. Dan was singing, Reggie Young was strumming, Jimmy Johnson played guitar with his shoulders. My eyes rested on Spooner, an amp partially blocking my vision. His eyes were closed and his head swayed slightly and it would be obvious to a dead person that he was playing his guts out. I leaned to the right to see him better, and I saw his feet dangling from his stool, not touching the floor, not touching the foot pedals. I followed his legs up to his hands, aware I'm witnessing a master at work, a ballet of the greatest depth and dimension: His hands were neatly folded in his lap. His eyes were still closed, his feet still dangled, his palms were together and fingers interlocked: For Spooner, the notes he plays are so big that the space between them can extend for a whole verse. Another chorus passed before he moved, and when he did, David Briggs at the electric piano with his back to Spooner suddenly laid out. No words were exchanged. Spooner stepped into the song like a ghost, as forceful as when he was sitting out, summoning spirits from the vastness.

Oh, you should see him smoke a cigarette.

Spoon was in his late twenties when he came to Memphis, and he stayed for about three years. He and Penn were side by side when the Box Tops took off. "Weeks and months had rolled past since 'The Letter,' and the record company from New York is calling Dan regularly," remembers Oldham. "They keep asking, 'Where's the follow-up? We need a record yesterday.' After this went on for a while, Dan approached me and said, 'Spooner, people have sent me songs, but I really don't like any. All I know to do is you and I just try to write them a song.' So we went to American one evening and each pulled out our list of dozens of titles and ideas and spent ten minutes on each one and there was nothing, really."

Penn: So me and Spooner stayed up a couple of nights lookin' for a song for the Box Tops' session. I had already booked the band for Saturday, which was like day after tomorrow, at ten o'clock in the morning. I need the song and I don't have a clue. Spooner don't either, and we're just working ourself into nowheres. So then it comes to tomorrow! And about dawn Saturday, we ended up over at Porky's, a restaurant right across from 827 [American's address].

Oldham: So daybreak, we go to this little cafe to eat breakfast and consider what to do next because Dan had booked all the musicians for a ten o'clock session to do our song. And we didn't have one yet. We were really getting tired, and considering the possibility of canceling everything.

Penn: We were just settin' there with the comin' downs. We'd ordered our little bite to eat and figured we'll just mosey on home and crash, because it's been a long two days and we didn't get nothing. I'm looking at Spooner and he's looking at me, big old empty looks. And finally ol' Spooner just laid his head on the table and said, "I could cry like a baby."

I set there a minute and I said, "What'd you say, Spooner?" He still had his head down, he said, "I could just cry like a baby." And it hit me. I said, "That's it, Spooner!" Ha! He said, "That's it?" And it hit him 'bout between the booth and the cash register. Magic time had just got here and it was one hundred percent on. Suddenly the air had changed! Just that fast.

Oldham: I guess we paid our tab and walking across the street, just shoulder to shoulder talking, we had the first verse of that song written before we got to the door. And we got the instruments, piano and guitar, and I think about an hour and a half later we had finished the song, put it on a little demo tape.

Penn: Spooner's on the way to the organ, I'm on the way to the board to turn it on, throwin' on a piece of tape, he's got the Hammond whirling. We had been ready to give up, there had been no doubt in my mind that the session would not occur that morning, but it did. We stayed in the studio—from that moment I would not leave for nothing. When the band got there, we were fresh as a daisy. The song actually gave us eight hours of sleep and I never felt better in my life.

Oldham: Alex Chilton came walking in at nine A.M., heard the song and I didn't know what we had at that point. We were just exasperated. Alex listened and he just reached his hand out to me and said, "Thank you." That was the first glimpse I had that maybe we'd done something right. And then at ten we recorded it.

Penn: And it was a hit record.

Jerry Wexler with David Ritz

THE QUEEN OF SOUL

Signed to Columbia Records at the dawn of her career, Aretha Franklin languished until her contract expired and she signed on with Atlantic Records. Atlantic executive and producer Jerry Wexler had production and distribution deals arranged with Stax Records in Memphis and Fame Records, run out of a little studio in Muscle Shoals, Alabama. Wexler's arrangement allowed for a cozy recording relationship in those studios. In Memphis, the Stax house band was the always-in-the-groove Booker T and the MG's. In Muscle Shoals, Rick Hall's house band was a bunch of rednecks with an intrinsic understanding of rhythm and blues. Wexler wanted to rescue young Aretha Franklin from the syrupy style she had affected during her five years with Columbia. He decided to commandeer the tense Muscle Shoals session himself.

WHEN SHE was 14, Aretha Franklin sang "Precious Lord" in her father's church. The Reverend C. L. Franklin was spiritual leader of the New Bethel Baptist Church, one of Detroit's biggest congregations. The live recording, a favorite of mine, came out on Chess in 1956. The voice was not that of a child but rather of an ecstatic hierophant. Since the days of covering Mahalia Jackson and Sister Rosetta Tharpe for *Billboard,* I'd been a fan of gospel, realizing that the church, along with the raw blues, was the foundation of the music that moved me so much. On Aretha's first recording, her singing was informed with her genius. From the congregation a man cried out, "Listen at her . . . Listen at her!" And I did.

From 1961 through 1967, Aretha made over a dozen albums for Columbia. She'd been signed by John Hammond, who called hers the greatest voice since Billie Holiday's. John cut superb sides on her, including "Today I Sing the Blues." Eventually she became the ward of the pop department, which turned out gems like "If Ever I Should Lose You." But as producer Clyde Otis said, "No one really knew what to do with her."

503

There were minor hits such as "Running Out of Fools," but mostly Aretha languished.

I always had my eye on her, although in 1967 there were a million other matters that seemed more important. I was in Muscle Shoals, still dealing with Pickett which was never easy. As the records got better, Wilson became more obstreperous. Early one afternoon, we were having trouble finishing a vocal when Percy Sledge walked in. "You sound good, Pickett," he said. "Man, you sounding like Otis."

"I don't sound like nobody," Wilson fired back, "except me."

Knowing Pickett's temperament, I shooed Percy out, and we got back to overdubbing. An hour later, we still didn't have the vocal when Percy popped in again. He was a sweetheart but the last person I wanted to see just then. And before I could get him out of there, he said, "It's sure enough Otis in there, Pickett. But now I'm hearing some James."

That was the red flag that enraged the bull. Wilson hated James Brown—for years there'd been bad blood between them over a woman. Suddenly Pickett charged. I stepped between them, a huge mistake. Wilson lifted me—and mind you, I'm no featherweight—and flung me against the wall across the room. He didn't want to hurt me, just wanted to get me out of the way. Percy was dumbfounded, but not afraid; after all, he'd been a professional boxer. I stepped in between them again, and luckily that stopped it.

In the middle of this madness, the phone was ringing. When the combatants finally cooled, I grabbed it. It was Louise Bishop: "Aretha's ready for you," she said. "Here's her phone number." Louise was a gospel deejay in Philly. In those days, Aretha ran with the gospel crowd, and Louise was the mutual friend I'd hoped would bring us together.

I called Aretha that minute and set up a meeting in New York. Her Columbia contract had expired. Within the week, she and Ted White, her husband, sat down in my office—no lawyers, managers, or agents in sight—and we made a handshake deal. It was beautiful.

My first instinct was to offer her to Jim Stewart and have the Stax team produce her. Stax was steaming, and no one figured to produce Aretha any better than those good folks in Memphis. I told Jim that if he went for the $25,000 advance, Aretha could be a Stax artist with Atlantic promotion and distribution, the same arrangement we had with Sam and Dave. Stewart passed. Thank you, Jesus.

That left it to me. Don't get me wrong: I was pleased to produce Aretha; I admired her talent and felt her strength. But at the time of her signing I was swamped, running back and forth between Muscle Shoals and Manhattan. The work was overwhelming. I was not only pushing for the sale of our company but considering moving out of New York altogether. I was toying with a crazy idea that wouldn't go away, the notion of getting a house on the North Fork of Long Island and another place in Miami, with a boat in each backyard—spend the winters in Florida, the summers on the Sound, and break the monotony of the Great Neck grind, maybe even set up a studio down South.

Because I was always doing 12 things at once, I was also always on the lookout for producers for my artists. In Aretha's case, fate, fortune, or the pull of my own passion led me into the studio with her to work in a more involving way than I had ever worked before. John Hammond, more friend than competitor, had encouraged me from the outset. "You'll do good things with Aretha," he assured me. "You understand her musically." Personally, John tipped me, she was enigmatic and withdrawn.

I knew that her preacher father was respected by his community as a civil rights leader and early advocate of black pride. He was a close friend of Martin Luther King, whom he brought to Detroit for the famous 1963 march up Woodward Avenue. He had recorded dozens of sermons for Chess which were rhetorical and metaphorical masterpieces, "The Eagle Stirreth Her Nest" being a classic of the genre. He had the gift of Good Book storytelling, never failing to rouse his church to fevered pitch. Franklin was a national leader, a charismatic character who reputedly took an occasional walk on the wild side. He'd been busted for pot possession and liked to party. Under unexplained circumstances, his wife had left him and their five children Vaughn, Erma, Cecil, Aretha, and baby Carolyn when Aretha was six. When Aretha was 10, her mother died. Some say the preacher used his children, especially the precocious Aretha, as props and pawns; others called him a devoted father. Aretha generally avoided the subject.

She started touring as a teen-ager, an opening act on her father's gospel show along with Lucy Branch and Sammy Bryant. C. L. also sang. In addition to loving religious song, Reverend Franklin loved jazz and R&B. Aretha's early education was formed by both the gospel greats of her day—Clara Ward, the Staple Singers, the Soul Stirrers, James Cleveland, the Mighty Clouds of Joy—and the secular stars as well. On the road and in his spacious mansion in Detroit, Reverend Franklin entertained artists like Art Tatum and Dinah Washington, R&B luminaries like Sam Cooke, Fats Domino, and Bobby Bland. In a world filled with musical and sexual excitement, Aretha heard and saw everything at an early age. By age 17, she herself had given birth to two children. And in a twist on the old myth where the preacher wants his child to sing only for the Lord, C. L. helped Aretha go pop. After all, he was something of a pop preacher himself and lived the pop life to the hilt. When members of his congregation objected to Aretha's secular songs, the Reverend set them straight in a hurry.

John Hammond signed her in 1960. "Sam Cooke was desperately trying to get Aretha for RCA," Hammond remembered. "I'm glad I prevailed. I cherish the records we made together, but, finally, Columbia was a white company who misunderstood her genius."

"Genius" is the word. Clearly Aretha was continuing what Ray Charles had begun—the secularization of gospel, turning church rhythms, church patterns, and especially church feelings into personalized love songs. Like Ray, Aretha was a hands-on performer, a two-fisted pianist plugged into the main circuit of Holy Ghost power. Even though we produced Aretha in a way that we never produced Ray, she remained the central orchestrator of her own sound, the essential contributor and final arbiter of what fit or did not fit her musical persona.

Writing at the start of the nineties, it's easy to forget that a quarter century ago there was no one else like Aretha Franklin. Pop music today is rich with glorious gospel voices and women singers in the mold cast by Aretha. As Bird gave birth to decades of altoists, Aretha became a model for people like Chaka Khan, Natalie Cole, Donna Summer, Martha Wash, Whitney Houston, Miki Howard, Marva Hicks, Vesta, Sharon Bryant. The list of her disciples is long. From the start—at least after our first experience in the studio—I saw she had raised the ante and upgraded the art form.

After Jim Stewart declined the opportunity, my instinct was to take her south anyway and bring her to Muscle Shoals, where I was still in the first flush of exhilaration with that wonderful rhythm section of Alabama white boys who took a left turn at the blues.

Before the trip we naturally mapped out a strategy. I had no lofty notions of correcting Columbia's mistakes or making her into a Mount Rushmore monument. My idea was to make good tracks, use the best players, put Aretha back on piano, and let the lady wail. Aretha, like Ray, was an inner-directed singer as opposed, let's say, to Mary Wells, who came to us after her Motown successes. We soon realized that we could do nothing with Mary. The fault wasn't hers, nor was it ours; she was an artist who required the idiosyncratic Motown production, which was simply out of our ken. There was something unique about that little Detroit studio—the attitude, the vibes, the energy that couldn't be duplicated elsewhere. The same is true of Memphis and Muscle Shoals.

It's interesting to consider why Aretha, a Detroiter, never signed with Motown herself, especially given that she was of the same generation as such Motown friends as Smokey Robinson, Diana Ross, and Martha Reeves—you'd think the connection inevitable. It's important to remember, though, that Berry Gordy's empire was built on a new phenomenon. In the early sixties, when his records started hitting, he had expanded the market. Like Phil Spector before him, Gordy was selling to white teenagers. This was a new formula—black music, produced by a black man and sold to white youth—and it became the backbone of Gordy's fortune.

Even though Atlantic and Motown were the only labels where the owners made the records, our approach was entirely different. I've never been interested in confecting teen-age music. Ever since Ahmet began recording Stick McGhee in 1949, the gut of the Atlantic R&B catalogue was pointed at black adults. If white people went for it, fine; if not, we'd survive. But I've always been amazed by Berry Gordy. His music was incredible—the ethereal Smokey Robinson songs, the Temps, the Tops, Marvin Gaye, the Marvelettes, the Supremes, Stevie Wonder. And he pulled off a miracle of marketing that never even occurred to me: he made his music acceptable, carefully covering it with a gloss and glamour that enabled his artists to become fixtures on "The Ed Sullivan Show." The sons and daughters of white-bread America became the children of Motown, and even today that generation, now middle aged, remains loyal to the sound of Gordy's energetic sexuality, a mixture of charm and innocence.

When Aretha arrived at Atlantic, she was not innocent. She was a 25-year-old woman with the sound, feelings, and experience of someone much older. She fit into the matrix of music I had always worked with—songs expressing adult emotions. Aretha didn't come to us to be made over or refashioned; she was searching for herself, not for gimmicks, and in that regard I might have helped. I urged Aretha to be Aretha.

I was happy with the songs for the first album, most of which she either selected or wrote herself. Preproduction went smoothly. Aretha worked on her Fender Rhodes at home, doing a rough outline of the songs. I would never dream of starting tracks without Aretha at the piano; that's what made her material organic. She'd find the key, devise the rhythm pattern, and work out the background vocals with either her sisters, Carolyn and Erma, or the Sweet Inspirations.

The Sweet Inspirations became one of the pillars of the Atlantic Church of Sixties Soul. Led by Cissy Houston (Whitney's mom), Estelle Brown, Sylvia Shemwell, and Myrna Smith were fabulous background singers who, like Aretha, instinctively understood harmonies; they could match vibratos, switch parts, and turn on a dime. And like the great King Curtis—our sax man, arranger, and in-house bandleader—they were always relaxed, fun, and ready to offer a suggestion or innovative passage. Ultimately, it was only a matter of common decency to put them under contract as a featured group. I suggested the name Inspirations, which unfortunately turned out to be already registered (to a group of acrobats!), so I added the "Sweet." In 1968, they had a top twenty hit, the eponymous "Sweet Inspirations," produced by Tom Dowd and Chips Moman in Memphis. In 1969 they sang background on Elvis's "Suspicious Minds," also in Memphis. They spread soul all over the album *From Elvis in Memphis.*

Aretha was a natural for the Southern style of recording. Once she had the basics—rhythm groove and vocal patterns—I knew she'd get off on the spontaneity of the studio. I took her to Muscle Shoals with only a modicum of doubt. I was a little anxious about presenting Aretha and Ted with a wall-to-wall white band, and consequently I asked Rick Hall to hire a basic black horn section—either the Memphis Horns or a section led by Bowlegs Miller. In addition to the racial mix, I also wanted a certain sonority that the brothers would bring to the horn section. Hall goofed and hired an all-white section. Aretha's response was no response. I never should have worried—about her. She just sat down at the piano and played the music.

Tension between Rick and myself had been slowly but surely building. When deejay Daddy Sears handed me the duo Clarence and Calvin, for example, I turned them over to Rick for production. Calvin got into an auto accident, and Clarence went solo as Clarence Carter. Tremendous hits ensued on Hall's Fame label—"Slip Away," "Too Weak to Fight," "Patches," and "Thread the Needle," with its irresistible groovegrind. I adored Clarence, but at renewal time Rick conveniently forgot our agreement and brazenly cut us out.

Hall could be belligerent. So could Ted White. And so, as it turned out, could one of the trumpeters. The session began smoothly enough. The rhythms Aretha had worked out on "I Never Loved a Man (the Way I Love You)" were super-smooth, salty enough to bring out her soul, loose enough to let the head arrangement fall into place. Aretha was on acoustic piano, Spooner Oldham on electric. In the corner, saxist Charlie Chalmers unobtrusively worked out the horn parts. This was the first of 11 tunes. All Aretha's vocals were scheduled to be completed in a week; the second week would be for sweetening. For this initial session, though, I decided to record everything live—which turned out to be both a blessing and a curse.

The minute Aretha touched the piano and sang one note, the musicians were captivated. They caught the fever and raced for their instruments. "I've never experienced so much feeling coming out of one human being," says drummer Roger Hawkins. "When she hit that first chord," adds Dan Penn, "we knew everything was gonna be all right."

But everything wasn't. The trumpeter was getting obnoxious and drawing Ted White into a "dozens" duel; they were ranking each other out while drinking out of the same bottle. A redneck patronizing a black man is a dangerous camaraderie. I dreaded a flash point, but somehow we completed the song. Listening to the playback, I couldn't believe how good it sounded.

"It took two hours," Penn recalls, "and it was in the can. It was a killer, no doubt about it. The musicians started singing and dancing with each other, giddy on the pure joy of having something to do with this amazing record. That morning we knew a star had been born."

That evening euphoria turned to horror. It was *Walpurgisnacht,* a Wagnerian shitstorm, things flying to pieces, everyone going nuts. Back at the motel it was footsteps up and down the hall, doors slamming, and wild cries in the night. I don't know what touched it off.

"I was drinking pretty heavy," Rick Hall recalls. "And so was Ted. I was in his motel room trying to straighten things out while things were only getting worse. 'I should have never brought Aretha to Alabama,' he kept shouting, and I kept shouting back, and finally we did get into a full-blown fistfight."

At six that morning I was in Ted and Aretha's room, with Ted screaming at me for getting them mixed up with "these fuckin' honkies." There was no way to reason. By noon, Ted had taken Aretha and split for New York. I was left with one completed song and a piece of another, Chips Moman and Dan Penn's "Do Right Woman—Do Right Man," for which we had only drums, bass, and rhythm guitar, no Aretha keyboards, no Aretha vocals. (While we were recording "I Never Loved a Man," Chips and Dan had been in Rick's office struggling with "Do Right Woman," and I helped them break up a lyric logjam. They were stuck on the first part of the bridge—"They say it's a man's world"—when I came up with the quasi-Jewish line "But you can't prove that by me.")

I got back to New York and ran off two dozen acetates of "I Never Loved a Man" for my key deejays. Before long it was prime time. It was burning up the radio, phone lines were jumping, the thing was a smash, and there I was with my adenoids showing: we had a stone hit, but only half a single. An auspicious way to kick off the Aretha epoch!

I needed Aretha to finish "Do Right"—in a hurry. And I couldn't find her. Not in New York. Not in Detroit. She's having love problems, I heard; she and Ted had split up. This separation turned out to be temporary (later, permanent), but for a couple of weeks Aretha might as well have fallen off the face of the earth. Meanwhile, the pressure was building; with the dee-jays wailing on "I Never Loved a Man," the distributors were screaming for the record.

Finally Aretha materialized. In fact, she came to the studio at 18 Broadway and made a miracle. She overdubbed two discrete keyboard parts, first playing piano, then organ; she and her sisters hemstitched the seamless background harmonies; and when she added her glorious lead vocal, the result was perfection. Moman and Penn like to shit a brick when they heard the final rendition.

Gerri Hirshey

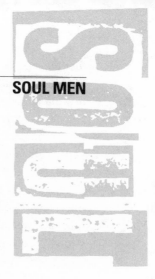

SOUL MEN

Known as "Double Dynamite," Sam Moore and Dave Prater were a hit-making machine for the Stax/Volt–Atlantic juggernaut in the 1960s. They recorded most of their major hits, "Hold On, I'm Comin'," "Soul Man," and "When Something Is Wrong With My Baby," with Booker T and the MG's, the Stax house band in Memphis. Their relationship onstage was friendly and boisterous. For much of their career, they had *no* relationship offstage. Gerri Hirshey finds Sam and Dave not in their glory days, but in the early 1980s, grateful for any kind of booking, owing to Prater's erratic behavior.

Prater died but Sam Moore is still active, occasionally appearing with fellow partnerless soul disciple Dan Aykroyd, and recording occasional duets (with Bruce Springsteen and Conway Twitty, to name an odd couple).

Hirshey's love for soul music dates from her childhood, when she watched James Brown perform on *The Ed Sullivan Show*. As a journalist, she wrote about sports and business, but decided, "Why not write about something you really care about?" Soul also played a part in Hirshey's marriage. At a college fraternity party, David Hirshey ceremoniously removed a Cream album from a turntable and replaced it with Aretha. Partygoers booed, but Gerri Hirshey fell in love with her future husband.

WHEN I CAUGHT up with soul man Sam Moore, he was singing the . . . blues. . . .

At the time he and Dave Prater were still Sam and Dave—they have since split for the umpteenth and last time—and they were enjoying a resurgence just after the Blues Brothers covered "Soul Man" on *Saturday Night Live*. Sam and Dave were invited to appear on the show, and they did, but John Belushi would not sing *with* Messrs. Double Dynamite.

"I asked him, and he went pale and said, 'Aw, no, man.' Cat wanted us to come out, do two bars of our song 'Soul Man,' then turn it over to the Blues Brothers and leave the stage. The four of us, okay. But not that way, not Sam and Dave as emcees. No, I don't need that. I am grateful for the chance again, don't get me wrong. But I won't do nothin' that is disrespectful to myself."

"Where's Dave?" The staff at Manhattan's Lone Star Café was nervous. Ten minutes to showtime, and still, only Sam had shown up. For years Sam and Dave were given to arriving separately, often from vastly distant places. I'd spoken to them several times, but they never sat for an interview together; it was impossible even to photograph them together unless it was onstage. As far back as 1969 I'd gone to a show of theirs that ended up being the Sam Revue. The weirdness persisted for nearly thirteen years. That night, at the Lone Star, would turn out to be one of their final appearances together. Still, Sam stonewalled on the subject of offstage relations. "Let's just say I need the work. *Have* to work. And leave it at that."

"Who gets the pitcher?"

A busboy had come in with a beer pitcher filled with water and a dishtowel. Sam reached for them, shaking his head.

"Twenty-six years on the road and still shaving out of a beer pitcher. Shee-it." He laughed, and set about unpacking what he called the soul man's one-nighter kit. It was a worn small Leatherette bag with a shoulder strap, packed with an engineer's precision. He extracted clean socks, toilet articles, and a straight razor rolled in a clean pair of Jockey shorts. A pearl-gray three-piece suit hung in a garment bag from a nail.

Though he regrets, bitterly, the excesses of his life within show business—booze, drugs, fortunes lost—Sam insisted he was still sure he had made the right choice when J. J. Farley, manager of the Soul Stirrers, approached him one night in 1956 in his hometown of Miami. Farley had heard him in a club, knew Sam was the gospel-trained deacon's son, grandson of a Baptist preacher. Farley offered him a chance to go out with the Soul Stirrers to see if he could replace Sam Cooke, who had left to sing pop. Sam was ready to leave Miami that Monday morning, but over the weekend Jackie Wilson came to town.

"I went to see him, and his show that night changed the course of my life," Sam said. "I saw what he could do with his voice in the broad range of songs he could do, and I was hooked. I went back and told Farley I couldn't go with them. I loved gospel, but I wanted to do like Jackie."

He stayed in Miami, working small clubs. He was onstage one night at the King of Hearts Club, trying to emcee an amateur show over the bar clamor, when he was joined onstage by a guy in baker's whites. Dave

Prater was a laborer's son from Ocilla, Georgia. He had lit out for the city, hoping to sing for pay. He was working as a short-order cook and baker's assistant when he hopped onstage during one of his breaks. A little fumphering around, and Sam and Dave found in each other a pleasing counterpoint. Dave had a gritty, hoarse bottom to his voice; Sam could wail at the top of the register, and together, their harmonies were sweet and jelly-smooth. Dave was so nervous, he dropped the mike; Sam caught it in mid-air and the crowd went berserk.

They talked and realized they could be part of a very specialized partner tradition. There had been Don and Dewey and Sam Cooke's protégés the Simms Twins. The duet tradition was furthered, in the sixties, by Don and Juan, by the blue-eyed soul of the white Righteous Brothers, and by James and Bobby Purify. The latter got their first hit, "I'm Your Puppet," in 1965, the year Sam and Dave left Roulette Records for Atlantic. Veteran R & B producer Henry Glover had them recording in New York for Roulette. But it wasn't until Jerry Wexler sent them down South, to Stax, that anything solid came together for Sam and Dave. He had signed them in Florida, where he found them, then made a handshake deal with Jim Stewart to record Sam and Dave with the Stax studio band and production team.

"Those guys were like Siamese twins when they came to us," Steve Cropper remembers. "They were incredibly tight."

So was their production team. When they arrived, they found a sheaf of songs composed by Isaac Hayes and David Porter, who established themselves at Stax largely on the strength of their work with Sam and Dave.

During the years when nearly every session yielded a hit, from 1966 to 1968, a big silver bus ferried the thirty-five-member Sam and Dave troupe to clubs, colleges, arenas, and dance halls. THE SAM AND DAVE REVUE, the destination sign read, in white lights. They carried red suits, white suits, three-piece lime green suits, all with matching patent boots and coordinated silk hankies woefully inadequate to absorb a soul man's nightly outpourings. Both Sam and Dave talk a lot about sweat. To Dave, it's proof that he's worked for his pay. For Sam, it's essential, almost mystical. He says he can't work without it.

"Unless my body reaches a certain temperature, starts to liquefy, I just don't feel right."

Outside the dressing room someone hollered, "Five minutes," and I left Sam to shave in his pitcher.

"Where's Dave?" The booking agent was sweating. Downstairs, on the tiny stage, the eight-piece band was setting up. A trombone slide narrowly missed a waitress. Sugar Bear, a mammoth keyboard player in flaming orange polyester, settled gingerly on a tiny stool. The drummer's elbows knocked the back wall. He nodded, then drew screams as he counted the band into the familiar rumble that signals the start of a brassy soul revue: *thunka-thunka* from the drums and bass; advance heat lightning off a poised tenor sax. A trumpet kicked into the opening strut of "Hold On, I'm Coming," and the announcer bawled showbiz soulspeak over it all: "The one, the only, the HEATERS of 'Hold On, I'm Coming,' the sultans of SWEAT, DOUBLE DYNAMITE, Sam and . . ."

At last, Dave. He was looking older, tiny corkscrews of gray in his hair, but once he had grabbed the mike, ten years fell off his face and landed somewhere in the front row. It was a good, happy crowd, pressing up against the stage, faces upturned to the almost instant mist of sweat. In unison, the gray jackets flew off, then the vests. After ten minutes the white shirts clung like sandwich wrap, nearly transparent. Fifty wet minutes later they were climbing the curved stairway to the second-floor dressing rooms, running a gauntlet of upturned palms, slapping five, ten, twenty before they made it past the bar and into the stairwell. Dave had stepped into his dressing room to towel off when Sugar Bear filled the doorway, looking puzzled.

"Where's Sam?"

Seconds later someone spotted him, a flash of gray silk heading out the downstairs exit, to a waiting car and the airport.

"Yo," Sugar yelled. "Soul man Sam, what you know about that Buffalo gig?"

The only answer was the sweep of traffic noise in the stairwell.

Six months after his last appearance with Dave Prater on New Year's Eve of 1981, Sam Moore was free of heroin for the first time since 1968. Over the years he had overdosed twice; the second time nearly killed him. At one point his weight dropped to 120 pounds. He says he was always depressed and bloody, full of holes, reduced to stealing methadone at times, working, as he'd said he had to, just for the next fix, which, he claims, show business "friends" were only too happy to provide.

"Word got out," Sam says, "Sam and Dave are bad news. We were reduced to playing toilets. I'd lie, I'd miss shows, I'd find guys in my dressing room who'd heard about my habit. And they were always there with more. You become scum, you deal with scum. I had a phone book with every dealer from Harlem to Kalamazoo. Got to a point they'd charge me more because of who I was. That night we talked at the Lone Star, why you think I left so fast? I'd shot enough to do the show, but I came off that stage *hurtin'*."

He admits he hadn't the strength to stop it himself. Having seen a TV program on experimental treatment with an opiate blocker called naltrexone, Sam's new manager. Joyce McCrae, got him into a program. Slowly, hellishly, he kicked. His weight went back up to a healthy 200; he was working out in a gym, counseling addicts on a hot line, and singing. Beautifully and alone. He talked, too, about addiction and shame and depression and, finally, about the longtime freeze-out with his former partner. In 1968, Dave Prater shot his own wife in the face during a domestic scuffle. She lived, but Sam's respect for Dave was dead.

"I told him I'd work and travel with him, but that I would never speak or look at him."

When he explained all this, Sam and Dave were speaking to each other only through attorneys. Having found another "Sam," Dave was billing his act as "The Sam and Dave Revue." Sam was getting solo bookings, but it was problematic.

"You get club owners questioning why they should pay Sam Moore twenty-five hundred dollars a night when they can pay 'Sam and Dave' eight hundred dollars a night with a band. Who cares about the original when a club owner has to pay eight hundred dollars for two shows?"

By January of 1984, Sam Moore was back in a recording studio. Alone. His voice was strong enough, he said. Strong enough to bust a beer pitcher.

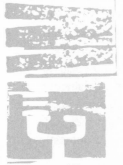

THE COMMITMENTS

The beauty and splendor of soul music, as debated and delineated by the Irish, white, working-class heroes of Doyle's novel.

THE TIME flew in.

Those Commitments still learning their instruments improved. The ones ready were patient. There was no group rehearsing. Jimmy wouldn't allow it. They all had to be ready first.

Derek's fingers were raw. He liked to wallop the strings. That was the way, Jimmy said, Derek found out that you could get away with concentrating on one string. You made up for the lack of variety by thumping the string more often and by taking your hand off the neck and putting it back a lot to make it look like you were involved in complicated work. He carried his bass low, Stranglers style, nearly down at his knees. He didn't have to bend his arms.

Outspan improved too. There'd be no guitar solos, Jimmy said, and that suited Outspan. Jimmy gave him Motown compilations to listen to. Chord changes were scarce. It was just a matter of making yourself loose enough to follow the rhythm.

Outspan was very embarrassed up in his bedroom trying to strum along to the Motown time. But once he stopped looking at himself in the mirror he loosened up. He chugged along with the records, especially The Supremes. Under the energy it was simple.

Then he started using the mirror again. He was thrilled. His plectrum hand danced. Sometimes it was a blur. The hand looked great. The arm hardly budged. The wrist was in charge. He held his guitar high against his chest.

He saved money when he could. He wasn't working but on Saturday mornings he went from door to door in Barrytown selling the frozen chickens that his cousin always managed to rob from H. Williams on Friday nights. That gave him at least a tenner a week to put away. As well as that, he gave the man next door, Mr Hurley, a hand with his video business. This involved keeping about two hundred tapes under his bed and driving around the estate with Mr Hurley for a few hours a couple of times a week, handing out the tapes while Mr Hurley took in the money. Then, out of the blue, his ma gave him most of the month's mickey money. He cried.

He had £145 now. That got him a third-hand electric guitar (the make long forgotten) and a bad amp and cabinet. After that they couldn't get him away from the mirror.

Deco's mother worried about him. He'd be eating his breakfast and then he'd yell something like Good God Y'Awl or Take It To The Bridge Now. Deco was on a strict soul diet: James Brown, Otis Redding, Smokey Robinson and Marvin Gaye. James for the growls, Otis for the moans, Smokey for the whines and Marvin for the whole lot put together, Jimmy said.

Deco sang, shouted, growled, moaned, whined along to the tapes Jimmy had given him. He bollixed his throat every night. It felt like it was being cut from the inside by the time he got to the end of Tracks of My Tears. He liked I Heard It through the Grapevine because the women singing I HEARD IT THROUGH THE GRAPEVINE NOT MUCH LONGER WOULD YOU BE MY BABY gave him a short chance to wet the stinging in his throat. Copying Marvin Gaye meant making his throat sore and then rubbing it in.

He kept going through. He was getting better. It was getting easier. He could feel his throat stretching. It was staying wet longer. He was getting air from further down. He put on Otis Redding and sang My Girl with him when he needed a rest. He finished every session with James Brown. Then he'd lie on the bed till the snot stopped running. He couldn't close his eyes because he'd spin. Deco was taking this thing very seriously.

All his rehearsing was done standing up in front of the wardrobe mirror. He was to look at himself singing, Jimmy said. He was to pretend he had a microphone. At first he jumped around but it was too knackering and it frightened his mother. Jimmy showed him a short video of James Brown doing Papa's Got a Brand New Bag. He couldn't copy James' one-footed shuffle on the bedroom carpet so he practised on the lino in the kitchen when everyone had gone to bed.

He saw the way James Brown dropped to his knees. He didn't hitch his trousers and kneel. He dropped. Deco tried it. He growled SOMETIMES I FEEL SO GOOD I WANNA JUMP BACK AND KISS MYSELF, aimed his knees at the floor and followed them there.

He didn't get up again for a while. He thought he'd knee-capped himself. Jimmy told him that James Brown's trousers were often soaked in blood when he came off-stage. Deco was fucked if his would be.

There was nothing you could teach James Clifford about playing the piano. Jimmy had him listening to Little Richard. He got James to thump the keys with his elbows, fists, heels. James was a third-year medical student so he was able to tell Jimmy the exact, right word for whatever part of his body he was hitting the piano with. He was even able to explain the damage he was doing to himself. He drew the line at the forehead. Jimmy couldn't persuade him to give the piano the odd smack with his forehead. There was too much at stake there. Besides, he wore glasses.

Joey The Lips helped Dean Fay.

—My man, that reed there is a nice lady's nipple.

For days Dean blushed when he wet the reed and let his lips close on it.

—Make it a particular lady, someone real.

Dean chose a young one from across the road. She was in the same class as his brother, third year, and she was always coming over to borrow his books or scab his homework. It didn't work though. Dean couldn't go through with it. She was too real. So the saxophone reed became one of Madonna's nipples and Dean's playing began to get somewhere.

Joey The Lips was a terrific teacher, very patient. He had to be. Even Joey The Lips' mother, who was completely deaf, could sense Dean's playing from the other side of the house.

After three weeks he could go three notes without stopping and he could hold the short notes. Long ones went all over the place. Joey The Lips played alongside him, like a driving instructor. He only shouted once and that was really a cry of fright and pain caused by Dean backing into him while Joey The Lips still had his trumpet in his mouth.

Billy Mooney blamed away at his drums. His father was dead and his brothers were much younger than him so there was no one in the house to tell him to shut the fuck up.

Jimmy told him not to bother too much with cymbals and to use the butts of the sticks as well as the tips. What he was after was a steady, uncomplicated beat: —a thumping backbeat, Jimmy called it. That suited Billy. He'd have been happy with a bin lid and a hammer. And that was what he used when he played along to Dancing in the Streets. Not a bin lid exactly; a tin tray, with a racehorse on it. The horse was worn off after two days.

The three backing vocalists, The Commitmentettes, listened to The Supremes, Martha and the Vandellas, The Ronettes, The Crystals and The

Shangri-las. The Commitmentettes were Imelda Quirk and her friends Natalie Murphy and Bernie McLoughlin.

—How yis move, yeh know———is more important than how yis sing, Jimmy told them.

—You're a dirty bastard, you are.

Imelda, Natalie and Bernie could sing though. They'd been in the folk mass choir when they were in school but that, they knew now, hadn't really been singing. Jimmy said that real music was sex. They called him a dirty bastard but they were starting to agree with him. And there wasn't much sex in Morning Has Broken or The Lord Is My Shepherd.

Now they were singing along to Stop in the Name of Love and Walking in the Rain and they were enjoying it.

Joined together their voices sounded good, they thought. Jimmy taped them. They were scarlet. They sounded terrible.

—Yis're usin' your noses instead of your mouths, said Jimmy.

—Fuck off slaggin', said Imelda.

—Yis are, I'm tellin' yeh. An' his shouldn't be usin' your ordin'y accents either. It's Walking in the Rain, not Walkin' In De Rayen.

—Snobby!

They taped themselves and listened. They got better, clearer, sweeter. Natalie could roar and squeal too. They took down the words and sang by themselves without the records. They only did this tho when one of them had a free house.

They moved together, looking down, making sure their feet were going the right way. Soon they didn't have to look down. They wiggled their arses at the dressing table mirror and burst out laughing. But they kept doing it.

Jimmy got them all together regularly, about twice a week, and made them report. There, always in Joey The Lips' mother's garage, he'd give them a talk. They all enjoyed Jimmy's lectures. So did Jimmy.

They weren't really lectures; more workshops.

—Soul is a double-edged sword, lads, he told them once.

Joey The Lips nodded.

—One edge is escapism.

—What's tha'?

—Fun. ———Gettin' away from it all. Lettin' yourself go. ———Know wha' I mean?

—Gerrup!

Jimmy continued: —An' what's the best type of escapism, Imelda?

—I know wha' you're goin' to say.

—I'd've said that a bracing walk along the sea front was a very acceptable form of escapism, said James Clifford.

They laughed.

—Followed by? Jimmy asked.

—Depends which way you were havin' your bracing walk.

—Why?

—Well, if you were goin' in the Dollymount direction you could go all the way and have a ride in the dunes. ——That's wha' you're on abou', isn't it? ——As usual.

—That's right', said Jimmy. —Soul is a good time.

—There's nothin' good abou' gettin' sand on your knob, said Outspan.

They laughed.

—The rhythm o' soul is the rhythm o' riding', said Jimmy. —The rhythm o' ridin' is the rhythm o'soul.

—You're a dirty-minded bastard, said Natalie.

—There's more to life than gettin' your hole, Jimmy, said Derek.

—Here here.

—Listen. There's nothin' dirty abou' it, Nat'lie, said Jimmy. —As a matter o'fact it's very clean an' healthy.

—What's healthy abou' getting' sand on your knob?

—You just like talkin' dirty, said Natalie.

—Nat'lie ——Nat'lie ——Nat'lie, said Jimmy. —It depresses me to hear a modern young one talkin' like tha'.

—Dirty talk is dirty talk, said Natalie.

—Here here, said Billy Mooney. —Thank God.

—Soul is sex, Jimmy summarized.

—Well done, Jimmy, said Deco.

—Imelda, said Jimmy. —You're a woman o' the world.

—Don't answer him, 'melda, said Bernie.

Jimmy went on. —You've had sexual intercert, haven't yeh?

—Good Jaysis! Rabbitte!

—O' course she has, a good-lookin' girl like tha'.

—Don't answer him.

But Imelda wanted to answer.

—Well, yeah ——I have, yeah. ——So wha'?

There were cheers and blushes.

—Was it one o' them multiple ones, 'melda? Outspan asked. —I seen a yoke abou' them on Channel 4. They sounded deadly.

Derek looked at Imelda.

—Are yeh serious?

He was disappointed in Imelda.

Deco tapped Imelda's shoulder.

—We could make beautiful music, Honey.

—I'd bite your bollix off yeh if yeh went near me, yeh spotty fuck, yeh. There were cheers.

Imelda ducked her shoulder away from Deco's fingers.

—I might enjoy tha', said Deco.

—I'd make ear-rings ou' o' them, said Imelda.

—You're as bad as they are, 'melda, said Bernie.

—Ah, fuck off, Bernie, will yeh.

—I thought we said slaggin' complexions was barred, said Jimmy. —Apologise.

—There's no need.

—There is.

———Sorry.

—That's okay.

—Spotty.

—Ah here!

Deco grabbed Imelda's shoulders. Bernie was up quick and grabbed his ears.

—Get your hands off o' her, YOU.

—As a glasses wearer, said James, —I'd advise you to carry ou' Bernie's instructions. Yeh might need glasses yourself some day and a workin' set of ears will come in handy.

—That's a doctor gave yeh tha' advice, remember.

Deco took the advice. Bernie gave him his ears back. Imelda blew him a kiss and gave him the fingers.

—Annyway, Imelda, said Jimmy. —Did yeh enjoy it?

—It was alrigh', said Imelda.

More cheers and blushes.

—This lady is the queen of soul, said Joey The Lips.

—Wha' 're you the queen of? Imelda said back.

—Then you agree with us, Jimmy asked Imelda.

—It's oney music, said Imelda.

—No way, 'melda. Soul isn't only music. Soul——

—That's alrigh' for the blackies, Jimmy. —They've got bigger gooters than us.

—Speak for yourself, pal.

—Go on, Jimmy. ———At least we know tha' Imelda does the business.

—Fuck off, you, said Imelda, but she grinned.

Everyone grinned.

—Yeh said somethin' about a double-edged sword, said James.

—I s'pose the other side is sex too, said Derek.

—Arse bandit country if it's the other side, said Outspan.

—I'm goin' home if it is, said Dean.

—Brothers, Sisters, said Joey The Lips. —Let Brother Jimmy speak. Tell us about the other side of the sword, Jimmy.

They were quiet.

—The first side is sex, righ', said Jimmy. —An' the second one is ————REVOLUTION!

Cheers and clenched fists.

Jimmy went on.

—Soul is the politics o' the people.

—Yeeoow!

—Righ' on, Jimmy.

—Our people. ——Soul is the rhythm o' sex. It's the rhythm o' the factory too. The workin' man's rhythm. Sex an' factory.

—Not the factory I'm in, said Natalie. —There isn't much rhythm in guttin' fish.

She was pleased with the laughter.

—Musical mackerel, wha'.

———Harmonious herring.

—Johnny Ray, said Dean, and then he roared: —JOHNNY RAY!

—Okay —Take it easy, said Jimmy.

—Cuntish cod, said Deco.

———Politics. ——Party politics, said Jimmy, —means nothin' to the workin' people. Nothin'. ——Fuck all. Soul is the politics o' the people.

—Start talkin' abou' ridin' again, Jimmy. You're gettin' borin'.

—Politics ——ridin', said Jimmy. —It's the same thing.

—Brother Jimmy speaks the truth, said Joey The Lips.

—He speaks through his hole.

—Soul is dynamic. (—So are you.) —It can't be caught. It can't be chained. They could chain the nigger slaves but they couldn't chain their soul.

—Their souls didn't pick the fuckin' cotton though. Did they now?

—Good thinkin'.

—Fuck off a minute. ——Soul is the rhythm o' the people, Jimmy said again. —The Labour Party doesn't have soul. Fianna fuckin' Fail doesn't have soul. The Workers' Party ain't got soul. The Irish people——no. —— The Dublin people —fuck the rest o' them. ——The people o' Dublin, our people, remember need soul. We've got soul.

—Fuckin' righ' we have.

—The Commitments, lads. We've got it. ——Soul. God told the Reverend Ed ——

—Ah, fuck off.

They loved Jimmy's lectures. His policy announcements were good too.

—What're they? Derek asked after Jimmy had made one of these announcements.

—Monkey suits, said Jimmy.

—No way, Rabbitte.

—Yes way.

—No fuckin' way, Jim. No way.

—I had one o' them for me mot's debs, said Billy. —It was fuckin' thick. The sleeves were too long, the trunzers were too fuckin' short, there was a stupid fuckin' stripe down——

—I puked on mine at our debs, remember? said Outspan.

—Some of it got on mine too, Derek reminded him.

—Oh, for fuck sake! said Dean. —I'm after rememberin'. ——I forgot to bring mine back. It's under me bed.

—When was your debs? Bernie asked him.

—Two years ago, said Dean.

They started laughing.

—Yeh must owe them hundreds, said Outspan.

—I'd better leave it there so.

—Jimmy, said James. —Are yeh seriously expectin' us to deck ourselves out in monkey suits?

—Yeah. ——Why not?

—Yeh can go an' shite, said Billy.

—Well said.

—Yis have to look good, said Jimmy. —Neat ——Dignified.

—What's fuckin' dignified abou' dressin' up like a jaysis penguin? Outspan asked.

—I'd be scarleh, said Derek.

Deco said nothing. He liked the idea.

—Brothers, Sisters, said Joey The Lips. —We know that soul is sex. And soul is revolution, yes? So now soul is ——Dignity.

—I don't understand tha', said Dean.

—Soul is lifting yourself up, soul is dusting yourself off, soul is ——

—What's he fuckin' on abou'?

—Just this, Brother. ——Soul is dignity. ——Dignity, soul. Dignity is respect. ——Self respect. ——Dignity is pride. Dignity, confidence. Dignity assertion. (Joey The Lips' upstretched index finger moved in time to his argument. They were glued to it.) —Dignity, integrity. Dignity, elegance. —Dignity, style.

The finger stopped.

—Brothers and Sisters. ———Dignity, dress. ———Dress suits.

—Dignity fuck dignity off dignity Joey.

—Dignity slippers, dignity cardigan.

—Ah, leave Joey alone, said Natalie.

Joey The Lips laughed with them.

Then Jimmy handed out photocopies of a picture of Marvin Gaye, in a monkey suit. That silenced them for a while.

———He's gorgeous, isn't he? said Imelda.

—Yeah, said Natalie.

Joey The Lips looked up from his copy.

—He's up there watching, Brothers.

—Now, said Jimmy when they all had one. —What's wrong with tha'?

—Nothin'.

—He looks grand, doesn't he?

———Yeah.

—We'll get good ones. Fitted. ———Okay?

Outspan looked up.

—Okay.

One of the best was the night Jimmy gave them their stage names.

—What's wrong with our ordin'y names? Dean wanted to know.

—Nothin', Dean, said Jimmy. —Nothin' at all.

—Well then?

—Look, said Jimmy. —Take Joey. He's Joey Fagan, righ'? ——Plain, ordin'ry Joey Fagan. An ordin'ry little bollix.

—That's me, Brother, said Joey The Lips. —I'm the Jesus of Ordinary.

—But when Joey goes on-stage he's Joey The Lips Fagan.

—So?

—He's not ordin'y up there. He's special. ——He needs a new name.

—Soul is dignity, Joey The Lips reminded them.

—What's dignified abou' a stupid name like The fuckin' Lips?

—I bleed, said Joey The Lips.

—Sorry, Joey. Nothin' personal.

Joey The Lips smiled.

—It's part o' the image, said Jimmy. —Like James Brown is the Godfather of Soul.

—He's still just James Brown though.

—Sometimes he's James Mr Please Please Please Brown.

——Is he? said Outspan. —Sounds thick though, doesn't it?

—Ours won't, said Jimmy.

He took out his notebook.

—I've been doin' some thinkin' abou' it.

—Oh fuck!

—Listen. ——Okay, we already have Joey The Lips Fagan, righ'. Now ——James, you'll be James The Soul Surgeon Clifford.

There were cheers and a short burst of clapping.

—Is tha' okay? Jimmy asked.

—I like it, said James.

He liked it alright. He was delighted.

—The Soul Surgeon performs transplants on the old piano, he said.

—That's it, said Jimmy. —That's the type o' thing. Everyone in the group becomes a personality.

—Go on, Jimmy.

They were getting excited.

—Derek.

—Yes, Jimmy?

—You're Derek The Meatman Scully.

They laughed.

—Wha' the fuck's tha' abou'? Derek asked.

He was disappointed.

—Are you fuckin' slaggin' me?

—You're a butcher, said Jimmy.

—I know I'm a fuckin' butcher.

—Yeh play the bass like a butcher, said Jimmy.

—Fuckin' thanks!

—It's a compliment, it's a compliment. ——Yeh wield the axe, —— know wha't I mean?

—I'll wield your bollix if yeh don't think of a better name.

—Hang on. —You'll like this. ————Over in America, righ', d'yeh know wha' meat is?

—The same as it is here.

—'cept there's more of it.

—No, listen, said Jimmy. —Meat is slang for your langer.

There were cheers and screams.

—That's fuckin' disgustin', said Natalie.

—Hang on a minute, said Derek. —Is Meatman the American way o' sayin' Langerman?

—Yeah.

—Why not call him Langerman then?

—Or Dickhead, said Deco.

—Fuck off, you, said Derek.

He wasn't happy at all.

—Listen, he said.

This wasn't going to be easy, especially with the girls there.

—There's nothin' special abou' my langer.

—YEEOOW, DEREK!

—Gerrup, Derek, yeh boy yeh!

—A bit of quiet please, Brothers, said Joey The Lips.

—It's the image, said Jimmy. ————Annyway nobody'll know wha' the name stands for till we break it in the States.

—It's a good name, said Joey The Lips. —Ever band needs its Meatman.

————I don't know, said Derek. —Me ma would kill me if she knew I was called after me gooter.

—She won't know.

—I'll tell her, said Outspan.

—Fuck off.

—Righ', said Jimmy. —Next ————Deco.

—Can I be Meatman too, Jimmy?

—No, said Jimmy. —You're Declan Blanketman Cuffe.

—That's a rapid name, said Outspan.

—Politics an' sex, said Jimmy. —Wha' d'yeh think, Deco?

—Yeah, said Deco.

—Billy.

—Howyeh.

—Billy The Animal Mooney.

—Ah deadly! Animal. ————Thanks, Jimmy.

—No sweat. ———Okay, Dean next. ——Dean.

Dean sat up.

—You're Dean Good Times Fay.

Cheers.

—That's grand, said Dean.

—Wha' abou' us? said Imelda.

—Hang on, said Jimmy. ——Outspan, we can't call yeh Outspan.

—Why not?

—It's racialist.

—WHA'!

—It's racialist. ——South African oranges.

—That's fuckin' crazy, Jimmy, said Billy.

—It's me jaysis name, said Outspan.

—Not your real name.

—Even me oul' one calls me Outspan.

—No she doesn't, said Derek.

—Fuck off you or I'll trounce yeh.

—I saw a thing on telly, said Dean. —It said they make black prisoners, righ', pick the oranges.

—I don't make annyone pick fuckin' oranges! said Outspan.

—Soul has no skin colour, Brothers and Sisters, said Joey The Lips.

—I don't even like oranges, said Outspan. ———'cept them satsumas. ——They're nice.

—Does soul eat oranges, Joey?

—Leave Joey alone, Fuckface, said Jimmy. —Listen, ——your name's Liam, righ'?

—I fuckin' know tha', thanks, said Outspan.

—It's not a very soulful name.

—Aah ——fuckin' hell! I can't even have me real name now.

—Shut up a minute. ——What's your second name?

—Wha' d'yeh mean, like?

—I'm James Anthony Rabbitte. What're you?

—Liam, said Outspan.

He went scarlet.

————Terence Foster.

—Howyeh, Terence, Imelda waved across at him.

He was going to tell her to fuck off but he didn't because he fancied her.

(Along with Jimmy, Derek, Deco, Billy, James and Dean, Outspan was in love with Imelda.)

—Righ', said Jimmy. —You are L. Terence Foster. —Listen to it, said Jimmy. —It sounds great. L. Terence Foster, L. Terence Foster. Doesn't it sound great?

—It sounds deadly, said Derek. —Better than bleedin' Meatman.

—Swap yeah, said Outspan.

—No way, said Jimmy.

—Wha' abou' us? said Bernie.

—Righ', said Jimmy. —Are yis ready, girls? ——Yis are ——Sonya, Sofia, an' Tanya, The Commitmentettes.

The girls screamed and then laughed.

—I bags Sonya, said Imelda.

—I'm Sofia then, said Natalie. —Sofia Loren.

—With a head like tha'?

—Fuck yourself, you.

—You've the arse for it anyway, Nat'lie.

—Fuck yourself.

—Wha' abou' me? said Bernie.

—She'd forgotten the last name.

—You're Fido, said Deco.

—Fuck yourself, said Natalie.

—Fuck yourself, Deco said back at her.

Natalie spat at his face.

—Here! Stop tha', said Jimmy.

—Hope yeh catch AIDS off it, said Natalie.

Deco let it go because he was in love with Natalie too.

—You're Tanya, Bernie, said Jimmy.

—Why can't I be Bernie?

—It's the image, Bernie.

—You'll always be Bernie to us, Bernie, said James.

—I must say, Jimmy, said Joey The Lips. —You've got a great man- agerial head on your shoulders.

—Thanks, Joey, said Jimmy.

—Brothers, Sisters, said Joey The Lips. —Would you please put your hands together to show your appreciation to Brother James Anthony Rabbitte.

They clapped, all of them.

David Ritz

WHAT'S GOING ON

What tortured Marvin Gaye was the same thing that tortured so many other great rock and roll and soul singers who came from a life in the church: the constant struggle between the sacred and the profane. David Ritz, who collaborated with Ray Charles, Jerry Wexler, Etta James, and Smokey Robinson, intended to collaborate with Gaye on an autobiography, but Gaye's father messed up that plan.

ONE THEORY of the life of Marvin Gaye could view his personal history as a carefully predetermined work—a play, a novel, a suite of songs—consciously constructed by the singer himself. Marvin liked to give the impression that he was calling the shots, creating wild twists and turns in order to keep himself amused. He possessed a highly developed sense of drama which, to some degree, shaped the very events of his existence. Gaye made himself into the author and principal actor in an incredible adventure which took him to the very top, then threw him to the bottom, only to have him rise again even higher, so that in the end his final fall would be his most spectacular.

The deeper truth, though, is that Marvin was only partially in control. His script had been written long before he appeared on the planet in Sophocles' play *Oedipus Rex,* produced four hundred years before the birth of Christ. The murderous relationship between father and son was a theme known to both the soul singer and the Greek playwright, and this classical sense of tragic inevitability hung over Gaye's life like a dark cloud. Guilty of another tragic failing, that of hubris—wanting too much, reaching too far, confusing himself for a god—Marvin fought his fate in vain.

The fundamentalist Christian view of Marvin Gaye would see him as a fallen preacher. Born with the sacred power to transmit Jesus' love through heavenly song, his religious responsibility was, at least in Marvin's own mind, clear. According to his own testimony, he'd felt the calling as a small child. But Marvin's electricity, like Al Green's, generated two sorts of reactions, sexual and spiritual, depending upon which switch Gaye chose to pull. "When Marvin defied God," a member of the House of God told me, "he understood the terrible price he'd have to pay."

The proof of his ability to preach is found in *What's Going On*. Along with Gaye's *In Our Lifetime,* written a decade later, *What's Going On*, like Ellington's sacred work, has the unmistakable sound of divine inspiration. But even more than Ellington, Gaye's gift was to reach out to millions on Top Ten radio, to wrap his holy messages in irresistible swathings of richly colored musical cloth.

What's Going On was the quiet moment in the raging storm that swept through so much of Marvin's life. In searching for subject matter, Gaye wisely chose to write about someone he knew—his brother. He made Frankie the main character of his work, looking back at America through the soul of his sibling.

With his sloped eyes, soft speaking voice, and lilting intonation, Frankie bears a striking resemblance to his brother. He also shares Marvin's acute sensitivity.

"The death and destruction I saw in Vietnam sickened me," Frankie told me. "The war seemed useless, wrong, and unjust. I relayed all this to Marvin and forgave him for never writing to me while I was over there. That had hurt, because he was a big star and none of my buddies believed he was my brother. 'Wait,' I told them, 'he's going to write me back and prove it to you.' He never did."

The tenuous relationship between the brothers would continue through the seventies, with Frankie gently pushing Marvin to let him sing while Marvin gently pushed Frankie into the background. For a short while, Frankie became one of Marvin's background vocalists. His contribution to *What's Going On,* though, was one of inspiration, not participation. Frankie's religious disposition set the record's tone. Far less troubled than his brother and father, Frankie was the perfect persona, adopted by Marvin, to express the sorrows and offer the solutions to what was ailing a war-torn America.

"I know this sounds strange," Frankie told me, "but I think that Marvin was always envious of my war experience. He saw it as a manly act that he had avoided. It's even stranger because while Marvin was always my hero, I was also his hero. I really believe he wanted to be me."

To some degree, there were musical precedents for *What's Going On*. Curtis Mayfield had long been intrigued by social themes, incorporating Christianity into "People Get Ready," a pop hit in 1965. Isaac Hayes, whose

Hot Buttered Soul profoundly influenced Marvin, was voicing strings and writing his quasi-symphonic score for *Shaft* at about the same time Gaye was composing *What's Going On.*

As with almost all Marvin's major projects, he himself didn't initiate the musical action. He needed help to get past his inertia. The title song, "What's Going On," was composed by Renaldo "Obie" Benson of the Four Tops and Al Cleveland, though there are somewhat conflicting explanations of its specific origins.

"We argued over the credits," Obie told me. "Marvin was funny when it came to credit, but basically it went down like this: I gave Marvin one-third of the song to sing and produce it. Naturally he put his own touches on it, being the master that he is. But all the music was already there."

"One day after Lem, Marvin, and I played golf," Mel Farr remembered, "we went back over Marvin's house on Outer Drive. We'd hit the ball especially good that day and we were all feeling good, sitting around and kibitzing, when I said, 'Hey, what's going on?' Marvin said, 'You know, that'd be a hip title for a song. I think I'll write it for the Originals.' He started fooling at the piano and when we dropped by to see him the next day he was still fooling with it. 'That's not for the Originals, Marvin,' we told him. 'That's for you.' "

Marvin wrote most of the songs in conjunction with others. Though he never stopped worrying that he wouldn't receive enough credit, Gaye still preferred company in the early creative stages. The major work, however, was essentially his.

"From Jump Street, Motown fought *What's Going On,*" Marvin claimed. "They didn't like it, didn't understand it, and didn't trust it. Management said the songs were too long, too formless, and would get lost on a public looking for easy three-minute stories. For months they wouldn't release it. My attitude had to be firm. Basically I said, 'Put it out or I'll never record for you again.' That was my ace in the hole, and I had to play it."

The ploy worked. Marvin won, and the winnings were bigger than even he had imagined. His first self-produced, self-written album altered not only his career but his very life. From now on, he'd be perceived—by the white community as well as by the black, in Europe and in America—as a complex and serious artist.

Everything about the album was different. The back cover showed a bearded, distraught Marvin standing in the rain, wearing a tie he had sworn never to wear. For the first time on one of his records, lyrics were listed and musicians credited. In spite of the fact that, according to his sister Jeanne, he had long ignored his family in Washington, D.C., he dedicated the work to his parents, among others—"thanks to the Rev. & Mrs. Marvin P. Gay Sr. for conceiving, having and loving me"—his sisters, brothers, wife, son, and friends, Clarence Paul and Harvey Fuqua among them. Berry Gordy was not mentioned, nor would Marvin ever thank him on the back of an album.

Vince Aletti spoke for a number of critics when, reviewing the record for *Rolling Stone,* he admitted that he had underestimated Marvin Gaye. *Time* magazine wrote a two-column review of the work: "After listening to . . . *What's Going On,* the Rev. Jesse Jackson informed its creator, Soul Crooner Marvin Gaye, that he was as much a minister as any man in any pulpit." The article quotes Marvin: "God and I travel together with right-eousness and goodness. If people want to follow along, they can."

The *Time* reviewer went on: "The LP laments war, pollution, heroin and the miseries of ghetto life. It also praises God and Jesus, blesses peace, love, children and the poor. Musically it is a far cry from the gospel or blues a black singer-composer might normally apply to such subjects. Instead Gaye weaves a vast, melodically deft symphonic pop suite in which Latin beats, Soft Soul and white pop, and occasionally scat and Hollywood schmaltz, yield effortlessly to each other. The overall style . . . is so lush and becalming that the words—which in themselves are often merely simplistic—come at the listener like dots from a Seurat landscape."

From the opening alto riffs of the title song, the listener was ushered into new musical territory. The establishment of a groove—lightly swinging, sweetly mellow, deeply relaxed—became Gaye's hallmark. For all the emotional and literary complexity, the effect was easy listening. Marvin sang to please the ear.

His multitracked voices were startling. He'd become a one-man Moonglows, a one-man Originals, singing duets and trios with himself, juxtaposing his silky falsetto and sandpapery midrange, weaving the fabric of his voices into a tapestry of contrasting shapes and colors.

"I felt like I'd finally learned how to sing," Marvin told me. "I'd been studying the microphone for a dozen years, and suddenly I saw what I'd been doing wrong. I'd been singing too loud, especially on those Whitfield songs. It was all so easy. One night I was listening to a record by Lester Young, the horn player, and it came to me. Relax, just relax. It's all going to be all right.

"I also saw that I wanted to treat the album as an album, not as a string of small songs. So I found a theme, and I tried to explore it from several different angles. At first, I was afraid, because I didn't know whether this had ever been done before, but when I got started I actually found that the process came naturally. It was easy. Don Juan was right: I was traveling down a path of the heart."

Marvin's instincts were to write from his immediate experience. Thus *What's Going On* was set in America's black urban neighborhoods, the territory of his childhood. The title song began with party sounds. Marvin's friends—Lem Barney, Mel Farr, Bobby Rodgers of Smokey's Miracles, and Elgie Stover—created an intimate atmosphere in which Marvin felt most comfortable. They were family.

"Later on," Mel Farr told me, "Motown convinced Marvin to re-record the tune with a group of professional backup singers. But it didn't sound as natural as the original, and Marvin stuck to his guns."

The first two songs set the scene and stated the sermon's thesis, combining an urgent 1971 political plea with a personal note to his own father. He cried out to his mother, to his brother, to all the brothers dying in the war, and finally pleaded with Father, singing that there's no need to "escalate."

"If I was arguing for peace," Marvin said, "I knew I'd have to find peace in my own heart. All the time since I'd been in Detroit, Father and I had little to say to each other. It was still hard for me to even look at him, even though I knew that he'd been collecting articles on me for the last ten years. He kept everything—more for his ego than mine. He might have been proud, but he was more jealous than anything else. Secretly I was wishing Mother would throw him out and divorce him, but I knew that could never happen. I didn't want him living off me, but how could I stop him when I had to support Mother? Basically, I was supporting the whole family. I resented that. But now was the time to put those resentments behind me. Jesus said forgive, and I needed to forgive, and be forgiven. Love should be unconditional. To be truly righteous, you offer love with a pure heart, without regard for what you'll get in return. I had myself in that frame of mind. People were confused and needed reassurance. God was offering that reassurance through his music. I was privileged to be the instrument."

In "What's Happening, Brother," Marvin spoke through brother Frankie, just back from Vietnam, facing a divided country and an uncertain future. The central character admitted confusion, not understanding what was happening "across this land."

Uncertainty led to escape. Drugs—its pains and pleasures—were the subject of the eerily seductive "Flyin' High (in the Friendly Sky)." Containing the seed of *Trouble Man,* Gaye's next major work, the song not only lamented the spread of dope in the ghetto, but echoed Gaye's concern with his own growing cocaine habit, calling it "self-destruction" and admitting he was "hooked."

The despair expanded to the horror of a nuclear holocaust. "Save the Children" became the album's most poignant piece, as Marvin asked a series of questions in a speaking voice filled with melancholy: Will all the flowers fade? Can the world be saved? Is humanity destined to die? Are our children fated to suffer? Do we care enough to save ourselves?

Based on Revelations and the state of the world, Gaye was convinced that the end was imminent. As time passed and his own fortunes fell, those convictions deepened. Now, though, after his doomsday vision, his depression was suddenly assuaged: Affirmation arrived in perhaps the single most emotional moment he ever reached on record. He spoke the words, "Let's save all the children," and then answered himself in song, pleading, "Save the babies, save the babies!" In the transition between the plainly spoken word "children" and the impassioned cry of "babies," Gaye's clarion call was clear as the light of day.

With lifted spirits, the suite continued seamlessly. The rhythm quickened. Hope was offered. "God is love." Marvin mentioned Jesus, whose only demand was that we "give each other love."

"I respect the Eastern religions," said Gaye. "Their philosophies are beautiful and wise. They've taught me to root myself in the present. I also believe in reincarnation. We're destined to return to repeat our mistakes if we don't grow toward God in this form. I respect Islam, though I worry that the Koran makes it too easy to kill. I respect all he great religions. But my own beliefs come down to two simple points. One, believe in Jesus, and two, expand love. Both points, you see, are really the same."

I said that I was surprised, given how he had rebelled against his father, that he had never rebelled against his father's Christianity.

"I could see the truth," Marvin explained, "not in Father's example, but in the words he preached."

Even at the bottom of his bluest funks, Gaye was clear about the lessons of Jesus. At some point Marvin lost the way—he himself said he didn't deserve to be called a practicing Christian—but God was always the light toward which he longed to travel.

"One of the reasons I love my father," said Marvin in one of his preaching moods, "is because he offered me Jesus. He made Jesus come alive for me, and that's reason enough to be grateful to him for the rest of my life. It's not about this church or that church. Almost all churches are corrupt. My church lives within my own heart. Jesus is there when you call him, whether you're strolling through a garden or caught in a storm at sea. He's a lifeline. He's a healer. His name is magic. His example is eternal. His hope is a beacon of light, and with him there is no fear, no death. When we don't follow his example and turn to exploitation and greed, we destroy ourselves. That's what 'Mercy Mercy Me' is about."

The song catalogued the ecological nightmares plaguing the world—mercury in our fish, oil spills, radiation, endangered species. How much more, he asked, can this "overcrowded" nation endure.

But in "Right On," Marvin turned away from the world—at least for a moment—to describe his own condition with characteristic candor. He admitted to a life of privilege, money, and "good fortune." And yet with so much wealth surrounding him, he saw himself as a man who "drowned in the sea of happiness." Such was the story of his life.

If he was to be spared, only love could save him, a unity of spirit expressed in the song "Wholly Holy."

Moving full circle, the suite ended where it began, back in the neighborhood, describing the plight of the poor through an ancient black blues—"Inner City Blues"—measured by the cadence of an urban bongo beat. The burden of taxes was a theme that ran through Marvin's work, just as it ran through Marvin's life. He viewed the obligation with adamancy and anger: Why pay taxes to buy moon rockets when we can't feed our poor? Why are we sending innocent sons off to die in wars that make no sense? Why have the cops gone "trigger happy?" Why has the world gone mad?

What's Going On concluded by repeating a small section of the title song in which Gaye expressed his sympathy with the rebellious youth of the early seventies, arguing against the injustice of judging people by the length of their hair.

Despite what Marvin called Motown's skepticism, the response in the marketplace was immediate and overwhelming. The album was the most successful in Gaye's recorded history. Between February and October of 1971, three of the songs—"What's Going On," "Mercy Mercy Me," and "Inner City Blues"—hit the Top Ten on the soul and pop charts.

It's easy to forget how radical the work was by 1971 standards. Structurally, the songs were not typical Top Ten fare. They owed as much to jazz as to soul or pop. "Wild Bill" Moore's raging tenor, for instance, was mixed under many of the tracks, an ongoing jazz counterpoint to the rest of the musical action. Song lengths were unconventional. "Inner City Blues" was over five minutes. Commercially, the notion of a black bitterly criticizing America was thought to be risky. For instance, James Brown's message songs, like "I Don't Want Nobody to Give Me Nothing (Open the Door, I'll Get It Myself)," had a conservative bent. Brown was basically patriotic; Gaye was not. There was also the old adage that, lyrically at least, gospel and pop never mix. Jesus simply wasn't mentioned in secular songs, not if you were aiming for a pop market.

In one fell swoop, Marvin disproved these theories. He revolutionized soul music by expanding its boundaries. He changed the direction of Motown by showing the sales potential of thought-provoking inner monologues. In winning the fight for his own integrity, others—equally talented and capable of creating their own art—benefited: Stevie Wonder, who since age ten had been studying Marvin, and now another Motown preteen, Michael Jackson, who would eventually follow Gaye's artistic lead as a singer, writer, and producer.

"When I was struggling for the right of the Motown artist to express himself," Marvin told me, "Steve knew I was also struggling for him. He gained from that fight, and the world gains from his genius. Don't get me wrong—Stevie would have made it big without me. His talent is cosmic. But as it turned out, Stevie's really a preacher like the rest of us. I like to think I helped show him the light. Now every time I hear him, in between my twinges of jealousy I thank God for Stevie's gift and the privilege of feeling his energy at such close range.

"The biggest result of *What's Going On,* though, had to do with my own freedom. I'd earned it, and no one could take it away from me. Now I could do whatever I wanted. For most people that would be a blessing. But for me—with all my hot little games—the thought was heavy. They said I'd reach the top, and that scared me 'cause Mother used to say, 'first ripe, first rotten.' When you're at the top there's nowhere to go but down. No, I needed to keep going up—raising my consciousness—or I'd fall back on my behind.

"When would the war stop? That's what I wanted to know . . . the war inside my soul."

Even with his creative breakthrough accomplished, Marvin's soul remained split. His ego demanded that he return to center stage, but his insecurities made him want to hide. As a result, Gaye alternated between two extremes, seeking love and rejecting love, realizing success and throwing it away, assuming the attitude of a prince while living with the fears of a pauper.

Rickey Vincent

THE MOTHERSHIP CONNECTION

George Clinton once said that his avowed purpose as leader of Parliament Funkadelic was "to rescue dance music from the blahs." He has been largely successful.

> "Funk . . . created the gods."
> —*Dr. Funkenstein*

GEORGE Clinton and his P-Funk band developed something far greater than their simple identity as a musical ensemble. P-Funk was and is more than a music style; it is a philosophy of life that for some approaches a religious creed.

Clinton himself maintains that P-Funk was never meant to be taken seriously, but its followers often did anyway. From the hard-core "maggots," "clones," and "funkateers" to the typical fan, P-Funk articulated a new worldview, often more relevant than the religious practices of their relatives in the detached decade of the 1970s. Those who chose to pay attention found that one could get deeper and deeper into P-Funk and never reach the bottom. Clinton's entourage ritualized The Funk into a metaphysical phenomenon of self-development not unlike the mystery systems of Africa and the Caribbean. Radio personality and funkateer Ashem "The Funky Man" Habaragani claims that "P-Funk is a Mystery System, like the ancient Mystery Systems of Kemet (Egypt); there's a rites of passage, and a way to better yourself."

The religiosity of P-Funk has never really been taken seriously, perhaps because of the lack of religious significance Clinton himself attributes to his music. However, with the many reincarnations of P-Funk philosophies in the rap music of the 1990s, and the growing awareness of the understanding of African religious systems, the deepness of the P is more relevant than ever. (It should be understood, however, that there are as many interpretations of The Funk as there are funkateers, and what follows is just one of them.)

The cool style of P-Funk scored a series of No. 1 dance singles from 1975 to 1980, which spawned a series of platinum-selling albums, which in turn drew thousands of fans to elaborate concerts filled with black cartoon characters, painted people, million-dollar props, loud music, and a series of chants told over a nasty, nasty groove. The long jams often "spaced out," in which obscure, eerie synthesizer tones and the offbeat philosophical ranting of Clinton and others in the band compelled listeners to absorb the meanings and the feel of the sounds. Visually, the band's look suggested—and the huge show created—an alternate reality, "dressed in diapers and leotards, as genies and wolfmen . . . looking like a cross between 'Star Trek' and 'Sanford and Son'." The music and concepts drew listeners into a coded philosophy of black nationhood, of freedom of expression and personal salvation through the use of symbols and double meanings that had deep roots in black music and religious traditions.

Bandleader George Clinton and writer-artist Pedro Bell were the primary sources of an endless flow of offbeat black philosophy that mocked the self-importance of religious and political doctrines while subtly creating their own. Clinton's use of operatic vocals and church-based funk chants were common, but they became subversive when the lyrics reprised well-known themes in black religion, while affirming the present-day circumstances of blacks. . . . Without polemics, militarism, or racially charged code words, Clinton's P-Funk placed the African-American sensibility at the center of the universe, and ultimately at the center of *history.*

Presaging by a decade the controversies surrounding historical accounts of the African origins of civilization, Clinton's crew circulated the notion that the pyramids were not only built by Africans (probably from outer space), but that these Africans were some bad mothas who could "Tear the Roof off the Sucker." By extension, P-Funk was claiming that symbolically, blacks *were responsible for civilization.* . . .

The mob later toyed with the notion of the Big Bang, claiming that a P-Funk party in "the Black Hole" was the cause of the *entire universe,* proclaiming, "That fuss wuz us." Parliament continued to link the story lines of every album, beginning with *Mothership Connection* in 1975, followed by *Clones of Dr. Funkenstein* in 1976, and the live recording *P-Funk Earth Tour.* A series of cartoon characters were introduced, beginning with "Star-Child" (alias the long haid sucka), one of the first clones of "Dr. Funkenstein"—the body-snatching doctor of funk played by George Clinton. On *Funkentelechy vs. the Placebo Syndrome* in 1977, an evil nemesis of funk was created, "Sir Nose D'Voidoffunk" (a character first conceived by P-Funk manager Tom Vickers, and overheard as usual by Clinton). This unfunky and overdressed character refused to dance, and spread the "Placebo Syndrome" everywhere he went. "Sir Nose," along with a growing cast of characters, followed the band around the universe in liner-note stories and on the recordings of the subsequent three albums: *Motor Booty Affair* in 1978, *Gloryhallastupid* in 1979, and *Trombipulation* in 1980.

Funkadelic album artist Pedro Bell was also guilty of perpetrating a bizarre, Afro-centric mythology on long Funkadelic album cover essays, which complemented his felt-tip-marker-drawn mutant-scapes of urban black life. Bell's visual imagery had the seamless layering of twisted symbols from the unconscious that Salvador Dali was known for, while Bell's dark ghetto eroticism and hyperbolic grammar forged a new realm of black language:

> *AS IT IS WRITTEN HENCEFORTH . . . that on the Eighth Day, the Cosmic Strumpet of MOTHER NATURE was spawned to envelope this Third Planet in FUNKACIDAL VIBRATIONS. And she birthed Apostles Ra, Hendrix, Stone and CLINTON to preserve all funkiness of man unto eternity . . . But! Fraudulent forces of obnoxious JIVATION grew. Sun Ra strobed back to Saturn to await his Next Reincarnation, Jimi was forced back into basic atoms; Sly was co-opted into a jester monolith . . . and only seedling GEORGE remained. As it came to be, he did indeed, begat Funkadelic to restore Order Within The Universe. Nourished by the Pamgrierian mammaristic melonpaps of Mother Nature, the followers of FUNKADELIA multiplied incessantly!*
>
> Standing on the Verge of Gettin' It On, liner notes (1974)

The fact that the entire P-Funk experience, the entire scene, the entire thang was too preposterous to be taken seriously allowed the funk mob to make all sorts of claims about the inherent qualities of Africans—and reach millions of listeners without the traditional hassles of spokesperson status. It also kept Clinton from the pop star visibility that might have kept his band in the black countless times.

The importance of these silly stories is the fact that Parliament, Funkadelic, and Bootsy's Rubber Band sold over ten million records in the last half of the 1970s by hitting first with the music, then drawing listeners into elaborate fantasyscapes that influenced a generation of urban youth. Clinton and his associates drew such far-reaching scope for their silly stories and cartoon characters that one can conceive of their works as folklore, and perhaps some of the first postindustrial black American mythology. Science fiction has often been associated with a religion or mythology for the technological age, by posing a backdrop for the major questions of creation and the destiny of mankind. Clinton and crew developed their own creation myths and their own black science-fiction, which placed the streetwise homeboy in the center of a series of inter-galactic parables, in which whites did not exist and the values and attrib-utes alluded to by The Funk constituted the resolution of each tale.

The mythic character of the many players in P-Funk served as ideals—albeit freaked-out ideals—of people inhabiting an imagined universe of total funkativity. The characters provided a framework for young people to imagine themselves in the image of their "Super Funky Heroes." In his 1987 Thesis on "The P-Funk Aesthetic," Michael O'Neal discusses the use-fulness of the P-Funk aesthetic as positive imagery for black children:

> Sir Nose and Starchild, and Dr. Frankenstein, as animated (as op-posed to real) superheroes, give black children a sense of animation in their own likeness that previously they have been denied—espe-cially by the media. These superheroes offer them a mythic sense of possibility.

The importance of inverting the negative associations with black-ness, darkness, funkiness, and stoopidness cannot be underestimated. The relentless barrage of negative information about black people por-trayed in the media, the absence of visible black advocates in the public eye, and the very semantic foundation of the language that associates white with "good" and black with "bad" can be overwhelming to a black child. P-Funk began to turn these notions on their heads.

The rise of P-Funk was part of a new era in black culture that devel-oped after the civil rights movement. The concept, and the myth, of black liberation since the days of slavery has been centered on the strong Christian-based notion of an Exodus from Babylon to the "Promised Land." The powerful speeches of Martin Luther King were based on this religious and cultural theme. "We Shall Overcome" was the theme song of the civil rights movement (with P-Funk the chant had become "Got to get over the hump!"); by the early 1970s, it was becoming clear that the reli-gious imagery of the past was inadequate for many of the black youth of the day. Youngsters who grew up in the 1970s never witnessed Dr. King on television or in person, and the most prominent blacks were often sports stars, including the Muslims Muhammad Ali and Kareem Abdul Jabbar. According to record producer and funkateer Anthony "Dave-ID K-OS" Bryant, there were many blacks who could see that the conditioning of traditional religion was "not happening" for them, could also see that "P-Funk was deeply religious, but also speaking to the way they are living today."

In the largest and most expensive black concert tour to date in 1977, Clinton and his entourage had a spaceship prop built, which would descend from the rafters of any large stadium. The performance preceding the descent of the Mothership was laden with funky ritualism, meditative chants, a series of massive symbolic stage props brought onstage, and a gospel churchlike invocation to bring the ship down. After a considerable frenzy had been built up, the chant "Swing down, I wanna ride" signified it was time for the landing.

The thunderous spectacle of lights, smoke, relentless music, and mystical symbolism was a profound example of black tradition in its unrestricted state. While the show was primarily designed as entertainment, and "Dr. Frankenstein" comes out of the ship to join the party, the landing of the Mothership serves as a metaphor for the "chariot" responsible for bringing "the chosen" to the Promised Land. The "chariot" is a myth, yet this chariot was *real.* The decade of the 1970s indeed represented that "Promised Land" of equality, a period of experiment in "integration" and "equality" for which the civil rights movement had worked for so long. P-Funk attempted to bring meaning and catharsis to that paradoxical realization of freedom. The Mothership was a celebration of the infinities of which blacks were now capable.

While raised with a traditional black Christian background, George Clinton was disinclined to associate with it. Clinton claims that the drug experience is what transformed his beliefs. "I didn't really believe in religion until I took acid in 1963. I didn't hear the Ten Commandments until then," he once said. Ultimately his mission was to "take rock until it becomes what the church was." By using nontraditional methods to attain a spiritual expression, Clinton used P-Funk to open the boundaries to spirituality—as a true *universalist.* Journalist Abe Peck concluded after a 1976 interview that "Clinton's spirituality has more to do with cosmic oneness than this earth's religions."

Many of the world's religions (particularly African ones) emphasize a "cosmic oneness" with everything, rather than the Western Christian concepts of man "fearing" God, man *versus* nature, mind versus body, intellect versus intuition. The African spiritual root of The Funk is important because the essence of funk music, as well as the *funk attitude,* is a return to certain traditional ways, among which are the basics of music-making; a celebration of the earthy, funky, emotionally vital way of life; and a cosmology of "oneness" in which everything and everyone in the universe is interconnected.

In ancient African cosmology—as well as in The Funk—everything lives and is connected. Locked on the one-count of the beat, Clinton's band regularly uses the chant "Every-thing-is-on-the-One" to express more than the unity of the band, the beat, and the rhythm. "On the One" means the oneness of everything. When The Funk is in full effect, every participant is a part of the Rhythm of the One.

The humanistic, inviting realm of many of the black bands of the 1970s consistently explored and advocated the idea of oneness, by maintaining large ensembles that could groove together, and by preaching songs of nondenominational spiritual and political unity. Their specific ideologies were often vague, but musically, most funk bands in the seventies had an implicit understanding of the groove, the essential *funk lock.* Funk bands accomplished rhythmically what few could say literally: that a diversity of rhythms represents a diversity of individuals, and that they all can be united—through the rhythmic groove of The Funk. Clinton's P-Funk not only grooved harder, longer, and deeper than the rest; they codified the thematic trend into an all-encompassing concept: P-Funk. By expanding the unity amid diversity concept beyond the small band—to a large band—to an entire collective—a modern tribe—a community—or a universe—P-Funk music offers a symbolic basis of organizing a *real community.* This was the ideal behind "One Nation Under a Groove." Clinton described the impulse of his biggest hit "One Nation" as: "Everybody on the One, the whole world on the same pulse." Thus the Rhythm of the One is the key to a collective spirit.

Michael Gonzales

MY FATHER NAMED ME PRINCE

**Here's a portrait of that enigmatic musician *Code* magazine
called "the artist who did that fucked up thing with his
name." Once again "Prince," he has survived critical
dressing-downs, record company squabbles, and fans who
couldn't pronounce the symbol that was his name.**

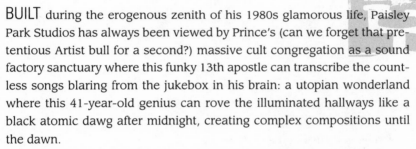

BUILT during the erogenous zenith of his 1980s glamorous life, Paisley
Park Studios has always been viewed by Prince's (can we forget that pretentious Artist bull for a second?) massive cult congregation as a sound
factory sanctuary where this funky 13th apostle can transcribe the countless songs blaring from the jukebox in his brain: a utopian wonderland
where this 41-year-old genius can rove the illuminated hallways like a
black atomic dawg after midnight, creating complex compositions until
the dawn.

Inside the spacious Paisley Park, the only rules that apply are Prince's
own—and since he never wears a watch, recording sessions can happen
whenever the mood slaps him. As Prince would later inform me, "My dad
was a musician, so I learned how to play the piano to please him. Our parents can be like gods to us, so I wanted to make him happy. But the only
voices I admired at the time were Smokey Robinson's and Blue Magic's.
Those were the brothers I wanted to sound like when I sang." One can almost imagine the kid humming "The Tears of a Clown" to himself while
being bused to a rich, white school in the fifth grade.

Located in the small burg of Chanhassen, about 30 minutes from
downtown Minneapolis—bordered by massive trees, nearby fast-food
joints and private homes—Paisley's waiting area has the playful appeal of
a circus funhouse as designed by the surreal eye of Salvador Dali. Chilling
on one of the colorful overstuffed chairs, I can hear soft music drifting over
the gentle cooing of the caged doves upstairs; next to the birdcage are
racks of multicolored, flamboyant costumes, while on the main floor
purple-hued walls are covered with framed platinum albums. Ivory birds
and fluffy clouds are painted on the upper part of the same wall.

"Hello," a bassy voice says, snapping me instantly out of a daydream queendom where Apollonia rules with a golden lasso. Dressed in sharp black pants, a thin bronze-colored sweater and matching boots, Prince glides across the blue carpet with the style of a runway model. Although he's a mere five foot three (without the heels, of course), Prince has a seductive, ocean-deep voice that would make Barry White proud. The only obvious oddity is the excessive facial foundation on his grill. Extending his long piano fingers into my hand, Prince has the grip of an all-true man. "Let's go into the studio," he says, leading the way.

Depending on whom you speak with, especially former employees who have dealt with Prince's madness on various levels, "His Royal Badness" can either be especially charming or the most bugged bastard since Batman took residence inside a cave. Indeed, from being asked to sign a confidentiality agreement upon entering Paisley Park to being informed that taping devices are off-limits within his domain (forcing me to scribble notes like a tanned Jimmy Olsen from *Superman*), it's obvious that a sense of control is important to Prince's ego. Since breaking with his former distributor, Warner Bros. Records, in 1996, preaching a personal sermon of artistic control and emancipation has been his favorite pastime. He's even decided to go so far as to rerecord new master versions of his entire 17-album Warner Bros. catalogue for his own NPG Records label, which he launched in the mid-1990's.

Prince slides a DAT of "The Greatest Romance Ever Sold" into a nearby tape machine. Lounging in a small studio chair and resting royally on his bony elbow like a St. Louis pimp macking at a riverboat blackjack table, Prince leans over and mumbles, "I wanted this song to be my answer to the sad state of current soul music." With its mesmerizing Arabic guitar sounds and robust choruses, this was the first single from his latest release, *Rave Un2 the Joy Fantastic,* an 18-track disc featuring cameos by Chuck D. Maceo Parker, Gwen Stefani, Sheryl Crow and Ani DiFranco. It represents Prince's first dealings with a major label in more than three years.

Damn near whispering, as though his observation is top secret instead of common knowledge, Prince says, "I've been tripping lately on how wack Rhythm & Blues sounds these days. It's either [songs like] 'Bills, Bills, Bills' or 'No Pigeons.' If that's the way men and women speak to each other, no wonder relationships are such a mess." Prince shakes his head and laments the lack of real romance in today's music.

"Yeah, but back in the day you sang about getting pussy as much as some of these young dudes," I remind him. "You just had a more poetic way of putting things."

Staring momentarily with a heated gaze that could melt cotton candy, Prince slowly relaxes and busts out laughing.

What is it that troubles him most about today's producers? "It bothers me when I see Missy Elliott and Timbaland on television whining 'People have stolen our sound.' Hey, if you're so bad, change your sound," he says, without missing a LinnDrum beat. "The only way people will stop biting is if you flip your style. That's what I've always done."

Seventeen years before the premillennial mojo visions of Y2K became the latest paranoid chant for a *Strange Days* generation obsessed with wild, in-the-streets rebellion, a freaky black boy from Minneapolis emerged from a dank basement—cluttered with discarded musical equipment and sticky porn magazines—with an important lyrical dispatch for the world to absorb. Decked out in sheer pop-life panties, a glimmering purple-hued maxi coat, designer high-heel boots borrowed from his older sister's closet and dragging a spooky synth to an abandoned studio, the blackadelic dissident forever known as Prince wailed: ". . . But when I woke up this morning / I could have sworn it was judgment day."

In my own science-fiction-captured imagination, I projected images of Prince cruising through a postapocalyptic wasteland (recklessly zooming in a little red Corvette, bopping his processed perm to an electro beat) while overdosing on crazed celebrations, dizzy dancers and sanctified nookie. Prince's Armageddon anthem "1999"—first introduced in 1982—has since become a vivid booming-system soundtrack for cosmic cowboys dashing toward destruction, wild-boy hedonism and an explosive New Year's Eve. "I was having lots of futuristic visions at that time in my life," he recalls. "There are some people of the lighter persuasion—that's what I call white people—who might tell you that I was reading Nostradamus, but that's not true. I just kept having these dreams that something was going to happen, and that the world might be a little scary at the end of the '90s." Despite this year's legion of natural disasters— major earthquakes in places like Turkey, Taiwan, Greece and Mexico; the *Their Eyes Were Watching God*–like rapture of Hurricane Floyd; and innumerable acts of senseless violence—Prince will brave his own prophetic musings and salute the millennium by performing at an unannounced location on New Year's Eve.

While the chilly city of Minneapolis has been best known as the home of mumble-mouth Bob Dylan and Mary Tyler Moore's goofy news crew, it was this Twin Cities homeboy who happened to renew my faith in the power of soul. By juxtaposing his sound with any subterranean style that might tickle his electric booty—swooning show tunes ("Sometimes It

Snows in April"), banging ballsy ballads ("Adore"), glittering glam ("Kiss"), horny harmonies ("Head") and paisley psychedelic pop ("She's Always in My Hair")—he could create his own eclectic ecstasy.

With Prince's '80s masterpieces *Dirty Mind* (1980), *1999* (1982), *Purple Rain* (1984), *Parade* (1986) and *Sign 'O' the Times* (1987), this self-described "little mother——— with the high voice" redefined the sound of blackness by creating his own aural universe for himself and others—including the stereo porn of Vanity 6, the gut-bucket soul of the Time, the new-age funk of the Family and the new-jack fusion of Madhouse. Although wacko Michael Jackson might have been more thrilling to a few, it was always obvious that Prince, who transformed into a Dolby-fueled Renaissance cat in the studio, often playing all of the instruments himself, was the more talented freak in the MTV sideshow.

Impressed by his musical diversity, live-evil jazzbo Miles Davis referred to his new pal as "the Duke Ellington of modern day black pop" in the pages of his autobiography. "I loved Miles, because he was more of a music fan than most people would expect," gushes Prince. "Miles loved good musicians and cool people, but he was also the type of guy to invite Mick Jagger to his house and make him sit outside. He was the type of guy who would tell you to meet him in the dressing room, then be sitting there butt naked. But I loved him."

With a massive back catalogue of 30 discs, which doesn't even include the hundreds of bootlegs on the market, Prince also influenced the latest wave of cyber-funk warriors (Dallas Austin, Timbaland and Tricky, among others), giving them the courage to experiment with music without fear. When I was much younger, I used to sit in my bedroom in Richmond, Virginia, surrounded by Prince posters . . . just blasting his records and absorbing his sound," neo-soul-stirrer D'Angelo said, before taking a drag from his Newport. On his much anticipated sophomore joint, *Voodoo,* brother D has even composed a moving tribute to The Artist Who Will Always Be Prince. Before his name change and disillusionment with the record industry, Prince was just another funk junkie trying to get his groove on. "When I was a kid I used to ride my bike over to Dee's Record Center and buy the latest releases," remembers Prince. "Dee weighed about 400 pounds and had hair like Al Sharpton. He would play the records for me, those little 45s with the big hole in the middle, and I would ride over there every three days. James Brown was putting out a single every three weeks, and I would buy them all. I would slide the discs on my handlebars so I could watch them spin as I rode home."

Prince went from being mesmerized by spinning 45s to perfecting his own nasty onstage spins, enhanced by his signature freaky shrieks. Still, it was more than James Brown–like moves that inspired this purple wonder. In the badass spirit of the Godfather of Soul, the li'l man's initial battle with his former "slave master" Warner Bros. Records began with his prolific desire to release more records than the label was willing to support, which later snowballed into a war over ownership of his master recordings. In his new international distribution arrangement with Arista, he will retain ownership of his master tapes. "Any creation should belong to the artist," says Prince. "I'm not a brat, but I do know that Western society is based on taking without giving back. The record companies are protected against everything. What began with me wanting to record when I felt like it, slowly became about my legacy as an artist."

Yet for someone who once had the word *slave* scribbled on his face, Prince has put his money where his mouth is by forming NPG Records as an outlet for his own muse and the talents of singer Chaka Khan and bassist-singer Larry Graham. "It's not always about just getting paid, but about respect. People like Chaka and Larry get beat down, because people don't support their art," says Prince. "Artists like Ruth Brown, Al Green, George Clinton and Sly Stone are our musical cornerstones, but the kids today just dismiss their elders so easily.

"If somebody like Babyface wanted to rent my studio, I would charge a lot of money, but what would it look like if I asked Chaka or Larry for any money? If I help support them, then it sets an example for others. For me, it's more about a sense of community and friendship."

Although not everyone has the artistic leverage that Prince now enjoys in his business arrangements, his struggle for freedom has seemingly left a paranoid impression on his psyche. "I don't believe in contracts anymore, because the word *con* has a deep meaning. So I don't have a contract with Arista—I have an agreement. Nor do I still have a marriage contract with Mayte, although we're still together." In December 1998, Prince had their then three-year marriage "annulled." They shared a "symbolic" ceremony last Valentine's Day to celebrate their love for each other. In fact, nowadays, it seems that he is more concerned with reconnecting to the real meaning of love in each of his lifetimes.

As our interview slowly comes to a close, a reflective man looks at me and says, "My father named me Prince because he wanted me to go further in the world, and that's what I strive to do every day."

HIP-HOP DEFINED

Here we are, on the road with Public Enemy.

GRANTED, Charlie Parker died laughing. Choked chickenwing perched over '50s MTV. So? No way in hell did Bird, believing there was no competition in music, will his legacy to some second-generation beboppers to rattle over the heads of the hiphop nation like a rusty sabre. But when Harry Allen comes picking fights with suckers adducing hiphop the new jazz, like hiphop needs a jazz crutch to stand erect, I'm reminded of *Pithecanthropus erectus,* and not the Charles Mingus version. B-boys devolved to the missing link between jazzmen and a lower order species out of Joseph Conrad. "Perhaps you will think it passing strange, this regret for a savage who was of no more account than a grain of sand in a black Sahara. Well, don't you see, he had done something, he had steered; for months I had him at my back—a help—an instrument. It was a kind of partnership."

Hiphop being more than a cargo cult of the microchip, it deserves being debated on more elevated terms than as jazz's burden or successor. Given the near absence of interdisciplinary scholarship on the music, the conceptual straits of jazz journalism, and hiphop's cross-referential complexity, the hiphop historian must cast a wider net for critical models. Certainly Public Enemy's *It Takes a Nation of Millions to Hold Us Back* (Def Jam) demands kitchen-sink treatment. More than a hiphop record it's an ill worldview.

Nation of Millions is a will-to-power party record by bloods who believe (like Sun Ra) that for black folk, it's after the end of the world. Or, in PEspeak: "Armageddon has been in effect. Go get a late pass." In *Roll, Jordan, Roll: The World the Slaves Made,* Eugene Genovese offers that the failure of mainland blacks to sustain a revolutionary tradition during slavery was due to a lack of faith in prophets of the apocalypse. This lack, he says, derived from Africa's stolen children having no memories of a paradise lost that revolution might regain. Machiavellian thinking might have found its way into the quarters: "All armed prophets have conquered while all unarmed prophets have failed." But the observation that blacks were unable to envision a world beyond the plantation, or of a justice beyond massa's dispensation, still resonates through our politics. Four decades after Garvey, the cultural nationalists of the '60s sought to remedy our Motherland amnesia and nationhood aversions through dithyrambs, demagoguery, and a counter-supremacist doctrine that pressed for utopia over reform pragmatism. Its noblest aim was total self-determination for the black community. For PE, that, not King's, is the dream that died.

The lofty but lolling saxophone sample that lures us into the LP's "Black Side" could be a wake-up call, a call to prayer, or an imitation Coltrane cocktease. Since we're not only dealing with regenerated sound here but regenerated meaning, what was heard 20 years ago as expression has now become a rhetorical device, a trope. Making old records talk via scratching or sampling is fundamental to hiphop. But where we've heard rare grooves recycled for parodic effect or shock value ad nauseam, on "Show Em Whatcha Got" PE manages something more sublime, enfolding and subsuming the Coltrane mystique, among others, within their own. The martial thump that kicks in after the obbligato owes its bones to Funkadelic's baby years and Miles Davis's urban bush music. But the war chants from Chuck D and Flavor Flav that blurt through the mix like station identification also say, What was hip yesterday we save from becoming passé. Since three avant-gardes overlap here—free jazz, funk, hiphop—the desired effect might seem a salvage mission. Not until Sister Ava Muhammad's tribute-to-the-martyrs speech fragments begin their cycle do you realize Public Enemy are offering themselves up as the next in line for major black prophet, missionary, or martyrdom status. Give them this much: PE paragon Farrakhan excepted, nobody gives you more for your entertainment dollar while cold playing that colored man's messiah role.

PE wants to reconvene the black power movement with hiphop as the medium. From the albums and interviews, the program involves rabble-rousing rage, radical aesthetics, and bootstrap capitalism, as well as a revival of the old movement's less than humane tendencies: revolutionary suicide, misogyny, gaybashing, Jewbaiting, and the castigation of the white man as a genetic miscreant, or per Elijah Muhammad's infamous myth of Yacub, a "grafted devil."

To know PE is to love the agitprop (and artful noise) and to worry over the wack retarded philosophy they espouse. Like: "The black woman has always been kept up by the white male because the white male has always wanted the black woman." Like: "Gays aren't doing what's needed to build the black nation." Like: "White people are actually monkey's uncles because that's who they made it with in the Caucasian hills." Like: "If the Palestinians took up arms, went into Israel, and killed all the Jews it'd be alright." From this idiot blather, PE are obviously making it up as they go along. Since PE show sound reasoning when they focus on racism as a tool of the U.S. power structure, they should be intelligent enough to realize that dehumanizing gays, women, and Jews isn't going to set black people free. As their prophet Mr. Farrakhan hasn't overcome one or another of these moral lapses, PE might not either. For now swallowing the PE pill means taking the bitter with the sweet, and if they don't grow up, later for they asses.

Nations of Millions is a declaration of war on the federal government, and on that unholy trinity—black radio programmers, crack dealers, and rock critics. . . . For sheer audacity and specificity Chuck D's enemies list rivals anything produced by the Black Liberation Army or punk-rallying for retribution against the Feds for the Panthers' fall ("Party for Your Right to Fight"), slapping murder charges on the FBI and CIA for the assassinations of MLK and Malcolm X ("Louder Than a Bomb"), condoning cop-killing in the name of liberation ("Black Steel in the Hour of Chaos"), assailing copyright law and the court system ("Caught, Can We Get a Witness?"). As America's black teen population are the core audience for these APBs to terrorize the state, PE are bucking for first rap act to get taken out by Washington, by any means necessary.

Were it not for the fact that *Nation* is the most hellacious and hilarious dance record of the decade, nobody but the converted would give two hoots about PE's millenary desires. One of the many differences between *Nation* and their first, *Yo! Bum Rush the Show,* is that *Nation* is funkier. As George Clinton learned, you got to free Negroes' asses if you want their minds to bug. Having seen *Yo! Bum Rush* move the crowd off the floor, it's a pleasure to say only zealot wallflowers will fade into the blackground when *Nation* cues up. Premiered at a Sugar Hill gala, several *Nation* cuts received applause from the down but upwardly mobile—fulfilling Chuck D's prediction on "Don't Believe the Hype" that by treating the hard james like a seminar *Nation* would "teach the bourgeois and rock the boulevard." But PE's shotgun wedding of black militancy and musical pleasure ensures that *Nation* is going to move music junkies of all genotypes. "They claim we're products from the bottom of hell because the blackest record is bound to sell."

PE producer and arranger Hank Shocklee has the ears of life, and that rare ability to extract the lyrical from the lost and found. Every particle of sound on *Nation* has got a working mojo, a compelling something other-ness and that swing thang to boot. Shocklee's reconstructive composition of new works from archival bites advances sampling to the level of mi-crosurgery. Ditto for cyborg DJ Terminator X. who cuts incisively enough to turn a decaying kazoo into a dopebeat on "Bring the Noise." Putting into effect Borges's rule that "the most fleeting thought obeys an invisible de-sign and can crown, or inaugurate, a secret form," PE have evolved a songcraft from chipped flecks of near-forgotten soul gold. On *Nation* a guitar vamp from Funkadelic, a moan from Sly, a growl abducted from Bobby Byrd aren't just rhythmically spliced in but melodically sequenced into colorful narratives. Think of Romare Bearden.

One cut-up who understands the collage-form is PE's Flavor Flav. Misconstrued as mere aide-de-camp to rap's angriest man after *Yo! Bum Rush,* he emerges here as a duck-soup stirrer in his own right. Flav's solo tip, "Cold Lampin with Flavor," is incantatory shamanism on a par with any of the greats: Beefheart, Koch, Khomeini. . . .

Those who dismiss Chuck D as a bullshit artist because he's loud, pro-black, and proud will likely miss out on gifts for blues pathos and black comedy. When he's on, his rhymes can stun-gun your heart and militarize your funnybone. As a people's poet and pedagogue of the op-pressed, Chuck hits his peak on the jailhouse toast/prison break movie, "Black Steel in the Hour of Chaos." The scenario finds Chuck unjustly under the justice. . . . Chuck and "52 brothers bruised, battered, and scarred but hard" bust out the joint with the aid of PE's plastic Uzi protec-tion, "the S1Ws" (Security of the First World). Inside the fantasy, Chuck crafts verse of poignant sympathy for all doing hard time. . . . His allusion to the Middle Passage as the first penal colony for blacks is cold chillin' for real. . . .

As much as I love this kind of talk, I got to wonder about PE's thing against black women. And my dogass ain't the only one wondering—sev-eral sisters I know who otherwise like the mugs wonder whassup with that too. Last album PE dissed half the race "Sophisticated Bitches." This time around, "She Watch Channel Zero?!" a headbanger about how brain-less the bitch is for watching the soaps, keeping the race down. ". . . Revolution a solution for all our children/But all her children don't mean as much as the show." Whoa! S.T.F.O.! Would you say that to your mother, motherfucker? Got to say, though, the thrash is deadly. One of those riffs makes you want to stomp somebody into an early grave, as Flav goes on and on insinuating that women are garbage for watching garbage. In light of Chuck's plea for crack dealers to be good to the neighborhood on "Night of the Living Baseheads," it appears PE believe the dealers more capable of penance than the sistuhs. Remember *The Mack?* Where the pimp figures it cool to make crazy dollar off his skeezes but uncool for the white man to sell scag to the little brothers? This is from that same mentality. And dig that in "Black Steel in the Hour Of Chaos," the one time on the album Chuck talks about firing a piece, it's to pop a *female* corrections officer. By my homegirl's reckoning all the misogyny is the result of PE suffering from LOP: lack of pussy. She might have a point.

"In the twentieth century, that's all there is: jazz and rock-and-roll."

Writing about rock and roll? Isn't that sort of like writing about sex? What kind of loser would want to write about it rather than *do* it? Why try to explain the mystical process that made Elvis move and the nation groove? Doesn't writing about it spoil everything?

Nah. Criticism of art can intensify the artistic experience. Paul Williams reminds us that Hendrix was, like Elvis, a musical mutant from another galaxy. Lester Bangs, as the geezer he never got to be, bounces us on his lap and tells us about the wild old rock and roll days of the last century. And J. R. Young spins short stories that mention albums only tangentially, as they relate to the life and the culture he so ably chronicles at the end of the 1960s. As with the rest of rock and roll, it's all about attitude.

One of the great things about rock and roll is its sheer egalitarianism. We're all rock and roll critics.

Joe McEwen

LITTLE WILLIE JOHN

McEwen does what any good critic should: make us appreciate what we have lost.

WHEN I was young, I had a gut feeling that energy and swing could transcend even the most lingering (and banal) adolescent traumas and depressions. As a teenager, I was often morose, though the music that attracted me—"Cool Jerk," "Shotgun," "Papa's Got a Brand New Bag"— rarely ever was. I liked ballads well enough, but with few exceptions (James Brown's "Lost Someone") such songs were either overwrought or slight. Mood music, even "Tracks of My Tears," was never moody enough.

Little Willie John was a teenager when he recorded his first hit, "All Around the World," for King Records in 1955. When he faded in 1962, he was a grizzled veteran of 23. Though rock and roll singing was once the province of the young, few under-twenty singers have been able to communicate more than jittery restlessness or poignant ache. Little Willie John's records are filled with much more. The songs on *Little Willie John*, a collection of his fifteen biggest hits, are dark and mature; sometimes messy, sometimes desperate. John sounded old, but his music was also delicate and vulnerable—he wasn't afraid to show his age. But more than anything, John's songs seemed to speak for every growing pain and young adult awkwardness. His music was an expression of longing and desire beyond physical love and romance. Little Willie John understood.

Little Willie John, Sam Cooke, Jackie Wilson, and (to a lesser extent) James Brown changed the manner of black popular singing. Each was a stand-up, church-reared vocalist who had a high regard for the stock tools of the trade: technique, presentation, and flair. That alone made them different from most, though older rhythm and blue singers like Ruth Brown and Roy Brown had similar upwardly mobile concerns. But the real difference was in style, and the very manner of a Little Willie John or Sam Cooke suggested a measured cockiness and self-assured presence that was inescapably black and soulful, no matter what the song. The new music, more gospel-derived and personal than that of the forties and early fifties, also implied a new stance, for each of the singers, in his own way, mastered the art of Cool.

Cool had been a part of black popular music before: in the zany antics of Cab Calloway; in the style of Billy Eckstine, the urbane Mr. B. But the jive of Calloway and the dapperness of Eckstine never left a lingering impression, maybe because emotional expression was never a part of the package: Calloway had his Hep Dictionary and Eckstine made women swoon with rococo Tin Pan Alley ballads that melted, one after the other, like landscapes on the open road. The implications of Cool for Cooke, John, Wilson, and Brown went beyond the surface, combining polished talent with swagger and acumen. Cool offered the potential for self-determination, and even irresponsibility. Above all, it meant a new day for black people. Cool, for one, meant you didn't have to answer to anybody. For two, it meant you had what it takes.

Though most soul singers in the sixties aspired to the mantle of Cool, only Aretha Franklin really possessed the breadth of talent necessary to support it. Soul music itself required a kind of clumsy involvement: Solomon Burke needed a witness and raising your hand just wasn't a part of Cool. There was always Motown, of course, but Motown was primarily teenage music. And when Motown singers tangled with anything other than Motown music, the results were usually contrived and embarrassing. *The Four Tops on Broadway* converted few people. Besides, the choreography, which was part of Motown's flash, also helped confine its practitioners to the ghetto. A few years past its time, choreography could look awful corny. Cool knew no such restrictions, save race perhaps, in its appeal. In 1971, when the last Soul Man, Al Green, surfaced, he registered Cool's lingering influences: Cooke, Wilson, and John were ticked off as favorites.

Cool was indisputably urban, and, in a sense, Sam Cooke was its epitome. Cooke sang like an urbane, soulful crooner, projecting feeling without seeming to sweat and often giving the impression that his sad songs were only momentary dissatisfactions with the state of things. Cooke ran his own show and even had his own record label. Above all, Sam Cooke exuded class in everything he did.

For Jackie Wilson, Cool was a magnificent voice that could tackle blues, rock'n'roll and the most unregenerate schmaltz; Cool was a hair-raising stage show that aroused audiences with splits, spins, slides, and knee-drops. Though Wilson was almost as active as James Brown on stage, he was never as intense—and besides, Wilson was much better looking. But it wasn't the sexual hysteria Wilson aroused that made him cool; Jackie Wilson overwhelming "Danny Boy" or "Night" for a black audience—that was Cool.

James Brown had much to overcome. He had a rural Georgia background; he was a fierce performer on stage. But Brown invented new dance steps and spoke the hippest slang. Like Cooke, he also ran his own operation, designed his own clothes, produced his own records, and made sure he got his money. Brown could get away with screams and grunts, and an occasional gauche outfit, simply because he was James Brown. But for real Cool, James Brown was too kinetic, too down, too black.

Jackie Wilson had more range and Sam Cooke more purity and grace, but no one had a voice like Little Willie John. While he did share a nasal, cigarette rasp with James Brown, John could punctuate even the harshest of phrases with a wild falsetto or suddenly retreat into a muffled, choked sob. John also had a fullness that Brown never possessed—a quality that gave his blues and ballads a heavy, drenching kind of melancholy. At the same time he was capable of great delicacy; his phrasing on the subdued "Let Them Talk" is meticulous and tender. At his best, John's voice simply sounded eerie. He wore snap-brim hats, smoked a pipe, and stood inches over five feet; like Sam Cooke, he could move an audience without acrobatics or show. Little Willie John had style.

Little Willie John was born in Camden, Arkansas, but moved to Detroit at an early age: R&B bandleader Johnny Otis remembers eyeing a 13-year-old John at a Detroit talent show in 1951. Otis passed the word to Syd Nathan of King Records, who ignored John and signed a group of entrants from the same show, Hank Ballard and the Royals. Through the early fifties, John made brief appearances fronting the bands of Duke Ellington and Count Basie, and toured more extensively with tenor saxophonist and R&B hitmaker Paul Williams. Little Willie John didn't lack for proper schooling. Though precious little has been written about John and his influences, those listed by Jackie Wilson (who also grew up in Detroit) serve the point well enough: Al Jolson, the Mills Brothers, the Ink Spots, Clyde McPhatter, the Dixie Hummingbirds, Louis Jordan.

When "All Around the World" was released, Little Willie John was seventeen and sounded thirty. Pop audiences didn't pay much attention. In fact, through his career, John nudged only two songs—"Talk to Me" and "Sleep"—into the Top 20. He hasn't been treated particularly well by rock historians either. He receives only passing mention in both *The Rolling Stone Illustrated History of Rock & Roll* and Charlie Gillett's *The Sound of the City,* the two most comprehensive works in the field. In other, lesser treatments, John is simply ignored altogether; the only sustained reference to the singer that I know of (liner notes aside) is the 200 word biography in Norm N. Nite's entertaining *Rock On.* The best tribute accorded Little Willie John came from a surprising source: James Brown, who recorded an album called *Thinking of Little Willie John and a Few Nice Things.*

But such oversights are understandable. If rock historians are drawn to anything, they're drawn to commitment, and a glance at the range of material John recorded in his career (the fifteen songs on *Little Willie John* span just seven years) reveals a noticeable lack of commitment to any form or genre. The commitment is to Making It, and a song as awkward as "Autumn Leaves" (recorded by John on *The Hot, The Sweet, The Teen-Age Beat*) was probably regarded by John as every bit as appropriate a vehicle as "Need Your Love So Bad," probably his most moving record. It was cynicism of a sort, though that attitude was more confined to record company presidents, A&R men, and producers. No doubt for John it was just a way out.

The songs on *Little Willie John* don't quite evidence the jumbled variety of material that can be found on his oddball King LPs. He recorded everything: squeaky pop-rock, "Flamingo," blues, soul ballads, punchy funk, novelty songs, and even one funny record called "Spasms," on which he hiccups like Jerry Lee Lewis. "All Around the World" was different; a jaunty, big-band piece that sounded like any number of Joe Turner's pre-rock'n'roll records for Atlantic. But such variety was all part of Cool, and mastering the least likely material only added to the singer's worldly luster. The Copacabana and the Apollo weren't mutually exclusive. A few years later, soul singers like Wilson Pickett and Al Green would try to mix the same oil and water, with much less success. The bottom of soul, after all, *was* commitment.

In a way, listening to a Little Willie John album is like listening to any number of post-Sun Elvis Presley records. Somewhere, amidst the show tunes and schlock, are moments of great passion and clarity. Such moments come, go, and come in bright flashes, like a dazzling move from some lazy or bored playground basketball legend. For the most part, the hits were the best of Little Willie John's work, as if to remind us that all the trendy contrivances and weird gimmicks were only so much album filler between the Real Thing. But that wasn't always so: the intensity of "Suffering with the Blues" is still a scary thing to listen to, and the gently shuffling "Home at Last" has the same doomy flavor that saturates "Need Your Love So Bad." Neither were hit 45s. On the other hand, "Sleep," a bizarre mismatch of bad orchestration and a song that had previously been associated with Fred Waring's Pennsylvanians, became John's biggest pop hit, as if to confirm all the industry's worst instincts.

Little Willie John is an uneven album, yet it's a record that stands quite alone. It was rhythm and blues, but when inspiration struck, John (and producers Henry Glover and Ralph Bass) locked into emotions that were more complex than those in stock blues and more mature than Utopian, Boy-meets-Girl, teenage love stuff. Though his best records run a gamut of emotional expression, rarely did John ever sound happy. For a mature adult, a performance as dark and knowing as "Need Your Love So Bad" would have been an achievement worth a lifetime; for a recently turned seventeen-year-old, the song is staggering in its depth and sensitivity. "Need Your Love So Bad" is rendered as a spare blues ballad, with no accompaniment other than a light rhythm section. The tinkling triplets of the piano are simple and familiar, but what John sings is no mere recitation of words. The phrasing is deliberate, marked by fuzzy slurs and sighs, and at times it seems as if the plea is so desperate, and the singer so lonely, that he's beyond verbal expression. It's a despair that hovers near some cavernous, internal abyss.

Occasionally John was able to transfer his brooding pathos to uptempo songs, and the staccato, James Brown-inspired "Heartbreak (It's Hurtin' Me)" is a worthy successor to better-known ballad hits like "Talk to Me" and "Let Them Talk." There's one moment in "Heartbreak" when it all seems to pour out: "This morning I was happy / Tonight I got 'em bad. . . ."

It's hard to say what effect all this heartbreak and fever had on someone who had yet to turn twenty-two. After "Heartbreak" came "Sleep," and then a quick slide downhill. The spark that flourished in a late adolescent never quite returned after "Sleep" (released in mid-1960), and even straight-ahead ballads like "The Very Thought of You" lack the glimmer and taut emotionalism present in John's work only a year earlier. Maybe the psychic trauma of being a very young man caught up in a fantasy world of hit records and cross-country touring took its toll. Or maybe the juice was just drained dry. By the end of 1961, Little Willie John was off the charts for good. Seven years later, after a conviction for manslaughter, he died in prison, of pneumonia, in Walla Walla, Washington, the stuff of legend.

Little Willie John is an album full of ambiguities. It doesn't define its time the way the early Sam Cooke hits did and it doesn't offer the apocalyptic drama of a James Brown song like "Please Please Please" or "I'll Go Crazy." It contains more mediocrity than it should (though even the mediocre songs prove to be illuminating, like the failures of all great artists), certainly more than the singer deserved in a retrospective album of this type. But the songs that move me on this record reach private emotions that I've kept sealed off since I was a teenager. When John sings "Need Your Love So Bad," I think of the lonely weekends I spent in high school wishing for a girl who not only combined a dozen mythic qualities, but who also felt the same battery of desires, fears, and depressions that haunted me. Naturally such a girl would be quite different from the rest, and "Let Them Talk" (with that wonderful phrase, "Idle gossip comes from the devil's workshop") is my bravado answer to sticking out like a sore thumb. "Fever" is surging sexual passions, and "Heartbreak (It's Hurtin' Me)"—well, that speaks for itself. Some of these emotions were simple and laughable, some poignant, and some worthy of the inarticulate rage I felt at the time. All remain as fresh and vivid as last night's dinner.

For the playground legend, the sum of the parts is always more important than the whole. And while self-sacrifice, drive, and hustle are the all-important ingredients of a successful team, there's a thrill beyond words in watching an athlete display skills that he alone owns, even if such gifts are eventually self-destructive. When thinking of Little Willie John, I'm reminded of that. When listening to *Little Willie John,* my life passes before me.

Robert Christgau

ROCK LYRICS ARE POETRY (MAYBE)

In the early years, rock and roll magazines were mostly fan
rags, such as *16, Datebook,* and *Tiger Beat.* By the late 1960s,
there was a need for something that took rock seriously and
Paul Williams's *Crawdaddy!* was born. Then *Rolling Stone*
came along. A couple of other short-lived magazines, *Cheetah*
and *Eye,* were also ready to agree that the kids were all right.
Among the subjects debated in the rock press was the nature
of rock and roll lyrics. The lyrics were *different,* but how
good were they? After Dylan, Simon and Garfunkel seemed to
be the most "serious" of the new artists because, well . . .
shucks, they sang about alienation. John Phillips of the
Mamas and the Papas also peppered his tunes with some pop
relevance. Jim Morrison was off on some Oedipal trip and
then there were those ever-changing Beatles.

Some writers, such as Richard Goldstein, sought to
claim legitimacy for rock composers ("The Poetry of Rock").
Others, like Robert Christgau, appreciated the changes, but
maintained enough perspective to realize that the new songs
were still American popular songs, even if they strayed a bit
far from the Tin Pan Alley tradition. Christgau published this
piece in 1967.

I WANT to say right now that none of the categories I'm going to be
using are worth much. All but a few artists resist categories; the good
ones usually confound them altogether. So a term like "rock" is impossibly vague; it denotes, if anything, something historical rather than aesthetic. "Mass art" and "kitsch" are pretty vague as well. Let's say that mass
art is intended only to divert, entertain, pacify—Mantovani, Jacqueline
Susann, *Muscle Beach Party,* etc. Kitsch is a more snobbish concept, and
a more sophisticated product. It usually has the look of slightly out-of-date
avant-garde in order to give its audience the illusion of aesthetic pleasure,
whatever that is. An important distinction, I think, is that many of the
craftsmen who make kitsch believe thoroughly in what they are doing.

That may be true of the creators of mass art, too, but their attitude is more businesslike—they don't worry about "art," only commercial appeal.

*   *   *

The songwriter who seems to sound most like a poet is Bob Dylan. Dylan is such an idiosyncratic genius that it is perilous to imitate him—his faults, at worst annoying and at best invigorating, ruin lesser talents. But imitation is irresistible. Who can withstand Paul Nelson of *Little Sandy Review,* who calls Dylan "the man who in every sense revolutionized modern poetry, American folk music, popular music, and the whole of modern-day thought"? Or Jack Newfield of the *Village Voice,* wandering on about "symbolic alienation . . . new plateaus for poetic, content-conscious songwriters . . . put poetry back into song . . . reworks T. S. Eliot's classic line . . . bastard child of Chaplin, Celine and Hart Crane," while serving up tidbits from Dylan's corpus, some of which don't look so tasty on a paper plate? However inoffensive "The ghost of electricity howls in the bones of her face" sounds on vinyl, it is silly without the music. Poems are read or said. Songs are sung.

*   *   *

"My Back Pages" is a bad poem. But it is a good song, supported by a memorable refrain. The music softens our demands, the importance of what is being said somehow overbalances the flaws, and Dylan's delivery—he sound as if he's singing a hymn at a funeral—adds a portentous edge not present just in the words. Because it is a good song, "My Back Pages" can be done in other ways. The Byrds' version depends on intricate, up-tempo music that pushes the words into the background. However much they mean to David Crosby, the lyrics—except for that refrain—could be gibberish and the song would still succeed. Repeat: Dylan is a songwriter, not a poet. A few of his most perfect efforts—"Don't Think Twice," or "Just Like a Woman"—are tight enough to survive on the page. But they are exceptions.

Such a rash judgment assumes that modern poets know what they're doing. It respects the tradition that runs from Ezra Pound and William Carlos Williams down to Charles Olson, Robert Creeley, and perhaps a dozen others, the tradition that regards Allen Ginsberg as a good poet, perhaps, but a wildman. Dylan's work, with its iambics, its clackety-clack rhymes, and its scattergun images, makes Ginsberg's look like a model of decorous diction. An art advances through technical innovation. Modern American poetry assumes (and sometimes eliminates) metaphoric ability, concentrating on the use of line and rhythm to approximate (or refine) speech, the reduction of language to essentials, and "tone of voice."

Dylan's only innovation is that he sings, a good way to control "tone of voice," but not enough to "revolutionize modern poetry." He may have started something just as good, but modern poetry is getting along fine, thank you.

*   *   *

Dylan's influence has not always been so salutary. Lennon-McCartney and Jagger-Richard would have matured without him. But had there been no Dylan to successfully combine the vulgar and the felicitous, would we now be oppressed with the kind of vague, extravagant imagery and inane philosophizing that ruins so much good music and so impresses the Kahlil Gibran fans? I doubt it.

*   *   *

Not much better is the self-indulgence of the Doors' Jim Morrison. "Twentieth Century-Fox," "Break on Through," "People Are Strange" and "Soul Kitchen," listed in ascending order of difficulty, all pretty much succeed. But Morrison does not stop there. He ruins "Light My Fire" with stuff like "our love becomes a funeral pyre"—Ugh! what does that mean? Nothing, but the good old romantic association of love and death is there, and that's all Morrison wanted—and noodles around in secondhand Freud in "The End." Morrison obviously regards "The End" as a masterwork, and his admirers agree. I wonder why. The music builds very nicely in an Oriental kind of way, but the dramatic situation is tedious stuff. I suppose it is redeemed by Morrison's histrionics and by the nebulousness that passes for depth among so many lovers of rock poetry.

*   *   *

Paul Simon's lyrics are the purest, highest, and most finely wrought kitsch of our time. The lyrics I've been putting down are not necessarily easy to write—bad poetry is often carefully worked, the difference being that it's easier to perceive flaccidly—but the labor that must go into one of Simon's songs is of another order of magnitude. Melodies, harmonies, arrangements are scrupulously fitted. Each song is perfect. And says nothing.

What saddens me is that Simon obviously seems to have a lot to say to the people who buy his records. But it's a shock. Like Kahlil Gibran all he's really doing is scratching them where they itch, providing some temporary relief but coming nowhere near the root of the problem. Simon's content isn't modern, it is merely fashionable, and his form never jars the sensibilities. He is the only songwriter I can imagine admitting he writes about that all-American subject, the Alienation of Modern Man, in just those words. His songs have the texture of modern poetry only if modern poetry can be said to end with early Auden—Edwin Arlington Robinson is more like it. Poets don't write like Robinson any more because his technical effects have outlived their usefulness, which was to make people see things in a new way. And even in such old-fashioned terms, what Simon does is conventional and uninspired. An example is "For Emily, Wherever I May Find Her," in which "poetic" words—organdy, crinoline, juniper (words that suggest why Simon is so partial to turn-of-the-century verse) and "beautiful" images (softer-than-the-rain, wandered-lonely-streets) are used to describe a dream girl. Simon is no dope; he knows this is all a little corny, but that's okay because Emily is an impossible girl. Only in order for the trick to come off there has to be an ironic edge. There isn't, and "For Emily" is nothing more than a sophisticated popular song of the traditional-fantasy type.

This kind of mindless craft reaches a peak in Simon's supposed masterpiece, "The Dangling Conversation," which uses all the devices you learn about in English class—alliteration, alternating concretion and abstraction, even the use of images from poetry itself, a favorite ploy of poets who don't know much of anything else—to mourn wistfully about the classic plight of self-conscious man, his Inability to Communicate. Tom Phillips of the *New York Times* has called this song "one of Paul Simon's subtlest lyrics . . . a pitiless vision of self-consciousness and isolation." I don't hear the same song, I guess, because I think Simon's voice drips self-pity from every syllable (not only in this song, either). The Mantovani strings that reinforce the lyric capture its toughness perfectly. If Simon were just a little hipper, his couple would be discussing the failure of communication as they failed to communicate, rather than psychoanalysis or the state of the theatre. But he's not a little hipper.

*   *   *

It is by creating a mood that asks "Why should this mean anything?" that the so-called rock poets can really write poetry—poetry that not only says something, but says it as only rock music can. For once Marshall McLuhan's terminology tells us something: rock lyrics are a cool medium. Go ahead and mumble. Drown the voices in guitars. If somebody really wants to know what you're saying, he'll take the trouble, and in that trouble lies your art. On a crude level this permits the kind of one-to-one symbolism of pot songs like "Along Comes Mary" and "That Acapulco Gold." "Fakin' It" does other things with the same idea. But the only songwriters who seem really to have mastered it are John Phillips and Lennon-McCartney.

Phillips possesses a frightening talent. "San Francisco—Flowers in

Your Hair," catering to every prurient longing implicit in teenage America's flirtation with the hippies without ever even mentioning the secret word, is a stunning piece of schlock. A song like "Once Was A Time I Thought" (as if to say to all those Swingle Singer fans, "You thought that was hard? We can do the whole number in fifty-eight seconds") is another example of the range of his ability. You have the feeling Phillips could write a successful musical, a Frank Sinatra hit, anything that sells, if he wanted to.

Perhaps you are one of those people who plays every new LP with the treble way up and the bass way down so you can ferret out all the secret symbolic meanings right away. Personally I think that spoils the fun, and I suspect any record that permits you to do that isn't fulfilling its first function, which pertains to music, or, more generally, noise. The Mamas and Papas' records are full of diversions—the contrapuntal arrangements, the idiot "yeahs," the orchestral improvisations, the rhyme schemes ("If you're entertaining any thought that you're gaining by causin' me all of this pain and makin' me blue. . . ") and Phillips' trick of drawing out a few words with repetitions and pauses. Perhaps this isn't conscious. In songs like "California Dreamin'," "12:30" and many others, Phillips is obviously just a good lyricist (with a lot of tender respect for the fantasy world of pure pop that critics like Hayakawa derogate so easily). But his lyrics are rarely easy to understand. Maybe it's just me, but I wonder how many of you are aware that a minor track on the second album, "Strange Young Girls," is about LSD. No secret about it—there it is, right out in the open of the first stanza: ". . . Walking the Strip, sweet, soft, and placid / Off'ring their youth on the altar of acid." But you don't notice because there's so much else to listen to.

*　　*　　*

Phillips achieves rock feel with his arrangements. The lyrics themselves are closer to traditional pop—Rodgers and Hart's "My Heart Stood Still," on the second album, sounds less out of place than Bobby Freeman's "Do You Wanna Dance?" on the first. Lennon-McCartney do it with diction. Their early work is all pure rock—the songs are merely excuses for melody, beat and sound. Occasionally it shows a flash of the subtlety to come, as in the sexual insinuation of "Please Please Me" or the premise of "There's A Place." . . . More often it is pure, meaningless sentiment, couched in the simplest possible terms. By the time of *A Hard Day's Night* the songs are more sophisticated musically, and a year later, in *Help!,* the boys are becoming pop songwriters. *Help!* itself is a perfect example. Words like "self-assured" and "insecure" are not out of rock diction, nor is the line: "My independence seems to vanish in the haze." This facet of their talent has culminated (for the moment) in songs like "Paperback Writer," "A Little Help from My Friends," and "When I'm Sixty-four," which show all the verbal facility of the best traditional pop and none of the sentimentality, and in deliberate exercises like "Michelle" and "Here, There and Everywhere," which show both.

Other songs like "Norwegian Wood," "Dr. Robert," "Good Morning, Good Morning" are ambiguous despite an unerring justness of concrete detail; little conundrums, different from Dylanesque surrealism because they don't fit so neatly into a literary category (Edward Lear is their closest antecedent). Most of the songs since *Rubber Soul* are characterized by a similar obliqueness. Often the Beatles' "I" is much harder to pin down than the "I" in Donovan or Jagger-Richard, a difficulty that is reinforced by their filters, their ethereal harmonies, and their collective public identity. This concern with angle of attack is similar to that of poets like Creeley.

Lennon and McCartney are the only rock songwriters who combine high literacy (as high as Dylan's or Simon's) with an eye for concision and a truly contemporary sense of what fits. They seem less and less inclined to limit themselves to what I have defined as rock diction, and yet they continue to succeed—the simultaneous lushness and tightness of "Lucy in the Sky with Diamonds," for instance, is nothing short of extraordinary. They still get startling mileage out of the banal colloquial—think of the "oh boy" in "A Day in the Life," or the repeating qualifications in "Strawberry Fields Forever." But they have also written two songs which are purely colloquial—"She Said She Said," and "All You Need Is Love."

"She Said She Said" is at once one of the most difficult and banal of Beatle songs. It is a concrete version of what in "The Dangling Conversation" (despite all those details) remains abstract, a conversation between a hung-up, self-important girl who says she knows "what it's like to be dead" and her boy friend, who doesn't want to know. (If Simon had written it, the boy would have argued that he was the one who knew.) The song uses the same kind of words that can be found in "She Loves You" (the quintessential early Beatles song), yet says so much more. Its conceit, embodied in the title, is meaningless; its actuality is a kind of ironic density that no other songwriter (except Dylan at his best) approaches. One of its ironies is the suggestion that callow philosophizing is every bit as banal as the most primitive rock-and-roll.

"All You Need Is Love," deliberately written in basic English so it could be translated, makes the connection clearer by quoting from "She Loves You" while conveying the ironic message of the title. Is love all you need? What kind of love? Universal love? Love of country? Courtly love? "She

Loves You" love? It's hard to tell. The song employs rock-and-roll—dominant music, big beat, repeated refrain, simple diction—and transforms it into something which, if not poetry, at least has a multifaceted poetic wholeness. I think it is rock poetry in the truest sense.

Maybe I am being too strict. Modern poetry is doing very well, thank you, on its own terms, but in terms of what it is doing for us, and even for the speech from which it derives, it looks a bit pallid. Never take the categories too seriously. It may be that the new songwriters (not poets, please) lapse artistically, indulge their little infatuations with language and ideas, and come up with a product that could be much better if handled with a little less energy and a little more caution. But energy is where it's at. And songs—even though they are only songs—may soon be more important than poems, no matter that they are easier too.

Once there were bards and the bards did something wondrous—they provided literature for the illiterate. The bards evolved into poets and the poetry which had been their means became their end. It didn't seem to matter much after a while, since everyone was literate anyway. But semi-literacy, which is where people go when they're not illiterate any more, is in some ways a worse blight.

The new songwriters think there should be bards again and they're right, but the bardic traditions are pretty faint. Too many of them are seduced by semiliteracy—mouthing other people's ideas in other people's words. But they are bards, and that is very good. Maybe soon it will be a lot better.

Paul Williams

ALL ALONG THE WATCHTOWER

Bob Dylan's original "All Along the Watchtower" on his 1967
John Wesley Harding was an apocalyptic tune in black and
white with just Dylan on guitar and harmonica, accompanied
by a flawless rhythm section. Hendrix's version, however, was
full fury, in Technicolor.

Paul Williams was the founder and editor of
Crawdaddy!, the first great magazine to take rock and roll
seriously. It grew from a mimeographed newsletter produced
when Williams was still an undergraduate, to a slick
magazine in the 1970s when it left his hands. He revived it as
a newsletter again in the 1990s. Williams has always been
one of rock and roll's most respected critics, with his books
Outlaw Blues and the whole *Performing Artist* series that
examines Dylan's onstage career. This is from Williams's
tribute to the one hundred greatest rock and roll recordings.

SO IF THE earnest strumming of an acoustic guitar is the primary source,
inspiration point, for rock's rhythmic excitement—and I think it is—what's
an electric guitar for? The answer, of course, is *sound,* and nowhere is that
answer more obvious than in the music of Jimi Hendrix. In 1966/67, with
the Beatles and the Stones working to expand the possibilities of rock
and roll sound by introducing new instruments, Hendrix came along and
expanded those possibilities more strikingly and with more lasting impact than any of his contemporaries by reinventing the instrument that
was already there. Electric guitar, phase II. Welcome the Other. This is not
black music. It is certainly not white music. Not a clever or even brilliant
incorporation of eclectic material or avant garde ideas into familiar
pop/rock/folk structures. Nossir. This is a new sound under the sun, obviously and inescapably Something Else, from first listen till the very end
of time. Jimi Hendrix's music, especially his guitar-playing, takes off in directions other folks can't even point toward.

"Seen a shooting star tonight, and I thought of you." All lives are brief,
some briefer than others, and in this little corner of eternity known to us

as the second half of the twentieth century a hit single is an effective way of making some nonharmful noise, proclaiming and calling attention to one's existence, telling whoever in the world may be listening that you have lived and that this fact makes a difference. The light flashes and is gone. But put enough of yourself into that light and it may just burn with a color seldom or never seen, something haunting and awakening, not soon forgotten by those who witness. In this way we beat the clock, if only slightly. In this way we express our desire to join the screaming that comes across our sky.

Two Hendrixes, forever yoked, scream their presence through this record: one personified as the most animate guitar that ever deigned to talk to you or me, and the other, equally powerful but so simple we fail sometimes to notice its impact, his human voice. Jimi twice. Each colors and intensifies the other, flirting and fighting, communicating a complex and extraordinary interdependence, constantly exchanging roles, set and ground, fire and fuel. All framed and supported by the genius of Noel Redding's bass playing, Mitch Mitchell's drums, Bob Dylan's song structure and vision and imagery. The scene is set. A reality captured, constructed. Brilliant preparation. And then Jimi begins to howl.

With a spectroscope we can read the colors in the light of distant suns and learn new truths about our universe. This 45 from another planet offers similar possibilities. Play it loud.

J. R. Young
REVIEWS OF *AFTER THE GOLDRUSH* AND *LIVE DEAD*

J. R. Young's *Rolling Stone* record reviews were more like short stories than album critiques. Several reviews, in fact, made only tangential reference to the album being discussed.

STEVEN no longer attempted to understand just what it was his father did in the den at night. The TV was on, that was a fact, but that wasn't the point. Steven knew his father didn't like the shows because his father could never tell Steven what it was he had seen as he sat in the big leather chair watching the color screen. Many times at breakfast over cups of Ovaltine and coffee, Steven had asked his father how he had liked "the show last night."

"The show?" his father would ask without looking up.

"Sure, Dad. On TV."

"Oh, that one. It was OK." Then he was off to work, leaving Steven alone at the breakfast nook with his mother. Her kitchen TV was always on and her eyes were always on it.

"Don't be late, hon," she said every morning at 8:15 as she stuffed a Mr. Goodbar or something special in his pocket and Steven would be off to school. He was a good boy. He was glad to get to school. He was growing up.

Steven had taken to sitting on the edge of his bed at night, surrounded by his own recent childhood, when his father took to the den. He had also taken up records and hi-fi stuff over the summer, but hadn't moved very far in that direction. He listened to nothing but the two records he owned, both Neil Young albums. He liked Neil Young; something about his voice. Steven's equipment was an old RCA piece, and he played his records very softly. As time passed, as his father spent more time in his den, Steven played them softer and softer until Neil Young was no more than a whisper next to the bed. Soon afterwards, he quit Neil altogether and took up the even tones of the Johnny Carson show from the den below. Before long, he knew the show well, knew the different voices, the names, and the same laughter. It was, however, the silence of his father he knew best, the strange glowing room filled with nothing but his father's silence. Steven listened to it every night, and every night had the same vision of his father sitting in the den, the old eyes level and steady and his tired mouth set tight as Carson ran through his light patter, as Newhart did his best bits off some old album, and as Shirley Bassey brought the audience to their feet with her own inimitable version of "Hey Jude." The eyes of his father never moved.

Steven was usually in bed when Johnny thanked his assembled each night, and it was then that Steven waited for the sounds of his father making his way to his mother's side down the hall. Somehow he never quite heard it, falling asleep somewhere in the midst of his quiet solitude and concentration.

The pattern developed slowly, and it was one which knew no easy course. Steven found his sitting place at the end of his bed earlier and earlier each night, it seemed, as autumn progressed so that soon Steven sat as his father sat before the eleven o'clock news. Then it dropped to a loud violent show at ten, a tuneful hour with a giant pop star at nine, and soon so that by the first frost it was down to Hazel at 7. His two albums had been tucked away long ago.

The breakfasts had changed, too, in this time. No longer did Steven's father read the newspaper, nor did Steven ask how he liked the show. It had gone beyond that, until now the two sat facing one another across the table, their backs straight and their lips closed. Steven didn't really understand any of it, but he knew enough to know that there was nothing to ask anymore. That's how it went for weeks.

One night, fully ten minutes before the Carson show gave way to the evening prayer, Steven heard the sharp click of the TV, and then nothing. Just the silence and then the old man took away even that.

"Steven. *Steven?* I know you're up there son. What is it? What do you want?"

Steven didn't answer right away, suddenly empty of all reason and coherence. His mind jumped at the voice and then raced insanely out of control as his shoulders quivered, and in the next moment it was only with the greatest of all efforts that he finally reined in those blind thoughts outside the living room spectrum of his old backyard. He opened his eyes carefully.

"Dad, can I talk to you? Can I come downstairs?" His voice wavered.

"Don't move, son. I'll come upstairs," and then as a poignant afternote as he searched the side table for his cigarettes. "Sure we can talk. You're my boy."

That night, over coffee and whipped cream, which the two had trooped downstairs and made with great hysterical flourishes, the man and his son talk for the first time as if all plugs had been pulled from their brains, paced and gesticulated with their whole bodies as they searched out a path ahead, punched and jabbed each other, laughed and cried like old Italian fishermen, and in the end resolved absolutely nothing.

When the two finally called it a night and shook hands at five thirty, they felt immediately better about things, although it is possible they didn't know why. Both fell asleep within minutes.

Perhaps it would be best not to dwell on the father's dream. Suffice it to say that it was still a matter of confused sexuality in which his wife always ended up being his younger sister, in this case much older somehow, and even at that he wasn't sure if at times it wasn't his mother. Whoever it was, the dream always ended up on a slow boat to China. Sometimes he was a nanny to the whole crew.

Steven's dream, on the other hand, was a good dream for a change. But he, alas, could never remember them. Even the good ones.

When they awakened the next day, they met at the breakfast nook well into the early afternoon. It was a brisk day. They also met with an apparent new understanding.

"Mornin', Steve," the father laughed as he sat down at the table rubbing his hands. "Got a lot of work to do around here, you and me, son. Better button up the old jacket. You and me, son, we'll take a day off and do a little work around the yard, huh, boy? And we'll rake," and he stole a glance around the room, "the *goddamned* leaves." He winked at Steven.

"Sure, Dad," Steven said, and he went back to eating his cereal. The father whistled a happy tune and buttered his toast. He spread a thick coat of marmalade and he grinned from ear to ear at Steven as he ate. Steven couldn't help but look up at him and smile.

"You know, Dad," Steven finally said, putting his spoon down, "you're a funny guy."

"Oh, yeah? What do you mean?" He poured a bowl of cereal.

"The TV, Dad. What was that TV thing all about? All those shows?"

"The shows?" his father said without looking up.

"Sure, Dad. On TV."

"Oh, those. They're OK." And he lapsed into silence.

Steven sat perfectly still for a few minutes and then, without announcement, left the table. He put on his coat and went downtown and hung around for most of the day. When he came home in the early evening, he carried the new Neil Young album under his arm and he was with it for a long time afterwards.

Marsha Steinburger and her best friend, Starglow Peterson, had hitch-hiked into Mill Valley from Sacramento in the early afternoon and were now sitting in Sheila Titterwell's front room on the hillside of Mount Tam. Sheila lived with some guy neither Marcia nor Starglow knew, but about whom they had heard nice things. He was at work now and would be home shortly. In the meantime, the three young lovelies were smoking some very potent dope, and were sitting on Sheila's floor watching the orange sun go down. By dusk, they were all four joints to the cosmos, and everything was a barrel of laughs.

"And that crazy fart is going to be home any minute," Sheila laughed as she took the toilet paper roll from Starglow. "You know what he does now? He comes screaming up that hill each night with Hugh Jardon, hollering as loud as he can like an asshole, 'GET OUT THE PIPE, PUT ON THE DEAD, AND SPREAD!' And like the cat is stark raving naked by the time he hits the front door." Sheila laughed again and shook her head, and then inhaled deeply on the roll.

"Put on the dead, and spread?" Marcia looked puzzled. Sheila raised one slim finger, held her breath a few seconds longer, and then exhaled slowly.

"Right. As in the Grateful Dead and legs. Real George thinks that it's the greatest to . . ."

She was interrupted as the quiet of the early evening disintegrated around them in a confusion of sound and squalor as the high whine of a VW wound down to a quick halt, and a huge voice called up to them.

"PUT ON THE DEAD AND SPREAD, 'CAUSE I'M LOADED AND READY TO GO!"

"It's Real George now," Sheila said jumping to her feet. "Excuse me." She pulled her sweater up over her head and off her arms, and then slipped out of her jeans. She was naked in a jiffy. "It's been like this for a week now, almost two."

She quickly crossed the room to the tape deck, threaded a reel, and turned the machine on.

The two visiting girls peered at her for a long moment, and then turned their attention to the strange shadowy figure charging up the front steps and leaving a trail of clothes strewn wildly behind him. He was going like sixty.

"Ever since he got that album," Sheila said as she opened the bedroom door, "Real George likes nothing better than to fuck to the Grateful Dead. It makes him on fire." She winked. "It's groovy." Sheila then disappeared in the darkness of the bedroom. And just as the Dead began "Dark, Star," Real George hit the front door with his naked pink and hairy body and crashed through into the living room.

"Da da!"

Marcia's and Starglow's mouths fell open as the fleeting vision swept through the room for a brief moment before disappearing along with Sheila in the darkness.

"Ahhh," someone said in there as Marcia and Starglow exchanged quizzical glances. "Ahh." The music grew louder.

"That's far out," Starglow said.

"Very far out," Marcia nodded.

The two girls turned around and looked back out into the hills. Already lights were beginning to come on as the land grew blacker.

"Gee, I wish I had a date tonight," Marcia finally said.

Cintra Wilson

OF COCK ROCK KINGS AND OTHER DINOSAURS

The New Yorker ran a cartoon of a somber-looking briefcase-toting fellow in business suit shuffling to work. The caption read "Man the same age as Mick Jagger." And that was over a decade ago. Cintra Wilson here muses on the phenomenon of the grandpa rock and roller.

THERE IS an important thing that kids today don't really know about. I don't really know about it either, even though I was kind of around for the tail end of it. It is a historical event I'm talking about, and it is commonly referred to as Mick Jagger.

Growing up, I mostly knew about Mick through Sam Shepard plays that made references to him, like *The Tooth of Crime* (in which a character is based on Keith Richards) and *Cowboy Mouth,* a play that Sam wrote with Patti Smith, which evinces a nearly mythological reverence for early Jagger. I didn't realize until a recent viewing of the video "Cocksucker Blues" by photographer Robert Frank what a king hell phenomenon young Mick Jagger was. By the time I was alive enough to notice Mr. Jagger, he looked like a desiccated version of Don Knotts and his laughably antique rock tours were sponsored by Pepsi. *Tattoo You* had just come out. In my junior high, only the back parking lot loadies with the feathered hair and plastic combs in the back pockets of their bootleg cords cared about the Stones at all, and then even they mostly cared about the older albums. The loadies were baked all the time so nobody trusted their taste anyway; they also liked Ronnie James Dio and Styx and all of the other shit nobody listened to except other very, very stoned people. When *Tattoo You* came out, I was into Devo and had about 80 buttons up either side of my shirt. The Stones meant nothing because they were not New Wave.

This video made me realize that cock rock was once very alive and is now dead, and rock'n'roll has really lost its supply of frightfully charismatic young front men. Bowie, Mick, Iggy, Lou Reed . . . hell, even Steve Tyler, if you dare mention such fluff as the Aerosmith legacy in that dubious lineup—they're all old, old, old, and it's a shame that most folks my

0 seconds

age never had a chance to see those grand old gentlemen of rock when they were at their blow-dried, blow-snorted, blow-jobbed peak.

The late '60s/early '70s is one era that will never really be able to repeat itself. It was an ignorant, selfish, sexist, self-destructive time. You could never repeat any of the backstage action featured in "Cocksucker Blues"—even the lowest slag-level of coke and cum-famished groupies have more self-respect than that now. It was an era with no boundaries whatsoever, and Mick navigated the ungainly sea of IV drug accidents and weepy orgies and omnipresent star-struck coke-gabbling morons better than any other lacquer-pants glam King of yore. It is amazing that Mick was ever Mick, looking at him now, and it is doubly amazing that he wasn't found dead years ago in a hotel room with needles in his feet and the remains of some horrible sex act stuck to his person.

It was crazy watching that video: Nobody (except Prince) could get away with that much genital focus these days. Let's say no white man could do it. The Red Hot Chili Peppers sort of did it, but it was more tongue-in-cheek, or rather, dick-in-sock. Ha ha, they were cutely saying about the male sex object phenomenon. There was nothing cute and reasonable about Mick at his gangly big-haired best, when he was wearing spangled body socks with extra codpiece sections for his legendary cod and long chiffon scarves and numerous cloth belts, with Lady Bianca pouting around the dressing room, smoking in Halston dresses.

He was completely non-ironic; there was something very powerfully unconscious and self-contained about his outrageous sexual persona that made men and women of the '60s and '70s just die wanting to lick his velvet hems. He was, perhaps, the most sexually sought-after human on the planet at one point, a male Helen of Troy. The entire band was cadaverous from sweating off eight pounds a night and eating nothing but narcotics; they were blown into wraiths from all that attention, all that masturbation aimed at them, the whole writhing mass of hippy culture imploding into death and debasement right in their hotel rooms. The Stones were a massive gale force that blew sideways the clothes and cash of anyone who came near, and Mick was the dervish at the epicenter, and it is hard to tell if he meant it that way or not.

I was asking a DJ from this really cool independent radio station an important question I've always had, which is: "Why Lou Reed?" Or more precisely, why is Lou Reed considered to be among the major arcana of perennial rock icons? The only reason I ever paid any attention to Lou Reed at all was because men whom I respected loved him: Lester Bangs, for one, and some angry punk rock guys from Detroit I knew in the early '80s. Coming from a jazz upbringing, I always thought his music was retardedly simplistic, and when I was in college, around the time his hit "I Love You Suzanne" came out, he was wearing a motorcycle jacket on an American Express poster, which pretty much fossilized my opinion of him in the negative. "OK, I'll tell you why Lou Reed," said the big Swede, in between alternate sucks of Guinness and American Spirit. "Imagine Mike D. of the Beastie Boys walking down the street. He's got beautiful new $300 sunglasses on. The exact right flat vintage Pumas. The big pants. He has beautiful vintage sound equipment he picked up in England. OK, so here comes Lou Reed down the street. He's wearing lizard-skin boots, tight, acid-washed black jeans, a leather jacket with elastic around the waist, a mullet hairstyle all short in the front and long in the back and carrying a brand new, state-of-the-art Japanese electric guitar. Now Mike D. might say, 'Hey, Lou, why are you so wack?' and Lou would be able to say, 'I don't need to do anything. I'm Lou Reed.' And it would be absolutely true."

I got what he was saying, but it still didn't explain anything I didn't already know. Lou, for some reason, has the Luminous Male Rock Charisma, which forgives everything. We don't have anybody like that around anymore. Since the big music corporations have decided who gets famous or not, there really haven't been a whole lot of fearless persona innovators.

My fiancé and I were on a plane recently, and on the way to the restroom, I noticed that a short guy with an ugly hat covered with pheasant feathers was pestering the stewardesses. Then I became aware that the guy was pulling a trumpet out. Then I realized that the guy was Chuck Mangione, going through his entire Chuck Mangione repertoire right there on the plane next to the restroom. We guessed that he was trying to make time with one of the stewardesses. We were treated to a long version of his recognizable hit, then heard him segue into "Spain" and even lesser-known hits of quiet-storm listening such as "Land of Make Believe." Poor Chuck. I only knew those songs because my mother played the Fender Rhodes 88 in a bar band that played covers of that stuff in the '70s. I don't think anybody else knew anything but his top-40 hit. The stewardesses nodded and clapped politely. You'd never see Mick in the back of the plane, strutting out a little version of "Gimme Shelter" for some United Airlines bint. You might catch Lou doing "I Love You Suzanne," but hey, he's Lou Reed.

I was at a rock show the other day. A friend of ours has just been signed to a major label with his tight-black-shirt-and-hair-in-the-face alternative goth boy band, and their black limousine was waiting with sinister promise out in front of the East Village venue, and hottie girls with long blond hair and silver boots were waiting for our friend to get offstage so they could casually smother him with girlish attentions. The lead singer was kind of a cross between David Byrne and Perry Farrell with just a skosh of Iggy, all of the boys were exceptionally cute and the music was loud, but the night was distinctly tame.

It was funny how innocent it all was. One of the band boys got offstage and told me fearfully that he thought he might have smoked too much pot. People were barely drinking. Wow, I realized . . . this is practically the '50s! Twentysomething people are worried about getting up in the morning. They were all carefully monitoring their substance intake and responsibly choosing the right condoms.

There was a woman older than me in the club hanging out with her dad, whom you knew had been used to far more intense party scenes than this polite little evening of hard rock. Was Dad disappointed? Or was this new scene just pleasantly middle-aged enough for him to deal with, after the abject chaos of 1971?

I wonder if I'll ever see it in my lifetime—a whole generation of naked people too high to say no to anything, with some legitimate Rock Lord at the center of it all, driving it all like a many-limbed Magic Bus. If I do, I'll probably disapprove.

Ellen Sander

INSIDE THE CAGES OF THE ZOO

Led Zeppelin had its beginnings in the British Invasion of 1964, when the Yardbirds offered themselves as candidates for best wannabe bluesmen. That band was a finishing school of sorts for guitarists, with Eric Clapton, Jeff Beck, and finally Jimmy Page filling the first chair. Clapton left when he felt the Yardbirds were turning away from the blues to pop music. Beck left because he was notoriously disorganized. Page, who had come into the band in the Beck era, assumed the leadership role and, gradually, the Yardbirds became the New Yardbirds and that band became Led Zeppelin, the quintessential, arena-filling heavy rock band.

From the start, Led Zeppelin was pasted by critics and the band kept a distance from rock journalists. Ellen Sander was an exception. Invited into their circle while on assignment for *Life,* Sander may have gotten too close. The *Life* article never appeared, but she wrote about her time in the Zeppelin Zoo in *Trips.*

Sander stopped writing about rock and roll and became a software designer.

SOME YEARS later, a group called Led Zeppelin came to America to make it, taking a highly calculated risk. The group had been put together around Jimmy Page, who had a heavy personal following from his previous work with the Yardbirds, an immensely popular British group that generated a great deal of charisma in the States. They got a singer from another group, a knockabout band on the English club circuit, a raw ferocious guttersinger, Robert Plant.

John Paul Jones joined next, one of the foremost young sessions bass players in London, then drummer John Bonham, who had been working on a construction job to earn enough money to feed his family when he was asked to join the group. Jimmy Page and his guitar fame, together with Peter Grant, a burly ex-wrestler, ex-bouncer, a manager who knew the business from the tough side in, set out to put together the top group in the world. It is every musician's and manager's intention, but this band pulled it off. In 1970 they would knock the Beatles off the top of the Melody Maker popularity chart in England and would be the top touring group in the United States. It was a carefully laid-out strategy involving carefully chosen people, carefully made deals, carefully contrived music, all of which worked. A little luck, timing, and experience and a lot of talent pulled the troupe all the way to the undisputed top of the heap.

In the beginning they barely played England at all. The real money, they knew, was in the States. They had put together a first album, a spirited, crisp breath of freshness at a time when rock and roll was really getting bogged down. They released it in England, then in America, and followed it over the Atlantic to play.

*   *   *

For a rock and roll band on the road in this raw naked land, the trip is not entirely a barrel of yuks.

They lived and worked and struggled to survive from day to day, from place to place, through unspeakable nightmares just to play music. It was loud, hard, gutsy rock, violent and executed with a great deal of virtuosity. Robert Plant, woolly, handsome in an obscenely rugged way, sang as if the songs had to fight their way out of his throat. Jimmy Page, ethereal, effeminate, pale and frail, played physically melodic guitar, bowing it at times, augmenting it with electronic devices, completely energizing the peak of the ensemble's lead sound. John Bonham played ferocious drums, often shirtless and sweating like some gorilla on a rampage. John Paul Jones held the sound together at the bass with lines so surprising, tight, and facile but always recessive, leaving the dramatics to the other three who competed to outdo one another for the audience's favor.

No matter how miserably the group failed to keep their behavior up to a basic human level, they played well almost every night of the tour. If they were only one of the many British rock and roll groups touring at the time, they were also one of the finest. The stamina they found each night at curtain time was amazing, in the face of every conceivable kind of foul-up with equipment, timing, transportation, and organization at almost every date. They had that fire and musicianship going for them and a big burst of incentive; this time around, on their second tour, from the very beginning, they were almost stars.

*   *   *

The group awoke to the Detroit late afternoon and munched on grilled cheese sandwiches in the motel snack shop, blocking out the next few hours before they'd have to play. Robert split for a brief walk and some shopping. As he crossed the street a motorist screeched to a stop beside him and spat in his face. He returned to the motel for a ride, all upset. "I'm white," he mused; "I can imagine how a spade feels here."

Detroit. The lowest.

He returned from the drugstore with shampoo, a comb, and some creme rinse for his copious mane, but no deodorant, which he needed regularly and badly.

During that evening's performance at the Grandee Ballroom, a converted mattress warehouse which was one of the country's oldest established rock halls, equipment failures plagued their music. The house was packed and restless, warmly appreciative, and relentlessly demanding. The vibes were heavy, the audience and crowd were infested with armed police who took a grim view of the scene. Even the groupies crowding the large dingy dressing room seemed particularly gross.

*   *   *

They were leaving for a concert at Ohio University on a two-stop flight from Detroit to Columbus. The sixty-mile drive from the airport to the campus in Athens, Ohio, was beautiful, lush in the height of springtime, but the group was too disoriented to enjoy it. Geography had been ripped past them at an unbelievable rate, so many time zones had been crossed and double crossed that the date, even the time, became irrelevant. The road manager kept it all together in between his own schedule of sexual sorties. He arranged reservations, arrival times, picking up money, waking the lads up in time. An equipment man was responsible for the thousands of pounds of instruments and sound equipment which had to be shipped, flown, expressed, driven, or otherwise transported from place to place intact. "How much time till the gig?" was the only question the group ever cared about at that point. Everything else was too fast, too complicated, or too troublesome to deal with. It got to the point by the time they got to Boston, where they asked a local disc jockey they knew to get girls for them, they didn't even want to bother wending their way through the groupies' come-hither games anymore.

Check into the hotel. A quick swim in the springtime chill. A bit of a drink at the hotel bar, crawling with conventioneers who pointed at them and guffawed. A sound check at the auditorium. Another nip at the bar. No supper.

They played a set, an encore, another. They were tired, keyed up, not knowing whether to shit or go blind, and they tumbled back to the hotel where they had to take pills to get to sleep. In the morning there was a mad, almost-missed-the-plane dash to the airport.

* * *

Robert was first onto the plane, galloping down the aisle like a de-mented ape, his armpit hair hanging from his sleeveless open-knit shirt, yelling at the top of his lungs, "Toilets, TOILETS! *Toilets* for old Robert!" The dear little Middle America passengers went into a state of mild shock.

Nerves frayed when they reached Minneapolis and the driver kept losing his way to the Guthrie Memorial Theatre. They arrived somewhat late; the performance nonetheless was spectacular, the audience laugh-ing in polite embarrassment at Robert's orgasm sequence onstage, and applauding lustily afterward. It was a sit-down crowd, all natty and urban, country-club hip. Part of this particular engagement, it turned out, was the obligation to attend a party at the lady promoter's country house, full of young locals in blazers and party dresses who gaped at the group for sev-eral unbearably dull hours. Comparing notes afterward, other groups who had been through Minneapolis said that every group playing there had to go through the same lame scene.

The road manager called a meeting the next day. There was a deci-sion to be made. There were four days until Led Zeppelin were due to play in Chicago. Nobody liked Minneapolis very much so it was decided by Jimmy Page and the road manager that the group would fly to New York for a few days of rehearsals and interviews by day, recording sessions (the second album was only partially finished) by night. They were re-minded that the second album should be out by their third tour to stack the cards in favor of their success.

Their success was built on a well-engineered promotional strategy. Recordings, airplay, personal appearances, and publicity have to be coor-dinated for the greatest impact. A constant flow of albums, the release of a new one timed with the dénouement of the current one is desirable. Their names must appear somewhere at all times in some sort of press, columns, fan magazines, critical journals, underground papers—no pos-sible exposure is left untried. Their English manager, American lawyer, road manager, and publicity agency, one of Hollywood's heaviest, con-spired to pack the heaviest possible punch.

* * *

Jimmy Page fell seriously ill twice on the tour but played every night. "That's how you know you're a pro," he chirped on the plane.

Two nights in Chicago and one night in Columbia, Maryland. A day off? No, surprise, Atlantic Records was throwing them a party at the Plaza in New York. At the party they were informed that their album had to be ready in time for a marketing convention during the next few weeks. That meant another session that night and they dutifully trooped off to the studio.

Jimmy Page was getting snappy, ragged, and pathologically work-oriented. John Paul Jones seemed to let the bedlam bounce off a carefully cultivated hard shell. John Bonham was often bitterly silent and horribly homesick. Robert Plant who, much to the pique of Jimmy Page, was emerging as the star of the group, talked constantly about buying a christening gown for his infant daughter back home. Slugging down a glass of imitation orange drink one morning after a night of clowning around so loud the motel manager checked out his room to see what was happening, he sighed, "God, I miss my wife," to no one in particular.

But the depression never lasted very long. Conversations were livened by riotous accounts of the previous night's misadventures and the group developed a remarkable flair for irritating waitresses and airline hostesses who ogled over them. In flight they would collapse in their seats, their eyes dull, faces slack, finally falling into uncomfortable sleep. They were coming stars, but they looked like something the cat dragged in.

Everyone was wrecked, drained, moody, jet-shocked, and almost sick. They were advised that the tour was going extraordinarily well, better than even expected, but it did not seem to affect them, or perhaps they didn't realize the implications of what they'd been through. But each time they faced an audience (and they never disappointed an audience the whole time) they knew. This music they played, these people who loved them, no matter how gut-bustingly horrible that tour was, made it all worthwhile. In those few hours the boys would be transformed from tired carping brats into radiant gods. Whatever happened, it never took the joy out of playing and playing well.

The tour came off in the black that time around. In a fairly typical arrangement, the group traveled with a paid road crew. The money they earned had to support those salaries, transportation, lodging, food, repair or loss of equipment, and every other road expense incurred. They retained a publicity firm, lawyers in both countries, a manager, and an accountant. Managers' and booking agents' fees are deducted from the gross, and by the time the accounting was done they might have gotten to divide among themselves one-third of the more than $150,000 that tour grossed. The fees they were able to get, from a flat $5,000 a night to over $15,000 for the particularly successful two-day Chicago engagement, were good, but not top money in the field.

The scheme had worked. That tour was a setup for the next one, the superstar trip, where they would gross $350,000 to $400,000 for less time, fewer dates, and much more comfortable living and traveling arrangements.

When Herman's Hermits, for instance, were at the height of their career, they chartered a private jet for a month at a time, stocked it with their favorite food, and played poker with their agent, often betting their evening's earnings in the game. From airports they would charter helicopters to the city and limousines to the gigs, never rumpling their soft teddy suits on the way, always sending the road manager out to cull and deliver the right kinds of girls. For more sophisticated groups there are the world's finest hotels, chauffeurs, managers, agents, and local rock and roll bigwigs to squire them around town through pesty crowds of clawing fans into the most lavish of private homes with all their needs provided for. Past all this scuffling, it's clear sailing for the duration of rock and roll stardom. Get it while you can, pop is fast and fickle, and scorn for fallen stars is merciless.

"In this business," commented John Paul Jones, "it's not so much making it as fast as you can but making it fast *while* you can. The average life of a successful group is three years. You just have to get past that initial ordeal. The touring makes you into a different person. I realize that when I get home. It takes me weeks to recover after living like an animal for so long."

*   *   *

I had been covering this tour on assignment from *Life* magazine, living through the last three weeks of it with them, through the miles of exhaustion and undernourishment, suffering the company of the whiny groupies they attracted, the frazzled rush of arriving and departing, the uptightness at the airports, and the advances of their greasy road manager. I had been keeping a journal of our discomfort to document this unbelievably wearing and astoundingly exciting slice of professional life so germane to the rock and roll Sixties.

At the Fillmore East, on the last date of the tour, I stopped in to say good-bye and godspeed. Two members of the group attacked me, shrieking and grabbing at my clothes, totally over the edge. I fought them off until Peter Grant rescued me but not before they managed to tear my dress down the back. My young man of the evening took me home in a limousine borrowed from an agent friend and I trembled in exhaustion, anger, and bitterness all the way. Over the next week I tried to write the story. It was not about to happen. It took a whole year just to get back to my notes again with any kind of objectivity.

If you walk inside the cages of the zoo you get to see the animals close up, stroke the captive pelts, and mingle with the energy behind the mystique. You also get to smell the shit firsthand.

Dave Hickey

THE DELICACY OF ROCK AND ROLL

Dave Hickey likes the word *wank,* so with all due respect, he does a lot of wanking around in this essay before he gets to the point. Bear with him; it's a point worth waiting for.

IN THE MID nineteen sixties, when I was attending the University of Texas at Austin, Thursday nights were "Underground Flick Nite" at the Y on the Drag. The movies were supposed to start promptly at 7:00 P.M., but the projectionist was also a dedicated revolutionary, so they never really started until the New Left cabals, which also met at the Y, had adjourned for the day. So we always went. After a hot afternoon plotting the destruction of bourgeois society—and barring some previously scheduled eruption of spontaneous civil disobedience—Flick Nite was sort of radicals' night out. Imagine *Mystery Science Theater 3000* with a hot Texas *mise en scène:* The clatter of the projector in the glimmering darkness. Smoke curling up through the silvered ambiance. Insects swooping. The ongoing murmur of impudent commentary from the audience. References to Althusser, Marcuse, group sex. Like that.

On the evening I want to tell you about, the evening I experienced the paradigm shift, the program began with a couple of Stan Brakhage films. I don't remember the titles, but they might be characterized thematically as "very nervous" and sort of about "film itself." As I recall, there was a great deal of panning, swooping, jiggling, dipping, and zooming—a great many explosions (the "film itself" seeming to catch on fire, at one point)— and overall, a bit more montage than I would have preferred. A young woman sitting in front of me in the darkness kept waving her cigarette languidly on the pivot of her wrist and muttering, "Boy, boy, boy, boy, boy, boy, boy," in a very bored voice.

She had a point. I can imagine these films coming back into vogue now, in this revisionist *momento macho.* Today, they would be minimalist action flicks—*Die Hard* sans Bruce Willis. Back then, they were the same old apocalypse—kinetic action paintings. People tended to mention Jackson Pollock when they talked about them. They were doing this when the second half of Flick Nite began—*and we thought Brakhage was dull!* In this new flick, the camera just *sat there,* trained on this guy who just sat there, too, sideways to the camera in a chair, like Whistler's mother's gay nephew, getting a haircut. That was it. The barber was out of the frame. All we saw were his hands, the scissors, and the comb, fluttering around this guy's head. *Clip-clip! Clip-clip-clip!*

We couldn't fucking believe it. This was *really* boring. Mesmerizing, too, of course, but not mesmerizing enough to keep us from moaning, keening almost, and swaying in our chairs. *Clip-clip!* But we kept looking at the screen even though we knew, after the first minute, that this was going to be it: that it was just a guy getting a haircut. Still, we watched, and it just went on and on. *Clip! Clip-clip-clip!* In truth, it was no more than five or six minutes, but that's a long time in a movie, approximately the length of a Siberian winter. So, I began thinking about *theory.* "What about the *clip-clip* of the scissors and the *clip-clip* of the projector?" I wondered. "The analogy of the 'actual' and 'represented' white noise? What about that?"

Then it happened. The guy getting the haircut reached into his shirt pocket, pulled out a pack of cigarettes and casually lit one up! *Major action!* Applause. Tumultuous joy and release! Chanting even. And the joy may have been ironic (it almost certainly was), but the release was quite genuine. I remember every instant of Henry lighting up that cigarette and the laughter I could not suppress. Because it was fun, and amazing to realize how seriously you had been fucked with. The haircut continued at that point *(clip-clip!),* but we were alive now. Fifteen minutes earlier we had been dozing through Brakhage's visual Armageddon. Now we were cheering for some guy lighting a Lucky Strike.

Clearly, Mr. Warhol was onto something here. It was stupid, but it was miraculous, too. His film had totally recalibrated the perceptions of a roomful of sex-crazed adolescent revolutionaries into a field of tiny increments. It had restored the breath and texture to things and then, with the flip of a Zippo, had given us a little bang in the bargain—and by accident, I have no doubt. We all knew, of course, that the events in a work of art are only large or small relative to one another, but our bodies had forgotten. Our bodies had become inured to explosions. The delicate increments of individual response needed to be reinscribed, and *Haircut* did that. When the lights came up, we were all looking at one another with new eyes.

"There has got to be some political application," the projectionist said to me as we stood around on the porch, finishing our beer. I doubted it, but I didn't say so, because I wanted to see more Warhol flicks, and I feared that once the critical instrumentalities of dialectical materialism were unleashed upon *Haircut,* it would become only too clear that Andy's film dissolved the idea of history and narrative into something tinier, more complicated and contingent. And for us, at that time, there were no politics without history. Politics *were* history—and vice versa—although, in truth, I found myself preferring the political morality of Warhol's film to Brakhage's. It was sadder and funnier, too.

Today, I know this wasn't quite fair to Brakhage, but at that moment the rhetoric of expressionist freedom had reached the point of rapidly diminishing returns. It just wasn't working anymore. I think I was correct, however, in assuming that Brakhage's practice (if it was not purely formal) was essentially tragic. His films strove toward a condition of freedom and autonomy, fully aware that the work itself, for all its abstract materiality, could never free itself from cultural expectations. Nor could the artist, for all the aleatory and improvisatory privileges he granted himself, free his practice from the traditions of picture-making. So, no matter how much you admired Brakhage's bird-on-a-wire lungings toward existential freedom, you had to admit, finally, that all the energy was in the wire.

Warhol's film turned that energy on its head. Warhol could not *invent* enough wires, nor try hard enough to impose normative simplicity—to avoid freedom at all costs—nor fail more spectacularly. The static camera, the static subject, the idiot narrative armature, the tiny non-individuated events *(clip-clip!),* only served to theatricalize the inherent imperfection and disorder of the endeavor, only served to foreground the sheer, silly ebullient *muchness* of the image moving in time. Thus, Warhol's self-inhibiting strategies liberated him as an artist and liberated his beholders, as well, into an essentially comic universe.

Brakhage told us what we already knew as children of the Cold War, that no matter how hard we tried, we could not be free—thus inviting us, paradoxically, into the rigors of utopian political orthodoxy. Warhol's film, on the other hand, told us what we needed to know, that, no matter how hard we tried, we could not be ordered—that insofar as we were tiny, raggedy, damaged and disorganized human beings, we probably *were* free, in some small degree, whether we liked it or not. All of this is probably self-evident to anyone who has lived through the past thirty years. The effect of these films on me, on that hot, Texas night, however, was nothing short of cataclysmic.

I knew, you see, that my encounter with Brakhage and Warhol was not, in any sense, a "high art" experience. It couldn't have been. I didn't know anything about high art—I knew about radical politics, jazz, rock-

and-roll, and linguistics—and understanding this, I have gradually come to distrust the very *idea* of high art in a democracy. I mean, what would it be like? Aristocratic cultures have a high and low. They have higher-ups and lower-downs, and consequently they may, on occasion, create a socially engaged, commercially disinterested high art that trickles down to instruct and inform the "lower orders." In a mercantile democracy, however, the only refuge from the marketplace is in the academy. So democracies, I fear, must content themselves with commercial, popular art that informs the culture and non-commercial, academic art that critiques it—with the caveat that, even though most popular art exploits the vernacular, some popular art redeems it—even though it's still for sale.

To reach this conclusion, I asked myself these questions: Is a painting by Jackson Pollock or a film by Stan Brakhage high art? Yes? Well, if so, could the art of Pollock or Brakhage exist without the imprimatur of Dizzy Gillespie and Charlie Parker? Could I have understood it without its being informed by the cultural context of American jazz? Without the free-form exuberance of bebop? My answer: No way, José. And, conversely, could bebop exist without Jackson Pollock and Stan Brakhage? You betcha. And could rock-and-roll exist without Warhol? Yep. And could Andy Warhol exist without rock-and-roll? I don't think so. These answers, of course, tend to confirm my own predisposition to regard recorded popular music as the dominant art form of this American century. My point is that Pollock and Warhol do not exploit the lumpen vernacular, they redeem it—elevating its eccentricities into the realm of public discourse. As a consequence, the work of Pollock and Warhol, like that of Rembrandt or Dickens or David, is the best that popular, commercial art can be—doing the best things it can do.

So now I think of that evening in Texas as marking the end of the Age of Jazz and the beginning of the Age of Rock-and-Roll—the end of tragic theater in American popular culture and the beginning of comic delicacy. Both ages make art that succeeds by failing, but each exploits failure in different ways. Jazz presumes that it would be nice if the four of us—simpatico dudes that we are—while playing this complicated song together, might somehow be free and autonomous as well. Tragically, this never quite works out. At best, we can only be free one or two at a time—while the other dudes hold onto the wire. Which is not to say that no one has tried to dispense with wires. Many have, and sometimes it works—but it doesn't feel like *jazz* when it does. The music simply drifts away into the stratosphere of formal dialectic, beyond our social concerns.

Rock-and-roll, on the other hand, presumes that the four of us—as damaged and anti-social as we are—might possibly get it *to-fucking-gether,* man, and play this simple song. And play it right, okay? Just this once, in tune and on the beat. But we can't. The song's too simple, and we're too complicated and too excited. We try like hell, but the guitars distort, the intonation bends, and the beat just moves, imperceptibly, against our formal expectations, whether we want it to or not. Just because we're *breathing,* man. Thus, in the process of trying to play this very simple song together, we create this hurricane of noise, this infinitely complicated, fractal filigree of delicate distinctions.

And you can thank the wanking eighties, if you wish, and digital sequencers, too, for proving to everyone that technologically "perfect" rock—like "free" jazz—sucks rockets. Because order sucks. I mean, look at the Stones. Keith Richards is *always* on top of the beat, and Bill Wyman, until he quit, was always behind it, because Richards is leading the band and Charlie Watts is listening to him and Wyman is listening to Watts. So the beat is sliding on those tiny neural lapses, not so you can tell, of course, but so you can feel it in your stomach. And the intonation is wavering, too, with the pulse in the finger on the amplified string. This is the delicacy of rock-and-roll, the bodily rhetoric of tiny increments, necessary imperfections, and contingent community. And it has its virtues, because jazz only works if we're trying to be free and are, in fact, together. Rock-and-roll works because we're all a bunch of flakes. That's something you can *depend* on, and a good thing too, because in the twentieth century, that's all there is: jazz and rock-and-roll. The rest is term papers and advertising.

Jeff Gomez

FANZINE

Hey, it's a tough life being a rock and roll critic.

AFTER a handful of phone calls, Chipp is sitting in The Scene, nursing a beer and looking over his questions. He's waiting for The Deer Park to arrive and set up their gear for a soundcheck. It's a little after seven, and the club, which won't open for another three hours, is empty except for Chipp, Todd (the owner), and Jack (the day bartender) who's waiting anxiously to get off his shift. Jack is staring at Chipp, waiting for him to finish his beer and leave, or else sip faster and order another. Chipp keeps his eyes trained on the carved surface of the bar. Nervously he checks his questions again. He feels for his pen, wallet, watch, and tape recorder. As he eases the recorder back onto the stool next to him, his hand brushes the spare console and it starts blaring, "Testing, one, two, three, testing . . ." seguing into a not-so-on-key rendition of "Rid of Me" by Randy until he's silenced by Chipp in the background shouting, "Shut up, asshole!" Chipp quickly shuts it off, but not before Jack is glaring at him again, this time harder than before.

At the back of the bar, to the right of the stage, a large door opens, the last rays of sunlight suddenly streaming into the dank, cavernous room. Chipp spots a medium-sized guy with black hair who lugs in two guitar cases and drops them unceremoniously on the raised stage. He's followed by a short blond guy who drops his load of a bass drum, returning in a few seconds with a handful of cymbals and two pedals. The two of them continue like this for about half an hour, bringing in tomtoms, a snare, a small seat, amps, two more guitars, as well as a backpack full of accessories: distortion pedals, strings, three straps, tuning keys, electronic tuner, and half a dozen cords.

Chipp finally recognizes the guys as Stoner and Johnny, the rhythm section for The Deer Park. They mill around for a second and Chip keeps quiet, waiting for the rest of the band to arrive. They don't. Chipp is just about to say something when another guy comes through the back door, but he's not in the band, either.

"What took you so long, Dave?" Stoner calls out as he's setting one of the amps on a folding chair and positioning a microphone against the glittery fabric facade. "We have half the stage set up already."

"Don't start with me, Stoner. I'm not having a good week. Uh, Jack, is Todd around?" the guy calls out to the bartender. "I want to talk to him about the guarantee."

"Guarantee?" The bartender laughs. "Since when does Todd give guarantees to local acts? Hell, if the Beatles re-formed and played a reunion show here on a Friday night, Todd wouldn't guarantee them anything, and that's *including* John."

"I know, I know," Dave says, pulling up a stool a few spaces away from Chipp. "He's a slimeball, but that's why he's a promoter. So is he around or what?"

"He's in the back." Jack puts down the mug he's been rinsing. "Let me go get him."

Dave suddenly turns to Chipp, who's been staring at him, trying to remember where he's seen him before.

"What do you want, kid?"

"Oh, I'm here to interview The Deer Park."

Dave looks him over.

"The fanzine, right? What was the name of that thing? '*Goddamn*?' "

Chipp clears his throat. "No, that's, uh, *Godfuck.*"

"Ooh, that's great." Dave laughs. "Send me extras for my sister. I'm Dave. We spoke on the phone."

"Yeah." Chipp smiles. The stranger's face finally falls into place. "You run the label. I thought I'd seen you here before. So how's it going?"

"Don't ask, sport." Dave sighs and pats down his pockets for something that isn't there. "You ever have one of those days?"

"Sure, I guess."

"Well"—Dave pauses, flashing a pair of bloodshot eyes—"I'm having one of those lives." He moves on. "The band is in the van. They're waiting for you."

"They are?" Chipp swallows nervously.

"Who else walks around with a tape recorder?"

Chipp nods sheepishly and starts to gather up his stuff when Todd comes through the side door that leads out to the alley. He's eating a huge orange and streams of juice are caught in his thick goatee.

"What's this I hear about a guarantee?" he says with his mouth full, spitting out the words along with little bits of pulp and seeds; a white fleshy vein sticks in his beard.

"Todd, you promised me. Now don't even try to . . ."

As Chipp heads for the back door, he can still hear the conversation, both voices starting to rise, filling with anger.

"I told you," Todd continues with his mouth full, "I'd split with you what I got at the door. If you don't trust me, then why don't you—"

Once outside Chipp spots The Deer Park's van parked in the corner of the empty lot. The back doors are open, and he can see two pairs of legs hanging out. Puffs of smoke appear every few seconds. He approaches the van slowly.

"Hey, I'm Chipp." He pokes his head around one of the rusting doors. "Uh, I'm from *Godfuck*. Didn't Dave tell you?"

They both nod, one of them taking a deep drag from a dove-tailed joint.

"Let's see, you're Johnny." Chipp points to the one who is not smoking. "And you're Stoner, right?" He points to the other. They both look at Chipp dumbly. "Just, you know, making sure."

Just as Chipp sits down, Johnny says, "There are two questions we refuse up front to answer, and they are 'What are your influences?' and 'How has the success of Nirvana affected you?' *Capisci*?"

"Sure, sure." Chipp fake-laughs, getting out his list of questions and scratching off the first two. He places the recorder on the floor of the van between them. He tries to press PLAY and RECORD together, but when he presses the buttons of the recorder, it slips into the steel grooves of the floor and only one of the buttons catches.

" 'LICK MY LEGS OF DESIRE! LICK MY—' " Chipp stabs the thing with a clenched fist as Randy's voice hangs in the air for a few seconds.

"Sorry."

Chipp straddles the recorder over the grooves, presses PLAY and RECORD, and begins the interview.

"So how long has The Deer Park been around?"

"Um"—Johnny fields the first question since Stoner is preoccupied with picking at a WE'RE THE MEAT PUPPETS AND YOU SUCK! sticker on the door handle—"since about '90. Neither of us came aboard until about six months ago. I'm not really sure how Ben and the first couple of guitarists got together. You'd really have to ask them."

"Okay," Chipp says, checking the question off his list and moving on to the next. "Where'd you get the name from?"

"From a book," Johnny says, wiping a long greasy strand of jet black hair out of his sallow face. "But the guy who wrote the book got it from somewhere. Ben explained it to me once, what it was, just in case somebody asked. It was something like the Deer Park was this big place in France where the aristocra . . . arista . . ." He struggles with the word for a few seconds before giving up. "Where the rich people brought all the virginal girls from the small villages, and guys just did whatever they wanted to them."

"The loss," Stoner deeply intones, "of innocence."

"Yeah," Johnny agrees. "That, and it also sounded good."

"Next question," Chipp mumbles, trying desperately to read his list in the dank half-dark of the van. "If you were trapped on a desert island and could bring only ten records, what would they be?"

Chipp tosses the question, and it lands on the other side of the van, sitting there for a moment as Stoner releases another lethal blast of smoke from his recently lighted skull bong, and Johnny rolls his eyes a couple of times, formulating his answer. In the downtime between yelling into the canyon and waiting for the echo, Chipp's eyes scan the van.

Filling the steel grooves on the floor of the van is a clear, sticky goo that most likely is some hybrid of assorted liquors and sweat, the snail trail of slime starting toward the driver seat and emptying out onto the bumper. Stickers and *Hustler* pinups line the inside of the van, which, as Chipp is beginning to notice, smells like a trash can with moldy food at the bottom. He checks the barely lit corners of the vehicle for perhaps a carton of month-old Subway sandwiches or a green pizza with growing fuzz anchored on a guitar stand. Johnny is sitting on a case of beer, and Stoner is leaning against the door with a curled-up and stained *Star Wars* blanket.

"Raw Power," Stoner begins his desert island disc list, adding, *"Raw Power, Raw Power, Raw Power, Raw Power, Raw Power, Raw Power, Raw Power, Raw Power* . . ."

"Well," Chipp says with a sigh, "that's only nine, but, whatever. Johnny? How about yours?"

"Stupid question." He shifts his weight. "Ask something else."

"Okaaaayyyy," Chipp draws out the word as he scrambles for the next question on his increasingly short list. "How do you guys come up with the lyrics?"

"We don't," Johnny burps, ripping off a leg of his chair and drinking it. "Ben does."

"How about the music? Where does *it* come from?"

"You'd have to ask Ben," Stoner says, trying to act out of it.

You'd have to ask Ben. You'd have to ask Ben. How many times have I heard that in the past half-hour? Jesus, what do these guys know? So when you're alone with a girl, how do you know she cares for you as much as you

care for her? Chipp imagines Stoner doing his best Syd Barret imperson-
ation: *You'd like, wow, have to ask Ben.*

"What are your goals for The Deer Park?"

"To keep making good music, plain and simple," Johnny answers.

The more frustrated Chipp gets with the rote answers, the angrier he
gets at himself for asking such lame questions.

"Well, that's all the questions I have," Chipp says, leaning forward to
turn off the recorder. Johnny says thanks and politely shakes his hand,
while Stoner just sits there taking hit after hit off his bong.

Back on the sidewalk, Chipp exits the parking lot and heads for the
street. It's nearly dark, the sky colored like a bruise, dark blue, purple,
black. Walking is difficult. The few bong hits he took (not to mention being
cooped up with Stoner for almost a half hour) slowly take hold, and he
finds it hard to resist a grin and begins laughing out loud.

The streets of Kitty are nearly empty. Chipp walks quickly along the
uneven sidewalks, kicking at cans and debris in his path. He thinks of
Stoner and Johnny back at the van, preparing for later in the evening
when they'll spend an hour pounding on their drum skins and bass. *Why
do they do it? What possesses them? Why bother?*

He stumbles loudly up the stairs to his apartment and finds Randy
lying on the couch. Randy is listening to Chipp's records, using Chipp's
headphones, with an empty bag of Chipp's Cheetos by his side. Chipp sits
down at the kitchen table, pulls out the recorder along with a pad of paper,
and a pencil, and gets ready to transcribe the conversation. He giggles
again and Randy twitches, as if he is being electrocuted. Chipp rewinds the
tape, presses PLAY.

"So, how long has The Deer Park been around?"

To his own ears his voice sounds strange, tinny, not at all how he
thinks it sounds. He laughs again, tries to concentrate, and begins writing
down their answers.

It's a quiet night, and Chipp can hear the music seeping from the seal
between the headphones and Randy's ears. He figures he'll transcribe the
interview, order a pizza, and then see if Randy and Sarita want to go to
The Scene with him and Heather. Why not?

PSYCHOTIC REACTIONS AND CARBURETOR DUNG

Greil Marcus, who edited the collection of writings by Lester Bangs for which this was the title piece, wrote this about his friend: "Lester published more than a hundred and fifty reviews in *Rolling Stone* (from 1969 to 1973, when editor Jann Wenner banned him for disrespect toward musicians; again in 1979, when record-review editor Paul Nelson demanded his reinstatement), but *Rolling Stone* was never his place of freedom. *Creem,* the rock'n'roll magazine that grew out of the milieu around John Sinclair's White Panther Party, was that place, at least for a time: it gave Lester space for the farthest reaches of invective, scorn, fantasy, rage, and glee. First as a contributor and soon as an editor, he made the magazine work as a subversive undertow in the inexorable commercial flow of the rock business. . . ."

RUN HERE, my towhead grandchillen, and let this geezer dandle you upon his knee. *While you still recognize me, you little maniacs.* You know the gong has tolled, it's that time again. Now let me set my old brain a-ruminatin', ah, what upbuilding tale from days of yore shall I relate today?

"What's all this shit about the Yardbirds?"

Ah, the Yardbirds. Yes indeedie, those were the days. 1965, and I were an impetuous young squirt, just fell in puppy love first time, she used to push my hand away and sniff, "I'd like to but I don't wanna turn into a tramp." The girls were actually like that in those—

"Ah, cut the senile drool an' get on with the fuckin' archaeology or we gonna de-dandle off yer knee an' go scratch up some action! *Oldster!*"

Okay, kids, okay, just bear with me; no reason to get excited . . . now, as I was saying, it was glorious 1965, and I was starved for some sounds that might warp my brain a little. You see, there wasn't much going except maybe "I'm Henry VIII, I Am"—no, I won't get that one out, I know it sounds good, but believe me . . . we were just stuck in one of those musical recessions we used to have every once in a while, back before we started trading Intra-Solar System package tours. . . . I recollect another mighty sad downer stretch long about the beginning of the seventies . . . except *that* one lasted so long we damn near dried up an' boycotted records entirely till Barky Dildo and the Bozo Huns showed up to save our souls . . .

"Ahhh, man, how could you like those guys? That stuff was the most reactionary, chickenshit fad in history! I mean, what's so big deal about playing buzzsaw fiddle an' catgut snorkbollerers? Jammin's fine, but those cats even resorted to 4/4 time and key changes! Now I ask you, Grandud, what kind of shit is that?"

All right, all right, I know I shouldna digressed again! From here on out I'm stickin' to the straight facts, and if you sassy tads interrupt me one more time I'm gonna paste one o' yuz right in the mouth!

"Which one?"

Random choice, O seed of my seed, random like everything else in this fuckin' madhouse of a world you guys got which I shall soon be gratefully bowing out of.

"Ahright, go head an' bruise yer knuckles so you can go soak 'em in hot beer, but don't say we didn't warn ya. You oughta know that yer the only old sod around here that Skewey, Ruey and Blooie'll take any crap off of . . . and what's this bowin' out shit? Who's grateful to be dead?"

Well, as a matter of fact, at one time there were a whole lot of marks who were just that. But that's another story. I've gotta get down to this Yardbird saga or we gonna digress ourselves right into the ozone. So listen now an' listen good, and hold your questions till the end.

The Yardbirds, as I said, were incredible. They came stampeding in and just blew everybody clean off the tracks. They were so fucking good, in fact, that people were still imitating 'em as much as a decade later, and getting rich doing it I might add, because the original band of geniuses just didn't last that long. Of course, none of their stepchildren were half as good, and got increasingly pretentious and overblown as time went on until about 1973 a bunch of emaciated fops called Led Zeppelin played their final concert when the lead guitarist was assassinated by an irate strychnine freak in the audience with a zip gun just fifty-eight minutes into his famous two-and-a-half-hour virtuoso solo on one bass note. Then they grabbed the lead vocalist, who was so strung out on datura be couldn't do much but cough "Gleep gleep gug jargaroona fizzlefuck" type lyrics anymore anyway, and they cut off all his hair and stomped his harmonica, gave him a set of civvies (an outsized set of Lifetime Chainmail Bodyjeans, I think it was) and ran him outa town on a rail. Last we heard he was trying to sing "Whole Lotta Love" to a buncha sentimental old hashheads in some Podunk club. Maudlin as hell.

But the Yardbirds, you know, even though they turned it all around they only lasted a coupla years. And some of the imitators they had! Man, I used to get my yuks just lookin' at those records! Like when they did "I'm a Man" and made the Top Ten with a mixture of Bo Diddley (ahh, he was this old fat cat cooked up this sorts famous shuffle beat . . . I think it was already passé before you guys were even born. Yeah, fact, when they finally junked the whole idea of a steady bottom pulse altogether I think you guys were still too young to remember the big cultural civil war about it, Jagger ambushin' Zagnose right in the streets and Beefheart taking to the hills of Costa Rica to hide till things cooled down some . . .) and feedback, everybody just blew their wads and flopped over, because all that electro-distort stuff that rocked you guys to sleep when you were first tokin' in your cradles was really unheard-of then, a real earthquake mindfuck. Some people found it vaguely indecent, like the naked nerve inside a wire gleaming all crazy at 'em, but us smokestack whizzband jive cats were bip to the cultural shift right from the start. We were just waitin' for somebody to come along and kick out the jams, yessir . . . oh, that phrase? Yeah, well, that's another one. Yeah, it does have a nice jagging ring, doesn't it. You'll laugh again, but we had a lotta zingy lingo when I was a tad—sharp riffs like "Right on!" and "Peace, brother!" . . . not like all this simpleminded telegraphic shit that passes for communication among you banal brats today. Why, I recall when I was in high school (oh, I told you—that was kind of where they put you when they didn't know what to do with you—when you were too big for the Kiddie Kokoons and too young to go out an' hafta assume what we used to call Manhood, which involved going at the same time every day to some weird building and doing some totally useless shit for hours on end just so you could get some bread and have everybody respect you)—when I was in high school, we used to have some mighty snappy patter. For instance, if somebody did something stupid, we used to say, "Whattaya got, shit for brains?" And another good one was, when you were mad at somebody, you could call 'em "You rotten sack o' shit!" Or a bunch of us, a gang of hoodlums about like you guys, would be driving up to a liquor store to get some Cokes and potato chips, the guy riding shotgun—later, later—would groan, "Mack down!" which meant the act of eating, of course. A few years later some imaginative souls started to call food "munchies," but luckily that moronic term didn't last long.

And even years before that we had a very mysterious incantation: "I don't make trash like you, I burn it!" You could say that and people would get confused. Or kids would, at any rate. I forget just what it signified—I kinda think it was a sort of Zen koan so when you were having a disagreement with somebody you could shoot that 'un their way and their analysis of it could either make peace or end up in a fist fight.

But I'm digressing again. Shit, you kids are right, I'm turning into a waxy-eyed old goat. With shit for brains. Soon as we finish this here anecdotal session I'm gonna go get under the Morphones and sedate my fevered brain an hour or two. I got a date with Delilah Kooch tonite an' I gotta be refreshed if I wanna still be bangin' when the cock crows, Organoil or no Organoil . . . ninety is a year for moderation. But as I was recounting before I wandered down the fleecy path, the Yardbirds themselves didn't hold together for many moons, and when they hit with "I'm a Man" they'd already started gettin' raided (someday I'll tell ya 'bout Paul Revere and the Raiders; hah, you wouldn' even believe me . . .) by little Teeno groups everywhere who immediately recorded windup versions of "I'm a Man" to fill out their debut albums, bands like the Royal Guardsmen, who had two Number One hits with the gimmick of this dog named Snoopy shootin' down old Germans in antique planes, I swear to God, and then punk bands started cropping up who were writing their own songs but taking the Yardbirds' sound and reducing it to this kind of goony fuzz-tone clatter . . . oh, it was beautiful, it was pure folklore, Old America, and sometimes I think those were the best days ever.

No, I don't just think so, I know they were, been havin' that feeling ever since about 1970 when everything began to curdle into a bunch of wandering minstrels and balladic bards and other such shit which was already obsolete even then. Man, I used to get up in the morning in '65 and '66 and just love to turn on that radio, there was so much good jive wailing out. Like there was this song called "Hey Joe" that literally everybody and his fuckin' brother not only recorded but claimed to have written even though it was obviously the psychedelic mutation of some hoary old folk song which was about murderin' somebody for love just like nine-tenths of the rest of them hoary folk ballads. And a group called the Leaves had a killer (that's another word you ought to add to yer little yaksacks) hit with "Hey Joe" and then disappeared after a couple of weird albums, though they did have one other good chart, "Doctor Stone" it was, a real heavyhanded double-entendre dope song. Every other fuckin' record was cram fulla code words for getting stoned for about a year there cause people were just starting to in a big way and it was a big furtive thrill, but the stupid government didn't figure the codes out, FBI and CIA and all, until about four or five years later, at which time they came out with this pompous exposé, this dude who looked like a cross between a gopher and the American Eagle and had a real killer vocal sound took off for this geriatric resort in the desert where people went for the jaded thrill of tossing their money away, he shot out there and delivered this weighty oration intended to let the country in on the secret that drugs and music were related when everybody already knew it anyway, and the whole shebang was hilarious because all the songs he used for examples were old as hell and everybody was already so stoned by that time they didn't need to serenade people into getting high anymore.

But for me and a lotta other folks that point, when nobody cared because everybody'd been converted to the new setup, was precisely where things started to go downhill. Instead of singing about taking tea with Mary Jane and boppin' yer dingus on ol' Sweet Slit Annie it was Help me God I don't know the meaning of life or I believe that love is gonna cure the world of psoriasis and cancer both and I'm gonna tell the people all about it 285 different ways whether you like it or not. And Why is there war well go ask the children they know everything we need to know, and Gee I sure like black folks even if my own folks don't and endless vinyl floods of drivel in similar veins. At that point I started to pack in and resort back to my good old '66 goof squat rock. I got out records like *96 Tears* by Question Mark and the Mysterians, who were mysterious indeed, and rewhooped to jungle juju cackles like "Wooly Bully," which is indescribable and was recorded by a bunch of guys who drove around in a hearse wearing turbans.

That was also when I got back into those junior jiver Yardbirds imitations in a big way. Like there was *Back Door Men* by the Shadows of Knight, who were really good at copping the Yardbird riffs and reworking 'em, and *Psychotic Reaction* by Count Five, who weren't so hot at it actually but ripped their whole routine off with such grungy spunk that I really dug 'em the most! They were a bunch of young guitar-slappin' brats from some indistinguishable California suburb, and just a few months after "I'm a Man" left the charts they got right in there with this inept imitation called "Psychotic Reaction." And it was a big hit, in fact I think it was an even bigger hit than "I'm a Man," which burned me up at the time but was actually cool now that I think about it, yeah, perfectly appropriate. The song was a shlockhouse grinder, completely fatuous. It started out with this fuzz guitar riff they stole off a Johnny Rivers bit that escapes me just now— it was the one just before "Secret Agent Man"—then went into one of the stupidest vocals of all time. It went, let me see, some jive like: " . . . I can't

get yer love, I can't get affection / Aouw, little girl's Psychotic reaction. . . ."
and then they'd shoot off into an exact "I'm a Man" ripoff. It was absolute
dynamite. I hated it at first but then one day I was driving down the road
stoned and it came on and I clapped my noggin: "What the fuck am I
thinking of? That's a great song!"

The album (Double Shot DSM 1001) had a killer cover, too—the photo
was taken from the bottom of a grave, around the rim of which stood the
members of the group, staring down atcha in the sepulchre with bug-eyed
malice. Really eerie, except that they were all wearing madras shirts and
checkered slacks from Penney's. Which was not so eerie, but a nice touch
in the long run. The colors and lettering were nice, too.

The back had four pictures of them: Count Five standing rather awk-
wardly in Lugosian capes on the lawn in front of an old mansion, trying
to look sinister; Count Five on some L.A. dancetime show ravin' it up
while a crowd of blooming boppers, presumably cordoned off from their
idols, pushed eagerly toward them from the right side of the picture; Count
Five in the TV studio; and Count Five loading luggage into the trunk of
their car with proper sullen scowls on their faces, gettin' ready for the Big
Tour as all popstars must (they probably took it in the manager's wife's
station wagon).

Unlike the many asininely obfuscating album jackets of the lamer latter years, when groups started forgetting to put any kind of information on
the back except maybe song titles and some phony Kodachrome nature
study which would have them passing around a dying redwood or something, Count Five's first eruption was on its backside just packed with all
the essential info. Like the names, nicknames, instruments played, and
ages (the oldest were nineteen) of everybody in the band. The song titles
looked promising too: aside from two ripoffs from the Who, they were all
originals, and with names like "Double-Decker Bus," "Pretty Big Mouth"
and "The World," to name only the first three, they could hardly seem to
miss.

But chillen, I'm tellin' ya that it took me many weeks of deliberation,
and many an hour's sweat hunched over a record counter, before I finally
got up the nerve to buy that album. Why? Well, it was just so aggressively
mediocre that I simultaneously could hardly resist it and felt more than a
little wary because I knew just about how gross it would be. It wasn't until
much later, drowning in the kitschvats of Elton John and James Taylor, that
I finally came to realize that grossness was the truest criterion for rock 'n'
roll, the cruder the clang and grind the more fun and longer listened-to the
album'd be. By that time I would just about've knocked out an incisor,

shaved my head or made nearly any sacrifice to acquire even one more album of this type of in-clanging and hyena-booting raunch. By then it was too late.

I tried and tried to buy the *Psychotic Reaction* LP—I'd go down to the Unimart stoned on grass, on nutmeg, vodka, Romilar or coming glassyeyed off ten Dexedrine hours spent working problems in Geometry (I was a real little scholar—when I had the magic medicine which catapults you into a maniacal, obsessive craving for knowledge), I tried every gambit to weaken my resistance, but nothing worked. Shit, I had a fuckin' split personality! And all over a fuckin' *Count Five* album! Maybe I was closer to the jokers' jailhouse than I ever imagined! On the other hand, what else could I or any other loon from my peer group ever possibly become schizoid over *but* a lousy rock 'n' roll album? Girls? Nahh, that's direct, simple, unrationalized. Drugs? Sure, but it'd be them on me, "Yer gonna pay for messin' with us, boy!," not my own inner wrack of dualistic agony. Nope, nothing more nor less than a *record,* a rock 'n' roll album of the approximate significance of *Psychotic Reaction* (who could contract barking fits from a Stones platter, much less the Beatles?), could ever pulverize my lobes and turn my floor to wormwood. I knew, 'cause I had a brief though quite similar spell of disorientation once over the Question Mark and the Mysterians album! I was at a friend's house, and I was high on Romilar and he on Colt 45, and I said: "Yeah, I bought the Question Mark and the Mysterians album today," and suddenly the equilibrium was seeping from my head like water from the ears after a sea plunge, a desultory vortex started swirling round my skull and gradually spun faster though I couldn't tell if it was a breeze just outside or something right between the flesh and bone. I saw my life before my eyes, and that is no shit—I mean not that I saw some zipping montage from birth to that queasy instant of existential vertigo, but that I saw myself walking in and out of countless record stores, forking over vast fortunes in an endless chain of cash-register clicks and dings at $3.38 and $3.39 and $3.49 and all the other fixed rates I knew by heart being if never on the track team unquestionably an All-American Competitive Shopper, I saw litter bins piled high with bags that stores all seal records in so you won't get nabbed for lifting as you trot out the door. I saw myself on a thousand occasions walking toward my car with a brisk and purposeful step, turning the key in the ignition and varooming off high as a hotrodder in anticipation of the revelations waiting in thirty-five or forty minutes of blasting sound soon as I got home, the eternal promise that *this* time the guitars will jell like TNT and set off galvanic sizzles in your brain "KABLOOIE!!!" and this time at least at last blow your fucking lid sky-high. Brains gleaming on the ceiling, sticking like putty stalactites, while yer berserk body runs around and slams outside hollering subhuman gibberish, jigging in erratic circles and careening split-up syllables insistently like a geek with a bad case of the superstar syndrome.

But that's only the fantasy. The real vision, the real freaking flash, was just like the reality, only looped to replay without end. The real story is rushing home to bear the apocalypse erupt, falling through the front door and slashing open the plastic sealing "for your protection," taking the record out—ah, lookit them grooves, all jet black without a smudge yet, shiny and new and so fucking pristine, then the color of the label, does it glow with auras that'll make subtle, comment on the sounds coming out, or is it just a flat utilitarian monochromatic surface, like a schoolhouse wall (like RCA's and Capitol's after some fool revamped 'em—an example of real artistic backwardness)? And finally you get to put the record on the turntable, it spins in limbo a perfect second, followed by the moment of truth, needle into groove, and finally sound.

What then occurs is so often anticlimactic that it drives a rational man to the depths of despair. Bah! The whole musical world is packed with simpletons and charlatans, with few a genius or looney tune joker in between.

All this I saw whilst sitting there in the throes of the Question Mark and the Mysterians frieze, and more, I saw myself as a befuddled old man holding a copy of the *96 Tears* album and staring off blankly with the slack jaw of a squandered life's decline. And in the next instant, since practically no time had elapsed at all, my friend said with obvious amazement: "You bought *Question Mark and the Mysterians?*"

I stared at him dully. "Sure," I said. "Why not?"

I realize that this sounds rather pathological—although I never thought so until laying it out here—and the Freudian overtones are child's play, I guess. But what I don't understand is what it all signifies. Don't get the idea that my buying of and listening to records per se has always been marked by such frenzy and disorientation, or even any particular degree of obsession and compulsion. It's just that music has been a fluctuating fanaticism with me ever since—well, ever since I first heard "The Storm" from the *William Tell Overture* on a TV cartoon about first grade. And riding in the car through grammar school when songs like "There Goes My Baby" would come on the radio, and getting a first record player in fifth grade, and hearing for the first time things like John Coltrane and Charlie Mingus's *The Black Saint and the Sinner Lady* and the Stones and feedback and *Trout Mask Replica.* All these were milestones, each one fried my brain a little further, especially the *experience* of the first few listenings to a record so total, so mind-twisting, that you authentically can say you'll never be quite the same again. *Black Saint and the Sinner Lady* did that, and a very few others. They're events you remember all your life, like your first real orgasm. And the whole purpose of the absurd, mechanically persistent involvement with recorded music is the pursuit of that priceless moment. So it's not exactly that records might unhinge the mind, but rather that if anything is going to drive you up the wall it might as well be a record. Because the best music is strong and guides and cleanses and is life itself.

So perhaps the truest autobiography I could ever write, and I know this holds as well for many other people, would take place largely at record counters, jukeboxes, pushing forward in the driver's seat while AM walloped you on, alone under headphones with vast scenic bridges and angelic choirs in the brain through insomniac post-midnights, or just to sit at leisure stoned or not in the vast benign lap of America, slapping on sides and feeling good.

So I finally got the courage of my lunacy and bought Count Five. I guess the last straw was when I read in a Teen Fan magazine (the only recourse then for some hardy listener trying to figure out what's going on with each new sluice of product) that Count Five claimed to have turned down "a million dollars in bookings" because it would have meant that they would have to drop out of college and, said their manager, all the boys realized that getting a good education was the most important thing they could do. What a howl! That really appealed to me, so the next time I perused the album in the racks I snorted, "The boys who went back to school. . . ." That's a certain claim to distinction—imagine Mick Jagger suddenly tripped by an attack of remorse, and right in the middle of a glug of champagne at some jet-set hot spot the ineluctable truth hits him: *You've got to get an education, boy.* You may have millions, but do you think you'll be a popstar all your life? Decidedly not. *What* will you do in those long years of dark autumn? Do you want to end up like Turner in *Performance,* having someone come up and blow your brains out because you can't think of any other diversions at the moment? It's not too late! Get back to the London School of Economics and get that degree. Man must have some form of constructive work to do; otherwise he's an ignoble weasel without meaning. So Mick gulps the rest of his champagne, disengages himself from the sweet thing at his side, and runs off to register. Eventually he earns a degree in Art and when the Stones fold he settles down to teach the drawing of the straight line to a succession of eager moppets. What an example that would be! He might even get blessed by the Pope, or invited to the White House! But of course that will never happen, because Mick Jagger is made of baser clay than Count Five.

I bought the album. It was the same day I got *Happy Jack* by the Who. I rushed home, found in *Happy Jack* a mild satisfaction, gagged at *Psychotic Reaction.*

But *Psychotic Reaction* was the album I kept coming back to. I played it gleefully and often for a year or so until it was ripped off by some bikers, and when I finally found it once more in 1971 in a used record store, man, I up and danced a jig. Then, however, I did something oddly petty and avaricious. It was in the $1.98 rack, right next to things like *Cosmo's Factory* and *Deja Vu,* and somehow that seemed inappropriate to me—it should have been in the 89¢ grab-bag rack where it belonged, right there with all the other down-and-out relics of yore, between *Doin' the Bird* by the Rivingtons, which I also purchased, and *96 Tears,* which was actually there and proved my point, the clerk having the bad sense this time to file it where it would be most comfortable (if this personalization bothers you, don't worry: once when I was in the seventh grade I went back to visit the town where I'd lived the year before and get back a copy of the Henry Mancini *Mr. Lucky* soundtrack album which I'd loaned to a friend and failed to retrieve before moving. When I got back home, I put the *Mr. Lucky* album into the record rack next to its old neighbor, the *Peter Gunn* album. Looking down on them sitting there like that, I felt glad for them. I was thinking that the two old friends, among the very first albums I ever bought, must be delighted to see each other again after so long. Maybe they even had some interesting tales to relate).

What I did, then, was to take the Count Five album, the one I'd dug so cool before and wished I still had so many times, and hold it up in the air and say to the store's manager: "What the hell is this thing doing in the $1.98 rack? Nobody's going to pay $1.98 for this!"

He looked at it a second, musing. I seized the time: "How long has this thing been sitting here? I bet it musta sat here a year or two at least, while other albums came and went. It belongs over there! 89¢!"

"Hmmm, I think you're right," he said. "I believe that record—no, the whole band, that's right—is one of the all-time clunkers of history. Yeah, put it over in the 89¢ rack."

"Sold!" I hollered, went over and threw him a buck and rushed out. I had it! The artifact! A stone tablet from Tutankhamen's tomb! A long-lost gem! Priceless—and *I got it for only 89¢!*

Well, rest assured, kids. Time hadn't dimmed the greatness of the Count Five album. In fact, it still hasn't. It sounds just as grungy and jumbled now as it did way back in 1967. I may not have played *Happy Jack* more than five times since that day I bought it, even though I never got rid of it (those Class albums that you just don't get any kicks out of will all reveal their worth and essential appeal someday, you always reason perhaps you yourself must become worthy of them), but I'm gonna rock it up and kick out the jams with *Psychotic Reaction* forever. In the first month after reacquiring it I must've played it ten times, and that's saying something. A poorboy of Port or Tokay, *Psychotic Reaction* blasting off the walls and I would hum with pointless joy as I hopped and stomped around the turntable and couldn't have sat down if I'd tried.

Track for track, you couldn't have found a better deal in a whole year's releases from Warner/Reprise. "Double-Decker Bus" and "Peace of Mind" mashed the Yardbirds into masterpieces as vital as the title bit, the latter for one of the most perfect examples of the rigidly mechanical riff in history, the former for its truly cosmic lyrics. . . .

But the real classics on the first Count Five album, while ignored in their own time, might have proven vastly influential if more people had been able to comprehend what the band was doing. "Pretty Big Mouth" was a crunching Tex-Mex street jam, somewhat reminiscent of a Caucasian crew of Red Mountain mariachis, which anticipated the even earthier excursions of their second album and scored with some of the greatest male chauvinist lyrics of all time: "I ended up in the deep deep South / Makin' love to the woman with a real big mouth!"

"They're Gonna Get You," somewhat similarly, was a sprung-rhythm essay in barbershop paranoia, particularly shining by a vocal which veered deliriously between a sullen plaint anticipating Iggy and a cartoon falsetto. But the real crusher was "The World," a clatter whose very monotony buckled under your feet like one of those moving ramps in the crazy house at an amusement park, while the lyrics consisted of a spartan minimum of phrases—" . . . you're so fine, you are mine" crowed in a series of whoops and gnashings goggle-eyed with glee and lunatic pride.

Unfortunately, *Psychotic Reaction* was the only Count Five album to be widely disseminated and recognized in its own time. Double Shot, a company nearly as erratic in promoting West Coast talent as ESP-Disk was handling New York innovators like the Godz, all but buried their second and third releases, giving them promotion and distribution equaled in its myopia and indifference only by Decca's handling of the early Who. The band was lucky enough, however, to have a dynamite manager with the vision to comprehend their potential and enough hardnosed hucksterish drive to eventually land them a contract with Columbia, where they made two more fine albums which, though given the production and promotion they had always merited, still fell flat sales-wise. Ignorant people were still writing them off as nothing more than a Yardbirds rip-off, critics ignored or smeared them with their snidest categorizations, and the sad result was that their most important work has never been given the attention it truly deserves.

Ironically enough, even as the "underground" press and self-appointed arbiters of public taste maintained their conspiracy of silence, it was the very despised trade journals of the "establishment" which first recognized Count Five's achievement in its initial flowering: "Evolving like so many others from their crude beginnings, Count Five has at length distinguished itself as a subtle, sophisticated integration of solid musical workmen creating some of the freshest and least grating sounds in recent memory." That's *Billboard,* talking about Count Five's fourth album, *Ancient Lace and Wrought-Iron Railings* (Columbia CS 9733).

But when *Snowflakes Falling on the International Dateline* (Columbia MS 7528) came out, it blew everybody with *ears,* all the kids fresh and free enough to flip the opinion-mafia the bird, right out the door and all the way to the corner. It featured the unparalleled "Schizophrenic Rainbows: A Raga Concerto," which no one who's sat through its entire 27 minutes will ever be able to forget, especially the thunderous impact of the abrupt and full-volumed entry of George Szell and the Cleveland Orchestra in the eighteenth minute. On this basis alone it must be considered the master-piece among their albums, though the melancholy "Sidewalks of Calais" which closed side one was also superb, with its remarkable lyrical matu-ration: "Pitting, patting, trying not to step on the cracks / In Europa, where we saw no sharecropper shacks. . . ."

Unfortunately, that was their last release. After investing so much technology and money in such an ambitious project and being repaid with such total public indifference, both the band and Columbia grew despon-dent at last, their contract lapsed, and the musicians themselves split for parts unknown, though one, the incredible guitar stylist John "Mouse" Michalski, later emigrated to England and formed the legendary though short-lived Stone Prodigies with several ex-members of John Mayall's Bluesbreakers and Ginger Baker's Air Force. That clutch of titans, as everybody remembers, made one incredible album, *To John Coltrane in*

Heaven, then embarked on their record-breaking ten-month tour of the States which was so grueling that afterwards the entire band were committed to rest homes for the rest of their lives.

Between *Psychotic Reaction* and the *Snowflakes* swan song, Count Five produced three other albums, each equally great and each a sevenleague step ahead of the last. My favorite has always been their third, *Cartesian Jetstream* (Double Shot DDS 1023). Here we had the fullest development of Count Five as a band that was intrinsically and still unqualifiedly rock 'n' roll (one need only give ear to the old Anglo-Saxon madrigals and Felicianoan pseudo-Flamenco of *Ancient Lace and Wrought-Iron Railings* to realize where their true strength lay). Fine and professional, yet intensely driving and almost grungy (sophistication, like history, cannot be braked), it was truly exhilarating music, filled with the wild pulsebeat of creation. Such dynamic originals as "Cannonballs for Christmas," "Her Name Is Ianthe," and "Nothing Is True / Everything Is Permitted" bring me back to it again and again, as does the addition of Marion Brown, alto sax, Sun Ra, piano, and Roland Kirk, bass pennywhistle, on the last track, "Free All Political Prisoners! Seize the Time! Keep the Faith! Sock It to 'Em! Shut the Motherfucker Down! Then Burn It Up! Then Give the Ashes to the Indians! All Power to the People! Right On! All Power to Woodstock Nation! And Watch For Falling Rocks!" That one was a true brain-blitz, and spotlighted some of the most original lyrics of the year.

The only Count Five album to fall totally flat was their second, *Carburetor Dung* (Double Shot DDS 1009). It can truly be said that this was Count Five at their grungiest. In fact, it was so grungy that on most of the songs you could barely distinguish anything except an undifferentiated wall of grinding noise and intermittent punctuation of glottal sow-like gruntings. I suppose the best way to characterize the album would be to call it murky. Some of the lyrics were intelligible, such as these, from "The Hermit's Prayer": "Sunk funk dunk Dog God the goosie Gladstone prod old maids de back seat sprung Louisiana sundown junk an' bunk an' sunken treasures. . . ." Lyrics such as those don't come every day, and even if their instrumental backup sounded vaguely like a car stuck in the mud and spinning its wheels, it cannot be denied that the song had a certain value as a prototype slab of gully-bottom rock 'n' roll. Other songs, such as "Sweat Haunch Woman," "Woody Dicot," and "Creole Jukebox Pocahontas" validated themselves by emerging slightly from the uniform one-dimensional sloppiness of the rest of the material.

On the other hand, you might be better off not to take my word, but just go into my record library and check the album out for yourself. Dave

Marsh loved it (he said: "It's one answer to just how far-out rock can go, one branch's end, and one of the most humanly primitive sets I've *ever* heard. You'd have to be crazy to make music like this, and I'm glad they did it"). Ed Ward told me he'd keep it forever because "It's one of the funniest albums in the history of rock 'n' roll, right up there with *Blows Against the Empire* and *Kick Out the Jams;* how can you pass up something like that?" Although Jon Landau absolutely refused to print a review of it in *Rolling Stone:* "Look man, I'm not in this business in the spirit of some kid who hides in an alley, sticks his feet out and trips the first person who walks by, then laughs his ass off when they fall on their face. Everything connected with this album is wrong. In the first place, it's absolutely horrible, one of the worst monstrosities ever released. Secondly, the group who recorded it are just a front for studio musicians; I know this for a fact. You can't tell me that the same group that recorded 'Iron Rainbows on the International Dateline' or whatever the name of that thing was, whatever it was it was a beautiful piece of work—pretentious, overarranged, overproduced, verbose, egotistical and gauche, but beautiful nonetheless— the glockenspiel player was wailing his ass off for twenty-seven minutes—but you can't tell me that that and *this* pile of crap were done by the same people. This probably is the band . . . good riddance. Another thing is that they're on a terrible label. Who ever heard of Double Shot Records? What kind of promotion and publicity do they get? Nada! How many records do they release a year? Who the fuck knows? The last decent act they had was Brenton Wood and that was four years ago. This album, I guarantee, will sell no copies. Just look at the cover: a rusty wheelbarrow, the body of an old Ford with no wheels or engine, and a cottonwood tree in the background. The sun has almost gone down and it's so dark you can hardly see a fuckin' thing. So the title's up there in oxblood-colored letters. Oxblood! And now you come to me and you say we gotta print a review of this album in *Rolling Stone* because it's the only one of its kind and if people don't get it now they may never have a chance to again. And you send this review comparing it to Louis Armstrong, Elmore James, Blind Willie Johnson, Albert Ayler, Beefheart, and the Stooges! All so people will buy it when there's no earthly reason why anybody interested in *music* should. Send the review to *Creem.* Make it the album of the year. Jesus Christ, I used to have some respect for you guys. Now I think you must all be either losing your minds or turning against rock 'n' roll. It's getting to where *Creem* won't even cover an album unless it's either free jazz or so fucking metallic, mediocre and noise-oriented that you'd do as well to stick your ear over a garbage dis-

posal or a buzzsaw. Remember, man: the public ain't buyin' it. No response at all."

Neither Jon nor I nurtured any bad feelings over this, however—it was
just that he couldn't stand ineptitude of any kind in music, which was perfectly reasonable, while I dug certain outrageous brands of ineptitude the
most! *Carburetor Dung* just may have been the most inept album I ever
heard—certainly it was right up there with *Amon Duul and Hapshash and
the Coloured Coat Featuring the Human Host and the Heavy Metal Kids.* Yes,
kids, that was the real title of a real record—I'm given to fabrication of albums sometimes, like if I wish a certain album existed and it doesn't I just
make it up, but that one's authentic. *Carburetor Dung* is authentic, too, but
Double Shot didn't give it any promotion for a combination of reasons
(title, attitudes of various people in both the press and industry, public indifference, and the fact that not one person at Double Shot was ever even
willing to talk about it it was so embarrassing). I think it just quietly faded
away, like Alexander Spence's *Oar* and so many other notable albums.
And as for Count Five, they finally went where all good little bands go—
to that big Gas Station in the sky.

"Well, that's all very interesting, keeping us here for the last four hours
telling us about the meteoric career of the Carburetor Dungs—"

No, no, *Count Five, Carburetor Dung* was the—

"YEAH, FINE, BUT WHEN THE FUCK ARE YOU GONNA TELL US
ABOUT THE YARDBIRDS?!"

Uh, hrmp—hmmmmm, yes . . . well, that story'll always be in reserve
for another day. Besides, when you get right down to it, Count Five were
probably about as important as the Yardbirds, in the long run. It's just that
some people are recognized in their own time, and some aren't.

"Because when he was alive, he could not walk, but now he is walking with God."

Creating art allows us to beat the odds and find immortality, without having to do the whole Doctor Faustus thing.

Buddy Holly, though dead two generations, is still young and hiccuppy. When Elvis sings "Baby, Let's Play House," he is still beautiful and undeniably the King. When dancers gaze into each other's eyes, they still hear the Drifters' yearning, soaring voices tearing into the soul of a Doc Pomus lyric. Somewhere, someone is hearing Jimi Hendrix for the first time and realizing that rules are for losers. And somewhere else, the greatest musician you've never heard of just died.

This section is a benediction for a few residents of rock and roll heaven; they're not really gone. They're still with us in their recordings, forever young, to be discovered by new generations of listeners. The sun also rises, you know.

Lewis Shiner

SAVING JIMI

Well . . . what *if* Brian Wilson had been able to pull it off and finish the *Smile* album? What *if* Jim Morrison hadn't drunk himself to death? What *if* Jimi Hendrix had made it through that night alive? How would those changes have altered the course of the moon and stars in the last three decades? Shiner's rock and roll fantasy novel, *Glimpses,* allows its hero, Ray Shackleford—a stereo repairman from Austin, Texas—to step into the dream world and fix what's gone wrong with rock and roll.

I GOT TO Ronnie Scott's club at midnight to see the show. It was a jazz venue, guys in suits and turtlenecks, guys in goatees and berets. The tables were all taken and I had to stand by the bar. I ordered a lemonade and checked the setup: Lonnie Jordan's Hammond B-3 and the drums and congas and the stacks of amps completely filled the stage. A roadie made a last pass to duct-tape anything that moved, and then the lights went down.

War had been gigging for ten years in San Pedro, now they suddenly had a gold record and a European tour. It didn't matter that front man Eric Burdon had been in the spotlight forever. They were hot. I saw the excitement and longing and bravado roll off them like sweat.

And tonight, for me, there was something extra. A chance to see Jimi perform again, and the knowledge that, in another world, this was the last time he would ever play in public.

The band tore into "They Can't Take Away Our Music." There's a sound a well-miked snare drum makes on stage that you can never get on record, like an ax splitting wood. That sound alone was reason enough to be there. Burdon had shag-cut hair past his shoulders, looking younger than I would have thought, rejuvenated by the band's energy. A spotlight hit Howard Scott for his guitar solo and the notes he played cut through the rhythm section like lasers. He fired them out of a blond-neck, sunburst Telecaster, looking fierce in sideburns that came down to meet the ends of his mustache.

As the spotlight tracked him I saw Jimi in the audience down front. Monika was with him, and a woman I thought was Devon Wilson, and five or six others crowded around. Jimi had on a shirt that looked like it was made out of peacock feathers.

I didn't see Erika. I wouldn't have a chance to talk to Jimi until after the show anyway. I stayed where I was and listened to the band. They did about half their album, standards like "Midnight Hour" and a couple of Animals tunes. They finished off with "Spill the Wine" and by this point the jazz crowd was on its feet.

Burdon gestured to Jimi and he got up on stage. He already has his black Strap up there, and he strapped it on and they went into "Tobacco Road." It was awkward at First. Jimi seemed to expect to run things and the rest of the band wasn't interested. When the time came they gave him a solo and Jimi cranked up and played hard.

Once Jimi started to play the personality clashes didn't matter. It was loud enough that I thought my eardrums might bleed. His feedback went inside me and left me ringing like expensive crystal.

When he was done he built up to a big finish. The band played right over him and took their own solos. Jimi looked pissed off. He took his guitar off and started to walk away but Burdon grabbed him by the shoulder and yelled in his ear. Jimi shook his head resignedly and put the guitar back on and comped rhythm chords. He had a look on his face like "why am I doing this" but he stayed out the song. Burdon introduced him and he got a big round of applause, which seemed to cheer him up.

They went into "Mother Earth," a traditional blues from the album, and things really caught fire. Howard Scot traded licks with Jimi and they both played blistering solos. People stood on their chairs and shouted and drank everything in sight. About this time some guy, either the manager or Ronnie Scott himself, came out and made frantic throat-cutting signals. It was the same thing I'd seen in my club days, managers terrified that somebody might have too good a time.

The band wound the song up and said their thank-yous and split. The house lights came up and the magic disappeared, leaving spilled drinks and cigarette butts, the knowledge that the last train had already run and there would be long queues for a taxi. For me it was worse, it was the sudden fear that this would after all be Jimi's last show. There was no sign of Erika, and I started to panic. What if Jimi went out the back door and disappeared? A heavyset guy in leathers refused to let me backstage.

I was contemplating an all-night vigil on Lansdowne Crescent when

Erika finally showed up. She was breathtaking in a strapless cream-colored dress. I had seen that body naked, had spent the night next to her, and never really touched her. I knew I wouldn't get another chance. She had a young guy with her in leather pants and a white shirt and a pony-tail like mine. She saw me as I stood up and the two of them made their way over. "Have they already finished then?" Erika asked.

I nodded. I wanted to apologize for the night before, but it wasn't the time or place, even if she'd wanted to hear it. She introduced me to the guy, whose name I immediately forgot.

This time there was no problem getting backstage. The dressing room was mobbed, and a line of young women stood against the wall, like they were there for an audition. Monika and Devon guarded Jimi from either side. Now that he was through playing he looked drained. His eyes were narrow and lined and there was no light behind his smile.

After all the hours I'd tried to imagine this moment, I was speechless. I knew Jimi was lost by looking at him. I was an idiot to think I could change that.

Then he saw Erika. He came to life and hurried over to hug her. He was not quite as tall as me and there was a shyness in the way he moved that was the opposite of the way he was on stage. He kissed Erika on the lips and said, "Baby, you look so *tired*. I'm not trying to put you down, I'm just worried, you know, I want to be sure you're okay and everything."

"I'm fine. Listen, this is a friend of mine, Ray, from the States. He needs to talk to you and I think you should listen."

I tried to swallow what felt like a ball bearing, stuck halfway down to my stomach. Jimi shook my hand and said, "Hey, Ray, brother, what's hap-pening?" The grip was familiar, large and dry and powerful, like his fa-ther's. Everything about him was familiar. It was like I had known him all my life. "So did you like see the show and everything?"

"Yeah, it was really good. I saw you in Dallas, too, the first two times."

"Oh yeah, Dallas, wow, man, that place is a real hassle sometimes. That first show everybody got real uptight over a little lighter fuel, you know?" He turned to Erika to bring her in. "They wouldn't let me burn my guitar or anything so I kind of put out this row of footlights."

"With the head of his guitar," I said.

"See? The man was there."

Erika touched Jimi's cheek. Over her shoulder I saw the young guy in leather pants talking with Eric Burdon. She said, "Jimi, I really think you're pushing yourself too hard."

"Well, you know how it is, this and that, I got that trial thing coming up Friday. And there's always somebody wants you to be somewhere, you know, it's hard to get away."

"Could you get away with me?" I said, finding my nerve again. "Just for a couple of minutes?"

Jimi looked at Erika and she said, "Go ahead, Jimi, I'll wait here."

We went through a fire door into an alley behind the club. It was red-brick and dark and the night had turned chilly. "Wooo, man," Jimi said. "I don't know if I'll ever get used to the weather over here. This is supposed to be September, can you dig?"

I nodded. "Look, this is going to sound weird to you however I say it. I don't know any way to do this except just blurt it out, okay?"

"Yeah, okay, whatever."

I squatted down and Jimi squatted next to me, his huge hands tucked into his armpits. I looked at the bricks at my feet and said, "I know you're open to things that most people aren't. UFOs and magic and spiritual things. So if I sound crazy maybe you'll give me a chance to, I don't know, a chance to convince you."

I knew I had to go ahead and say it or I would lose him. "I'm from the future and I can prove it."

"Oh, man."

"I know things nobody could possibly know. I know you want to get with Chas Chandler again. I know you're planning to fly to New York after court on Friday, to get the tapes for *First Rays of the New Rising Sun,* and bring them back here for you and Chas to work on, to finish the record, so you can go play with Miles Davis."

Jimi looked genuinely terrified. I hated to scare him, hated to look like some obsessed lunatic. "Who are you?" he said.

"My name is Ray Shackleford. I'm from 1989. I want to save your life."

"Mike Jeffery sent you, right? Oh God, I knew this was gonna happen."

"I'm not from Jeffrey, I swear to you. I want you to finish the record. I saw a list you wrote out for it. Side one: 'Dolly Dagger,' 'Night Bird Flying,' 'Room Full of Mirrors,' 'Belly Button Window,' 'Freedom'; side two: 'Ezy Rider,' 'Astro Man,' 'Drifting,' 'Straight Ahead'; side three: you started out with 'Night Bird Flying' again—how could I know all this?"

"I don't know."

"Because I'm who I say I am. And in the world I come from, you die Friday morning because you take a few too many of Monika's sleeping pills and choke to death in your sleep."

"Oh, man." He looked at me sideways, like half of him wanted to laugh and the other half wanted to run away. "Oh, man."

I rubbed my hands over my face, tried to relax. "Don't make up your mind yet. Just listen. I know your rooms at the Cumberland are a cover and you're staying with Monika at 22 Lansdowne Crescent. I know you just sent Billy Cox home because of an acid freak-out. I know you can't trust any of these people who are all over you because they all want something."

Jimi balanced himself with one hand and turned until his back rested against the wall of the club. "Man, it's like, I just don't know anymore, you understand? There's all these people and there's this new thing, like peace and love, right, and maybe these people really do love me, but . . ."

"Maybe they just need what you have. They see you on stage and they see how that music makes you so alive, and they all want that. Even if they have to take it away from you to get it."

Jimi didn't say anything.

"That's not what I want. I want to save your life. I want to see *First Rays* finished."

Jimi shook his head. "So tell me again what's supposed to happen? I mean tell me exactly."

I told him. I told him what the inside of Monika's flat looked like, I told him the pills were called Vesperax and he shouldn't take more than two, I described the attendants who picked him up.

"Man," he said, "you're really not bullshitting me are you? You really know something. You're from when?"

"1989."

"And I never finished *First Rays* or *Straight Ahead* or anything?"

"No. They did a single album called *Cry of Love* and a soundtrack for this really stupid movie called *Rainbow Bridge,* from that concert you did in Maui. Reprise threw them together from whatever was lying around. But everybody still knows who you are. You still win guitar magazine polls as favorite guitarist. They put music on these computer discs now, they call them compact discs, and they've reissued all your stuff, plus live albums and interviews and studio jam everything they could find."

"So I guess they've got computers playing everything, right? Is that what the music is like?"

"It's like Led Zeppelin, mostly, only heavier. Heavy metal, they call it. That's what most kids listen to."

"Man."

"The Beatles never get back together, but the Stones are still touring. And the Who."

"I don't know, man, this all sounds so weird and everything, all these old guys playing rock and roll. Did everything just like stop after I died?"

"Pretty much. There was something called punk at the end of the seventies, that was pretty exciting, only it got commercialized too fast. Now there's rap, which is drum machines and chanting, not much music in it at all. But if you live, see, you can change it. With *First Rays*, by playing with Miles—"

The back door of the club swung open. Monika and Devon were there, and a black man in an expensive suit and a neatly trimmed beard. "Jimi," Monika said, "shouldn't we be maybe going home now?"

For a minute I'd had him. Now Monika had brought him back to earth, the real world of food and bed and court cases. He stood up and dusted at his velvet trousers. "Yeah, okay, whatever."

I stood up too. "Listen," I said. "I want to come see you. Thursday night, at Monika's place. To make sure nothing happens, okay?"

"Sure, man, come over about twelve or something, all right? We can talk some more, that'll be real nice."

As they went inside I heard Monika ask, "Who was that funny man? What was he wanting?"

I stayed in the alley for a minute or two to get my breath. Okay, I thought. I can't miss this time. Everything is going to be okay. I went back in. Jimi was gone, and so were Erika and her new boyfriend. That was okay too. Everything was going to be okay.

I was at Lansdowne Crescent at midnight sharp Thursday night. I knocked on the door downstairs and when nobody answered I tried to see in the darkened window, and finally sat on the steps to wait. It hadn't rained all day but the air was damp and the chill got into my bones. I was wearing new clothes that I'd bought on Oxford Street and I'd been to see Sly Stone at the Lyceum. I'd seen Eric Clapton in one of the box seats, but Jimi didn't show.

When he wasn't at Monika's flat by two I started to worry. He might have decided I was crazy and gone to the Cumberland Hotel to avoid me. He could take the same Vesperax at the Cumberland as he could at Monika's and wind up just as dead.

I heard Monika's sports car a little before three. A minute or so later the two of them came down the metal stairs, Monika in the lead. "Jimi," she said, "that strange man is again coming around."

Jimi looked disappointed to see me. "I'm really sorry," he said, "there was this thing at this rich cat's flat I had to go to."

"You just have to promise me one thing and I'll get out of here. Promise me you won't take more than two of Monika's sleeping pills. They're stronger than anything you're used to."

"If I don't sleep tonight I swear I'll go out of my mind."

"Just take one or two, and if they don't put you out right away, give them another few minutes. I promise you they'll knock you out. And you'll still be alive tomorrow."

Monika had only been half listening. "Is this man making threats to you?" she asked.

"No, be cool, baby, he wants to help me."

"Everybody is wanting to help you."

"I just want him to promise," I said to her. "If he takes any of your Vesperax, he shouldn't have more than two."

"Okay, all right, already, I promise." He laughed with no feeling in it. "I promise."

I shook his hand and said good-night. Monika watched me suspiciously all the way up the stairs, but that was okay. Watch over him, Monika, he needs a guardian angel tonight.

I stood outside in the cold knowing there was nothing more I could do. Finally I caught a cab on Ladbroke Grove and went back to my hotel.

I was outside the flat at ten the next morning. My heart was in my mouth. I hadn't fallen asleep until after sunup and it seemed like only seconds later that I got my wake-up call. I felt like a knife that had been sharpened over and over for a single job, and now the job was nearly done but I was worn away to nothing. I sat and stared at my watch, and every few seconds my eyes would flick back to the wrought-iron gate at number 22.

At 10:13 Monika came up the stairs, looking rumpled. She headed down the street toward the local market. It took all I had not to bolt down the stairs to see if Jimi was okay.

Monika was back at 10:24. I was wound so tight that I jumped to my feet when I saw her. I hadn't meant to say anything to her but now it was too late. She froze and stared at me as I ran across the street to her.

"You again," she said.

"When you go back to bed, please, please make sure Jimi's okay. If it looks like he's been throwing up, come get me. I know what to do."

"I only gave him the two pills. Like you said."

"He might have gotten up in the night and taken some more. Just check him, please."

"I will check him. Now please go."

I nodded and walked away so she wouldn't call the cops. She went downstairs, I circled the block, and sat on the curb again. Worst case, the ambulance would be here at 11:30. It was a long wait. I spent it in weird, violent fantasies in which I fought the ambulance attendants for Jimi's life.

Eleven-thirty came and went, and I started to breathe easier. By 11:45 I was light-headed, ecstatic. By noon the fatigue caught up to me. I walked back to Notting Hill Gate and found a bakery with sweet rolls and orange juice and lingered over them as long as I could stand it.

At one P.M. I made a last pass by the flat. All was quiet. No ambulances, no police, Monika's car parked where it had been.

Jimi was alive.

I had a long, deep sleep, then went down to the lobby, where there was a television. There was nothing on the news about Hendrix, just train strikes and the ongoing hostage crisis in Jordan, where three hijacked airlines had been blown up. A newsreader asked if we had entered the Age of Terrorism and I didn't want to be the one to tell him yes, we had. The *fedayeen,* the men of sacrifice, were sharing their sense of helplessness with the world. Just like the rest of the starved and desperate people picking up guns and knives in Southeast Asia and Latin America. Could Jimi Hendrix change that?

I walked down Southampton to a nice Italian place I'd found. It was a beautiful evening, too beautiful to spend giving myself the third degree. Hendrix could do as much good as anyone, and I'd given him some time to do it in. It might take him weeks to come up with a final mix of the album, and I would hang around until he did.

I lingered over dinner and took a cab to the Speak after midnight. There was always the chance that Erika would show up, or somebody else that I might want to meet. I was ready for something. The room was crowded, and Rod Stewart and the Faces were playing loud enough to rattle the glasses on the bar. I got a lemonade and let the movement of the crowd take me toward the stage.

I wasn't too surprised when I saw Jimi holding court at a row of table down front. He saw me on the sidelines and beckoned me over. "Heyyy," he said, shaking my hand. "My man. Future man. What did you say your name was?"

"Ray. Ray Shackleford."

"Ray. Cat that knows his drugs. That shit of Monika's, like, I took a couple and I was laying there, thinking, 'Man, this is not happening,' and I was gonna get up and take some more and then remembered what you said so I just lay there awhile longer and then pow, it just laid me *out*. Hey, you got to meet my people. This is Mitch, and Sly Stone, you know Monika, this is Devon and this is Eric Clapton. Next to Eric there is the Queen of Sheba. Yes, the Queen of Sheba, thank you very much." Actually it was Pattie Boyd, still married to George Harrison. Clapton would write "Layla" for her next year in Miami.

I shook hands all around and somebody brought me a chair. I'll never forget the next two hours. Part of it was the glamour, of course. They were all beautiful and rich, talented and famous. None of that was as important as the way music mattered to all of them. The conversations were hard to follow, three or four of them going at once, Eric earnest and adamant, Sly full of revolutionary fervor, Jimi laid-back, saying, "Well, you know, like, dig, brother," while the music blasted all around us. Like in a song, the words didn't matter as much as the feeling, the community, the warmth. Jimi seemed renewed. Maybe things had gone well in court, maybe on some level he knew he'd cheated death. Maybe all he'd needed was a good night's sleep.

After the Faces finished, Jimi and Eric got up to jam. Jimi wanted to play "Sunshine of Your Love" and Eric didn't. Jimi started it anyway, laughing and saying, "Oh come on, don't act like you don't know it, it goes just like this here," and they ended up trading solos for ten minutes while Ron Wood and Kenny Jones backed them up. They did "Key to the Highway" and then Sly got up and sang "Land of a Thousand Dances." A part of me knew that it would never have happened without me, and it was all the thanks I needed.

The jam broke up a little after two. It could have gone on forever and been all right with me. Monika and Devon, still jockeying for position, went backstage. I stayed and talked with Pattie Boyd, mostly about her sister and Mick Fleetwood. She was surprised I knew so much about the band, since they hadn't really broken in America yet.

Jimi and the others came out carrying guitar cases. I stood around with them and when I had a chance I asked Jimi about New York and the tapes.

"Oh yeah, for sure, man, I talked to Chas this afternoon. He's got me a flight over on Monday and then I'm going to come back and we're going to see if we can do a thing with them. He's really groovy about it, I think it's going to happen. Listen, when I get back, you should really come down with us and hear what we've got."

"I'd like that," I said.

I guess I wanted him to give me addresses and phone numbers on the spot, and it took me a second to realize he was only being polite. "Sure, man, you can like come by the studio or something, it'll be real nice."

"Okay," I said. "Thanks." I shook his hand. I didn't want to leave, but the time had clearly come.

Jimi felt it and let me off the hook. "If you're not doing anything, you could come along over to this party. Probably be some, I don't know, like free booze or food or girls or something."

It's the kind of thing he must have done all the time, one more little act of kindness, like all the others that had eaten him up, chipped away pieces of him until there was nothing left. At that moment I didn't care. I was grateful for the piece he'd offered me. "Yeah. I'd like that."

The group moved slowly toward the stairs. Jimi handed me his guitar case while he put on a trench coat. One more thing to make me feel like I belonged. Monika kissed him quickly and went ahead to get her car. We went upstairs into the cold light of Margaret Street. There were only a few people left on the sidewalks.

"Christ, we'll never get a cab," Eric said.

"I'll go ring one up, shall I?" Pattie said. She moved in close to him and he put his arm around her. It made me lonely to look at them.

"Give it a minute," Eric said. "Something will turn up."

Some kid with shaggy hair over his ears and collar came up to talk to Jimi. I couldn't hear any actual words, but the rhythm was American and sounded harsh and unpleasant. Jimi stood there with his hands in the pockets of his trench coat, but guitar at his feet, smiling and answering the kid's questions. I looked away for a second, trying to spot Monika or a cab.

When I looked back the kid had a gun.

"Look out!" I yelled.

I started to run toward him. Jimi was looking at the gun. He didn't try to run or knock it away. There wasn't time. The kid fired five times, point-blank, into Jimi's chest.

WHERE WERE YOU WHEN ELVIS DIED?

**For the record, I was in a Wendy's in
Bowling Green, Kentucky.**

WHERE were *you* when Elvis died? What were you doing, and what did
it give you an excuse to do with the rest of your day? That's what we'll be
talking about in the future when we remember this grand occasion. Like
Pearl Harbor or JFK's assassination, it boiled down to individual reminiscences, which is perhaps as it should be, because in spite of his greatness,
etc. etc., Elvis had left us each as alone as he was; I mean, he wasn't exactly a Man of the People anymore, if you get my drift. If you don't I will
drift even further, away from Elvis into the contemplation of why all our
public heroes seem to reinforce our own solitude.

The ultimate sin of any performer is contempt for the audience. Those
who indulge in it will ultimately reap the scorn of those they've dumped
on, whether they live forever like Andy Paleface Warhol or die fashionably
early like Lenny Bruce, Jimi Hendrix, Janis Joplin, Jim Morrison, Charlie
Parker, Billie Holiday. The two things that distinguish those deaths from
Elvis's (he and they having drug habits vaguely in common) were that all
of them died on the outside looking in and none of them took their audience for granted. Which is why it's just a little bit harder for me to see Elvis
as a tragic figure; I see him as being more like the Pentagon, a giant ar-
mored institution nobody knows anything about except that its power is
legendary.

Obviously we all liked Elvis better than the Pentagon, but look at what
a paltry statement that is. In the end, Elvis's scorn for his fans as manifested in "new" albums full of previously released material and one new
song to make sure all us suckers would buy it was mirrored in the scorn
we all secretly or not so secretly felt for a man who came closer to god-
hood than Carlos Castaneda until military conscription tamed and revealed him for the dumb lackey he always was in the first place. And ever
since, for almost two decades now, we've been waiting for him to get
wild again, fools that we are, and he probably knew better than any of us

in his heart of hearts that it was never gonna happen, his heart of hearts so obviously not being our collective heart of hearts, he being so obviously just some poor dumb Southern boy with a Big Daddy manager to screen the world for him and filter out anything which might erode his status as big strapping baby bringing home the bucks, and finally being sort of perversely celebrated at least by rock critics for his utter contempt for whoever cared about him.

And Elvis was perverse, only a true pervert could put out something like *Having Fun with Elvis On Stage,* that album released three or so years back which consisted *entirely* of between-song onstage patter so redundant it would make both Willy Burroughs and Gert Stein blush. Elvis was into marketing boredom when Andy Warhol was still doing shoe ads, but Elvis's sin was his failure to realize that his fans were not perverse—they loved him without qualification, no matter what he dumped on them they loyally lapped it up, and that's why I feel a hell of a lot sorrier for all those poor jerks than for Elvis himself. I mean, who's left they can stand all night in the rain for? Nobody, and the true tragedy is the tragedy of an entire generation which refuses to give up its adolescence even as it feels its menopausal paunch begin to blossom and its hair recedes over the horizon—along with Elvis and everything else they once thought they believed in. Will they care in five years what he's been doing for the last twenty?

Sure Elvis's death is a relatively minor ironic variant on the future-shock mazurka, and perhaps the most significant thing about Elvis's existence is that the entire history of the seventies has been retreads and brutal demystification; three of Elvis's ex-bodyguards recently got together with this hacker from the New York *Post* and whipped up a book which dosed us with all the dirt we'd yearned for for so long. Elvis was the last of our sacred cows to be publicly mutilated; everybody knows Keith Richard likes his junk, but when Elvis went onstage in a stupor nobody breathed a hint of "Quaalude . . ." In a way, this was both good and bad, good because Elvis wasn't encouraging other people to think it was cool to be a walking *Physicians' Desk Reference,* bad because Elvis stood for that Nixonian Secrecy-as-Virtue which was passed off as the essence of Americanism for a few years there. In a sense he could be seen not only as a phenomenon that exploded in the fifties to help shape the psychic jailbreak of the sixties but ultimately as a perfect cultural expression of what the Nixon years were all about. Not that he prospered more then, but that his passion for the privacy of potentates allowed him to get away with almost literal murder, certainly with the symbolic rape of his fans, meaning that we might all do better to think about waving good-bye with one up-raised finger.

I got the news of Elvis's death while drinking beer with a friend and fellow music journalist on his fire escape on 21st Street in Chelsea. Chelsea is a good neighborhood; in spite of the fact that the insane woman who lives upstairs keeps him awake all night every night with her rants at no one, my friend stays there because he likes the sense of community within diversity in that neighborhood: old-time card-carrying Communists live in his building alongside people of every persuasion popularly lumped as "ethnic." When we heard about Elvis we knew a wake was in order, so I went out to the deli for a case of beer. As I left the building I passed some Latin guys hanging out by the front door. "Heard the news? Elvis is dead!" I told them. They looked at me with contemptuous indifference. Maybe if I had told them Donna Summer was dead I might have gotten a reaction; I do recall walking in this neighborhood wearing a T-shirt that said "Disco Sucks" with a vast unamused muttering in my wake, which only goes to show that not for everyone was Elvis the still-reigning King of Rock'n'Roll, in fact not for everyone is rock'n'roll the still-reigning music. By now, each citizen has found his own little obsessive corner to blast his brains in: as the sixties were supremely narcissistic, solopsism's what the seventies have been about, nowhere is this better demonstrated than in the world of "pop" music. And Elvis may have been the greatest solipsist of all.

I asked for two six-packs at the deli and told the guy behind the counter the news. He looked fifty years old, greying, big belly, life still in his eyes, and he said: "Shit, that's too bad. I guess our only hope now is if the Beatles get back together."

Fifty years old.

I told him I thought that would be the biggest anticlimax in history and that the best thing the Stones could do now would be to break up and spare us all further embarrassments.

He laughed, and gave me directions to a meat market down the street. There I asked the counterman the same question I had been asking every-one. He was in his fifties too, and he said, "You know what? I don't *care* that bastard's dead. I took my wife to see him in Vegas in '73, we paid fourteen dollars a ticket, and he came out and sang for twenty minutes. Then he fell down. Then he stood up and sang a couple more songs, then he fell down again. Finally he said, 'Well, shit, I might as well sing sitting as standing.' So he squatted on the stage and asked the band what song they wanted to do next, but before they could answer he was complaining about the lights. 'They're too bright,' he says. 'They hurt my eyes. Put 'em out or I don't sing a note.' So they do. So me and my wife are sitting in total blackness listening to this guy sing songs we knew and loved and I ain't just talking about his old goddam songs, but he totally *butchered* all of 'em. Fuck him. I'm not saying I'm glad he's dead, but I know one thing; I got taken when I went to see Elvis Presley."

I got taken too the one time I saw Elvis, but in a totally different way. It was the autumn of 1971, and two tickets to an Elvis show turned up at the offices of *Creem* magazine, where I was then employed. It was decided that those staff members who had never had the privilege of witnessing Elvis should get the tickets, which was how me and art director Charlie Auringer ended up in nearly the front row of the biggest arena in Detroit. Earlier Charlie had said, "Do you realize how much we could get if we sold these fucking things?" I didn't, but how precious they were became totally clear the instant Elvis sauntered onto the stage. He was the only male performer I have ever seen to whom I responded sexually; it wasn't real arousal, rather an erection of the heart, when I looked at him I went mad with desire and envy and worship and self-projection. I mean, Mick Jagger, whom I saw as far back as 1964 and twice in '65, never even came close.

There was Elvis, dressed up in this ridiculous white suit which looked like some studded Arthurian castle, and he was too fat, and the buckle on his belt was as big as your head except that your head is not made of solid gold, and any lesser man would have been the spittin' image of a Neil Diamond damfool in such a getup, but on Elvis it fit. What didn't? No matter how lousy his records ever got, no matter how intently he pursued mediocrity, there was still some hint, some flash left over from the days when . . . well, I wasn't there, so I won't presume to comment. But I will say this: Elvis Presley was the man who brought overt blatant vulgar sexual frenzy to the popular arts in America (thereby to the nation itself, since putting "popular arts" and "America" in the same sentence seems almost redundant). It has been said that he was the first white to sing like a black person, which is untrue in terms of hard facts but totally true in terms of cultural impact. But what's more crucial is that when Elvis started wiggling his hips and Ed Sullivan refused to show it, the entire country went into a paroxysm of sexual frustration leading to abiding discontent which culminated in the explosion of psychedelic-militant folklore which was the sixties.

I mean, don't tell me about Lenny Bruce, man—Lenny Bruce said dirty words in public and obtained a kind of consensual martyrdom. Plus which

Lenny Bruce was hip, too goddamn hip if you ask me, which was his un-doing, whereas Elvis was not hip at all, Elvis was a goddam truck driver who worshipped his mother and would never say shit or fuck around her, and Elvis alerted America to the fact that it had a groin with imperatives that had been stifled. Lenny Bruce demonstrated how far you could push a society as repressed as ours and how much you could get away with, but Elvis kicked "How Much Is That Doggie in the Window" *out* the window and replaced it with "Let's fuck." The rest of us are still reeling from the im-pact. Sexual chaos reigns currently, but out of chaos may flow true un-derstanding and harmony, and either way Elvis almost single-handedly opened the floodgates. That night in Detroit, a night I will never forget, he had but to ever so slightly move one shoulder muscle, not even a shrug, and the girls in the gallery hit by its ray screamed, fainted, howled in heat. Literally, every time this man moved any part of his body in the slightest centimeter, tens or tens of thousands of people went berserk. Not Sinatra, not Jagger, not the Beatles, nobody you can come up with ever elicited such hysteria among so many. And this after a decade and a half of crappy records, of making a point of not trying.

If love is truly going out of fashion forever, which I do not believe, then along with our nurtured indifference to each other will be an even more contemptuous indifference to each others' objects of reverence. I thought it was Iggy Stooge, you thought it was Joni Mitchell or whoever else seemed to speak for your own private, entirely circumscribed situa-tion's many pains and few ecstasies. We will continue to fragment in this manner, because solipsism holds all the cards at present; it is a king whose domain engulfs even Elvis's. But I can guarantee you one thing: we will never again agree on anything as we agreed on Elvis. So I won't bother saying good-bye to his corpse. I will say good-bye to you.

Yoko Ono

STATEMENT TO THE PRESS

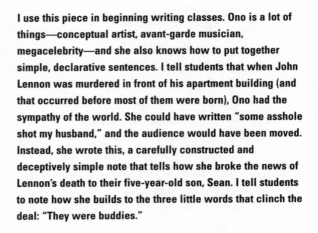

I use this piece in beginning writing classes. Ono is a lot of things—conceptual artist, avant-garde musician, megacelebrity—and she also knows how to put together simple, declarative sentences. I tell students that when John Lennon was murdered in front of his apartment building (and that occurred before most of them were born), Ono had the sympathy of the world. She could have written "some asshole shot my husband," and the audience would have been moved. Instead, she wrote this, a carefully constructed and deceptively simple note that tells how she broke the news of Lennon's death to their five-year-old son, Sean. I tell students to note how she builds to the three little words that clinch the deal: "They were buddies."

I TOLD Sean what happened. I showed him the picture of his father on the cover of the paper and explained the situation. I took Sean to the spot where John lay after he was shot. Sean wanted to know why the person shot John if he liked John. I explained that he was probably a confused person. Sean said we should find out if he was confused or if he really had meant to kill John. I said that was up to the court.

He asked what court—a tennis court or a basketball court? That's how Sean used to talk with his father. They were buddies. John would have been proud of Sean if he had heard this. Sean cried later. He also said, "Now daddy is part of God. I guess when you die you become much more bigger because you're part of everything."

I don't have much more to add to Sean's statement.

The silent vigil will take place December 14th at 2 P.M. for 10 minutes. Our thoughts will be with you.

Joel Selvin

MORE THAN "THE PIANO PLAYER"

**A death that registers barely a blip on the screen of *People*
magazine moves Selvin to study another, lesser known, rock
and roll tragedy.**

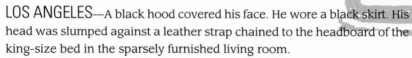

LOS ANGELES—A black hood covered his face. He wore a black skirt. His head was slumped against a leather strap chained to the headboard of the king-size bed in the sparsely furnished living room.

Kevin Gilbert, 29, was dead. That much his manager could see peering in at the front door that morning last May.

The Los Angeles County coroner's office sees four or five such deaths a year—"autoerotic asphyxiation," caused when people go one small step too far in depriving their brains of oxygen while they reach orgasm. It was a death without dignity, a random fall through the cracks of a secret life.

Gilbert was a prodigy musician from San Mateo who could play any instrument; colleagues invariably called him "the most talented musician I ever met." To the rest of the world, though, his only real claim to fame lies in the credits to *Tuesday Night Music Club,* the 1993 debut album by Sheryl Crow.

"I saw something in *Entertainment* magazine that said Kevin Gilbert, the piano player on Sheryl Crow's record, had died," said songwriter David Baerwald, a member of the Tuesday club of the album's name. He paused, sadly shaking his head. "He hated that Sheryl Crow record and that's all he's going to be known for. The piano player? Roll over, Kevin Gilbert."

*　　*　　*

When Gilbert first brought his girlfriend Sheryl to informal Tuesday night songwriting sessions with his friends, he played a pivotal role in shaping an $85 million megahit. For her, the album brought three Grammys, stardom and an industry buzz that makes her forthcoming CD one of the most eagerly anticipated releases this fall. But for him, it was hardly a triumph. "I don't know if I can ever forgive her," he wrote in his journal. "I don't hate her—I'm just sooo disappointed."

In a way it's a classic Hollywood tale: Gifted boy artist meets girl artist, mentors her to success and is left in the dust—equal parts "Sunset Boulevard," "A Star Is Born" and "All About Eve." By any measure, Gilbert's career was a fitful tumble of brilliance and happenstance, a series of near misses and one hit that wasn't his. And his Tuesday night cohorts describe Crow—who refused to be interviewed for this story—as a marginally talented singer who exploited his skills and theirs in a ruthless grab for success.

But this wasn't a movie, and so the real story is inevitably messier and more complex. As the circumstances of his death suggest, Gilbert had a dark side, a hidden face making him an enigma to his friends. There was a history of antidepressants, a string of journal entries registering acute self-loathing and doubt. Once, he wrote about feeling intimidated when meeting a well-known session musician at a concert. "I suck," he wrote, circling the words for emphasis.

He had a promising start. As a South Bay teenager, Gilbert was given the run of Sunnyvale's Sensa Sound studio after hours; there, he recorded tracks with his progressive rock group, Giraffe. In 1988 he won the U.S. and worldwide finals of a talent contest run by the Yamaha piano company. One of the judges—Pat Leonard, a producer for Madonna—invited Gilbert to make a record in Los Angeles.

That album, *Toy Matinee,* sold nearly 200,000 copies in 1991, thanks in part to an MTV video featuring actress Rosanna Arquette (whom Gilbert had dated). Gilbert put together a road version that included his then current girlfriend on background vocals and second keyboard—Sheryl Crow.

Making that album, Gilbert, at 21, met another record producer, Bill Bottrell, who became a kind of father figure. Bottrell brought him to sessions for Madonna and Michael Jackson; before long, Gilbert had sublet the space adjacent to Bottrell's Pasadena studio, Toad Hall. From there he set about recording his solo debut.

Drawing on all his perfectionist instincts, along with his ingrained self-doubts, Gilbert didn't just work on his record; he suffered over it, recording and rerecording, polishing, tweaking, rethinking, redoing.

"It was a long process," said Bottrell, who used to hear Gilbert thumping away through the common wall. "He sat over there endless nights."

In August 1992, Bottrell convened Gilbert and other musicians at Toad Hall with the simple agenda of collaborating for the fun of it every Tuesday night. "We were all good, not to be immodest," Baerwald said. "We were all all cynical, embittered by the process of pop music. We were trying to find some joy in music again."

A party atmosphere predominated—"Bill would sift through (the music) the next morning while we were all nursing hangovers," drummer Brian MacLeod recalled. Then Bottrell introduced a project he thought might force a little focus onto the freewheeling, chaotic sessions.

Sheryl Crow had finished an album for A&M Records, but despite the $500,000 spent on it, nobody at the label was thrilled with the results. Hoping for a quick fix, A&M hired Gilbert to remix the album, which was, in the immutable illogic of the record industry, already scheduled for release. Crow's manager asked Bottrell to step in as well.

On Crow's first Tuesday night with the club, Baerwald showed up with musical sidekick David Ricketts (from the 1986 David and David album), both of them high on LSD, with the first verse already written to a song, "Leaving Las Vegas." Baerwald picked up a guitar, Ricketts the bass, and the band fell together to pick up where it had left off.

Baerwald "couldn't function," said Bottrell. "Sheryl started to get drunk. I was looking for that moment when the good take would happen."

For most of that year, Bottrell and his Tuesday crew—now working all week long—scrupulously fashioned and reshaped Crow's album. Because everything was a collaboration, songwriting credits were equally shared. "Everybody was equal," said Baerwald, "except Sheryl. She wasn't one of us. We helped her make a record."

Gilbert's name wound up on seven of the 11 songs; he sang and played keyboards, guitar, bass and drums.

His relationship with Crow was kept separate and even a secret from the group. "I'd see long conversations in the parking lot," Baerwald said.

"Kevin challenged her," MacLeod said. "He was trying to get her to be honest and sing from her heart."

Unsure of herself, professionally in over her head, Crow went home with Gilbert after sessions and listened to him rant about the industry's failings. "She had Kevin filling her with doubts," Bottrell said.

When he wasn't with Crow or the club, Gilbert struggled with his solo album, playing most of the instruments on his supple but powerful pop-rock tracks—polished productions that showed the gleam of countless studio hours. A proposed deal with a major label fell apart, so he made do with a tiny custom label.

After nearly a year of working together, all for one and one for all, the Tuesday Night musicians were shocked to learn they didn't figure into any more of Crow's plans. Bottrell got the news when he met her to hand over the finished master in a Sunset Strip coffee shop. Although there had been much talk of hitting the road together to promote the record—bassist Dan Schwartz even bought a new bass for the tour—"she essentially told me to get lost," Bottrell said.

"I add Sheryl Crow to a long list of people in Hollywood who told me they were my friend until they got what they wanted from me," Schwartz said.

As Crow's relationship with Gilbert deteriorated—apparently she turned her attentions to an executive at the record label, Baerwald said—an increasingly bitter Gilbert threw himself deeper into his own album.

"I think I'm a tinge jealous over her upcoming release," he wrote in his journal. "It's probably going to be huge so I have to prepare myself mentally for that. If she gets what she wants after behaving this way, she'll be absolutely intolerable."

For Gilbert, the final straw came when Crow sang "Leaving Las Vegas" on the David Letterman show. Afterward, when Letterman asked her if the song was autobiographical, a flustered Crow blurted out, "Yes."

"I've never been to Las Vegas," continued Crow, who nobody remembers having contributed greatly to the writing of the song. "I wrote it about Los Angeles. It's really metaphorical."

The next day, she and Gilbert exchanged angry words over the phone. He wasn't the only one furious. Author John O'Brien—who wrote the novel that inspired both Baerwald's early song lyrics and the movie starring Nicolas Cage—was still grumbling about Crow's gaffe to his literary agent on the day he blew his brains out, a scant few weeks before the movie deal was complete.

As Crow's album soared on the charts (her nod to Gilbert in the liner notes says, "I owe you big for two years of musical and emotional support. Thanks"), Gilbert's solo album, a masterful but underpromoted effort titled *Thud,* disappeared almost immediately on release. At the same time, ironically, a tape he recorded for the Led Zeppelin tribute album, dropped from the disc at the last minute, exploded on Los Angeles radio, leaving his little custom label ineptly scrambling to capitalize.

Despite their new notoriety the Tuesday Night Music Club never could quite regroup. The members did play one guest appearance with Crow at an out-of-town club, but the record company made it clear they would not be included in the more prestigious Hollywood show.

Gilbert threw himself into other projects: helping Baerwald produce a solo album by Susannah Hoffs of the Bangles, working with Bottrell on an album by Linda Perry of 4 Non Blondes (the Tuesday night gang dubbed her "the anti-Sheryl"), writing and recording scores for TV shows under a pseudonym. He even produced a movie soundtrack song for which Crow sang vocals—a version of Steve Miller's "The Joker"—although they were never in the studio at the same time.

In November 1994, Gilbert met playwright Cintra Wilson at a party in San Francisco; two months later she moved to Los Angeles to live with him. "He was massively depressed over the whole Sheryl debacle," Wilson said. "I was a basket case. We were perfect for each other."

Despite the tension with Crow, most of the Tuesday Night Music Club attended the Grammy Awards in March 1995. To show irreverence, Wilson rented 19th century funeral regalia for Gilbert and her to wear: a morning coat and top hat for him, ostrich plumes and a bustle for her. Crow sat in the row in front of them. "They were not on good terms," Wilson said. "She was tensely gracious. It was a furtive, tense, real glitzy night."

Crow picked up three awards, including Record of the Year for "All I Wanna Do," a Tuesday Night instrumental with lyrics borrowed from verses in a little-known volume by a poet in Vermont. A week later, Gilbert was still wearing his Grammy medallion around his neck like a badge of valor.

From there, he set out to recapture the creative anarchy he felt was the authentic legacy of the club. He and MacLeod produced some startling records, far removed from anything either of them had ever done.

They were scary, dense, pop-industrial recordings, with Gilbert whispering ominous, almost threatening processed vocals. "They gave me nightmares," Bottrell said. Gilbert envisioned a new band, Kaviar, clad in fetish rubber gear. He pulled other musicians into the plan. At the same time, Gilbert could toss off simple, beautiful, sentimental tunes. In Baerwald's last memory of Gilbert, the pianist was noodling around on the keyboard, plaintively singing Randy Newman's "Marie." Baerwald had briefly dozed off. "I woke up crying," he said. Bottrell, who played perhaps the largest role in Gilbert's career, doesn't think he ever really knew him. "There were tremendous areas of his life I was not privy to," he said. "There were motives I could never quite figure out."

But Bottrell's wife, Elizabeth, remembers sensing a powerful mood of peace and reconciliation in a phone conversation with Gilbert the afternoon before he died. They talked about attending an industry dinner together; Gilbert kidded her about wearing rubber. They never spoke again.

On an afternoon this summer, several hundred of Gilbert's friends and associates gathered for a memorial service at the Bottrells' Glendale home. Cintra Wilson, dressed in white, sat next to MacLeod as Sheryl Crow walked up to say hello. "I barked at her," Wilson recalled. Wilson knew the titles of the album's songs well enough. "Run, baby, run," she yelped at Crow, who fled in tears.

Although Crow is reluctant to discuss Gilbert, she has been openly vocal in interviews about the rift over the album with the Tuesday Night Music Club. "There were guys in the group who were feeling bitter about the record doing so well," she recently told *Billboard* magazine. "Maybe I should have called it something else."

Later this month, she will release her follow-up album, titled, not insignificantly, perhaps even defiantly, *Sheryl Crow*—a two-word title that doubtless speaks volumes on her behalf. Clearly, this singer wants to prove that she's an act and a talent all her own—not the smoke-and-mirrors creation of a savvy, multitalented backup band.

She did mention Gilbert to a Dutch journalist in an interview last month. "I wasn't surprised by his death," Crow told Edwin Ammerlaan of *Orr Magazine*. "Kevin was one of the most self-destructive people I've ever met. I don't want to go into this too much, but it wasn't a nice story."

Mikal Gilmore

KURT COBAIN'S ROAD FROM NOWHERE

A friend of mine told me that he was on his way to a used CD store when he heard on the radio that Kurt Cobain's body had been found. When he got to the store, the clerks had stacked all of their Nirvana albums in the front of the store, under a sign that read. "Buy them before the body gets cold." Cobain's death was as cataclysmic to his generation as perhaps Lennon's had been earlier, but as this anecdote shows, it was not universally greeted with reverent lip-trembling hush. Here's a variation on the whole can't-go-home-again theme.

THERE IS LITTLE doubt that Kurt Cobain did not have an easy time of life in this town. He was born in nearby Hoquiam in 1967, the first child of Wendy Cobain and her auto mechanic husband, Donald. The family moved to Aberdeen when Kurt was six months old, and by all accounts, he was a happy and bright child—an outgoing, friendly boy who, by the second grade, was already regarded as possessing a natural artistic talent. Then, in 1975, when Kurt was eight, Don and Wendy divorced, and the bitter separation and its aftermath were devastating to the child. Instead of the sense of family and security that he had known previously, Kurt now knew division, acrimony, and aloneness, and apparently some light in him began to shut off. He grew progressively introverted, and to others, he seemed full of shame about what had become of his family. In the years that followed, Cobain was passed back and forth between his mother's home in Aberdeen and his father's in nearby Montesano. It was in this period that the young Kurt became sullen and resentful, and when his moods became too much for either parent, he was sent along to the homes of other relatives in the region—some of whom also found him a hard kid to reach. (There are rumors that Cobain may have suffered physical abuse and exposure to drug abuse during this time, but nobody in the family was available to confirm or deny these reports.)

In short, the young Kurt Cobain was a misfit—it was the role handed to him, and he had the intelligence to know what to do with it. Like many youthful misfits, he found a bracing refuge in the world of rock & roll. In part, the music probably offered him a sense of connection that was missing elsewhere in his life—the reaffirming thrill of participating in something that might speak for or embrace him. But rock & roll also offered him something more: a chance for transcendence or personal victory that nothing else in his life or community could offer. Like many kids before him, and many to come, Kurt Cobain sat in his room and learned to play powerful chords and dirty leads on cheap guitars, and felt the amazing uplift and purpose that came from such activity; he held music closer to him than his family or home, and for a time, it probably came as close to saving him as anything could. In the process, he found a new identity as a nascent punk in a town where, to this day, punks are still regarded as either eccentrics or trash.

The punishments that he suffered for his metamorphosis were many, and are now legend. There are numerous stories that make the rounds in Aberdeen about how Cobain got beat up for simply looking and walking differently than other kids, or got his face smashed for befriending a high school student who was openly gay, or got used as a punching bag by jocks who loathed him for what they saw as his otherness. Hearing accounts like these, you have to marvel at Cobain's courage, and even at his heroism. It's a wonder he made it as far as he did without wanting to kill the world for what it had inflicted on him for so many and long seasons.

Though Cobain is now Aberdeen's most famous native son, and though many people recall him from his time here, there's something about his presence here that proves shadowy and inscrutable to the locals. Lamont Shillinger, who heads Aberdeen High School's English department, saw as much of Cobain as most people outside his family. For nearly a year, during the time he played music with the teacher's sons, Eric and Steve, Kurt slept on Shillinger's front-room sofa, and in those moments when Cobain's stomach erupted in the burning pain that tormented him off and on for years, Shillinger would head out to the local Safeway and retrieve some Pepto-Bismol or antacids to try to relieve the pain. But for all the time he spent with the family, Kurt remains a mystery to them. "I would not claim," says Lamont Shillinger, "that I knew him well either. I don't think my sons knew him well. In fact, even to this day, I suspect there are very few people that really knew Kurt well—even the people around him or the people he was near to. I think the closest he ever came to expressing what was inside was in his artwork, in his poetry, and in his music. But as far as personal back and forth. I seriously doubt that he was ever that close to anybody."

Another Aberdeen High teacher, Bob Hunter, affirms Shillinger's view. Hunter, who is part of the school's Art department, began teaching Cobain during his freshman year, and worked with him for three years, until 1985, when Cobain quit school. Though the two of them had a good relationship, Hunter can recall few revealing remarks from his student. "I really believe in the idea of aura," says Hunter, "and around Kurt there was an aura of: 'Back off—get out of my face,' that type of thing. But at the same time I was intrigued by what I saw Kurt doing. I wanted to know where he was getting the ideas he was coming up with for his drawings. You could detect the anger—it was evident even then."

Hunter lost track of Cobain for a while after Kurt dropped out of school, until he had Cobain's younger sister, Kim, in one of his classes. From time to time, Kim would bring tapes of her brother's work to the teacher and keep him informed of his former student's progress. Says Hunter: "Even if Kim had never come back and said that Kurt was really making it as a musician, I would have kept wondering about him. I've taught thousands of students now, but he would have been up there in my thoughts as one of the preeminent people that I hold in high esteem as artists. Later, after I heard the contents of his suicide note, I was surprised at the part where he said he didn't have the passion anymore. From what I had seen, I would have thought the ideas would always be there for him. I mean, he could have just gone back to being a visual artist and he would have remained brilliant."

In time, Cobain got out of Aberdeen alive—at least for a while. In 1987, he formed the first version of the band that would eventually become Nirvana, with fellow Aberdonians Krist Novoselic on bass and Aaron Burckhard on drums. A few months later, Cobain and Novoselic moved to Olympia, and eventually Burckhard was left behind. Nirvana played around Olympia, Tacoma, and Seattle, and recorded the band's first album, *Bleach,* for Sub Pop in 1988. The group plowed through a couple more drummers before settling on Dave Grohl and recording its groundbreaking major label debut, *Nevermind,* for Geffen in 1991. With *Nevermind,* Cobain forced the pop world to accommodate the long-resisted punk aesthetic at both its harshest and smartest, and did so at a time when many pundits had declared that rock & roll was effectively finished as either a mainstream cultural or commercial force. It was a remarkable achievement for a band from the hinterlands of Aberdeen, and the whole migration—from disrepute on Washington's coast to worldwide fame and pop apotheosis—had been pulled off in an amazingly short period of time. Back at home, many of the kids and fans who had shared Cobain's perspective were heartened by his band's accomplishment.

But when Cobain turned up the victim of his own hand in Seattle on April 8, 1994, those same kids' pride and hope took a hard blow. "After the suicide," says Brandon Baker, a fifteen-year-old freshman at Aberdeen High, "all these jocks were coming up to us and saying stuff like: 'Your buddy's dead. What are you going to do *now*?' Or: 'Hey, I've got Nirvana tickets for sale; they're half off.' "

Baker is standing with a few of his friends in an alcove across the street from the high school, where some of the misfit students occasionally gather to seek refuge from their more conventional colleagues. The group is discussing what it's like to be seen as grunge kids in the reality of post–Nirvana Aberdeen. Baker continues: "I realize that Kurt Cobain had a few more problems than we might, but him doing this, it kind of cheated us in a way. We figured if someone like him could make it out of a place like this . . . it was like he might have paved the way for the rest of us. But now, we don't want people to think that we're using his path as our guideline. It's like you're almost scared to do *any*thing now. People around here view us as freaks. They see us walking together in a mall and they think we're a bunch of hoodlums, just looking for trouble. They'll throw us off the premises just for being together. I don't know—it's sad how adults will classify you sometimes."

The talk turns to the subject of the summer's upcoming Lollapalooza tour. In the last few days, Aberdeen's *Daily World*'s headlines have been given to coverage of a major local wrangle: the Lollapalooza tour organizers have proposed using nearby Hoquiam as the site for their Washington show, in part as a tribute to all that Cobain and Nirvana did for alternative music and for the region. Many residents in the area, though, are incensed over the idea. They are worried about the undesirable elements and possible drug traffic that might be attracted by such an event, and even though the stopover would bring a big boom to the badly ailing local economy, there is considerable resistance to letting such a show happen in this area.

"You would think," says Jesse Eby, a seventeen-year-old junior, "that they would let us have this one thing—that the city council would realize we might appreciate or respect them more if they let something like this show come here. It would be such a good thing for the kids around here."

"Yeah," says Rebecca Sartwell, a freshman with lovely streaks of magenta throughout her blond hair. "I mean, can't we just have *one* cool thing to do, just one day out of the year? I mean, besides go to Denny's and drink coffee?"

Everybody falls silent for a few moments, until Sartwell speaks up again. "I don't know how to explain this," she says, "but all I want is *out.* Maybe I'll move to Olympia or Portland or someplace, but when I get there I don't intend to say, 'Hey, I'm from *Aberdeen,'* because then everybody's going to assume I'm an alcoholic, manic-depressive hick. It's bad enough having to live here. I don't want to take the reputation of the place with me when I leave."

Everybody nods in agreement with Rebecca's words.

SAVE THE LAST DANCE FOR ME

Doc Pomus wrote songs until the end of his life. He also became a comforting shoulder for other songwriters when they faced writer's block. John Lennon, Bob Dylan, and a number of others turned to him for advice.

Pomus died in 1991 and not long afterward, his old friend Phil Spector made the induction speech as Jerome "Doc Pomus" Felder was enshrined in the Rock and Roll Hall of Fame.

IT GIVES me great pleasure to thank you for the privilege and honor of inducting my dear and beloved friend, mentor, and teacher, Doc Pomus, into this illustrious Rock and Roll Hall of Fame—without question the greatest hall of fame in the world. And Pete Rose, if you're listening and they don't want you in *that* hall of fame—yeah, we like guys who've done some time, gambled . . . And it's obvious the Baseball Hall of Fame doesn't give a damn how well you played the game, so why the hell should we? Come on!

First of all, to put things in perspective, I should mention the fact that I imitate Doc's voice and I think I was the only one he'd allow do it; he said I made him sound like a cross between Daffy Duck and Elmer Fudd, but folks, he sounded like that. So you can better understand the Doc Pomus I knew, I'll tell you a short story about me and Doc that occurred soon after I met him in 1960. While I know it is not a serious way to start this, I know he would not mind if I shared it with you, and you will excuse my imitation of him. I lived in New York and Doc used to call me up on the telephone. He befriended me and took me in; he would invite me to dinner and he'd take me to Joe Marsh's Spindletop. Now, Joe Marsh was an alleged, you know, an alleged, an alleged, an alleged—but I don't know. Doc would say to me, "I'll buy you a steak. C'mon." So I would go down to this restaurant for the finest meal in the world and conversation and memories that were lovely. His wife at that time was working in *Fiorello*; she was a big star on Broadway. One day we're sitting in there eating and

I don't know, but out of the corner of my eye I saw something happen—I thought it took five hours, but it took like a second—a guy in a raincoat walks in with a hat, walks in and goes up to a guy and BOOM BOOM BOOM, three booms in the head and the guy slumps over dead, just like that. I mean I couldn't believe it. I'd never seen a murder, an execution in a restaurant. When Doc called me up the next time, I told him, "I can't go back in that place ever." And Doc says, "What's the matter babe?" "There was a murder! In the Spindletop Restaurant." I came from Los Angeles, and I was born in New York, but I'm telling you, . . . And the scene was ten years before the *Godfather!* So Doc says, "You gotta understand something babe. You see life is up and down, up and down." I said, "What does up and down have to do with it? A man got murdered." He said, "The place is incredible, right, the salads, I mean how about the service in that restaurant? You have to look at the up side." I said, "I don't get it, I don't get it at all, a man got murdered, man, his brains were splattered all over." He said, "You're looking through those funny glasses babe, you gotta see things on the up side, up up up." I said, "I don't see anything up about a man being murdered. I don't see anything up and I don't know what it has to do with the murder. How do you explain anything that has to do with the murder." "Well the murder—that's the down side of the restaurant, you understand, that's the down side." As I said before, I met Doc in 1960, he befriended me at that time. While he was alive, he was the light of my life. Now that he's gone that light has gone out. His passing has made me realize much I don't understand. See, I know that love comes from the heart, but I have no idea where love goes when the heart dies. Nor do I know what it is within the heart that breaks so badly that it's impossible to repair. Doc's love was of a higher standard than that which I had ever previously known. He was uncompromising and totally committed, and I'm going to be a better person because of Doc Pomus, if you can believe that. What was so remarkable about Doc's love was that it came from the body of a person who never experienced a childhood or even a life on a physical level as we know it. Nor did he have much about which to be physically joyful, grateful, or even loving, if you will, since most of his life was spent in physical discomfort. It was not nearly fulfilled and I will be remiss if I do not mention how personally upsetting and distressing this was to him, and how completely inexcusable it is to me that Doc Pomus during his lifetime was never inducted into The Songwriters' Hall of Fame. The Hall of Fame generally seems to be sponsored by BMI and ASCAP and has been in existence for years. This giant of a songwriter, one of the world's finest, the songwriter I wanted to meet when I came to New York, the songwriter John Lennon wanted to meet, was not in The Songwriters' Hall of Fame. They ignored Doc Pomus. This is a man who before the end of 1960 had already written such classics as "Lonely Avenue," "Youngblood," "Teenager in Love," and "Save The Last Dance For Me." And this man was more than a songwriter. He was a poet, for I need not remind you that while he wrote "Save The Last Dance For Me," he never experienced the thrill or the emotion of that wonderful feeling. For him not to have been admitted during his lifetime into The Songwriters' Hall of Fame is inexcusable, and shame on those people who allowed it to happen. It hurt his zeal and kept his life unfulfilled. But you know, even with his life unfulfilled and all the physical discomfort, he still approached life and lived every day with the happiness, the spirit, and the giving of love and friendship, which he gave to each and every life he entered, and everyone who knew him knows that's true. It was then and still is beyond my comprehension, something I've never seen before. Therefore I now know that that kind of love and strength and desire exists and I will settle for giving or receiving no less.

At this time, I would like to briefly mention and discuss something which I think is relevant to Doc Pomus the lyricist and Doc Pomus my friend; it is inside of me and I have to say it. Doc knew my two youngest twins; named Philip, Jr. and a little girl Nicole, aged nine. Doc was their friend as well and often sent them gifts and spoke to them on the phone. He was particularly fond of little Philip, Jr. as they had a camaraderie—little Philip, Jr. suffered a great deal of physical discomfort from an illness and he knew that Doc too had an illness he got as a little boy and was unable to walk. I mention this because on Christmas Day, 1991, my little son, Philip Jr., aged nine, passed away after a nine-year battle with leukemia. It was Philip, Jr., who, with his sister Nicole, told me not to be sad when my best friend Doc Pomus died. Because when he was alive he could not walk and now that he had died he was in heaven, walking with God. Well, I hope Doc and his little friend, my son Philip, Jr., are walking together.

You know it was years before I realized that Doc Pomus was what we referred to as "handicapped," or "physically challenged." He just never made me aware of it. He spoke, lived, and moved with such grace and such command of his life that I never saw him as handicapped in any way. I'm telling you he made it a privilege to be in his presence and to receive his love and friendship—what I would not give for one more time to share the pleasure of that company. And if the little we know about the universe and life can be simplified, perhaps there is something to be learned or gained by Doc's passing. We know, for example, that when the sun moves down it leaves its beautiful warmth on the land, and we most assuredly know, as Irving Berlin said, if I may paraphrase him, that when the song is ended, the beauty of the melody lingers on. So by that knowledge we know that for every joy that passes, something beautiful remains, and when I think of Doc Pomus, I will find, as should you, comfort in the beauty of his memory and his songs. Yes, he was taken away, but more important than the fact that he died, which took but an instant, is the fact that he lived, and because he lived, we are much better.

As a final thought, when you go home tonight, each and every one of you say to yourselves, for the noble deed you have done this evening, "Score one for the good guys," for that's what Doc Pomus was. That's what all of you are.

Bangs, Lester, both articles from *Psychotic Reactions and Carburetor Dung.* Copyright © 1987 by the Estate of Lester Bangs. Reprinted by permission of Alfred A. Knopf, a Division of Random House, Inc.

Berry, Chuck, from *The Autobiography of Chuck Berry.* Copyright © 1989 by Chuck Berry. Reprinted by the permission of Crown Publishers, Inc.

Booth, Stanley, from *Dance with the Devil.* Copyright © 1984 by Stanley Booth. Reprinted by permission of Random House, Inc.

Brown, James, with Bruce Tucker, from the book *James Brown: The Godfather of Soul.* Copyright © 1990 by Thunder's Mouth Press. Appears by permission of the publisher.

Browne, Jackson, "The Load-Out" from *Running On Empty.* Copyright © 1977 by Swallow Turn Music/Warner/Chappell Music, Inc., and Gianni Music. Reprinted with the permission of Warner/Chappell Music, Inc. All rights reserved.

Burroughs, William, and Devo, "William Burroughs Meets Devo" © 1982 Scott Isler. All rights reserved.

Christgau, Robert, "Rock Lyrics Are Poetry (Maybe)" from *Cheetah* (December 1967). Copyright © 1967 by Robert Christgau. Reprinted by permission of the author.

Cleave, Maureen, "How Does a Beatle Live? John Lennon Lives Like This" from [London] *Evening Standard* (March 4, 1966). Reprinted with the permission of the *Daily Express.*

Cohn, Nik, "Tribal Rites of the New Saturday Night" from *New York* (June 7, 1976): 31–43. Copyright © 1976 PRIMEDIA Magazine Corporation. All rights reserved. Reprinted with the permission of *New York* Magazine.

DeCurtis, Anthony, "A Life at the Crossroads" from Eric Clapton, *Crossroads.* Reprinted with the permission of the author.

DeLillo, Don, excerpt from *Great Jones Street* (Boston: Houghton Mifflin, 1973), pp. 1–4, 20–24. Copyright © 1973 by Don DeLillo. Used by permission of the Wallace Literary Agency, Inc.

Des Barres, Pamela, text, pp. 133–43 of *I'm with the Band: Confessions of a Groupie.* Copyright © 1987 by Pamela Des Barres. By permission of William Morrow and Company, Inc.

Didion, Joan, reprinted by permission of Farrar, Straus and Giroux, LLC, excerpt from "The White Album" from *The White Album.* Copyright © 1979 by Joan Didion.

Doyle, Roddy, from *The Commitments.* Copyright © 1987 by William Heineman, Ltd. Reprinted by permission of Random House, Inc.

Dylan, Bob, "Blind Willie McTell" (1983) and liner notes for *Bringing It All Back Home* (Columbia Records, 1965). "Blind Willie McTell" Copyright © 1983 by Special Rider Music. *Bringing It All Back Home* Copyright © 1965 by Special Rider Music. All rights reserved. International copyright secured. Reprinted by permission.

Escott, Colin, and Martin Hawkins, *Good Rockin' Tonight: Sun Records and the Birth of Rock 'N' Roll* by Colin Escott and Martin Hawkins. Copyright © 1991 by Colin Escott with Martin Hawkins. Reprinted by permission of St. Martin's Press LLC.

George, Nelson, from *The Death of Rhythm and Blues.* Copyright © 1988 by Nelson George. Reprinted by permission of Pantheon Books, a division of Random House, Inc.

Gillett, Charlie, from *The Sound of the City: The Rise of Rock 'n' Roll* (New York: Da Capo Press, 1983). Reprinted by permission of Da Capo USA and Souvenir Press, Ltd.

Gilmore, Mikal, from *Night Beat: A Shadow History of Rock and Roll.* Copyright © 1998 by Mikal Gilmore. Used by permission of Doubleday, a division of Random House, Inc.

Goldstein, Richard, "Gear." Originally published in the *Village Voice,* and "Next Year in San Francisco" from *Goldstein's Greatest Hits: A Book Mostly About Rock 'N' Roll* (Englewood Cliffs, NJ: Prentice-Hall, 1970). Originally published in the *Village Voice* (1968). Reprinted with the permission of the author.

Gomez, Jeff, from *Our Noise.* Reprinted with the permission of Scribner, a division of Simon & Schuster, Inc. Copyright © 1995 by Jeff Gomez.

Gonzales, Michael, "My Father Named Me Prince" from *Code,* December 1999. Reprinted by permission of LFP, Inc.

Gordon, Robert, excerpts from *It Came from Memphis.* Copyright © 1994 by Robert Gordon. Reprinted by permission of the author.

Shaar Murray, Charles, from *Crosstown Traffic*. Copyright © 1989 by Charles Shaar Murray. Reprinted by permission of St. Martin's Press, LLC and Faber & Faber Ltd.

Shiner, Lewis, from *Glimpses,* pp. 270–81. Copyright © by Lewis Shiner. By permission of William Morrow and Company, Inc.

Siegel, Jules, "Goodbye Surfing! Hello God!" Reprinted by the permission of Russell & Volkening as agents for the author. Copyright © 1967 by Jules Siegel. Copyright © renewed 1995 by Jules Siegel.

Smith, Patricia, excerpt from *Life According to Motown* (New York: Tia Chucha Press, 1991). Reprinted by permission of the author.

Smith, Patti, "dog dream" from *Early Work: 1970–1979*. Copyright © 1994 by Patti Smith. Used by permission of W. W. Norton & Company, Inc. "Rise of the Sacred Monsters." From *Creem* (1973). Reprinted by permission of the author.

Southern, Terry, "Riding the Lapping Teague." Copyright © 1972. Reprinted by permission of the Estate of Terry Southern.

Spector, Phil, Induction Speech (The Rock and Roll Hall of Fame) for Doc Pomus reprinted by arrangement with Phil Spector International.

Spector, Ronnie, with Vince Waldron, excerpt from *Be My Baby: How I Survived Mascara, Miniskirts and Madness, or My Life as a Fabulous Ronette* (New York: Harper Perennial, 1990), pp. 143–150. Originally published by Harmony Books. Copyright © 1998 by Vince Waldron.

Tate, Greg, "What Is Hip Hop?" from *Vibe* (1993). Reprinted by permission of the author.

Thomas, Robert McG. Jr., "11 Killed and 8 Badly Hurt in Crush Before Rock Concert in Cincinnati" from the *New York Times* (December 4, 1979): A1, A13. Copyright © 1979 by the New York Times Co. Reprinted by permission.

Tosches, Nick, "Jerry Lee Lewis Sees the Bright Lights of Dallas" from *Hellfire*. Copyright © 1982 by Nick Tosches. Used by permission of Grove/Atlantic, Inc.

Townshend, Peter, from *Rolling Stone,* December 9, 1971. Copyright © by Straight Arrow Publishers, Inc. 1971. All rights reserved. Reprinted by permission.

Turner, Tina, with Kurt Loder, text from pp. 72–3, 74–5, 75–6, 77–9, 81–3, 83–7 of *I, Tina: My Life Story*. Copyright © 1986 by Tina Turner. By permission of William Morrow and Company, Inc.

Uhelszki, Jaan, "I Dreamed I was Onstage with Kiss in My Maidenform Bra" from *Creem* (1975). Copyright © 1975 by Jaan Uhelszki. Reprinted with the permission of the author.